THE DRAGON TWINS

THE COMPLETE SERIES

MICHELLE MADOW

DREAMSCAPE
PUBLISHING

For Cocoa, my sweet, beautiful dog who was with me through every book I've written.

THE DRAGON TWINS

DARK WORLD: THE DRAGON TWINS 1

1

GEMMA

We were best friends, and now, he hates me.

Tears welled up in my eyes as I stared at the last sentence in my journal entry. I inhaled the salty air and looked up to where the waves lapped the sand, and then out to the ocean to gaze off into the horizon. A light breeze blew around me, and the sun shined high in the sky. It was almost noon, so the sunlight brightened my entire cove.

My cove. That was how I'd always thought of it. By some miracle, no tourists had found the rickety wooden steps that led from the scenic road down the cliff to where the cove provided me my own private paradise. The locals didn't come here, either. It was like the cove gave off an aura that told them to turn away and find another beach to hang out at.

According to my family history, my great-great-great-great-great grandmother—or something of the sort—had cast a spell around the cove with her sisters to make it so no one wandered into it. The beaches in Australia were Crown land, owned by the Queen of England for public use. But no one came near it but us.

My twin sister, Mira, hated it here. She said it was spooky, since there were no people around. She saw no point in hanging at the beach alone.

Which left it empty—just the way I liked it.

I wiped away my tears and refocused on my journal. Well, technically it was a sketchbook, since I didn't like to stay in the lines while writing. Half of the page was already filled with my messy handwriting. But so far, I didn't feel any better than I had when I'd first sat down.

I lowered the pen back down to the paper and continued writing.

I tried to make it work. I wanted it to work. But love can't be forced. It either exists, or it doesn't.

I stopped and stared at the words.

Then, something moved ahead and to the right.

I startled and looked up, and my eyes met those of a guy around my age. He was tall and tan, muscular without being bulky, had brown hair that fell in waves across his forehead, and hazel eyes so intense that it was like they were seeing into my soul. He looked out of place in jeans, a black t-shirt, and sandals—like he hadn't planned on coming out to the beach.

"What are you drawing?" His accent was distinctly American. A tourist. September was the start of tourism season in Australia, although it normally drew an older crowd, since American families waited to visit until winter or spring break when school was out of session.

"I'm not drawing," I said. "I'm writing."

He walked forward until there were only two meters between us. "Writing what?"

I placed the pen between the pages and closed the journal. "Stuff."

"Wow." His eyes twinkled in amusement. "Stuff. Sounds exciting."

I smiled, since yeah—I couldn't have been more generic than that. "I'm writing about my life," I said. "Figuring things out. Soul searching. You know how it goes."

No, he probably doesn't "know how it goes." My cheeks heated, and I glanced back out at the ocean. *Most people don't keep journals so they can try to make sense of their innermost, angsty, brooding feelings that they're too self-conscious to share with anyone else—even their twin sister.*

"So it's a diary?" he asked.

"A journal," I said quickly.

"Isn't that the same thing?"

"Diaries are for kids," I said. "Journals are different. They're more reflective."

"Ah," he said. "I see."

The air crackled with energy between us. I wiggled my toes in the sand, aware of every grain between them. The sand always calmed me, and despite the mid-day sun bearing down on it and heating it up, it never burned.

He held his gaze with mine, and his hazel eyes with a sunburst of orange around his pupils were so familiar. I could have sworn…

"Have we met before?" I asked.

"I just got in last night," he said. "I'm Ethan. And you are…?"

"Gemma."

"Gemma." The two syllables sounded like music as he spoke them. "Pretty name."

"Thanks." I smiled and tucked a loose strand of my long brown hair behind my ear.

Ethan walked closer and situated himself beside me. He sat on my left—so he couldn't peek into my journal—leaned back on his palms, and gazed out at the horizon. I waited for him to jump up and say something about how hot the sand was, but it was like he didn't notice at all.

Just like me.

Realizing I was staring at him, I turned my eyes back down to my journal. "I broke up with my boyfriend," I said. "Well, *ex* boyfriend."

Why am I telling him this? I pressed my lips together and glanced around, as if searching for a way out even though I knew every inch of the cove like the back of my hand.

"Let me guess," he said, and when I looked back up at him, my skin tingled with electricity. "You broke his heart?"

My chest panged at the reminder. "Something like that."

Silence again, but a comfortable one.

"We were best friends," I continued with a small sigh. "Now, he hates me."

"I'm sure he doesn't *hate* you. You don't seem like the type of person who's easy to hate."

"Thanks, I think?" I shook my head slightly and smiled again, watching the way his silky hair moved in the breeze. I wanted to run my fingers through it to see if it was as soft as it looked.

"You wouldn't be writing in your journal to figure out your feelings if you didn't care about *his* feelings," he said simply.

"Maybe," I said, although I knew Joey didn't see it that way. He thought I'd been heartless. That I didn't care about him at all. That I'd used him and then abandoned him.

As my best friend—*ex* best friend—he should have known me better than that.

"So, why'd you break up with him?" Ethan asked.

Why do you care? I wanted to ask in return. I was just some stranger on the beach.

But for some reason, he *did* care. And who knew—maybe talking about it would help me get rid of the weight I'd been carrying on my shoulders since the breakup.

"He just wasn't the One," I said. "When we kissed for the first time, I felt nothing. Absolutely *nothing*. And I didn't want to lead him on. So I broke up with him."

"Right after you kissed?"

"Yeah." I bit my lower lip. "Not the most tactful way to go about it, was it?"

"I can think of worse ways," he said. "But that one probably wasn't the best."

"At least I know you're honest."

"I try to be." He glanced down at the sand, his eyes suddenly distant. "When I can."

I set my journal down and turned to face him. "You can always be honest," I said. "It's not always easy, but long-term, it's always better than lying."

He brought his focus back to me, as intense as ever. "Have you ever had to keep a secret?" he asked. "A big one, for the greater good? One that other peoples' lives depend on?"

"Not really," I said, since my family's belief that we had witchcraft in our veins would sound crazy. Especially since none of us had ever been able to cast a spell. And because we'd sworn to tell no one. "Have you?"

A shadow crossed his eyes, and he stood up and brushed the sand off his jeans. "I've gotta go," he said. "Maybe I'll see you around again, Gemma."

"Yeah," I said breathlessly, my head spinning from the sudden way he'd come into my life, and the sudden way he was apparently leaving it. "Maybe."

He spun around, jogged out of the cove, and turned the corner before I could ask how long he was staying in town and where he was heading off to so quickly.

2

GEMMA

"You'll never guess what happened at the beach today," Mira said as she grabbed the bowl of mashed potatoes and dumped a huge spoonful onto her plate. Her cheeks were flushed pink, and her bright blue eyes twinkled with excitement.

That was the only genetic physical difference between me and my twin—her eyes were blue, and mine were green. It shouldn't have been scientifically possible, since we were identical. The doctors had no explanation for it.

My mom called it magic.

Mira was also tanner from all her time surfing, and her hair was shorter and dyed blonde. But those were choices—not something she was born with.

I took the bowl of mashed potatoes and spooned a more sensible portion onto my plate. "You caught your biggest wave yet?" I asked.

"Nope." She smirked mischievously. "I met someone."

"Let me guess," my mom said as she placed the bowl of mashed potatoes back in the center of the table. "This 'someone' is of the male variety?"

"Duh." Mira rolled her eyes. "He was walking by, and we got to talking. He just moved to town, and he's never surfed before. So starting tomorrow, I'll be giving him lessons."

"He'll be a pro by the end of the year," my mom said.

"You'll have forgotten about him by the end of the year," I teased my sister.

That was how it always went with her. A guy struck her interest, she got him to fall halfway in love with her, and then she got bored and dumped him.

I'm not much better. My mind instantly went to Joey.

But that was different.

Or was it?

"Not with this one." A dreamy look crossed Mira's face. "He's different. I've never believed in love at first sight, but with him..." She trailed off, smiling as she cut into her meatloaf and took a bite.

My mom raised an eyebrow. "You can't be in love with him already," she said. "You just met him."

"Come on," Mira said. "You think we're descended from an ancient line of witches, but you don't believe in love at first sight?"

"Maybe I'd believe it if Gemma said it," she said. "But you fall 'in love' with a new boy every month. Also, I don't *think* we're descended from an ancient line of witches. I *know* we are."

"Ooookay," Mira said, and she took another bite of her food.

"You'll find out in three months," my mom said confidently.

Because we were part of a witch circle called the Gemini circle, and she claimed Mira and I were the twins of an ancient prophecy. In three months—on our seventeenth birthday—we were going to receive dragon magic that had been gifted to our ancestors and passed through our bloodline for generations.

I *wanted* it to be true. But every time I tried a spell from our family spell book, nothing happened. Mira had stopped trying with me back when we were thirteen, calling it a stupid family superstition.

I was excited for the night of our birthday, but at the same time, I was trying not to get my hopes up. It was better to be surprised than disappointed.

"Anyway." Mira straightened, still smiling despite my mom's mention of magic. "Back to the guy. We'll be an official couple by the start of next term. Just you wait."

"I'm sure you will," I said, since when Mira set her sights on something—especially when that something was a guy who'd caught her interest—she was a force to be reckoned with.

I felt kind of sorry for the poor guy whose heart she was bound to break.

"Does this mysterious guy have a name?" my mom asked.

"Ethan," she said, and I froze, my fork halfway to my mouth.

"He said he passed you on his walk down the beach," Mira continued. "He's gorgeous, right?"

His intense, hazel eyes flashed in my mind. The way he'd sat down next to me, and how easy it had been to talk to him in those few minutes that had passed far too quickly.

Gorgeous was an understatement.

He was perfect.

"He's American," I said instead. "You can't date a tourist."

"He's not a tourist," she said. "He just moved here from North Carolina. His dad got a super amazing job offer, so they picked up and moved across the world. He's starting school with us next term."

What?

I stared at her, mind blown.

Ethan was going to our school. I was going to see him again. Maybe we'd have a class or two together.

"How long did you hang out with him?" I sounded far more nonchalant than I felt.

"All day."

Hot jealousy raced through my veins. Why did Ethan have time to hang out with Mira, and not with me?

"Just the two of you?" I asked.

"No." She frowned. "It was me and my friends. Ethan and I actually went back to find you to see if you wanted to join us, but when we got to the cove, you were gone."

"It was hot out," I said quickly.

Her brow furrowed in confusion. "The heat never bothers you."

It was true. But it was better than admitting that after Ethan left, I couldn't focus on anything other than him. After ten minutes of staring out at the ocean hoping he'd come back, I went back home to read for the rest of the day to try to stop thinking about him.

It hadn't worked.

Regret hit me hard, and I wished I could go back in time and tell myself to stay at the cove. Then Ethan *would* have come back, and today would have played out completely differently.

It's not like Ethan and Mira are actually dating, I told myself. *And he asked to come back to get me. That has to mean something, right?*

"Why didn't you text me?" I asked.

"I did," she said. "I asked if you wanted to hang out with me and my friends at the beach. You said you were reading, so I figured that was that."

"You didn't say anything about Ethan."

"Would that have changed your mind?"

Yes.

"Maybe."

She looked at me like she didn't recognize me. "You're not interested in him, are you?" she asked. "Because he said you guys only talked for like, five minutes. And you're never interested in *anyone*. Well, except for Joey, and we all know how *that* worked out."

I flinched at the mention of my ex.

"Sorry," she said. "Is he still not replying to your texts?"

"Nope," I said, inwardly fuming about how she'd changed the subject before I could answer her question about Ethan.

But like she'd pointed out, I'd never really been interested in *any* guy. Including Joey, if we were being honest. And she was right—Ethan and I had only talked for five minutes. Maybe less.

Just because I was attracted to him, it didn't mean I was *interested* in him. And I hated fighting with my twin. Which was exactly what was going to happen if I admitted to being interested in Ethan.

Give it time, I thought. *She'll be bored with him in a month. Then, if it's meant to be between me and Ethan, it'll happen naturally. She won't even care, because she'll have already moved on to someone new.*

I needed to be patient and let fate take its course.

"Earth to Gemma." Mira snapped her fingers to get my attention. "Did you hear a word of what I just said?"

"Sorry. I was thinking."

"Of course you were. But back to Joey. You're the one who broke up with him. So if anyone should feel awkward at the start of next term, it should be him—not you."

"You were never friends with any of your exes before you dated them," I said. "It's different."

"Maybe." She shrugged. "But whatever happens next term, you know I've got your back. Right?"

"Right," I said, although for the first time, I wasn't sure I truly believed it.

3

GEMMA

THREE MONTHS LATER

I STOOD in front of the mirror, studying the jeans and burgundy tank top I'd chosen for tonight.

For my seventeenth birthday.

But most importantly, for the Gemini circle twins ceremony.

I ran my hands over the front of my jeans. There were no instructions about what to wear for the ceremony, so my mom had told Mira and me to wear whatever we were most comfortable in.

For me, that was always jeans and a tank.

I brushed my hair, and then looked around my room. Books lined the shelves on every wall. Fantasy, science fiction, historicals, thrillers, mysteries, and even the occasional contemporary romance. You named it, I had it.

My window was a perfect reading nook where I could sit and look out at the ocean. It would have been expensive real estate, if generations of my family hadn't owned the café below the small apartment and passed it down the family line.

I zeroed in on the shelf of my favorite books—the one close to my bed—and read the titles on the spines. The majority were fantasies. As I studied them, I was reminded of each wonderful story I'd read and enjoyed, which calmed my racing heart.

Two knocks on the door, and Mira opened it and pranced inside. She wore high-rise jean shorts that barely covered her butt, and a pink crop top that showed a sliver of skin above her belly button. Her short, blonde hair was perfectly wavy, in the way I knew meant she'd curled it first, then brushed it out to make it look more casual.

She examined her reflection from multiple angles. "How do I look?" she asked.

"Cute shorts," I said. "Are they new?"

"Yep." She turned around to look at herself from behind, and pouted at her reflection like she was a model posing for a photoshoot. "But I'm going for more than 'cute.' I want to be irresistibly sexy."

My heart dropped. Because I knew what that meant.

She had plans with Ethan after the ceremony.

"You do realize that if the ceremony works, we're going to be there all night," I said. "Right?"

"The ceremony's not going to work." She rolled her eyes, turned to face me, and crossed her arms over her chest. Her push-up bra was so tight that she was nearly spilling out of her top. "It's all a bunch of craziness."

"It might not be," I said, even though we'd had this conversation a million times.

Mira wasn't going to believe in magic until she saw it herself.

I, on the other hand, had faith. Because I always felt the tingle of magic in the air around me. It was right there, but if I tried to grasp it, it slipped through my fingers.

It felt the strongest at the cove. I could have sworn that sometimes I saw a shimmer of green or orange dance across my skin. I could never make it happen when anyone else was there, but I knew what I saw.

And then, there was something else. Some other proof I knew I'd seen before. But whenever I tried to remember, it slipped away like a forgotten dream.

"Ethan's already on his way." Mira dropped her arms back down to her sides and smiled. "And I need to look perfect. Because tonight's *the* night."

My chest tightened, because I knew what she meant. She'd only been talking about it for the past month.

She wanted to lose her virginity to him.

The thought of it tore me up inside. But I kept my expression blank, like I always did when she brought up Ethan. Then I swallowed down the lump in my throat and asked, "Where are you guys going?"

"Not sure yet. But we'll figure it out once I tell him it's what I want for my birthday."

"You mean he doesn't know?"

"He knows that I love him," she said. "I told him last week, on Christmas. So now, it's time to seal the deal."

I stared at her, shocked.

How had she not told me she loved him until now?

"And he said it back?" I asked.

Please say no, please say no, please say no...

Guilt slammed down on me, because I shouldn't have been wishing that for my twin. Mira *loved* Ethan. Hoping he didn't love her back was selfish and cruel.

But I couldn't help it. Every cell in my body buzzed with *wrongness* at the thought of Ethan being in love with Mira.

"He doesn't have to," she said coolly. "I know he loves me. Tonight, he'll finally be able to show me. And that's what's important."

He doesn't love her.

I relaxed and sat on the edge of my bed. "When's he getting here?" I asked.

"He just left his house. So, around half an hour."

"We'll still be doing the ceremony."

"He knows that," she said. "He asked where we'll be, so I told him. He's gonna wait for me in the parking lot nearby."

"You told him about the ceremony?"

I couldn't believe it. No one but the witches in the Gemini circle was supposed to know.

"It's just Ethan." She shrugged. "It's fine."

"No, it's not 'fine.'" I glanced at the door, knowing Mom was getting ready in her room down the hall. She wouldn't be able to hear us—she always kept music on—but I was paranoid anyway. "What if he sees something?"

"All he'll see is a few people gathered around a bonfire."

"You know that might not be true." I didn't care how much Mira claimed to love Ethan—she shouldn't have told him our family secret. "Give me your phone."

"What?" Her hand went to the back pocket of her shorts, and she stepped back. "Why?"

"Because I need to text Ethan. I'll tell him we're going somewhere different, and to meet you in the parking lot of the café."

"You're *not* texting Ethan." She stared me down like a cat whose territory had been breached.

"Then you do it," I said. "What's the difference if you meet up with him there or here?"

"Because I can jump right into his car if I meet him there. It's easier."

"The cove is *five minutes away*," I said. "Just have him wait here."

"No."

"Are you seriously putting him before me? Before Mom?" I glanced at the door again. "Because if you don't text him to meet you here, I *will* tell her."

"You wouldn't."

Guilt washed over me. Because Mira and I had always had each other's backs. It was part of the twin code.

But this ceremony was bigger than all of us.

"Family first," I said. "And Ethan's not our family."

She held my gaze for a few more seconds. Then she let out a long, defeated sigh. "Fine." She pulled out her phone and tapped furiously on the screen. "Done," she said, and she raised her eyes to meet mine. "Happy?"

"Let me see." I held out my hand so she could pass over the phone.

She did, and I glanced at the screen.

Change of plans—meet me at the café. So excited for tonight! Cya soon <3 <3 <3

Three moving dots appeared underneath the message. He was typing.

I held my breath as I waited for his response to come through.

Sounds good.

Simple and to the point. Plus, he didn't return her heart emojis.

Or maybe he just wasn't the type of guy to send hearts.

It was such a stupid thing to care about. But I couldn't help but wonder if it meant something. That maybe he didn't love her, and that he never would.

I blinked, sickened by my thoughts—again. Hoping he'd never love her back was a terrible thing to want for my twin. I was awful just for thinking it. I hated myself for it.

It had been this way since that day at the beach.

Which was why I avoided Ethan as much as possible. Whatever I felt for him was just a stupid crush. And I refused to let it grow. I refused to do that to Mira.

Those five minutes we'd spent together in the cove had meant nothing.

At least, that was what I kept telling myself.

"Gemma," Mira said, and I snapped my head up to look to her. "My phone."

"Oh. Right." I held it out to her, and a physical weight felt like it lifted off me when she took it back.

She glanced at the screen, then put the phone back into her pocket. "Are you happy now?" she asked.

"Very." I forced a smile and held my hand out for her to take. "Now, let's go. We have a ceremony to attend."

4

GEMMA

WATER LAPPED at my bare feet as I stared out at the ocean, watching as the bottom of the sun touched the horizon. The sky was a perfect mix of purples and pinks, and the puffy clouds created one of the most beautiful sunsets I'd ever seen. I inhaled the salty air, more at peace in the cove than ever before.

A breeze blew around me, and energy flowed through me, buzzing from my head to my toes.

There was magic in the air. I could feel it.

"Gemma," my mom called from behind me. "It's time."

I turned around to look at where Mira, Mom, my cousins Sasha and Rebecca, plus Sasha's daughter Kelly were waiting around the unlit pyre.

The six of us were the only witches left in the Gemini circle. At least, the only ones we knew of, since we'd lost touch with our more distant relatives over the past few decades.

I'd only met the three of them a few times. Kelly was a few years older than us, and was studying biology at the University of Sydney. Her mom was some high-powered attorney. The other cousin was a doctor's wife, and she stayed at home to take care of their son.

They had only slightly more interest in our family's history than Mira, but they'd flown in from Sydney for the ceremony, thanks to my mom's insistence.

In their designer clothes, they looked out of place in the cove. But they all shared our naturally wavy hair—even though they'd all highlighted theirs, like Mira. Their rounded, youthful-looking faces were similar to ours, and we all had the same straight, aristocratic noses with a few freckles scattered out to our cheeks.

Mira and I were the only ones with bright-colored eyes. Theirs were brown, like my mom's.

I walked over to the pyre, anticipation in every step, and stopped in front of the tall teepee of firewood and sticks. I faced the cliffs in the back of the cove, and Mira stood across from me, looking out to the ocean.

Kelly crossed her arms over her chest and snapped her gum. "What do we do now?" she asked. She wore all black, her jeans and long sleeve shirt so tight that it could pass as a bodysuit.

My mom was already halfway across the cove, examining the sticks scattered across the sand. She picked up two of them. "We light the fire," she said as she headed back to us. She came to me first and held out the sticks, both about thirty centimeters long. I grabbed the curvier one from her left hand. Then she went to Mira and handed her the other stick.

I held the stick in front of me like a wand and studied it. Was it just me, or was it pulsing slightly in my grip?

My mom pulled two lighters out of her satchel, handed one to Sasha, and the other to Rebecca. "I'll let the two of you do the honors," she said. "You'll light the girls' sticks when I give you the go."

She didn't say it, but I knew she was having them do it because the sticks needed to be lit at the same time, and she didn't want to choose between me and Mira.

"What about me?" Kelly asked.

"Focus on giving your energy to the circle," my mom said.

"Whatever that means," she mumbled, and then she spat her chewed gum out onto the sand next to her feet.

Irritation rippled through me at her casual pollution of the beach. But the wind blew sand over the gum, hiding it from sight.

Rebecca walked over to me, and Sasha went to Mira. "Do you really believe in all this?" she asked softly.

"Yes." I stood straighter. "I do."

"I hope you're right." She gave me a small smile.

I nodded in return, as if saying, *we've got this.*

If this worked, and the three of them saw magic with their own eyes, we'd have three more active witches in the Gemini circle. Not that me, Mira, and my mom were truly "active" witches, since every spell we tried failed, but maybe this would be the turning point for all of us.

My mom pulled the Gemini spell book out of her satchel. The pages were so worn that the thick book looked ancient, and she opened it to a marked page near the end. "Lighters ready," she said, and Rebecca flicked the lighter on. The small flame danced on its surface, and I could have sworn the tip of it leaned toward me, like it was drawn to me. "And... go."

Rebecca lowered the lighter to the end of the stick. The flame immediately caught, growing bigger as it danced across the wood. The stick buzzed with energy, and the fire strengthened.

I pulled my gaze away from the fire to look across at Mira. The top of her stick was also aflame, although her fire wasn't as large as mine. Her expression was serious, and her hair blew around her face, light and shadows dancing like ghosts across her features.

But somehow, the air around me was still.

"I'm going to count to three, and then you'll lower your sticks to light the pyre," my mom said.

Mira and I nodded.

"One, two," she said, and anticipation built inside me with each number she counted off. "Three."

THE DRAGON TWINS

I kneeled down and touched the fiery end of my stick to the wood at the bottom of the pyre. The flame caught hold, whooshing along the pyre in seconds. I dropped the stick, and it disappeared with the wood surrounding it.

The bonfire lit up the beach, and the flames crackled and popped as they climbed toward the sky. Warmth emanated from the fire onto my face, the heat curling toward me and begging me to move closer.

I did. Sparks flew out, and I was vaguely aware of them landing on my arms. They were warm, but it didn't hurt.

"Gemma." Rebecca's sharp voice pulled me out of the moment. "Be careful. You'll burn yourself."

I took a small step back and looked around the fire at Mira.

My twin stood over a meter away from the flames, watching me with wide, scared eyes. A breeze blew around her, and she drew in a long, deep breath of the salty air.

She and the others stood around the fire in an even circle. I was the only one out of place, standing so close to the flames. So I took a few steps back and completed the circle. I glanced over my shoulder as the top of the sun disappeared behind the horizon, making way for twilight.

My mom nodded at me, and continued. "Now that the fire is ready, all four elements are with us in the cove," she said. "It's time to call them into our circle. As I speak the name of each element, focus on it and picture it joining us. Once the elements are fully present, I'll proceed with the spell."

"How will we know when they're present?" Kelly frowned.

"Trust me," my mom said. "You'll know." She looked to Mira and then to me. "If you're the chosen twins, then once the ceremony is complete, one of the four elements will claim you. Absorb your element, and control it. Understood?"

"Understood," I said, and Mira repeated the same.

My mom waited a few seconds, and then she began. "Earth," she said, and I burrowed my toes in the sand.

A deep, resounding buzz traveled up through the bottoms of my feet and through my body. The sand grounded me, and it felt like roots grew up through my feet, holding me steady and fusing me with the earth.

"Air," she continued, making me hyper-aware of the breeze brushing against my skin. "Water," she said, and I closed my eyes to listen to the waves lapping the shore behind me. "Fire."

The bonfire popped and burned higher. Sparks flared out of it like fireflies. The sharp smell of smoke filled the air, and the warmth coming off the flames caressed my skin like a blanket.

The others also gazed into the fire, as if they felt it, too. Even Kelly had uncrossed her arms and dropped the attitude.

"Welcome to our circle," my mom said, as if the elements were living beings that could hear and understand.

The fire danced higher, the sand warmed, the breeze stirred, and the waves crashed louder.

My heart was pounding so fast that I barely remembered to breathe.

It's happening. It's really, truly happening.

My mom raised the book and started reciting the spell. It was in Latin, but the foreign language flowed off her tongue so easily that she sounded like she spoke it fluently. The light of the flame flickered over her skin, and I could have sworn I saw a slight sheen of yellow magic shimmer around her.

She said the final word, then looked back up.

Thunder rumbled so loudly that the ground vibrated, followed by an ear-splitting crack and bright white lightning.

And then, chaos.

Heat seared through my veins, my blood bubbling to a boil. Wind rushed around us, and the sand slithered over my feet. The fire grew so tall that it looked like it was trying to touch the stars, and rain fell from the sky in buckets, soaking me in an instant. The rain was so heavy that it blinded me, yet the fire still burned strong.

"Claim your elements!" my mom screamed over the howling wind. "Absorb them into your bodies!"

I threw my head back, closed my eyes, and opened up my palms. *Earth, fire, wind, water*, I thought, trying to connect with them like we'd done in the beginning of the ceremony. *Which one of you is mine?*

The heat intensified and surrounded me. The sand crawled over my ankles, then up my legs and over my body, covering me completely. I should have been suffocating. I should have burned. But the sand burrowed inside me, followed by the heat that warmed my skin.

Fire and earth.

They were *mine*.

I opened my eyes and saw the final bits of flames surrounding my arms before they died out.

Except they hadn't died out.

They'd fused with my soul.

The bonfire still burned, but at a normal height, like it had been before we'd done the spell. And the rain had stopped falling—everywhere but where Mira was standing.

I walked slightly around the fire to get a better look at my sister. Except I could barely see her. The rain had joined with the wind, so she was standing in the center of a waterspout that touched the sky.

"Mira!" I screamed. "Stop fighting it! Close your eyes and relax! Let your elements inside!"

My mom rushed over to me and took my hands, her eyes wide with fear.

What would happen if Mira failed?

Was it possible to fail?

Terror coursed through me, and my mom yelped and yanked her hands out of mine like I'd scalded her.

I glanced at her hands—they were red. I *had* scalded her.

Before I had time to contemplate what I'd done, the rain stopped falling around Mira. The wind slowed, revealing my sister on her knees in the sand. Tears streamed down her face, and she ran her hands along her arms, as if making sure she was still in one piece.

I ran to her, fell down to my knees next to her, and wrapped my arms around her. She was dry, despite the downpour that had surrounded her moments ago. She trembled as she cried.

"You did it," I said. "*We* did it."

"Yeah." Her voice shook. "We did."

Then a piercing squawk sounded from above, and a giant red-eyed bird tucked its wings to its sides and dived toward the cove.

5

GEMMA

I cursed and pulled Mira to the side.

But the bird wasn't heading toward us.

It flew straight down to Kelly, who stood there frozen, her mouth open in surprise. It dug its claws into her shoulders, opened its wings, and Kelly screamed as it flew her up to the top of the cliffs. Her shrieks filled the air as she dangled between the bird's hind legs—legs that looked like they belonged on a giant cat. Its fur-tipped tail whipped around behind her.

That thing was no bird.

"Kelly!" her mom—Sasha—screamed, and then she looked to me and Mira. "DO SOMETHING!"

Do what?

Flames from the bonfire flickered in the corner of my eye.

Fire.

One of my elements.

I raised my hands toward the monster, heat coursed through me, and a line of fire shot out of my palms.

But I redirected my aim and shot the blaze of fire into the empty sky. Because if I burned the bird, then I burned Kelly.

The fire hit nothing and fizzled out.

And what was I supposed to do with earth? Throw rocks at the bird? Even if I *could* do that, there was a chance I'd hit Kelly, too.

"Mira," I said, and I turned to my sister. She cowered in fear as she stared up at Kelly dangling from the creature's talons. They were getting higher by the second. "Use the wind to force it back down."

"How?"

"I don't know. Just focus on the wind and *use it.*"

She didn't move, and for a moment I worried she wasn't going to try. But then she raised her hands, palms out, and narrowed her eyes as she focused.

A breeze stirred—Mira's magic.

"Good," I said. "Now, push the monster down from above."

I had no idea what we were going to do once the creature was back in the cove. But we needed to get Kelly closer. We'd figure out the rest from there.

Mira pressed her lips together, bent her knees to steady herself, and cried out as she tried to use her magic. Wind rustled the tree leaves, but the bird-like creature continued flying upward.

Then the creature released Kelly from its talons.

She shrieked as she plummeted down toward us.

"Use your wind to cushion her fall!" I screamed at Mira.

Mira pushed again. A gust of wind shot out of her palms, and it flung Kelly into the side of the cliff.

She smacked into the rocks with a sickening thud and tumbled down in a free fall, hitting the cliff twice more and landing on the sand like a rag doll. Her limbs twisted in angles that shouldn't have been physically possible.

No.

I grabbed Mira's arm and stared at Kelly's body.

No one could have survived that.

Sasha screamed Kelly's name and rushed to her side. She fell down onto her knees, wrapped her arms around her daughter's body, and collapsed into a heaving, sobbing mess.

Another squawk sounded from above.

The monster was dive-bombing again.

I raised my hands and shot out a stream of fire. But the bird was moving so quickly that I missed it by meters. I shot out more fire, and missed again.

The creature flew diagonally, toward the ocean.

Rebecca was shoulder deep and swimming off to the side. Maybe she thought birds hated water? But she couldn't swim fast enough, because the monster grabbed her shoulders with its talons and plucked her out of the ocean.

It flew up and over us, and water dripped off of Rebecca. A few drops landed on me.

"Try again." I grasped Mira's arm so she wouldn't try to run.

"I'm going to," she snapped, and she yanked her arm out of my grip and raised her palms so they faced the bird.

The wind pushed the bird slightly off-course.

"Force it down!" I said.

"I'm *trying!*"

She pushed out another gust of wind, which smacked into the bird and pushed it out toward the ocean.

The bird raised its wings and rode the wind, like it was hang-gliding.

"Use your water!" I told Mira.

"I don't know how!"

The bird released Rebecca over the ocean, and my heart plummeted into my stomach.

It was nearly impossible to survive a fall into water at that height. I'd learned that during a family trip with Mom and Mira to Sydney, when we did a tour to climb to the top of the Sydney Bridge. During construction of the bridge, some of the workers lost their balance, fell into the water, and died. At that height, the impact with the water was as strong as an impact with concrete.

And Rebecca had been much higher up than the height of the bridge.

I stared helplessly out at where she'd fallen.

Then someone came up from behind and grabbed my hand.

I turned around.

"Ethan?" I said at the same time as Mira threw her arms around him and buried her head in his shoulder.

"I brought your mom to the cave at the other side of the cove," he said, and he reached for me, pulling me toward the cliffs. "We need to hide."

"No." I jerked to a stop and looked over my shoulder at Sasha collapsed over Kelly's body. "We can't leave her there. It'll get her next."

"We don't have time," Mira said. "It's already coming back."

"I'll get her," Ethan said. "The two of you get to safety."

"You don't have magic," I told him sharply. "I'm getting her."

He released my arm and shot a blaze of fire out toward the ocean. "You were saying?" he asked with a self-satisfied smirk.

I stared at him, shocked. "What *are* you?"

"I'll explain later," he said. "Go with Mira."

I glanced over my shoulder again. Sasha's back was toward the ocean, and she was oblivious to the chaos around us. If she stayed with Kelly, that monster would surely kill her next.

But why should I trust Ethan? His loyalty was to Mira—not to some distant cousin of mine.

"Get Mira to the cave," I told him. "I'm getting Sasha."

I spun around and sprinted toward her before he could argue.

I stopped once I was behind her and swallowed down disgust at the sight of Kelly's twisted, mangled body. Jagged bones stuck out of her skin, and her blood soaked the sand. Her neck twisted at an unnatural angle, and her eyes stared blankly up at the sky.

I reached for Sasha's arm and pulled. "Come on," I said. "We have to go."

"No." Sasha yanked her arm out of my grasp. "I'm not leaving her here."

"You have to. That thing's already on its way back. If we don't hide, it'll come after us next."

"Fine," she said. "Let it."

"You can't mean that." I reached for her again.

"Don't touch me!" She pulled back and narrowed her eyes. "You're just as much of an abomination as that thing is."

I stepped back, shocked.

She couldn't mean that.

"We have to go," I repeated. "Please. Come on."

"No."

I bit my lip and turned around to see the monster's progress. It was a stadium's length away. Its eyes glowed red, getting brighter by the second.

Even if I tried to run to the cave, I wouldn't have time to get there before the monster reached the cove.

Panic rushed through me. If I didn't fight, I'd be dead. Sasha, too.

So I raised my hands, screamed with everything in me, and shot twin beams of fire at the monster.

The flames were so bright that I couldn't see if I'd hit it or not.

Suddenly, two matching beams of fire shot out from next to me. They joined mine, and the four beams fused together to form a burning blaze of magic.

I glanced over my shoulder at Ethan. His gaze was intense as he stared straight ahead, and the light from the flames danced across his perfect features.

He was focused, determined, and deadly.

He glanced over to meet my eyes, and I could have sworn he looked *proud* of me. "Keep going," he said. "We've almost got it."

I swallowed and refocused on putting as much magic as I could behind the fire.

Feathery wings extended out over the flames, and the creature squawked, the sound chilling my bones like nails on a chalkboard. The scent of burnt flesh filled the air.

"On three, gather your magic and shoot out as much as possible—a giant ball of it," he said, and I nodded. "One, two, THREE!"

Heat seared through my veins, and I pushed out my magic in a single blow. The flames blasted out in a ball of bright light, like an exploding sun.

Another squawk, and the bird monster thudded to the ground at the same time as my magic fizzled out.

I sucked in a long, painful breath and sank down onto the sand. Exhaustion hit me like a train. It was like my magic was a well, and there was nothing left inside.

Ethan knelt down and took my hands. Sparks flew over my skin where he was touching me. "We did it," he said. "You're amazing."

Electricity buzzed through the air so intensely that I couldn't focus enough to speak.

He moved closer and rubbed circles on my palms. Embers glowed in his hazel eyes, like they were reflecting fire.

Footsteps pounded on the sand, and he yanked his hands out of mine as Mira and Mom ran toward us. He stood up, and Mira wrapped her arms around him in a tight hug.

Sharp, hollow pain exploded in my chest.

Mom cleared her throat, and Mira pulled away, her cheeks flushed red.

I glanced over at Sasha. She'd turned her back to Kelly and was sitting in the sand, focused on something in front of her.

The charred remains of the bird-like monster lay a few meters away, right where the bonfire had been. It was huge—the size of an SUV—and its features were barely recognizable under its cracked, blackened skin.

"What *was* that thing?" I turned to Ethan, since he obviously knew more than he'd previously let on.

"A griffin," he said.

"A *what*?" Mira's eyes were as large as saucers.

"I'll tell you everything once we're back at my house," he said. "My car's parked at the top of the cliffs. Let's go."

My mom nodded, took Mira by the shoulders, and guided her toward the steps that meandered their way to the top of the cliff.

I knelt down next to Sasha, praying she'd listen. "Kelly's gone," I said softly, my eyes filling with tears. "We have to go with Ethan."

She just sat there, catatonic.

Ethan reached into his pocket and pulled out a small tranquilizer dart filled with dark blue liquid. "We don't have time for this," he said, and then he bent toward Sasha and pricked her arm with the tip of the dart.

She blinked a few times, and her expression relaxed.

"Sasha," Ethan said calmly. "Go up the steps as quickly as you can, get into my car, and let me drive you to my house."

She nodded, stood up, and hurried to the steps, taking them two at a time to make her way to the top of the cliff.

"What'd you do to her?" I asked.

"Complacent potion," he said simply. "I'll explain later."

Before I could reply, he took my hand, and we scrambled up the steps to follow Sasha to the parking lot.

6

GEMMA

"What the hell *was* that thing?" I said after jumping into the back seat of Ethan's car.

Mom was also in the back, and a drugged-up Sasha sat between us. Mira had taken shotgun.

"A griffin," Ethan said calmly. "One that was somehow possessed."

"A what?"

"A sort of bird-lion hybrid," he said. "But it shouldn't have had red eyes. There was something wrong with it."

"There was a lot wrong with it." Mira's voice rose in panic. "Like the fact that *it shouldn't exist*."

"Well, as you just saw, it does exist," he said. "Welcome to the world of magic."

Energy coursed through me. I was buzzing with it. Because while what had happened tonight was scary as hell, it also meant that what I'd always believed to be true was correct.

Magic existed.

I studied the center of my palm, where fire had burst out of it when I'd defended myself against that monster.

"Don't use your magic," Ethan snapped. "We can't risk them tracking you down and attacking again."

"Who's 'them?'"

"I'll explain once we're back at my house. But right now, I need to focus on getting us there as quickly as possible."

He put the pedal to the metal as he sped down John Astor Road—the scenic drive that wound around Australia's southern shoreline. I gripped the armrest to keep myself from sliding into Sasha.

None of us spoke during the drive. All I could do was replay the events in the cove in my mind. It had happened so quickly that it didn't feel real.

The image of Kelly's mangled body bleeding out in the sand would forever haunt me. And that red-eyed creature…

Ethan had saved our lives. And he had magic like mine.

How?

I'd hoped my life would be changed forever tonight, but never in my wildest dreams had I imagined it would happen like *that*.

We made it to Ethan's house in just over twenty minutes. Although calling it a "house" would be a disservice. Because as he pulled into the long driveway, it was clear that it was most definitely a mansion. A modern, airy mansion with floor to ceiling windows, situated high enough on a hill that it had a killer view of the ocean.

We followed him inside, and the moment he opened the door, my mouth watered at the delicious smell of cooked meat.

"I hope you're hungry," he said. "Because Grandma Rose prepared dinner, and she always makes far too much for us to finish on our own."

Mom walked by my side behind Ethan and Mira. She was calm given everything that had happened tonight, but Mom was always cool and collected, especially in times of crisis.

Sasha followed, not saying a word.

We entered the dining room, which had a banquet table in the center and huge windows that looked out to the ocean. A dark-haired woman stood with her back to us. She was putting the finishing touches on setting the table. A platter with slices of lamb, and another with a massive chicken, sat in the center of it. She carefully touched the rim of the plate and the handles of the utensils, as if feeling to make sure they were in place.

She spun around to face us, and I startled and stepped back. Because her cloudy, white eyes stared straight ahead.

She was blind.

Then she smiled, which brought her from creepy to friendly in less than a second. "Welcome," she said, and she motioned to the table. Her voice was low and warm. "I'm Rosella. Please sit down and help yourselves. I've made more than enough for all of you."

She'd set the table for six.

As if she'd known we were coming.

Had Ethan texted her when we left the cove?

"Don't be shy," she added. "I'm sure you have many questions. Ethan and I will explain everything while we dine."

"Thank you." I walked to the table and sat down. I was so hungry that my bones felt hollow, and I stared hungrily at the chicken as the others made themselves comfortable.

If I wasn't concerned about table manners, I would have ripped the leg off that chicken and devoured it without bothering to use utensils.

My stomach rumbled—loudly—and I wrapped my arms around it.

Ethan smiled at me and reached for the serving tools beside the chicken. "Which part do you prefer?"

"The leg," I said quickly.

I inhaled the chicken leg in what must have been a minute. I went in for seconds, but with the bottomless pit of hunger taken care of, I could finally focus on the reason *why* Ethan had brought us here.

He sat directly across from me, and I zeroed in on him, surprised when his eyes were already on mine.

He was looking at me like he had after we'd killed that monster. Like he was amazed.

"You have magic," I said simply.

"An astute observation."

I made a face in annoyance.

Mira turned to him, since she was sitting next to him. "How long have you had magic?" she asked.

"My entire life."

Her face crumpled, and she looked at him like she didn't know him. "After everything I told you, how could you keep this from me?"

My mom's sharp gaze went to Mira. "What did you tell him?"

My twin pressed her lips together, refusing to meet Mom's eyes. "Not much," she finally said. "Just about the ceremony, and how you thought Gemma and I would get magic tonight."

"That was a family secret," my mom scolded her. "Not something you tell a guy you've only known for a few months."

"That's what I told her," I said.

"You knew about this?"

I flinched back slightly, since she was right—I'd lied to her by keeping Mira's secret. But that was how it had always been between me and Mira.

Twins before anyone else. Even before Mom.

"I only told her a few hours ago," Mira came to my rescue. "And I'm sorry I told him, but I never actually thought anything would *happen* tonight."

"How did he even know where we'd be?" she asked.

Mira quickly told her everything I already knew from when we'd talked in my room before the ceremony.

"Don't blame Mira," Ethan cut in, and from the way he moved, I could tell he'd reached for her hand beneath the table. The twinge of jealousy that I felt whenever I saw them together passed through me, but I did what I always did and pushed it down. "I knew about the ceremony, even before she told me. And I steered our conversations in ways that ensured I'd know where you'd be tonight, in case you needed my help."

"Against the griffin," I said, still processing the fact that the monster had been *real*.

"Precisely. You used your magic well, but your abilities are still raw. If I hadn't been there to help you, things wouldn't have happened the way they did."

We'd be dead.

The implication hung in the air, although none of us wanted to say it out loud.

Mom raised her chin proudly. "So you're a witch, too," she said to Ethan, continuing before he could confirm it. "But how? Male witches barely have any magic."

"I'm not a witch," he said simply. "I thought you'd have already figured that out, since no witches—besides the chosen Gemini twins—have elemental magic."

"Then what are you?" I asked.

He kept his eyes locked on mine, and said, "A dragon."

7

GEMMA

I stared at him, speechless.

Obviously I'd always known the story of my ancestors being gifted with dragon magic over a thousand years ago. And if dragon *magic* existed, then actual dragons had to exist, too.

But that didn't make it sound any less crazy.

"A dragon," I repeated, trying to get it through my head. *"How?"*

"Yeah," Mira chimed in. "Because you don't look like a dragon. Thank God for that."

"I was born a dragon," he said. "Same as my dad and sister."

Mira glanced at the stairs. "Lizzie's asleep?" she asked.

"Yep."

"And your father?" my mom asked.

"Away on supernatural business."

"Hm." She pressed her lips together, not looking pleased with his answers. Then she looked to Rosella and asked, "You're a dragon, too?"

"No," she said. "I'm Ethan and Lizzie's guardian. I'm from a peaceful place in India called the Haven, where many supernaturals live."

I sucked in a sharp, amazed breath. Because there was an entire *place* where supernaturals lived, assumedly undetected by the rest of the world.

Incredible.

"What sort of place?" Mira looked completely dumbstruck.

"More on that later," Rosella said. "Because when Ethan and his family journeyed to Earth from the dragon realm, I was assigned to look after them to help them assimilate to life here. That was seven years ago."

"Back up." I stared at Ethan. "You're from a different *realm?*"

"What's a realm?" Mira asked.

"Another world connected magically to Earth," I said, since I read about this all the time in fantasy novels. "Like the place they went in the *Narnia* series when they walked through the wardrobe."

"Correct." Ethan nodded. "Although it's far more difficult to journey to Ember than to Narnia."

"You mean Narnia exists?"

"No." He chuckled. "But like Rosella said, I've been here for seven years. I've read the books, too."

"Oh." That was the last thing I'd expected him to say. "You read?"

"Yes, I read." His eyes sparkled with amusement.

Mira looked back and forth between us and frowned. "The two of you can continue your little book club later," she said, and she turned back to Ethan. "I thought dragons were big scaly monsters with wings."

"We can shift into 'big scary monsters with wings,'" he said. "At least, my dad can."

"But you can't?" I asked.

"We're only able to shift after our eighteenth birthday."

"But you turned eighteen last month," Mira said.

"The magic that grants us the ability to shift is unique to Ember," he said. "We must be on Ember's land the first time we shift. Once I return home—if I'm ever able to return home—then I'll be able to shift."

"If you can't prove it to us by shifting, how do we know anything you're saying is true?" I asked.

"Once my father returns, he'll shift for you," he said. "But like you saw in the cove, I have elemental magic."

"Fire magic."

"And air." He glanced at Mira, then back at me. "Although fire's my strongest element."

"Does this mean that Mira and I are dragons, too?"

"You're witches whose ancestors were gifted with dragon magic," he said. "I thought you already knew that."

"That's what we've always been told." Mira sounded like she was in a trance.

"But all we've known is that the chosen twins in the Gemini line would be blessed with elemental dragon magic," I said. "We were never told anything about being able to shift into dragons."

"Because you won't be able to shift into dragons," he said. "You're either born a dragon shifter, or not. The two of you aren't shifters. You're witches."

"So how come we've never been able to perform any spells or brew any potions?" I asked. "Because trust me, I've tried."

"I'm sure you have." Ethan looked amused.

Rosella set her silverware down on her plate, and we all looked to her. "The Gemini circle has extremely diluted witch magic," she said. "In the eyes of most supernaturals, witches with such low levels of magic are considered basically human. It's why the supernatural world has never sought you out. You didn't register on our radar."

I bristled, not liking the idea of being viewed as powerless.

Especially after what I'd done tonight.

"I'm guessing it wasn't a coincidence that you moved here," I said. "You knew about us, and you *did* seek us out."

"We did."

"But how did you know to move here just in time for our ascension ceremony?"

"Because I'm gifted with future sight," Rosella said. "I knew to move here with Ethan and his family because I knew when—and had a general idea of where—you and your sister would receive your magic."

8

GEMMA

"So you're a witch," I said.

"A prophetess," she corrected me. "And I'm here to help you."

"How? Shouldn't we be getting help from Ethan? Or his dad? Or the other dragons living on Earth?"

Excitement crawled over my skin at the thought of dragons living on Earth. And prophetesses, and griffins, and whatever else was out there.

Werewolves? Fae? Vampires? Mermaids? I'd read books featuring all of those supernatural creatures. The possibilities were endless.

"My dad, sister, and I are the only dragons living on Earth," Ethan said sadly.

"Where are the others?" I asked.

"Back on Ember."

"You miss it there?" I couldn't imagine what it must have been like to pick up with his family and leave his entire *realm* for a world where they were the only ones of their kind.

His expression hardened. "There's nothing to miss."

"What do you mean?" Mira asked.

"Ember's changed over the past few centuries. It's no longer a safe place for my kind. Luckily, my family was gifted passage out of Ember—to help *you*. It's my job to protect you."

Mira shifted in her seat, her eyes downcast. "What do you mean, it's your *job*?" she asked.

"It's my duty to ensure the survival of the Gemini twins gifted with dragon magic. In Ember, we call you the Dragon Twins."

"So your people have heard of us?" I asked.

"You and Mira are something of a legend there. We've been waiting for you to ascend into your magic for a long time."

"But we're just witches with dragon magic. We can't shift. Why would actual dragons care about us?"

"Because you're not *just* witches with dragon magic," he said. "According to legend, one of you will eventually be gifted with power over the fifth element."

"What's the fifth element?" I'd read a few fantasy books where the main character was gifted with the fifth element. In the most recent one I'd read, it was the ability to heal or kill with a touch.

"I don't know," he said. "No dragon in history has ever had power over it. But it's my job to protect you and help you learn how to use your magic. Then, once you're strong enough, we'll find out what the fifth element is and figure out how to use it for our benefit."

Mira sniffed and brushed a tear off her cheek.

"What's wrong?" Ethan's voice was soft with concern.

"This is why you dated me, isn't it?" she asked. "Because it's your *job*."

I could have sworn that guilt flashed over his eyes.

But then he took Mira's hands. "No," he said. "Of course not."

"You mean it?"

Of course he means it, I thought. *Because he met me first. If his goal was to find us and date one of us, he would have stayed with me that first day in the cove.*

"Yes, I mean it," he said, and Mira relaxed, seemingly accepting his answer.

They both settled back into their seats, and all was well between them again.

"As much as Mira shouldn't have told you about the ceremony, I'm glad she did," my mom said. "You saved our lives, and I'll never be able to repay you for that."

"You owe me nothing," he said. "It's my duty to protect your daughters. You have my word that I'll be here for them, always."

Warmth settled over me at the certainty of his words. Because despite how distant he'd been since that first day in the cove, I believed him.

My mom nodded, sat straighter, and turned to Rosella. "Since you're gifted with future sight, I assume you know why the griffin attacked us?"

Rosella stared in Mom's general direction with her cloudy eyes. "I don't know much," she said. "But I can tell you this—there's someone out there who wants to get to your daughters before they're able to access the fifth element."

"You mean they want us dead," I said.

Mira scooted closer to Ethan and held onto his arm, her face pale.

"Perhaps," Rosella said. "Or they might want to keep you alive so they can force you to use the fifth element to their advantage."

"As if we'd ever do that."

"There are forces out there far more powerful than you've yet to realize," she said. "There's no saying what they—or you—might do if they get ahold of you."

I swallowed at her ominous tone.

What does she know that she isn't telling us?

"What sort of forces?" I asked instead.

"Dark ones," she said. "And they can track you whenever you use your magic. You won't be safe until we learn how they're doing it and stop them."

"Who's 'we?'"

"The three of us," Ethan said. "I can't use my magic without leading them to us, either. Which means I want to figure out how we're being tracked and put an end to it as badly as you do."

"But how are we supposed to 'put an end to it' if we can't use our magic?" I shuddered as the image of the monstrous griffin flashed through my mind.

If we hadn't used our magic against it, we'd be dead.

"We'll use it when the time's right," he said. "Until then, you and Mira need to train so you're ready when that time comes."

"But we can't use our magic," I said flatly. "So how are we supposed to train?"

Rosella chuckled. "The Haven—the place where I usually live—is one of six supernatural kingdoms on Earth," she said. "But like I said, it's a peaceful kingdom. The witches there aren't as skilled with using their magic for battle as those in the other kingdoms. Which means you must go to one of the other five kingdoms to train."

"But the person who's after us will still be able to track us."

"The magical domes around the kingdoms should block them from doing so," she said. "But not all of the kingdoms are welcoming. There are some you'll want to avoid at all costs."

"Which ones?" Mom asked, as if she knew of these kingdoms.

"That's not for you to worry about. Because I've reached out to the queen of one of the safe kingdoms—Utopia. She's agreed to take you in. All four of you."

"Wow." I exhaled, unsure what else to say.

"We can't just pick up and leave," Mira said in a rush. "This is our home. We have friends here. And what about school? And the café?"

"You're not safe here," Ethan said. "We have to go."

Mira's lower lip quivered. "But I don't want to. I don't want magic, either. And I don't want these *monsters* tracking us."

"I know you don't," he said. "But this is your destiny."

The word sent shivers up my spine.

"Well, I don't want it." She slid her chair back, stood up, and marched out of the room.

Ethan hurried after her and blocked her path.

"Move," she commanded.

"No."

She stepped to the side, but he mirrored her, blocking her again.

"School doesn't start up for another few weeks," he said. "Come to Utopia. If you still feel this way after a few weeks of training, we'll discuss other options."

"What kind of options?"

"None that are good. But give Utopia a chance—for me. Can you do that?" He gazed down at her like he was trying to convince her just by looking at her.

I held my breath, waiting.

The others were silent, too.

"Fine," she said after a few long, tense seconds.

He nodded, took her hand, and they re-joined us at the table.

"What about her?" I glanced at Sasha, since we couldn't just leave her here.

"I've made arrangements for a witch to transport her to the Haven," Rosella said. "The supernaturals there will help her adjust to the changes in her life."

She said it so simply—like Sasha was going through a career change instead of witnessing magic for the first time and watching a monster brutally kill her daughter and cousin. And thanks to the complacent potion, Sasha didn't even twitch.

"Lizzie will also come with me to the Haven," Rosella added.

Ethan's expression hardened at the mention of his sister. "I trust you'll keep her safe there," he said.

"I view Lizzie as my own daughter," she said. "And the Haven is the safest place she can be."

He nodded, like he'd been prepared for this possibility. "And my dad?"

"He plays an important role in this, too," she said. "He's unable to reach us right now—as usual when he's away on supernatural business—but you'll learn about that role in due time."

He pressed his lips together, but didn't ask for more information. He must have been used to Rosella's cryptic way of speaking.

"So." I bounced in my seat, trying to quell the adrenaline rushing through my veins. "When do we leave?"

"Soon," she said, and from there, she explained the basics of what to expect when we got to Utopia.

9

GEMMA

THE NEXT TWO days passed in a blur.

Rosella convinced one of the witches from the Haven to watch the café while we were in Utopia. Her name was Shivani, and she was more than happy to take on the task.

Every time we asked Shivani about the dark forces Rosella had been referring to, she shut down and said we'd learn more in Utopia. She was impossible to crack, so I eventually stopped trying, since we'd be in Utopia soon enough.

Ethan had been camping out on the couch in our living room. He only left the house once, and that was to say goodbye to his sister before Rosella took her and Sasha to the Haven.

Mira had asked him to stay in her room, but he'd refused. And he'd been as closed off as ever, especially when we asked him to tell us about Ember. So Mira hung out in the living room with him, watching mindless reality TV shows. I stayed in my room, trying—and failing—to focus on reading.

What books would I bring with me to Utopia? I eventually settled on a few I'd already read and *knew* I loved, because it would be nice to have a sense of familiarity and comfort in such a strange, new place.

The next morning, I waited in the living room with Mira, Mom, Ethan, and Shivani. Mira's suitcase was the largest, but mine was the heaviest, thanks to the books. Everyone always told me to get a Kindle—Mom even bought me one for Christmas a few years ago—but I preferred holding an actual book in my hand. Not like it would matter in Utopia, since they didn't have the internet *or* cell service there.

Mira stood next to Ethan, tapping furiously on her cell phone.

"Who are you talking to?" I asked her.

"Just replying to comments." She didn't look up from the screen. "I posted on Facebook that we were going on holiday to New Zealand and wouldn't have cell service, and the post is blowing up."

I reached for my cell to check my messages. I'd texted my closest friends the same cover story, and had heard back from everyone—even Joey. Things were still shaky between us, but at least he'd started talking to me again over the past few weeks.

I had one new message, from my closest friend, Jillian.

Have fun in the mountains! Don't do anything I wouldn't do ;)

I chuckled, and responded, *Thanks! I'll do my best.*

Then I unzipped the front pocket of my suitcase and placed the phone inside. Just because Utopia didn't have internet didn't mean I wasn't going to bring my phone with me. I might not have been as attached to it as Mira, but I still couldn't imagine leaving it behind.

Suddenly, a ball of fire lit up in Shivani's hand.

Mira stopped typing mid-sentence and dropped her arm to her side.

I stared hungrily at the fire. Its warmth called to me, and the tip of the flame tilted in my direction.

"Gemma," Ethan said my name tightly. "Stop."

Right. No magic.

I centered myself and forced myself to look away from the flame.

Once the fire was gone, I looked back at Shivani's hand. She held a letter—parchment inked with cursive, like it had come from the past.

"How come you can use magic but we can't?" Mira asked.

"Fire messages are sent with witch magic, not elemental magic," Shivani said in that calm, patient way of hers. "Whatever's tracking you can only track dragon magic."

"Which is why we need to learn how to use our witch magic," I said.

She frowned—looking at me in pity—then wiped the expression from her face. But I knew what she'd been thinking.

Our witch magic was too weak to be useful.

"The witches from Utopia will be arriving any moment." She looked to Mira, who was still holding her cell phone. "It's time to put that away."

Mira frowned and kept typing.

"Mira," Mom said sternly, but she just typed faster.

"You don't want to get off on the wrong foot with these witches." I raised an eyebrow at my twin. "Do you?"

Mira stopped typing, and she shoved the phone into her suitcase without clicking the lock button.

She was still zipping her bag shut when four people appeared at the side of the room.

Two girls around my and Mira's age, and two women around Mom's age. One of the girls had brown shoulder-length hair and small, serious eyes. The other girl had shiny, jet-black hair that hung straight down to her waist. The women looked like older versions of each of them—I guessed they were their moms. And they all wore fitted animal skins, like they'd time traveled in from the Stone Age.

The girl with long black hair smiled warmly and bounced on her heels. "You must be Gemma," she said to me, and then she turned to Mira. "And Mira."

"Yep," I said, already feeling like she and I would get along well.

"Hi," she said. "I'm Harper."

The older woman who I guessed was her mom introduced herself as Tanya.

"And I'm Carrie," the other woman said. "With my daughter, Alice. We've been sent to bring the four of you to Utopia." She gave away no emotion as she appraised us. Then she turned to Ethan, and suspicion filled her fish-like eyes.

Supernatural men weren't allowed in Utopia. The queen of Utopia—Elizabeth—had made an exception for Ethan because Rosella had requested it, but Rosella had already warned us that the women of Utopia would be less than friendly to Ethan.

Ethan held Carrie's gaze until Carrie looked away.

"I'm Rachael," Mom said, breaking the silence.

Carrie nodded, then glanced at our bags. "Those won't be coming with us," she said.

Mira rested her hand protectively on top of her suitcase. "But we need our stuff."

I moved closer to my suitcase, too. Not because of the clothes inside of it, like I knew Mira had done, but because of my books.

"Everything you need will be supplied by the queen," Carrie said. "Now, let's join hands in a circle—one of us between each of you—and we'll teleport you to Utopia."

10

GEMMA

The ground disappeared under my feet, and my stomach dropped, like it did on a roller coaster. But the feeling only lasted a second, and the next thing I knew, I was standing on soft, grassy land.

We were on top of a mountain so tall that it nearly reached the clouds. Fields stretched out in the valleys between the mountains, and I saw the ocean in the distance. The ocean should have been familiar and comforting, but with the mist rolling off the water, it was so different from the bright blue ocean at home.

"Welcome to Mount Starlight," Harper said. "What do you think?"

"It's beautiful," I said, continuing to gaze around in wonder.

"Just wait until you're inside." Her eyes sparkled in excitement, and she looked at the crater on the top of the mountain.

Mira followed Harper's gaze to the rim, and she stilled. Anxiety radiated off her skin.

Because Utopia was *inside* the volcano. The volcano was dormant, which I knew simply from the fact that I couldn't feel the warmth of magma below. According to Rosella, the witches who'd found the volcano a thousand years ago had used their magic to clear out the magma chambers so they could build the kingdom inside.

The witches led us to the crater, and the ground hummed under my feet, like it was welcoming me to the kingdom.

Mira trudged behind. She looked wary, but Ethan held her hand, and soon, we were all standing around the crater's rim.

An open, steel contraption that looked like a rustic freight elevator hung in the center. Cables held it to the top, and it appeared to operate by a crude rope and pulley system.

"Don't worry." Alice smirked and stepped onto the platform. "It's safe."

My mom walked up to it warily. "Why can't we teleport into the kingdom?" she asked.

"Utopia has multiple levels of protection," Tanya explained. "The dome around

Mount Starlight keeps out everyone except those transported inside by the witches who live here. Then there's another spell cast inside the volcano, to stop teleportation to and from the kingdom's chambers. So even if someone managed to break through the dome—which has never happened—they'd still have a ways to go before reaching our home."

"Utopia is the safest place in the world," Harper added, and she walked over to the platform and gracefully hopped down into it. It creaked under her weight, but she didn't seem to notice.

"And this is the only way inside." Carrie motioned to the platform. "Please, after you." She watched us in amusement, like she was waiting for us to chicken out.

I gathered my hair over my shoulder and shot her a small smile. "Thanks," I said, and the ground cushioned my steps as I walked toward the edge of the crater with what I hoped was as much ease as Harper.

Harper smirked up at me in challenge, and I hopped down onto the platform.

It moved a bit, and I reached for the rail to steady myself, a thrill passing through me.

"Not so hard," Harper said.

"Nope," I agreed. "Not hard at all."

I looked up at the others, caught off guard by the way Ethan's eyes blazed as he gazed down at me. Was that... admiration?

He turned to Mira before I could figure it out.

My twin had stepped back, and she'd crossed her arms over her chest, like she was protecting herself.

Ethan rested his hand on the small of her back. "I'll be behind you the entire time," he assured her. "And Gemma will help you inside." He glanced at me when he said my name, and I nodded.

"It's completely solid," I assured her as the platform creaked under my feet. "If you can stand on a surfboard, then standing on this is a breeze."

She closed her eyes and took a deep breath, inhaling the crisp mountain air. When she opened her eyes again, they glinted with the same determination as when the surf was particularly strong and she was set to conquer the waves.

She made her way toward the crater, and Ethan and I helped her onto the platform. She was shaking a bit, and her face was pale, but she did it.

Mom went next, followed by Harper and Alice's moms, then finally, Ethan. He hopped onto the platform like it was nothing, and didn't even reach for the railing. Instead, he made his way to Mira's side.

"You okay?" he asked her.

"Yep." She nodded, even though she looked like she was about to be sick.

With everyone finally on the platform, I glanced down. Lights like stars twinkled below, leading into the abyss.

"How far down does this thing go?" I asked.

"A bit over two hundred meters," Alice said as she stepped to the lever on the side of the platform. "The ride can be a bit jerky, so you might want to hold onto the rails."

She pulled the lever, the platform shook, and we descended into the volcano.

We quickly reached the tiny stars, and I looked around in awe. Because they weren't stars—they were glowworms. Living organisms that hung from the rocks by strings of their own creation. They glowed a soft blue, and it felt like we were traveling into another universe.

"I've always wanted to visit the glowworm caves in New Zealand," I said as I looked around.

"So you know what they are," Harper said. "Not all of our visitors do."

"I've never heard of them," Ethan said.

"That's because you're American," Mom said, as if it were some kind of insult.

"I'm not American," he said. "I'm from Ember."

We all silenced at the mention of his home realm.

"From where?" Harper asked.

"Ember," I repeated. "The dragon realm."

She looked just as confused as before.

"You haven't heard of it?"

From the way Ethan and Rosella had spoken of Ember, I'd assumed all supernaturals knew of the realm.

"We don't know much about dragons," she said. "Except for—"

"Harper," Alice cut her off. "Don't ruin it."

Harper pressed her lips together, like it was taking all of her energy not to continue.

"Ruin what?" Curiosity brewed inside me.

"If we tell you now, then it won't be a surprise," Alice said, and then she pushed the lever, slowing the elevator down.

I glanced over the rail, and leaned forward to get a better look at the city below. The stone buildings were natural extensions of the walls, and they continued down for what must have been over a kilometer. They were linked by rickety wooden bridges, and orbs of orange light lit up the city like small suns. And straight down the center, at the bottom of the vertical city, was a large, crystal clear lake.

Mira relaxed at the sight of the water.

"How many witches live here?" I asked.

"Thousands," Tanya said. "And there are about a thousand vampires, too."

I spun around to face her and gripped the rail behind me, waiting for her to say she was joking.

She didn't.

Mira and Mom looked as shocked as I felt. Ethan, of course, seemed unfazed.

Like he knew about this.

The elevator landed on top of the tallest building in the city, but I made no move to hop out.

"Vampires," I said, like I was testing out the word on my tongue. "You're joking. Right?"

"Why would I be joking?" Tanya asked.

"Because vampires..." I almost said, *because vampires don't exist*, but I stopped myself. Because witches existed, and dragons existed, and prophetesses existed, and monsters like the griffin existed. I'd wondered about other supernaturals, but I didn't think we'd be descending into a den of *vampires*.

"Vampires are dangerous," Mom said, and she walked over to stand protectively in front of me and Mira. "They're murderers. Take us back to the surface. *Now*."

"We're not going anywhere," Carrie said. "The vampires in Utopia pose no threat."

"Witch blood tastes terrible to them," Tanya added. "Don't worry. We're safe."

Mom didn't budge, so I walked around her. "What about dragon blood?" I asked.

"I don't know," Tanya said, and she looked to Ethan. "Has Rosella tasted your blood?"

No way.

All eyes went to Ethan, who looked as stoic as ever.

Mira stepped away from him. "Why would Rosella want to taste your blood?"

"Because Rosella's a vampire," he said simply. "She didn't want to mention it to you—and she asked me to say nothing—because it would delay your decision about coming to Utopia. And we needed to get you here quickly."

"So you lied to us."

"I did what I had to do to keep you safe," he said, and then he glanced at me. "Both of you."

Warmth heated my core at his protective gaze.

Mom's eyes swirled with anger. "You sent my daughters into a *pit full of vampires* without bothering to warn us about what we were walking into," she said, loudly enough that the women walking the paths below looked up to see what was going on.

"You're causing a scene," Carrie said.

"You bet I am."

Carrie stared at my mom, then nodded in what might have been respect. "Arguing about this here will do no good for any of us," she said. "Let us escort you to your quarters. Then, once we're there, we'll explain everything."

11

GEMMA

The witches walked us down a flight of steps, to a rickety bridge. I held onto the rope railings the entire time, hoping it wouldn't snap. Once across, we walked down a path lined with simple stone houses.

Everyone cleared the way for us, watching us curiously.

Their gazes were mainly on Ethan.

Tanya stopped in front of a wooden door identical to the others. "These guest quarters are reserved for witches from other kingdoms when they visit," she said.

Carrie removed a bone-colored skeleton key from her satchel, unlocked the door, and swung it open. The walls of the small living room were stone, and the simple wood furniture matched the flooring. The only pop of color was the faded red rug beneath the sofa and armchair surrounding the fireplace.

A platter of bread, cheeses, and sliced meat sat on the coffee table, and an orange ball of magic lit the hearth with a warm, welcoming glow.

I loved it.

There were also three open doors along the walls that led to bedrooms. Each was decorated in a similar sparse manner as the living room.

"Looks like me and you are sharing a room," I said to Mira.

"The three of you will each have your own room," Carrie said stiffly. "We'd never allow such valued guests to share."

"But there are four of us," Mira said.

"There are three *women*." Carrie raised her chin. "The boy will stay in the men's chamber."

"I will not." Ethan stepped forward, and the specks of orange around his pupils glowed. "I'm the twins' protector. I need to remain as close to them as possible at all times."

"The twins are well protected in Utopia," she said. "You should be grateful that the queen is allowing you to stay here at all."

"A bit of extra safety never hurt anyone," he said. "I'll sleep on the couch."

"It's against protocol. However, you're free to take the matter up with the queen when we take you to see her."

"And when will that be?"

"Today." She glanced at me and Mira. "After they're prepared for what to expect."

He nodded, apparently understanding what she meant. "Great. I will."

Mira rested her hand on his arm, but he didn't move or look at her.

Tanya clicked the door shut and walked to the center of the room. "Before we introduce you to the queen, I believe we have a conversation to continue." She motioned to the sofa and armchair. "Please, sit. Harper and Alice—bring over the chairs from the table so there are enough seats for all of us."

The girls did as instructed, and the four witches sat on the kitchen chairs. Ethan took the plush armchair, and Mom, Mira, and I made ourselves comfortable on the sofa.

Tanya motioned to the platter of food. "All our food is grown and produced in the kingdom," she said. "Help yourselves."

Ethan leaned back in his chair and crossed his arms. "I'm not hungry," he said.

"Very well," she said. "But I hope you're able to work up an appetite before meeting the queen. It's customary in all kingdoms to break bread before entering into an important discussion or deal."

He nodded, although he made no move for the food.

But I *was* hungry, so I made myself a small cheese and meat sandwich. The bread was still warm, and it was delicious.

"You say the vampires here pose no threat, since they don't drink witch blood," my mom launched back into the previous conversation. "But I assume they must feed somehow."

"Correct," Carrie said. "Thus, we have the men's chamber."

I nearly choked on my sandwich, but I forced the bite down. "You keep the men here as *sacrifices* for the vampires?" I asked.

"Of course not." Tanya chuckled. "It's illegal for the vampires in Utopia to drain humans dry. They drink until they're satiated, and no more."

"And how do the men feel about their role as living blood banks?"

"They're grateful," she said. "All of the human men in Utopia were rescued from dire living situations. They have a home here, and they're taken care of for life. They want for nothing."

"In exchange for being fed on by vampires," my mom said darkly.

"The experience is pleasurable for everyone involved," Tanya said with a small smirk. "And there's no lack of women for our men to choose from. In fact, there's no need for anyone to choose at all. The majority of us don't mind sharing."

Mom raised an eyebrow, but said nothing.

"I'm interested in seeing the men's chamber." I wanted to see where Ethan would be living, so I'd know where to find him for any reason.

"Looking to have some fun during your time here?" Harper asked.

"No." My cheeks warmed, and I looked down at the half-eaten sandwich in my hands. "Nothing like that."

"Oookay." She didn't sound like she believed me. "Maybe you'll change your mind after you meet them. Our recruiters only select the most attractive men."

Ethan sat straighter and glared at her. "Gemma and Mira can't afford any distractions."

"I thought you were their protector," she said. "Not their keeper."

"I'm here to help them learn how to use their magic. To do that, they need to stay focused."

"I think they can decide what keeps them focused." She smirked, clearly baiting him, but he stared her down until she looked away.

Tanya looked back and forth between Harper and Ethan, amused. Then she looked to me and Mira. "There are clothes for you in your wardrobes," she said. "Rosella passed along your sizes. You'll need to change so you blend in. Then we'll get Ethan situated in the men's chamber, and take the four of you to meet Queen Elizabeth."

12

GEMMA

The animal skin skirt and top were surprisingly comfortable. So were the shoes. They reminded me of moccasins, and they were lined with wool.

Mira hated the clothes, but I didn't mind them.

Once we were dressed, Carrie led us to another elevator platform. The front doors were made of bars, and they clasped together in the center, like elevators from the early twentieth century.

Alice pulled the lever, and we started our descent. We didn't stop until we reached the bottom.

Brightly colored fish swam in the crystal clear lake, which reflected the city, making it look twice its actual size. There were even small parks with short bushy trees.

People chatted happily as they walked, many of them carrying baskets of what smelled like freshly baked bread and sweet fruit. Mainly women, but I spotted some men, too. The ground floor was all restaurants and shops, just like most major cities, and they were busy with customers.

"Quit dallying," Carrie said. "You'll have plenty of time to explore later."

We walked along a path next to the lake, then branched off and headed toward a wide entrance to a cave.

Mira stopped and bit her lower lip. "We're leaving the city?" she asked.

"As its name implies, the men's chamber is in a separate magma chamber from the main city," Carrie said. "We have to walk through a lava tube to get there."

Mira nodded, put on a brave face, and we continued forward.

The dampness inside the tunnel clung to me as we walked, and the surrounding rocks hummed with energy that warmed my skin. Orange orbs along the ceiling lit the way.

Three women passed by on the right. They smiled politely, and as I nodded back in greeting, I inhaled a sharp, metallic scent. I recognized the scent—from Ethan's house.

Ethan's house that he'd lived in with Rosella.

Rosella, who was a *vampire*.

I waited until the women were far enough away, then turned to Harper. "They're vampires, aren't they?" I asked.

"The smell's impossible to miss." She crinkled her nose and smiled.

"So vampires smell metallic, and witches smell floral," I said, guessing that the sweet smell of the witches wasn't perfume. She nodded, and I continued, "What do dragons smell like?"

"Spicy," she said. "You and Mira smell mainly like dragon. It covers up your witch smell so much that I wouldn't realize you had witch blood if I didn't know otherwise."

"Spicy," Mira repeated. "Like Ethan's cologne?"

"I don't wear cologne," he said with an amused smirk. "Never needed it. This spiciness is all natural."

"You've gotta be kidding me." Mira groaned. "I'm gonna be walking around smelling like *cologne?*"

"Would that be so terrible?" Ethan asked.

"Yes. It absolutely would." She ran her fingers through her hair, as if trying to mask her dragon scent with the lavender smell of her shampoo.

"Then it's a good thing that all supernatural scents can be either masculine or feminine," he said. "You and Gemma smell like fresh cinnamon rolls. It's nice."

Mira reached for my arm, held my wrist up to her nose, and sniffed. "It does smell nice." She smiled. "I suppose I can live with that."

The tunnel widened, and we stepped out into another chamber—a much smaller one than we'd been in before. Like the other chamber, stacks of stone houses climbed up the walls. In the center of it all was a park.

Men strolled along the pathways with women—sometimes with one woman, but many with two or three. A few women walked with multiple men, too. And the men only wore animal skin pants—their chests were bare. Their perfectly defined bodies had to either be from hitting the gym, or from magic.

"I told you they're all attractive." Harper grinned.

My cheeks heated, and I yanked my gaze away from a man in his twenties who was passing by with a woman on each arm.

Tanya led us down a path to the tallest stack of houses, although it was only a fraction of the height of the ones in the main chamber. "This is where we house the older teens," she said. "Let's head in and get Ethan situated."

13

GEMMA

We entered into the common area of the building, which had the same hardwood floor, low ceiling, and stone walls as the quarters where I'd be staying with Mom and Mira. But this space was much larger, with multiple groupings of sofas and chairs. Men in their twenties sat around some of the tables, and they all turned to look at us as we entered.

But I didn't pay them much attention. Because bookcases lined the walls, and I hurried to the nearest shelf to examine the spines.

They were mainly thrillers, mysteries, and what looked to be military science fiction. I'd read a few of them, but none of the military stuff, since that wasn't a genre I liked.

Someone walked up beside me—Harper. "Come on," she said, and she tugged on my hand. "I want you to meet one of my best friends, Benjamin."

She dragged me to one of the central seating areas, where Alice was standing with a tall, blond guy who looked to be a few years older than us. He was so muscular that he could have been a cover model for a male fitness magazine.

The adults had all stepped to the side, giving us our space.

"Benjamin," Harper said excitedly when we reached him. "These are my new friends—the twins I was telling you about. Gemma and Mira."

"Welcome to the man cave." He flashed us a pearly white grin.

Despite still not knowing what I thought about the whole "human men's chamber" thing, I couldn't help it—I laughed.

His blue eyes twinkled, like my amusement made him happy. "How are you liking Utopia so far?" he asked.

"It's... different," I said slowly.

"It's cold," Mira said. "And cramped."

"I take it you're not a city girl?" he asked.

"I'm not an *underground* girl."

"Ah." He nodded. "Earth must not be one of your elements."

45

"You know about our magic?" I asked.

"Harper filled me in." He smiled at her, and she nodded encouragingly. "I needed to know what I was getting into, since Ethan and I will be sharing a suite."

"We'll see about that," Ethan said.

"Damnnn." Benjamin clutched his hands to his heart, like he was wounded. "We've only known each other for a few minutes, and you're rejecting me already?"

"Nothing personal," Ethan said smoothly. "But I'm going to be staying with the twins."

"Really?" Benjamin's confidence gave way to confusion.

"No." Alice sighed and crossed her arms. "He's going to ask the queen if he can stay with the twins, and she's going to say no."

Benjamin's lips curved up into a small smile. "Don't be so sure of that, little witch," he said.

"Why not?"

"Because this chamber is for the *human* men. And our new heartbreaker here is far from human."

Mira stepped closer to Ethan and reached for his hand. "Ethan won't be breaking any hearts here," she said.

Benjamin raised an eyebrow. "The two of you are together?"

"I'm the twins' protector," Ethan said before Mira could answer. "My focus is making sure the twins are safe, and teaching them how to use their magic. My place is with them. With *both* of them." He glanced at me after saying that last part, as if making a point that I was just as important to him as Mira.

My eyes locked on his, but Mira frowned, and I looked away.

"The answer to your question is yes," Mira said to Benjamin. "Ethan and I are together. Which is another reason why he shouldn't be living in this... place." She looked around in distaste.

"No problem," Benjamin said. "I prefer brunettes, anyway." He winked at me, and I froze.

Ethan took his hand out of Mira's and stepped closer to me. He said nothing, but the way he stared Benjamin down said it all.

Don't even think about it.

"Whoa." Benjamin held his hands up in defense. "I didn't realize you were with both of them. My bad."

"He's not with both of us." Mira sneered. "He's *my* boyfriend."

"But I'm here—in this realm—with both of them," Ethan said. "To protect them."

Harper glanced worriedly between the four of us. "Gemma's single," she said quickly. "Right?"

A sharp tug at my chest wished I could say no. With Ethan standing so close to me, and with the pull I felt toward him, it *felt* like I should say no.

But Benjamin was watching me, waiting for an answer.

They were *all* waiting for an answer.

"I am," I said, and I forced what I hoped was a pleasant smile. "But we really *are* here to learn how to use our magic. Our lives depend on it."

"I get it." Benjamin quickly regained his cool, confident air. "But if you ever need to take a break and are up for grabbing a drink, just let me know."

Ethan watched me closely, and his jaw muscle tightened.

"Maybe," I said, getting a small thrill from the annoyance that crossed Ethan's eyes. "I'll see how things go."

"Great." Benjamin's smile widened. "You know where to find—"

He stopped speaking mid-sentence, and his gaze went to the entrance of the building.

A tall, commanding woman stood at door. A vampire, judging by the metallic scent that overpowered the room. She wore animal skins like the rest of us, but she also had multiple belts around her waist, with dried, shrunken *heads* dangling from them. And her lips were stained red with blood.

Revulsion passed through me, but I swallowed it down. Because a crown of bone and teeth sat on her head.

She had to be the queen of Utopia.

Everyone in the room stopped talking, stood, and faced her.

She focused only on me, Mira, and Ethan.

Alice hurried forward and lowered her head in respect. "Your Highness," she said.

"Alice," the queen replied, and Alice looked back up. "I just finished a meal, and I heard you were here."

"What can we do for you?"

"Since I was already passing through, I've come to fetch you, Harper, and our new guests. Because now that they've settled into their quarters, it's time for me to welcome them to the kingdom."

14

GEMMA

The queen escorted me, Mira, Ethan, Mom, Harper, and Alice out of the men's chamber, and through a lava tube that tilted downward, deeper into the volcano. Mira's breathing shallowed, and beads of sweat formed on her forehead.

I desperately wanted to know why the queen only wanted Harper and Alice to come with us, and not their moms. But Harper and Alice said nothing as we walked with the queen, and the three of us did the same. I had zero intention of breaking royal protocol around a vampire queen with bloodstained lips and shrunken heads hanging from her belts.

All of the shrunken heads were male. If she tried anything against Ethan...

Fire sparked inside me at the thought.

Because if she tried anything against Ethan, I'd burn her like I'd burned that griffin.

The lava tube gradually became larger, and we emerged into a small cavern held up with columns of rock. An arched stone bridge with no handrails led the way over a narrow canyon, to a throne inside an open-mouthed dragon skull.

The skull was huge—about three times the height of the throne. Its sharp teeth pointed downward, and the roof of its mouth created a canopy above the throne.

"The dragon bones were gifts from your ancestors," the queen said as she made her way across the bridge. She stopped a few meters away from the throne, her back toward us, and admired the massive skull.

"Our ancestors knew dragons?" I asked, my voice amplified by the acoustics of the cavern.

The queen turned around, smiled, and sat on her throne. "I will answer your question," she said. "But first, we must break bread. Rosella is a trusted friend of mine, and I've promised her that I'll keep you safe during your time in my kingdom. So come closer, and stand before me."

Mira's grip around my hand tightened. Her face was so pale that she looked like she was about to pass out.

"It's okay," I whispered to her, softly enough that I hoped the queen couldn't hear. "She wants to help us. Plus, we have our magic. And there's air and earth all around us."

If it hadn't been for the slight breeze against my skin, I wouldn't have thought she'd processed my words.

She inhaled, and together, we walked across the bridge. The others followed, until we stood in front of the queen.

She reached into a satchel hanging next to one of the shrunken heads and pulled out a few small crackers that looked like communion wafers.

Harper walked forward, her long black hair shining under the magical orange light, took a cracker, and popped it into her mouth. Alice did the same.

Ethan pushed ahead of me and Mira to go next.

Probably to make sure the crackers weren't poisoned.

He finished his cracker, then turned to face us, and nodded.

Mira and I approached the queen together. My heart pounded so quickly that she must have been able to hear it.

"Gemma." She looked at me, then at my sister. "Mira. Welcome to Utopia." She held out the crackers, and Mira and I each took one. I tried to stop myself from shaking as I popped it in my mouth.

The cracker tasted as bland as it looked.

The queen nodded, and we joined the others. Mom took her turn, and then the queen popped the final cracker into her mouth, chewed, and swallowed.

"Back to your question," the queen said, her hard gaze focused on me. "The witches of the Gemini circle bonded with dragons for the short time that dragons lived on Earth. They were dragon riders, and they helped the Nephilim kill the last of the demons."

Demons. Nephilim.

How many types of supernaturals *were* there?

"What year was this?" Mom asked.

The queen opened her mouth to answer, but Ethan jumped in first. "My ancestors ventured out of Ember to explore Earth in the late fifth century," he said. "But once the demons were gone, the Nephilim turned on us. So, after only a brief time on Earth, we were driven back to Ember. We've been trapped there ever since." His eyes darkened, like they did every time he mentioned his home realm.

Why are the dragons trapped in Ember?

But I knew Ethan wouldn't answer.

So I turned to Mom. "Was that when the dragons gifted our ancestors with their magic?"

"Much information was lost between then and now," she said. "But yes, that would make sense."

"My people started talking about the prophecy of the Dragon Twins after they were driven out of Earth," Ethan said. "It lines up."

"It does." The queen nodded. "And speaking of the prophecy, I'd like to see what the two of you can do."

"I was gifted with control over fire and earth," I said. "Mira has air and water."

"I didn't ask you to *tell* me what you can do," she said. "I asked you to show me."

"We haven't trained. I don't want to accidentally hurt anyone…"

"I'm an original, immortal vampire." She bristled. "Nothing you can do will hurt me."

I thought back to how I'd charred that griffin down to the bones, and wasn't entirely sure that was true.

Ethan turned his palm up to face the sky, and a small flame danced in his hand. "You're a natural," he said to me. "You've got this."

I took a deep breath, turned my palm to the ceiling, and stared at it. I imagined a flame dancing on my skin, like it had for Ethan.

Nothing.

Why isn't it working?

The queen crossed one leg over the other and leaned back in her throne. "I'm waiting," she said.

A spark lit up inside me, and I reached for it, pushing it up toward my hand. A tiny flame emerged from my palm... but it died out a second later.

I sucked in a sharp breath, shocked and embarrassed.

Then something cracked to my right.

I looked over just as a few stones broke off the nearest column and tumbled to the bottom of the canyon.

I shuffled my feet and rubbed my still warm palm against my skirt.

"Fire and earth. You have work to do," the queen said, and she turned to Mira. "Your turn."

Mira stood completely still. She was barely even breathing.

"Ethan," I said quickly. "Light up your fire again, and let Mira use her air magic to blow it out."

He nodded and did as I asked. The fire lit up his eyes—or his eyes were glowing from using his magic.

"Think about what it felt like when we fought the griffin," I said to Mira. "You can—"

"I can do this." She sounded stronger now—more like the Mira I knew. "I know." She raised her arm so her palm faced Ethan's flame, stared at the fire, and narrowed her eyes in concentration.

I thought the fire swayed toward Ethan, but I couldn't be sure.

A breeze prickled my arm, and the fire moved again. It nearly blew out, but like those trick candles Mira had bought for our birthday one year, the flame didn't extinguish completely, and it rose back up.

Ethan closed his fist, and the fire snuffed out.

"I suppose that was good enough for now," the queen said with a bored sigh. "You said you can control water, too?"

"There's no water in here." Mira looked around helplessly.

"There's water in the air. Humidity. Do something with that."

"That's highly advanced water magic," Ethan said. "She's not at that level yet."

"Yet, Gemma was worried about losing control of her magic and possibly hurting me." She raised an eyebrow. "Why such confidence when you clearly have much to learn?"

"I shot blazes of fire at the griffin," I said. "Ethan and I burned it to a crisp."

"And now you can barely create a flame?"

"It could have been the adrenaline." I shrugged. "I don't know."

"That played a part," Ethan said. "But you'd also just gotten your magic."

"So shouldn't it have been *harder* for us to use?"

"Not necessarily," he said. "Dragons are born with elemental magic—it's pretty weak until we reach our teens, but it's there. But when we receive our shifting magic, it's intense. The magic hasn't fully settled in yet—it's new and volatile—so we immediately and uncontrollably shift into our dragon form. But it only takes a few hours for the magic to settle. Then, once it does, we have to learn how to dig into the magic, harness it, and control it. It's not easy. It takes some dragons up to a year to learn how to fully control their shifting—some even more. It would make sense for your elemental magic to behave in a similar way."

"Like I said, the two of you have work to do," the queen said, and then she zeroed in on Mira. "And you still haven't demonstrated your water magic."

Mira looked to Ethan for help.

"You'll eventually be able to control water," he said. "Including the droplets in the air. But when water elementals create their element—like Gemma and I did with fire—it's almost always in the form of ice."

"Why?" she asked.

"There aren't scientific reasons of *why* behind magic," I jumped in, since this had always been one of the biggest differences between me and my twin. She trusted logic, and I trusted intuition. "It just exists."

"That's not an explanation."

"Gemma's right," Ethan said, and Mira's face fell. "There's no scientific formula behind this. Ice is the opposite of fire. It's the most natural for water elementals to use."

"So what am I supposed to create?" she asked. "An icicle?"

"That would be useful," he said, and the corner of his lips curled up into a knowing smirk. "Especially to hurl into an enemy's heart."

Mira looked at Ethan like she didn't recognize him. Then she turned back to face the queen, held her hand in front of her, and stared at it in intense concentration.

Come on, I thought. *You can do it.*

Finally, just when she looked about to give up, a thin sheen of ice formed across Mira's palm. It crystalized, so it looked like snow.

"Stop," the queen said. "You're straining yourself."

Mira let out a short breath and dropped her hand back down. The ice disappeared instantly.

I walked to her side, also facing the queen, and said softly, "You did great."

"You did better," she said.

I nodded, since I *had* done better, and we both knew it.

"Neither of you did well," the queen said, and I pressed my lips together. "If you want to beat whatever's coming after you, then you'll need more magic than that. Luckily, you have Ethan, Harper, and Alice to train you. Ethan with dragon magic, and Harper and Alice with witch magic."

I turned to look at Harper and Alice. "*You're* our teachers?" I asked.

"Yeah." Harper smirked. "Why so surprised?"

"I thought we'd be taught by someone older. Someone with more experience."

"We're two of the strongest witches in Utopia," Alice said. "Any witch here would be thrilled to train with us. And judging by how weak your witch scent is, any one of them probably has more potential than either of you."

"But can they do this?" I opened my palm again, and a fire danced along the top of it —more than I'd been able to call forth when the queen had asked. The flame grew taller, then puffed out.

"No." Alice's expression was as stern as ever. "They can't."

Harper's eyes gleamed with excitement, and she rubbed her palms together. "This is going to be fun," she said.

"GIRLS," the queen said, and our attention zipped back to her. She was standing, and she looked down at us with authority. "Harper, bring the twins and their mother back to their quarters. Alice, see the boy back to the men's chamber."

"About that," Ethan said, and the queen's attention snapped to him. "I'm the twins' official protector. Due to the exceptional circumstances, I want to stay with them in their quarters while we're here."

"Absolutely not," she said.

"The order for me to protect them was issued by the King of Ember," he continued. "I insist that you reconsider."

"We're not in Ember." Her voice was tight, like it was taking all her restraint to stop herself from attacking him. "We're in Utopia, where *I'm* queen. And every male here lives in the men's chamber. No exceptions."

"Every *human* male," he said. "This situation is different."

"You're correct—it's different." She took a few snake-like steps toward him, then stopped and rested a hand on top of one of the shrunken heads hanging from her belt. "You're the most powerful male currently residing in this kingdom. Which makes it even more important that you not lodge in the main chamber, where our women sleep and are therefore most vulnerable."

"I'd never try anything against—"

"ENOUGH." The word echoed throughout the cavern. "I assume you trust that the twins will be safe in Utopia. Otherwise, why did you bring them here?"

He pressed his lips together, standing completely still. "I do believe they're safe here," he finally said. "However, they'd be extra safe with me by their sides at all times."

"Are you asking me to endanger my women by allowing you to live in the main chamber?"

"I wouldn't be endangering your women. I'm not going to hurt *anyone* here."

"According to you." She looked at him like he was no better than dirt. "Is it not enough that I'm letting you stay here? To *train* here?"

"It's more than enough."

"Good. Because if I sense anything but gratitude, I won't hesitate to have you removed from my kingdom."

Stop fighting her, I thought. *This is getting us nowhere. Actually, it's* hurting *us.*

After a few extremely tense seconds, Ethan clenched his fists by his sides and lowered his gaze. "I appreciate your generosity, Your Highness," he said, although the words sounded forced. "I'll sleep in the men's chamber at night, as you insist. But I'll be by the twins' sides at every moment while awake."

She raised her chin, appearing satisfied with his submission. "We're done here," she said. "Go with Harper and Alice to continue getting settled into your quarters. Your lessons start tomorrow, and not only will I need a progress report each week, but I require that this progress be made quickly. Understood?"

"Yes, Your Highness," Harper and Alice said in unison, and then they led the way out of the throne room.

15

GEMMA

Mira made a *huge* deal of telling Ethan goodbye when we reached the tunnel that led to the men's cavern, wrapping her arms around his waist, kissing him, and telling him how much she'd miss him.

"You know he's not sailing across the Pacific, right?" Alice asked. "You'll see him in the morning."

I bit the inside of my cheek to stop from chuckling.

Mira rolled her eyes and turned to the witch. "Have you ever even had a boyfriend?" she asked.

"That's none of your concern." She bristled. "Let's go."

Mira kissed Ethan again—for an extra long time—and then Ethan walked with Alice down the tunnel that led to the men's chamber.

Harper's shiny, dark hair swung back and forth as she led the way back to the main chamber. "Your books are in your rooms," she said. "Look them over tonight—especially the one about history. That's the boring stuff, and I'd rather get it out of the way so we can move onto the fun stuff."

"You mean magic?" I asked.

"What else would I mean?" She smiled, and I did, too.

Harper's energy was contagious, which was more than welcome, since Mira kept looking around like something was going to jump out at her at any moment.

We stepped into the elevator, rode it back up to the top of the city, and returned to our quarters. Like Harper had promised, Mira and I each had a pile of old, dusty books waiting on our nightstands.

"As long as you don't need anything else, I'll leave you to it." Harper glanced at the books. "Because you've got a lot of reading to do."

Mira, Mom, and I walked into my room, and Mom and I started flipping through the books the moment Harper left. The thickest one was about the history of the supernatural world—the one Harper wanted us to focus on tonight. There was one for spells, one for potions, and more.

Mira didn't touch any of the books. It was like she thought they were dusted with poison.

I reached for the spell book and started skimming through it. It was far more descriptive than the spell book that had been passed down the Gemini line.

Mom reached for the book and eased it out of my hands. "Harper told you to start with history," she said. "Not spells."

"I was just curious."

"I'm sure you were. But so am I. So I'll be taking over that book for the night."

We shared a smile, and I was sure she'd be up all night reading, too.

Sure enough, she walked into the living room, made herself comfortable in the big armchair, and started digging into the book.

Mira still stood in the corner, her arms crossed over her chest.

"I'll give you a summary of the history before we go to sleep," I said, and then I grabbed the book on potions and held it out to her. "Why don't you start with this?"

She made no move to take the book. "You're just saying that because I like chemistry."

"Yeah. I am. But it's not like we have much else to do. You might as well start with something you like."

"We could always leave," she said, and she glanced at the door. "We know where the men's chamber is. We could get Ethan, and get out of here."

"We can't leave," I said.

"Why not? We're guests—not prisoners."

From the way her voice wavered, I knew she knew the truth as much as I did. She just wasn't ready to face it. So I sat down on the bed and patted the spot next to me.

She sighed and sat down.

We crossed our legs and faced each other, like we'd done during serious conversations since we were kids.

"You know what's out there," I started. "That griffin could have killed us. We have to stay here so we can learn how to defend ourselves—and learn how to stop whoever's tracking us from finding us."

I'd say it a million times if that was what it took to drill the truth into her ridiculously thick skull.

"I know," she said, and she looked around the plain, wooden room. "But I don't like it here. It's stifling—it's hard to breathe."

I pulled in a long breath, finding the earthy air as refreshing as ever. "We only got here a few hours ago," I said. "You just need some time to get used to it."

"I'll never get used to it."

"Maybe not," I said. "But we'll be safe here. That's what matters."

"We'll be safe in a city inside a volcano that's filled with witches, vampires, and the human men they feed on for blood?"

We looked at each other for a long second, then broke out into unrestrained laughter.

"This is all crazy," I said when we eventually stopped laughing.

She wiped away a tear from the side of her eye. "Finally, something we agree on."

"Here's the thing," I said, serious again. "We *can* get out of here. But first, we need to learn how to use our magic. So what do you say?" I held the potions book out to her again. "Do you want to get out of here, or what?"

She took a deep breath, and her eyes filled with newfound determination. "I do," she said, although she stood up and headed out of my room without taking the book.

"Where are you going?" I asked.

"To get the history book from my room. Harper said we should start there, so that's what I'm going to do."

16

GEMMA

WE READ until it was so late that we were about to fall asleep in the living room.

The next morning, the orange orbs in my room grew gradually brighter—like the sun rising—to gently wake me up. It was much more pleasant than being jolted awake by an alarm.

A platter of homemade bread, cheese, jam, meats, and fruit waited on the kitchen table.

"Did you let someone in?" I asked Mom.

"No," she said. "Someone must have dropped it off while we were sleeping."

I was famished, so I dug in. So did Mira and Mom. There was even a fresh pot of coffee on the counter. It wasn't as good as what we brewed at the café, but it did the job.

We were polishing off the loaf of bread when there was a knock on the door.

I jumped to my feet and hurried to see who was there.

Harper and Alice. Alice looked as pristine as ever, but Harper's hair was pulled up in a messy bun, her eyes glazed over.

"Is everything okay?" I asked.

"Besides the fact that it's *way* too early for anyone to be awake?" she said with a giant yawn.

"Not a morning person?" I asked.

"That's the understatement of the century."

I let them in, and Harper went straight for the coffee. "Is it okay if I have some?" she asked, already pouring a cup.

"Go ahead," I said, and she proceeded to drink it black.

"Since you didn't have time to go to the market yesterday, my mom brought you breakfast this morning," Alice said. "I see you enjoyed it."

"It was delicious," I said.

"Good," she said, and she looked to Mom. "My mom will be by in a bit, and she'll show you around the shops so you can stock up."

Worry crossed my mom's face. "What kind of currency do you take?"

"No currency," Alice said. "We all contribute to the kingdom, and we're allowed to take what we need."

"Interesting," my mom said, nodding in approval.

Harper placed her now-empty coffee mug down on the table, her eyes already sparkling with some of the life I'd seen in them yesterday. "How'd your reading go last night?" she asked.

"Good," I said. "I got to the part where the dark witches cast the spell on the fae to make them allergic to iron."

"You're a fast reader," she said in approval. "Now, gather your books, and we'll bring you to the training room."

The training room had a long table in the center, a fireplace, and paintings of various places in Utopia.

Ethan was already there. He stood when we entered, and his eyes locked on mine. "How'd you sleep?" he asked.

I froze, unsure why he was asking me instead of Mira.

Mira walked to the chair next to him and dropped her bag of books onto the table. "Fine, given that we're stuck in this stuffy volcano," she said, and then she looked up at him and pouted. "I missed you."

Alice rolled her eyes.

"You, too," Ethan said, although he didn't sound convincing.

But it must have been enough for Mira, because she smiled and situated herself in the seat next to him. She scooted her chair as close to his as possible, their shoulders nearly touching.

Harper reached for a book at the end of the table—the spell book. "Since you got ahead on your history reading last night, we can jump into some of the fun stuff," she said with a mischievous smile. "We've decided to focus on witch magic in the morning, and then Ethan will take over with training your elemental magic in the afternoon. So take out your spell books and turn to chapter one. We'll start with the easy spells, and continue from there."

17

GEMMA

The "easiest" spell involved putting calming energy into a purple and white crystal. Then tonight, we'd place the crystal on our nightstands to help us sleep better.

No matter how hard we focused, neither Mira's nor my crystal glowed.

We were just as unsuccessful with the spell to cleanse our energy, and with what Harper called the "pretty spell"—a spell to smooth out any imperfections on our faces.

"Practice these tonight," Alice said once it was finally lunchtime. "After an hour of history reading."

After lunch, Ethan took over so we could work on our elemental magic, although Harper and Alice stayed in the room. They were curious to see how our elemental magic worked.

Unfortunately, they didn't see anything more than what we'd done yesterday in front of the queen.

"Technically, you should be good with crystal magic, since crystals are part of the Earth," Harper said to me at the end of the day. "Along with any spells that involve candles."

"And you should be good with water and air spells," Alice said to Mira. "And potions. We'll start working on potions next week."

Mira's eyes lit up. "I've always been good at chemistry," she said. "And customers at the café like my drinks way better than Gemma's. Mom just has me work the register because I'm friendlier."

"Not true," I said.

"It is, and you know it."

I shook my head and smiled, since there *were* customers who specifically requested that Mira make their drinks.

"Speaking of the café," Harper said. "Some of our friends stopped by a few weeks ago. Selena, Torrence, Reed, and Julian. Did you meet them?"

"Doesn't sound familiar," Mira said. "But tourists are always coming in and out of the café. We're a famous destination for people to stop at for a drink and pastry at the start of their scenic drive down John Astor Road."

Harper's brow creased. "You would have remembered these four. They're supernaturals who had questions about dragons. Queen Elizabeth sent them your way."

"That *didn't* happen." Mira laughed. "We definitely would have remembered if it did."

But there was something familiar about those names…

"Was this a few days before Christmas?" I asked.

"Yes." Harper sat straighter, and she smiled. "You met them?"

I thought harder, but couldn't put my finger on it. It was like the memory of them ordering drinks at the café was there, but blurry.

"One of the girls had brownish-reddish hair, right?" I asked. "And the other was blonde. With unusual colored eyes…"

"Violet eyes," Harper said. "That's Selena. She's half-witch, half-fae. Only fae have eyes like that."

"I think we talked to them," I said. "But they just came in for a drink and left."

"Hm." Alice sat back and pursed her lips. "Interesting."

"They must have gotten their answer somewhere else," Harper said. "Anyway, it's time for dinner. I heard a certain someone will be at one of my favorite places tonight…" She looked to me and gave me a mischievous smirk.

A pit formed in my stomach.

"Benjamin?" Mira asked.

"Got it in one." Harper smiled at her, then looked back to me. "He asked about you."

Ethan also looked to me, his eyes glowing with sparks of ember. "Do you think that's a smart idea?" he asked. "You have a lot of reading to do. Dinner in your quarters would be far more sensible."

Mira frowned. "A short dinner out won't hurt."

"No." I sighed, hoping I sounded disappointed. "Ethan's right."

"You're no fun." Mira pouted, and then she looked to Ethan for approval. "But fine. We'll do our reading."

"Good choice."

With that, we packed up our books and headed back to our quarters.

And I didn't care how long it took—I wasn't going to sleep tonight until I got that dream spell to work.

18

GEMMA

By the end of the week, I was finally able to do the "easy" spells. But I was still no better at using my fire and earth magic than I'd been when I'd arrived in Utopia.

Mira, on the other hand, was improving. She could create a small icicle in her hand, although it melted pretty quickly.

I needed to catch up.

So I held my hand up in front of myself and steadied my breathing, feeling the embers spark inside me and willing them to come to life.

A small flame ignited in my palm. Excitement rose inside me, and I imagined tethering the flame in place so it wouldn't go out.

"That's it." Ethan watched the fire flicker and dance. "Feed more magic into it, and picture it growing bigger."

I inhaled, imagining that my breath was feeding oxygen to the fire, and pushed more magic into the flame.

It expanded to the size of a tennis ball, and the fire grew taller. The goal was to get it to eye-level. Ethan said that once it got that high, there was enough magic in the fire to keep it under better control.

So I held steady, as focused as ever, watching the flame inch up. Almost to neck-level. Just a bit more...

The cord that connected the magic inside me to the fire in my hand snapped apart, and the fire snuffed out.

I cursed and tried to gather the magic again, but nothing happened.

"All right." Harper brought her feet down from where they'd been resting on the table. "We've pushed ourselves enough for the day."

"I almost had it," I said. "I'll get it next time."

"That's what you said the last five times," Mira said.

"This time felt different. I was so close..."

"Which means you should definitely be able to do it tomorrow," Harper said brightly. "But Friday's the best night to go out. Are you guys in?"

Excitement danced across Mira's face. "Can we go to one of the restaurants by the lake?"

"The *best* restaurants are by the lake." Harper smiled, looking like she was about to bounce out of her seat.

They both looked to me, waiting.

I studied my palm. I'd been so close to getting that fire under control. Just a few centimeters more, and I would have had it.

"You're right about your magic," Ethan said to me before I could answer. "With another try or two, you would have had control over that flame."

"I know."

He held my gaze for another few seconds, and I had to remind myself to breathe. Then he nodded, satisfied, and looked to the others. "The three of you should go to dinner tonight," he said. "I'll stay back with Gemma and help her train."

Mira sat back, shocked. "You don't want to come?"

"I do want to come," he said. "But training comes first. It's my duty to protect the two of you *and* to make sure you can protect yourselves. So I'll stay back and help Gemma."

"I'll stay back, too," Mira said. "It never hurts to practice more. Right?"

"I'd normally agree. But you've been improving steadily this week, which is amazing," he said, and she smiled at the compliment. "Gemma hasn't improved. I feel like it might be easier for her with fewer people watching."

Mira pouted, but she quickly got ahold of herself. "I'm her twin," she said. "I don't count as 'people.'"

I smiled, since it was true.

At the same time, my stomach fluttered at the thought of being alone with Ethan.

Maybe if we were alone together again, I'd know for sure if the connection between us in the cove had been real.

But I shouldn't have been thinking those things about Mira's boyfriend. It was wrong on so many levels.

Why wouldn't my feelings for Ethan just *go away?*

"Mira's right," I forced the words out. "She can stay."

Ethan didn't even look at Mira. "I think it would be best if it were just the two of us," he said.

My heart leaped. "Why?"

"Because Mira doesn't have fire magic. I do. And I can feel her water and air magic in the room even now. It might be easier for you to harness your fire without other elements in the room distracting you."

Mira frowned at the last part.

"It's just a theory, but it's worth a try," he continued. "If it doesn't work, we'll call it a night and meet up with everyone at the restaurant."

I bit my lower lip as I thought about it. Because Mira definitely wanted me to say no.

But if this worked, maybe I could make some forward progress with my magic.

"All right," I said, and Ethan's eyes brightened—like he'd been worried I wasn't going to stay. "Let's do it."

19

GEMMA

ONCE WE WERE ALONE, Ethan walked around the table and sat down in the chair next to me. His skin burned so hot that I felt the warmth against mine.

He was sitting so close that I couldn't bring myself to meet his eyes.

Breathe, I told myself. *Focus.*

"Gemma," he said, his voice soft and soothing. "Look at me."

I did.

Electricity buzzed through me and filled the space between us, just like it had when we'd sat close together on the beach.

If I felt like this from simply being near him, what would it feel like to *touch* him?

Stop.

I moved my chair away to put a few more centimeters of space between us.

He blinked, then snapped back into focus. "I didn't want the others to know until we test it out, but there's more to my theory than I said before," he said. "Because sometimes, dragons who share the same type of elemental magic can boost each others' magic."

"Like when we killed that griffin at the beach," I said, and he nodded. "But why don't you want the others to know?"

"It's not that I don't want the others to know," he said. "It's that I don't want *Mira* to know."

I held his gaze for a few seconds, waiting for him to elaborate.

He didn't.

"You're asking me to keep something from my sister," I said. "I need to know why."

He exhaled slowly, looked off to the side, and then refocused on me. "You and I both have fire magic, and Mira and I both have air magic," he started. "Your magic and my magic boosts each other's. I'm sure of it after what happened at the beach. But my air magic doesn't interact with Mira's the same way. If she knows it didn't work with her and that it worked with you…" He trailed off, like he didn't know how to say it.

"You think she'll be jealous," I said.

"More than that. I think she'll be angry. And you know how she gets when she's angry."

I nodded slowly, since when Mira got angry, things got messy. Like that time Kenny Tannen called me the boring sister, and Mira told our entire class that Kenny was the worst kisser ever. Or the time Pamela Bains tried cheating off one of my tests, so Mira "accidentally" crashed into her while they were surfing. Pamela sprained her ankle so badly that she couldn't surf for months.

"Why would your magic boost mine and not Mira's?" I asked.

"I don't know. But Mira's making good progress, and I don't want to throw her off. Anyway, do you want to try this? Again?" He smiled slightly, as if he was sure it was going to work.

Why wouldn't it, since it already had?

"We're going to have to tell Mira eventually," I said. "You know that, right?"

"I do. But the time has to be right."

"It does." At least we agreed on that. "So, what do I have to do?"

"Exactly what you were doing when you created the flame earlier. Try to get it to eye level."

"And what will you be doing?"

"The same thing." He moved his chair toward me, closing the space I'd created earlier.

Heat swirled through me. Embers of it ignited in my core, ready to be set loose. My magic felt more *alive* than ever.

I sat forward, held my hand out in front of me, and focused. He did the same.

I barely had to tug at my magic before a flame burst out of my palm. Excitement rushed through me, and I glanced over at Ethan.

The flame in his hand was a mirror image of mine. Everything about it was identical, down to the way it flickered and moved.

"Good," he said steadily. "Now, make the flame grow."

The magic warmed within me, and as it did, it fed fuel to the fire. The flame grew to my eye level, and the cord that bonded me to my magic strengthened.

Grow higher.

The flame shot up—all the way to the ceiling. The smell of scorched wood filled the air.

Crap.

I pulled back on the magic, and the fire shrank and disappeared.

Two identical scorch marks had charred the ceiling. One where my fire had been, and another next to it, where Ethan's had been.

"Gemma," Ethan said slowly. "Don't make any sudden moves. Just look at the table."

I did.

The table was levitating a few centimeters off the ground.

The *wooden* table.

I sucked in a sharp breath, my muscles strained, and the table thumped back down onto the floor.

I stared at it in silence. Because the table was huge and heavy, and until I was aware of what was happening, I hadn't felt its weight at all.

I turned my head slowly to face Ethan.

He was watching me with pride. But it was beyond pride. He looked positively mesmerized.

"I did that, didn't I?" I asked, even though I already knew I had.

"You did," he said. "With your earth magic."

"But it wasn't just me. You helped with your magic. I wouldn't have been able to do that if it wasn't for you."

"Yes, you would have," he said. "My magic helped, but that power is inside you. And the earth magic was all you."

My blood heated, and my heart pounded. I heard the faint pulse of another heart, too.

Ethan's.

His heart was beating in time with mine.

A thrill buzzed through me, and we sat there, eyes locked. It was the same way he'd looked at me on the beach. Our magic connected us like magnets, and I didn't want to pull away. Every instinct in my body urged me to move closer, to feel his skin against mine.

It was like Ethan had reached into my soul and left his fingerprints on my heart.

Then my sister's face flashed in my mind. Because if Mira were to walk in and see Ethan and me sitting like this, what would she think? What would she do?

As if he knew what I was thinking, Ethan stood up so quickly that his chair nearly tumbled backward.

"I'd call that a success." He didn't look at me as he spoke. "We should head down to the restaurant to meet up with the others. I'm sure you're hungry."

My stomach rumbled, as if responding on command.

But I couldn't face my sister right now. The guilt would be splattered all over my face, and Mira knew me well enough to see it. And the buzz between Ethan and me was a living, tangible thing. I didn't trust myself to hide it.

I needed time to cool off—to get my feelings back under control.

Especially because these feelings were only a result of Ethan and me sharing the same element.

I couldn't let myself believe anything else.

"I'm actually heading back to my quarters," I said. "I want to practice the spells from this morning. Maybe the increased control over my elemental magic will help with my witch magic, too."

"Good plan." He sounded relieved, and my heart fell. "I'll walk you back."

"No." I stood up and backed away. "Go join the others. I'll be fine."

I spun around and headed out before he could respond.

Leaving him, just like he'd left me that first day at the beach.

Every bone in my body ached to turn around and go to him.

But I ignored it.

And when I got back to my room, I didn't practice any spells. Instead, I got into bed, curled up into a ball under the covers, and cried until falling asleep.

20

GEMMA

Ten days passed, and even though Ethan and I didn't train privately again, I felt the heat of his gaze during our lessons. He helped guide me as much as he helped Mira, but the connection buzzed between us every time he got close to me.

The scorch marks stayed on the ceiling, along with plenty of new ones I'd made during our lessons. Getting a flame to touch the ceiling was easy now. My earth magic had been improving, too. I'd been able to get the table to levitate to right below the ceiling.

Which was exactly what I was doing now. I felt a slight strain on my muscles, but it was nothing I couldn't handle.

"How long do you think you can hold it?" Alice asked.

"An hour?" I guessed. "Maybe more?"

"Well, we don't have an hour, and I'm hungry," Harper said. "Let's stop for the day. We can test out your table-levitating stamina tomorrow."

I was hungry, too. I was always famished after training. So I lowered the table to the ground.

"Gemma," Harper said, sounding much more serious than usual. "I think it's time."

"Time for what?"

"For you to come out to dinner." She smiled, and I sighed in annoyance, since this wasn't the first time we'd had this conversation. "It can't be any good for you to stay cooped up in your quarters," she continued. "Come out. Live a little. Have some *fun*."

"I have fun," I said, although I wasn't even convincing myself. Because since coming to Utopia, I hadn't even *read* for fun, despite knowing where the library was. All I'd been reading were textbooks.

And while it was interesting to learn about the supernatural world, the textbooks were so dry that it wasn't exactly *fun*.

"Fine," I gave in. "I'll go."

"Yes!" Harper pumped a fist in the air, and she gave Mira a high five. "Victory!"

Even Alice smiled.

The only one who didn't look happy was Ethan.

We ended up at a Mexican restaurant overlooking the water. Harper ordered two pitchers of margaritas the moment we sat down.

"Make one of them a virgin," Ethan said.

Harper rolled her eyes, but did as he asked. "Don't worry," she said to me. "You can drink from our pitcher."

"You shouldn't drink," Ethan said. "You need to be on your A-game with training."

His bossy tone stirred up a fire inside me. So when the pitchers came, I reached for the one with alcohol and poured myself so much that it nearly spilled over the top of my glass.

"Maybe you *do* know how to have fun," Harper said with a smile.

Ethan's eyes hardened, and I moved my glass as far away from him as possible, not wanting him to take it from me.

Mira also went for the margarita with alcohol. The only ones who had the virgin drink were Ethan and Alice.

"One of us has to stay sober to keep you protected," Ethan muttered as he poured his drink.

Mira rolled her eyes.

I sat back and took another sip of my drink. I hadn't felt this relaxed since before the ascension ceremony, and Harper was right—it felt good. Like things were normal for a change.

Except that everyone in the restaurant kept glancing over to look at us. They were trying to be discreet, but it wasn't working.

"Have they been doing this every time you go out?" I asked Mira.

"Yep," she said. "Eventually one of them will come up to the table and ask us to show them our magic."

"And you do?"

"No one ever complains about a little ice added to their drink." She pulled an ice cube from the air, plopped it into my margarita, and smiled.

I matched my sister's smile with one of my own, and said, "I guess if anyone needs their food warmed up with a bit of fire, I'm your girl."

The food arrived, and we dug in, barely speaking as we inhaled our tacos.

"What do you think?" Harper asked once we were done eating. "Best tacos you've ever had?"

"For sure," I said, and it was true. The food in Utopia was some of the best I'd ever had, period.

We were hanging out chatting, when just like Mira had said, someone approached the table.

Benjamin.

He smiled at me, then looked at Harper. "You never miss a Margarita Monday, do you?" he asked.

"Never." She sat back in her chair and grinned. Then she looked at me, to Benjamin, and back again.

She'd set this up.

My cheeks heated, my stomach sank, and I wanted to run back up to my room. But I was trapped.

Benjamin ran his fingers through his blond hair and focused on me. "I just finished up, but saw you guys and wanted to say hi," he said. "I hear you've been making incredible progress with your magic."

"I don't know if I'd call it 'incredible,'" I said. "But it's definitely progress."

"I've already seen Mira's." He playfully raised an eyebrow. "Want to show me yours?"

I chuckled, because even though that line would have sounded slimy from most guys, Benjamin was clearly joking. He actually reminded me a bit of Joey, and I understood why he and Harper were friends.

"Sure." I flipped my palm to the ceiling and created a small fireball in my hand. After a few seconds, I snuffed it out.

"Neat," Benjamin said. "I wish I could do that."

"You just wish you weren't human," Harper teased.

"Can you blame me? What you all can do is amazing," he said, and I smiled at how right he was. "Anyway," he continued, returning his attention to me. "Now that you're venturing out, what do you say about that drink we talked about the other day?"

All eyes went to me, and I shifted uncomfortably in my seat.

Especially because one pair of eyes felt heavier than the rest.

Ethan's.

He sat rigidly in his chair, and waves of heat emanated from his direction.

He wanted me to say no.

And it pissed me off. Because he had no right to care.

What harm could come from one drink with a friendly, attractive guy?

"Sure," I said quickly, before I could change my mind. "Sounds good."

"Cool." Benjamin smiled. "I'll pick you up on Wednesday at eight?"

"I'm not busy." I chuckled, given my complete lack of a social life recently. "But can we do seven? I've been getting up early for training."

"Seven it is." He gave me one last smile, then headed back to where he was sitting with a group of women.

"Yes!" Harper squealed. "You made the right choice. And it's a good thing you've figured out how to do the pretty spell. You can do it Wednesday night."

"Hey." Mira frowned, offended. "We don't need a pretty spell to look hot."

"Of course you don't," Harper said. "But it doesn't hurt."

But I was barely paying attention to what they were saying.

Because the smell of burnt wood filled the air, and it was coming from Ethan's direction.

He tore his angry gaze away from me and focused on Mira. "Speaking of getting up early, it's time we head back for the night," he said, and then he leaned over and kissed her. "And you're right. You don't need a pretty spell to look hot."

Keeping his eyes locked on hers, he stood up, draped his arm around her shoulders, and led her out of the restaurant. The rest of us followed.

But as we got up, I glanced at his chair.

Both armrests were charred black—right where his hands had been wrapped around them.

21

GEMMA

Benjamin showed up to our quarters exactly at seven on Wednesday night. He wore animal skin pants and no top, like most of the men in Utopia. He even came with a bouquet of tulips.

Mira must have told him that tulips were my favorite flower.

I thanked him, took the bouquet, and fumbled around to find a vase in the cabinets. Then I met him back at the door.

"You look beautiful." He eyed the short skirt and tight top that Mira had insisted I wear.

"Thanks." I grabbed Mom's coat off the rack next to the door and put it on. It was slightly big, but it worked.

Benjamin was a natural at small talk, so we chatted easily back and forth on the walk to the restaurant.

"The place we're going isn't super crowded, but I thought that would be good, so we could actually hear each other while we chat," he said as we neared the restaurant. "Unless you want to go somewhere more popular?"

"No," I said quickly. "Quiet's good."

"Cool. That's what I thought."

The restaurant looked like something out of the American Old West. We stepped through the swinging saloon doors, and I followed Benjamin to a seat at the bar.

There was only one other person sitting at the bar—an older man with crazy white hair a few seats down.

The bartender came over, dressed in a corset tied so tightly that her breasts nearly spilled out of the top. "What can I get you?" she asked with a smile.

"Whiskey for me," Benjamin said, and then he looked to me. "Pick your poison."

The white haired man chuckled and placed down his beer. "Watch yourself with that whiskey, boy," he said, his tone open and friendly. "It's strong stuff. Just one of them knocks me straight out."

The bartender laughed and looked back at us. "Emmett can't hold his whiskey, but you should be fine," she said. "It's our specialty."

"Sounds good," I said, since it was clearly *the* drink to get at a Wild West themed bar.

"Good choice," Benjamin said.

"We'll see about that," the white-haired man said. "But if it's too strong for you to handle, Clara makes a mighty fine wake-up juice."

"Can't you see they're on a date?" Clara said with a smile as she poured our whiskey. "Give the kids some privacy, or I'll say you're drunk and send you home." She winked at him, he raised his beer in a toast, and she placed the glasses of whiskey down in front of us. "Enjoy," she said, and then she poured herself a glass of whiskey and walked over to chat with Emmett.

Judging by how close she leaned in to him, they were clearly an item.

Benjamin and I clinked our glasses and each took a sip. The whiskey was strong, but smooth.

He rotated his seat to face me. "So, how's your training been going?" he asked, his eyes taking on a new level of intensity.

I leaned back and crossed my legs away from him. "Some days are better than others," I said, and I summarized what Mira and I had been up to with our training since arriving in Utopia.

As we continued chatting, Benjamin slowly moved his bar stool closer and closer to me.

Each time he did, I moved mine a bit farther away. Eventually, after he finished his whiskey, he placed his hand lightly on my arm.

I quickly pulled away.

He frowned, then sat back. "You're not really feeling this, are you?" he asked.

I glanced down at my hands, feeling terrible. Because when Benjamin had asked me out, I'd known I wasn't interested. I didn't even know why I'd said yes.

Wrong. You said yes because Ethan wanted you to say no, and you wanted his attention.

Disgust rolled through me. Disgust at myself for hurting Benjamin because of my feelings for Ethan. It was selfish and thoughtless. Benjamin was a nice guy who deserved better.

He sat there patiently, waiting for my answer.

"I'm sorry," I finally said. "I just have a lot on my plate. After what happened with the griffin, and now having to focus on training..." I trailed off, unsure where to go from there.

"It's okay," he said. "I get it."

"Really?"

"Yeah." He smiled, and just like that, his disappointment was gone. "You're here to learn how to use your magic. And I mainly just wanted to show you a fun time. If that means hanging out as friends, that's cool. If you need to get back to your quarters to keep studying, I can walk you back. No pressure."

"Thanks," I said. "That's really nice of you."

"What can I say?" He smiled again, although he did sound slightly bummed. "I'm a nice guy."

"You are," I agreed. "And it's refreshing to not be studying for a change. Let's stay for another drink? As friends."

"Sounds great." He held up a hand to signal Clara to come back over, and ordered us two more drinks.

She chatted with us as she poured our drinks, as if we'd known each other for years.

I could get used to this. Because Utopia was safe. It was full of people like me—with magic. People I could be myself around.

Maybe, in the future, Utopia could feel like home.

22

GEMMA

After two more weeks of practice, we were back in the queen's cavern.

She watched us from her throne inside the dragon's mouth, her head held high. "Show me what you've learned," she said.

Harper, Alice, Ethan, and Mom were there, along with about twenty witches on guard to protect the queen if necessary. They stood in a circle around us, stone-faced and intimidating, with swords strapped to their backs.

Mira went first. She bent her arms at the elbows, palms facing the ceiling. She took a deep breath, and then ice flowed out of her palms, wrapped around her hands and wrists, and traveled down to her elbows. Rows of icicles dropped down from her arms to the floor.

She looked like living artwork.

The ice cracked and broke apart, and she shot it out in all directions. Wind blew around us as she made sure the ice crystals swerved around everyone, although the witches reached for their swords to shield themselves, just in case.

The wind picked up, and the icicles shot toward the ceiling. They stopped mid-air, melted, and water rained down on us in slow motion.

I stood there as the last of the water droplets splashed on my face, shocked.

Mira had never done anything that extreme in practice.

Either she'd been practicing without telling me, or the pressure from the queen had pushed her to the next level. Given that we were together nearly every time we practiced, I assumed it was the latter.

The queen remained silent for an incredibly slow few seconds.

"Nice job," she finally said, and then she turned to me. "Can you perform as well as your sister?"

I swallowed, feeling the pressure of all eyes in the room on me. I'd intended to create a few fireballs and raise rocks from the ground. Nothing as spectacular as what Mira had just done.

Time to up my game.

I said nothing, since obviously the queen didn't want me to answer with words.

Instead, I walked forward, stopped a few meters away from the queen, and glanced around to make sure the general area around me was clear. After confirming that it was, I bent my arms at the elbows like Mira had done, turned my palms up to the ceiling, and called on my magic.

Heat filled me, pressing against my skin and begging to be set free. Taking inspiration from Mira's icicles that surrounded her, I envisioned the fire shooting up out of my palms and joining together to arc over my head.

The magic burst forth, and as I held the fire in place, burning embers fluttered down around me. They fizzled out into ash, and the orange light from the flames danced across the queen's impassive face.

She looked completely unimpressed.

I can change that.

Still holding onto the arc of fire above my head, I called on my earth magic. It bloomed inside me, filling me, and I pushed it out like a sonic wave.

The cavern shook like the first rumblings of an earthquake. Pieces of rock dislodged themselves from the stone columns and fell to the floor, plumes of dust puffing up as they hit the ground.

The shaking intensified, and the queen widened her stance, her eyes wide in alarm. "Stop," she commanded. "I've seen enough."

I snuffed the fire out and let go of my earth magic.

The fire disappeared.

But the cavern continued to rumble.

"I said stop." Her voice was low and threatening.

"I stopped." I looked around, confused. The witches stood with their swords ready, and Mira's eyes were wide and frightened.

Ethan held his gaze with mine. "Hold onto your magic," he said steadily. "*Control* it."

I reached for my earth magic again and focused on stabilizing it. But something pushed back, smothering me and fighting me.

Something that *wasn't* my magic. Something so dark that my stomach dropped in fear.

Ethan rushed to me and took my hands. He squeezed them tightly, his intense gaze focused on mine.

He was trying to join his magic with mine to help me.

The connection between us opened, and power filled me at the same time as shock crossed his face.

He dropped my hands and spun around to face the queen. "Dark magic," he said. "It's inside the kingdom."

She shook her head. "Impossible."

Then her eyes went blank, she flipped her hand so her palm faced the sky, and a flaming letter appeared in her hand. A fire message.

The flames extinguished as quickly as the message had arrived.

She nearly ripped the letter apart as she opened it. She read it quickly, then looked back up at everyone in the cavern, fierce and strong. "Utopia's been breached," she said. "We're under attack."

23

GEMMA

ETHAN PULLED Mira over and stood in front of us, one hand in each of ours, like he was blocking us from attack.

"This cavern is the safest place in the kingdom," the queen said. "It's the last place they'll reach."

"Who's 'they?'" my mom asked, panicked.

"Dark witches. Accompanied by an army of demons." She focused on me, Mira, and Ethan while saying the final part, and my stomach fell.

Because Utopia's barrier dome was impenetrable, even by greater demons. And demons could only be killed with holy weapons. Holy weapons were rare, and since Utopia wasn't supposed to need them, there were none here.

We could fight the demons, but we couldn't kill them.

There was only one way in and out of Utopia—the volcano's crater. And we couldn't get there without facing an army of dark witches and demons.

An army that we didn't have the proper weapons to kill.

Screams echoed through the tunnel that led to the main chamber, and terror filled me to the core.

"They're here for Gemma and Mira," Ethan said. "The breach happened when they used more magic than ever before. It can't be a coincidence."

The queen stared us down so intensely that I feared she'd rush at us and break our necks so the dark witches couldn't get what they wanted.

I moved to the side, so half of me was blocked by Ethan's sturdy frame. My sister's shoulder brushed mine—she'd done the same. She trembled with fear.

More screams from the main chamber, and this time, they were louder.

The queen's focus snapped to the guards. "I'll send a fire message to Avalon so they can dispatch the Nephilim army to help us. Harper, Alice, Rita, Betty, and Taylor—stay back here with the twins, Ethan, Rachael, and me. Jennifer, Marie, and Vicky—guard the cavern's entrance to keep the attackers at bay. The rest of you—slow the attackers in any way possible. Even if that means using dark magic."

"Yes, Your Highness," the witches said in unison, and then they hurried out of the throne room to follow through on the queen's command.

For the first time since arriving to Utopia, the walls felt like they were closing in around me. Because the throne room might be the hardest chamber in the kingdom to penetrate, but it was also a dead end.

We were trapped.

The queen rushed to her throne, took a piece of parchment and a pen from one of the wooden boxes next to it, and scrawled out a message. She handed it to Harper, who made it disappear in a ball of fire.

"The Nephilim will come to help us. But once they defeat the demons, this chamber will be the last place they'll be able to reach," the queen said. "We have to pray that they get here before the demons."

More screams. So close that they had to be nearing the entrance of the tunnel that would bring them to the throne room.

The queen focused on me and Mira. "Rosella risked Utopia to help the two of you," she said. "I can only think of one reason why."

Before she could continue, a narrow stream of black, smoky magic shot out of the tunnel and struck Alice's chest.

Alice's eyes widened, she fell back, and her head smacked to the ground. Her blank, empty eyes stared up at the ceiling.

Dead.

I spun around, reached for my earth magic, and flung it at the tunnel.

The walls rumbled, and the tunnel shook. Rocks broke loose from the ceiling, and the entire thing collapsed in on itself from the center outward. An avalanche of earth and stone poured out of what used to be the entrance, then stilled and settled down.

Dust rose up and out, so thick that it entered my nose and lungs. My eyes burned with it.

The others coughed and tried to wave the dust away from their faces, but it was everywhere.

Then a rush of wind pushed it out to the walls, clearing the area.

Mira.

Or Ethan. His fire magic was so strong that sometimes I forgot he had air magic, too. And from the way my sister trembled and cowered, and Ethan stood as strong as ever, I'd bet it was him.

The wind stopped, and then, silence. With the tunnel filled in, I could no longer hear the screams from the main chamber.

One of the other witches assigned to stay back with us spun around and pointed her sword at me. "We can't teleport out of here." She sneered, although she didn't move forward. "You destroyed our only escape."

"No, I didn't," I said steadily. "Because I'm going to create a new one."

24

GEMMA

I FOCUSED on the ground beneath my feet, and Ethan's hot skin so close to mine. The magic from both of them flowed into me, strengthening me, replenishing me like water being poured into a well.

I could do this.

I *had* to do this.

Otherwise, we'd all end up dead.

I spun around to face the wall opposite of the caved-in tunnel. Deep in the magma chamber, I felt the life of the earth surrounding us. The earth was a part of me. I felt the location of every chamber in Utopia, and the shape of the volcano, as clearly as I could feel my own limbs.

The soles of my feet connected with the ground, roots of magic growing out of them and connecting with the earth. I dug deep and pulled the warm magic through the rocks and dirt so it flowed inside me.

I collected as much magic as I could, raised my arms with my palms outward, and shot a blast of magic at the wall.

My magic slammed into the packed rock, nearly knocking me over with the impact. But I stood strong and dug the magic through the earth like a giant drill on super speed. I held onto it, pushing and pushing for kilometers until exhaustion took over.

I released my hold on the magic, let out a long breath, and fell onto my knees. My brain was so foggy that all I heard was white noise. Beads of sweat ran down my face, droplets landing on the ground.

I focused on my breathing, relieved when the magic from the earth filled me again, replenishing me with every breath I took.

But that wasn't all that was replenishing me.

Ethan had kneeled to my side, and he'd wrapped an arm around me to keep me propped up. His fire magic radiated off of him, also filling me with renewed power.

"Gemma," someone said from my other side—Mira. "What did you do?"

I steadied myself and looked around.

Everyone was staring at me, their expressions awestruck. Even the queen.

I stood up, not bothering to brush the dirt off my knees. "I couldn't create a tunnel to the surface, because we don't know if whoever attacked us left some of their people up there to guard it. So I created an underground tunnel that goes past the kingdom's borders. Once we're past the border, the witches should be able to teleport us out of here."

A bang sounded from the closed-in tunnel behind me. Then another, and another.

The dark witches and demons. I felt them blasting through the dirt and rocks, clearing the tunnel.

How did they have magic strong enough to do that? It shouldn't be possible.

"They're coming for us." I slowly spun in a circle to look at everyone in the cavern. "At the pace they're going, we have a few minutes, tops. We have to go. Now."

"Where, exactly, are we going?" the witch who was still pointing her sword at me asked.

"To the Haven," Ethan said, and I nodded, since it was exactly what I'd been thinking.

"And what's to stop the dark witches from blasting through their protection dome, too?"

"They find us by tracking our magic," I said. "They can't track our magic if we don't use it." I ran to the tunnel, stopped at the entrance, and motioned for the others to pile in. "We have to go."

No one moved.

The thumping as the witches and demons cleared out the collapsed tunnel got louder and louder.

My chest tightened. Did they not trust that the tunnel wouldn't collapse in on us?

Just when I was getting ready to assure them it was safe, my mom rushed forward, stepped inside the tunnel, and turned to face us. "You heard my daughter," she said. "This is our best chance to get out of here. Let's go."

The witches didn't move. Instead, they looked to Queen Elizabeth, waiting for her command.

The queen stood inside the jaws of the dragon skull, like she was waiting to eat the dark witches and demons alive. "Go with the twins," she said. "Bring them to the Haven."

"And you, Your Highness?" Harper asked.

"I'm staying in my kingdom. The dark witches and demons can fight me, and they can hurt me, but they can't kill me. Only a Nephilim can do that. And after the Nephilim arrive and fight off the demons, the survivors will need their queen. Now, I'm ordering you to escape through the tunnel and bring the dragons to the Haven. Do everything possible to keep them safe."

The witch holding her sword lowered it and looked to me. "You heard the queen," she said. "Dragons—go through the tunnel first. We'll be right behind you."

"I'm going last," I said quickly. "I need to seal the entrance from the other side to stop the demons from following us."

Another bang from the collapsed tunnel, closer now.

Ethan pulled Mira toward the tunnel, to where Mom was standing. "Go," he told her, pushing her to the entrance. "I'll be right behind you."

"You're not coming with us?"

"I'm staying behind with Gemma. To make sure both of you are safe."

She pulled him in quickly for a hug, then followed Mom into the tunnel. The four witches followed, and Ethan and I went after them.

When we were about thirty meters inside, I turned around. The queen was still waiting in her dragon skull. The booms of the dark witches throwing their magic at the caved-in tunnel sounded like they were moments away from breaking through.

The queen nodded at me.

I reached for my magic, threw it at the entrance, and the opening of the tunnel crumbled in on itself.

Ethan and I joined the others, lit up the way with our fire, and ran. Every fifty or so meters, I turned around and collapsed the tunnel behind us.

I'd love to see the witches and demons try to break through *that*.

As we ran, my breathing shallowed. Because while I'd been training with my magic, I hadn't been doing any physical training. And sports had never been my thing.

I was going to need to work on that.

Just when I was running out of steam, Harper came to a sudden stop. The rest of us stopped as well.

"We should be beyond Utopia's border by now." She grabbed my hands, then looked at the others. "Witches, pick a dragon. It's time to teleport to the Haven."

25

GEMMA

THE WITCHES of the Haven let us in the moment we appeared outside their protection dome. Apparently, they'd been expecting us.

The tall, green mountains in the middle of the lush, Indian jungle were positively breathtaking. But I didn't get to look around much before they teleported us into a colorful tearoom.

"Wait here," one of the Haven witches instructed. She and the others wore matching white tunics and pants, like they were at a yoga retreat. "We'll send for food and refreshments, and Mary will be with you shortly."

Mary—the original vampire who was the leader of the Haven. Unlike the rulers of the other kingdoms, she didn't use a royal title.

She also wasn't with us "shortly." After three hours, we were still waiting in the tearoom.

The witches attempted to make conversation, but they were all tense with worry for their family and friends back in Utopia. Since we'd only heard the fighting, we had no idea how bad it actually was. We were trying to be positive, but it was forced, and we all knew it.

Because we'd all heard the blood curdling screams.

They were going to give me nightmares for the rest of my life.

After what felt like another hour, there was a knock on the door, and a female vampire—presumably Mary—let herself inside. Like the witches, she wore all white. Her long, brown hair flowed down her back, and her eyes held wisdom far beyond her youthful appearance.

"I'm sorry for making you wait so long." She took a deep breath, then fidgeted slightly, composing herself. "I had to convene with the leaders of the other kingdoms so we could decide on a course of action."

"You spoke with our queen?" Rita—the witch who'd pointed the sword at me—asked.

"I'm sorry," she said sadly. "But no. According to the reports of the Nephilim, Queen

Elizabeth was gone by the time they arrived in Utopia. They hoped you might know where she was, but if you're asking about her now..."

"She stayed behind to fight with our people," Rita said. "But she's an original vampire, and can only be killed by the Nephilim. So unless one of the Nephilim turned on us, she's out there somewhere."

"We're doing our best to find her," Mary said. "Once we do, she *will* be rescued. Although, knowing Elizabeth, she'll save herself before we have a chance." Her eyes twinkled with fondness—clearly, she and the queen of Utopia were friends.

"What about the rest of Utopia?" Harper asked. "How many survived?"

"The Nephilim are getting a headcount as we speak, and we have witches on the scene to heal the injured. Once we have an official list, you'll be among the first to see it."

"So there are survivors." Harper relaxed and let out a long, relieved breath.

"Yes." Mary glanced down, then met Harper's gaze again. "But not many."

Worry crossed Harper's eyes, and she looked smaller than ever.

"None of our prophets saw this coming." Mary bit her lower lip, troubled. "If they had, Utopia would have been prepared. But now that we know the dark witches can break our boundary domes, we're reinforcing them as much as we can, and Avalon's sending Nephilim to each kingdom to ensure we're protected. What happened in Utopia will not happen again. You *will* be safe in the Haven."

"You're letting us stay?" I held my breath as I waited for her answer.

"The Haven is a safe haven for all supernaturals," she said. "Of course you can stay. But I do have one condition."

"What's that?"

"Rosella told me that the dark witches are able to track your dragon magic. I'll do everything I can to figure out how they're doing that—and how they broke Utopia's protection dome. In the meantime, you'll have to refrain from using your dragon magic while here. The dark witches don't know where you are, and I intend to keep it that way."

"We already planned on it," Ethan said. "Especially since the twins now have excellent control over their elemental magic. Without them, we wouldn't have escaped Utopia. So I think it's safe to say that they've completed their training."

"I'm glad to hear it." Mary gave me and Mira a small smile. "However, you will be continuing your training in the Haven."

"But we can't use our magic," Mira said, confused.

"I never said you'd be training with your magic," she said, and Rita smirked, like she knew where Mary was going with this. "Because demons are after you, and they can only be killed with holy weapons. Do either of you know how to use a dagger? Or a sword?"

"No," Mira and I said in unison.

"As I thought. But don't worry—we'll have that fixed in no time. Because Avalon's sent the best swordswoman in the world to teach you."

26

GEMMA

Raven Danvers.

The Queen of Swords.

I'd read about Raven in the history of the supernatural world textbook. She was a legend, along with the two other queens destined to help win the war against the demons—the Queen of Cups and the Queen of Wands.

The Queen of Cups was also known as the Earth Angel. Her magic had founded the mystical island of Avalon, where she used the Holy Grail to turn humans who'd proven themselves into Nephilim, so they could join the army that was battling the demons.

The Queen of Wands had the most magic of anyone in the world. Only gods were more powerful than the Queen of Wands. She was on a mission to save her best friend from a magical, hidden island where she was being imprisoned by the conniving goddess Circe.

Then there was the Queen of Swords. The most badass swordswoman on Earth, with bright red hair to match her fiery spirit. The Holy Sword Excalibur—yes, *the* Excalibur that had previously belonged to King Arthur—had chosen Raven to wield it. With Excalibur's magic, the Queen of Swords could beat any opponent she faced.

Not only had she come to protect the Haven, but she was also our new teacher.

For the past ten days, whenever we weren't passed out in a dead sleep, we were training with a sword or dagger. The witches gave us healing potion each night for our daily injuries so we were ready to start fresh the next morning.

If only healing potion could cure exhaustion. Because by the intense way Raven trained us from sunrise until nightfall, I would have sworn she didn't need any sleep.

She claimed that if you wanted to stay awake and alert badly enough, you could will yourself to do so.

"Watch your form!" Raven yelled as I sparred against Mira. "Stay on the balls of your feet. Anticipate your opponent's next move!"

In one swift motion, I knocked Mira to the ground and pointed the tip of my sword at her chest.

THE DRAGON TWINS

My sister glared at me. "Again," she said, and she rolled over and pushed herself up from the ground.

Thanks to our recent training, the grass in the field near the outskirts of the Haven where we'd been practicing was totally trampled upon.

The clean, crisp air and the mystical mountains made me feel like a Jedi apprentice. Except unlike the Jedi, I couldn't use my magic.

"Maybe it's time for a break?" Ethan asked from where he was sparring with David, one of the other Nephilim who'd come to help protect the Haven. He spun around and blocked David's sword with his own. They stayed like that, swords locked together, both of them looking at Raven to make the call.

"One more round," Raven said. "Then we'll break for a quick lunch."

Mira and I faced each other, holding up our swords as we waited for Raven to tell us to begin. Mira eyed me, her gaze hard and steady, determined to take me down.

Part of me wanted to let my sister win this round.

But she always knew if I let her win.

And I hated giving anything but my best.

"You've got this," Raven said to Mira. "That's not just any sword—it's a holy weapon. Feel your sword's energy. Connect with it. Make it a part of you."

"But don't use my air magic to help," Mira muttered.

"With the right technique, you don't need elemental magic to fight with weapons."

Mira huffed and tightened her grip around the handle of her sword.

"One," Raven started to count down. "Two—"

"Stop," someone said from behind us.

I spun around and saw Mary making her way up the hill.

I hung my sword to my side, its tip facing the ground so it wasn't pointed at the original vampire. The others—including Raven—did the same.

"Mary," Raven said brightly. "Do you want to see the twins' progress? They're doing well, if I do say so myself." She squared her shoulders proudly.

"I'm sure they are," Mary said. "But that's not why I'm here."

"What's up?" Raven asked.

Ethan was by my and Mira's sides in a flash.

I watched Mary, wondering what had brought her out this way. She'd been busy working with the other kingdoms to provide relief for what remained of Utopia, and to figure out how the demons had breached its protection dome.

By the time the Nephilim had arrived in Utopia, there were barely any survivors. Harper's mom, Benjamin, and most everyone else I'd met while there were dead.

And Queen Elizabeth was still missing.

Since we'd been training around the clock, Mom had been staying with Harper, trying to keep her busy.

"The Haven's archives have been thoroughly checked," Mary said. "As have the other vampire kingdoms', along with the Devereux circle's extensive library and the Bettencourt vampire coven's digital database. We can't find an answer to how the dark witches broke through Utopia's protection dome. The most powerful witches in the world—even the *mages*—don't have magic strong enough to do that. The only person who does is the Queen of Wands, and she was with the Supreme Mages on their mission to find Circe's island at the time of the attack."

"What about the prophets?" Raven asked.

"We wouldn't have had to go to the archives if the prophets had an answer," Mary said. "They were the first ones we consulted."

"Were you able to find anything about how they're tracking dragon magic?" Ethan asked.

"No. But there's still one last place we haven't checked."

"Where?" I asked.

"A place few know about, and where fewer have entered."

Chills traveled up my spine at the cryptic way she was talking about this place. "And you're going to check there?"

"No," she said. "*You're* going to check there. Specifically, you and Mira."

Ethan stepped forward, standing straight as a soldier. "Wherever the twins go, I go."

"I'm afraid that won't be possible."

"Why not?"

"I'll explain in private," she said. "The three of you, follow me. Raven—take a rest for the day. After how hard you've been working, you deserve it."

"Seriously?" Raven shook her head in irritation. "You say all this stuff about a mystery place, and you aren't going to let me in on the secret?"

"It wouldn't be a secret if everyone knew about it." She smiled, clearly enjoying herself.

"Fine." Raven rolled her eyes. "But I'm the Queen of Swords. I'll find out about this place one way or the other."

"Given how you get when you put your mind to something, I'm sure you will," Mary said. "But that day isn't going to be today."

With that, Mary led us back to the main building, so we could learn where she was sending us next.

27

GEMMA

I'D EXPECTED Mary to bring us to the tearoom. Instead, she led us to the residential area, its streets lined with small, stilted houses.

"I thought we'd chat in my house," she said, offering no further explanation for her decision.

She led us to a house that looked no different from the others, and opened the door. No key necessary—in the Haven, they believed locks took away the sense of community. Ethan hadn't been happy about that when we'd been given our rooms in the hotel, but his room was right next to mine and Mira's, so he didn't complain *too* much.

He'd asked for a connecting door, but Mom wouldn't hear of it.

Mary's house was the size of an average one-bedroom apartment. The decorations were simple and functional—nothing to make it look like the living space of the leader of the kingdom.

"This is really where you live?" Mira asked.

"Yes." Mary smiled. "As you know, the Haven shares all of our resources equally. Being the leader of the kingdom doesn't mean I need more living space than anyone else." She said it so simply—like it was common sense—and strolled into the small kitchen. "Would you like anything to drink? Water, juice, soda?"

"Coffee?" I'd quickly become addicted to South Indian filter coffee, and intended on adding it to the Twin Pines Café menu whenever Mira, Mom, and I were back home.

If we ever made it back home.

I swallowed down anxiety at the thought. Because with each day spent away, home felt more and more like a distant memory.

A life that no longer belonged to me.

A life I no longer had a place in.

"Gemma?" Ethan's voice pulled me out of my trance. "Everything okay?"

"Yeah," I said. "Just tired from all our training."

He nodded, although I could tell he didn't believe me.

Mary brought the coffee into the living room, and we sat down in the sofas and chairs. We all helped ourselves—except for Mary, who'd brought herself a mug of blood. The blood had a distinct metallic scent, although there were also some added spices, since the vampires in the Haven drank animal blood instead of human blood. They said it tasted better that way.

"So," Ethan said to Mary. "Tell us about this place where the twins and I are going."

"It's called Hecate's Eternal Library," she said. "And only the twins are going."

"I'm their protector." He sat straighter and squared his shoulders. "I go where they go."

"I'm afraid that won't be possible," she said. "Hecate is the goddess of witches, so only witches can enter her library. The library is at the top of Moon Mountain. Witches start the journey at the bottom of the mountain and hike up. You'll be rejected at the first roadblock."

"Roadblock?" I asked.

"Witches must prove themselves before entering the library," she said. "And they only have one chance to try."

Mira's face paled. "You mean these roadblocks could kill us?"

"No." Mary chuckled, although I didn't see why it was funny, since everything in the supernatural world seemed like it was out to kill us. "The mountain's magic will heal you before you die, and send you back to where you came from. In your case, back to the Haven."

I sighed, since I had zero interest in *almost* dying. But I supposed I shouldn't be too picky.

"What are the roadblocks like?" I asked.

"I can't tell you," she said. "You'll have to find out on your own."

"But you know?"

"Yes. I went to the Eternal Library, many centuries ago."

"But I thought you said only witches could go to the library."

"I used to be a witch," she said. "Before becoming a vampire."

"Right." I nearly smacked myself on my forehead. I should have remembered that from my history textbook.

"Back to the roadblocks," Ethan said, his eyes blazing with intensity. "I assume they'll have to use magic to get through them."

My lips parted when he said "they'll" instead of "we'll."

If he'd stopped fighting to come with us, then he must truly trust Mary, and know this was our final option to figure out who was tracking us.

"Hecate designed the trek up the mountain to test which witches will earn the right to enter the library," she said. "Take from that what you may."

"Then we have a problem," he said. "Because their strongest magic is their *dragon* magic—not their witch magic. And if they use their dragon magic, they'll lure the demons straight to the mountain."

"Unless they can't track us on the mountain," I said.

His eyes locked on mine. "Are you willing to bet your life on that guess?"

I pressed my lips together and said nothing. Because no matter how much better Mira and I had gotten with our elemental magic, the demons and dark witches had magic beyond what we understood.

They had magic that shouldn't exist.

We needed to be as careful as possible. Which meant only using our limited witch magic, and our basic skills with swords.

"What about Harper?" I said. "She was one of the strongest witches in Utopia. She could come with us and help us up the mountain."

"Not a bad idea," Mary said. "I'll send someone to bring Harper here. Then we can fill her in, and see if she wants to join you on the quest."

28

GEMMA

Three witches from the Haven teleported me, Mira, and Harper to the base of the mountain. They flashed out immediately after we arrived.

"Whoa." Harper's eyes were as wide as saucers as she gazed over my shoulder. "Look."

I spun around and gasped.

Ahead of me stood a tall, narrow mountain framed by the purplish-blue night sky. The stars shined like gemstones, and the moon hung so low that it looked five times its normal size.

A tall, slim palace grew out of the mountain's peak. Wispy clouds surrounded the palace's base, and its crystal turrets reflected the starlight.

Hecate's Eternal Library.

Mist cleared around our feet, revealing a dirt path lined with moon-colored stones. A muffled howl echoed through the air, followed by another, and another.

Dogs.

Or wolves.

Shivers ran up and down my spine. I wanted to call on my fire magic to warm up, but of course, I resisted.

"Looks like we're supposed to follow the path," I said. "Come on. Let's go."

I'd been nervous about being around Harper—after losing her mom and her home, I didn't want to say anything that upset her. But Harper was as talkative as ever, peppering us with questions about the Queen of Swords as we walked down the moonlit path.

She looked so different in her Haven whites than she did in the animal skins worn in Utopia. Softer, and younger.

"Did the Queen of Swords say anything about the Angel Trials?" Harper eventually asked.

"Nothing more than I read in the history book," I said, and Harper sighed in disappointment. Because the Angel Trials—the test a person took to see if they were worthy of entering Avalon to join the Earth Angel and her army—were as mysterious as the journey up Moon Mountain. "From what Raven said, she doesn't remember much. Most people who complete the Angel Trials remember nothing."

"I can't believe you're on first name basis with the Queen of Swords," Harper said.

"She's pretty relaxed about formalities," I said. "Not so much with training."

"I'd love to take a lesson from her when we're back."

"Sure. I'll ask." I had a good feeling Raven would say yes—she loved showing off her abilities with a sword.

The moonlight beamed down on us, its energy like whispers brushing my skin. I gazed up and took a deep breath, drinking in its magic.

Then I glanced at Mira, who'd been uncharacteristically quiet. "Hey," I said to my twin. "You okay?"

"I'm fine," she said, although her ocean blue eyes were dark and moody, a storm raging within them.

Something was upsetting her. And it was *really* upsetting her, because she wasn't usually one to hold her tongue.

It had to do with Ethan. I could *feel* it. Mainly because I also felt like he should be with us, helping us on this quest.

I felt safer with him nearby. As distant as he could be, he'd slowly become a steady force in my life, and I trusted that he'd do anything for me and Mira.

"Are both of you gonna be all broody the whole way up the mountain?" Harper asked.

"No." I immediately felt bad, because if anyone had a reason to be broody, it was Harper. "Sorry. I think I'm just tired. Training with Raven was exhausting."

"Sounds like it," she said as we turned around a curve in the path. "But it might be time to put that training to use. Because I think we've found our first roadblock."

29

GEMMA

A NEON blue river wound like a moat around the mountain. The path led to an arched wooden bridge... and a black wolf sat calmly in the center of it. It was way larger than a normal wolf—it was about the size of a car. Its eyes glowed white, and the blue light from the river reflected off its sharp, pointed teeth.

We stared at the wolf, and it stared straight back at us.

Challenging us.

I took a deep breath and reached for the handle of my sword. "I guess we're supposed to fight this thing."

"Hell, no, we won't," Mira said. "The bridge isn't the only way across." She stepped over the stones that lined the path and walked to the river.

Of course.

Why fight our way past a monstrous wolf when we could swim instead?

Harper and I looked at each other, shrugged, then hopped over the stones and followed Mira. Pink lily pads covered the water, and purple frogs ribbitted as they leaped from pad to pad.

"Are you sure it's safe to go in there?" I eyed the strange, glowing water. "It looks toxic." I looked to Harper, since she had far more experience with witchcraft than I did.

Mira looked to Harper, too.

"How would I know?" she asked. "This is the first time I've seen neon blue water, too."

"Maybe there's some sort of spell to test—"

Before I could finish the sentence, Mira kneeled down and dipped her hand into the water.

"Mira!" I grabbed her arm and pulled her hand out of the water. "We can't use our elemental magic."

"I'm not using my elemental magic." She narrowed her eyes and yanked her arm out of my grip. "But I'm naturally in tune with water. I can already feel that the river forms a ring around the mountain. If any of us can get a sense of if we can swim through it safely, it's me. Besides, it's less dangerous than going past *that* thing." She glanced at the wolf, which was sitting down and watching us curiously.

The wolf didn't look as dangerous now that it was sitting with its head tilted to the side—like a dog more than a wolf.

But I'd seen those pointy teeth.

"Go ahead." I nodded to Mira, although her hand was already submerged in the water again.

She closed her eyes, and all was still. I didn't want to breathe—the only sounds were the ribbiting frogs and the distant howls of wolves.

"The water's safe," Mira said. "It *looks* strange because of the color, but otherwise it's no different than regular water. We can swim through it."

She removed her slippers and put them inside the small satchel along her weapons belt. Then she jumped into the river like a cannonball. The water splashed up and hit me in the face, and I backed away on instinct.

She resurfaced and treaded in the water. "Come on in," she said with a giant smile. "It's the perfect temperature."

"Every temperature of water is perfect to you," I said, since she'd be comfortable in water that was nearly freezing—or boiling.

"You know what I mean," she said. "It's like a bathtub."

Harper and I removed our shoes and tucked them away.

Then Harper jumped in just like Mira had done.

I sat down on the edge and dipped my feet in, so the water lapped around my knees. Mira was right—it felt no different from regular water. And it *was* the perfect temperature.

Slowly, I lowered myself into the river so I was treading water with Mira and Harper. My white top bubbled up around me, and my sword was heavy by my side. But with my new supernatural strength, it didn't drag me down.

Something rubbed against my ankle, and I flinched my foot away. A pink lily pad floated next to me. A vine curled down off of it into the water near where my foot had been. The purple frog sitting on the lily pad stared at me, then it ribbited and shot its tongue out to catch a fly.

"Everything okay?" Mira asked.

"Yeah. There's just stuff at the bottom of the river."

"You mean the vines?" Harper asked, and I nodded. "But isn't earth your element?"

"It just caught me by surprise," I said, and then I pushed off to swim across the river.

But I couldn't swallow past the tight unease in my throat. Because Harper was right—earth *was* my element.

And something about the vines didn't feel right.

We swam around the lily pads, but no matter how much we tried to keep our distance from them, their vines kept creeping around my ankles. Judging by the way Mira and Harper occasionally paused, they were having the same problem.

We were nearly to the center of the river, where the lily pads got the thickest. They continued in both directions, so there was no getting around them.

Mira led the way, pushing through the blanket of lily pads.

They surrounded her, like she was a lily pad magnet. She stopped moving forward, and from her jagged movements, I could tell she was thrashing with her ankles.

She looked around, panicked.

"Mira!" I called, and I swam as quickly as I could to reach her.

But the vines curled around my feet until they were so tight that I couldn't move. My heart raced, my pulse quickening. I treaded water to keep afloat, swallowing the least amount of water that I could, and tried pulling my feet free. But the harder I pulled, the tighter the vines became.

Harper stayed back where the lily pads weren't so thick. "There's no way through," she said. "We have to turn around."

"They're not letting us move." I tried to pull one of my ankles free again, but it was useless.

"They're enchanted. They don't want you getting to the other side," she said. "Tell them you're turning around. See if they listen."

"You want me to talk to the lily pads?" Mira asked.

Before Harper could answer, I closed my eyes and reached out to the pink plants. Not with my magic, but with my thoughts.

We mean no harm. We just need to get to the library. Let us go to the other side. Please.

A vine wrapped around my waist and tightened so much that it hurt to breathe.

Panic shot through my body, and I opened my eyes.

Sorry, I thought this time, desperate for any way to get free. *We'll turn back around. Just let us go.*

The vine loosened around my waist, followed by the ones around my ankles. I sucked in a sharp breath of relief at no longer having to fight to stay afloat.

But Mira was still struggling.

I touched the lily pad closest to me, and its neon pink color pulsed slightly, as if it was telling me it was listening.

Mira, too.

My sister's thrashing stopped.

She swam back to the shore like a bullet through the water.

Harper and I followed, and we pulled ourselves up out of the river, where Mira was already standing.

My twin gathered her hair over her shoulder and squeezed out the excess water. "What did you do?" she asked me.

"I tried to get the lily pads to let us across. But Harper was right—they're enchanted not to let anyone through. So I promised them we'd turn around, and they let us go."

"You used your magic?"

"No," I said. "I might have been able to control them with my magic, but I didn't do that. I just talked to them. Like Harper said."

"Hm." Mira didn't look convinced.

Then a breeze blew past us, and suddenly, we were dry.

"Did *you* just use your magic?" I asked my twin.

"No." She held her hands up in defense. "I swear it."

"It's the mountain," Harper said. "It's enchanted. It was telling us that we did the right thing by turning around."

"How can you tell?" I asked.

"I'm a witch," she said simply. "So are you. Push aside your frustration about not being able to use your elemental magic, and focus on your witch magic."

I closed my eyes, centered myself, and took a deep breath.

Warmth tingled in my core and spread to my arms and legs.

Magic.

It was everywhere.

I smiled, content for the first time since arriving at Moon Mountain. When I opened my eyes, Harper was watching me with approval, like she had every time I'd successfully completed a spell in Utopia.

Mira looked more at peace, too.

Harper glanced at the bridge. "With swimming across the river out of the question, it seems like there's only one way to the other side."

"The wolf." Dread filled my stomach.

"I don't think it's just any wolf," she said.

"No kidding," Mira muttered. "It's a monster."

"It's Hecate's," Harper said. "All her animal familiars are black. And it's just been sitting there—it hasn't moved to attack."

"Maybe it's bound to the bridge," I said.

"Maybe," Harper said, and then she started walking toward the bridge, as confident as ever. "But there's only one way to find out."

30

GEMMA

We stood shoulder to shoulder at the start of the bridge, with Harper in the middle.

The wolf stared back at us with bright white eyes that looked like miniature moons.

"Be ready to draw your swords if necessary." Harper's voice was low and steady, as to not startle the wolf. "But don't threaten it unless it threatens us."

My heart beat so intensely that I could feel it pounding in my head.

What happens if we can't draw our swords fast enough?

I shook the thought away. Mary had promised that this journey wouldn't kill us. We'd just *almost* die, be healed, and sent back home.

But I refused to let that happen. We needed to get to that library.

"Maybe we should keep walking around the mountain," I said. "See if there's another way forward."

"There's not," Mira said. "I felt the river the same way you felt those lily pads. It surrounds the mountain. This is our only way across."

I took a deep breath, letting the magic in the air fill me and calm me. Then I stepped forward, my foot landing on the first plank of wood on the bridge.

The wolf's ears perked up, but it remained seated.

I brought my other foot forward, so I was fully standing on the bridge. Mira and Harper followed my lead. Keeping my breaths steady, I slowly approached the wolf.

It continued sitting there peacefully, observing us as we got closer.

Howls echoed in the distance.

The wolf stood up slowly.

I tensed, ready to reach for my sword if necessary.

Anticipate your opponent's next move, Raven's voice filled my mind. *Be ready if they're about to attack, but be equally aware if they want to yield.*

The wolf showed no outward signs of aggression. Instead, it took a slow step forward, and then another, and another, until it stood centimeters in front of Harper.

She stood perfectly still.

The wolf lowered its snout to the top of her head and sniffed. Its eyes glowed soft green, like the Northern Lights. Then it did the same thing to me and Mira. After each sniff, its eyes glowed green again.

I stayed still, afraid that any sudden movement would cause it to attack. I barely even breathed.

The wolf made a sound that seemed like approval, turned on its paws, and walked to the other side of the bridge. It stepped off, then turned back around, watching us.

"I think it's letting us pass," I said softly.

"Agreed," Harper said. "But we should still be ready, just in case."

Ready to fight.

We walked carefully and softly to the other side of the bridge. The wolf stayed where it was and moved its head up and down, as if telling us it was okay to pass.

Harper stepped onto the path first, and I followed. Mira stepped off last.

Once across, it felt like someone wrapped me in a blanket, binding me. The ground no longer pulsed with life. The embers inside me dimmed and snuffed out.

"My dragon magic," I gasped. "It's gone."

"Mine, too," Mira said softly.

But warm light still shined down on me, comforting me. The moon.

Whatever had happened to me when I'd stepped off that bridge had done something to my elemental magic—but not to my witch magic.

Harper shushed us and looked at the wolf. It was still staring at us.

None of us said a word as we continued forward. But I kept an eye on the wolf, until I was watching it over my shoulder.

It returned to its post on the bridge and turned its back to us.

We quietly walked around a bend in the path. Instead of being surrounded by moonstones like the path that had led us to the bridge, it was surrounded by shrubbery. It was like we were in a labyrinth, but one with a single way forward.

The bushes smelled warm and welcoming. I ran my fingers along the leaves, but the energy I normally felt while touching the earth was gone. It was like the leaves were dead, although from their vibrant green color, they were obviously very much alive.

It was my connection with them that was dead.

Suddenly, it felt hard to breathe.

"What happened to my elemental magic?" I looked at Harper, hoping she might have an answer.

"I don't know," she said. "Maybe Hecate's protecting her mountain from whoever's trying to track you down."

"Maybe," I said. "But she better give us our magic back when we're out of here." I stood straighter, hoping the goddess heard me. "At least we have one roadblock down. And who knows how many more to go." I looked up at the mountain, disheartened by what little progress we'd made.

"We'll be up there before we know it," Harper said. "Look—the path is starting to incline."

It was subtle, but she was right.

And so, we continued forward, starting the gradual ascent to the top of Moon Mountain.

31

GEMMA

"He's been so distant," Mira complained. "And I don't understand why."

We'd been hiking up the winding path for hours, unable to tell how far up we were because of the tall hedges lining the sides.

The entire time we'd been talking, Mira kept turning the conversation back to Ethan.

"It's probably nothing personal," Harper repeated for what felt like the millionth time. "He has a lot to worry about since you and Gemma got your magic. It's his responsibility to keep the two of you alive. Imagine how stressful it must be for him."

"But that doesn't mean he should push me away every time I try to get close to him."

"He's protecting you because he loves you." Harper had far more patience than I did. Or maybe I was just annoyed because whenever Mira talked about her relationship with Ethan, it was like a punch to the gut.

"He doesn't love me." Mira sniffed and wiped the corner of her eye.

"Of course he does," Harper said.

"No. He doesn't. He acts like it—at least, he did before we got our magic. But he's never said it."

Hope filled my chest.

Is he pulling away from Mira because she's not the one for him?

"Why do you look so smug about it?" Mira sneered.

"Sorry." I wiped all emotion from my face. "I'm just surprised."

"That's not what you look like when you're surprised."

Sometimes it was really annoying when someone knew you almost as well as you knew yourself.

"Fine." I scrambled for a lie. "I guess I agree with him that we need to be focused on learning how to use our magic. By not progressing your relationship, he's helping keep you—and me—alive."

"That doesn't make any sense."

I shrugged, because she was right—it probably *didn't* make any sense. It was just the first excuse that popped into my mind.

Harper glanced at me, suspicion in her eyes, then refocused on Mira. "Have you slept with him?" she asked.

I nearly stumbled on the dirt at the bluntness of her question.

Mira's cheeks reddened. "We've gotten close, but no," she admitted. "Dragons abstain from sex until after their first shift. So we have to wait until he returns to Ember and gets his full dragon abilities." She sighed. "Whenever that might be."

"He's talked to you about Ember?" Harper perked up, as curious as she'd been when we were telling her about the Queen of Swords.

"Nothing more than that," she said.

"Do you know *why* dragons wait until after their first shift?"

"He says it's because of some old dragon myth," Mira said. "But he won't say more than that."

"Interesting." Harper nodded, and I had a feeling she was going to probe Ethan for information once we returned to the Haven.

"But even though we can't be together physically, I don't understand why he's pulling away emotionally," Mira continued, and just like that, we were back at square one, trying to explain to Mira that Ethan was just as—or more—stressed than we were. After all, he was away from his home, living in a strange realm, and responsible for keeping us alive when we were literally magnets for trouble.

We were far from home, too, but at least we were still on *Earth*.

Sort of. Because Moon Mountain didn't feel like Earth. Especially because even though we'd been walking for hours, the moon still hung in the same place in the sky.

"Does the sun ever rise here?" I asked, switching the conversation away from Ethan.

"No idea," Harper said. "But since Hecate's also a goddess of the moon, she might have spelled it to be eternally night."

"Is that even possible?" Mira asked.

"Anything's possible with magic." I smiled and tilted my head up, closing my eyes as the moonlight soaked into my skin. With my elemental magic muted, it was like my soul was opening to receive witch magic. Like I was being blessed by Hecate.

My eyes were still closed when something furry brushed my ankle.

I jumped to the side and fell into Harper.

She grabbed my arm and steadied me. "Relax." She chuckled. "It's just a cat."

A black cat with glowing eyes and a crescent shaped white spot on its forehead looked up at me expectantly.

Another cat crawled out of the bushes—this one with a crescent shaped spot in the other direction on its forehead. It circled Mira's ankles and sat down, looking at her in the same way my cat was looking at me.

A third cat emerged. Its white spot on its forehead was a complete circle, and it nuzzled Harper's legs.

"They're Hecate's," Harper said confidently. "The symbols on their foreheads come together to create the triple moon."

I nodded, since I also recognized the witchy symbol.

Harper kneeled and held her finger out toward her cat's face. The cat looked at it for a second, then rubbed its cheek against her finger.

Mira and I did the same. Our cats nuzzled our fingers, too.

I felt instant affection for my cat, as if it had decided to accept me.

We'd never had animals in our house, but after our interactions with the wolf and the cats, I was feeling much more like a cat person than a dog person.

Harper's cat turned around and started walking down the path, its tail held high. Mira and my cats followed.

"Come on," Harper said. "They want us to follow."

"Did you communicate with your cat?" I hadn't read about that type of magic in the spell book. But witches also had private family spells, so there was no way to know what each witch was capable of doing.

"Telepathically?"

"Yeah. I guess."

"No." She chuckled. "Don't be ridiculous. But it's obvious that the cats want us to follow them. And I'm gonna bet they're leading us to our next roadblock."

32

GEMMA

We didn't have to follow the cats for long before they stopped at a fork in the road. Well, multiple forks, since the path split into three.

Each cat walked to the start of one of the paths. My cat was in front of the path on the right, Harper's in the center, and Mira's on the left. The white markings on their foreheads glowed under the moonlight.

"I think they want us each to take a different path," Harper said.

"Bad idea," I said. "Whenever people split up in books and movies, it never ends well."

"But this is a roadblock," she said. "We're supposed to be brave and face challenges to prove we deserve access to Hecate's Eternal Library. And the cats want us to face this challenge on our own."

"I'm with Gemma," Mira said. "You came with us because we need your help. You can't give us your help if we split up."

"But this is what the goddess wants."

"I thought you didn't have telepathy," Mira snapped.

"I don't." Harper crossed her arms and glared at Mira. "But I'm intuitive. Especially with magic. Like you said, that's why I came here with you. And our cats want us each to go down a separate path."

Mira looked to me, waiting for me to defend her.

But the magic in the moonlight prickled my senses, and I knew Harper was right.

"Each of the cats chose one of us," I said, slowly and carefully. "They led us down the path, and now they want us to follow them down different paths. Like Harper said, we're here to show Hecate that we deserve access to her Eternal Library. If we're too scared to walk down a path alone, what does that prove?"

Mira's nostrils flared. "It proves that we're smart and cautious."

"Or it proves that we're unworthy to enter the library," I said. "And yeah, I *am* scared to walk down that path alone. But if we don't do this, we'll fail, be sent back to the Haven, and be just as lost as we were before."

"You can't know that."

"I'm not sure how," I said. "But I can feel it."

Mira frowned, but she didn't refute my statement.

"You feel it, too, don't you?" I said. "The magic in the air. The *witch* magic."

My twin shifted on her feet, refusing to meet my eyes. "Maybe."

Her cat purred, as if saying she was on the right track.

"We need to do this," I said. "And remember—no matter what happens here, we can't die. So whatever's waiting at the ends of the paths can't kill us."

"But they can almost kill us."

Agony flashed in Harper's eyes. "*Almost* dying is a hell of a lot better than being dead," she said.

She'd been perky so far during our journey, but in that moment her grief over her mother's death hung in the air so heavily that it pulled at my heart.

Mira pressed her lips together and said nothing.

"So it's decided," I said. "We'll follow our cats down our paths, and find each other when we're back out."

If we got back out.

But I must have sounded more confident than I felt, because Mira simply nodded, and then the three of us wished each other luck and followed our cats down our assigned paths.

33

GEMMA

The path narrowed, the tall shrubbery on both sides of it making it feel more like a labyrinth than ever. My cat occasionally looked back, checking to make sure I was following.

"Lead the way," I said. "I'll go where you go."

When I spoke, a delicious smell flooded my senses. Sweet, mystical, fantastical. Calmness settled around me, and my stress melted away.

The smell was coming from up ahead, and I hurried forward, curious to see what it was.

I rounded a curve, and smiled at the beautiful purple flowers growing out of the hedges. Their petals curved downward, and narrow yellow bulbs burst forth from their centers. A few dark blue berries surrounded them, but the fruit wasn't nearly as gorgeous as the flowers.

What type of flower are they?

The name was at the tip of my tongue, but I couldn't put a finger on it. It also didn't help that the textbook on plants and herbs was the one I'd paid the least attention to in my studies. I had a natural grip on nature because of my earth magic, so instead, I'd focused on learning spells and training my elemental magic.

But the flowers were filling me with such happiness.

Maybe they were breaking past whatever spell was muting my earth magic?

I stepped closer to the hedges, entranced, and reached forward to touch the largest flower.

A needle darted out of the bulb and pricked my thumb.

I gasped and pulled my hand back. A drop of blood bubbled out of the tiny hole. But it didn't hurt.

It felt tingly. Numb.

Cold.

Ice cold.

I instinctively raised my thumb to my lips and sucked off the blood. Then my tongue numbed, and my mouth dried. As I swallowed, the flower's name popped into my mind.

Nightshade.

Poison.

I swayed on my feet, and the flowers blurred. My heart raced, and fear seized my throat, squeezing until I struggled to breathe.

No.

I needed to resist. I needed to stand strong.

Earth is one of my elements. I shouldn't be able to be poisoned by an element that's part of me.

Colors swirled around me, and I closed my eyes, trying to focus on my earth magic. It had to still be there, inside me. But no matter how deep I reached, there was nothing.

Letting go, I collapsed on the ground in a heap. I wanted to cry, but tears refused to form. My tear ducts had dried out.

Without treatment, nightshade was deadly.

This was it.

I'd failed the test.

Failed at the hand of my own element.

Pathetic. I didn't deserve access to Hecate's Eternal Library.

But all wasn't lost. Hopefully Mira or Harper would succeed where I'd failed.

I rested my head on the ground and stared up at the stars streaking the sky like a time-lapsed photo.

My lids grew heavy, and I could barely keep them open.

No, I thought. *Fight it.*

My skin grew hot. Burning hot.

My fire magic?

Maybe it was there. If I could find my fire, maybe I could find my earth magic, too.

I smiled at the thought.

Then I closed my eyes, inhaled the sweet, delicious air, and sank into darkness.

34

GEMMA

"What are you drawing?" Ethan's melodic voice echoed in my mind.

My journal appeared in my lap, and my pen in my hand. I sat cross-legged on a comforting blanket of hot sand. Waves lapped the shore, and I tasted the salt air on my lips.

I was back in the cove.

On the day I'd met Ethan.

He was crisp and clear, wearing his black t-shirt and jeans that looked out of place on the beach. But the rest of the world was hazy. It was like I was seeing everything but Ethan through a curved lens.

How did I get here? Why was I here?

I wanted to ask. But my body wouldn't obey my command.

"I'm not drawing," I said against my will. "I'm writing."

I'd never forget the first words I'd spoken to him. I'd played that conversation around in my mind ever since, wondering what I could have said differently to make him want to stay.

He walked forward, his hazel eyes so focused on me that he took my breath away all over again. "Writing what?"

"Stuff." I inwardly cringed at my reply. I would have changed it to say something more eloquent, but I was apparently a parasite in my own body, along for the ride in this dreamlike memory.

"Wow." He smiled, and from the amused look in his eyes, I wondered if my reply had truly been as bad as I'd thought. "Stuff. Sounds exciting."

From there, the conversation continued exactly as I remembered it. His asking what I was writing about, and my telling him about Joey and the terrible way I'd broken up with him.

"Have you ever had to keep a secret?" he finally asked. "A big one, for the greater good? One that other peoples' lives depend on?"

In the conversation that had happened in the real world, I'd said, "Not really."

But those words didn't come out of my—well, dream-Gemma's—mouth. Instead, I looked out to the horizon, at the sunlight sparkling on the ocean.

"You can tell me," he said softly. "I don't know anyone here, except for you. I promise I won't tell anyone."

I took a deep breath, then looked back at him. The flakes of orange surrounding his pupils glowed softly—embers of magic.

Somehow, I felt what this other version of me was feeling.

She was experiencing the magical connection between me and Ethan. The same bond I felt when he helped me use my fire magic.

She instinctively knew she could trust him.

I leaned closer and lowered my voice. "My sister and I are supposedly descended from an ancient line of witches," I said. "We can't use any magic, but according to legend, that might change in January, on our seventeenth birthday."

"Your sister." He watched me with wonder. "You're one of the Dragon Twins."

"I never said anything about dragons."

"But I'm right." He scooted closer, his eyes locked on mine so intensely that I couldn't have looked away if I'd wanted to. "You're one of the twins from the prophecy."

"How do you know all this?"

"Because I'm not really from America. I'm from the dragon realm—Ember. And I'm here on Earth to protect you and your sister after you're gifted with elemental dragon magic."

Nothing from that moment forward was anything like I remembered.

Instead of Mira mentioning Ethan that night and saying she wanted to date him, I brought Ethan to dinner. He told us everything that in my memory, he'd explained in his house with Rosella.

Initially, Mom was angry that I'd spilled our family secret. But Ethan defended me, saying my intuitive connection with magic must have known he could be trusted.

Mom accepted the explanation and left it at that.

During dessert, Ethan's fingers brushed mine, and he held my hand under the table. His touch felt so natural.

Mira noticed and smirked. The look she gave me clearly said, "Give me all the dirt later."

Mom smiled at Ethan in approval. "If you're going to be around my daughters all the time, then I expect you to make yourself useful," she said. "The café is hiring. Any chance you're looking for a job?"

"I already have a job—protecting your daughters," he said seriously, and his grip tightened around mine. "I'd say that's pretty useful."

"Agreed," Mom said. "But it'll look suspicious if you sit around the café staring at them all day. So, what do you say? Are you up for learning how to brew the best coffee in South Australia?"

"I've never been much of a chef..."

"It's not that hard," I teased, surprised at the lightness in my tone. "I'll teach you."

He smiled in return, looking at me like I was the most important person in the world. "I can't say no to that," he said. "When do we start?"

"Now," Mom said. "Gemma—teach your new friend how to make an after-dinner cappuccino."

Mira waggled her eyebrows as Ethan and I stood up.

Did she not feel jealous? At all?

This had to be a figment of my imagination. There was no world that could be this perfect.

But as long as I was here, I was going to enjoy every single second of it.

The next few weeks passed in a blur of kisses with Ethan when we thought no one was watching, and deep conversations in my room that lasted late into the night.

Falling into a pattern of loving each other was as natural as breathing.

Unlike when Ethan had dated Mira, Mom let him stay over as long as he wanted. Many times, that meant he stayed all night, the two of us talking until we fell asleep in each other's arms.

Mira wasn't home much. When we weren't working, she was either with her friends or with whatever guy she was dating that month.

When the three of us were together, Mira treated Ethan like a brother.

No one would have guessed that in another world, she'd been complaining for hours about how she'd told Ethan she loved him, but he hadn't said it back.

Because Ethan's heart belonged to me, and mine belonged to him.

Forever.

"Do you feel ready?" Ethan asked on the night before the ascension ceremony.

We were in the cove, sitting exactly where we'd been when we'd first met. He'd brought a dozen candles and lit them with his fire. The flames flickered, and the space filled with magic.

He sat next to me in the sand. Our legs were pulled up to our chests, and he brushed his shoulder against mine.

My heart danced at even the smallest of his touches.

"I was born ready," I said. "This is the moment I've been waiting for my entire life."

"And the moment I'd been waiting for my entire life happened months ago," he said. "On the day I met you. I love you, Gemma."

My breath caught in my chest. Because no matter how often I heard him say it, it still amazed me that it was true.

Ethan loved me.

No one had ever loved me like he did, and no one else ever would.

Except it wasn't real. For the weeks I'd been in dream-Gemma's body, I'd had to constantly remind myself of that heartbreaking fact.

This wasn't reality.

At least, it wasn't *my* reality.

But that didn't make my feelings any less true.

"And I love you," I said. Because real or not, I loved Ethan with every cell in my body. We were perfect together. Our souls vibrated on the same frequency—like we'd been made for each other. "I'm the luckiest person in the world to have met you."

He leaned forward, looked into my eyes, and kissed me like he'd never get enough of me.

Even though I wasn't in control of dream-Gemma's body, every movement of hers reflected what mine would have been, down to the involuntary pounding of her heart.

Slowly, he lowered me down until my back pressed against the warm sand, his body hovering on top of mine. Desire warmed his skin, making it hot to the touch. It might have burned anyone else, but not me.

Our matching elements connected us on a spiritual level so intense that it was impossible to put into words.

I arched my back and traced my fingertips along his neck, my body aching for him to come closer.

He groaned softly, but he didn't move. Instead, we stared at each other, silent, our eyes saying more than words ever could. It was like he was seeing into my soul. His chest rose and fell in deliberately controlled breaths, and mine did, too.

I wanted to be with him, fully and completely. I wanted our bodies to meld into one.

From the love burning in his eyes, I knew he wanted that, too.

But this was normally the point where he brushed his cheek against mine, held me, and reminded me that we needed to wait until he returned to Ember and he received his ability to shift. It was an oath all dragons made—to wait to be intimate with anyone until receiving their shifting magic.

He still hadn't told me why.

"I don't want to wait," I said slowly, as if speaking too quickly would ruin the moment.

"Neither do I. But it's my duty to honor the vow made by my ancestors." *His voice was strained with every word he spoke, as if he was going to break that vow at any moment.*

I swallowed, and tears prickled my eyes. "But why did your ancestors make that vow?"

He breathed steadily for a few more seconds, silent. Then he rolled over and sat up. Saying nothing, he raised his hands and ignited a flame in each palm. They mirrored each other, completely identical, down to the way they moved.

"Twin Flames," *he said, the light of the dancing fire reflecting in his eyes.* "Centuries ago, most dragons had a Twin Flame out there, somewhere. A mirrored soul they were destined to find, and would search for until they did."

As I looked into the flames, I saw my face reflected in one, and Ethan's in the other.

But I blinked, and the images were gone.

"Over time, as conditions in Ember worsened, fewer and fewer dragons found their twins," *he continued.* "Now, Twin Flames are more of a myth than a reality. But still, we wait to be intimate with anyone until receiving our shifting magic. Because only when we've become whole—when our dragon side unites with our human side—are we ready to find and connect with our twin. Before that moment, even if we met our twin, we'd be attracted to them but we wouldn't know for sure if it was a Twin Flame connection. Our first shift changes that. At least, that's what the legend says."

He snuffed out the flames, his eyes so pained that my lungs tightened around my heart.

As if his pain were my pain.

"But I'm not a dragon." *I could barely get the words out.* "So I can't have a Twin Flame."

"You'll have dragon magic," *he said.* "That's what connects Twin Flames—our magic. Every twin shares at least one element with the other."

"And I get my magic tomorrow."

"Yes." *He watched me carefully, as if he were thinking the same thing as me, but wanted me to say it first.*

"Do you think there's a chance—"

I didn't hear the rest of dream-Gemma's question.

Because her voice muffled, and the world blurred.

"Ethan," *I cried out, and I tried to reach for him, but there was nothing there.*

I was floating, no longer in a body at all. I might as well have been fire itself, existing to the human eye but not solid enough to grasp.

No, I thought. I want to go back.

But I wasn't totally in limbo. Because there was dirt beneath my back, grounding me to the earth. I was lying down on it... had I passed out?

"Gemma," someone said my name.

A voice I'd know anywhere. Because I'd heard it every day of my life.

Mira.

35

GEMMA

"It's working," someone else—Harper—said as I groaned and forced my eyes open.

Harper and Mira's faces came into focus. Both of them looked down at me in concern. But there was something else in Mira's eyes—anger.

It was the same way she'd looked when she'd been complaining about Ethan.

Ethan.

I felt the ghost of his touch on my skin, and the sweet taste of his lips kissing mine.

I could still hear him telling me he loved me.

And the memories of those weeks spent with him weren't fading like a normal dream.

They felt *real*.

Harper held something to my lips—a small bowl filled with a sweet, herbal drink. "I already injected some of this into your system," she said. "But drinking more can't hurt."

I finished it all, then asked, "What is it?"

"Healing potion," she said, like it should have been obvious. "How do you feel?"

I pushed myself up and looked around. We were back at the place where the main path split into three.

"Okay, I guess." I pressed my index fingers to my temples and rubbed away a slight headache.

It felt like a lifetime ago that I'd been on this path with Mira and Harper, making our way up the mountain to Hecate's Eternal Library. Half of me felt like it was here with them, and the other half felt like I was back in the cove with Ethan.

The moment I'd been waiting for my entire life happened months ago. On the day I met you.

Tears welled in my eyes at the memory of his words.

But the memories I had of him—of *us*—weren't real.

A wave of heartbreak crashed over me at the reminder that in the real world, Ethan didn't love me. He barely even *knew* me.

Those months with him were only a dream. A long, detailed, extremely realistic dream.

One I'd never truly wake up from, because no matter how much it hurt, I'd live it over and over in my mind, unable to let go.

I needed him to hold me again. To tell me he loved me. To look at me like I mattered more than anyone else in the world.

But he never would.

And it pained me down to my soul.

"Gemma?" Harper asked softly.

I rubbed the tears away, did my best to swallow down the pain, and looked up at her concerned face. "What happened?" I asked.

"You were poisoned. By nightshade."

Of course.

How could I forget the purple, sweet-smelling flowers with the yellow bulbs? The needle pricking my finger, and tasting my poisoned blood?

It had been so long ago. Everyone back at the Haven must be so worried. Mom, Mary, Raven... and Ethan.

They probably thought we were dead.

"You both stayed here this entire time?" I asked.

"You really think we'd leave you alone?" Harper said, stunned.

Mira eyed me warily, like she was afraid to speak.

She was looking at me like she didn't know me.

"It's been weeks..." I said slowly. "Months."

"What are you talking about?" Mira scoffed. "It's only been a few hours."

What?

"That's not possible," I said.

"It's true—nightshade usually puts people out for much longer, if they wake up at all," Harper said. "If you'd eaten the berries, you'd probably be back at the Haven by now."

"What were you thinking, getting so close to nightshade?" Mira asked. "You of all people should know it's poisonous."

"Having earth magic doesn't mean I know the details about every single flower," I snapped back. "It shouldn't have been something I even had to worry about, since normally, my magic would have protected me."

I looked down at the ground, ashamed. Because if I'd studied plants and herbs as much as I'd practiced spells, this never would have happened.

"What were on your paths?" I asked, wanting to change the subject away from how close I'd come to failing the roadblock.

"Mine was hemlock," Harper said. "I immediately recognized it and turned around. Mira's path was the only one that was safe. It had all the herbs and materials necessary to brew healing potion."

"I'm guessing you brewed it?"

"No." Mira stuck her nose in the air. "I did. At least, I made most of it."

"How'd you know...?" I looked at my sister in awe. Because brewing healing potion was high-level magic.

It took witches years to reach that level, if they ever did at all.

"I figured it was a test, so once I realized what the ingredients were for, I got started on making the potion. I assumed the two of you were on similar paths and making potions of your own. I was a bit more than halfway done when Harper came running down the path. She told me about the nightshade, and that she'd carried you out of your path, back to where we'd started. I hurried back to sit with you, and she finished up the potion."

"Ah." I nodded, since of course Harper had helped. Mira might have been good with potions, but the final steps in potion making were always the most difficult.

"At least I was doing something productive while you were getting poisoned by your own element," Mira snapped again, like she could read my thoughts.

"Why are you so angry?" I asked.

My twin stared at me like she hated me. "Because while you were sleeping, you kept saying his name."

"Whose name?" The words nearly got stuck in my throat. Because I already knew the answer.

"Ethan's," she said.

Just hearing his name hurt.

I love you, Gemma, the memory of his words echoed through my mind.

But it wasn't a memory. It was a hallucination. Because that was one of the effects of nightshade—vivid hallucinations.

And during the hallucination, I'd definitely told Ethan that I loved him, too.

Crap.

I hadn't said that while I was asleep... had I?

It would certainly explain why Mira was so mad.

"What, exactly, did I say?" I asked, refusing to panic until I had more details.

"You were saying his name. Over and over and over again."

I exhaled in relief that it hadn't been anything more than that. Then I scrambled for an explanation.

"I was dreaming about the night of our ascension ceremony," I said the first thing that came to my mind. "When Ethan saved our lives."

"Oh." Mira frowned.

"We were attacked," I continued. "He and I fought the griffin."

"I know what happened," she said. "I was there, too."

Guilt flooded through me. "I know," I said. "But it was a dream. I'm sorry. I don't remember much beyond that."

Lies.

Sort of. Because hallucinations were similar to dreams. I just remembered this hallucination a lot more clearly than a dream. Almost like it had actually happened.

My heart ached again at the memories.

No. Not memories.

Hallucinations.

I couldn't allow myself to think anything else. It would hurt too badly. Those weeks with Ethan were a figment of my imagination.

I'd never get *my* Ethan back.

Living with the hope of anything else would break me.

"Fine," Mira said. "Sorry for snapping. It's just... the way you were saying his name..."

"What?" I could barely get the word out.

"It's nothing." She shook it off and pasted on a small smile. "I'm just glad you're okay."

I nodded, even though it definitely *wasn't* nothing. I knew it, and I had a sense that Mira knew it, too.

But Mira and Harper needed to sleep. I could use some sleep—some *actual* sleep, not drugged up hallucination sleep—too.

So we lit a fire, gathered leaves to create makeshift, lumpy mattresses, and didn't speak of my dream again.

36

GEMMA

THANKFULLY, I didn't dream that night.

When I woke up, my cat was curled up next to me, and the moon was still in the same place in the sky. I had no idea what time it was—or if time passed on Moon Mountain at all.

At least I felt rested. My elemental magic was still muted, but my witch magic felt stronger than it had before.

I'd heard it said that if someone lost one of their senses, their other senses became stronger. Maybe that was what was happening with my witch magic.

Unable to fall back asleep, I rubbed my eyes and sat up. The leaves crinkled beneath me, and I removed the ones that had gotten pressed onto my skin during the night.

Mira and Harper stirred at my movements and woke up, too. Mira was slow to wake, but Harper was up in an instant.

Leaves dangled in her long black hair, but she didn't seem to notice or care. "Look." She smiled and pointed at the fire. "Hecate's looking out for us."

A basket of breads, meats, and cheeses sat by the fire. My stomach rumbled, and we rushed toward the basket and dug in. Each bite filled me with energy, like the food was full of magic. We shared bits of the meat with our cats, too.

Once all the food was gone, we sat back and drank from the water bladders that had been next to the basket.

No matter how much I drank, the water bladder remained full.

"I didn't know witch magic could do this," I said as my water bladder refilled itself again.

"It's not a spell I've ever heard of," Harper said. "But Hecate's the embodiment of magic. She can do spells far beyond the skills of witches *and* mages."

Mira took another swig of water. "Must be nice," she said.

We sat there in silence and stared up at the palace. We were about halfway up the mountain, or maybe more, since the winding path shrank in diameter as we made our way up.

"How are you feeling?" Harper asked me.

"Better," I said. "Thanks."

She nodded, satisfied, then stood up and brushed breadcrumbs off her pants. Our Haven whites weren't so white anymore, thanks to our night sleeping on the dirt. I rubbed off the dirt that I could, but it was pretty hopeless.

Not that we had anyone around here to impress, anyway.

Harper opened her water bladder and dumped the water over the fire, snuffing it out.

Smoke drifted up from it, and I stared sadly at the charred sticks and logs. Because I should have been able to *feel* the fire with my magic. But there was nothing there.

"Your elemental magic's still blocked?" Harper asked.

"Yep." I didn't look away from the smoke.

"Bummer."

Mira faced the path she'd gone down yesterday—the one with the healing herbs. "We should keep going," she said. "The faster we get to the top of the mountain, the sooner we can get back to the Haven."

And the sooner we'll get back to Ethan.

I imagined running up to him and kissing him, and how he'd smile at me with pure happiness, like I lit up his world.

No, I reminded myself. *Ethan will kiss* Mira *when we return to the Haven—not me. I'll be basically a stranger to him.*

My chest hollowed at the thought of him looking at me like he didn't know me—of the lack of affection I'd see in his eyes. It was like someone had carved out a piece of my heart, and I felt the hole with every breath I took.

Will the pain ever go away?

It had to. Because Ethan had chosen Mira. I was the one who didn't fit into the equation.

I never would.

Another wave of pain crashed through me. All I wanted was to curl into a ball and cry. Or better yet—fall asleep and wake up in *my* Ethan's arms.

"You okay?" Mira asked me.

"Yeah." I shook away my thoughts of Ethan and met her eyes. "Why?"

"You look like you just saw a ghost."

My stomach dropped. Because that was what my memories of Ethan were—a ghost. No, not even that. Because ghosts had once been alive. The love that Ethan and I had shared was a figment of my imagination.

Hopefully the memories—and the pain they brought me—would fade in time. If not, perhaps I could drink memory potion when we were back at the Haven. I wasn't sure if memory potion could erase memories of something that hadn't actually happened, but it couldn't hurt to try.

In the meantime, I needed to focus on the task at hand—finishing the hike up to Hecate's Eternal Library.

And I refused to let my dream of Ethan distract me from completing that mission.

37

GEMMA

We walked a few kilometers, and the mist intensified up ahead.

It swirled like an angry storm cloud and came together until it was about the size of a door. It thickened until it was impossible to see through, then solidified into a naked woman with three heads.

One of the heads was a dog—a hound. The other was a horse. And the final one was a serpent.

All six eyes zeroed in on us, and they looked *hungry*.

I grabbed the handle of my sword, yanked it out of the holster, and held it out in front of me.

"What are you doing?" Harper hissed.

"Preparing to defend us."

"But that's Hecate."

"That's not Hecate." I stayed focused on the creature. Either Harper was blind, or I was hallucinating again. "That's a monster."

The dog growled, the horse bared its teeth, and the snake hissed.

Mira also reached for her sword. She was shaking, and she gripped the handle so tightly that her knuckles turned white.

"Stop," Harper said. "We shouldn't—"

The monster rushed toward us, and we hurried out of the way just in time.

Harper and Mira went left, and I went right.

The monster spun around, dirt flying up from underneath its feet. The dog and horse snarled at us, and the snake hissed again, its forked tongue sliding in and out.

I glanced at Harper and Mira to try to see what they were thinking, while also keeping an eye on the monster.

Mira stood behind Harper, scared. But Harper held up her sword and stared determinedly at the monster, as if sizing up the best angle of attack.

She glanced at me and nodded.

It was go-time.

Harper and I ran at the monster and swung our blades toward its mid-section. But the monster was quick—it did a front flip over our swords and landed on the other side.

I spun and swung again, but it dodged my blade.

Each time we swung at the monster, it danced around us, moving in a blur. I followed all of Raven's instructions, but no matter what I did, I couldn't land a blow.

And while the monster was moving fast, it wasn't trying to bite us.

Did it not want to harm us?

Each time I paused, thinking it might end up being peaceful like the wolf, it rushed at me again.

Clearly *not* peaceful.

Sweat poured from my brow. I did my best to steady my breathing, grateful for all the high intensity interval training Raven had put us through during our time at the Haven. The supernatural strength I'd gotten during the ascension ceremony had surely expedited my training progress, too.

Harper and I kept at it, although neither of us could get in a strike.

Suddenly, another sword came out of nowhere and sliced through the monster's midsection.

All three of its mouths opened in surprise, and it dissolved into mist.

The mist spread out, revealing Mira. She held onto her sword, staring at it in shock.

"You did it." I dropped my sword and pounced on her, engulfing her in a hug.

"Ew." She backed away, her nose scrunched in disgust. "You're drenched in sweat."

I laughed like it was the funniest thing I'd ever heard. Because sure enough, her clothes were damp where I'd been touching them.

"That was *awesome*," Harper said to Mira. "I thought you were just gonna hang back and let me and Gemma do the hard work. But no—you showed that monster what you were made of."

"I had no choice." Mira shrugged. "You and Gemma clearly weren't getting anywhere."

"Or your joining in was part of the test," I suggested. "Because it was impossible to beat that thing until you jumped in."

Her eyes flashed with annoyance. "Or maybe I'm better with a sword than you give me credit for."

Harper glanced at me, because we both knew Mira wasn't better with a sword than either of us. "You blended into the background, got the monster to think you weren't a threat, then attacked when it wasn't expecting it," she said to Mira. "Smart strategy."

"Thanks." Mira shook out her hair and smiled.

She definitely hadn't intended it to be strategy, but it made her happy to let us think it, so I wasn't going to argue.

"Want to take a rest to cool off?" Harper asked.

"I'm ready to keep going if you are," I said.

"I'm always ready."

"Me, too," said Mira, even though she'd barely exerted herself during the fight.

Our cats must have agreed, because they jumped out of the mist and continued walking down the path. They didn't even look behind to make sure we were following. It was like they *knew* we were there.

Eventually, after a few more kilometers, something else took shape in the mist.

Horses. Three of them.

They were the most magnificent horses I'd ever seen. Swirling galaxies of purple stars dotted their silky black fur, making them look like the embodiment of night. Silver streaked their tails and manes, and their eyes glowed white like the moon.

They watched us patiently, then walked toward us. The one in front of me lowered her head and nuzzled my arm.

Get on, she seemed to be saying.

"Have you ridden a horse before?" I asked Harper, since I already knew Mira had just as much horse riding experience as I did.

"None."

"Did you see any horses in Utopia?" Harper's eyes saddened after saying the name of her now-destroyed kingdom.

"Nope."

Mira ran her fingers through her horse's mane. "They're gentle," she said. "It can't be any harder than riding a surfboard."

"Maybe," I said, not convinced. Because surfboards were *things*. Horses were living creatures.

Hopefully I'd fair better on a horse than on a surfboard. But probably not. Because if I thought surfboards were unpredictable, what was going to happen with a horse that could throw me off its back at any moment?

Mira jumped, swung one leg over her horse's back, and landed gracefully on it. "That was easy." She grinned and shook her hair out. "Just do what I did."

Harper walked to her horse's side and easily mirrored Mira's movements.

My horse huffed, like she was asking what I was waiting for.

I ran my fingers along the side of her face. Her fur was supernaturally soft, like silk. Magic poured off her, its warmth entering my fingertips and spreading through my body.

"Come on," Mira said. "We don't have all day."

I moved to stand on my horse's side and took a deep breath. Her back was higher than my head. How had Mira and Harper jumped up there so easily?

Supernatural strength, I reminded myself. *You've got this.*

But supernatural strength didn't make up for my hesitation, or for the clunky sword hanging by my side.

First I didn't jump high enough. Then the sword banged against my knee, catching me off-guard and knocking me down to the ground.

I fell down on my butt, and Mira laughed.

I glared at her, and she pressed her lips together, still smiling. So I stood up, wiped the dirt off my backside, and jumped with no hesitation.

I swung my leg up—this time aware of my sword—landed on the horse's back, and wrapped my arms around her neck to steady myself. I was nowhere near as graceful as Mira or Harper, but at least I'd gotten up there.

Why could I move better with a sword than Mira, but not jump onto a horse?

I didn't have time to think about it, because my horse turned around to face forward, and then we were off.

38

GEMMA

I HELD onto my horse's mane for dear life, but the ride was surprisingly smooth. It was like she was running on air.

I glanced over at Mira and Harper, saw that their horses' hooves were a few centimeters above the ground, and realized they *were* running on air.

A thrill passed through me at the amazingness of Hecate's magic, and I settled into my horse's back to enjoy the ride. Before I knew it, we broke past the cloud line. We were so close to the crystal palace that I had to crane my neck up to look at it, and the moon was so huge that it took over the night sky.

As I was taking in the palace's beauty, my horse slowed to a stop. Mira's and Harper's did, too.

"Do you need water?" I asked the horse gently. "Food?"

It neighed and shook out its silvery mane. Then, the three cats jumped down onto the path—I had no idea where they'd come from—looked at us, and meowed.

"I think this is as far as the horses will take us," Mira said.

Her horse bobbed its head up and down, as if nodding to say Mira was right.

Mira jumped off gracefully, landing like the earth was a cloud beneath her feet. Harper did the same. I looked down at the ground, more ready than ever to get back on it.

The dirt welcomed my feet, cushioning my landing.

I stroked my horse's cheek, said goodbye, and joined Mira and Harper in the middle of the path. Our cats walked up to us and nuzzled our ankles. Magic flowed through me, and while I couldn't see the magic, I could somehow *feel* that it was silver.

Our horses ran by us and flew into the sky. The stars on their black coats twinkled, their bodies became transparent, and then, they were one with the night.

I reached for the handle of my sword, as if making sure it was still there, then glanced back up at the crystal palace. "Looks like it shouldn't be much longer," I said.

"Depending on how many more roadblocks Hecate throws our way," Harper said.

Mira and I nodded, and we continued walking forward along the path. As we walked, Harper quizzed us on spells and potions we'd learned in Utopia. I did better on the questions about spells, and Mira did better on the ones about potions.

I'd always thought potions were boring... until I'd needed one after the nightshade. When we got back to the Haven, I planned on practicing more.

Eventually, we turned around a bend and reached the end of the path.

Except it wasn't the true end. Because the path continued into a dark, gaping cave that led into the mountain.

Two tall, matching pillars of a beautiful woman stood on the sides of the cave's entrance. The woman had hair as long as Harper's, and the triple goddess symbol—the full moon surrounded by two crescent moons—was etched on her forehead. Her stone eyes glowed white, like all the animals we'd encountered so far.

Three lit torches waited on the ground between the pillars. Assuming they were for us, I walked forward and picked one of them up.

"Gemma," Mira hissed. "What if that was a trap?"

"It's not." I shrugged and spun back around to look into the cave. It was dark inside, although starry lights that reminded me of Utopia's glowworms twinkled along the ceiling.

"You had no way of knowing that," she said.

"The torches were left for us by Hecate," I said. "They're here so we can continue down the path that'll lead us to the library."

"How do you know that?" My twin's eyes narrowed into slits.

"I'm not sure," I said, since I'd spoken without having to think. "I just do."

"You're connected to the goddess." Harper picked up a torch. "I feel her magic, too."

Mira stomped toward the final torch and grudgingly picked it up. "How come I don't feel it?" she asked.

"You need to open your mind to her magic," Harper said. "Let it flow through you."

Mira closed her eyes and took a deep breath. She stayed like that, completely still, for a few seconds. Then, she opened her eyes.

"Do you feel it now?" I asked.

"A bit," she said. "It feels... silver. I'm not sure if that makes any sense."

"It makes perfect sense." I smiled, glad that my twin was getting better at this.

She smiled back at me, and the three of us stepped inside the cave to continue down the path.

39

GEMMA

Our cats disappeared into the night, just like the horses.

As we walked deeper into the cave, crystals grew out of the ground, getting thicker and taller. Purple and blue magic swirled inside them, the colors bright like the night sky.

Eventually, we reached a large, crystal door. It was slightly translucent, but not enough to see what was on the other side.

"How do we get inside?" Mira asked, since unlike a door, the smooth crystal had no handles.

I placed my torch on the ground—making sure to dig it into the dirt enough that it would remain upright—stood back up, and touched the crystal.

My hand passed through it, and was surrounded by magic. I gasped at how warm and welcoming it felt. A breeze stirred around me and caressed my skin.

Welcome, the crystal seemed to say. *Come inside.*

But I couldn't go without the others. We'd started this together, and we'd go through the crystal together, too.

So I pulled my hand back.

Mira and Harper crowded around me and examined my hand. Luckily, it looked no different than it had before I'd touched the crystal.

"You should have tested that out first," Mira said. "With a stone, or with your sword. Not with *yourself*."

"I knew it would be okay," I said.

"With what?"

"My intuition."

We glared at each other, locked in a standstill. Mira would never understand my magical intuition, just like I'd never understand her lack of one.

"What's done is done," Harper said. "The crystal door is our only way forward. And we didn't come all this way to stop now."

"Hell no, we didn't," I said, and I held my hands out for them to take. "Are you both coming or what?"

Harper stepped up and took my hand.

Mira stayed stubbornly in place.

"Come on," I told my twin. "Do you really want to stay here alone in this cave?"

"You wouldn't leave me here."

"I wouldn't," I agreed. "But where would that get us?"

"Nowhere," Harper said.

"Exactly."

We both stood strong, our eyes locked on Mira's big blue eyes. She looked so scared and small. Like the cave was about to swallow her whole.

"I know this is hard for you," I continued, speaking softer now. "Earth's my element—not yours. But it's safe. I promise."

"Says what? Your intuition?" she said, like it was a dirty word.

"Says the fact that I stuck my hand through the crystal and was fine."

She glanced at the hand I was holding out to her. The same hand I'd pulled out of the crystal unharmed.

Mira never denied cold, hard logic.

"Fine." She stepped up and took my hand. "I'll come."

"I knew you would." It took all of my effort not to stick my tongue out at her, like I'd done when we were kids.

We counted down to three, and then we glided inside the crystal. It was like stepping into pure, warm light.

I wasn't sure if seconds or minutes passed before we stepped out of the warmth and into a massive, ivory hall. The ceiling had been carved to look like beautiful upside-down flowers that reminded me of the nightshade, and wood benches lined the marble floor.

The breathtaking architecture would have stolen my attention if not for the stunning, dark-haired woman at the opposite end of the hall.

Her deep purple gown flared out and gathered at the floor, and keys dangled from a chain wound loosely around her waist. Her eyes shined with moonlight, and the mark of the triple goddess glowed on her forehead.

Hecate.

"Gemma, Mira, and Harper." Her voice was like music, and her eyes dimmed out until they looked relatively normal—although her irises were a dark shade of purple that sparkled with the occasional tiny star. "Welcome to my Eternal Library."

40

GEMMA

THANK YOU?
It's an honor to be here?
Is this real?

I had no idea how to respond. All I could do was stare as I searched for the proper first words to say to the goddess of witchcraft.

"Does this mean we passed the roadblocks?" Harper was the first to speak.

"With flying colors." Hecate smiled. "Minus that unfortunate run-in with nightshade." She glanced at me, and disappointment flared in my chest.

"I know." I lowered my eyes. "I'm sorry."

"You don't need to apologize," she said, and when I looked back up at her, the corners of her lips turned up in a small smile. "There's a reason why witches work in threes. When one messes up—and mortals always make mistakes—they have two others ready to help them back on their feet. Just like Harper and Mira did for you."

"And like Mira did when she helped us beat that monster," I said.

Hecate bristled. "That *monster* was a version of me," she said. "But yes, I placed myself in your path to ensure that all three of you were brave enough to gain entrance to my library."

"I thought so." Harper perked up with curiosity. "What about the horses? And the cats? And the wolf?"

"We could discuss your journey here for days." Hecate brushed off Harper's questions. "However, that's not why you came. So tell me—what knowledge do you seek to gain?"

I opened my mouth to respond, but she continued before I could.

"Be careful, because each of you can only ask me one question per visit," she said. "After that, you're on your own. And visitors have been known to get stuck in my library for years—or longer—if they try to find information without my guidance. So I recommend you make your questions good ones."

No pressure or anything.

"Think as we walk." Hecate turned and glided toward the door at the end of the hall.

The door opened without her touching it, and she led us into a room completely opposite of the ivory one we'd just left. Rows and rows of dark, wooden bookshelves lined the red-carpeted hall.

In the center of the hall, a banquet table covered with food and drink extended as far out as I could see. An old woman in a poodle skirt emerged from behind one of the bookshelves and walked slowly toward the table. She didn't acknowledge us standing nearby. Instead, she reached forward, picked up a sandwich, and started to eat.

"Remember my warning," Hecate said.

My heart plummeted into my stomach, and I couldn't bring myself to ask how long the woman had been wandering around the library, searching for information amongst its many shelves.

"Does the hall ever end?" I asked instead.

Hecate raised an eyebrow. "Is that your one question? The one you ventured all the way here to ask?"

"No." I pressed my lips together and tried again. "I meant to simply observe that the hallway doesn't appear to end."

The goddess nodded, like she was proud of me. "It's called the *Eternal* Library for a reason," she said. "As you noted, the hall has no end in sight. And the books are organized in a way that only I understand. Thus, it's imperative that you have my help while searching for information." She glanced sadly at the old woman, who finished her sandwich and walked away from the table to continue her futile search through the library's endless shelves.

"She should give up and go home," Mira said.

"She can go home at any time she pleases," Hecate said. "She chose to stay. By now, she's been wandering the library for so long that she likely doesn't remember the information she sought in the first place."

I swallowed down a lump in my throat. Because what could this woman have needed to know so badly that she thought it worth getting stuck in limbo for the rest of her life?

Farther out in the distance, a man wandered to the table and helped himself to food and drink.

Chills ran up and down my spine.

How many of them were there? Were they as endless as the library's hall? Was there any way to help them?

But as important as those questions were, they weren't answers I immediately needed to know. I'd ask eventually—but not now.

So I shook myself out of it and remembered why *I* was there.

Three questions. One each.

How was I supposed to only pick *one?*

"Can the three of us discuss—" Harper stopped speaking and clamped her hand over her mouth. Then she lowered her hand and continued, "What I meant to say was that the three of us are going to step aside to discuss what we're going to ask, to make sure we get the information we need."

"Very wise, young witch," Hecate said. "But don't take too long. The sooner you return to your realm, the better."

Goosebumps rose along my arms at the knowing way she said it.

THE DRAGON TWINS

The three of us huddled next to one of the columns and discussed what we were going to ask.

As we talked, I looked at the spines of the books. None of them were titled. No wonder it was nearly impossible to find one without Hecate's help.

We reached a decision, then rejoined Hecate.

"What do you wish to learn?" she asked.

Harper and Mira looked to me. Hecate did, too.

"Who—or what—can sense my and Mira's dragon magic?" I asked.

Hecate stared forward, and her eyes glowed again. Swirling, sparkly smoke drifted out of them and down the hall, filling the library with its magical mist. A breeze circled around us, and the mist tingled against my skin, cooling my lungs as I breathed it in.

Five minutes passed before Hecate's eyes sucked the mist back inside them, like a vacuum. A plain, red book floated into her hands, and opened to a page about two-thirds of the way in.

I leaned forward to get a better look, but Hecate pulled the book closer to her chest and angled it so I couldn't see the pages. "You ask the question," she said. "I find the book, I read the information, and then, you listen. I'll tell you what you need to know."

What we *need* to know.

Not what we *wanted* to know.

There was a difference.

But we didn't have any other options right now, and Hecate was helping us, so I'd take what we could get.

"This book contains a list of the gifted vampires that were turned in the last century," she said. "One of them—Jamie Stevens—is a distant relative of yours. Her gift is the ability to feel when dragon magic is being used, and to locate where the magic is coming from."

"So she's the one who's after us."

"It seems so."

"Why?" I asked, since it didn't make sense. Why would a relative of ours—one who was clearly attuned with dragon magic—want to hurt us?

"You've already asked your question." Hecate slammed the book shut, and it disappeared into starry purple mist. "Who's next?"

"Me." Harper looked as fierce as ever, and Hecate nodded for her to proceed. "The demons destroyed my home. They killed my family. They never should have gotten past Utopia's boundary. So I need to know—how did they do it?"

It was a tough one for her, because she also wanted to know *which* demon—or dark witch—had done it. But everyone in every vampire kingdom was already trying to figure that out. The thing that baffled them was *how* they'd pulled it off.

If Harper could get that information, it would be a game changer.

Hecate's eyes glowed again, her mist filled the library, and another book flew into her hands. The book was thick and dark gray—it had probably been black when it was new. Something *evil* leaked out of its pages, and I shivered in its presence.

It opened itself, and its pages flipped to the center.

Hecate's eyes widened.

"What is it?" Harper asked.

"The Dark Wand," she said, and when she looked back up at Harper, it was with sorrow—and with fear.

"What's the Dark Wand?"

"It's one of the four Dark Objects," the goddess explained. "As you know, magic always balances itself. Light and dark. One can't exist without the other. There are the four Holy Objects—the Holy Grail, the Holy Sword, the Holy Wand, and a final object that will reveal itself in time. Each of those objects has a dark counterpart that can only be used by a demon or dark witch. They were buried away thousands of years ago, but it seems they're back. The Dark Wand—which is the specific object in question—allows its wielder to use an unnatural amount of dark magic. Whoever broke past Utopia's boundary dome did so with the Dark Wand."

Harper cursed. "Shouldn't a prophet *somewhere* have picked up on this and warned us?" she asked.

"I'm sorry," Hecate said. "I can only answer one question."

"I didn't expect you to answer," Harper said. "But at least now we know what we're up against."

"You do." Hecate nodded, then turned to Mira. "Twin of Ice and Air," she said. "Tell me—what is your question?"

41

GEMMA

My twin looked up at Hecate, took a deep breath, and froze.

Come on, Mira, I thought. *You know what to ask.*

She swallowed and composed herself. "Where can we find the gifted vampire who's hunting us?" she asked. "Jamie Stevens."

Hecate called another book into her hands. It was dark like the previous one, and just as thick. It also had that sludgy feel of evilness leaking out of it.

It flipped open and settled on a page near the front.

Concern crossed Hecate's eyes. "Lilith," the goddess said softly.

Harper swallowed. "What about her?"

"The gifted vampire is with her," Hecate said. "Either by choice, or as a captive. Find Lilith, and you'll find Jamie Stevens."

"But Lilith is *impossible* to find," Harper said. "The Nephilim army has been trying and failing to find her for years."

"Lilith is using extremely dark magic to remain hidden," Hecate said. "Even I don't know where she is."

Dread swept from my head to my toes. Because I'd been prepared for us to go against nearly any type of monster out there.

Lilith was a whole other ballgame. I'd learned about her during my studies in Utopia. She was a greater demon, which meant only a Nephilim could kill her.

"How are we supposed to kill *Lilith?*" I asked, mainly to myself, since we'd already used our three questions for Hecate.

"We can't," Harper said. "But we don't have to kill Lilith to stop that gifted vampire from tracking your dragon magic. We just have to locate her… even though the Nephilim army has been failing at that for nearly two decades."

"We don't have to do anything except bring this information back to the Haven," Mira said. "They're the ones with experience. They can handle it from here."

I startled at my twin's response. "We can't just sit back and do nothing."

"Why not?"

"Because *we're* the ones they're after. If not for us, the others in our circle would still be alive. Everyone in Utopia would still be alive. Mary's risking her people and her kingdom by allowing us to stay in the Haven. We owe it to them to help."

Mira glanced at the floor and pressed her lips together. "How are we supposed to do that if we can't use our elemental magic?" she asked.

"My moon realm is spelled so only witch magic can be used by those who enter," Hecate replied. "All other types of magic are muted the moment a person crosses the bridge. Your dragon magic will return once you're back in your realm."

"And this vampire is tracking that magic…" Harper trailed off, looking like she was onto something.

"What're you getting at?" I asked.

"Nothing. At least, nothing yet," she said, and then she looked back to Hecate. "Thank you for answering our questions. Now, we need return to the Haven to share what we've learned. Mary said the way out of the library is far more simple than the way in?"

"I assume you mean that as a statement, not a question," Hecate said with a knowing smile.

"Of course."

The goddess unclasped the chain belt around her waist and held it out so the keys dangling from it were displayed in front of us.

The keys were about the height of my palm, and each one was unique. There must have been thirty of them in all, in metals like silver, bronze, copper, and gold. Intricate designs decorated each one, complete with crystals and symbols, and they each pulsed with magic.

"These keys take their owner from the library to any place they've been before," she said. "They also work the opposite way—you can use them in any door, and that door will open into the library. No one will be able to follow you. And you can't take anyone with you, either. One key, one person."

I itched to reach for a key—I'd always liked pretty things—but forced myself to resist.

Mira's eyes sparkled as much as the crystals.

Harper was more focused on Hecate than on the keys. "Are you giving us a key?" she asked.

"Each key is magically bound to its owner," she said. "The owner is the only one who can use the key. And I'm giving *each* of you a key. I'll be giving you a key to bring back to Ethan, too."

"I thought only witches could come to the Eternal Library," I said.

"Ethan has a trace of witch magic in his soul," she said simply. "Not enough to use, but it's there."

I glanced at Harper and Mira, but they looked just as confused as I felt.

"He has no idea that he's descended from witches," I said, sure of it. If he'd known, he would have insisted on coming with us to Moon Mountain.

"He doesn't have a witch ancestor," Hecate said.

"Then how does he have witch magic?"

"I've already answered your three questions," she said. "Now, do you want your keys, or not?"

"Of course we want them," I said.

"As I thought," she said. "Mira—pick your key first."

Confusion rushed through me. Because why did Hecate choose Mira first? Harper had far stronger witch magic than the two of us. And I cared more about being a witch than Mira did.

Give Mira more credit, I thought. *She's my sister. My twin. She's capable of just as much as I am.*

"I just pick the one I think is the prettiest?" Mira asked.

"No," Hecate said. "Close your eyes. Then focus on your magic and let it guide you to the key that matches your soul."

"Right." Mira sighed and blew a stray bit of blonde hair off her face. "Easy."

She pushed her hair behind her ears and closed her eyes. We were all silent as she reached forward.

At first, nothing happened.

Then her palm glowed silver, and the magic pulled her forward until her hand brushed against a key in the center. She wrapped her hand around the key and plucked it off the chain.

She stepped back and opened her eyes. Wonder filled them, as if she'd been touched by Hecate's magic.

"Well?" I bounced on my toes, eager to see which key my twin had chosen.

She opened her palm and revealed a silver key with a sky blue crystal at its head. Decorative swirls curled down its body until reaching the rectangular grooves at the bottom.

"It's perfect," Mira said, breathless.

"Of course it is." Hecate smiled, and a delicate chain that matched the key appeared out of thin air. "So you can wear it, always," the goddess explained. "But be sure to wear it under your shirt. Even though the key will only work for you, and even though only those who have a key know what they can do, that won't stop others from trying to steal it."

"How can you be so sure that only people with keys know what they can do?" Harper asked.

"Try again?" Hecate raised an eyebrow.

"Right. No questions." Harper cleared her throat. "You must have put an enchantment on the keys."

"A memory spell," Hecate confirmed. "You can tell anyone about the keys, but they'll forget a second later. Only those with a key can retain the knowledge of what they can do."

"So, only witches," I said.

"Or those who were once a witch and who still have a key," she said. "Like the leader of the Haven kingdom, Mary. She still has her key, although after being turned into a vampire, she has no more witch magic inside her. So she can no longer use it." Sadness passed over her eyes, like she was grieving the witch Mary had once been. But the emotion passed quickly, and she was back to business. "Now—Harper. Your turn."

Harper closed her eyes, and her palm glowed silver. In what must have been only a second, she stepped forward and grabbed a key near the edge of the chain.

Her key was silver, with a crescent moon and a small star on its head. A purple gem sat in the center of the star, and more stars formed a helix down its body.

"Witchy." Harper's eyes glinted in approval. "I like it."

The key's chain appeared out of nowhere, and Harper draped it around her neck. The gem pulsed with magic, and she played with the bottom of the key with her fingers, looking thoroughly satisfied.

"Finally, Gemma." Hecate looked to me. "Step forward and select your key."

42

GEMMA

I looked at the keys hanging from the chain, sizing them up. They were all intricate and beautiful, but some had bigger, brighter gems that sparkled more than others.

I wanted a sparkly one.

"You don't choose your key," Hecate reminded me. "Your key chooses you."

"I know." I stepped forward, closed my eyes, and focused on my witch magic. It flared to life, and I could practically see its bright orange color dancing like a flame inside me. But when my hand tingled, it was cool, not hot.

Hecate's silver magic. It pulled me forward so strongly that there was no point in trying to resist. The keys' magic pulsed outward, like each key was a living, breathing thing.

But one of their heartbeats was louder than the rest.

That one, I thought. *It's mine.*

I reached forward and wrapped my fingers around the key. It was warm, and the pointy edges of the metal dug into my skin. Its magic rushed through me and down to my core, binding itself to me like a breath of fresh air.

"Well?" Mira asked. "What'd you get?"

I opened my eyes and looked down at the key in my hand.

Disappointment coursed through me.

Because I'd chosen the plainest key in the bunch.

Its gold color was all right, although it was a dull compared to the other gold keys. And it didn't have any crystals. Instead, its head was a clock with two large wings coming out of the top, and two smaller ones coming out of the bottom.

"I guess you've always been good at keeping time," Mira finally said.

"I don't understand." I looked to Hecate, who was clasping the chain back around her waist. "Shouldn't I have gotten one that has to do with my magic?"

"Are you not pleased?"

The key's magic dimmed, like it was disappointed with my disappointment. And I immediately felt bad. Because while it wasn't sparkly, the metalwork was still pretty. At a closer look, it was actually more intricate than the others. The attention to detail was extraordinary.

As if the key could read my thoughts, its magic hummed to life again.

I put on the necklace, and the key fell happily onto my chest, like it was making a home there.

"I just don't understand what the key means," I said. "I was expecting something to do with my elements, or with witchcraft." I glanced at Harper's pretty moon and stars key.

"A key can reflect its wearer's magic," Hecate said. "But not always. I'm sure its meaning will be revealed in time."

I pulled at the key, and the chain stretched like a rubber band. When I let go, it returned to its original size.

"Cool spell," Harper said.

"I figured it would be inconvenient to have to remove the necklace every time you needed to use the key," Hecate said. "And I didn't want any witches to choke themselves if they needed to escape a situation quickly."

I glanced at the door that led to the Ivory Hall. "So I just stick this key in the keyhole, think of the Haven, and the door will open to the Haven."

"That's how the keys work," Hecate said. "But before you go, you still need one more key. Since Ethan isn't here, I'll pull his key for him."

"You can do that?" I asked.

"I'm the goddess of witchcraft," she said. "My magic is connected to all the witch magic in the world. Of course I know which key is his."

"And you knew which keys were ours before we pulled them?"

"I did." She didn't explain further. Instead, she picked a key hanging from her belt and held it up. "This one is Ethan's."

My lips parted as I took in its beauty. It was such a bright gold that my key looked dull in comparison. A gemstone with orange and green swirls took over the majority of its head, and above it was an intricately carved dragon with strong wings spread high.

"He'll love it," I said, and I stepped forward to take it.

Mira's hand pushed mine out of the way. "I'll take it for him," she said snidely.

I dropped my hand and let Mira take the key, crushed by the reminder that Ethan was with her and not with me.

Hecate looked at me with pity.

Does she know...?

It was a question I'd have to ask another time, since I'd already used my question for today. Besides, what did it matter if she knew about my dream? Her knowing about it wouldn't make it real.

It would *never* be real.

Agonizing grief pulled at my heart again.

"Gemma?" someone said—Mira. "What are you doing?"

I blinked, realizing I'd been staring into space. "Just... thinking."

"I'm sure you have a lot to think about." Hecate smiled in understanding. "But now that you've asked your questions and have received your keys, it's time you leave my library and return to the Haven."

43

GEMMA

We walked to the door, and Harper volunteered to go first.

"Go ahead," I told Mira after Harper was gone. "I'll be right behind you."

Mira clicked her key into the lock, and its blue gem glowed. Then she turned the key and opened the door. It *looked* like it led back into the Ivory Hall, but when Mira stepped through, she disappeared.

I reached for my key and looked to Hecate, who was watching calmly by my side. "Thank you. For everything," I said. "Hopefully I'll be back soon."

"I'm sure you will," she said. "And Gemma?"

"Yeah?"

"Do yourself a favor and put more trust into Fate. She'll show you the way in time."

I nodded and said okay, since I wasn't going to say no to a goddess. But internally, I cursed Fate. Because if Fate were on my side, wouldn't she have had Ethan stay with me that first day at the cove? Like he had in my dream?

Unless Ethan and I weren't supposed to be together.

Maybe he *was* meant for Mira. And maybe I was so torn up about it because I was the one who'd always longed for a fated romance—not Mira. I'd been waiting to meet my One for as long as I could remember.

Maybe I was just plain jealous.

Disgust at myself prickled through me. Because Mira was my twin. My true loyalty was to her—not to Ethan.

I straightened and focused on the door.

When I walk through, I'll leave my feelings for Ethan behind.

I *had* to do it. Because if I sat around pining for a version of Ethan that didn't exist, I was going to make myself miserable.

And I deserved so much better than that.

Satisfied with my decision, I slid the key into the keyhole. Its wings moved up and down, and the clock rotated in a circle.

The key clicked to the side, I swung the door open, and stepped into the tearoom in the Haven.

44

GEMMA

Hecate had sent a fire message to Mary to let her know we'd be arriving, so Mary, Mom, and Ethan were already there, along with Mira and Harper. Mira was already at Ethan's side.

His familiar hazel eyes were the first ones I saw.

The eyes I'd looked into every time he'd told me he loved me. Everything about him was as I remembered from the dream, down to the curve of his lips and the wave in his hair.

Except he'd always been happy when we were together.

Now, his expression was hard, and angst darkened his eyes.

But when he saw me, he lit up with the adoring smile I remembered, and love for him consumed me. It caressed my skin like a gentle breeze, and ignited like a flame inside me. It crashed down like a wave and settled on my soul like sand at the bottom of the ocean. And, whether those months with him were a dream or not, I knew I'd love him for all of time.

I froze, overwhelmed with emotions, and someone engulfed me in a hug.

Mom.

"Gemma?" She pulled away and placed her hands on my shoulders. "Did something happen?"

"Yeah." I blinked to bring myself back into focus. "A lot happened."

"Clearly. But you look…" She paused to contemplate it. "Something's different."

I lived through an alternate past few months that only I remember.

"I'm fine." I shrugged off her hands and looked to Harper. "What have you told them so far?"

"We got here less than a minute before you did," she said. "We haven't told them anything yet."

"But that's about to change," Mary said, and she made herself comfortable on one of the colorful sofas. "Because we need to discuss everything you learned from Hecate. Assuming you asked the proper questions?"

"You knew," I said.

"I did. But I trusted you'd know what to ask, and I didn't want your mind to be on anything else but crossing the roadblocks while you hiked up the mountain. Because if you didn't make it to the Eternal Library, we wouldn't be any closer to getting answers than we were when you left."

I felt Ethan's heavy gaze on me the entire time she spoke, so much that I could barely focus on what she was saying. And I couldn't help it—I met his eyes again.

He was totally still. And he was looking at me like I was the only person in the room. Like he was longing for me. Yearning to hold me.

My heart stopped, pain crashed through me, and I looked away.

Because Ethan looked at me that way whenever he told me he loved me.

"Gemma?" Mom yanked me out of my thoughts again. "Are you sure you're okay?"

"Yeah." I forced a small smile, despite the hollow cavern expanding in my chest. "Just thinking about everything that happened on the mountain."

I also felt the weight of someone else's stare—Mira's. But I couldn't bring myself to meet my twin's eyes.

"We have *so* much to fill you in on," Harper said, although her voice was tight, like she also knew something was off. She sat down near Mary, and the rest of us followed.

It took every conscious cell in my body not to look over at Ethan again.

"It started soon after we were dropped off at the base of the mountain," Harper said. "We didn't have to walk far—" She stopped speaking mid-sentence and reached for her throat. "Why can't I keep talking?"

Mary simply smiled. "The journey up Moon Mountain is something only witches who've done it are able to know," she said. "Rachael and Ethan haven't hiked up the mountain. You're unable to speak of your journey in their presence."

"So should they leave…?"

"No," Mary replied. "Because it isn't the journey we're concerned about. It's what you learned from Hecate in the Eternal Library."

"Of course." Harper sat straighter. "We were only allowed to ask Hecate one question each. Gemma went first."

We each explained what we'd asked, and the answer we'd been given.

"We came back using our keys," Mira finished, and then she removed Ethan's key from around her neck and handed it to him. "This one's yours."

He took it and studied it, looking pleased. "It's perfect," he said, and he looked to Mary. "But there's no witch magic in my heritage. I don't understand why Hecate gave it to me."

"It's very pretty," Mom chimed in from next to me. "What does it do?"

"We just told you," I said, but I didn't continue.

Because Hecate's words echoed in my mind.

You can tell anyone you want to about the keys, but they'll forget a second later. Only those with a key can retain the knowledge of what they can do.

Mom didn't have a key. And she'd already forgotten what we'd told her about them.

"It's a token from Hecate," Mary said. "She's done Ethan a great honor by gifting it to him."

Mom nodded, but her eyes were blank. It was like everything we said about the keys went in one ear and out the other.

Ethan was focused on her, concerned, and Mary explained Hecate's memory spell on the keys.

"Got it," he said once she was done. "But I still don't understand why I have a key. I have no witch magic."

"Hecate doesn't make mistakes," Mary said. "There must be something you don't yet know."

Ethan frowned, but he didn't say any more.

"The Dark Objects," Mary continued, and she shook her head, like she was still getting it through her mind. "No one's ever spoken of such things in the entire thousand years I've been alive. And as far as I know, there's no record of them in any archive. Surely if there were, someone would have mentioned it by now."

"Their existence could have been covered up," I suggested.

"Perhaps." She nodded thoughtfully. "I'll inform the other kingdoms. As for this gifted vampire in Lilith's lair…"

"I have an idea about how we can find her," Harper said.

"You have an idea about how to find the greater demon we've been trying and failing to hunt down since before you were born?"

"Yes." She actually *smirked* at Mary. "It'll be dangerous. But if we can pull it off, I think it just might work."

45

GEMMA

AFTER HEARING HARPER'S PLAN, Raven got to work sorting out the details. Four days later, we were about to turn the plan into reality.

Harper stood across from me, bundled in a jacket and wearing winter boots that had no place in the mountainous, Indian jungle.

Since my fire kept me warm even when I wasn't actively using the element, I wore regular Haven whites. No need to get bogged down in extra clothing when it wasn't necessary.

The others had already teleported out. Me, Harper, Mira, Ethan, and the two witches transporting them were the only ones left.

I checked on Mira, and her eyes were wide in terror.

I'd tell her to stay behind, but both of us were essential to the plan.

"You good?" I asked my twin.

"No," she said, and she swallowed down her fear. "In and out. Right?"

"Yep," Harper chirped, although from the way she bounced on her toes, I could tell she was anxious, too. She took my hands, and said, "I'll go when you tell me to."

"Let's do it." The words left my lips before I could think twice.

The ground disappeared, my stomach swooped, and then, I was standing on land again. But when I opened my eyes, it wasn't the mountains I was looking at.

Packed snow blanketed the plain for as far as the eye could see. Our group of Nephilim and witches stood together, about fifty of them in all. The Nephilims' tight black Avalon uniforms stood in stark contrast against the witches' Haven whites. And while the golden-rimmed eyes of the Nephilim all watched us, none of them spoke.

Instead, they looked ready to attack at any moment.

They didn't trust us.

Raven was closest to us, her sword in hand, and she was the only one who smiled. "Welcome to Aurora, Nebraska," she said, and then she tossed her sword in the air, catching it with her other hand. "Needless to say, I haven't missed it."

She glanced over her shoulder at the abandoned, white farmhouse in the distance. It was the farmhouse where she'd once been held captive by the demons. Her rescue had revealed that the demons were hunting gifted humans, turning them into vampires, and draining them of their blood.

Over the years, the Nephilim army had located some of the bunkers and freed the captives. But they'd yet to learn what the demons were doing with the gifted vampire blood.

Add that to the list of questions I wanted to ask Hecate. *If* Hecate decided to show up the next time I returned to the Eternal Library. Because we'd used our keys to visit the library every day since returning to the Haven, and she hadn't been there any of those times.

I had a feeling that getting an audience with Hecate was a lot more rare than it had initially seemed.

One of the witches—a short one with spiky brown hair—stepped forward and smirked. "Are you going to finally show us this dragon magic of yours, or what?" she asked.

Fire warmed my core, the earth grounded my feet, and I smiled at finally being able to sink into the comfort of my elemental magic.

Mira's face paled in the moonlight.

Fiery sparks of determination flared in Ethan's eyes.

"Let's get in formation," he said, and Raven repeated his statement loudly enough for the Nephilim in the back.

Within seconds, the Nephilim and witches formed a circle around me, Ethan, Mira, Harper, and the witches who had teleported with Ethan and Mira.

Harper checked to make sure everyone was in place, then she closed her eyes and chanted in Latin. It was a spell I knew from our lessons—a boundary spell. It was one of the most advanced spells in the book. I was nowhere close to being able to do it, but magic flooded out of Harper's hands and surrounded us in a dome. The dome dimmed out, but it was still there, protecting us.

It was a much smaller version of the protection domes around the kingdoms. We would be able to leave and re-enter as we pleased, but no one else would be able to enter unless teleported in by one of the witches currently inside.

The Nephilim faced out with their swords drawn. Raven was the most magnificent of all of them, with orange magic swirling around her sword.

If she were to have an elemental affinity, I had a feeling it would be fire.

"Well?" She tilted her head and smirked. "You ready to get one step closer to magical freedom?"

My fire sparked inside me, as if it could answer her question. But the air around me chilled.

"You really don't think Lilith will come?" Mira asked.

"No way will she come." Raven rolled her eyes. "In all the years we've been fighting this war, Lilith has never put herself in the path of danger. She has minions for that. *Expendable* minions."

Minions she's been sending to kill us.

The spiky haired witch narrowed her eyes at Mira. "Are you scared?"

"Of course she's scared." Ethan came to Mira's defense. "But she has me. And Gemma." He looked to me, and I nodded. "We can do this."

"Yes." My eyes didn't leave his. "We can."

"Then stop staring at each other and do it," the witch said, and she shivered. "It's freezing out here."

"I can do something about that." I raised my arms, fire erupted from my palms, and I pushed it up, aiming for the stars.

After keeping my elements trapped for so long, it felt incredible to let loose. And while the snow melted around my feet, and the earth filled me with energy, it was my fire that fueled me.

Air circled around my fire—Mira. I glanced over at my twin, happy to see her smiling as the wind whipped around her. Flakes of snow swirled at her feet, flew up into the cyclone, and spiraled around as well.

Then another burst of fire lit up the sky—Ethan. He stood like I was, arms raised, blasts of fire pouring out of his palms. Flames danced across his skin, just like they did across mine.

As if he knew I was watching him, he glanced over and gave me a small, confident smile. The type of smile that gave off the impression that we'd already won... or that we knew we *would* win.

"We're waiting, Lilith!" Raven yelled, holding her sword up to the sky. "It's time to send your friends out to play!"

Her voice echoed across the snow-covered field.

Then, silence.

But the Nephilim and witches stayed in position, so I kept my fire burning, too. I had so *much* fire inside me—like not using it for so long had stored it up, and it was finally getting the release it craved.

Either that, or I'd been getting stronger.

Suddenly, people appeared out of nowhere around the circle. Some of their eyes glowed red—demons. Like us, they teleported to the field in pairs, each of them holding onto a witch. Many of them had swords strapped to their side.

The Nephilim pounced.

Raven was a blur as she zipped from demon to demon, leaving piles of ash in her path. The other Nephilim weren't quite as fast, but they seemed to be putting up good fights against the demons and witches.

Mira, Ethan, and I reined our magic back in.

Our job was done.

I looked to Harper and stepped toward her.

But her eyes were dark and haunted as they stared out at the Nephilim fighting the demons and witches, their cries and grunts accompanied by the clashing metal of their swords.

It was chaos.

Then, Mira screamed.

I spun around and gasped at the sight of a demon standing in front of my twin, only centimeters between them.

The demon shouldn't be in here. It shouldn't be able to get through the boundary dome.

A frail woman in a white dress stood next to the demon. Her skin was as pale as the snow, and her hair as black as Hecate's. She held a long, silver wand by her side, and the crystal at the top of it glowed red.

She smiled wickedly, spun around, and blasted red magic at the witches surrounding us.

Mira's mouth was still open, and blood dripped out of the corner of her lips.

"NO!" I yelled, and before I could think twice, I pulled the dagger out of my weapons belt, jumped at the demon's back, and rammed the dagger though its heart.

The demon disintegrated to a pile of ash at my feet.

Mira collapsed into my arms, narrowly missing my weapon's blade.

Something pressed into my stomach, and I looked down to see what it was.

The steel handle of the demon's dagger.

It was sticking out of Mira's stomach. Blood leaked out around it, staining her white tunic red.

I fell to my knees, tears streaming down my face as I cradled my twin in my arms. She didn't cry.

"We'll get you out of here," I said. "You'll be okay." I held her tighter, my heart racing as I looked around for someone—anyone—for help.

Ethan emerged from the fighting—he'd been helping the Nephilim and the witches—and rushed to our side. He was all business as he examined Mira. "Leave the dagger where it is, and don't move her," he told me, and then he rushed for the nearest witch—the one who'd brought him here—and pulled her down to kneel next to us in the snow. "Bring her to our destination and get her to a healer."

The witch created a boundary dome around the four of us, grabbed Mira's hands, and flashed out.

I stared down at Mira's blood on my palms, shocked and unable to move.

Ethan reached down and took my hands. "Gemma," he said my name calmly. "We have to get out of here."

"I don't have strong enough witch magic to teleport. And what about the others…" I looked out to where the pale witch had been blasting our witches with that wand.

It had to be the Dark Wand.

Many of our witches were collapsed onto the ground. Some of their eyes looked blankly up at the stars—dead. Others kept jumping out of the way of the wand's blasts.

I let out a breath of relief when I didn't see Harper amongst the fallen.

The witch with the wand strode forward, to where Raven finished off two demons at once.

Raven spun to face her. "Lavinia," she said. "I should have known you'd come."

"I've been waiting for this moment for years," Lavinia said. I could only see her back, but the red crystal in the wand glowed as she spoke. "When I can finally take down the indestructible Queen of Swords."

She raised the Dark Wand and blasted red magic at Raven.

Raven held up her sword with both hands and blocked the wand's magic. The magic reflected off the blade and up into the sky, where it disappeared into nothing.

Lavinia kept the magic aimed at Raven, and Raven continued to hold it off with her sword, although she trembled from the effort.

"I have the Dark Wand." Lavinia took slow, forced steps toward Raven, like she was walking through sludge. "I'm stronger than you."

"No. You're. Not." Raven narrowed her golden eyes, then rotated the angle of her blade and redirected the wand's magic so it knocked down one of the demons fighting a Nephilim. She did the same to another demon, and another. Once there were no more clear targets in range, she turned back to Lavinia. "Where's Lilith?"

"As if I'd tell you."

"I didn't think you would. But it was worth a shot."

Lavinia threw more red magic at Raven, and Raven stumbled back, although she quickly found her center again. "My wand is more powerful than your sword," Lavinia said. "You can't beat me."

"Watch me." Raven changed the angle of the sword so the magic bounced off right above the original beam.

Lavinia's own magic struck back at her.

The witch slammed backward into the snow.

Raven ran toward her and jumped, her sword raised and ready to strike.

But when she was mid-air, Lavinia flashed out with the Dark Wand.

Raven's sword struck the snow instead. She cursed, then looked around at the Nephilim and witches still fighting the demons and dark witches.

Lavinia had killed too many of our people with the Dark Wand. The demons and dark witches outnumbered us.

But Raven was quickly moving again, and before I knew it, she'd already turned four more demons to ash.

I rose to stand, and Ethan did, too. I called on my fire, ready to char a demon or dark witch, but they were all fighting our people. And while Raven had supernatural reflexes with her sword that made her fast enough to aim at our enemies while they were engaged in combat with one of our own, I wasn't comfortable risking it.

So I reached for my dagger instead.

Ethan wrapped his fingers around my wrist. "What are you doing?"

His touch warmed my skin, but I forced myself to focus. "They need help," I said.

"The Nephilim have it covered. And Mira needs you. You can't risk yourself." He paused, his voice strained, and he added, "*I* need you."

I swallowed and focused on breathing, even though it was close to impossible with him looking at me like he valued my life more than his own. "So what do you want to do?" I asked. "Stand here and watch, and do nothing?"

"That was always the plan."

I sighed, since he was right. With Lilith tracking our dragon magic, the three of us were the Nephilim army's best bait to find the greater demon.

Our job was to stay alive. Because bait was no use if it was dead.

Like Mira...

No, I shook the thought away. *She's getting treated right now. The knife was still inside her, so she didn't lose too much blood. She's going to be okay.*

Suddenly, somebody appeared in front of me, on the opposite side of the boundary dome.

Harper.

And she looked... happy.

"Did you do it?" I asked.

"I found the perfect one." She smiled wickedly. "When I brought her in, the witches were already getting started on healing Mira."

Relief rushed through me, although I wouldn't be completely relaxed until Mira was in the clear.

Harper looked around at the battle still happening on the field. The numbers were smaller—on both sides—but the Nephilim appeared to be getting an upper hand on our enemies.

Whenever it looked like one of our people was about to lose to one of theirs, Raven zipped to their side to take over.

"We need to get out of here," Harper said. "Gemma, I'll bring you first."

I looked to Ethan. "Promise you won't do anything stupid?"

"Like jump back into the fight once you're gone?"

"Yeah." I lowered my eyes, my cheeks feeling hot, then looked back up to him. "I need you, too."

My heart pounded so loudly I could hear it in my head. And despite the battle around us, it felt like Ethan and I were the only ones on the snow-covered field.

I felt like I'd just poured out my soul to him.

"My job is to protect you and Mira," he said. "With neither of you here, I have no reason to stay. Besides, Raven has it covered."

I glanced at the Queen of Swords just as she turned two more demons to ash.

"Good." I smiled, relieved. "I'll see you soon?"

"See you soon."

I took Harper's hands, nodded to let her know I was ready, and she flashed us out.

46

GEMMA

We landed on the outskirts of an African village, where the soft pinks and oranges of sunrise bathed small huts with straw roofs pointed up like teepees in its light.

A barrier dome separated the village from the tundra beyond it. And three black women in jeans and colorful tops stood inside the dome, waiting for us.

They teleported to our sides and smiled warmly. One of the women was older, although I could only tell by the strands of gray in her hair. Her skin barely had any wrinkles. All three of them wore wood bangle bracelets up their arms, and the distinct, floral smell of witch radiated off their skin.

The older woman introduced herself as Makena. The witches with her were her daughters, Lissa and Kessie.

"You must be Gemma," Makena said, then she looked to Ethan. "And you are...?"

"Ethan Pendragon."

I startled at his use of his true surname. He'd mentioned that he'd only taken the surname of Walker to better fit in on Earth, but he'd never said his true surname until now.

"Ah, yes." She smiled. "A descendent of—"

"Never mind that," Ethan cut her off. "Where's Mira?"

"She's recovering in her room."

I looked to the closest hut and shuddered at the thought of my twin being treated in such a primitive structure.

"And the witch?" Harper asked.

"In an inquisition cell. Now, come inside." She walked to me and held her hands out, and the other two witches walked to Harper and Ethan. "We'll bring you to your sister."

I took her hands, and she teleported me to the center of the village, in front of the largest hut there. Although that wasn't saying much, since none of the huts were particularly large. And the hut didn't appear to have an entrance. In fact, *none* of the huts had doors or windows.

"This is the guest hut?" I asked, hoping I didn't sound rude.

THE DRAGON TWINS

"No," she said with a small, knowing smile. "This is the entrance to the kingdom." She stepped forward, and metal probes came out of the straw roof, directly at eye level. Laser beams shot out of them and into Makena's eyes.

"Identity confirmed," a robotic voice said from somewhere near the scanner.

The roof twisted up and around like a corkscrew, revealing a thick steel tube beneath it.

I stepped back and stared, my mouth open in shock. Because that thing belonged on a space station—not in a village in Africa.

It creaked as the roof continued to move upward, then stopped at the top. The door in front of us whooshed to the side automatically, opening into a giant, industrial elevator.

Makena strode inside. "Gemma, Ethan, and Harper," she said, looking at each of us as she said our name. "Welcome to the Ward."

The elevator took us down a few floors, and opened into a steel hall.

Makena exited the elevator, although her daughters stayed inside. "Lissa and Kessie have business to attend to," she said. "But first, hand them your weapons."

Harper's hand went protectively to the handle of her sword. "Our kingdoms are allies," she said. "You can trust us."

"And we're offering you safety," replied Makena. "In exchange, we ask that you trust us in return."

I handed over my dagger first, in a gesture of good will. Ethan handed over his weapons next, followed by Harper, although Harper looked less than pleased.

"My daughters will ensure your weapons are stored in a safe space. When you leave, we'll return them to you," Makena said. "Now, come with me."

I exited the elevator, then looked back at Makena's daughters. Neither had said a word since we'd met. "Nice to meet you," I said.

"Have a safe stay," Lissa replied.

Kessie remained silent.

The doors hissed shut behind us, leaving us with Makena in the cold hall.

She'd looked so friendly up in the open air. Now, her strong cheekbones were as hard as the metal walls surrounding us.

"This is the guest hall." She spun around and led the way, the taps of her clunky boots echoing with each step. "You'll each have your own room for the duration of your stay."

Judging by how close the doors were to each other, the rooms were the sizes of prison cells.

She motioned to a large door in the center of the hall, spaced farther away from the others. "This is the communal washroom."

"We're sharing?" Harper balked and looked uneasily at Ethan.

"The only people who have private facilities are the prisoners," Makena said. "And I can assure you that the hall washrooms are far more luxurious than what they're forced to use in their cells."

"I'm sure they are," she said. "But are there separate areas for the women and the men?"

"Of course. It's easy to forget that you were born and raised in Utopia, since you're wearing Haven whites," Makena said more kindly. "Security is our highest priority in the Ward. While the wash stations are grouped close together for efficiency, you'll have privacy at all times. Would you like to see, or should we go check on Mira?"

"We'll check on Mira," I said quickly, and Harper gave the door to the washroom a dirty look as we passed it.

Makena led us to a door on the far end of the hall. She pressed her thumb to a fingerprint scanner, and the door whooshed open.

As I expected, the room was tiny—only about twice as wide as the twin bed where Mira was sleeping. It was as plain and industrial as the elevator and the hall, but at least it was clean.

"Mira." I rushed to my twin's bedside and kneeled on the floor, so we were at the same level. She was pale, but breathing. I wanted to reach for her—to touch her to make sure she was warm and alive—but I didn't want to hurt her. So I looked back at Makena. "How's she doing?"

"She's holding up well," she said. "The dagger didn't hit any vital organs. It was like that demon was trying not to kill her."

"Then why's she unconscious?" I knew enough about healing potion to know it didn't knock people out like this. She should have woken up when we'd come in.

"She was extremely panicked, so we gave her a sedative to help her relax. She kept fighting us and begging us not to drag her underground again. I tried to explain that the Ward is the safest kingdom in the world, but she refused to believe me. So I thought it best that she sleep until she was surrounded by people she trusts."

"She does hate being underground," I said, remembering how stir crazy she'd been in Utopia.

At least Utopia tried to make their kingdom welcoming with their trees, gardens, and lakes.

The Ward just felt like a cold spaceship. The metal was so thick that even though we were underground, I couldn't feel the Earth's magic through the walls.

"Can we see the wound?" Ethan asked. "So we can verify that she's healing."

"Of course." Makena walked over to Mira and lifted the bottom of her pajama top up to show her abdomen.

There was a red, mangled scar where she'd been stabbed, but the wound was closed.

"It will continue to heal during the day," Makena said. "By nightfall, there will be no evidence left of the injury."

"Thank you," I said. "If there's anything we can do for you in return..."

"We want what you want—to stop Lilith, and to win this war against the demons," she said, and she looked to Harper. "You've already helped by delivering what we desired. You said she was weak?"

"I studied the dark witches in the battlefield and selected the one who looked the most scared," Harper said. "She was easy to overpower and deliver to you."

"Which means she should break easily." Makena smiled. "The High Warden is getting acquainted with her in an inquisition cell as we speak. Now, I'll show you to your rooms."

Harper yawned. From the dark circles under her eyes, she looked ready to collapse into a deep sleep the moment she got into bed.

"I'm staying with Mira," I said. "I need to be here when she wakes."

"Me, too," Ethan said.

"Understandable," Makena said. "But I need you to scan your fingerprints into the entry system so you can access your rooms. It will take less than a minute."

We followed her down the hall. My room was next to Mira's, and Harper's and Ethan's were across from ours. Getting our fingerprints in the system was simple. I peeked inside my room, unsurprised to find that it was identical to Mira's.

"We take our meals together in the mess hall," Makena told us. "But if you require any sustenance while in your room, there's a tablet on the nightstand where you can place your order."

"And then it appears out of the wall?" I joked, since there were definitely walls that created anything you wanted out of nothing in the sci-fi novels I read.

"How would it be created by the wall?" Makena looked at me quizzically. "A human will deliver it as promptly as possible."

"Of course." I nodded, back to being serious.

"And you can reach me by fire message for anything else."

Another advanced spell I'd yet to come close to mastering. I'd tried back at Utopia, but all I'd ended up doing was burning the letter with my elemental magic.

My elemental fire was *very* different from the harmless fires witches created while sending fire messages.

"You can also send me a message via the tablet," she continued, likely for Ethan's benefit. "Everyone will be turning in for bed soon. The bugle will sound before breakfast, and Mira will be healed by then, so I expect to see you all there."

She teleported out, leaving the three of us in the hall.

Harper yawned again and stretched her arms. "I need sleep," she said. "But first, a hot shower." She glanced at the door to the washroom, and then to Ethan.

"I won't go in there until you're done," he said. "You have my word."

She nodded, apparently satisfied, and headed for the washroom.

"Let's see if that tablet has white hot chocolate with extra whipped cream and marshmallows," Ethan said once Harper was gone.

"What?" I blinked, confused about where that had come from.

"Your comfort drink," he said. "Right?"

"How do you know that?" I hadn't had white hot chocolate since before we'd left for Utopia. And definitely never when Ethan had been around.

At least, not when *this* Ethan had been around.

The other Ethan—the one who loved me—always knew when I wanted my favorite drink.

Don't think about him like that, I chided myself. *The "other Ethan" isn't real.*

The reminder hurt as much as always. Especially since I loved this Ethan as much as the "other Ethan," despite him not returning my feelings.

"You've told me before." Now, Ethan was the one who looked confused.

"No. I definitely haven't." I watched him closely, every nerve ending feeling like it had been electrified.

What if those months we'd had together weren't a dream? I wasn't sure what else they could be, but in a world full of magic, wasn't anything possible?

"Maybe Mira mentioned it," he said, and just like that, the moment was broken. "Anyway, we both need sleep for tomorrow. I'm going to get some blankets and set them up on her floor. We'll sleep in shifts?"

"Yeah," I said, and then I shuffled back into Mira's room, picked up her tablet, and placed an order for two white hot chocolates.

Because if my memories—or whatever they were—served correct, then Ethan loved my comfort drink just as much as I did.

47

GEMMA

Five days.

That was how long it took for the dark witch Harper had brought to the Ward to talk.

The four of us were studying in the guest common room when Makena sent us a fire message to let us know that the prisoner wanted to speak with us. She sent vampire wardens to get us, and they escorted us into the elevator, which took us deeper into the ground than I thought possible.

Mira fidgeted more and more as we continued down. Even though she was fully healed, she'd been struggling to breathe while we'd been in the Ward. She was having panic attacks, which were mental instead of physical, so healing potion couldn't do anything for her. And she refused any type of sedatives, since we needed to always be aware in case we were attacked.

Well, *Ethan* had told her to refuse sedatives, and she'd listened to him.

He'd been staying in her room every night, sleeping with her on that small twin bed to help her relax. I'd walked in on them once, snuggled up together with his arms wrapped around her, protecting her. I couldn't get the image out of my mind.

Seeing him with her felt so *wrong*.

Especially when I could still feel the ghost of his arms around me from when he'd held me every night for weeks.

Finally, after we must have been hundreds of meters below ground, the elevator hissed to a stop.

It opened, and Makena waited for us in a hall nearly identical to the guest hall. Except the doors in this hall were closer together—practically next to each other—and they shimmered with the glow of boundary domes. But these boundary domes weren't the bright colors of a light magic spell that kept people from getting in.

They were gray and black. Dark magic spells to keep whoever was inside imprisoned.

Because the Ward was home to the highest-level security supernatural prison in the world, where the worst of the worst were locked up. None had ever escaped.

We stepped out, and the two vampire wardens—who hadn't spoken a word to us—followed.

Makena barely acknowledged them before turning around and leading us down the hall.

The vampire wardens stayed in front of the elevator.

"We cast multiple layers of protection spells around each cell, to guarantee that the prisoners have no chance of escape," Makena explained, motioning to the doors. "Each layer is cast by a different witch." She walked a few more doors down. "Here we are. Cell six thousand and eighty-two."

I glanced at Mira, and her eyes were just as wide as I knew mine were.

"How many prisoners are in the Ward?" I asked Makena.

"That's top secret information only known by the king and the high wardens." She stepped forward and pressed the pad of her thumb on the fingerprint scanner.

The scanner turned green.

"High Witch Makena," a robotic female voice said from the speaker next to the door. "What is your request regarding prisoner six thousand and eighty-two, category mid-level dark witch?"

"I'd like to see and speak with the prisoner," Makena said.

The door shimmered and disappeared.

Illusion magic.

But witches didn't *have* illusion magic. So it had to be advanced technology.

A girl in a gray jumpsuit lay on a thin mattress on the floor. She stared emptily at the ceiling, her jet-black hair spread out in tangles around her head. The only other things in the small cell were a chamber pot, a rusted spigot coming out of the wall, and a tray with an empty glass and a bowl of untouched mush.

"Isobel," Makena said. "Sit up and face the ones who captured you."

The witch—Isobel—groaned as she pushed herself up. She was frail, with tan skin and watery gray eyes. She had metal cuffs around her wrists, although they weren't linked together with a chain. Blood crusted her hairline, but other than that, there wasn't a mark on her.

Most disturbingly, she appeared to be younger than me and Mira. Fourteen, or fifteen at the most.

Harper stepped forward, her gaze locked on the girl's, her rage so intense that I could physically feel it. "You destroyed my home," she said, her voice low and hard. "You killed my family."

Isobel continued to stare blankly ahead. If she hadn't obeyed Makena's command to sit up, I wouldn't have thought she could hear through the boundary.

"Why did you do it?" Harper slammed her fists against the boundary, and Isobel flinched backward. "Why are you working with those *monsters?*"

Isobel turned her gaze down to her lap and picked at her fingernails. They were also crusted with blood. "I'm sorry," she said, her voice barely louder than a whisper.

"Sorry isn't good enough."

Isobel only shrugged.

"You turned on your own kind," Harper continued. "Your circle may have gone dark, but you're still a witch. And you turned on us."

It was true—witches who used dark magic weren't inherently evil. There were some witches in every kingdom that used dark magic. They simply needed witches around them who used light magic to balance them out.

It only became problematic when an entire circle went dark, like the Foster witches and whatever circle Isobel was a part of.

"Once they get what they want, the demons will turn on you," Harper said. "You do realize that. Right?"

"Harper," Makena said firmly. "Isobel has already been interrogated. She's ready to make a deal with you."

"What kind of deal?" I asked. Because the scared girl cowering in the corner of her cell hardly looked ready to do much of anything.

"She's agreed to teleport you to the gifted vampire who's tracking you. In return, she'll live the rest of her life in the Ward as a citizen instead of as a prisoner."

Harper's eyes narrowed. "So you're letting her go free."

"Not free," Makena said. "She'll have to teleport back here immediately after dropping you off. Then she won't be allowed to leave the Ward, ever. If she gives us any trouble, she'll be sentenced like any other citizen."

"She deserves to stay locked up," Harper muttered.

Isobel raised her head, and her gaze sharpened. "Do you want my help or not?" she asked.

"We do," I said before Harper could get a word in. "I assume we'll make a blood oath to make sure you stick to the deal?"

Blood oaths were one of the first things Harper and Alice had taught us. They could be done by any supernatural, no matter how strong their magic. And there was no going against a blood oath. If you did, your blood would turn against you and kill you in one of the most painful ways possible—by boiling you alive from the inside.

Blood oaths weren't used often—a pure display of trust was preferred amongst potential allies—but certain situations called for them. Such as this one.

"Of course a blood oath will be necessary," Makena said. "Isobel has a long way to go before she can be trusted."

"She can never be trusted," Harper said.

"Don't let your grief harden you to the potential inside of everyone," Makena said kindly. "Other than the demons and angels, no one is purely good or purely evil. When guided by someone who believes in them, even the darkest of souls has the potential to see the light."

Harper paused, and for a moment, I thought she was going to agree. Then she glanced at Isobel, who looked all ratty in her cell, and her expression hardened again. "Just because they have the potential to see the light doesn't mean they will," she said.

"That's true. But we owe it to them to try."

"She deserves to rot in this cell," Harper said. "But do with her what you will. All I care about is that she brings us to the gifted vampire."

Isobel glared at Harper, and the cuffs around her wrists glowed. She trembled, her expression twisted in pain, and she dropped her hands back down to the floor.

Harper looked at the cuffs suspiciously. "What was that?"

"The cuffs stop witches from using their magic," Makena said.

"But there's no spell for that."

"No spell that you know of," she said. "Or that you're capable of performing."

"I'm a high witch of Utopia," Harper said. "I'm capable of performing any spell."

Makena raised an eyebrow. "Who says a witch performed the spell?"

Harper opened her mouth, then closed it. Her hand went to the chain around her neck—the one with Hecate's key dangling underneath her shirt.

I had a pretty good idea about what her question might be when we saw Hecate next.

"We're not accomplishing anything by standing around," Ethan said before Harper could speak. "What are the conditions of the blood oath?"

"I'll bring you, Harper, and one of the twins to the gifted vampire, Jamie Stevens," Isobel said. "Then I'll return to this cell immediately."

I stiffened. "Why only one of us?"

"No idea." Isobel shrugged and glanced at Makena. "Ask her."

I stared Makena down, waiting for an answer.

"You're going straight into Lilith's lair. She clearly wants something with you, and she wants you alive. If she didn't, then that demon wouldn't have missed all of Mira's vital organs," Makena said. "If something goes wrong, and both of you are captured, then Lilith will have what she wants. I can't allow that to happen."

"So why don't I go on my own?" Harper asked. "I'm perfectly capable of doing this myself."

"Because I didn't agree to that plan," Isobel said smugly. "It's you, the prince, and one of the twins, or nothing."

"The *prince?*" I repeated, staring dumbfoundedly at Ethan.

Ethan's hands curled into fists. "It doesn't matter," he said.

"You're a *prince?*" Mira asked. "And you don't think it matters?"

Isobel giggled, and I wondered if she was fully sane. "He's right," she finally said. "It doesn't matter. At least, not in the state that Ember's in right now."

"What do you mean?" I asked.

"The dragons have no power." She ran her index finger over the cuff on her other wrist. "They're slaves in their own realm. They haven't had power for centuries."

I glanced at Ethan to confirm if she was telling the truth. From his hard expression, and the way he wouldn't meet my eyes, she was.

"Then who *does* have power?" I asked Isobel.

"No one you ever want to meet," she said darkly. "Trust me on that."

I studied her, sizing her up.

Was she *scared* of whoever was ruling Ember?

And if she was scared, did that mean the demons and dark witches were scared, too? Could these rulers of Ember be the key to helping us bring down the demons?

"I know what you're thinking," Ethan said to me. "And no. Absolutely not."

"You don't know what I'm thinking," I said.

"You're wondering if we could ally with the rulers of Ember against the demons."

I narrowed my eyes at him. Because I wouldn't have been surprised if Mira had read me that easily, but Ethan wasn't my twin.

"How'd you know that?" I asked.

"It was obvious."

"Hm." I watched him, wondering. Because first there was the hot chocolate, and now he was reading me more easily than ever.

Just like the Ethan I remembered.

You didn't "remember" anything, I reminded myself. *You hallucinated.*

I wanted that other Ethan back so badly that I would probably grasp at anything to believe it was possible. Especially because every time this Ethan spoke to me like I was a stranger instead of someone he loved, it was like a knife to my heart, slashing it to shreds over and over and over again.

It physically hurt. So much that sometimes, I didn't think I'd ever be able to bear it.

I wished I'd stayed away from that nightshade. Whatever it had done to me was going to drive me crazy—if it hadn't already.

But I needed to control my emotions. Because right now, we had bigger issues to deal with.

"So," Harper said, glancing between me and Mira. "Which one of you wants to come with us to Lilith's lair?"

48

GEMMA

"Me," I said immediately. "I'm going."

I didn't expect Mira to argue.

I was right.

"No," Ethan said.

"What?" I stared at him, shocked. Mira was his girlfriend. He loved her. I thought he'd be happy with keeping her safe inside the Ward.

"Once we're with the gifted vampire, we'll be free to use our elemental magic against her," he said. "You and I have a stronger affinity with our fire magic than I do with air and you do with earth. Mira's strongest affinity is water. She complements my fire. And we need all the variety we can get."

"But I'm better with a sword," I said. "And when we combine our fire, we're stronger."

"You are?" Makena looked at us quizzically.

"It's both of our strongest affinity," Ethan said.

"Hm." Makena nodded, but said no more.

"Both are good points," Harper said. "But Gemma wants to go. Mira—what do you want?"

My twin's hand went to her stomach—to the spot where the demon had stabbed her. "Gemma's right—she's better with a sword," she said, speaking slowly. "And she has better control over her magic. She should go."

Harper nodded, like she'd expected that.

Ethan frowned.

Why doesn't he want me to go?

"Decision made," Makena said, and then she allowed us inside Isobel's cell so we could perform the blood oath.

Since blood oaths weren't witch magic—they were just *general* magic—Isobel could do it with the cuffs still on.

Part of the oath was that Isobel was never allowed to harm any of us or try to escape the Ward before the mission was complete, to make sure she wouldn't attack once the cuffs were removed. There were a bunch more clauses, too, to ensure Isobel didn't go rogue.

Makena had thought through everything to make sure the oath was airtight.

Ethan was the last to slice his palm, press the cut against an identical one on Isobel's palm, and seal the oath. The cuts healed immediately after they pulled away.

"It's done, then," I said.

"Yes," Makena said. "It's done."

"We need our weapons back."

"On it."

The elevator doors opened, and her daughters stepped in, carrying our weapons. One longsword and one holy dagger each. They handed them over silently, and stepped back.

Harper examined her sword—as if worried it had been tampered with—and placed it back in the sheath in her weapons belt. I took mine back without inspection, as a gesture of good will to our hosts.

"We should leave now," Ethan said. "We're well rested, and have done as much training and studying as possible. And the sooner we're done, the sooner the twins can resume practicing with their elemental magic."

Isobel held her hands out. "Who's first?" she asked.

"Me." Harper stepped forward. "I can make a sound barrier spell around the three of us—me, you, and the gifted vampire—when we arrive. That way she can't cry out for help."

"Smart," I said. "I'll go after you."

"No," Ethan said. "I'm after Harper."

"Why?"

"Because it's the safest."

"For who?"

"For you."

The ember flakes in his eyes burned with fire, and I knew he wasn't budging.

"Fine," I said, since I'd be there a second afterward, anyway. "We should get going." I didn't want to give Mira a chance to change her mind. She'd already almost been killed once.

The fear I'd felt when I saw the hilt of that dagger sticking out of her stomach... I'd never imagined a life without my twin. But in that moment, I had. And Mira was a part of me. The pit of emptiness in my soul at the thought of a life without her in it was unbearable.

I refused to let that become a reality.

"Harper?" I glanced at her.

She gave me a curt nod, then took Isobel's hands.

They were gone in a blink.

I held my breath, waiting for Isobel to return. My blood slowed, and all I could do was stare at the spot where they'd disappeared.

What if Isobel doesn't come back?

Based on the blood oath, that meant she'd be dead.

Which meant Harper would likely be dead, too.

Then Isobel reappeared, and I breathed easier. "The barrier spell is cast," she said, and she flashed out with Ethan. She returned a few seconds later and held her hands out to me. Her expression was stone cold.

I took a deep breath and placed my hands in hers.

The floor disappeared underneath my feet, my stomach flipped, and then I was back on solid ground.

I was in a small bedroom with Ethan, Harper, and a vampire in her thirties with short brown hair and red eyes.

Only demons had naturally red eyes.

"She's demon bound," Harper said, as if I didn't know that already from our studies on supernatural species. "To Lilith."

The vampire—Jamie—nodded after Harper said Lilith's name. She just stood there, in the depressing room with no windows and sparse furniture, staring at us with those creepy, demonic eyes. It was like she was a prisoner.

What more did our studies say about the demon bound?

They were forced to do whatever the demon they were bound to commanded. But they didn't have *zero* free will. And if Jamie was bound, then it meant...

"You're not willingly helping the demons," I said. "Are you?"

She shook her head slowly. "They took me," she said, her voice trembling. "They turned me into..." She paused and stared down at her hands in disgust. "Into this *monster*."

I shuddered, not knowing if she was referring to being a vampire, or to being demon bound.

"Are you here to help me?" she asked hopefully.

I swallowed, wishing I could tell her yes.

"We could only teleport in because Isobel brought us," Harper said. "But there's a boundary spell around this place. We can't teleport out."

The hope drained out of Jamie's eyes. "You're here to kill me."

"You've been tracking us." Ethan didn't answer her question. "You've been telling them where we are so they can find us and try to kill us." He flipped his hand around, opened it, and a flame burst out of his palm.

Jamie's mouth opened in an O of surprise. "You're one of them." She backed up, although she was forced to stop when she hit the inside of the boundary dome. "Dragons."

"I am." He nodded. "And it's my duty to protect the twins. As long as you're alive, you'll keep sending the demons after us. You're putting their lives in danger. Anyone who puts their lives in danger needs to be stopped."

"I'm only doing it because of *her*," Jamie said desperately. "Lilith. She's forcing me."

Harper removed the dagger from her weapons belt and stepped closer to Jamie. "The only way to unbind you from Lilith is to kill her," she said sharply. "We can't do that. At least, not yet."

The light left Jamie's eyes, and she nodded. "I understand," she said slowly. "But I'm not Lilith's only weapon."

"You're talking about the Dark Wand?" I asked.

"And the Dark Grail. That's how she bound me to her."

"No way." Harper sounded truly shocked. "The cup the demons use to bind supernaturals to them is the Dark Grail?"

Jamie nodded.

"What other Dark Objects does she have?"

I held my breath, waiting. Because every moment we stayed was more dangerous for us. But if we could get more information…

"I don't know," Jamie said. "But she has a dragon heart. It's how she's finding the Dark Objects."

Ethan brought out his dagger and pointed the tip of it toward Jamie. "Where did she get a dragon heart?" he asked calmly—*too* calmly. Like it was taking every effort to not ram that dagger into her heart.

Jamie's eyes flashed with fear. "Lavinia brought it to her," she said. "From a dragon she slayed in Australia."

Ethan stiffened, and his grip tightened around the handle of his dagger. "What was the dragon's name?"

"Bradon Pendragon," she said. "The king of the dragons."

All of the air left my chest at once.

Because Bradon was Ethan's father's name.

Ethan's father who was supposed to be away on supernatural business.

Before I could fully process the information, Ethan rushed at Jamie and buried his dagger deep in her chest.

She sucked in a sharp breath, her eyes glazed over, and she slumped forward.

Ethan removed the dagger, and I watched, speechless, as Jamie's body crumpled to the ground.

I couldn't move.

All I could do was stand there, staring.

I knew we were going to kill her. But I'd thought she was working with the demons by choice. I hadn't expected her to be bound. I hadn't expected her to give us information that could help us.

And Ethan…

I focused on him.

He glared down at Jamie's body, orange embers glowing in his hazel eyes, flames dancing along his skin. Rage radiated off him, and he breathed heavily, as if each breath pained him.

"Ethan!" Harper yelled. "The bond is severed. We have to leave."

Wind blew through the dome, and he didn't acknowledge that he'd heard her.

The door to the room opened, and three demons rushed inside. They ran at us, but the barrier dome stopped them in their tracks.

Ethan was just standing there, staring into nothing. Jamie's blood dripped off his dagger and onto the floor. The flames grew around his skin, and the wind whipped my hair against my face.

His body was there, but his mind was lost somewhere else.

I rushed toward him and placed my hands on his shoulders, forcing him to look at me. The flames that surrounded him engulfed my hands, but of course, they didn't burn me.

"Ethan," I said his name steadily, firmly. "We have to leave."

He didn't even see me.

I need to bring him back.

So I did the first thing that crossed my mind.

I leaned in and kissed him.

49

GEMMA

At first, it was like kissing a statue.

Then, his lips responded to mine. Warmth flickered through me, and he wrapped his arms around me, pulling me closer.

It was like I'd come home. Everything about him was so familiar, as if we'd done this a million times before.

Because we have.

Memories of all the times we'd kissed rushed through me, and his fingers brushed along my cheek, like he was memorizing the shape of my face.

I could have stood there kissing him forever.

But I pulled away slowly and looked up into his eyes. They were open and warm, just like I remembered.

The wind stopped, and the flames died down along his skin.

"Gemma," he said my name slowly, like he was coming out of a trance.

"Hey." My heart leaped, and I gave him a small, shy smile.

"I missed you."

"What...?" I shook my head, confused.

He looked down at me in awe.

With *love*.

For the first time since waking up from being poisoned, I was seeing *my* Ethan. And I never wanted to let him go.

"I'm taking down the boundary." Harper's panicked voice yanked me back into focus. "We need to get to that door."

I shook myself out of it and glanced around. I could talk with Ethan later. Because right now, demons prowled the boundary walls, blocking our way to the door. They circled us, staring us down like wolves eyeing their prey. Ten of them in all.

Ethan sized them up, and his expression switched to fight mode. He created twin balls of fire in his hands. "Gemma and I will hold them off with our fire," he said. "Harper—you go through the door first. We'll follow."

Ethan looked at me in a way that I knew meant, *I've got your back.* He'd hold off all the demons himself if it meant protecting me from getting hurt. And he was more than capable of doing so.

But I had my own magic.

And we worked best while fighting together.

"Since when were you the one in charge?" Harper asked.

"It's the best plan," he said. "Unless you have a better one?"

"Kill them all and show Lilith what we're made of?" She held up her dagger and grinned wickedly.

"We already did what we came here to do." Ethan glanced at Jamie's corpse. "Now we need to get out of here."

"I know." Harper frowned. "But it would be fun."

"We're sticking to the plan," he said, and then he glanced at me. "You ready?"

I called upon my fire and reflected his stance. "Let's do this."

Harper flung her hands out, and the boundary spell shimmered away. The moment it did, the demons ran through.

Ethan and I slammed the demons closest to us with fire. But the key was maintaining control. Because we weren't in a giant cavern like in Utopia. The room was small. And if it caught on fire, the flames could hurt Harper.

The demons caught in our blast grunted in pain, and their skin turned bright red. But they didn't burn like a human would have, or like the griffin had when we'd killed it.

Because there was only one way to kill a demon—with a holy weapon.

"GO!" Ethan screamed at Harper.

She stayed put and glared at the demons, who were howling as the fire charred their skin. "You're weakening them." Fire reflected in her eyes, and she held up her dagger, ready to attack. "I can easily take them down."

"Don't be stupid," I said. "Go to the door."

"*You* don't be stupid," she snapped. "Every demon killed is a small win for us in this war. These demons may only be pawns, but you have to eliminate the pawns to have a clearer shot at the queen."

I had no time to reply before she ran toward them, moving in a blur as she reached the first one and drove her dagger into its heart. It turned to ash, but before the ash hit the ground, she'd already ashed the one next to it, too.

She was fast, and good with a sword.

But the demons weren't dumb.

The moment they realized what she was doing, two of them circled around to come at her from behind.

I let go of my fire, reached for my dagger, and ran it through the back of a demon and into its heart. It turned to ash, and its sword clinked to the ground next to Harper's feet.

But I'd only gotten one of them.

The other pulled Harper to its chest and sliced a dagger across her neck.

Blood poured out like a waterfall.

A scream echoed through the room—mine.

Eyes wide, Harper dropped her dagger and pressed both of her hands to her throat, trying to stop the blood. But it poured past her fingers, and the demon let her go.

She collapsed to the ground.

Ethan rushed at the demon and ran his dagger through its heart.

There were two piles of ash behind him—he must have been fighting some of the demons while I'd jumped to save Harper.

Harper.

She'd fallen onto her stomach, so her dark hair covered her face, wet with the blood pooling around her. There was nothing I could do to help—there was no way that wound wasn't fatal—but I wouldn't leave her.

Before I could reach her, Ethan wrapped an arm around me, stopping me. He used his other hand to maintain control over his fire, creating a wall of it so the five remaining demons couldn't reach us.

"We need to get out of here," he said. "*Now.*"

I glanced at Harper, then at the demons, and then back to Harper. She lay there limply, her chest rising and falling in shallow breaths.

She was still alive.

How was that possible? There was so much blood...

"One key, one person," Ethan said. "We can't take her with us. And even if we could, we can't save her. Healing potion only heals non-fatal wounds."

I nodded, knowing he was right.

But I couldn't bring myself to leave her like this.

"I won't lose you." He eased me toward the door, still maintaining his hold on the fire. "I *can't* lose you."

Was he saying it because he was bound to protect me? Or because—

"Gemma." He let go of me and nudged me toward the door. "Use your key. I'll be right behind you."

I froze, numb from everything that had just happened. Fire blazed through the room, but I couldn't feel its warmth.

All I could feel was the pit of horror in my stomach at the knowledge that Harper was dying.

If I'd rushed to help a few seconds earlier, maybe I could have saved her.

"She was impulsive," Ethan said, as if he knew what I was thinking. "It wasn't either of our faults. She chose her own fate. Now, you need to choose yours." He looked to the door, then back at me, his eyes begging me to do as he asked. "I won't leave until you do."

I nodded slowly. Because every moment that Ethan and I stayed, we were putting ourselves in more danger.

We needed to get back to the Ward.

Back to Mira. And eventually back to Mom, who was still in the Haven and had to be worried sick about us.

I glanced at Harper. She'd stopped breathing.

Hopefully she was with her mom now, in the Beyond.

"You'll be right behind me?" I asked Ethan.

"Always."

I reached for my key, faced the door, and slipped it into the keyhole. It clicked to the side and the clock started rotating.

This is it.

I took a deep breath, opened the door, and stepped back into Hecate's Eternal Library.

50

HARPER

I sucked in a sharp breath and brought my hands to my neck.

I'd expected more pain.

But the skin there was soft and smooth. Like it had never been slashed so my life's blood could pour out of it.

I felt weak—as was to be expected—and I couldn't feel my magic.

But I was alive.

How...?

I pushed myself up and looked around. I was in a child's room with pink wallpaper, on a twin bed with a lacy white comforter. A woman with black hair and snow-white skin sat on a small rocking chair across from me, holding the Dark Wand.

Lavinia.

Her eyes met mine, and she smiled. "You're awake."

"What did you do to me?" I'd expected my voice to be raspy, after the slash to my throat. But it was the same as normal.

"I healed you," she said simply.

"But that wound was fatal," I said. "I was *dying*."

"You were." She nodded, continuing to rock back and forth. "I brought you back."

"That's not possible." My eyes went to the Dark Wand.

It had enough power to break down the boundary dome around Utopia.

Who was to say it couldn't have healed me from the brink of death?

"I didn't use the Dark Wand." Lavinia stopped rocking, sat straighter, and placed her feet on the ground. In her frilly white dress, she could pass as a child. An *evil* child. "I used another method."

"What method?"

"I had you turned into a vampire."

"What?" My stomach dropped, and I stared at her, willing her to take it back. This couldn't be happening. I was a witch. She couldn't have turned me into a vampire. Because if I was a vampire, it meant I'd no longer have my...

I reached for my magic.

There was nothing there.

My magic was gone.

I leaped off the bed to rip that wand out of her hand. But the moment my feet hit the floor, my knees buckled and my legs gave out like wet noodles from under me.

Lavinia walked over, picked me up, and set me back onto the bed.

I leaned against the wall, my chest heaving as I tried to catch my breath.

She studied me, amused. "You're in transition," she continued. "You need to drink human blood within three days to complete your change into a vampire. After that, you'll only be given animal blood, to keep you weak and under control."

"I won't do it," I said. "I'd rather die."

"We'll see about that." She raised an eyebrow, smirked, and made herself comfortable in the rocking chair again. She watched me, waiting, like she knew I had more questions.

I didn't want to give her the satisfaction.

But I *did* have more questions. And there she was, sitting so casually, waiting for me to ask them.

I might as well take as much advantage of the opportunity as I could.

"Where did you find the Dark Wand?" I asked.

"The question isn't *where* I found it," she said. "It's *how* I found it."

"I already know you found it with the dragon heart."

With Ethan's father's heart.

My heart broke as I remembered the devastation on his face when he'd found out. Because I knew that feeling—the icy numbness that rushes through your body as your heart shatters into pieces. It can never be glued back together, no matter how much time passes.

"I found it with help from the Queen of Wands." She smirked again.

I blinked, confused. Because the Queen of Wands—Selena—and her best friend Torrence had come to Utopia a few months ago. They'd needed to find a dragon heart to make sure Torrence wasn't taken prisoner by the goddess Circe. Queen Elizabeth had directed them to the Gemini circle for answers, and they'd been on their way.

But according to Gemma and Mira, Selena and Torrence had never talked to them. And everyone knew that Circe had taken Torrence, which was why the Queen of Wands was off on an adventure of her own, trying to rescue her best friend.

"The Queen of Wands failed to find a dragon heart," I said simply.

"Wrong," Lavinia said. "She and her friends found the dragon. They nearly killed him, although it didn't seem like they were going to go through with it. But then I stole him from under their noses and left them in the dust. Well, in the sand."

"Then you used the heart to find the Dark Wand," I said, and she nodded. "What other Dark Objects do you have?"

"Now you're asking the right questions." She looked at me approvingly. "So far, we have the Dark Grail, the Dark Wand, and the Dark Crown."

My mind spun.

Because we didn't have a Holy Crown. I'd never even heard of the Holy Crown.

It has to be the Holy Object for the Queen of Pentacles.

The queen who hadn't risen yet.

"What does the Dark Crown do?" I asked.

"Why would I tell you?"

"You don't know what it does." It was a guess. But she'd been pretty open with me so far, so calling her out seemed the best way to go.

Her eyes narrowed, and she pressed her lips together, like she wasn't sure she was going to say more.

I sat there silently, my eyes locked on hers, waiting.

"We *will* know, once the Dark Queen of Pentacles rises to claim it," she said. "Which is why we've been putting all our energy into bringing her here. You made it a lot more difficult by killing that vampire, but we'll figure out another way."

"The twins," I realized. "You think the Dark Queen of Pentacles is one of the twins."

"I don't just 'think' the Dark Queen of Pentacles is one of the twins," she said. "I have it on good authority that one twin will wield the Dark Crown, and the other the Holy Crown. The question is—which twin is which?"

"Neither of them will ever want to help you, no matter what this 'good authority' of yours says."

"I wouldn't be so sure of that, little witch," she said, and I balled my fists to my sides at how condescending she was being. "Oh, wait. You're not a witch anymore. It's a shame, really. I heard you were quite gifted with magic. You had to have been, to be a high witch of Utopia at such a young age."

"I'll be a strong vampire, too."

"So I was right." She laughed. "You'll complete the transition."

I said nothing.

"You'll get to see which twin joins me," she continued. "Which do you think it'll be? Gemma or Mira?"

"I already told you. Neither will join you."

"But one of them *will* step into the role of the Dark Queen of Pentacles."

"You don't know that."

"I do." She stood up, held the Dark Wand beside her, and raised her chin like a queen. "It's time for me to leave you on your own to get settled in. Don't bother trying to escape—I have demon guards stationed outside your door. And not only do you no longer have a holy weapon, but you're too weak to put up a fight."

Again, I didn't bother replying. Because we both knew she was right.

She gave me another smug smirk, and then left the room, closing the door behind her.

The door.

I reached to my neck, relieved to find the chain still there, and pulled my key out from under my shirt. My beautiful key with stars and the crescent moon. My gift from Hecate.

My ticket out.

Gathering as much strength as I could, I pushed myself out of the bed and crawled —slowly—to the door. My legs were too weak to stand, but I was able to reach up and get my key inside the keyhole.

I waited for it to click open.

Nothing happened.

I tried again, and again. But still, nothing.

My heart sank into my stomach.

Of course nothing happened. The key only worked for witches. And I wasn't a witch anymore.

Grief rushed through me as the loss of my magic became real. The loss of my identity. Because without magic, who *was* I?

Too weak to get back to the bed, I stayed on the floor and cried for what must have been an hour. But eventually, I got ahold of myself.

Because I couldn't change what had happened to me. But I'd been a strong witch. And while it was going to take work, I was going to stick to my promise to Lavinia and become a strong vampire, too.

And I wasn't going to rest until she and Lilith were dead.

THE DRAGON REALM

DARK WORLD: THE DRAGON TWINS 2

1

GEMMA

I stepped inside the Eternal Library, spun around, and stared at the door.

Come on, Ethan. I could barely breathe as I waited for him to come through. Time felt like it stood still.

There were five more demons in that room that we hadn't killed.

Had they gotten to him? Stopped him from leaving? Or worse?

Had he decided to stay back and kill them all himself? He'd been so angry. And after what he'd learned about Lavinia killing his dad, I nearly slapped myself for not considering the possibility that he might stay back for revenge.

You'll be right behind me? I remembered the words I'd spoken to him only seconds earlier.

Always.

I hadn't questioned his response.

Because I trusted Ethan with all of my soul. The Ethan in this reality… the Ethan in my dreams… he was the same. I'd felt it when I'd kissed him.

Finally, when I was seconds away from putting my key back in the lock and returning to that room, Ethan hurried out of the door.

I rushed into his arms and buried my face in his chest, inhaling his familiar, earthy scent. His arms tightened around me, warm after using his fire magic.

"What took you so long?" I asked after pulling away.

"It's only been a few seconds."

"Oh." It felt like it had been so much longer.

I stood there, speechless, my eyes locked on his hazel ones. Then, my focus drifted down to his lips.

The lips I'd kissed.

His breathing shallowed, as if he was thinking about the kiss, too.

"That wasn't the first time," he said slowly.

"What do you mean?"

"We've kissed before. I don't know how to explain it, but I *remember* it. Kind of. It's hazy, like a dream..." He shook his head and looked off to the side, then snapped his focus back to me. "I probably sound crazy."

"No," I said quickly. "You don't."

"Did you feel it, too?"

I swallowed, since where could I possibly begin? How was I supposed to explain my experience to him, when I didn't understand it myself?

"What do you remember?" I asked instead.

"The two of us, kissing in the cove," he said, his cheeks flushed. "In the library at school. In the back room in the café. In your room." His eyes roamed up and down my body, and heat rose to my cheeks, too.

Because what we'd done together in my room had been far more than kissing.

"It doesn't make sense." He scratched his head. "Unless..."

"Unless what?"

"Memory potion." He dropped his arm back down to his side and stood straighter. "Witches can make memory potion and use it to take away memories and replace them with false ones. Like what they did to Raven."

I nodded, since I knew all about what had happened to Raven—both from the textbook on the history of the supernatural world, and from the Queen of Swords herself.

She'd been taken by a witch and held captive in a prison for weeks. Afterward, she'd been given memory potion to make her forget the supernatural world. Her memories had been replaced, so she'd believed she'd jetted off to Europe and spent all of that time there, instead of being locked in a witch's prison.

Which would mean...

"You think your time with Mira wasn't real?" As I said it, I *wished* it were true.

I was a terrible sister.

"I don't know." He shrugged. "They feel real. More real than what I remember with you."

His words sent a sharp pain through my chest.

"What else do you remember with me?" I held my breath again, wishing for the impossible.

Wishing for him to remember *all* of it.

"No more than I just told you," he said. "And the memories are already fading. But maybe Hecate knows what's going on." He looked around the Library's ivory hall, but I'd already checked—Hecate wasn't there.

I'd been to the Eternal Library enough times by now to realize that Hecate usually wasn't there. It was like she was teasing us. Because the library contained endless knowledge, but only when she saw it fit to provide it to us.

"I'm sorry." Guilt filled me deep to the core as I thought about how I'd rushed up to him and kissed him. "I shouldn't have done it. I just didn't know what else to do..." I flashed back to Ethan standing there, staring at Jamie's corpse—at where he'd driven the dagger into her heart. He'd been lost in his mind, oblivious to the demons prowling the boundary dome around us. "I needed to bring you back."

He looked across the hall, and his grip tightened around the handle of the sword sheathed by his side. "She's going to pay for what she did," he said, his voice dark and deadly. "I'm going to carve out Lavinia's heart and make sure she's awake to feel every excruciating moment of it."

I wished so badly that I could take his pain away. Instead, I swallowed, unsure what to say.

"I'm the ruler of my people now—no matter how few are left of us." He still wasn't looking at me. It was like he was talking to himself, figuring out his thoughts aloud. So, despite my multitude of questions, I did what I thought he needed, and waited silently for him to continue. "I need to go to them. I need to free them. And then, we'll attack the demons. Rip them apart until there's not a single one of them left. They're going to beg for mercy, and they'll curse the day that they thought they could get away with bringing the dragons into this war."

He spun back around, and I flinched at the vengeful glint in his eyes.

Then he shook it off and was back to the warm, caring Ethan I knew and loved. "But first, we need to get back to the Ward."

I nodded and reached for my key.

The longer we stayed here, the more I feared that Ethan might want answers so badly that I'd lose him to the Library's endless halls.

"And Gemma?" he said, and I froze, waiting for him to continue. "Promise me something."

"Anything."

"Don't tell Mira. If she finds out, it'll break her."

"I know," I said, since while my twin was strong, she had one major weakness.

Ethan.

And I was going to make sure she never found out that he was my biggest weakness, too.

2

GEMMA

I STEPPED through the library door first, and emerged in the guest common room of the Ward.

As we'd discussed, Mira and Makena were waiting for us there. Mira paced around, running her fingers down a strand of her short blond hair. Makena sat at the head of the table, perfectly still.

Mira stopped walking, and her wide blue eyes met mine.

Guilt washed over me again. My chest hurt—it was like someone had taken a belt, wrapped it around my ribcage, and kept tightening it until I was going to explode.

I'd never be able to look at my twin the same way again. And if she knew about me and Ethan...

She'd hate me.

I wished I didn't think it possible that my twin could ever hate me. But she'd become so obsessed with Ethan that it was like she loved him more than me.

I didn't have much time to continue spiraling in my downward thoughts, because Ethan entered the room a few seconds after me.

Mira's eyes lit up, and she ran into his arms.

He hugged her back, but his eyes were blank, as if he felt nothing.

Finally, after a few painful seconds of watching the two of them together, Mira pulled away and looked up at Ethan. "Harper?" she asked, and she glanced to me, waiting for one of us to answer.

I shook my head no, unable to say it out loud.

Harper's dead.

I couldn't save her.

We left her behind.

But Harper had already stopped breathing when we'd left her. And she'd chosen to fight those demons, even though we had a clear path to the door.

Still, I should have reacted faster to help her. If I had, maybe she'd be here.

"Let's sit down." Ethan led Mira to the table, and they sat side by side.

I sat across from Ethan and stared down at my hands, unable to look at him. If I did, I was sure my sister would see my love for him splattered across my face.

Makena cleared her throat. "Explain what happened," she said.

Ethan took the lead, telling them everything that had happened from the moment we'd been dropped off in Lilith's lair.

"I'm sorry to hear about your father," Makena said once he was finished. "From what I've heard, he was an excellent king."

Ethan nodded. "His footsteps will be impossible to fill."

"It will be difficult," Makena said. "But every leader brings his or her people in a new direction. I have confidence that you'll make your father proud."

"I'll have to, eventually," he said. "But the Elders lead our people—*my* people—whenever my father's gone. And he was gone more than he was there, so he could be here on Earth looking after me and my sister. We were always his priority." He looked to Mira, and then to me. "Because my job is to look after the two of you. And the two of you are my people's priority."

"They believe we're destined to save them," I said, remembering what he'd told us after we'd received our magic. Then I remembered what Isobel—the dark witch being held captive in the Ward—had told us before we'd left. "The dragons in Ember are slaves. And they think we can free them."

"Which is why the two of you are a priority," Ethan said. "By keeping you alive, I'm ensuring the freedom of my people."

My first instinct was to say that Mira and I weren't strong enough to save a realm of enslaved dragons. But I pressed my lips together, keeping the thought to myself.

Because right now, Ethan needed something to believe in. He needed a purpose.

That purpose was me and Mira.

I stole a glance at him, surprised to find he was looking straight at me.

I looked away as quickly as possible.

Luckily, Mira was focused on the door we'd both came in through.

"Why did Harper do it?" she asked. "The two of you were holding off the demons with your magic. You gave her a straight path out of there. She knew you could hold them back long enough to follow after her. So why'd she fight them?"

"Harper was angry." Makena's voice was hard and firm. "Lilith's dark army destroyed her home and killed nearly everyone she knew. Harper was also an extremely strong witch—not just for someone her age, but for *any* witch. It made her arrogant. Anger and arrogance don't mesh together well."

"Don't talk about her that way," I snapped.

Makena barely reacted. "I'm simply answering your sister's question."

I glared at her in response.

Everyone in the Ward was so cold and unfeeling. I couldn't wait to get out of there.

"Harper was right to be angry," Ethan said, and from the steady way he spoke, I could tell it was taking him every effort to contain his anger, too. "But Makena's right. Harper was impulsive, and it got her killed. I won't let either of you make that same mistake."

"We won't," Mira said quickly. "Especially because we have no reason to go back there."

"I don't just mean there," Ethan said. "I mean *anywhere*. Lilith might not be able to track you through your magic anymore, but she's still after you. You won't be safe until she's dead."

"But only a Nephilim can kill a greater demon," Mira said. "We literally *can't* kill her. And neither can you."

"We might not be able to make the killing blow," Ethan said. "But there are other ways we can help."

"Such as what?"

"Firstly, by freeing the dragons in Ember," he said. "But more immediately, by going to the Eternal Library and asking Hecate."

Makena looked unsurprised by Ethan's statement.

It was like she hadn't heard him at all.

"Now that no one can track you when you use your dragon magic, your time is best spent practicing in the Haven," she said. "The three of you are too powerful to spend your time with your noses stuck in books. There are plenty of other supernaturals who have that task covered."

So, she didn't have a key.

The keys were spelled so that whenever someone with a key mentioned the secrets of the Library to someone without a key, the person without a key forgot immediately—or, in Makena's case, thought they'd heard something else.

She seemed to think that Ethan wanted us to search for information in various supernatural libraries, instead of getting information from Hecate in her Eternal Library.

"Don't worry," Ethan said. "We'll be practicing."

She nodded in approval.

"Thank you for letting us stay here these past few days," I added, in an attempt to change the subject.

"It was the least I could do to thank you for bringing us a witch from Lilith's army," Makena said.

I looked down at my hands.

Because *Harper* had been the one to bring Isobel to the Ward. Makena should have been thanking Harper—not us.

Ethan stood up. "It's best we be on our way," he said, and then he turned to me and Mira. "There's someone in the Haven who's going to be *very* happy to see you."

"Mom." I smiled, although it vanished a second later.

Because Mom would ask why Harper wasn't with us.

Telling her about what had happened would be like re-living it all over again.

"Is there anything I can get you before you teleport out?" Makena asked.

"No," I said, not bothering to say that we weren't strong enough witches to teleport—that we'd be using our keys. She'd simply forget a second later and return to her belief that we'd be teleporting away. "We're good."

And then, one by one, the three of us used our keys to step through the common room door and into the Eternal Library.

3

GEMMA

Hecate wasn't there.

Since it hadn't been long since we'd been in the Library, I shouldn't have expected anything else. But the keys couldn't be used to travel directly from one place to another—we always needed to stop in the Library as an in-between. So it didn't hurt to hope.

After doing a final look around to make sure Hecate wasn't hiding behind any bookshelves, we returned to the tearoom in the Haven.

The guard stationed outside the door sent a fire message to Mary to alert her of our arrival.

Minutes later, Mary entered the room, with Mom and Raven at her heels.

"Where's Harper?" Raven was the first to ask the question.

"She's gone," I said blankly, and then we sat down and told them everything that had happened in that room with the demons.

Mom was crying by the time we were done. Only a few tears—she quickly wiped them off her cheeks—but I didn't think I'd ever seen her cry. Parents were supposed to be the strong ones, and Mom had always been stronger than most.

She'd also always been the one to take care of me and Mira. But now that Mira and I had magic, and Mom still barely had any, we were the ones who needed to protect her.

The role reversal couldn't be easy on her.

"What's your plan from here?" Raven asked once they were caught up on what had happened.

"We're going to do everything we can to kill Lilith," Ethan said.

"So you want to go to Avalon."

"I thought Avalon only accepted the strongest supernaturals," Mom said.

"Avalon accepts anyone who passes the island's Trials," Raven said. "Usually that means the strongest supernaturals and humans—so the humans can train to become Nephilim. But not always. There's not an exact science behind it. But it doesn't hurt to try."

I glanced at the others, unsure what to say. Because since getting attacked in the cove, all we'd been focused on was learning how to use our magic and figuring out how Lilith was tracking us. We hadn't thought about where we'd go afterward.

Where *were* we supposed to go?

We wouldn't fit in at the café in Australia anymore. Going back there and pretending everything was normal would be impossible.

I'd started to think of Utopia as home—or at least as a place that could eventually be my home—but that had been yanked away when Utopia was destroyed.

Perhaps Avalon was a good choice.

But what if all four of us didn't pass Avalon's Trials? Then I wouldn't be able to stay. Because I wouldn't feel at home without Mom and Mira... and without Ethan.

Of course, that was assuming I'd pass the Trials. Maybe I'd fail.

"It's something to think about," Ethan finally said. "But first, we have some questions we need answered."

"No better place to get questions answered than at Avalon," Raven said. "We don't have anyone on the island with dragon magic. I'm sure Annika will be happy to sit down with you and chat."

Annika—the only full angel that lived on Earth. They called her the Earth Angel. She was also the Queen of Cups, which meant she could use the Holy Grail to turn humans into Nephilim. *And* she was the leader of Avalon.

She was probably even more intimidating than Raven.

"I thought Annika didn't know anything about the Dark Objects?" I asked.

"She doesn't," Mary said. "According to Annika, the Dark Objects aren't supposed to exist. She was more surprised to hear about them than I was."

Raven turned back to me and Mira. "By coming to Avalon, you'll be part of Avalon's Army," she continued, and then she focused on Ethan. "What better way to help us kill Lilith than that?"

"Dragons are strong fighters. I can help kill Lilith by freeing my people," he said. "And we can't do that from Avalon."

"You can't do that from here, either."

"I never said we intended to get our questions answered here."

"Then how do you plan to get them answered?"

"By using this." Ethan pulled his key out from under his shirt. "I'm going into Hecate's Eternal Library every morning until she shows up and tells me what I need to know."

Raven blinked, her eyes blank.

Mira fiddled with the chain around her neck.

"Raven," Mary said gently, and Raven looked to her, as if she hadn't heard a word Ethan had said. "The four of them have been on the run to stay alive for weeks. Give them time. This isn't a decision that needs to be made this exact second."

"I don't know about that," Raven said. "Even though Lilith doesn't have a vampire who tracks dragon magic anymore, she's not going to stop coming after the twins. And Avalon is the safest place in the world. Not even the Dark Wand can break through Avalon's barriers."

"How do you know that?" I asked.

"Because if it could, Lavinia would have used it already. Just like she did on Utopia."

"Unless Lilith has a bigger plan."

"A bigger plan than taking down Avalon?" Raven scoffed. "I highly doubt that."

"Raven," Mary said sternly. "We're tabling this discussion for now. They've been through a lot these past few days. Give them time to process."

I relaxed slightly, since Mary was right. The past few days felt like they'd happened in a blur. We needed time to think.

And time to talk to Hecate.

"Fine," Raven gave in. "Take time to think. But during that time, we're going to continue our training."

Mira groaned, and I couldn't blame her. Raven's sword fighting lessons were *exhausting*.

"Not as intensely as before, since I'm assuming you'll also be practicing using your elemental magic," she continued. "But you still need to train to fight. Because even though you can use your magic now without being tracked, it doesn't change the fact that the only way to kill a demon is with a holy weapon. Which means you have to get as good at using them as possible."

4

GEMMA

My thoughts were so consumed with my memories of Ethan that I couldn't fall asleep that night.

No, not memories.

Of my *dream* of Ethan.

Or my drug-induced hallucination of Ethan.

Whatever it was.

But even though he'd remembered, his memories had slipped away.

Maybe, if we kissed again, they'd return.

But what if they disappeared every time? I'd have my Ethan back for a few minutes, and then he'd disappear, over and over and over again.

It would be torture. Self-inflicted torture.

Maybe it would be worth it for those few minutes of happiness.

Maybe his memories would come back stronger each time, until they were ingrained in his soul as permanently as they were ingrained in mine?

But I'd never find out. Because what had happened in that room could never happen again. We'd both agreed on it.

I couldn't do that to Mira.

It would be so much easier if I could forget about the Ethan I'd loved, as easily as he'd forgotten about me.

Then, I gasped. Because maybe I could.

I instantly gave up on trying to sleep, got up, and got dressed. Because there was someone I needed to see.

And I needed to see her *now*.

The doors in the Haven didn't have locks, but when I held my key up to the doorknob, a lock magically appeared above it. I clicked it open, and stepped into the Eternal Library.

As always, I looked for Hecate.

She wasn't there.

So I opened the Library door again and walked through, ending up on the front step of the person's house I was going to see.

I felt bad for waking her up at noon, which was the equivalent to the middle of the night in the Haven, since all vampire kingdoms kept a nocturnal schedule. But this conversation couldn't wait.

So I knocked on the door.

Rosella answered in a second. She wore Haven whites, and her dark hair was secured in a loose braid that flowed down her back. Her milky eyes were pointed in my direction, although they were blank and unfocused.

"Come in." She opened the door wider and motioned for me to enter. "I've been expecting you."

Of course she'd been expecting me. I supposed that was one of the perks of having future sight.

I inhaled the sweet, sugary scent of pancakes and syrup, and smiled. The kitchen table was already set for two people, with a plate stacked high with pancakes in the center. I rarely ate pancakes—Mom said pancakes, waffles, and French toast were excuses to eat dessert for breakfast—so I welcomed the treat.

A cup full of blood sat next to Rosella's water glass, and a mug of white hot chocolate was next to mine.

"Given what you're going through, I figured you needed some comfort food," she explained as she sat down.

I also took my seat. "Do I even need to explain why I'm here?"

"Please do. I have a general idea about what's going on, but only from an outsider's perspective. For a better understanding, it would help to hear it from you. And since you haven't spoken with anyone about it yet, I feel like it would help you to talk about it, too."

And so, I launched into everything that had happened since being poisoned by the nightshade, talking so quickly that I barely had time to drink my hot chocolate, let alone eat pancakes. But the whole situation was making me so anxious that I didn't have much of an appetite, anyway.

"Have you ever remembered a dream so clearly before?" Rosella asked when I was done.

"No. I have intense dreams a lot, but they always fade, like dreams are supposed to."

"Then your experience doesn't sound like a dream."

"I know that," I said. "But if it wasn't a dream, then what was it?"

"What do *you* think it was?"

"I don't know." I let out a long, frustrated breath and stabbed my pancake with my fork. "That's why I'm asking you."

"Your intuition is strong. I'd like to hear what you think."

"My thought sounds crazy." I'd barely even let *myself* think it, since it was too out there to possibly be true.

She cocked her head to the side. "Crazier than everything that's happened in the past few months?"

"Yep," I said. "Definitely crazier."

"Then I'm all ears."

"All right." I said, sitting forward. "Have you ever heard about the multiverse theory?"

"The theory that there are an infinite number of worlds running parallel to ours, each the result of a different decision we've made."

"I guess that means you've heard of it."

"I can see the future." She smiled. "But I only see the future as it would turn out at that point in time. The moment I share a person's future with them, they can make a different decision and change the future I previously saw. So I know more than anyone that there are *many* ways life can play out."

"But is there only one way it can play out? Or does each decision cause a split, so it plays out in both ways, but in different worlds?"

"You think there's another world where you opened up to Ethan in the cove, and he ended up with you instead of your sister? And that the nightshade allowed you to experience that world?"

It sounded crazy when she said it out loud.

"Is it possible?" I asked.

"I wish I had an answer, but I'm afraid I don't know," she said sadly. "However, what I do know is this—you exist in *this* world, and the past is set in stone. You create your own future here. What point is there in wondering what your life would be like if you made a different decision in the past?"

"I don't know." I shrugged. "But maybe if nightshade brought me there once, it can bring me there again."

"If there are an infinite number of worlds, how can you guarantee that taking the nightshade would take you to the exact same world you experienced before?" she asked, although she continued before I could answer. "Even if you could return to that world, you had no control of your body in there. Would you want to be a parasite living inside this other version of yourself forever? And if you did choose that, what would happen to your actual body here?"

"You're making my head spin."

"I'd say I can't imagine it, but I see a future that's regularly changing, so I'm not one to talk," she said. "But tell me—how have these memories been making you feel?"

"Sad," I said without a second thought. "Alone. Confused. I'm grieving a relationship that no one else knows about. One that technically never existed—at least not in this world. And I can't talk about it with anyone. Except now, with you."

"And I'm more than happy to listen," she said. "But you came here to ask me a question."

"I just asked you a ton of questions."

"But you haven't asked *the* question. The one I can actually answer."

I took a deep breath. Because once I asked, there was no turning back from the decision I'd have to make.

"If I took memory potion, would it erase my memories of what I experienced with Ethan?"

I held my breath, unsure what I wanted the answer to be.

If she said no, then I wouldn't have to decide if I wanted to take the potion or not. It would be decided for me.

If she said yes… then I'd forget how incredible it felt to be loved by Ethan. How safe and cared for I was with him.

That would be a good thing, I reminded myself. *It's what I want.*

Was it?

"Yes," Rosella answered, giving me no sign if she thought this was a good idea or not. "It would."

"Do you have some for me?" I wouldn't be surprised if she did, since she knew why I wanted to talk to her before I'd arrived.

"I don't," she said. "Only an extremely powerful witch can brew a strong enough memory potion to do what you ask. And one of the ingredients she'll need will be a bit of your DNA, such as a strand of hair."

"I don't know the high witches here," I said. "At least, not well enough to make this request."

The only one I'd known well had been Harper. I swallowed down a lump in my throat at the thought of her.

I also knew Makena, but I had a sense she wasn't the type of person to do anything for free.

"Do you think you can introduce me to one here in the Haven?" I asked. "One you know I can trust?"

"I don't need to introduce you to a Haven high witch," Rosella said simply. "Because there's one you already know."

I wracked my mind trying to think of a high witch I'd had an actual conversation with in my time in the Haven. But for the majority of the time I'd been here, I'd either been training with Raven, or sleeping. I'd met some witches in passing, but that was all.

"She's not currently living in the Haven," Rosella continued. "And you met her before going to Utopia."

Where was I before going to Utopia?

Home.

"Shivani," I said the name of the Haven high witch who was watching the café while we were gone.

"Yes." Rosella nodded. "You'll get to her. I don't know how—since your magic isn't strong enough for you to teleport—but I know you will."

I reached for the chain around my neck. "I take it that means you don't know about Hecate's keys."

I assumed not—since she wasn't a witch—but it didn't hurt to try. Maybe her future sight gave her insight that no one else had.

Rosella was quiet for a second. Then she shook her head, as if coming out of a daze. "I'm sorry," she said. "What did you just say?"

"Hecate's keys," I tried again.

She said nothing. It was like she hadn't heard me at all.

"You're right," I said, giving up. "I can figure out a way to get there on my own."

"I know you will. But memory potion takes a bit of time to brew, so you should get going. You don't want anyone to realize you're gone. If they do, they might start asking questions."

She was right. I'd never been a good liar, especially when it came to lying to Mira.

Which was why I *needed* to take the memory potion.

If I didn't remember being in love with Ethan, then I wouldn't have to lie about it.

And I'd feel better, too. I wouldn't have this aching hole in my heart that no one would ever be able to fill.

But that nagging feeling still tugged at my soul. The one asking if I truly wanted to forget the greatest love I'd ever known.

"I'm going to decide to take the potion, right?" I asked Rosella.

If I knew what I'd do, then I could stop wondering and worrying.

"The decision is yours, and yours alone," she said. "If I tell you the future I see now, it could influence you to make a completely different decision. All you can do is what you feel is right. Not just for you, but for everyone involved."

I cursed inwardly. Of course it couldn't be as easy as her telling me the right choice to make.

"You best get a move on," she said, and she stood up to see me out. "The clock is ticking, and time waits for no one."

5

GEMMA

Rosella said goodbye, and she closed the door, leaving me on her doorstep.

I reached for my key necklace and stared at the lock.

I needed to get this over with. I'd feel so much better after I did.

So I stuck the key into the lock, turned it, and stepped into the ivory hall of the Eternal Library.

Hecate wasn't there. But I didn't mind, since she wasn't who I needed to see. Talking to her would waste time I didn't have.

I turned back around and stared at the door I'd just come in through. Using the key was easy—I just had to picture the place where I wanted to go. And, other than my room at home, there was no easier place for me to picture than the café downstairs. The old wooden floorboards, the shelves of books that lined the walls, and the tables surrounded by chairs and sofas. It was warm and homey—nothing like the chain coffee shops people loved in the city. When people came to Twin Pines Café, it was to sit down, *enjoy* their drink, and appreciate the view of the ocean from the back porch or outside the window.

I could almost smell the fresh coffee.

When I stepped through the door, everything was just as I remembered. It was dinner time, so the evening crowd was enjoying their sandwiches and drinks, along with plenty of tourists who'd stopped by at the end of their scenic drive along John Astor Road.

"Gemma!" someone said from one of the couches near the bookshelves. "You're back!"

My best friend from school, Jillian. She was up in a second, and nearly gave me a hug. Then she froze, her eyes running up and down my clothes.

"What are you wearing?" she asked.

I looked down at my Haven whites, feeling stupid for not remembering to change.

"Long story," I said, and I hurried toward the door to the back room. As far as I knew, Shivani had told everyone that my family and I had moved in with relatives in

New Zealand. I did *not* have time to coordinate with her cover story right now. "I'm only here for a bit. Sorry."

I disappeared into the back room, not giving her time to ask any more questions.

Hopefully Shivani could make a memory potion for Jillian, so she'd forget I was there. Slip it in her coffee or something. The taste of the coffee was strong enough that it might be able to mask the potion, especially on someone who wasn't expecting it.

I hurried upstairs to Mom's room/office. Shivani was there on the computer, managing the bookkeeping, just like Mom would have been doing if we'd been home.

She looked up from the computer, startled. "Gemma," she said, and she glanced around, checking to see if anyone else was there. "What are you doing here?"

"I need memory potion," I said quickly. "And I don't want anyone to know about it."

"So you came to me."

"Obviously." I was so eager to get this over with that I could barely stand still.

"All right," she said. "But if I'm making you memory potion, then I need to know what for."

"It's a long story," I said, hating that I had to go over it *again*.

It hurt too much to repeat. Talking about it was like opening a fresh wound.

"Then I suggest you tell me quickly." She leaned back and crossed her legs, clearly not going to budge. "Because I'm not making you a memory potion without knowing *why* I'm making you a memory potion."

I paced around the room and summarized the situation as fast as I could.

Once I finished, Shivani's expression was solemn. "I'm sorry for everything you're going through," she said. "And I'm more than happy to help. It's just…"

My heart dropped. "Just what?"

"I've never heard of nightshade doing such a thing."

"Oh." I frowned.

"But memory potion works on all memories." She forced brightness into her tone. "You have memories of these moments with Ethan. So it doesn't seem illogical to think you can drink memory potion and erase the false memories."

"So I'll replace the false memories with… different false memories."

"Ideally, you won't remember them at all," she said. "It'll be like your experiences while asleep were a forgotten dream. Although, the potion will only erase your memories of the time when you were knocked out from the nightshade. If you want to erase your memory of your kiss with Ethan, I'd have to create a separate potion. Although I don't see what good that would do, since *Ethan* would still remember it. But with your false memories erased, your emotions attached to the kiss should disappear, too."

"Good," I said, although the word felt empty. "That's good."

"I need a strand of your hair."

I plucked one out and handed it to her.

"Perfect," she said. "Now, you look like you could use some sleep."

I yawned, not realizing how tired I was until she said it. And the thought of lying down in my own bed sounded *really* nice.

I'd missed being home.

"Go get some rest," she said. "I'll wake you once the potion's ready."

6

GEMMA

I GOT BACK BEFORE SUNSET, so no one realized I'd left.

For the next two days, Ethan, Mira and I visited the Eternal Library to see if Hecate was there to answer our questions.

She wasn't.

So we continued with our training. Raven didn't give up on telling us about Avalon while we were practicing sword fighting with her. And while life on the island did sound wonderful, the thought of living there didn't feel right to me. I couldn't explain why, but it was like something was tugging me in a different direction. I didn't know where that direction was, but I could pretty confidently say it wasn't Avalon.

"He looks so hot when he fights with a sword," Mira said, ogling Ethan as he sparred with Raven. "Doesn't he?"

My heart slowed, and my blood froze.

Because it was the tone Mira used when she was egging someone on. But she wasn't even looking at me. Her eyes were glued on Ethan.

Ethan—who *did* always look attractive when fighting with a sword. Especially when he was fighting to keep us safe.

But he hadn't looked at me since we'd returned to the Haven. He'd look in my general direction, but he never met my eyes.

It was worse than when he'd acted like I was a stranger.

Because now I was a stranger whose existence he was purposefully ignoring.

Mira didn't seem to require an answer to her question, which was good, because my throat was so constricted that I wasn't sure I'd be able to speak.

Drink the potion. It'll all be better once you do.

The indestructible vial of memory potion was hidden in my undergarments drawer in my room in the Haven. A cliché place to keep it, but it would be safe there. Especially because everyone in the Haven respected each other's privacy.

Every morning and night, I'd taken it out and stared at it.

And every morning and night, I'd placed it back in the drawer.

I'd gone to all that trouble to get the potion. So why couldn't I do something as simple as *drinking* it?

"Nice job," Raven said, pulling me out of my thoughts. The tip of her sword was pressed against Ethan's chest. "If you'd been fighting anyone else, I bet you would have won."

She lowered her sword, and Ethan held out his hand, shaking hers.

"Good match," he said, and she smirked as she dropped her arm back to her side.

No one could beat the Queen of Swords when it came to fighting with blades. Especially when she was using the Holy Sword, Excalibur—the one she was holding now.

She never parted with it. I'd bet she even slept with it.

"Time to break for the day," Raven said. "I don't know about you guys, but I'm *starving*."

"Me, too," I said, and I turned to walk in the direction of the hotel. "I'll see you tomorrow!" I tried to sound as chipper as I could.

"You're having dinner in your room *again*?" she asked.

Mira waited for my answer, too.

Ethan, of course, wouldn't look at me.

"I'm tired," I said what I'd been saying every night. Training was exhausting, and fighting my feelings for Ethan was even more so. "And I want to do some reading before bed."

I also had zero desire to have dinner with Ethan and Mira. Lunch every day had been tough enough, but at least lunch was quick. In the Haven, they lingered and socialized in the dining hall long after finishing dinner.

Having dinner sent to my room so I could stare at the walls and brood over my feelings for Ethan and whether or not to take the memory potion was clearly a *much* better use of my time. Especially because if I'd just drink it, then I'd stop being so miserable. Maybe I'd even be able to relax and make some friends in the Haven, like Mira had been doing.

"You sure about that?" Raven's eyebrows knitted in concern. And while her reflexes were quick, I could have sworn she'd glanced at Ethan.

Does she know?

There was no way she could know. Except... Raven was observant. She had to be, to anticipate her opponent's every move.

And the sooner I drank that potion, the less there'd be for her to observe.

"I'm sure," I said, and then, like every night since getting back to the Haven, I hurried back to my room.

Except tonight, I intended to finally be able to sleep without tossing and turning over my unrequited love for Ethan.

Because with my memories gone, my heart could finally rest, and I could be at peace.

7

GEMMA

The next morning, it finally happened.

I stepped into the ivory hall of the Eternal Library, and Hecate was there.

She wore a sparkling purple gown, and her raven-colored hair flowed freely down her back. She was so ethereal that she took my breath away.

"You're here," I said, shocked.

"Yes." She gave me a close-lipped, knowing smile. "I'm here."

Mira stepped through the door next, followed by Ethan.

My twin stepped back the moment she saw Hecate, as if intimidated by the goddess's presence.

Ethan reached for her waist and steadied her.

I looked away, since for reasons I didn't understand, my chest always tightened at the sight of the two of them together.

Probably because of that kiss...

But that hadn't meant anything. At least, not to him. I'd just needed to snap him out of it, and he'd kissed me back because for a moment, he'd thought I was Mira.

It was an accident. I needed to forget about it.

He already had.

So I pushed the thought away and refocused on Hecate.

The goddess was as calm as ever. "I believe you have questions for me?" she asked.

"So many questions," I said quickly.

"Then I hope you've prepared your best ones."

I swallowed, then nodded. Because *Ethan* had his best question ready. From there, my best question depended on Hecate's answer to his question, and then Mira's on her answer to mine.

But I was ready to think on my feet.

"Come with me." Hecate spun around and led us through the door that opened to a never-ending hall lined with bookshelves from top to bottom. A buffet table ran down the center, displaying a variety of food and drinks for those who'd been too impatient to wait for Hecate and had gotten lost wandering the Library, trying to search for the answers to their questions on their own.

How long had they returned to the Library, day after day, before giving up on getting an audience with Hecate and venturing to find a book with the answer to their question themselves?

What question was worth risking the loss of what could be years of their lives?

And why did Hecate appear in the Library some days, and not on other days? And why would she only answer our questions if she met us in the ivory hall, and not if we were lost perusing the endless books on the shelves?

But I wasn't going to ask any of those questions. At least, not today. Because the answers wouldn't help the situation on Earth. And saving Earth was the number one priority.

"Who wants to go first?" Hecate asked.

She'd barely finished speaking before Ethan stepped forward.

"How do we kill Lilith?" he asked, his voice low and deadly. His eyes gleamed with spite—with his need for revenge.

I was grateful he was on my side, and not fighting against me. Because anyone in Ethan's path was bound to get burned by the dragon king.

It was so surreal that he was an actual *king*.

Hecate gazed down the hall. Her eyes swirled purple like the night sky, and mist poured out of them, ghostly tendrils reaching down the halls and shelves as they searched for the book with the answer.

It didn't take long for a dark gray book to fly out of the shelves and into her hand.

The mist retreated back into her eyes, the book opened, and a breeze blew the pages until landing on one in the center.

She looked at Mira, then at me, and then her gaze returned to Ethan's. "To defeat Lilith, you'll need the fourth Holy Object," she said. "The Holy Crown."

"Wow," I said, since the identity of the fourth Holy Object had been one of the questions I'd been contemplating asking. "Where can we find the Holy Crown?"

The mist swirled out of Hecate's eyes again, searching through the Library.

I'd asked a question.

I hadn't meant to ask it. But it had come out so quickly that I hadn't realized it.

Mira's lips were pressed into a firm line.

Ethan's expression betrayed no emotion. Although it was impossible to truly know, since he still wouldn't look at me.

The mist retreated, and a deep red book flew down the hall, smacking into Hecate's waiting hand. She must have placed the other book down while I'd been lost in my thoughts.

Just like before, the breeze opened the book to a page. Although this time, the page was near the end of the book.

"Hm," she said as she studied the page. As always, she didn't let any of us see what she was reading. "Very interesting."

I bounced on my toes and waited anxiously for her to continue.

"The first place you need to go to find the Holy Crown is in Ember," she said. "To the hidden dragon kingdom. Ethan knows where it is."

Ethan simply nodded.

"I didn't realize the Crown could be in more than one place." I made sure to phrase it as a thought instead of a question.

"Neither did I," she said. "But, you asked where to go to *find* it. Ember is the first place. It's likely that you'll figure the rest out from there."

"You say it like you know it for sure."

"There are many things I know," she said. "And many I don't."

It took all of my effort to stop from rolling my eyes and huffing.

Why were the people with divine knowledge always the most hesitant to share it?

"The journey to Ember is a one-way trip," I said, since I'd learned it in my studies. "Once you enter, you can't leave."

"That's because it's used as a realm for the fae and mages to send their prisoners," Ethan said, scowling. "The spell keeping them there is stronger than any barrier spell in existence. Not even the strongest, darkest supernatural prisoners can figure out to escape. My dad was the only one who could come and go as he pleased. But he never told me how..." Realization flashed over his eyes, and he reached for the chain around his neck.

"What?" Mira asked.

"My dad wore a similar chain around his neck," he said slowly, as if he were trying to recall something he'd learned long ago. "I can't remember what hung from it. But according to Hecate, I have witch blood in my veins. Which means either my father or mother had to have witch blood, too. What if it was my dad? And what if he also had a key?"

"You'd know if your dad wore a key like ours," Mira said. "Right?"

"Except I didn't have a key until recently," he said. "The magic of his key could have stopped me from knowing what it was, or even from remembering it was there."

"Maybe." Mira didn't look convinced. "But you said the spell on Ember is stronger than any other barrier spell. That *no one* can leave once they're there. What if the barrier blocks us from being able to use our keys, too?" She quickly glanced at Hecate. "That question was directed toward Ethan," she clarified. "Not to you."

If Hecate was put off by Mira's snapping at her, she didn't let it show. "I know," she said simply. "Now, what's your question?"

Mira didn't look at either me or Ethan. "Will the keys be able to take us to and back from Ember?"

Hot anger swirled within me. Why did Mira ask her question without consulting us first?

Don't be a hypocrite, I thought. *You asked your question without consulting either of them.*

But my question had slipped out. Which, I supposed, Mira's had, too.

Besides, it was information we needed to know.

"Since I created the keys, I don't need to consult a book to answer your question," Hecate said. "My keys allow to you walk through the door of the Library and into any place you've ever been. This applies to every realm, including Ember."

"But we've never been to Ember," I said. "So we can't use our keys to go there."

"Yes, that's how the keys work," Hecate said.

"So how are we supposed to get there?"

"I'm afraid you've used up your questions for the day," she said.

"Then it's a good thing I know the answer," Ethan said. "Because there are only two portals that lead to Ember. And I'm pretty sure we can get to at least one of them."

8

GEMMA

Instead of returning to our rooms in the Haven, we went straight to the tearoom.

I picked up the pen and notepad sitting on the coffee table.

Meet us in the tearoom, I wrote. *We have news.*

I ripped the paper off the notepad, folded it, and placed it in my upturned palm.

"There's a witch stationed outside this room," Mira said. "She can send fire messages to Mary."

"I know. But I can't get better without practice."

Every time I'd tried to send a fire message so far, I'd burned the letter with my elemental fire magic instead of sending it to the intended recipient with my witch magic. It was a medium-level spell—Mira still hadn't succeeded with it, either—but our phones wouldn't work outside of the Earth realm. And we needed to be able to communicate no matter where we were. Especially because we had no idea what was in store for us in Ember.

So I was determined to master this spell.

Put an imaginary barrier around your elemental magic, I remembered what Harper had said during our lessons. *Focus only on your witch magic.*

I stared at the paper and recited the incantation.

Magic tingled up from my core, traveled through my arm, and released out of my palm.

A small flame engulfed the letter, then disappeared.

No ashes remained on my palm.

"Yes!" I smiled. "I did it."

"Good job." Ethan nodded with respect. "This will be useful once we get to Ember."

"Thanks." My heart fluttered at the compliment.

Stop it, I told myself. *It was just a compliment. And he didn't even look me in the eyes when saying it.*

I needed to get him alone so I could propose my idea about both of us taking memory potion to forget about that kiss. It would be best for all three of us—me,

Ethan, and Mira. Because the kiss never should have happened. And if neither me nor Ethan remembered, it would be like it never *had* happened.

The guilt I was carrying would disappear. Ethan's, too.

I wasn't sure which Haven witch would help us out, but surely Mary could point us in the right direction.

At the thought of Mary, she opened the door and joined us in the tearoom, the letter I'd sent to her in hand. She looked back and forth between me and Mira and held it up. "One of you sent this?" she asked.

"I did." I smiled. "It was my first successful fire message."

"Well done." She walked over to one of the colorful chairs and sat down. "I assume you received an audience with Hecate?"

"We did," I said, and the three of us sat down as well and filled her in on what we'd learned.

She listened attentively, and from her calm expression, I had no idea what was going through her mind.

"There are two realms with portals to Ember," Ethan said. "Mystica and the Otherworld."

Of course, I knew about both realms from my studies. Mystica was the realm of the mages, and the Otherworld was the realm of the fae. The mages of Mystica kept mainly to themselves. But the demons had recently launched an attack on the Otherworld, so now the Otherworld was allied with Earth's supernatural kingdoms. The alliance was new—and apparently very tense and complicated—but at least it was something.

"None of us have ever been to the Otherworld," I continued. "So we can't use our keys to get there. We were hoping—"

"I can't guarantee what kind of reception you'll receive from the fae," Mary said before I could finish the sentence. "But I do have what you need to get to the Otherworld."

9

GEMMA

In all the weeks we'd spent with Ethan since getting our magic, he hadn't told us anything about his home realm. So, for the rest of the day, he prepared us for what to expect when we got to Ember.

At least, he told us what he could, since he'd left Ember when he was a small child. Most everything he knew about his home realm had been told to him by his father.

"We'll take the portal to Ember," he finished. "And then, I'll lead you to the kingdom. Well, what's left of the kingdom." A shadow crossed his eyes at that last part.

"But since you've been there before, you can use your key to go *straight* to your people," Mira said. "You can literally walk in the front door and be there. So why don't you go alone, get the Crown, and bring it back here?"

"Because it's my duty to protect you," he said. "I can't do that from another realm."

"We're safe in the Haven."

"We were supposed to be safe in Utopia, too."

She frowned and said nothing.

"Nowhere is safe," he continued. "But we have our keys. As long as there's a door nearby, we have a way out of whatever situation we find ourselves in."

And what if there's no door nearby?

I kept the thought to myself, since I didn't want to upset Mira.

"Fine," she said, still frowning. "But I'm tired. I'm going to take a nap." She used her key to exit the tearoom—presumably to go to her room.

Ethan watched her leave, his expression hard.

Whatever he was thinking, I couldn't read him. And I didn't know why I thought I'd be able to. He was one of those people who was near impossible to read.

But I could almost always read my twin.

"She wants you to go after her." I motioned at the door.

"She does." He sighed, then looked to me.

My chest tightened. Because this was the moment I'd been waiting for.

Time alone with Ethan to ask him the question that had been on my mind for days.

"Wait." I took a deep breath, glanced down at my feet, and spoke as quickly as possible. "I think we should take memory potion to forget about what happened in that room."

I nearly smacked myself. Could I have been any more generic?

I forced myself to meet his eyes, and he looked... amused.

It was the first time he'd looked me in the eyes in days. My breath caught at the intensity of his stare.

Why did his gaze have so much power over me?

"You mean the kiss?" he asked.

"Yes." My voice nearly got stuck in my throat. "That."

"No."

"What?" I startled.

"You heard me. No. I won't take the potion."

I froze, unsure what to say. In all the times I'd rehearsed this conversation in my mind, I'd never imagined he'd say no—and especially not so quickly.

I shook myself back into focus. "Why not?"

"Because it happened," he said quickly. "And, memory potion or not, we can't change that."

"But we're the only people who know. If we take memory potion, it'll be like it never happened. And that would be easier—for all three of us."

"What if I don't want to forget?"

Confusion rushed through me. Confusion... and a small thrill of happiness.

No.

I couldn't be happy about this. What we did was wrong. I wouldn't let myself feel anything else.

"We agreed that Mira should never know," I said.

"We did," he agreed. "But just because Mira will never know, it doesn't mean *we* have to never know."

"Why does it matter?" I asked. "It meant nothing. The only reason you snapped out of it was because you thought I was Mira."

"I never thought you were Mira."

"That's not true," I said. "When we kissed, you thought about all the times you'd kissed *Mira*."

"I never said that." His brow furrowed in genuine confusion.

"Yes. You did."

Silence for a few seconds as we stared each other down. Because I knew what had happened. He'd definitely said that he'd flashed back to all the times he'd kissed Mira—to all the memories they'd shared together.

Why claim otherwise?

"Fine," he muttered. "If that's what you want to think to feel better about it, then fine."

"Why are you doing this?" I asked.

"Doing what?"

"Being so... stubborn."

He let out a small chuckle. "You've known me for months," he said. "Haven't you realized? I'm always stubborn."

"You and Mira both," I said.

"And you, too," he said. "You're the most determined, focused person I've ever met.

Which, for the record, are nice ways of saying 'stubborn.'"

My breath caught again, and I took a step back to get ahold of myself. "Then you should know that I'm determined to take this memory potion. I have to do it. For Mira."

"You don't have to do anything," he said simply. "But fine. If it makes you happy, take the memory potion."

"So... you'll do it?" That was surprisingly easy.

"*I* won't do it," he said. "But I won't stop you from doing it."

I pressed my lips together. This wasn't getting us anywhere.

"You should get the potion made as quickly as possible," he said, and was it just me, or was there a twinge of pain in his voice? "It takes a few hours to brew, and we're leaving for Ember in the morning."

I stood there, confused. Because why did he want to remember that kiss? It couldn't have meant anything to him.

Could it have?

I nearly asked, but I stopped myself.

"Good point," I said instead. "Thanks."

Without a glance back at him, I spun around, turned my key in the lock, and stepped into the Library's ivory hall.

Hecate wasn't there.

Figured. I sighed in frustration.

Although it was probably a good thing that Hecate wasn't there, because in that particular moment, the only thing I wanted to know was why Ethan didn't want to forget that kiss. And that would be a waste of a question, given that there were so many more important things we needed to know regarding what we were about to face.

I stepped through the door again, and entered Mira's room.

She was lying in bed, staring up at the ceiling while spinning a strand of her hair around her fingers.

She knew I was there, but she didn't move.

I walked over to the bed, laid down next to her, and also stared at the ceiling. We stayed there like that for a few seconds, in the sort of comfortable silence that only happened with people you'd known your entire life.

"You seem happier," she finally said.

"I do?"

"Yeah. You seem... less burdened. Which makes zero sense, given what we're doing tomorrow."

I let out a long breath and kept staring at the ceiling. Because she was right—it made no sense.

"Maybe I like having a goal again," I said, trying to make sense of it by speaking it out loud. "We were in limbo before, not knowing what to do or where to go. Now, the decision's made. There's nothing else to do but focus on getting it done."

"I guess." She shrugged, and I could tell she didn't relate.

"You want me to sleep in here tonight?" I asked.

"You mean you're finally going to stop avoiding me?"

I sucked in a sharp breath. "What do you mean?"

"You've been avoiding me," she said simply. "It's like you're afraid to talk to me."

"Since when?" Panic filled me. It had to have been since the kiss. She'd noticed.

Of *course* she'd noticed. Mira might not be the most intuitive with magic, but she'd always understood people. Especially me.

"For *weeks*," she said. "Ever since you got poisoned by that nightshade."

"Huh." Something tugged at my thoughts—something important that had happened with the nightshade—but then it was gone. "I'm sorry."

"It's okay," she said. "I know it must have been scary to be that close to death."

"As if we haven't fought for our lives multiple times since getting our magic." I chuckled.

"Tell me about it," she said. "But you know what I mean. I knew we couldn't actually die on Moon Mountain… but seeing you like that… it was awful. There was nothing I could do to help you. I hated it."

"You made the healing potion," I reminded her.

"*Harper* made the healing potion. At least, she did the hard part."

"You started making it," I said. "If you hadn't, Harper might not have been able to finish in time."

"True." She smiled for the first time since I'd come into her room. "Thanks."

"For what?"

"For believing in me."

"I always believe in you," I said. "You're my twin."

"True." She finally moved her gaze away from the ceiling to look at me. "Like it or not, you're stuck with me."

"And I've always got your back," I said. "Just like I will in Ember. We're going to be okay there."

Hopefully the more times I said it, the more I'd believe it.

She nodded, saying nothing. Mira was never one to sugarcoat anything.

"We have a big day tomorrow," I finally said. "We should try to get some rest."

"I don't know if I'll be able to sleep," she said.

"Me, either. But we should try."

I hadn't expected to be able to fall asleep. I hadn't actually wanted to. Because I was going to do what Ethan had suggested and find someone to get me that memory potion. Probably Rosella. She wasn't a witch, but she'd know who to tell me to go to.

But I must have been more tired than I'd realized, because when I opened my eyes and glanced at the clock, it was the next day. Well, the next *night*, because of the Haven's nocturnal schedule.

Mira stretched and rubbed her eyes. "What time is it?" she asked.

Dread pooled in my stomach, and I said, "It's time to leave for Ember."

10

GEMMA

Saying goodbye to Mom was tough. She tried to be strong, like she'd been when we'd entered into battle with the demons and gone to Lilith's lair. But as strong as she was, she couldn't conceal her worry.

While we couldn't tell her about the keys, since she'd just forget a second later, we calmed her by telling her we could teleport between realms. We said it was an ability that only a rare number of witches had, which was relatively close to the truth.

Eventually, we hugged, said goodbye, and went to the tearoom, where Mary was waiting. Mary was in Haven whites, but the three of us wore brown tunics and pants made from rough cloth that made me feel like I belonged in a medieval village. A witch had procured the clothing for us after Ethan had explained what the people of Ember wore.

Because once we were in Ember, we needed to blend in. That wouldn't be possible in modern clothing or Haven whites.

Mary looked us over. "I was alive when clothing like this was commonplace," she said. "Back then, things were much more… primal."

"Ember is extremely different from Earth," Ethan said. "At least, from present day Earth."

Mary watched me and Mira with worry.

"We'll be okay," I said. "We have Ethan looking out for us."

Ethan nodded, looking pleased with my statement—with my trust in him. There was also a hint of question in his eyes.

He had to be wondering if I'd taken the memory potion.

Would he ask?

No, the answer came to me immediately. Because if he respected my decision, he wouldn't risk telling me and having me find out what I'd done. And I believed he did respect my decision—even though he didn't know what decision I'd made.

Mary walked to the back corner of the room, pressed her hand against the wooden panel, and pushed it open.

A secret door.

"Follow me," she said, and she led us into a dimly lit room hidden behind the tearoom.

A simple fountain—like the ones in the mall people threw pennies into for good luck—took up the majority of the room. Other than that, there were no decorations.

Mary reached into her pocket, pulled out three coins, and handed one to each of us.

I held the coin closer to examine it. Heavier than a regular coin, it was gold, with a portrait of a beautiful, doll-like woman carved into it. A delicate flower wreath sat on her head. I flipped it over and looked at the tall, elaborate crown carved on the back. Letters curved around the crown, spelling out the words "Empress Sorcha."

"Portal tokens," Mary explained. "Together, you'll toss your tokens into the water and jump into the fountain."

Nervous energy rushed through me, and I ran my fingers over the carved surfaces of the coin to calm myself.

"The Empress is waiting for your arrival," she continued. "She doesn't like to be kept waiting."

Ethan stepped up to the edge of the fountain. "We'll hold hands when we jump through," he said. "So we're never in different realms at the same time."

I stared at the water and didn't move. Because we'd be jumping *into* the water and not coming back up.

I hated having my head underwater. Just the thought made my lungs hurt, like they were already begging for air.

How did anyone *enjoy* the sensation of not being able to breathe?

"Gemma?" Mira asked, already standing by Ethan's side. "Are you coming?"

"Of course." I walked up to her side, so Mira was between me and Ethan.

Ethan's jaw tensed.

Had he expected me to stand next to him? Did he *want* me to stand next to him, so he could hold my hand when we jumped into the fountain?

It doesn't matter, I thought, shaking myself out of it. *Even if he wants to hold your hand, it's better for everyone if you don't want to hold his.*

"It'll be okay," Mira assured me. She must have thought I was still thinking about my dislike of the water, instead of beating myself up over my desire to hold her boyfriend's hand.

"I know." I couldn't look at her—or at Ethan. "Let's just get this over with."

Ethan counted to three, and we tossed our coins into the fountain.

Purple mist spread through the water, glittering like a galaxy of stars, and swirled around until it filled the fountain.

"It's time," Mary said. "Go now, before the portal closes."

Ethan and I grabbed Mira's hands at the same time, the three of us stepped up onto the edge, and I barely had time to suck in a deep lungful of air before we jumped into the sparkling purple water.

11

GEMMA

WE DIDN'T MAKE A SPLASH. I didn't even feel my feet hit the surface of the water.

Instead, we floated through nothingness. It was what I imagined it would feel like to float through space.

I opened my eyes, stopped holding my breath, and sucked in cool, crisp air. Bright lines of light surrounded us, and I gazed around in wonder. It looked like the scenes in *Star Wars* when they jumped their ships to light speed.

Before I could glance at Mira and Ethan, my feet hit solid ground, and the racing stars melted away.

I landed with so much force that I fell onto my knees, dragging Mira and Ethan down with me. Luckily, we all reacted in time to let go of each other's hands and catch ourselves with our palms. Otherwise, our faces would have smashed into the marble floor.

The quick reflexes were probably thanks to all that time training with Raven.

There was something under my hand—the gold coin. I grabbed it to place in my pocket, but stopped midway there.

Because there were two pairs of feet in front of us. One in simple, flat sandals, and the other in crystal heels.

I looked up and gasped at the sight of the women standing before us—mainly at their shimmering, iridescent wings that looked like they were made of holographic lines of light.

The woman with the crystal shoes wore a white gown with skirts that puffed out of her waist like Cinderella. Her face was unmistakably the same one as on the coin, and she wore the tall crown from the back of the coin on her pale blonde hair. Her wings were the color of diamonds, and they sparkled just like them.

She had to be the Empress of the Otherworld—Sorcha.

The other woman had gold wings, and she wore a green dress that was far less formal, although its colorful stitching looked intricate and expensive. She watched me with calm gray eyes that held decades of wisdom. Or perhaps centuries, given the immortality of the fae. She stood slightly back from the Empress, as if it weren't clear enough from the Empress's gown and crown that she was the one in charge.

Ethan hurried to his feet. Mira and I did the same.

We were in a large, open-air courtyard with Roman-styled columns lining all four sides of it. The tree leaves and flowers in the gardens were sparse and wilted, like they were barely holding onto life. Perhaps they had trouble getting enough sunlight through the light blue protection dome up ahead—the one that I knew surrounded the entire city.

I refocused on the Empress, who was eyeing Ethan in disapproval.

He bowed his head. "Empress Sorcha," he said.

"King Pendragon," she replied, and then she glanced at me and Mira, waiting.

I did as Mary had instructed us and curtsied. Hopefully the Empress didn't notice my legs shaking. "Your Highness," I said.

Mira curtsied and said the same.

"Gemma," the Empress said to me, and then she looked to my sister. "Mira."

The golden-winged woman gave me a small smile of approval, and I stopped holding my breath.

I hadn't messed up the royal greeting. At least, not terribly enough to cause offense.

"Welcome to the Otherworld," the golden-winged woman said. "I'm the Empress's advisor, Aeliana. We've been expecting you for quite some time."

"But you were only told we were coming yesterday," I said.

"True. However, I've known about your visit for longer than that."

Future sight. It had to be.

Ethan remained focused on the Empress. "Mary said you'd take us to the portal," he said.

"I will," she said. "But as I'm sure Mary also told you, the portal is a one-way trip to the prison world."

"We're aware."

"Very well. Then follow me."

The Empress led us out of the courtyard and up to the roof of the palace. There were marble, Roman-styled buildings on top of it—like a town on top of the roof.

The palace was the tallest point in the city, looking out over the densely packed buildings around it. The buildings closest to the palace were large, sturdy, marble structures. The ones on the outskirts were wood, and they looked like they might topple over at any second.

A few people we passed had wings of a variety of colors and wore stitched clothing like Aeliana. Most had no wings, and they wore gray uniforms that nearly blended into the marble floors and buildings. Red tattoos circled their right biceps, and they kept their gazes down as we passed.

Half-blood servants. The tattoos bound their magic, leaving them at the mercy of the fae.

Selena—the Queen of Wands—was also a half-blood fae. After becoming the Queen of Wands, she'd made a deal with the Empress—an alliance with Avalon in exchange for allowing her to free the half-bloods from their magical chains.

But she'd gotten so caught up in trying to save her best friend Torrence from a goddess that was keeping her captive that she'd yet to return to the Otherworld to free the half-bloods.

According to the witches in Utopia, Selena blamed herself for Torrence getting captured. But Selena was the only person in the world who could use the Holy Wand to free the half-bloods. And as I looked around at the servants we passed—all of them with downturned eyes—I wondered why Selena couldn't have put someone else in charge of rescuing Torrence so she could free the servants she supposedly cared so much about.

I didn't want to dislike someone I'd never met—especially not one of the Holy Queens. But how could Selena leave the half-bloods so helpless when she had the power to free them?

Eventually, we made it to the opposite side of the palace's roof, and the Empress stopped in front of a building that looked like a mausoleum. It was made of marble, and had columns leading to the door.

She reached into a pocket hidden in her skirts and pulled out a black key. She stuck the key into the lock, the key glowed red, like burning coal, and she opened the door.

Aeliana stayed back. "This is as far as I go," she said. "But before you leave, I have something for you." She reached into the satchel tied at her side and pulled out two gold coins.

"More portal tokens?" I said, confused. Because the three of us already had portal tokens. At least, we had the ones we'd borrowed from Mary.

"These are rare portal tokens," Mary said. "They were given to me by the only fae with omniscient sight who'd ever lived—"

"Prince Devyn," I said quickly.

She raised an eyebrow. "You know your history."

"Part of our training after receiving our elemental magic was learning the history of the supernatural world," I explained. "I learned as much as I could."

"Gemma's a great student," Ethan added, and I looked at him quizzically.

Why was he so eager to compliment me?

Mira's lips pinched with annoyance. She never liked when I received praise and she didn't.

I refocused on Aeliana, not wanting to look at Ethan *or* my twin. "Prince Devyn could do more than see the most probable future," I continued. "He could see *all* possible futures."

"Correct." Aeliana nodded. "Which meant he could prepare for more than one possible future. And when he gave these tokens to me, he told me they were the only two portal tokens in existence that connect Ember to the Otherworld. They can be used in any fountain in Ember to create a portal back here. Devyn told me to give them to you before you entered Ember."

"But there are three of us." I reached for the key around my neck, as if getting reassurance that it would work as promised.

Could Hecate have been wrong? And if she had, why were we only getting two tokens instead of three?

"He said the purpose of the tokens would eventually become clear," she said, and she placed them in my hand. "That's all I know, since I cannot see what will happen to you once you're in Ember. But I wish you the best of luck."

Her expression was grave, like she thought we were dead already.

Mira looked to me, worried, and I could practically read my twin's thoughts.

I'll back out of this if you will.

But we'd already come this far. So I shook my head, thanked Aeliana, and followed Sorcha through the door.

Ethan took Mira's hand and guided her forward.

Of course he did. It seemed like she needed his help with *everything*.

Maybe he liked the fact that she was always scared. Maybe it gave him a higher sense of purpose.

Except when he and Mira had started dating—before we'd gotten our magic—Mira had never been scared of anything.

Realizing I was getting lost in spiraling thoughts, I tore my gaze away from them and refocused on the task at hand.

Inside the mausoleum, a boundary spell the color of Sorcha's diamond wings surrounded a pit of tar. Red glowed out of it, providing the only dim light in the building.

"The portal to Ember," the Empress said. "No one has ever walked through voluntarily."

Ethan stepped forward, not looking scared in the slightest. "There's a first for everything," he said.

His fearlessness amazed me. But of course he wasn't scared. Ember was his home.

I needed to trust that he'd keep us safe there.

I also needed to trust my own ability to keep us safe. Because I had magic, too.

And I wasn't afraid to use it.

12

GEMMA

I'd expected it to hurt when I jumped through the portal.

It didn't.

Instead, it tingled, like the air was electrically charged.

It wasn't long before I tumbled out and hit the ground, landing directly on my shoulder. Pain shot up it, and I sat up and held it to relieve some of the pressure.

We were in a mostly flat desert with an occasional brown boulder along the ground. It reminded me of the Outback.

Ethan and Mira had been dumped near me. Mira looked frazzled, and Ethan was on his hands and knees, staring at the ground in a daze, like he couldn't stand up.

I didn't have time to ask him if it had started, because two groups of four people each walked around two giant brown rocks. The group to my left wore long black cloaks with hoods draped over their heads. They were like grim reapers without scythes.

The people in the other group all had wings. Green, red, blue, and yellow. Three of them were men, one was a woman, and they wore gladiator-style warrior outfits with swords strapped to their sides.

The first group was made up of dark mages, and the other was dark fae.

They represented the two major kingdoms in Ember—the Dark Allies. Their alliance was shaky at best, and was held together by one common enemy.

"Dragons." The female fae sneered, looking straight at us.

Mira hurried over to me, her eyes wide with question.

What should we do?

"How did they get loose?" the man next to the female fae said.

She drew her sword. "They don't have cuffs," she said steadily, and the other fae reached for their swords as well. Then she looked back at us and smiled, her red wings the same color as a demon's eyes. "Stay where you are," she said sweetly. "Don't use your magic on us—we won't hurt you unless we need to defend ourselves. You can trust us to keep you safe."

Her voice was calm and musical.

She was putting glamour into her tone.

But we'd been prepared for this. The tiny black stones attached to a thin chain around our ankles protected us from psychic attacks—which included fae glamour.

I stayed as still as possible, hoping it seemed like her glamour had worked on me. Then I glanced at Ethan. He was still on his hands and knees, and he took slow, forced, deep breaths, like he was straining for air.

It was happening.

I nodded at Mira, and she nodded back.

Then the mages reached up and pulled down their cloaks. Two men, and two women. Their eyes swirled with inky blackness, until they were totally dark. Like they had no souls.

"Come with us," the tallest man said. "We don't want to fight. You're more valuable to us alive than dead."

"Why do they get to go with you?" the female fae said. "We'll take the boy—he has the strongest scent. You can have the twins."

"No," the mage said. "We'll take one twin. You can have the other. We'll duel for the boy."

"A duel to the death?"

"A duel until first blood is drawn."

The female fae smirked and tilted her head. "You should take the twins and let us have the boy," she said. "He looks sick."

I squeezed Mira's hand, and we backed away from Ethan to give him space.

It shouldn't be long now...

The mages and the fae continued to watch each other, both groups on guard, apparently unsure how to proceed.

They didn't have time to figure it out, because Ethan's entire body shook with what seemed to be total agony, and then he exploded into dragon form.

He soared up into the air, his red scales glistening in the sunlight, his wings held up regally behind him. I gasped at the sight. Because while I knew dragons were big, I wasn't fully prepared for *how* big. He must have been at least six meters tall, and his wingspan twice that much.

He pulled his head back and breathed a line of fire directly at the leader of the mages.

The mage held his hands up, and black, smoky magic shot out of them, blocking Ethan's fire. The flames mushroomed out around the magic, but Ethan was stronger, and his flames pushed the thick black smoke back down toward the mage.

Then a sword flew through the air like a javelin and sliced through Ethan's right wing.

Ethan roared and pulled back on his magic, barely moving out of the way of the black magic flowing out of the mage's hands. He swung his head around and breathed a line of fire at the fae.

The blaze hit the yellow-winged fae, and he screamed as the fire ravaged his body, consuming his flesh and leaving behind the distinct smell of cooked meat.

Ethan spun back toward the mages and blasted fire at one of them. But like the first mage, she held him off with dark magic.

"We don't want to kill you!" the tall mage screamed up at him. "But we will if we have to."

The fae used this opportunity to lob another sword at Ethan.

He stopped attacking the mage and avoided the sword. Barely.

The fae with blue wings growled, raised his hands, and threw icicles at Ethan.

Ethan blasted the icicles with fire, and they melted before they reached him.

Water magic.

That fae wasn't a normal fae. He was a chosen champion—a half-blood fae chosen by a god to compete in the annual, gladiator-like competition the fae held each year called the Faerie Games. Given his water magic and the blue wings, I assumed he'd been chosen by the god of the sea, Neptune.

But I didn't have much time to think about it, because the tall, male mage shot more dark magic toward Ethan.

I did the first thing that crossed my mind—focused on the rocks surrounding the mage's feet, used my magic to raise them up into the air, and smacked them into the mage's head.

His black magic puffed out, he wobbled, then fell to the ground.

The woman standing next to him kneeled down, checked for his pulse, and let out a pained sob.

I flexed my wrist.

Did I kill him?

It felt like it should've been harder to kill a dark mage.

Hopefully it wasn't, because the other three mages spun to look at me and Mira, their inky eyes swirling with anger.

I cursed and reached for as much magic as possible—both my fire and earth magic.

I'd never taken on a mage. There *were* no mages on Earth to train with.

But there was no time like the present.

"Blast them," I said to Mira, and I blasted them with fire at the same time as my twin shot ice out of her palms.

The female mage—still on the ground—raised one of her hands and held off our elements with a cloud of black smoke. She screamed and pushed harder, and I strained against her magic.

Ethan was also sending fire toward the mages, but he was being held off by the other two.

I glanced to where the fae were standing—except there *were* no more fae standing. Ethan had burned them all to the ground.

But the mage aiming her magic toward me and Mira pushed harder, and I widened my stance, putting everything I had into holding her off with my fire. Mira was now using air, and holding off the other male mage, who'd joined the woman in trying to blast us down.

So much for them wanting to keep us alive. If that smoky magic reached us...

The strongest mages could use dark magic to kill on the spot.

It was closing in on us. And Ethan kept getting closer and closer to the ground.

The swords the fae had thrown into his wings had ripped through them. And while Ethan healed quickly, he didn't heal *immediately.*

Fear descended upon me.

The mages were beating us.

Not even ten minutes after landing in Ember, and we were failing in our mission. Maybe Mira had been right, and Ethan should have gone without us.

But it wasn't over yet. I needed to try using my earth magic again. Earth magic was trickier, because fire was my strongest affinity, and it was difficult to focus on using more than one element at a time.

Breaking from my fire magic—even for a second—could give the mage the time she needed to overpower me.

But I needed to try. Because what we were doing so far wasn't working.

I needed to reach for more rocks on the ground with my magic, like I'd done to kill that first mage.

I *felt* the rocks at their feet. But trying to raise them was like trying to raise a giant boulder.

"Gemma!" Mira yelled. "She's getting too close!"

Sure enough, there was only about a meter of fire magic between my palm and the black smoke, and she was gaining centimeters on me each second.

Suddenly, red light flashed in the corner of my eye.

Two plumes of dark smoky magic shot out from where the light had been and smacked into the mages who were attacking me and Mira.

They fell to the ground.

Dead.

The final mage must have been shocked, because Ethan cut through his dark magic and burned him to ash.

I wanted to jump in victory.

Instead, I pulled back on my magic and turned to see where the surprise dark magic had come from, ready to defend myself against whoever had wielded it if they tried to attack us.

Two people.

A girl around my age with long auburn hair, and a guy with jet black hair and skin so pale that I wouldn't have been surprised if he'd grown up underground in Utopia.

Judging from the magic they'd used, they were mages. Dark mages.

So why did they help us?

"Gemma," the girl said, as if we'd met before. "Mira. I take it the dragon is with you?" She motioned to Ethan, and I stared at her blankly.

Ethan lowered himself to the ground. Blood dripped out of the holes in his wings—I had a feeling it wouldn't have been long until he needed to land, anyway—and he shifted back to human form.

He looked exhausted, but his human form wasn't wounded. Thank God.

He hurried over to me and Mira and faced the dark mages. "Who are you?" he asked.

"I'm Torrence," the girl said, then she pointed to the dark-haired guy next to her. "This is Reed. Long story, but we've met the twins before. And we definitely weren't expecting to see you when we landed in Ember."

I stared at her, confused. Because how was Selena's best friend here? And why was she acting like she knew us?

"We haven't met before," I said simply.

"Yes, we have," she said. "Twin Pines Café. We dropped in a few months ago, but you don't remember because we made you forget. Well, *Selena* made you forget."

"The Queen of Wands?" Mira asked.

Torrence's eyes went hard, and she said nothing. Because of course she meant the Queen of Wands.

The Queen of Wands, who was currently on a mission to find Torrence and free her from Circe's island.

If Torrence had been thrown into Ember, and Selena wasn't with her...

"Selena didn't save you," I guessed. "Did she?"

"She tried," Torrence said. "But she shouldn't have. She should have known I could handle myself."

I glanced at Reed. He'd been silent so far, and from his intense expression, I had a feeling he wasn't going to be as open as Torrence.

"Something happened to Selena," Ethan guessed.

"It did." Torrence's voice was flat.

"Did Circe take her?" I asked. "Did Selena offer herself as a trade and take your place on Circe's island?"

It sounded like something one of the Queens would do. Something noble, to save someone they loved.

"Selena's not here because she's dead," Torrence said, her eyes so empty that it put me on edge. "The Supreme Mages killed her."

13

GEMMA

"Selena has the most magic of anyone in the world," I said, shocked. "That's not possible."

"Six Supreme Mages were there," Torrence said. "And they didn't just kill Selena. They killed Selena's soulmate Julian, too."

I shivered at her empty stare. Because Selena was Torrence's best friend. How was Torrence so unemotional right now?

It had to be shock. Selena's death must not have sunk in for her yet.

"Tell us what happened," Ethan said. "From the beginning."

Mira looked around, worried. "Shouldn't we get out of here?" she asked. "What if more of *them* come?" She tilted her head toward the charred remains of the dark mages and fae.

"They rotate the portal guards at nightfall." Ethan glanced up at the sun, which was high in the sky. "We have a while until then. Enough time to hear the two of you out."

I could practically hear the subtext in his tone.

Enough time to figure out if we can trust them.

It seemed crazy to not trust the Queen of Wand's best friend. But there was something *off* about Torrence. Something I couldn't put my finger on.

I barely remembered when she came into the café, but a gut instinct told me she was different than she was then. And if there was anything I'd learned since getting my magic, it was to trust my intuition. It hadn't steered me wrong yet.

"How do you know the guards' schedule?" Mira asked.

"I'm the King of Ember," Ethan said. "There might not be many dragons left, but this is our realm. We know what goes on in it."

She nodded, apparently satisfied with his answer.

I hadn't even thought to question him, because if Ethan thought we were in danger, he never would have suggested staying put.

There were only two people he thought could be putting us in danger right now—Torrence and Reed.

So I turned my attention to them, waiting for them to explain.

"What do you all know?" Torrence asked. "Because the last I'd seen the two of you, you were witches with barely any magic and no knowledge of the supernatural world. Now, you have elemental magic. *Strong* magic, from the looks of it."

"Dragon magic," I said.

"Right. Your mom said you were supposed to get dragon magic on your seventeenth birthday. I guess she was right."

I held up my hand and ignited a flame in my palm. "Dragon magic *is* elemental magic," I said, and I closed my fist, snuffing out the flame.

"Impressive," she said, although she looked anything but impressed.

"We've learned a lot since getting our magic a few months ago," I said. "We were educated on the entire supernatural world. We know you bargained with Circe, lost, and ended up a prisoner on her island."

"For all eternity," Torrence sneered.

"Right," I said. "You made the bargain to help save Selena from the Otherworld when she was held captive there. So, she felt obligated to save you in return. She, Julian, and Reed—" I paused to look at him when I said his name. He stared straight back at me, and I shuffled my feet uneasily, refocused on Torrence, and continued, "They created a search party with the Supreme Mages to find you and save you."

Torrence curled her hands into fists when I mentioned the Supreme Mages, and inky blackness swirled in her eyes.

The same inky blackness that I'd seen in the dark mages. And then, I realized...

"You used mage magic when you helped us fight the dark mages," I said. "But you're not a mage. You're a witch."

"Half-witch," she corrected me. "Half-mage. Apparently, I take after my dad." She paused, then clarified, "He was the mage. Well, he *is* the mage. Apparently he's still alive. And he's here, in Ember."

"That's why you're here?" I asked. "You want to find him?"

"Wait," Ethan said before Torrence could answer. "Let's backtrack a bit." He faced Reed. "How—and when—did you, Selena, Julian, and the Supreme Mages find Aeaea?"

Aeaea—the name of Circe's island. In Utopia, I'd learned that Circe had the ability to *move* the island. It made her nearly impossible to track when she didn't want to be found.

And she hadn't wanted to be found by Selena, Julian, Reed, and the Supreme Mages. That was what had been taking them so long to find the island.

"About two weeks ago, the Supreme Mages used their magic to find the island," Reed said coolly. "We were working on a bargain with Circe. Trying to find something she'd trade in exchange for letting Torrence go."

"How was that working out?" Ethan asked.

"Not well."

"Not surprised."

"We anchored our boat to her island, so that if she moved the island, we'd go with it," Reed continued. "Then, after about two weeks of unsuccessful discussions, Circe's palace exploded like a bomb had gone off. It took out the majority of the island. We were only safe because we were on the edge of it."

"She was trying to blast you out?" I guessed.

"No." Torrence's eyes were now completely black. "I did it. It was how I killed Circe."

THE DRAGON REALM

"*You* killed Circe? On your own?" I asked, baffled. Because Circe was far more powerful than Torrence. It shouldn't have been possible.

"Circe pissed me off," Torrence said simply. "She pushed me to a breaking point. So I killed her."

Her eyes returned to normal, and they were so haunted that dread filled my body.

"Circe was toying with me." Torrence's voice shook, but she straightened and got ahold of herself. "For weeks, she'd been trying to seduce me. But it wasn't working. She isn't my type." She glanced at Reed, then looked away when she saw he was already looking at her. "Eventually, she got impatient. You wouldn't think an immortal sorceress would get impatient, given all the time she must have on her hands." She chuckled darkly, then continued, "But she did. She tried to force herself on me. And when she did... I exploded." She motioned her hands outward and made a sound like a bomb going off.

"You blew her—and her island—up," I said, and Torrence nodded. "How?"

"I don't know." She shrugged. "But I did. I was the only thing alive on that island after the blast."

I studied her, confused. Because something didn't add up. If Torrence had been there, alive and free on the island, and the rescue party had survived the blast, then why weren't they all safe on Avalon right now?

Why had the Supreme Mages turned on Selena and Julian, and why were Torrence and Reed in Ember?

"Hm." Ethan looked as suspicious as I felt. "What happened after that?"

"Julian, Selena, Reed, and the Supreme Mages found me curled up where the palace had been, covered in ash. And then, the mages sentenced me to Ember."

"What?" I balked. "Why?"

"Because she went dark," Reed said. "Once a mage gives in like that, there's no coming back. All mages who give into darkness are sent to the prison world. Ember."

I waited for Torrence to deny it.

She didn't.

Instead, she smirked. "I didn't only kill Circe," she said. "Because I wasn't the only one she'd trapped there. She kept hundreds of men—men she'd turned into pigs. And when I turned that island to ash, the pigs went, too. All of them. Dead."

"So you murdered hundreds of people," I said darkly.

"Yes. And I don't regret it."

Reed gave us a look as if to say, *See? She's completely dark.*

Torrence stood there, unaffected by her admission.

At least there was one thing clear from her answers so far—she wasn't holding anything back. She felt no guilt for what she'd done. She didn't even seem to care that her best friend was dead.

"What happened to Selena?" I asked. "Why did the Supreme Mages kill her?"

"Right after rescuing me—while still on Circe's island—Selena tried to talk the Supreme Mages out of my sentence," she said. "When they didn't budge, she used her magic on them. Not dark magic—she wasn't trying to overpower them. I think she was just trying to scare them. She'd been working with them for weeks, so she didn't expect them to turn on her. So she was unprepared for all six of them to use dark magic on her at once. The type of dark magic that kills—the type you saw us use here today." She glanced at the dead mages nearby. "She probably could have defended herself with the Holy Wand—if she'd been ready. Then her soulmate—

Julian—was so torn up that he also attacked the Supreme Mages. They took care of him *real* quickly."

Chills ran up and down my spine at how calmly she was telling us this.

"And the Holy Wand?" Ethan asked.

"It's gone." Torrence shrugged. "Selena stored it in the ether in the final second."

Ethan's brow furrowed. "What do you mean?"

"Oh, right—you'd have no way of knowing about that. You know that Selena and Julian were gifted with magic from the gods," she said, and I nodded. "Selena received lightning and storm magic from Jupiter, the king of the gods. Julian received fighting magic from the god of war, Mars. One of Julian's abilities was that he could pull any weapon he wanted from the ether—an invisible space between worlds. Selena was able to amplify that ability with the Holy Wand and cast a spell that allows a person to store a weapon they chose in the ether." She reached into the air and pulled a sword out of nowhere. Her eyes glinted with excitement. "Cool, right?"

"Very cool." I nodded, not wanting to say anything that might provoke her to use that sword on me. Or on Mira and Ethan.

Luckily, Torrence pushed the sword back into that same invisible place in the air, like the ether was an invisible locker that was always by her side.

"I tried to use it to attack Circe a few times," she said. "It never worked. She let me keep it—probably because she didn't think I could hurt her with it."

"So the Holy Wand is locked in the ether, and the only person who can remove it—Selena—is dead," Ethan said, as if trying to get it all straight. Torrence nodded, and he continued, "Is there any other way to retrieve the Wand?"

"Not that I know of," Torrence said. "And good riddance to that. You should have seen Selena with that thing. No one should ever have that much power."

Was it just me, or did she sound *jealous*?

"The Supreme Mages followed through on their sentence and threw you into Ember." Ethan remained calm as he spoke—like he was also trying not to set Torrence off. Then he looked to Reed. "Why are you here?"

"I'm not dark, if that's what you're asking," Reed said. "But I love her."

Torrence flinched, but her expression remained stone cold.

"I couldn't let her come here alone," Reed continued. "So I attacked the Supreme Mages. But I'm the firstborn son of a highborn mage, so they wouldn't dare kill me. Instead, they sentenced me to Ember. Just like I wanted them to."

"I told him not to do it," Torrence said. "He didn't listen."

"Damn right I didn't listen."

From the fierce, determined way he looked at her, it was clear he loved her.

Before she'd gone dark, she'd earned this stoic, guarded mage's heart.

Torrence had been through a trauma. But before that, she'd been good. I knew it.

No one is ever purely good or purely evil, Makena's statement from back in the Ward echoed in my mind. *When guided by someone who believes in them, even the darkest souls have the potential to see the light.*

Reed loved Torrence. He *believed* in her.

And my intuition told me to believe in her, too.

"You saved us from those mages," I finally said. "What do you want in return?"

"Easy," Torrence said. "I want you to help *us* get back to Earth."

Us. Not *me.*

She cared about Reed enough to want him to go back with her.

It wasn't much, but it was a start.

"What do you want to do once you're back there?" Ethan asked.

"The witch Lavinia took something from me that I needed." Her eyes swirled with inky blackness again. "Once I'm back on Earth, I'm going to find her. And then, I want to kill her."

Ethan studied Torrence, like he was seeing her in a different light. "As do I," he finally said.

"Good." She smiled. "We're on the same side."

"Apparently so."

I nearly touched my pocket where I'd put the two portal tokens, but stopped myself. No need for Torrence or Reed to ask what I was hiding in there.

"We can help you," Ethan said. "But you were sent here for a reason. And as much as I'd love to fully trust you, we need to be careful."

Torrence raised an eyebrow. "Are you asking for a blood oath?"

"I am."

"Great." She removed her sword from the ether and examined its sharp edge. "Then let's get started."

14

HARPER

Three knocks sounded on the door.

I sat on the edge of the twin bed, glared at the door, and said nothing.

The person on the other side opened it anyway.

No, not a person.

A *demon*.

"Food delivery." The demon shoved a quivering human man into the room with me. The man fell down onto his knees. "Drink up."

Then the demon pulled the door shut and locked it, leaving me alone with the human.

My throat burned as I stared at the man, and an ache built in my gums. I barely saw what he looked like. All I could focus on was the pulsing vein on his neck as I inhaled the sweet, tantalizing scent of human blood.

I was so hungry that my bones felt hollow. I had no idea how much time had passed, but I was pretty sure Lavinia had kept me in transition for as long as possible, to torture me with starvation until right before I died from it.

Which explained why I wanted to sink my teeth deep into this human's neck and drink every drop of blood in his body.

But I clenched my fists and held my breath, blocking out the smell of the blood. Then, I moved my gaze away from the human's neck and met his dark brown eyes.

This scrawny, bearded man with deep circles under his tired eyes was a far contrast from the beautiful human men who'd lived in Utopia.

He watched me with resolve, like he was prepared to die.

I can't, I told myself. *I'm going to be a strong vampire. Strong enough to resist the temptation of human blood. My first act as a vampire* won't *be murder.*

Of course, I needed to drink his blood to complete my transition. But I didn't have to kill him. A full meal would suffice. The vampires in Utopia drank anywhere from one to three pints a day. A human could lose about three to four pints of blood before passing out.

If he passed out, I'd know I drank too much.
So I'd have to take it slowly.
Somehow.
"Hold out your wrist." I breathed in the least amount of air as possible as I spoke.
He blinked, confused. "You're not going to kill me?"
"Not if I can help it."
And I *could* help it.
He raised his arm to expose the inner part of his wrist, shaking. The thick vein there pulsed—not as much as the one on his neck—but enough. And I knew from the vampires in Utopia that while drinking blood from the wrist wasn't quite as satisfying as blood from the neck, it was easier to maintain self-control.
"This will probably hurt at first," I said. "Sorry." Not wanting to make this take any longer than necessary, I held my breath again and took slow, measured steps toward him.
He stayed still, apparently smart enough to know that sudden movements wouldn't fare well for him.
I lowered myself down onto my knees, grabbed his wrist, and sank my teeth into the vein.
Sweet, warm blood poured down my throat.
Euphoria.
My breathing quickened as I drank, and I tightened my grip around his arm. His blood flooded through me, and the hunger stopped gnawing my stomach and bones.
How much blood had I had so far? I had no idea. But the more I drank, the stronger I felt.
His arm grew limp.
I cursed and pushed him off me.
He lay on the floor, dazed, but alive.
I licked the remainder of his blood from my lips, watching as the puncture marks on his wrist started to heal. I expected to be hypnotized by the scent of his blood, but while it still smelled delicious, my stomach didn't hollow with pain like it had before.
I'd had enough, and my body knew it.
I backed into the corner of the room and stayed focused on the man, who was lying on his back, relieved tears streaming down his face.
I didn't know what to say to him. Ideally, I'd be able to tell him it would be okay—that I could help him. But he was trapped in Lilith's demon den just like I was.
Even though I hadn't finished him off, I suspected Lilith would send him off to another vampire who would. Of course, that was assuming she kept other vampires in this place. I hadn't seen anything but the room where she'd kept Jamie Stevens, and the room where she was keeping me. Both were small with no windows, so there was no way to know where in the world I was.
I was standing there staring at him when a familiar tingle rose in my core and expanded through my body.
Magic.
Impossible. When witches became vampires, they lost their magic. Whatever I was feeling couldn't be real. It had to be a phantom feeling, like when people lost a limb and felt like it was still there.
But I'd know my magic anywhere...
There was only one way to find out.

I closed my eyes, then teleported from one side of the room to the other.

I was still looking at the man on the ground—but from the opposite direction.

A thrill shot up my body, and it took everything in me not to spin around and cheer with victory.

I still had my magic. And I didn't intend on staying in this cramped, creepy room for a moment longer.

I hurried over to the man, took his hands, closed my eyes, and focused on teleporting to my destination.

Nothing happened.

Of course not. Like most places where supernaturals lived, Lilith had a boundary spell cast around her lair. I could teleport within this room, but I couldn't teleport *out*.

I reached for Hecate's key around my neck. Then, I looked sadly at the human man nearly passed out on the floor.

Because the keys only worked for their owners.

I wouldn't be able to bring him with me.

But I needed to get out of there. I had no idea what Lilith and Lavinia wanted with me, but they wouldn't have turned me into a vampire for no reason.

I thought back to Jamie Stevens and her red, demon bound eyes...

I refused to let them make me a slave to Lilith. I'd be of no help to *anyone* if that happened. I'd be able to save more people by leaving—even though it meant leaving this human man behind.

I *had* to do it. Because this was war. There were always casualties in war.

"I'm sorry," I said to him, and then I walked over to the door and took a deep breath.

Please don't reject me, I prayed to Hecate, since even though I still had my witch magic, I didn't know if she'd accept me now that I was a vampire.

I steadied myself and stuck my key into the lock. It glowed with magic, and I clicked it open, then stepped into the ivory hall of Hecate's Eternal Library.

The door shut behind me, and I could breathe again.

I was safe.

And I was definitely still a witch.

How?

As I thought it, Hecate walked through the door on the opposite end of the hall. She wore a long purple dress that glimmered like a galaxy of stars. Her long black hair flowed down to her waist, just like mine.

Other than the different eye color, the resemblance between the two of us hadn't passed my notice.

"Harper," Hecate greeted me. "You've changed."

I almost sarcastically said, *You noticed?* But I stopped myself.

No way was that going to be my one question.

"I almost died back there," I told her. "I *would* have died. But Lavinia had me changed into a vampire."

"She did." From the way Hecate spoke, it sounded like she was already aware of my situation.

"I shouldn't be able to use my witch magic," I continued. "I shouldn't still *have* my witch magic."

Hecate said nothing.

And I knew *exactly* what I wanted to ask her.

"Why do I still have my witch magic?"

"Come with me." She spun around and walked toward the doors that led to the never-ending hall of bookshelves. As always, a few people dressed in clothes from different decades wandered around, examining the shelves and occasionally taking a break to grab food or drink from the long banquet table in the center.

I followed Hecate to the podium at the start of the hall.

She stood in front of it, stared forward, and released starry mist from her eyes. It crawled through the hall, tendrils snaking along the shelves and brushing against the blank spines of the books as they searched for the one that held the answer to my question.

It didn't take long before the mist retreated, bringing a book with it. The book landed in Hecate's hands, flipped magically through the pages, and settled on one near the back. Once it did, the goddess's eyes returned to normal.

As she read what was on the page, she held the book at an angle so I couldn't see its contents.

"A book you've seen before," she finally observed.

"Really?" I couldn't believe it, given the endless number of books in the library.

"A list of the most recently turned gifted vampires, with your name at the end. Harper Lane—gifted with the ability to still use her witch magic."

I replayed her words in my mind, and joy rushed through me. "So my magic won't go away?"

"You've already asked your one question," she said.

I rolled my eyes, since obviously I wasn't asking a *question* question—the kind that required her to find a book on the shelves.

"Vampire gifts are permanent," I said instead. "I'll have my gift forever."

And now that I was a vampire, *forever* meant a lot more than it did when I was a witch. Because vampires were immortal.

I was *immortal*. I was going to stay seventeen forever.

The knowledge that I now had endless years ahead of me didn't feel real.

At least I looked mature for my age—easily able to pass as someone in their twenties.

"Are you all right?" Hecate asked.

"Yeah," I said. "It's just... a lot to process."

"It is. Now, I must take my leave. And I recommend you do the same." She glanced at the witches roaming the aisles, as if saying, *You don't want to stay here and end up like them.*

"Wait," I said, and she watched me patiently. "Thank you. For letting me keep my magic."

"I had nothing to do with it," she said. "It was all you. You've always been extremely gifted with magic. And, as you know, when people with an extraordinary ability are turned into vampires, that ability amplifies."

"Of course." I nodded slowly, still in shock that I had my magic. I'd spent days locked in that room while in transition, devastated about losing it.

Now, I had it back.

And I was going to use my gift to get revenge for the destruction of Utopia, by doing everything I could to kill Lilith, Lavinia, and every single demon and dark witch who walked this Earth, until the supernatural world was safe again.

15

HARPER

I USED my key to enter the Haven's tearoom. No one was there.

So I walked to the notepad, picked up the pen next to it, and wrote, *It's Harper. I'm alive and in the tearoom. Get the twins and Ethan, and meet me here.*

I folded up the paper and sent it as a fire message to Mary.

Minutes later, Mary, Rachael, and Raven rushed inside. They stared at me like I was a ghost.

"Where are the twins?" I asked. "And Ethan?"

"You're a vampire," Mary said, as if she hadn't heard my question.

"I am."

"But you just sent a fire message."

"I'm a gifted vampire. My gift is the ability to use witch magic. I'll explain more when the twins and Ethan get here."

"They're not coming," Rachael said flatly.

My stomach twisted, and I braced myself for the worst. "What happened?"

"They've left on a mission to Ember," Mary explained. "Now, I think we should all sit down. I'll send for food and refreshments. Because we have a lot to catch up on."

"Neither of my daughters will go dark," Rachael said for what must have been the fifth time.

"That's what I told Lavinia," I said. "But she sounded pretty convinced otherwise."

"She's wrong."

"I know."

Except there was no way to *really* know. Anyone could go dark if they were pushed to a breaking point. And we had no idea what was happening to them in Ember.

"Someone needs to go to Ember and warn them," I said. "I'll do it."

"No," Mary said sharply.

"Why not?"

"It's too dangerous."

"I'm a vampire gifted with witch magic," I said. "I can handle danger."

"And Ember is a prison realm full of dark mages and dark fae. Yes, you're strong, but they're stronger."

"You don't believe in me."

"I absolutely do believe in you. But this is their mission—not yours. And like you said, you're a vampire gifted with witch magic. That makes you incredibly unique."

"What's the point of being 'incredibly unique' if I can't do something to help?"

"Why do you think you can't do anything to help?" Raven asked.

"Because they're in Ember," I said. "And I'm here."

"I wasn't referring to helping Ethan and the twins," she said. "I'm talking about what's happening here on Earth. You said you want to help us win against the demons. So, figure out what you can do to help us *here*."

I sat back, frustrated. Because ever since Ethan and the twins had arrived in Utopia, I'd been in charge of overseeing their training. Their mission *was* my mission.

But what if it wasn't? Because as much as I hated to admit it, Mary had a point about the danger in going to Ember alone. And if there was anything I'd learned while in Lilith's lair, it was that I wasn't invincible.

My impulsive actions had nearly cost me my life. I didn't intend to make the same mistake twice.

"Where am I supposed to go?" I asked. "My home is gone."

"You know you always have a home here," Mary said.

"Thank you. But I can't stay here."

She didn't look surprised by my answer. "Why not?"

"Because I want to be the strongest vampire I can be. The only way to do that is by drinking human blood."

Part of the deal of living in the Haven was that the vampires agreed to survive on animal blood. I supposed it was noble of them. But it made them weaker.

And I refused to be weak.

"I understand," Mary said with a kind smile. "And I agree that you likely wouldn't be happy living in the Haven. But the offer is always there."

I sighed, thinking of my home once again. I'd give anything to go back. As a high witch of Utopia, I had a place and purpose there. I had family. I had friends.

Now, I had nothing.

"Why are we bothering debating this?" Raven cut in. "The answer's obvious."

"It is?" I perked up, ready for anything.

"Of course." She smirked. "You're powerful. You're unique. You want to become the strongest version of yourself, and you want to kill the demons as much as the rest of us. Which means you belong in Avalon, so you can get the best training in the world and join Avalon's Army."

16

GEMMA

We took the horses that had belonged to the dark mages and fae, and set off across the continent.

Thanks to Ethan's knowledge of the land, we didn't encounter anyone on our journey. Ember was mainly desert—not very hospitable to life—so the Dark Allies didn't roam far from their kingdoms. And the dragon kingdom wasn't far from the portal—only a day and a night by horse, with the horses going as quickly as possible.

Eventually, we rode so far that we reached the ocean.

Ethan stopped his horse in a cove that reminded me of my cove at home. "We're here," he said.

I looked around, confused. Ethan hadn't told us much about the dragon kingdom, in case we encountered any issues along the way. Meaning, in case any of us got taken by the dark mages or fae. He couldn't risk the Dark Allies discovering the dragon kingdom's location.

"There's nothing here," Mira said.

"Which is exactly what the Dark Allies think." He jumped off his horse and led it toward the entrance to a cave carved into the cliff. "And what we want them to believe."

We followed him inside, only having to walk about half a kilometer before reaching a pool of water. The inside of the cave would have been pitch black to humans, but thanks to our supernatural vision, it was like walking outside on a night when the moon wasn't shining. Dark, but doable.

Ethan stopped near the water and tied his horse to a rock. "Here's the entrance."

The cave didn't continue farther.

My attention went back to the water, and my chest tightened. "You're not saying…" I trailed off, unable to say it out loud.

"The dragon kingdom is underwater." Mira apparently had the same thought as me.

"Yes," Ethan said.

"How far underwater?" I asked.

"About three kilometers."

I stepped back until my palms pressed against the cave wall. The warm energy of the solid rock calmed my racing heart, helping me think clearly.

"How are we supposed to get down there?" I asked.

"We have powerful water elementals who keep watch through the water. They're able to watch the entrance of the pool as if gazing through a looking glass," Ethan explained. "They can hear through the water, too."

"Cool," Mira said. "I want to learn how to do that."

"It's advanced water magic. But I'm sure you'll master it in time."

She smiled at his belief in her.

"So they'll be able to hear us," I said. "Then what?"

"They'll send water elementals to get us," he said. "It'll be fine. You'll see."

I watched the water warily. I had no doubt we'd survive, but I couldn't imagine the journey down *kilometers* of water as being anything but terrifying. All of that water closing in around us, ready to drown us at any moment...

I shuddered at the thought of it.

This must have been what Mira felt like when we were in the underground kingdoms.

And we weren't even down there yet.

"What about the horses?" I asked.

"Water elementals will come up and bring them to a location far enough away that if the Dark Allies stumble across them, they won't be able to track them back here," he said. "From there, the water elementals will shift and fly back home. We're far enough away from both of the dark kingdoms that they won't be spotted."

"You've really got the hang of all this," Torrence said.

"The Dark Allies have lived in Ember for centuries," he replied. "During that time, we've learned how to stay safe and hidden. There wouldn't be any of us left otherwise."

She made a noise of what sounded like approval.

Ethan kneeled down next to the still water and dipped his finger into it. Ripples traveled outward.

Seconds later, an older woman's face appeared in the water. There was light behind her, and her features were decently clear—it was like we were looking in on her through old, foggy glass.

She studied Ethan, and her eyes widened. "Prince Pendragon?" she asked.

Ethan's expression turned solemn. "It's King Pendragon now."

The woman turned her eyes down and muttered a prayer. Then she refocused on Ethan. "I'll send an envoy for you immediately. How many are traveling with you?"

"There are four others," he said. "And five horses."

"Understood," she said. "Welcome home, and we'll see you soon."

Ten water elementals—five males, and five females—surfaced about ten minutes after Ethan spoke to Galinda. That was the name of the older woman who'd appeared to us in the water. He'd known her as a kid while living on Ember, which was how she'd recognized him.

Galinda wasn't in the envoy sent for us. All ten of the water elementals appeared to be in their twenties, or early thirties at the most.

They kneeled to Ethan after surfacing, with sadness in their eyes. "King Pendragon," they said, mostly in tandem.

"Rise," Ethan said, and they did as he commanded.

It was strange to see him treated this way, especially by people older than him. Back at home, he'd been just another guy around town. In Utopia, he'd been treated as less than even the human males. In the Haven, he was an equal.

Here, he was king.

It hadn't truly hit me until that moment.

A dark-haired woman glared at Torrence and Reed. "Who are they?" she asked.

"They're mages," Ethan said simply.

"Dark mages." Icicles formed in her hands, ready to attack.

He stepped in front of her and stared her down. "They're with us."

"They're our enemies."

"Are you questioning your king?"

She held his gaze, then backed down. "Of course not. But hopefully you understand my hesitation."

"I do." He nodded.

"I assume this has to do with the two of them." She motioned to me and Mira.

"The Dragon Twins of prophecy?" Ethan smirked.

"I thought that might be the case."

"It is," he said. "And we're wasting time standing here. We need to get down to the kingdom. Now."

"Very well," she said. "Who's first?"

Mira stepped forward. "I am."

The dark-haired dragon studied her in approval. "You'll go with Topher," she said, and a blond, male dragon stepped forward from the side. His hair was the same color as Mira's.

"I'm going to shift," he said kindly. "Then you'll hop on my back, and I'll swim us to the kingdom. You don't have to do anything but enjoy the ride." He waggled his eyebrows at the last part.

"Don't get any ideas." Mira glanced at Ethan and smiled. "I'm taken."

Ethan didn't look back over at her. In fact, Ethan had been quieter than usual since getting to Ember. He hadn't said much of anything to any of us during the journey to the cave.

Topher glanced at me, but I was already avoiding his gaze.

Every time Mira told a guy she was taken, their instinct was to move onto flirting with me. As if since we were twins, we were interchangeable.

It was tiresome, but I was so used to it that I was prepared.

Within seconds, Topher shifted into dragon form. His dragon was a bit smaller than Ethan's, and his scales a deep blue that shined like gemstones. He lowered himself down to the ground, and Mira easily climbed onto his back.

She situated herself, and then he dove into the water so smoothly that there was barely a splash.

I stared at the water with dread.

I did *not* want to do that.

"Gemma?" Ethan said my name softly, his eyes understanding and kind. "How about you go next, so you can get it over with?"

"Sure," I said, since he was right—it was best to get it over with. "Sounds good."

It sounded terrifying.

A girl with curly red hair stepped forward. "Let me guess," she said. "You're a fire elemental?" Her voice was bubbly and sweet, and I liked her already.

"And earth," I said.

"That explains it," she said. "I'm mainly water, but I have some fire in me, too. And I'd be honored to take one of the twins of prophecy to our kingdom. You'll be safe with me—I promise."

"What's your name?" I asked.

"Farrah."

"All right, Farrah," I said. "Let's do this."

Farrah's dragon form was mostly blue like Topher's, but with specks of orange scattered throughout. She was a bit smaller—it seemed like a shifter's dragon form was in ratio to their human form. She showed her razor-sharp teeth in what I assumed was an attempt at a smile and lowered herself down so I could get on.

Climbing onto her back was easy. And judging by the large spike protruding out of the bottom of her neck—right in front of the place where I sat—dragons were meant to have human riders.

I wrapped my hands around the spike, and without warning, she dove into the water.

I sucked in a breath, closed my eyes, and braced myself for the cold.

But there was nothing. No water against my skin.

Slowly, I opened my eyes.

I was still on Farrah's back. We were underwater, inside a giant air bubble. The bubble followed us as she flapped her wings, flying us through the water. It was so dark that I could barely see anything except the outlines of the fish around us.

Then, an orange light glowed in the distance. As we approached, the light grew bigger, until I could make out an entire city at the bottom of the ocean. A domed kingdom with a tall palace in the center and gradually smaller buildings spreading outward into a circle, like the lost city of Atlantis.

"Wow," I said, and Farrah flew through the water faster as we completed our approach.

We reached the dome, and she flew straight through it. The transition between being inside the air bubble around us to being inside the dome was seamless. Not even a single drop of water touched me.

People walking below paused to stare up at us. The streets were lined with blazing torches, which was why the city glowed orange. Fiery light came out of the windows, too.

We flew to the top of the central tower. There was a landing pad on the top of it—like the ones used for helicopters—and Farrah lowered us onto it.

I climbed off her back, and she shifted into human form.

"Where's Mira?" I asked.

"Down below," she said, and I noticed the start of a circular stairway at the corner of the roof. "Where our Elders are waiting to meet you."

17

GEMMA

I followed Farrah down to the top floor of the tower, where Mira, Topher, and two others—an older man and woman—were waiting. Despite their silvery hair and wrinkles around their eyes, they didn't look weak.

The high ceilinged, circular room was gothic in design, with dark stone walls and floors. Tall windows looked out of all parts of it to the city below, and guards stood silently between them. The city radiated orange light, and the water surrounding the dome glowed blue. Colorful, reptilian fishes swam outside the dome, like a reversed aquarium, with them looking in on us.

My chest tightened at the thought of all the tons of water pressing down on the dome.

"How was the ride?" Mira asked casually.

"Good," I said. "You?"

"Amazing."

Torrence and her dragon came down the steps next, followed by Reed, and lastly, Ethan.

The Elders dropped down to their knees when Ethan entered.

"King Pendragon," they said in unison.

"Darius," Ethan said to the man, and then he looked to the woman. "Hypatia. It's good to see you again."

"I wish it were under better circumstances," Hypatia said as she and Darius stood back up. "But it's good to see you, too."

Ethan simply nodded in response.

Darius, Hypatia, and all the guards watched Torrence and Reed, on high alert.

"I respect your authority as king," Darius said tightly. "But I expect you have an explanation for bringing two mages into our kingdom."

"I do," Ethan said, and he told them everything that had happened since we'd arrived in Ember.

"They'll be guarded at all times," Hypatia said once he finished. "And we won't hesitate to use force against them if they try anything against us."

"You don't have to talk about us like we're not here," Torrence said. "We can hear you."

"We will talk as we please," Hypatia snapped. "The two of you may have strong magic, but you're outnumbered here. Don't forget your place."

"You mean we shouldn't forget that we're miles under the ocean, in a kingdom full of dragons who want to kill us?" Sarcasm dripped from Torrence's tone.

Hypatia didn't bother with a reply. Instead, she focused on me and Mira.

"The twins of prophecy," she said warmly, sounding completely different than she had when she'd spoken to Torrence. "The ones who will free our people from their bondage."

The pressure that I already felt from being surrounded by water grew, and I shuffled my feet, nervous. "That's what we've been told," I said. "And we're happy to help in any way we can. But we're not full dragons. We have elemental magic, but we can't shift."

"They also have witch magic," Ethan added.

"A bit," I said.

"Interesting." Hypatia studied us and pursed her lips. "I wonder..." She glanced out one of the windows, then looked to the guard standing closest to the door. "Bring Janelle up to join us," she said. "It's time to see if the twins are the solution we've been waiting for."

18

GEMMA

The guard brought up a tall, middle-aged woman with long, thick, platinum hair. She was nearly as tall as Ethan—she looked like a warrior princess. Her eyes were sharp and intelligent, but there were shadows underneath them.

She was exhausted.

And around her wrists were matching black cuffs.

I'd seen cuffs like those before.

Isobel—the witch Harper had delivered as a prisoner to the Ward—had worn them. They'd stopped her from performing magic.

"Twenty years ago, Janelle and three others were rescued from the Dark Mage kingdom," Hypatia said. "It's the only rescue mission of our generation that's been successfully completed. But, just as the dragons before them who've been enslaved by the Dark Allies, we're unable to remove the cuffs that bind their magic. As long as the cuffs remain on their wrists, they're unable to shift or use their elemental magic."

"They say you can set me free." Janelle held up her wrists, her sharp gaze on me and Mira. "Want to have a go?"

"I don't know if we can," I said, and I looked to my twin. "But we can try."

"How?" Mira asked.

"With our intuition. Let's touch the cuffs and see what we can do."

Mira looked doubtful.

"Those cuffs were created by a Supreme Mage," Reed said simply. "You can't dismantle them."

"They're the dragon twins," Janelle said. "Of course they can dismantle them."

"Let them try." Reed shrugged. "It won't work."

Janelle glared at him, then faced me and Mira. "Come on," she said. "Prove him wrong."

All eyes were on us, and more pressure mounted in my chest. I couldn't look at any of them. All I could do was focus on the cuffs around Janelle's wrists.

How were we supposed to do this? There wasn't a spell like this in any of the books Mira and I had studied. There'd been no mention of magic binding cuffs at all.

"You *can* do it," Janelle said, although she didn't sound as confident as before. "Right?"

"We'll do our best."

I gave Mira a look that said, *you better try your best*, then stepped forward until I was standing in front of Janelle.

Mira joined me. She wouldn't meet Janelle's eyes. She wouldn't meet my eyes, either.

"I'll take one cuff," I told my twin. "You take the other."

I placed my fingers on the cuff closest to me, and Mira did the same with hers. The cuff hummed with magic, although the magic felt dark and draining. Like it was trying to suck out my soul.

No wonder Janelle looked so exhausted.

"I'll follow your lead," Mira told me.

"All right." I closed my eyes and cleared my mind.

Hecate, I thought, and I pictured the goddess, imagining she was there with me. *Guide me on what I need to do.*

I waited for something to click.

Nothing happened.

Silence hung heavy in the room.

"Gemma?" Mira asked, and I opened my eyes. My twin watched me, waiting.

"Focusing on neutralizing the magic." I hoped I sounded more confident than I felt. Because I'd totally made that up. "Draw it out of the cuffs."

"Okay."

I closed my eyes again, and pictured the magic flowing out of the cuffs and into my body.

Nothing happened. So I pulled at it harder.

Still, nothing.

"It's not working," Janelle said, her voice flat. Defeated.

I opened my eyes and took my fingers off the cuffs. Mira did the same.

"I'm sorry," I said. "I *want* to help. I promise I'll figure it out."

"How?"

My hand went to the key around my neck.

Add this to the ever-growing list of questions I had for Hecate. I needed to write down the questions sometime. List them in order of importance. Otherwise, I was never going to be able to keep track.

"I know someone who can help," I said. "I can't say any more than that, but I need you to trust me." I glanced at Mira, then at Ethan. "To trust *us*."

Hypatia watched me curiously. "Who's this 'someone?'" she asked.

"Someone who has answers—to everything."

"Hm." She pursed her lips, studying me. "When will you be able to get these answers?"

"I don't know," I said. "But I'll do my best to get them as soon as I can."

"You do that," she said. "Once you do, you know where to find us."

We all watched each other warily.

The Elders were losing their belief in us.

"We *will* help the enslaved dragons," Ethan said confidently. "You have my word, as your king. But unfortunately, we can't stay here for long."

"You brought the twins here safely," Darius said. "You returned to the kingdom you're destined to rule. Where else do you need to be?"

"We need to return to Earth."

"Now?"

"As soon as possible. As you know, demons threaten their realm. The supernaturals there are fighting, but they're losing."

"What does this have to do with us?" he asked.

"There's something here we've come to get—something we believe can turn the war in our favor," Ethan said.

"*Our* favor?" Hypatia raised an eyebrow. "You speak as if you're one of them, and not one of us."

"Our interests align with the supernaturals on Earth," he said, unfazed by Hypatia's doubt. "Like I said, there's something here we've come to retrieve. This object could be the key in beating the demons. But more than that—if freed, the dragons can help the supernaturals on Earth defeat the demons. We're stronger than any of their species. If we join them, their army will be nearly unstoppable. So it's in their interest to help us free our people—if we agree to help them in return."

"You're proposing an alliance with the supernaturals on Earth," Darius said.

"Precisely. And they'll be more likely to hear us out if we bring this object back to them."

"And what object is that?"

Ethan braced himself, held his gaze with Darius's, and said, "We're here for the Holy Crown."

19

GEMMA

"I'm afraid I can only halfway help you," Darius said.

"What do you mean?" I asked.

"Come with me and I'll show you." He glanced at Torrence and Reed. "The mages will stay here."

"The mages will come with us," Ethan said.

"You don't trust us with them?" Hypatia asked, and from her tone, it was clear that we *shouldn't* trust her with the mages.

She'd probably bring them to a torture cell, like the ones in the Ward.

"Quite frankly, no," Ethan said. "And I don't blame you for that. But I promised them that I'd do everything I could to get them back to Earth, and I intend to stand by that promise. So, they stay with us, wherever we go."

"As you wish." She sighed. "You are, after all, our king."

She didn't sound happy about it.

Darius led us to a lift that reminded me of the ones in Utopia and took it to the lowest possible floor—the basement.

We stepped out into a small room with stone walls, a sand floor, and a single steel door.

Darius removed a skeleton key from his robes and used it to open the door.

It swung open, revealing a huge room full of gold, gems, crystals, and more, in piles up to the ceiling and spilling out everywhere possible. It was like stepping into the Cave of Wonders.

"Are these all magical objects?" I asked, looking around in amazement.

"Mostly, no," Darius said. "They're treasures, but they're not magical. You see, dragons love beautiful objects. We keep them here and gift them to citizens who earn them. A reward system, per se. It gives everyone something to focus on—something bright and shiny to look forward to in such dark times."

"You're hoarding worthless treasure in your basement," Torrence said, like it was the most ridiculous thing she'd ever heard.

"These treasures are our currency. They ensure that everyone does their best to contribute to the kingdom. But not all of the objects here are non-magical." He spun around and led the way through the vault, meandering around the piles of treasure overflowing onto the path.

We followed him, and I *definitely* spotted Torrence eying up some of the bracelets. Mira, too.

Then I spotted a gold pen inlaid with rubies, and slowed down to stare at it. I'd *love* to write in my journal with that pen...

"Dragons," Reed muttered from behind us, and I quickened my pace.

Darius eventually stopped in front of a small, unremarkable wooden box with a tiny keyhole in the front. "Here we are," he said, and then he kneeled down, removed a tiny key from his robes, and opened the box.

Inside were clear crystals about the size of my pinkie finger, tied together at the bottom with wires of gold, in the shape of a half circle. At the end was a taller crystal and half a crescent moon, sawed off in the center.

"Half of the Holy Crown," I realized, and Darius nodded. "Why only half?"

"I don't know," he said. "But we've kept it safe here for centuries. Waiting to give it to you."

Mira's eyes were as wide as they'd been when she was looking at the bracelets, and she stepped forward to take the Crown.

Darius handed it to her, and I frowned at the fact that Mira got to hold it first.

She gasped as she took in its beauty, and her skin looked more radiant than ever. Her hair looked shinier, too.

It was like the Crown's light had rubbed off on her.

"Wow," she said. "What does it do?"

"No one knows," Darius said. "We thought you could tell us."

Another question to add to the list of things to ask Hecate. I was seriously going to lose track.

"We don't know yet," I said. "But we're going to find out." I reached for the Crown, prepared to pull it out of Mira's hands.

She grudgingly handed it over.

The moment I touched it, I was flooded with warmth. With *magic*. It was like a golden glow came out of the Crown and flowed through me. Pure, light, holy magic that filled me to the core.

"How do we know it's real?" Torrence asked.

"It's real," I said.

"How do you know?"

"Because I can *feel* it."

Before I realized what was happening, Torrence reached forward and wrapped her hand around the big crystal at the end of the Crown.

Ice rushed through my veins.

And Torrence fell to her knees, crumpled into herself, and cried.

20

TORRENCE

Agonizing pain hit me so hard that it knocked me over, like I'd been run over by a truck.

Selena was dead.

Julian was dead.

All of those hundreds of men who Circe had turned into pigs on the island were dead.

The only person I was happy to see dead was Circe.

Selena had risked her life to save me. Just like I'd risked my life to save her after the fae had taken her to the Otherworld. She'd trusted the Supreme Mages to help her find and free me.

But she was dead. I was never going to see my best friend again.

Because the Supreme Mages had *killed* her.

They were going to pay for this.

I needed to get to Avalon. Because Selena's parents—the leaders of Avalon—needed to know what had happened to their daughter.

And then it was going to be war against the mages.

But the need for revenge didn't cloud my grief. My heart ached with it. Selena was more than a best friend—she was like a sister to me. With her gone, I'd never feel whole again. A piece of my heart was gone forever.

Someone kneeled down next to me and wrapped his arms around me.

Reed.

I leaned into him, feeling more grounded with him holding me.

"Torrence?" He spoke my name like a question.

With eyes full of tears, I looked up into his dark, concerned gaze.

My heart burst with emotion.

I love you, I remembered him telling me, right before the mages had thrown us down the portal to Ember.

At the time, I'd felt nothing.

Now, love for him crashed over me like a tsunami.

"Reed." My voice cracked when I said his name. "I'm so, so sorry."

"You're back," he said quietly, like he was afraid to get his hopes up.

"I am. And I love you, too. More than you could ever possibly know."

His lips crashed down on mine, and I kissed him back like he was the only thing in the world keeping me alive. He tasted familiar and sweet, and I wished I could take back the pain I'd seen in his eyes ever since he found me on Circe's island. The pain I'd put there—by going dark.

Then, someone cleared his throat behind us.

Darius.

I pulled away from Reed, and we both stood quickly.

Darius watched us like a disapproving grandfather, and heat rose to my cheeks. But I kept a hand firmly in Reed's, and he held mine tightly back, like he never wanted to let go.

"Do either one of you want to explain what just happened?" Darius asked.

"I went dark," I said, although the words didn't feel real as I spoke them. The whole experience didn't feel real—I remembered it clearly, but it was like watching a movie instead of having truly lived it. I recalled everything that had happened, but not the emotions I'd experienced *while* it had happened. "The mages were right to send me to Ember. I was totally and completely dark. But now... I'm back."

"It shouldn't be possible..." Reed looked mystified. "No mage has ever come back after going dark."

Gemma held up the half of the Crown. "It happened after you touched this," she said.

There was something different about her. She looked harsher. Stronger. There was a hardness in her eyes that hadn't been there before.

Or maybe I'd been looking at her differently when I'd been dark. Maybe everyone had looked different then. Softer.

Then I glanced at Mira, and she looked the same as before. Hesitant and a bit scared, like she was uncomfortable in her own skin.

It was a miracle she'd survived that fight with the dark mages and dark fae.

They only survived because I helped them, I thought, although of course I didn't say it out loud.

They'd only gotten their magic a few weeks ago. They were new to it, so what they'd done was downright impressive. And I had faith they'd grow stronger from here.

I believed in them, just like I'd always believed in Selena.

Grief hollowed my heart at the thought of my best friend, and I leaned into Reed for support.

It didn't seem possible that I'd never see Selena again.

But I'd watched her die.

She was gone. Forever. And a part of my soul had died with her. I hadn't realized it then, but I felt it now.

"Touching the Crown brought you back," Reed realized. "The Crown's the key. If we can bring it to the dark mages, we can bring them *all* back."

"Assuming they want to be brought back," Mira said.

"They don't." I remembered the calmness that came with feeling no emotions. The feeling of control—of being unstoppable. Of having what felt like unlimited power and no qualms about what to do with it. "Once they figure out what it does, they'll kill you before you come close to them with it."

"We don't have time to strategize about how to turn an entire kingdom of dark mages good again right now," Gemma said harshly. "Let alone to organize ourselves to execute a plan—*if* we're able to come up with a feasible one that won't get us killed."

Ethan stepped back, like she'd slapped him. "If we can free the mages from the darkness, they might be willing to set the dragons free," he said. "How can we not *have time* for that?"

"Because this is only half the Crown." She spoke slowly, like she was talking to a child. "We need the rest of it. That's our mission, and it has to be our priority. Because if only half of the Crown can do this, imagine what'll happen when it's whole."

Ethan stood completely still, and I had a feeling he was going to fight her.

"She's right," Mira jumped in before he could. "Our mission is to find the Crown. Not *half* of the Crown. The *full* Crown. We have to stay focused on that."

"It's our best hope at defeating the demons." Gemma spoke immediately after her sister, like she was finishing her twin's thought. "It's our best hope at staying *safe*."

That final word snapped Ethan out of his anger. "Right," he said. "You're right. I just hate leaving them there when we have a way to save them."

"Our people have been enslaved by the Dark Allies for centuries," Darius said. "We can survive in their kingdoms for a few more weeks, or months, or even years. We have to think long term. And your plan about allying with the supernaturals on Earth is a good one. With them on our side—*and* with the full Crown, assuming you find the second half of it—we have the best chance of beating the Dark Allies and setting our people free."

21

HARPER

To get to Avalon, you needed to complete the island's entrance Trials.

Only one vampire kingdom could take you to the place where the Trials began—the Vale, which was located deep in the Canadian Rocky Mountains.

So, Mary sent a fire message to the ruler of the Vale, King Alexander. He quickly replied, saying a witch would meet me outside the entrance of the boundary dome.

Like all witches who'd grown up in one of the six kingdoms, I knew the entrance locations to the boundary domes of each one of them. It was part of our training. So I said my goodbyes and teleported out of the Haven, ready for whatever adventure awaited me next.

As promised, a witch waited for me outside the Vale.

Even though I'd been there before, the snowy kingdom built into the enormous mountain stunned me with its beauty. It was a winter wonderland that belonged in a giant snow globe.

"Come with me." The witch didn't bother with an introduction before teleporting me to the throne room inside the kingdom.

King Alexander—a pale skinned, dark-haired vampire—sat on the tallest throne. He looked intimidating, but then he smiled, and his smile was so warm and welcoming that it immediately put me at ease. His wife, Queen Deidre, sat on the throne next to his. They both wore formalwear and had golden crowns upon their heads.

A vampire with warm brown skin, dark hair, and bright blue eyes stood next to the king. He wore jeans and a button-down shirt, and he was startlingly attractive. He could have easily passed as a Bollywood movie star.

Who is he...?

"Harper," King Alexander said, and I turned my focus back to him. "Welcome to the Vale. Although, from your letter, it sounds like you won't be here for long."

"I've come to enter the Angel Trials," I said proudly.

"I'm sure the Earth Angel will be delighted to have you on Avalon."

As King Alexander spoke, my eyes strayed to the bright blue ones of the vampire next to him.

The corner of his lips turned up in a devious smile, and I lowered my gaze as heat flooded my cheeks.

Why was he watching me like I amused him so much?

"Harper." Queen Deidre snapped me back to attention. "Might I introduce you to our brother, Prince Rohan?" She motioned to the blue-eyed vampire, who still watched me with amusement. "He'll be escorting you to the location where you'll begin the Angel Trials."

"Your Highness," I said with a polite nod.

"Call me Rohan." His voice was smooth, like silk.

I was so hypnotized by everything about him that I nearly forgot to smile.

Come on, Harper, I told myself, shaking myself out of it. *You never get this worked up about a man. Especially one you're never going to see again.*

To make it worse, he was a *vampire*.

In Utopia, we were taught that male supernaturals were naturally power hungry—that they weren't to be trusted. We were supposed to be repulsed by all of them, or at least constantly on guard around them.

So why did Rohan's eyes make me feel like they were calling every cell in my body to come closer to him?

If I wasn't wearing an onyx ring, I would have sworn he was using compulsion on me.

He was so flawlessly good-looking that he had to know it. How many vampire—and human—women in the Vale had he swept off their feet, gotten to fall head over heels for him, and left heartbroken at the end of it? Probably countless amounts.

No way was I letting myself be alone with him. Nothing good could come from it.

I got ahold of myself and looked to Queen Deidre. "I'm sure you're aware of our beliefs and customs in Utopia." I swallowed away a small lump in my throat as I spoke of my destroyed home. "I think it would be most appropriate for you to lead me to the starting point of the Angel Trials. Or at least another woman who knows its location."

Rohan smirked and crossed his arms over his chest. "Afraid to be alone with me?" he asked.

"I'm not *afraid*." Annoyance stirred in me at how cocky he sounded.

"It sure sounds like you are."

Queen Deidre's gaze bounced back and forth between the two of us like she was watching a tennis match.

"I'm surprised," Rohan continued before I could respond. "From what I've heard, you're a vampire gifted with the ability to use witch magic. Surely I should be the one afraid of you?"

I raised an eyebrow in challenge. "*Are* you afraid of me?" I asked.

"I'm not."

"Maybe you should be." The words were out of my mouth before I realized they could be construed as a threat.

Threatening a royal of a vampire kingdom while you were a guest in said kingdom was never a good idea.

"Not like I would ever hurt you," I quickly covered up my mistake. "As long as you don't do anything to warrant it."

"I'd never dream of hurting you," he said, and I sucked in a sharp breath at how sincere he sounded.

Neither of us spoke for a few seconds. We just stared at each other, not wanting to be the one to look away first.

Had he left me speechless?

Queen Elizabeth would be ashamed if she saw me now. My mother would be, too.

But there was something about Rohan...

"I promise that my brother is no threat to you," Queen Deidre said. "But if you prefer me to escort you to the start of the Angel Trials, then I'm more than happy to grant your request."

Rohan watched me, challenging me.

After what he'd just said to me, I'd seem weak if I accepted the queen's offer—even though I was the one who'd asked her to be my escort.

But having the queen accompany me would be far more appropriate than going alone with Rohan.

Screw what's more appropriate, I thought. *What do I want?*

"Thank you for the offer," I said to the queen. "But I'll go with Rohan."

22

HARPER

Rohan led me down a huge hall more decadent than anything I'd ever seen. It was so beautiful that I wanted to slow down to take it all in.

"You coming?" he asked over his shoulder.

"Sorry." I hurried to keep up, although I kept looking around as much as possible as we walked.

"The palace is French in design," he explained, like he was giving me a tour. "This specific hall was inspired by the Hall of Mirrors in Versailles."

"Interesting." I nodded as if I knew what he was talking about.

He smiled, like he could tell I'd never heard of the Hall of Mirrors, but he didn't call me out on it. Instead, he slowed down and walked at my pace as I took in the beauty of the palace.

Eventually, he turned a corner into a smaller hall and stopped at a plain wooden door at the end of it. The door was the most unremarkable thing I'd seen in the palace so far. It looked positively medieval.

"This is the start of the Angel Trials?" I asked.

"You think we'd make it that easy?"

"No," I said, since when was anything in the supernatural world ever easy? "Of course not."

He took an iron key out of his pocket and unlocked the door, revealing a stone staircase that circled downward. Torches lined the walls to light the way. The path was so narrow that we'd have to walk single file.

"Follow me," he said, and he started down the stairs.

I followed, and jumped as the door shut loudly behind me.

"You spook easily?" he asked.

"No." I bristled.

"Don't worry," he said. "The door gets mostly everyone."

I was hardly "most everyone," but he was so full of himself that I didn't feel like arguing.

"It takes a bit of time to get to the bottom," he said as we walked. "How about I use that time to tell you about myself?"

I rolled my eyes, even though he wasn't looking back to see it. "By all means," I said, since it would be better than walking in awkward silence. "Go ahead."

"I was born in 1897, in India. But my life didn't truly begin until the summer of 1918, when a beautiful witch named Kavya moved to my village," he said, and while I couldn't see his face, it sounded like he was smiling. "Of course, I didn't know she was a witch at the time. She claimed to be a healer from the city, and she'd come to my village because the sickness that had been ravaging the country was headed our way. She wanted to try and save as many of us as possible."

"That was the year of the Spanish Flu," I said, since of course I'd learned about it. "Witches around the world tried to create a potion to cure it."

They hadn't been successful, since no potion had ever been created that could cure a naturally occurring human illness. But it hadn't stopped them from trying.

"You know your history," he said.

"Of course I know my history. I'm a high witch of Utopia."

Was a high witch of Utopia.

Past tense. Utopia didn't exist anymore.

I had a feeling he was thinking the same thing, and I braced myself for him to say it out loud to make some kind of point.

Instead he spun around and stared at me, still taller than me despite the fact that he was standing two steps below me. The fire from the nearest torch flickered across his eyes, and it was like he was staring into my soul.

"You're more than just a high witch," he said. "You're also a vampire. Which probably makes you the strongest witch in the world."

"It might." My magic tingled with happiness inside me.

Energy buzzed between us, and neither of us moved. My breathing shallowed. His did, too.

Then he spun around, breaking the moment, and continued down the stairs. "Anyway, back to the important stuff," he said, and I hurried to follow him. "Kavya fell in love with me at first sight."

I sighed and rolled my eyes again.

"As I did with her," he continued. "We were inseparable for a week. But the Spanish Flu hit the healthiest people the hardest. So it wasn't long before I got sick."

"Of course it wasn't."

How was he able to sound full of himself, even when talking about how he'd gotten sick with one of the worst flus in human history?

"She did everything she could to help me," he said. "Including teleporting me to the Haven and begging Mary to turn me into a vampire."

"I guess she was successful?"

"She was. Mary doesn't turn humans into vampires often, but she loved Kavya, and she could tell Kavya loved me. So, she gifted me with eternal life."

"But you're immortal." I had a feeling I knew where this story was headed, given that he was no longer living in the Haven. "Kavya wasn't."

"Kavya had no interest in turning into a vampire," he said sadly. "But we married anyway, and we spent every day together until the day she died."

I frowned, since I'd seen it happen before in Utopia. If a vampire in Utopia wanted to turn one of their human lovers into a vampire, they both had to leave the kingdom forever. So, sometimes vampire women chose to stay by their lover's side until he grew old and died.

The heads on Queen Elizabeth's belt were those of her greatest loves.

"You don't approve," Rohan said.

"No," I said, surprised he'd think that. "It sounds like you truly loved her."

"She was the love of my life."

"And now she's gone."

"She passed away thirty years ago."

"I'm so sorry." There had to be better words, but I couldn't find any.

"Thank you," he said, still continuing steadily down the steps. "I'd prepared for the moment for my entire life. But no type of preparation could make her death less painful."

We walked in silence for a few seconds, and I had no idea what to say. Because I knew women were capable of all-encompassing love. But for a male vampire to devote his heart to a woman he knew was going to age and die?

No one in Utopia would have believed it possible.

"I'd always stayed in the Haven for Kavya," he continued. "But once she passed, I told Mary goodbye, and I left. Roamed around the world for a few decades, spending time with a few rogue vampire clans along the way. Then word spread about Avalon and the Earth Angel's army. Like you, I came to the Vale to enter the Angel Trials."

"And you failed." I instantly felt bad about being so rude to him after he'd opened up about the death of the love of his life. "Or you chose to stay in the Vale."

I didn't see why he'd choose to stay here instead of going to Avalon, but I supposed it was always an option.

"You got it right the first time." He stopped and turned to face me. "I failed the Angel Trials. But King Alexander and Queen Deidre said it was meant to be, and they've been like family to me ever since." He paused and glanced down the stairs. "Now, wait here."

"I thought I was supposed to follow you?"

"I need to unlock the portal," he said. "The process can be… uncomfortable."

"What do you mean?"

"Do you trust me?" he asked.

"I just met you."

"That's not an answer."

I stared at him in challenge.

"You do trust me." He smiled. "Don't you?"

I searched my mind for an answer that wasn't a lie… and one that wouldn't give him the satisfaction of my saying yes. "I trust King Alexander and Queen Deidre," I said. "And they trust you."

"That means you trust me."

"Are you always this infuriating?" I asked.

"Do you always avoid answering questions?"

"So, yes," I said. "You *are* always this infuriating."

"I prefer the word charming, but I suppose 'infuriating' will do for now," he said. "Anyway, you're still avoiding my question."

"Why do you care?" I asked. "After I get to Avalon, we'll probably never see each other again."

Good riddance to that.

"Never say never," he said. "But I know you trust me. Otherwise, you would have said no."

"Why's it such a big deal?"

"It wasn't a big deal until you made it one."

I huffed in annoyance. He obviously wasn't going to back down. "I clearly trusted you enough to let you take me to the entrance of the Angel Trials," I said. "So are you going to take me there or what?"

"I told you—I need you to stay here for a moment." He zipped down the steps in a blur before I could argue, leaving me staring in shock at where he'd been standing.

What in the world had just happened between us?

I didn't have time to think about it, because a bright yellow light started glowing from below. It was like a bomb went off, and I turned away, closed my eyes, and used my arm to shield my face. The light was warm, and it enveloped me completely.

The warmth died down, and I lowered my arm.

"You can come down now!" Rohan called from below.

I hurried down the stairs, into a cave-like room, then froze. Because behind Rohan, a purple vortex swirled on the cave wall.

"A portal," I said in disbelief. "But what was that yellow light?"

"It was a security measure," he said. "We can't just leave the portal down here for anyone to find. As a royal of the Vale, I needed to unlock it for you."

"Great." I stared at the portal and took a deep breath in anticipation. I'd teleported all over Earth, but I'd never gone to another realm. "So, we just... go in?"

"The portal goes to an anchor island off of Avalon," he said. "To Sir Gawain's Cove. The Angel Trials begin there."

"So you're not coming any further."

"This is where I leave you," he confirmed, and surprisingly enough, he sounded sad about it. "Once you get to the cove, it's up to you to figure out how to start the Trials. Good luck, Harper."

"I'm a witch *and* a vampire. I don't need luck," I said. "But thank you."

"You're going to do great."

He still watched me sadly, like he wanted to say more. And something tugged at my chest, pulling me closer to him.

It was like the Universe didn't want me to leave.

But I resisted. Because I was here for one reason—to go through that portal and enter the Angel Trials. I didn't need some guy I'd just met holding me back... no matter how ridiculously gorgeous that guy might be.

What *was* it about Rohan that was so magnetic? It was like he had a supernatural hold on my heart.

"You're a gifted vampire," I realized. "Aren't you?"

"What makes you say that?"

"Nothing." My cheeks heated, and I shook the thought away. Because what exactly was I going to say? That he was gifted in the art of seduction?

All it would do was feed his ego. And his ego certainly wasn't in need of any feeding.

He cocked his head to the side. "You're blushing."

"I'm not," I lied, and I stepped closer to the portal, as if the purple glow could cover my red cheeks. "Bye, Rohan. I'll put in a good word for you once I get to Avalon. Maybe they'll reconsider and let you in."

"I don't think it works like that," he said. "Besides, the Vale is my home now. If I had an option, I'd choose to stay here."

"That makes one of us," I said, and then I tore my gaze away from his, spun around, and walked through the portal.

23

HARPER

I woke up slowly, my head heavy and hazy. I felt drugged, and only half awake, still unable to open my eyes.

From the gentle rocking beneath me, I assumed I was in a boat. I breathed in, surprised to find that the air was damp, like I was surrounded by mist.

Where am I? What happened?

Images and feelings flashed through my mind. A beach, a boat, a trident, rolling hills, a wyvern, some kind of monster I'd slain, a dark forest, a castle, and a tough decision to be made.

As I grew more and more awake, the memories disappeared. They were as impossible to hold onto as the mist in the air surrounding me.

Finally, I was able to open my eyes. Just as expected, I was surrounded by fog.

I sat up—I was in a wooden rowboat—but the fog was so thick that I could barely see a meter in front of me.

Is this it? Am I in Avalon?

I moved to the front of the boat, placed my hands on the sides, and glanced down at the water. It was dark, and it looked cold. I dipped a finger in it, unsurprised to find that it was as icy as it looked. But while I could tell it was cold, the cold didn't bother me.

One of the perks of being a vampire.

After about a minute, the mist parted.

I was in a forest. One with trees similar to the ones in Canada. Snow-covered mountains towered around me, so tall that they looked like they could reach the stars.

My stomach lurched.

It can't be possible.

The mist continued to clear, until it was gone.

I was at the end of a river.

Rohan stood at the riverbank, waiting for me. He watched me sadly as my boat floated up to the rocks and planted itself there.

He didn't move toward me. It was like he was afraid to get closer.

"I shouldn't be here," I finally said, holding tightly to the edges of the boat. "Something went wrong. I need to go back." I glanced behind me, but the mist was gone. It was just river, forest, and mountains as far as I could see.

"There is no 'back,'" he said. "But there is a grand plan. Which means you're exactly where you're meant to be."

"I'm meant to be on Avalon."

He said nothing.

Because what else was there to say? I looked up at the moon, which was a sliver away from being full, and felt Hecate's magic watching over me. I trusted Hecate, and I trusted Fate.

So why were they doing this to me?

I reached for my key necklace, wanting an answer. But in my heart, I already *knew* the answer.

My destiny wasn't on Avalon. If it were, I would have passed the Trials.

But that didn't make me feel like any less of a failure.

"How far are we from the Vale?" I asked.

"A few kilometers," he said. "Not a far walk—or run. Unless you want to teleport us back. Whatever you prefer."

"We can walk," I said, and I hopped out of the boat. "But I don't feel like talking."

He nodded, then led the way, respecting my wishes and walking back to the Vale with me in silence.

24

HARPER

I woke before sunset—again.

Despite the room fit for royalty that King Alexander had given me in the Vale, with a plush canopy bed far more comfortable than what I'd had in Utopia or the Haven, I was barely managing a few hours of sleep each day. I'd spent more time tossing and turning than actually sleeping.

In the precious hours that I did sleep, I dreamed of the Trials. But when I woke up, the memories always faded.

No one remembered the Trials. Not even those who'd passed them.

Giving up on falling back asleep, I picked up the book on my nightstand and opened it to the marked page near the center. It was a science-fiction book about a group of people who'd been transported by plane to a bleak future. I'd chosen it out of the many in the Vale's library because the main character shared my name. It seemed as good of a reason to choose a book as any, and reading it was keeping my mind off the fact that I'd failed the Angel Trials.

I'd *failed* the Trials.

I still couldn't believe it.

I read until there was a knock on the door. My morning glass of blood, always delivered at the same time by Lucy, a non-royal vampire who worked in the palace. She had a chipper attitude that no one should ever be allowed to have in the early morning.

I placed the book down and walked to the door, preparing myself for Lucy's bright smile and peppy greeting.

But Lucy wasn't there.

Rohan stood in her place. He held two glasses of blood, and he didn't look happy.

"You've been avoiding me," he said.

"I've been busy."

"Busy brooding in your room."

"What can I say? I'm good at brooding." I glanced at the glasses of blood in his hand. "I only need one."

Newly turned vampires oftentimes had less control over their bloodlust, so they were allowed more blood as they adjusted to their new life. But not me. I'd been doing fine with regular portions.

"These aren't both for you." Rohan gave me a devilish grin. "One's for me."

"Tell me you're not inviting yourself into my room for breakfast."

"I can't, because that would be a lie. And if there's one thing I'm not, it's a liar." He strode into my room, placed the glasses on the table, and made himself comfortable on one of the plush chairs. "Lucy's coming over any minute to drop off the pancakes," he continued, as if he hadn't just barged in without an invitation. "I heard you've only been living off blood. And while it's true that vampires don't need food to survive, the food here's amazing. Especially the pancakes."

I didn't have time to reply before Lucy rolled a breakfast cart inside. Not only were there pancakes, but there was bacon, hash browns, and maple syrup that smelled like it had been freshly drained from the tree.

Lucy was abnormally quiet as she arranged the plates on the table. She kept glancing at Rohan, and every time he met her gaze, she looked away and blushed.

"Smells amazing." He inhaled dramatically. "Thanks, Lucy."

"My pleasure." She smiled, as if speaking to him was a precious gift. "Is there anything else I can get for you? Orange juice, maybe? And some champagne? It's never too early for a mimosa."

"Great idea," he said, and he looked to me. "How do you feel about mimosas?"

It took every effort to stop myself from smiling. Because I *loved* mimosas with brunch. And margaritas with Mexican, and wine with Italian, and basically any drink meant to pair with a fun meal.

But I didn't want to give Rohan the satisfaction of knowing he'd arranged something for me that I liked. Because I *didn't* like him barging in without an invitation—no matter how much I loved a good boozy brunch.

"I have work to do today," I said instead.

He frowned, then looked back at Lucy. "We'll have mimosas—with the best champagne you've got," he told her, as if it wasn't a crime to ruin an expensive champagne by mixing it with orange juice.

"You've got it," she said, and she hurried out with the cart, closing the door behind her.

Rohan leaned back in his chair and watched me mischievously.

"That wasn't fair," I finally said.

"What wasn't fair?"

"You used your gift on her."

"What gift?"

"You know what gift." I pointed to the door. "The one that made her act like… *that*."

He chuckled, amused. "I have no idea what you're talking about."

I rolled my eyes. Did I have to spell it out for him?

Apparently so.

"You made her all skittish," I said.

"Are you saying that you think I have a gift to intimidate people?"

"Not *intimidate* people." I nearly stomped my foot at how aggravating he could be. He was definitely trying to make me say it out loud.

And I'd worked myself into such a corner that we both knew there was no getting around it.

"Then what, exactly, do you think I did to her?" he asked.

"You..." I moved my hands in exasperation, unable to meet his eyes as I said the next part. "Mesmerized her."

He studied me and smirked, getting more of a kick out of this by the second. "You thought I had this gift after I walked you to the portal to the Angel Trials," he said. "Does that mean I 'mesmerized' you, too?"

I shook my head, like he was being ridiculous. "Of course you didn't."

"Then why else would you think this was my gift?"

"Because you *tried* to mesmerize me. I resisted. Clearly."

He raised an eyebrow. "Did you?"

"Of course I did. You're the one who apparently can't resist *me*, given how you barged in here and insisted on having breakfast with me."

"Brunch," he said.

"What?"

"We're having mimosas. That means it's brunch."

"The sun just set." I motioned to the window, where the final pinks and oranges of sunset were disappearing behind the mountains. Because of the Vale's nocturnal schedule, sunset here was the equivalent of sunrise in the human world. Everyone was just waking up for the night. "It's nowhere near lunch time. And that's what brunch is—a combination meal between breakfast and lunch."

"You're really combative, aren't you?" he asked.

"Only because you're so..." I paused to think of a word.

"So what?"

"So *frustrating*."

Not wanting to talk about it anymore, I walked over to the table and picked up my glass of blood. It was still warm, but soon it would start to cool. We couldn't have that. And, since drinking meant I wouldn't have to talk to Rohan, I finished it as quickly as possible.

Rohan picked his up, but he sipped it much slower than I did.

I'd just placed my glass back down when Lucy knocked on the door and rolled in another cart—this one full of champagne, an assortment of juices, and two glasses.

"Is there something wrong with the food?" she asked.

"No," I said. "Why?"

"Because you haven't sat down. Is there something else you need?"

My stomach rumbled, as if answering the question for me. Because I hadn't eaten actual *food* since being turned into a vampire. And now that it was right in front of me, smelling absolutely delicious, I was famished.

"No, I'm good," I said. "I was just waiting for the mimosas." I quickly sat down, avoiding meeting Rohan's eyes.

Lucy left the champagne cart next to the table. "So you can mix your own," she explained. "I know everyone prefers their mimosas differently. Now, if you don't need anything else..."

"This is perfect." Rohan shot her a movie star grin. "Thanks, Lucy."

She beamed in return. "Any time," she said. "Enjoy!" She hopped around and hurried out of the room, closing the doors behind her.

"You did it again," I said once she was gone.

"Mesmerized her?" he asked.

"Yes."

"Maybe I did." He shrugged. "But I don't have a gift. It's all natural."

From his amused expression, I had a feeling he was telling the truth.

He was *beyond* frustrating.

No good response came to my mind, so I stood up, walked to the cart, and picked up the bottle of champagne. It was an expensive brand I'd only had once, for my sixteenth birthday.

"No way am I ruining this with juice." I easily popped the cork and poured myself a glass, not stopping until it reached the top.

"For someone who was iffy about having mimosas, you're sure going heavy on that champagne," Rohan observed.

"It's champagne—not vodka," I said. "I'll barely feel a thing."

"Is that a challenge?"

"No," I said, since I didn't want to let my guard down *too* much around him. "But I bet I can eat more pancakes than you."

"Challenge accepted," he said, and then we both dug in.

As we ate and drank, I ended up telling Rohan *everything* that had happened since Gemma, Mira, and Ethan had arrived in Utopia.

He was good, fun company. And it was refreshing to chat with him. I'd tried to spend time with the high witches of the Vale, but they'd been standoffish from the beginning.

They hadn't said it outright, but I knew it was because I was a vampire. Even though I could use my witch magic, they didn't consider me to be one of them. I was an outsider, and they'd made sure I knew it.

Breakfast with Rohan was the most relaxed I'd felt since getting to the Vale. Which was crazy, since a few weeks ago I *never* would have thought it possible that I'd feel at ease around a supernatural male. But after being rejected from Avalon and rejected by the witches, it felt nice to feel accepted.

Even if that acceptance was from an arrogant male vampire with more charm than should be legal.

"So Lilith has the Dark Grail and the Dark Crown, and Lavinia has the Dark Wand," he said once I'd finished telling him everything. "Who has the Dark Sword?"

It was a good question—one I was surprised I hadn't thought of yet.

Maybe he'd been right, and I'd been spending too much time brooding in my room instead of trying to do something productive.

"I don't know," I said, and just like that, an idea started forming in my mind. "But maybe…"

He leaned forward, intrigued. "Maybe what?"

"We know Lilith and Lavinia are trying to find the Dark Sword," I started. "But what if we got to it first?"

"And then what?" he said. "They'll track it down with that dragon heart and destroy the Vale like they destroyed Utopia?"

His words were a jolt to my heart.

"Sorry," he said. "I didn't mean it like that."

I swallowed down my grief. "I know you didn't," I said, then quickly returned to the subject at hand. "But they haven't tried attacking any other kingdoms now that we have Nephilim patrolling the borders."

"True. But they probably want that Sword more than they wanted the twins," he said. "If they know it's here, they'll figure out a way."

"So what if we don't keep it in the Vale?"

"Do you think you can convince the Ward to take it?"

"Not the Ward," I said. "It would be safest somewhere the demons and dark witches literally *can't* reach. Which means we need to find that Sword, and get it to Avalon."

25

GEMMA

STANDING in the empty ivory hall of the Eternal Library, I pulled off my key necklace and threw it on the marble floor.

I'd been coming here every day for a week.

Each day, Hecate wasn't there.

What use was endless knowledge when the person who was supposed to give it to you was never available?

I was so angry that I wanted to blast fire at the key. I wouldn't *actually* do it—I wasn't stupid—but it was probably a good thing I couldn't access my dragon magic while in Hecate's realm.

I glanced at the door to the hall with the endless shelves of books. Because I'd seen the book that had talked about the Dark Objects. I'd seen it when Hecate had told us about the Dark Wand.

Maybe I could find it again.

No, I thought, remembering the blank expressions of the others who were trying to find books in the shelves, and had gotten stuck in the Library for years. *Don't go there.*

Not wanting to risk giving into temptation, I picked up the key and returned to the throne room in the dragon kingdom where the others were waiting.

Mira frowned when she saw me. "She wasn't there," she said.

"Nope."

Darius's expression went blank. "Where were you?"

"Left something in my room," I said. "Sorry."

Everyone without a key nodded, easily accepting my excuse for leaving and returning. None of them thought to ask what I'd "left in my room."

A second later, they forgot it had happened entirely.

Such was the magic of the key.

"This isn't working." Ethan ran his hands through his tousled brown hair in frustration.

The motion made me remember how silky smooth his hair had felt when I'd kissed him.

Guilt twisted my heart at the thought.

"We need to figure out another way to find the second half of the Crown," Ethan said, focusing on Mira as he spoke.

Ever since we'd gotten to Ember, he'd been back to ignoring me. Whenever I was around him, I felt like I didn't exist. He was always near—he didn't like to leave my and Mira's sides—but he always spoke to Mira instead of me.

It was clearly on purpose, and it took all my effort to resist throttling him and demanding to know why he hated me so much.

"I could try another tracking spell," Torrence said.

"And what would you do differently this time?" Hypatia asked.

"Try harder?"

"It wouldn't change the fact that tracking spells only work for people—not for objects."

Torrence frowned, which was apparently as close as she'd get to admitting that Hypatia was right.

"There *is* another way for you to find the second half of the Crown," Hypatia said. "Landon—step forward."

A male guard with wild, dark curls walked from his post by the window to the center of the room. He kneeled down in front of Hypatia and met her eyes.

Hypatia gave him a knowing look, reached into her cloak, pulled out a gold dagger, and handed it to him.

I watched, not understanding.

Was that a magical dagger that could be used to find the second half of the Holy Crown? And if it was, why hadn't anyone said something sooner?

Landon looked to Ethan. "King Pendragon," he said. "This is for you—and for the future freedom of our people."

He raised the dagger to his throat and slashed it across his skin.

Blood poured out of the open wound and onto the stone floor.

It was like I was watching what had happened to Harper all over again.

I didn't move.

There was nothing I could do to help him.

The dagger slipped out of Landon's hand, and he collapsed to the floor, into the puddle of his blood.

Then, it hit me.

"His heart," I said, slowly and quietly. "You want us to use his heart to track the second half of the Crown."

Hypatia nodded. "He sacrificed himself so you could do so."

"We'll get to work immediately," I said. "His sacrifice won't be in vain."

"But why was his sacrifice necessary?" Mira asked. "Landon was young and strong. Surely you have the hearts of those who have already passed? Or someone older who could have made the sacrifice. Someone who didn't have so many years ahead of them."

"The stronger the dragon, the stronger their heart will be for tracking," Ethan explained. "And the heart must be fresh. Once it dries up, its magic is gone."

"But rest assured—we'll have a ceremony in three days to honor Landon and his sacrifice," Hypatia said.

However, I wasn't focused on a ceremony. My thoughts went to Lavinia, who was using Ethan's father's heart to locate the Dark Objects. "How long does it stay fresh?" I asked.

"A heart that's well taken care of can last for months," answered Hypatia.

I nodded and inhaled the intense, spicy scent of Landon's blood.

His heart would certainly be fresh.

I'd cut it out myself, except I had no experience with anything resembling surgery. The last thing I wanted was to mess up and accidentally slice the heart, making it useless.

"I don't think Landon would want us to waste any time," I said, since it seemed like the most diplomatic way to say, *what are we waiting for?*

"He wouldn't," Hypatia agreed. "Guards—take Landon's body, remove the heart, get it cleaned up, then bring it back here. As quickly as possible."

Two guards picked up Landon's body and carried it out of the room. Another two followed them out, then returned with cleaning supplies and got started on cleaning up the mess.

"How long will it take for the heart to be ready?" I asked.

"They'll work efficiently," Hypatia said. "It won't be long."

The guards finished cleaning up, and Hypatia and Darius gave me and Mira tips on how to use our elemental magic. Up until getting to Ember, Ethan had been the only person who'd been able to help us learn to use our dragon magic. And while Ethan was strong, it was helpful to learn from others, too. Especially ones who were so much older, simply because they'd had more time to master their skills.

Torrence and Reed watched from the side, both of them smart enough to know to stay quiet and in the background, to make sure the dragons didn't think they were any sort of threat.

A little over an hour passed before the guards returned. One of them carried a small gold box. He approached Ethan, kneeled, and held it up to him. "King Pendragon," he said.

Revulsion crossed Ethan's eyes as he stared down at the box.

Does he need me to take it for him?

I nearly did just that.

Then, I stopped myself.

Of course he's having a tough time, I thought. *This probably reminds him of what happened to his dad.*

"Thank you," Ethan finally said, and he took the box from the guard.

The guard stood and resumed his post by the wall.

Ethan opened the box and stared at the contents inside, his expression neutral.

"When you're ready, pick up the heart and think of the object you seek," Hypatia said. "If it locates it, you'll get a general sense of where it is. The fresher the heart, the more accurate the location will be."

Ethan took a deep breath, then removed the heart from the box. His hand covered most of it, sparing us the gory details. He closed his eyes and concentrated.

We watched him silently, waiting for him to locate the second half of the Crown.

After the longest minute ever, he opened his eyes and looked to Hypatia. "Nothing's happening," he said, and disappointment filled me to the core.

So much for that plan.

"I thought that might be the case," she said.

Mira's bright blue eyes widened. "If it might not work, then why did you let Landon sacrifice himself?"

Why did she care so much about Landon? She hadn't known him. And he hadn't been murdered. He'd *chosen* to sacrifice himself.

You'd think we'd seen enough death by now for her to start growing numb to it.

Like I have.

"A dragon heart can only track an object if that object is in the same realm as the heart," Hypatia explained. "If Ethan feels nothing, then the second half of the Holy Crown likely isn't in Ember."

"We've only been to two other realms," Ethan said. "Earth and the Otherworld."

"We've been to Mystica," Torrence chimed in. "Although after our experience there, I have no intention of ever returning."

"How many realms *are* there?" Mira asked.

"The only known realms are Ember, Earth, the Otherworld, Mystica, and Hell," Hypatia said. "And Avalon, although Avalon is anchored to Earth. But, might I suggest you start with the most likely one of the bunch?"

"You mean Earth?" I asked.

"Precisely."

"But if the second half of the Crown is on Earth, wouldn't Lavinia have found it already?"

"To find an object, you have to focus on what is it you're looking for," Hypatia said. "Lavinia doesn't know the Crown has been split into two. She doesn't know to look for *half* of it. She cannot find what doesn't exist. And the Crown in its entirety doesn't exist."

"But she can locate the other three Holy Objects," I said. "So why didn't she use the heart to track down Annika, Raven, and Selena?"

"Who says she hasn't?" Torrence chimed in.

Hypatia looked at her calmly. "Go on."

"Lilith has been extremely strategic in this war for the sixteen years she's been on Earth," Torrence continued. "We know she's on a mission to find all four Dark Objects, and that she hasn't acquired all of them yet. We also know she's been hunting gifted humans, turning them into gifted vampires, and draining them for their blood. We still haven't figured out *why* she's doing this, but it has to all be for some greater plan. She's probably waiting to attack until she has all her pieces in place."

"A logical conclusion," Hypatia said, and Torrence looked pleased with herself for getting the dragon Elder to agree with her.

"So it sounds like we should get going," I said. "Get our pieces in place before Lilith gets hers." I turned to Torrence and Reed. "Before we came to the Otherworld, the Empress's advisor gave us these." I removed the portal tokens from my pocket. "The only two tokens that can bring you out of Ember."

Suspicion dawned in Torrence's eyes. "How'd she know you'd need them?"

"Prince Devyn gave them to her."

Torrence nodded in understanding. She knew all about Selena's dad, and his gift of omniscient sight, so mentioning him was the only explanation necessary.

"Any chance she told you where they'd bring us?" she asked.

"They'll bring you to the Otherworld," I said.

"Figured," she said. "Good thing we're on good terms with the fae. We shouldn't have an issue getting back to Earth from there."

"What's your plan for when you're back?"

"We're going home—to Avalon," she said. "The Earth Angel needs to know what happened to her daughter."

I couldn't imagine how difficult that conversation was going to be. "Then I guess this is goodbye," I said, surprised by the twinge of sadness I felt at the thought. Even though Torrence had been dark when she'd saved us from the mages, there was a certain bond you developed with someone when they saved your life. And ever since the Crown had brought her back from the darkness, she was actually pretty cool.

"Goodbye for now," Torrence said. "You never know where the future might lead." She took the tokens and handed one to Reed. "Now, where's the nearest fountain?" she asked. "Because I'm ready to get out of here."

26

GEMMA

AFTER TORRENCE AND REED LEFT, the Elders brought us the half of the Crown. Ethan took it for safe keeping. He didn't explain why, but I guessed he didn't want to have to choose between giving it to me or Mira.

It was definitely the right call.

We said goodbye to the Elders, then used our keys to enter the Library.

As had been the case recently, Hecate wasn't there.

I walked back to the door and brought out my key.

Mira and Ethan didn't move.

"Are you guys coming?" I asked.

"There's something we need to talk about first," Ethan said.

I stilled, not liking his serious tone. "And what's that?"

"Ever since touching that piece of the Crown, you've been different."

"I don't know what you're talking about."

It was a lie. I knew exactly the moment he was referring to—it was when I'd handed the Crown to Torrence.

It was the ice that had flooded my veins when she'd touched it and returned from the darkness.

But I didn't mind. In fact, I liked it.

It numbed the pain I'd felt every time I looked at Ethan and remembered what it felt like to kiss him.

Whatever had happened when I'd touched the Crown had made me stronger. Less emotional. Less vulnerable.

"When Torrence touched the Crown, it brought her out of the darkness," he said. "But when you touched the Crown, it put darkness into you."

"When I touched the Crown, it gave me purpose," I said. "It gave me something to fight for."

"It changed you," Mira said. "And don't try to argue with me. I'm your twin. I know you."

"Maybe you don't know me as well as you think."

She backed away, like she'd been slapped. "You never would have talked to me like that before."

"Things change," I said. "Besides, you touched the Crown, too. Nothing happened to you."

"We have a theory about that," Ethan said.

"Now you've been 'theorizing' about me behind my back?"

"The change happened when you and Torrence were *both* touching the Crown," he continued. "We think some of your light magic went into her, and some of her dark magic went into you."

"That's impossible."

"So you wouldn't mind if we go in there and ask one of those witches wandering around the shelves if she's willing to try taking the dark magic from you? A more experienced witch, who's able to handle it?"

"It would be a waste of time. We need to get back to Earth and find the second half of the Crown."

"Wrong," Mira said. "We need to get you back to normal."

"I *am* normal."

"Then prove it."

"No," I said, and I walked up to the door, stuck the key into the lock, and left the Library before they could argue with me further.

The Haven's tearoom looked the same as when we'd left. I picked up the pad of paper and wrote to Mary to let her know we were back.

As I was writing, Ethan and Mira came in to join me.

They looked *pissed*.

But it was more than that. They also looked *worried*. They cared about me. Mira loved me. Ethan… I didn't know what he felt for me. But he cared about keeping me safe.

I straightened and took a deep breath. They weren't going to drop this. I wouldn't have dropped it if the situation were reversed and Mira had absorbed some of Torrence's dark magic.

I'd do everything I could to get that darkness out of my twin.

It was only a small bit of dark magic. Not nearly enough to consume me, like how Torrence had been when we'd met her.

But I was strong enough to handle my emotions without the dark magic numbing them. It was harder, but I could do it.

Because the most important thing was finding the second piece of the Crown. If getting rid of the dark magic meant it would be easier to work as a team with Mira and Ethan, then I guessed that was what I was going to have to do.

"Fine," I admitted. "You're right."

Mira looked stunned. "So you'll try getting rid of it?"

"How would you suggest I do that? Bring Mary in here and ask if any of her witches would mind absorbing some dark magic that accidentally got transferred into me while we were in Ember?"

"We already told you how we think you should do that," she said. "Most of the witches wandering around the Eternal Library are basically catatonic. You could transfer it to one of them."

"I won't do that," I said.

"Why not?"

"Because like you said—they're basically catatonic. And like I told you, I can control the dark magic. I won't force it on someone who can't."

"Then we'll go with your idea," Ethan said. "We'll ask Mary."

"Deal." I finished up the letter I'd been writing to her, folded it up, and sent it as a fire message.

Mary came alone—as we'd requested—and listened to everything that had happened to us on Ember. *Including* how I'd accidentally siphoned some of Torrence's dark magic.

"I don't think you should try giving that magic to another witch," Mary said once we were done.

Ethan sat back, shocked. "Why?"

"Because that magic is stronger than dark witch magic—it's dark *mage* magic," she said. "We don't know what'll happen if Gemma does this. It could kill the witch who tries to accept the transfer."

I should have been disappointed.

But I wasn't.

"So what should we do?" Mira asked.

"I think that question is better suited for Hecate," Mary said.

"If she's ever around to answer it," Ethan muttered.

"Hecate will be around when she needs to be around." Mary smiled knowingly, then looked to me. "In the meantime, most witches aren't either fully light or fully dark. Having dark magic doesn't make someone a bad person. The biggest difference with your case is that the dark magic inside of you was taken from someone else. But you appear to be in control of it."

"I am," I said steadily.

"And I trust you want to remain in control of it? That you don't want to give into the darkness?"

"I don't."

On a base level, I knew it was true. I wanted to help people. I wanted to love. I wanted to be happy.

I couldn't do any of that if my emotions were numbed.

"As I thought," Mary said. "I need you to understand—witches who turn dark do so because they give in to dark feelings. Pain, anger, jealousy, heartbreak, and fear, to name a few. Everyone experiences these emotions at points in their lives. But witches who go dark let these feelings consume them. They welcome the dark magic as an escape from their pain. It's like a drug, and they become addicted. But I can sense a strong soul, and I have full faith that this challenge is something you can handle."

"I don't like this," Ethan said.

"Neither do I," Mira agreed.

"You don't think I can control it?" I asked.

"I know you can control it," Ethan said. "But you shouldn't have to."

"I guess I'm not the only one doing things I shouldn't." I held his gaze, daring him to keep pushing.

Keep fighting me on this, and I'll tell Mira what happened.

He froze, and realization dawned in his eyes.

We still hadn't spoken about whether I'd drank that memory potion or not. But now, we wouldn't have to. Because I *knew* that he knew I hadn't.

Mira looked back and forth between us. "What are you talking about?"

"I'm talking about the fact that we should be using that dragon heart to locate the second half of the Crown," I said. "Instead, we're sitting here, wasting time talking about things we can't control."

Luckily, my twin appeared satisfied with that answer.

"Finding the second half of the Crown is certainly a priority," Mary said. "But first, there's something I need to tell you."

"What happened?"

"Nothing bad, I promise," she said. "In fact, it's good news. About Harper."

27

GEMMA

Harper was alive.

I couldn't believe it.

The weight I'd been carrying of feeling like I'd been partly responsible for her death lifted.

"I can't believe she didn't pass the Angel Trials," I said. "If there was anyone I thought would definitely get into Avalon, it was her."

"Fate works in mysterious ways," Mary said.

"So when can we see her?"

"You will see her again," she said. "But Harper is doing important work at the Vale. Rosella has advised that she isn't to be interrupted."

I sat back and frowned. "I understand," I said, since I trusted Rosella. "But shouldn't we at least let her know we've returned from Ember?"

"I'll make sure she knows you're back," Mary promised. Then, she looked to the golden box that Ethan had placed on the bench beside him. "But I believe the three of you have the second half of the Holy Crown to find."

"We do," I agreed, relieved that the conversation seemed to have shifted away from me and the dark magic.

Ethan pulled the box onto his lap, opened it, and reached inside. He didn't pull the heart out. Instead, he wrapped his hand around it while it was still inside the box.

He closed his eyes, deep in concentration.

None of us said a word.

Within seconds, his eyes snapped open.

"Bring me a map," he said.

Mary stood and walked to a cabinet on the side of the room. She opened it, pulled out a large roll of parchment, and laid it out on the coffee table.

It was a detailed, hand-drawn map.

Ethan closed the box and placed it back down next to him. Then he got up, kneeled next to the coffee table, and pointed to a spot on the bottom of the map. "That's where the second half of the Crown is," he said.

I eyed the spot where he was pointing and shivered. "Are you sure?"

"Yes. I'm sure."

"I've always wanted to go to Antarctica," Mira said with an excited smile.

Dread pooled in my stomach at the thought of the frozen continent. Ice. And water. Lots of it.

"Of course, I always imagined I'd go there on a cruise." Mira tilted her head, then looked to Mary. "How, exactly, *are* we supposed to get there?"

"I must say—I've never been. Nor do I know of any witches who have, so they can't teleport you there," she admitted. "But it seems you already have the answer."

"I do?"

"You've already looked into getting there by ship."

"I have," she said cautiously. "But those are cruises for people on vacation. And they're expensive."

"Do any of the kingdoms seem to lack money?" Mary asked.

"Well… no." Mira looked around at the expensive decorations in the tearoom. "I just didn't think you'd use that money to send us on a vacation."

"It wouldn't be a vacation. It would be a mission. Unless you have a more efficient idea of how to get to the Antarctic Peninsula?" Mary looked to me and Ethan, as if we might have the answer.

"By plane?" I said. "Or helicopter?"

Anything *but* a ship.

"Antarctica is the most preserved natural continent in the world," Mira said. She'd been so interested in Antarctica that she'd gone to a science center near our house a few years ago to check out a special exhibit they had about it. "There are no airports or helicopter landing pads. Well, there are on the research stations, but I don't believe there are any of those near where we're heading."

A quick search on Mary's phone showed that there weren't.

"Getting on board a ship heading to the Peninsula does sound like a solid way to get there," Mary said as she continued to do searches on her phone. "Mid-March is the end of the Antarctica touring season, but I see one or two cruises I can get you on."

"Leaving when?" I asked.

"In two days," she said. "Which gives us more than enough time to work out the details of your trip."

28

GEMMA

On the morning of our departure, we went to the lobby of the hotel in the Haven, where Mary and a dark-haired witch in high-heeled black boots were waiting for us. There was a significant amount of luggage next to them—the witches of the Haven had packed for us to make sure we were ready for our journey. Packing for Antarctica was apparently not an easy task, despite the fact that our elemental magic made us more resilient to extreme temperatures.

"Gemma, Mira, and Ethan," Mary said as we joined them in the center of the lobby. "Meet Bella Devereux, your chaperone for the trip."

"Aren't you Torrence's mom?" Mira asked.

"Torrence's *aunt*," Bella corrected her. "Torrence told me all about the three of you. When the Earth Angel told us about your mission, and that you were seeking a powerful witch to accompany you, my niece insisted I go."

I'd *wanted* Torrence to come, but one of the reasons for having a witch come with us was so she could pose as my and Mira's mom. We needed to do our best to blend in with the humans, and three teenagers traveling alone would draw too much attention. It would also be illegal, even though I was confident that Mary could have forged passports for us if necessary.

"You didn't want to stay with Torrence?" I asked, since they hadn't seen each other for months. She must have been worried sick about her niece.

"I did," she said. "But like I said, Torrence insisted. She said it was a token of appreciation for everything you did for her in Ember. And when she put it that way, I agreed. I don't know how you brought her back from the darkness, but I'll never be able to repay you. She's the closest thing to a daughter that I have."

"Bella's one of the most powerful witches in the world," Mary added. "There's no one else I trust more to accompany you."

"I've heard about this elemental magic of yours," Bella said. "Can't wait to see it for myself."

I immediately called a flame into my hand, and Mira did the same with an icicle.

Bella studied our elements with a determined glint in her eyes. "Neat," she said. "They're gonna love you once you get to Avalon."

"Assuming we get in," I said. Because if Harper got rejected from Avalon, none of us were guaranteed a spot.

"You'll get in," she said confidently, then she looked at her watch. "Anyway, we've gotta head out. If we're going to blend in, we need to try to be on time. Who's first?"

"I am," Ethan said, since we'd already discussed this. The first person to teleport out would only be at our destination alone for less than a minute, and he refused for that person to be either me or Mira.

Bella teleported out with Ethan, then with Mira, and then with me. Our drop-off point was a posh hotel room in Buenos Aires, Argentina. Bella had stayed at the hotel before—she and her sisters used to do some business in South America—so she'd teleported there and checked into the room last night.

Next, Bella teleported in with our luggage. Six large bags for four people. We also each had a personal backpack. Ethan was keeping the gold box with the heart, and another box with the half of the Crown, in his.

"Welcome to the Alvear Palace Hotel," Bella said after popping in with the final piece of luggage. "Come on. The rest of the group is already gathered in the lobby."

The ship we'd be going on was small—only 140 passengers—and as part of the vacation package, everyone on the trip stayed in this hotel the night before leaving.

We brought our luggage down into the huge, elegant lobby, which had marble floors and walls. There was a huge wine bar, but it was closed, due to the fact that it was four in the morning. The flight to the city where we'd be boarding the ship—Ushuaia—was ridiculously early.

Our luggage was loaded onto the bus, which took us to the airport, where a plane chartering waited for us. The others on the trip were mainly older couples—probably retired—but in good shape. There were also a few families with kids who looked around our age, or in their lower twenties. They were all eyeing each other, as if deciding if they'd become vacation friends or not.

I looked away whenever one of them looked my way. We weren't on this trip to make friends. The fewer people we chatted with, the better.

It would make Bella's job easier after our mission was complete.

The flight was about three and a half hours long. Mary probably could have found at least *one* witch who'd been to Ushuaia before, but since everyone on the trip was flying there together, going with them on the plane was part of our plan of blending in.

More busses met us in Ushuaia, and the cruise company provided us with a tour around the area until the ship was ready to board. We took photos with the mountain landscape behind us, had a delicious Patagonian lunch, and played with Siberian huskies at a local dog sanctuary.

Finally, the bus brought us to the port, where our ship—The Golden Explorer—was waiting.

While we waited in line to check in, waiters wearing white gloves presented us with champagne on silver platters—and juice for those of us underage. The ship went with the American law of having to be twenty-one to drink, but Bella also opted for juice, since we needed to keep our guard up at all times.

Just because this *felt* like a vacation, it didn't mean it *was* a vacation.

A mother and daughter stood behind us, and the mother smiled at us as she took a glass of champagne. "This is my daughter, Vera," she said before taking a long sip of her drink. "It looks like she might be the same age as the three of you...?"

"We're seventeen," Mira said quickly.

"Vera's twenty," the woman said, and Vera gave us a small smile. "Are you triplets?"

"We're twins," Mira said. "Ethan's my boyfriend."

My heart clenched, but I maintained what I hoped was a friendly smile.

"Are you gonna do the polar plunge?" Vera asked.

"You bet I am," Mira said, at the same time as Ethan and I said no.

"Cool." Vera focused on Mira. "Want to jump together?"

"Yes." Mira smiled, and the two of them chatted until it was our turn to check in. Bella kept glaring at her to stop, but Mira ignored her.

Finally, Bella stepped up to the check-in desk. "Bella Devereux," she said, and then she told the woman our names.

"We have you in the owner's suite." She gave us a friendly smile and handed us each a plastic key card. "Suite 734. Welcome aboard the Golden Explorer. Your butler is waiting in your suite to tell you about what the ship has to offer, and to get you acquainted with the amenities on board."

Butler? I thought as we took the elevator to the seventh deck. I knew this was a luxury cruise line... but each room had a personal *butler?*

Sure enough, a butler was waiting in the hall next to our door when we arrived. He introduced himself as Kent, and he gave us a tour of our suite, letting us know to call him whenever we needed anything.

Everything about the suite was pure luxury, down to the marble bathrooms, silk sheets, and large balcony overlooking the water. There was even a bucket with two bottles of fancy champagne waiting on the table.

"What are those for?" I motioned to the chains that bolted the table and chairs to the floor.

"They keep the furniture in place while crossing the Drake Passage," he said. "The forecast is looking rough for our crossing, so you'll be glad they're there. If you brought the patch with you, now's a good time to put it on."

Alarm bubbled up inside me. "What patch?"

"The seasickness patch," he explained. "Goes on your neck behind your ear. Most passengers wear them while crossing the Drake. If you didn't bring any, you can stop by the medical center and pick some up from the doctor."

"Did we bring the patch?" I asked Bella.

"Too many possible side effects," she said. "We're going to tough out the Drake naturally."

Kent raised an eyebrow, apparently wary of this decision. "As you wish," he said. "The medical center's hours are listed in the directory, in case you change your mind."

From his tone, it sounded like he was positive we were going to change our minds.

"There's a briefing each evening at 6:00," Kent continued. "Have you been on a Goldensea expedition cruise before?"

"Nope." I hadn't been on *any* cruise before. Why travel by sea when there were plenty of perfectly good hotels on solid ground?

"Since it's an expedition cruise, we have no set destinations," he explained. "The expedition crew analyzes the conditions each evening and figures out where we can safely anchor down for our daily shore excursions. Ideally, we'll have two landings per day—one in the morning and one in the afternoon. However, this is dependent on the ocean's conditions, since it needs to be safe to land." He looked at each of us, like he was making sure we were following, then continued, "If you need anything or have any questions, press the butler button on the phone, and I'll be of your assistance. Would you like to go to the restaurant for lunch while I unpack for you?"

"We'll unpack ourselves," Bella said. "And we'll be taking all of our meals in the room."

Kent looked taken aback, but he quickly masked his reaction. "As you wish," he said. "If you decide to check out the restaurant, it's in the aft of deck four."

"Thank you," Bella said, and it was clear from her tone that we were *not* going to check out the restaurant.

The fewer people we interacted with, the better. Which meant it would likely be the four of us, inside the cabin, ordering room service until the dragon heart told Ethan that we were close enough to jump ship.

Kent left the room, and I turned to Mira. "What's the Drake Passage?" I asked.

"It's the passage between the southern tip of South American and the Antarctic Peninsula. It's one of the roughest seas in the world," she said casually. "The Atlantic, Pacific, and Southern Oceans all meet in the Drake Passage. Throw a storm into the mix, and we'll get to experience the famous Drake Shake."

"Drake Shake?" I wrapped my arms around my stomach, baffled by how she sounded *excited* for this experience.

She glanced at the table and chairs. "It's why those are bolted to the floor," she said. "The ship will be *rocking!*"

"I figured," I grumbled, then I turned to Bella. "Maybe I should get that seasickness patch. I can't imagine any of its side effects being worse than being motion sick."

"Blurred vision?" She raised an eyebrow, and I sighed, since she was right—if we ended up having to use our magic, blurred vision would be worse than having my stomach all jumbled up.

"Time to unpack," she said. "I'm taking the master bedroom. Gemma and Mira, you get the other. Ethan, you'll be taking the couch. It's one of those that turns into a bed."

"Why don't Ethan and I take the second bedroom," Mira said. "You and Gemma can take the master."

"I'll be taking the couch," Ethan said, and Mira frowned, like she'd been punched. "It's in the center of the suite—the best place I can be to make sure everyone's safe."

"Makes sense," I said, even though I was actually just happy that Ethan wasn't jumping on the chance to share a bed with Mira.

"Then Gemma and I are in the master bedroom," Mira said to Bella. "There's one of you, and two of us. It's only fair."

"Deal," Bella said, and I was surprised—I'd thought she'd fight Mira more on it. "Also, no one touches that champagne. We're here on a mission, which means we have to be on alert at all times. We can't afford to be inebriated."

"My thoughts exactly," Ethan agreed.

Mira frowned again. "You all are no fun."

"I'm loads of fun," Bella said with a wicked smile. "I'm also alive. And I intend to keep the three of you that way, too. So let's unpack, and then, let's practice some magic."

29

GEMMA

THE DRAKE PASSAGE was *worse* than I'd expected. On the first night at sea, the ship rocked so much that it tossed me out of bed. I was so sick that I would have had to stay in the room whether Bella was letting us leave or not.

Not even Mira could go out on the balcony to "enjoy the Drake," as she'd crazily said. The captain had forbidden anyone to step out on deck, and even she was worried she'd fall overboard. And Mira's water magic was strong, but strong enough to save her from the angry, eight-meter tall waves? She *might* have been able to do it, but it wasn't something any of us wanted to risk.

At least my twin hadn't gotten sick. She was the only one of the four of us who hadn't. At one point, Bella had even moaned about wishing we were able to use the seasickness patch.

She and I both. Although the sea was so rocky that I doubted the patch would have made a difference.

It took two ridiculously long days to cross the Drake. I couldn't eat, I couldn't drink, and of course, I couldn't read. The only thing I could do was lay in bed and watch television.

Bella didn't have a key to the Library, so from her perspective, we were stuck on the ship, since witches couldn't teleport on board a ship. The place they were going had to be fixed in one spot. Try to teleport onto a moving ship, and you'd end up in the middle of the ocean.

There was always the Eternal Library, but Ethan insisted we spend the least amount of time there as possible. It was too tempting to walk into the hall of books and browse for answers ourselves. We couldn't risk getting lost there.

As much as I hated to admit it, he was right.

Plus, we *had* to stay on board the ship, in case the dragon heart picked up on the location of the second half of the Crown. But we still visited the Eternal Library every day—we had too many questions to not at least *try* to get answers from Hecate.

She was never there.

What on Earth did she have to do that was more important than helping us *save the world* from the demons? Didn't she *want* the world to be saved?

Judging by how little she made appearances in the Library, apparently not.

On the sixth morning of the cruise, I was jolted awake at 6:05 am by the captain making an announcement over the ship-wide intercom system. The intercoms were everywhere—even inside the suites—and it was impossible to turn them off or lower the volume.

Add that to the list of things that were making this voyage extremely unpleasant.

"In ten minutes, we'll be crossing into the Antarctic Circle!" He was elated, because cruises usually didn't make it so far south. *Especially* not ones that had such a rough crossing of the Drake.

Little did he know that we'd gained so much time because Mira had been coaxing the ocean currents and the wind to help us sail faster. After all, the more land we covered, the better the chance of the heart picking up on the exact location of the second half of the Crown.

"Our expedition guide Malcom is at the front of deck six with a GPS tracker," the captain continued. "Get bundled up to meet him there and see exactly when we cross the 66 degree south line!"

Of course, we didn't go to deck six. But Mira, Ethan, and I did step out onto the balcony, where we heard people cheering on the deck below when we crossed into the Antarctic Circle.

I gazed out at the icebergs sitting on the water in the distance. We'd passed some huge ones during our journey—the only way we'd been able to enjoy Antarctica so far was by stepping out onto the balcony and viewing the icebergs, snow-covered mountains, and the occasional whale spotting.

Bella had stayed inside the suite so far. It was *freezing* outside, which didn't bother me, Mira, or Ethan, thanks to our elemental magic. Bella, on the other hand, had to put on multiple layers of clothing to brave the cold. She said it wasn't worth the hassle, since she could see the same thing from the window.

After taking in the view, we went back inside. Like he did every morning, Ethan took the golden box out of the closet and brought it to the dining room table. He opened it and reached inside to touch the heart.

"We're getting closer," he said, which was what he'd been saying each day, the farther south we got. "Bring out the map."

Mira grabbed our Antarctica Atlas from the bookshelf, laid it out on the table in front of Ethan, and opened it to the zoomed-in page of the Antarctic Peninsula. The three of us—me, Mira, and Bella—gathered around Ethan, waiting.

Ethan pointed to an island on the page. "Here," he said, and I moved closer to get a better look.

Detaille Island.

"That's where the captain's trying to anchor down today," I said.

They hadn't stopped talking about it on one of the few channels we got on our TV —the Goldensea channel that discussed our journey through Antarctica. There were lots of educational segments on the history of the continent, and on the wildlife we might spot.

During my time in bed while seasick, I'd learned more about Antarctica than I'd ever wanted to know.

Detaille Island was the only place we were trying to land that had remnants of human settlement, thanks to the British scientific station—Base W—that had been occupied and then hastily abandoned in the 1950s.

"Do you think the second half of the Crown is at Base W?" I asked.

"I think it's worth a look."

"Me, too."

Mira bounced in excitement. "So we're finally leaving the ship?"

"That's the only way to Detaille Island," I said. "So, yes. We're leaving the ship. Then, hopefully, coming back on board with the second half of the Holy Crown."

30

GEMMA

THE OCEAN WAS rough when the ship anchored down—so rough that at first glance, it seemed like it was going to be impossible to get to the island. But with help from Mira, the water calmed enough for it to be safe.

We layered up in the appropriate clothing—including our bright red Goldensea jackets that every guest was required to wear while off the ship—and left our suite. We made our way down to the locker room where the ship kept the heavy-duty snow boots we needed to step foot on Antarctica, located the ones with our suite number on them, and put them on.

Next, we got in line to board a zodiac—an inflatable, raft-like boat that fit eight people, plus an expedition guide to drive. The waters were choppy, but thanks to our supernatural strength, we hopped on with no problem. The same couldn't be said for the other four people assigned to the boat with us. One of them—an older man—would have face-planted into the side of the zodiac if the crew hadn't been holding onto him to keep him somewhat balanced.

We all wore backpacks, and I glanced at Ethan's to make sure it was secure. His was the most important, since it held both the dragon heart and half of the Holy Crown.

He squeezed one of the straps, as if letting me know he had it covered. Not that I ever doubted him. I'd always trust Ethan to keep me and Mira safe.

Once all eight of us were loaded onto the zodiac, the driver pulled the motor, and we sped over to Detaille Island. The water was choppy, and Mira—who'd taken the seat in front—smiled and faced forward, enjoying the ride. The air was clean, crisp, and pure—untouched by humankind. This beautiful continent belonged to nature and the animals that lived there.

I held tightly onto the ropes, glad I'd opted for a light breakfast that morning.

Fifteen minutes later, the zodiac pulled up to Detaille Island. There was no dock—we just pulled straight up to the rocky ground, the front of the zodiac lodging on top of it. A steep hill with a narrow, winding footpath led up to a flat area on top, where I could just make out the small shack of Base W. Expedition guides lined the steep, slippery path, ready to help to make sure no one fell.

One by one, we hopped off the zodiac.

The moment my feet hit the ground, I nearly fell to my knees in relief. I wanted to lie down and thank every god out there that I was back on land. But I stayed focused, easily making my way up the path without needing help from the guides.

Once up to the top, I took a deep breath of the crisp air and admired the snow-covered mountains stretching out in the distance, reaching so high that they touched the clouds.

This was the most middle of nowhere I'd ever been in my life. If I didn't know any better, I would have thought I was in a mystical ice realm instead of on Earth.

Mira and Ethan stood next to me, also admiring the view.

"Beautiful, isn't it?" Ethan said.

"It is," I said, amazed by how everything here was so still, quiet, and perfect.

Then, Bella joined us. "We're not here to take in the sights," she said. "Any updates with the heart?"

Ethan removed the pack from his back, set it on the ground, and unzipped it. He reached inside, although he didn't take out the box. He moved his hand around inside the backpack like he was opening the box, then he closed his eyes and was still.

Even though I couldn't see, I knew his hand was around the heart.

He snapped his eyes open and looked out toward the mountains—the opposite direction of Base W. "We're getting closer," he said. "It's that way."

"Are you sure?" I'd been *so* sure that the second half of the Crown would be inside Base W. That there'd be some secret passage inside it that only supernaturals could enter.

"I'm sure."

"All right." Mira rubbed her hands together, her blue eyes glimmering with excitement. "Off to the mountains we go. Finally."

"We're not going *to* the mountains," I said. "They're across the water." I turned to Ethan, alarmed. "Right?"

"I don't know," he said. "All I know is that the heart is telling me to go that way."

"We can always hijack a zodiac," Bella said.

I nearly balked and said that was ridiculous, but then I realized it wasn't a terrible idea. The crew would still be able to get everyone back to the ship. It would just take a bit longer than it would have otherwise.

"Let's hold up on hijacking anything until we check out what's in that general direction," I said.

"Agreed," Ethan said.

"Bummer." Bella frowned. "You're no fun."

Mira rolled her eyes. "Says the person who wouldn't let us leave our suite for the entire first half of the cruise."

"That was different. It would have been a bad idea. *This* is a good idea."

Ethan zipped up his bag and put it around his back. "Zodiac hijacking is an option to consider later," he said. "For now, we walk."

"Hey!" One of the expedition guides—Malcolm, the one with glasses who'd held the GPS when the ship had crossed the Antarctic Circle—hurried in our direction. "You can't go any farther than this."

"Of course." Bella smiled. "Sorry." She gave us a look, and we followed Malcom back to the outer edge of the area we were allowed to be in.

He looked up at the sky, pointed, and started saying something about the birds.

"Very interesting," Bella said, clearly finding it anything but. "We can go over there, right?" She pointed in a general direction off to the side.

"Sure." Malcolm startled slightly at how she'd cut him off, like he was offended that she didn't want to hear more about the birds. "Just don't go any farther out than this."

"Thanks," Bella said. "Got it."

We walked off, staying in the acceptable area, and Malcolm hurried to another group of tourists to tell them more about the birds. Skuas. I'd learned about them on the TV while I'd been stuck in bed.

They loved hunting baby penguins during hatching season in January. They plucked them right out of their nests. I was glad we weren't there during that time, because that *wasn't* something I'd have wanted to witness.

Bella placed her backpack on the ground, unzipped it, and pulled out four vials of clear potion.

"Invisibility potion," Mira said before I had a chance.

"One for each of us," Bella said as she handed them out. "Cheers." She uncapped her vial and chugged it down.

The three of us did the same.

The potion tasted like air. I wouldn't have been sure I'd actually drank anything if the vial wasn't empty afterward... and if my arms hadn't turned ghostly sheer. A quick glance showed that my entire body looked like that.

Ethan, Mira, and Bella also looked like ghosts. Our backpacks, too, and assumedly everything in them.

"We can see each other because that was from the same batch," Bella said. "We're invisible to everyone else."

"Cool." I hadn't taken invisibility potion before, but it felt freeing. Like I was an observer instead of actually there.

Something about being an observer in my own body felt weirdly familiar. Like déjà vu.

"Now, we walk," Ethan said, and we continued forward without any guides bothering us again.

As we made our way to the opposite end of the island, the snow on the ground thickened. There were more penguins nearby, although we did as we were supposed to and stayed out of their way.

The island wasn't big, so it wasn't long before we reached the other side.

"Well?" I looked to Ethan, and he set the backpack down again and reached inside for the heart.

He was done in a second. "We're close."

"But not there yet?" I glanced out at the water. It was dark, and it looked *cold*. If we were going into another underwater kingdom...

I shuddered at the thought.

"We still have to go that way." Ethan pointed to the mountains across the water again. "Sorry."

Bella rubbed her hands together. "Zodiac hijacking it is."

"Not so fast." Mira held her hand over her forehead to block the sun. "Look."

I glanced out to where a short, flat-topped iceberg about a few meters long drifted in our direction. A beautiful woman with long, platinum hair stood on top of it. She looked like Elsa from *Frozen*, except her outer gear was made of thick layers of animal skins, like those worn by Alaskan natives.

She scanned the general area where we were standing. "Where are you?" she asked.

I glanced at the others, saying nothing. Invisibility potion made us invisible, but it didn't block sound.

"I know you're out here," she continued.

Invisibility potion also didn't hide footprints.

She caught sight of the trail of them behind us, smiled, and the iceberg floated to the edge of the island.

"I'm not going to hurt you," she said, her voice soft and soothing. A light metallic smell drifted over to us—she was a vampire. "You can show yourselves."

I nodded at the others. Because the dragon heart had led us here for a reason. And this woman was our only lead about what to do next.

If she attacked, it would be four against one. Besides, she already knew where we were from our trail of footprints.

Good thing Malcolm had been too involved in bird watching to have noticed those earlier.

Bella reached into her pack and pulled out four small tablets. They were the same ghostly color that we were—the same empty color of the invisibility potion.

We each took one and chewed. They were chalky, and within seconds, we were back to our visible selves.

The woman smiled as we shimmered into sight. "Much better," she said. "I'm Katherine. *Queen* Katherine."

I looked around the desolate landscape, then back to her. "Queen of what?"

"The Queen of the Seventh Kingdom."

31

GEMMA

I STARED AT HER, shocked.

The Seventh Kingdom was a myth.

I nearly said so, but stopped myself. Because up until a few months ago, I'd thought everything supernatural was a myth.

Why would the Seventh Kingdom be any different?

Bella, apparently, didn't feel the same way.

"The Seventh Kingdom doesn't exist," she said. "It's an imaginary place the Earth Angel said she was from so she could be accepted as a contender to win Prince Jacen's heart while he was choosing a bride."

"It's true that Annika Pearce—the Earth Angel, and the Queen of Cups—pretended to be a princess from my kingdom," Queen Katherine said. "But the Seventh Kingdom does, in fact, exist. I'm here to lead you there."

Ethan's fingers tightened around the straps of his backpack. "Why?"

"Because we have something you're looking for."

"How do you know what we're looking for?" I asked. "And how did you know we'd be here?"

"Avalon and the Haven aren't the only kingdoms with prophetesses and witches," she said. "We have our own. How else do you think we stayed hidden all this time?"

"I think you stayed hidden because if you're telling the truth that the Seventh Kingdom is real, then it's in Antarctica," I said flatly. "It doesn't get any more remote than this."

"I assure you that I'm telling the truth." She smiled again, like she was amused I doubted her. "Come with me, and you'll see."

I stayed put. "How long have you known we'd come here?" I asked.

"A while."

"Days? Months? *Years?*"

"Something like that. But all that matters is that I'm here for you now, ready to bring you to my kingdom."

"It seems too easy," Bella said what I was sure we were all thinking. "Shouldn't there be trials we need to pass, or something?"

"This isn't Avalon," Queen Katherine said. "I'm not recruiting you to join an army."

"Thank goodness for that," Mira muttered.

"I'm also only inviting the three dragons to the Seventh Kingdom," she said, and then she looked to Bella. "You and I will teleport back to the ship—while it's still anchored down—so I can compel everyone on board to forget you were there."

"I'm staying with the three of them," she said. "We already have vampire allies prepared to do reconnaissance once the ship lands back in Ushuaia."

"And until then, you intend to have them think you've gone missing on Detaille Island?" she asked, and none of us replied, since our plan hadn't actually gotten much further than locating the second half of the Crown. "They'll send out teams looking for you. It'll draw attention—possibly *supernatural* attention. Demonic attention."

"Fine," Bella said, and then she glanced at me, Ethan, and Mira. "But we can't leave them here while you handle the crew and passengers on the ship."

"They'll be perfectly safe here," Queen Katherine said. "The ship you came here on is small. This won't take me long. But obviously our time is limited, since we can only teleport onto the ship while it's anchored down. So I need you to take me there—now."

Bella said nothing. It was like she was waiting for me, Ethan, and Mira to make the decision.

"I have a question," I said, and all eyes went to me. "You say you're a queen of a vampire kingdom. That would make you an original vampire."

She nodded, and I continued, "But there are only six original vampires. Five, now that Queen Laila's dead."

"There were seven original vampires. Six, since Laila's passing." She frowned when she said the dead queen's name, as if they'd been friends.

They likely had been, since the original vampires had performed the long-forgotten spell that had turned them immortal together.

"Then why do the others never speak of you?" I asked.

"Because they don't remember me. I compelled them to forget."

"Impossible," I said. "Vampires with the ability to compel can't be compelled by other vampires."

The only vampires with the ability of compulsion were the original vampires and the vampires they'd personally turned—the vampire princes and princesses. It was why the original vampires were so particular about who they turned.

"I'm gifted with the ability of superior compulsion," she said. "I can compel anyone—including other original vampires."

I became suddenly aware of the onyx ring beneath my gloved finger. It was supposed to protect us from mind intrusion, including vampire compulsion.

Would it protect us against Queen Katherine's *superior* compulsion?

Bella shifted uncomfortably on her feet.

"We're running out of time," Queen Katherine said to Bella. "I need you to take me to the ship."

Bella pressed her lips together, not replying. Which was a good thing, since it meant Queen Katherine wasn't using her ability of superior compulsion to force Bella to take her to the ship. She was letting Bella make the choice on her own.

"Do it," I said. "We came here for a reason. We can't lose this chance."

I purposefully didn't mention the second half of the Crown, since Queen Katherine hadn't yet specified what she had that we were looking for. No need to show our cards this early.

"I agree with Gemma," Ethan said, and Mira nodded that she also agreed.

"Very well." Bella stepped toward the edge of the cliff, in front of Queen Katherine's iceberg.

Queen Katherine launched herself up with vampire speed and landed gracefully in front of Bella.

Then Bella took her hands, and they vanished into thin air.

32

GEMMA

"The Seventh Kingdom is real," I said once they were gone. "I can't believe it."

Ethan stared out at the mountainous horizon.

I glanced at Mira, who'd barely said a word since Queen Katherine had arrived. "You okay?" I asked.

"I'm fine," she said, although from her tone, she was clearly *not* fine.

"Are you sure?"

"Yes, I'm sure."

I bristled at her tone, then brushed it off. Mira had been moody since the ship had set sail. Being cooped up in our suite had really been getting to her.

Now, she stared at the iceberg Queen Katherine had arrived on, lost in her thoughts.

"Do you trust it?" I asked, motioning to the iceberg.

"It's ice," she said. "Of course I trust it."

Then, she was silent again. Ethan, too.

"Is there something you guys aren't telling me?" I asked.

"No," Mira said quickly—*too* quickly.

Ethan gripped the straps of his bag tighter, not looking at either of us.

"You still have the Crown," I said to him. "Right?"

"Of course I still have the Crown."

I nodded, since obviously he would have said something if he didn't. And there was no place he could have lost it. Plus, Ethan was too responsible to lose *anything*, let alone half of the Holy Crown.

So why were they both acting so strange?

"Is everything okay between the two of you?" I asked the first possibility that came to mind.

Mira snapped her head around to look at me and shot me a bright, forced smile. "Everything's great."

My breath caught. Because she was lying.

Mira and Ethan were having problems—again. Problems that, knowing my sister, could distract her from what we'd come here to do.

And I was *happy* about it.

My stomach twisted, even though my seasickness had gone away since stepping onto solid ground.

"I don't trust her," Ethan said suddenly.

My mouth nearly dropped open. "You don't trust Mira?"

"No." He looked confused that I'd say such a thing. "I don't trust Queen Katherine."

"Me, either," Mira said, although she still wouldn't look at Ethan. "She can use her gift to make anyone do anything she wants, regardless of any protection spells they have on them. At least, that's what it sounded like."

"That *is* what it sounded like," I agreed. "But if she wanted to use compulsion on us, why tell us she had it at all? Why not just use it and then make us forget she used it?"

"Maybe she *will* do that, after we leave the Seventh Kingdom," Ethan said. "She clearly doesn't want word out that it exists."

"Which means she could compel us to forget everything that's happened since she pulled up on that iceberg," Mira said. "She could compel us to forget everything that's happening *now*."

"We won't forget," I said.

"How do you know that?"

"Because I trust her."

"You can't just blindly *trust* her," Mira said, as if it were a dirty word. "You can't blindly trust *anyone*."

"I'm not blindly trusting *her*," I said. "I'm trusting my feelings."

"Same thing."

I swallowed down irritation. Because this was the same fight we'd had over and over again. Despite everything we'd learned about magic, Mira would never understand the power of intuition, and I'd never understand why she couldn't believe we had magic *inside* ourselves after seeing so much magic in the world around her.

Why was one so hard to believe, and not the other?

"What do you think?" I asked Ethan, since there was no point in continuing this conversation with my twin.

"I'm not sure," he said. "But the heart directed us here, which means the Seventh Kingdom must have the second half of the Crown. We need to go with Queen Katherine, whether we can trust her or not. If she tries anything, we've trained enough that we should be able to handle ourselves. Plus, we have our keys. I'm going to assume there are doors in the Seventh Kingdom. If things get bad and we need to leave, we'll use our keys and go to the Haven's tearoom."

"Assuming she doesn't compel us to forget about the keys and what they can do," Mira muttered.

"She won't," I said. "She can't. The keys are Hecate's magic."

"You have no idea what Queen Katherine can or can't do."

I took a long, slow breath to calm myself, since telling Mira to trust Hecate would be pointless.

Instead, I changed the subject, and we discussed the possibilities of what type of magic the Holy Crown might be able to do. The Holy Grail turned deserving humans into Nephilim, the Holy Sword increased fighting ability, and the Holy Wand amplified magic.

What could a *crown* do?

"Maybe it enhances intelligence," I suggested.

"Or allows mind reading," Ethan said.

I frowned at the thought. A lot of people would love the ability to read minds, but I'd always imagined it would be terrible. Thoughts were supposed to be private. A person's character should be judged on what they chose to say and do—not on their thoughts.

If anyone knew my thoughts about Ethan, they'd think I was a terrible person.

Maybe I *was* a terrible person. But I was doing my best to not let my heart control my brain, no matter how difficult it was. And that had to count for something. Right?

"Maybe mind control?" Ethan said, a moment before Queen Katherine popped back in.

She looked us over and nodded. "I told you you'd be safe."

"How'd it go on the ship?" I asked.

"Perfectly well. No one on board knows you were ever there."

"And what about Bella?"

"She's returned to Avalon. She's looking forward to being in warm weather again, so she can wear more flattering clothing."

I smiled, because that sounded like something Bella would say.

"Now, let's hop on board." Queen Katherine motioned to the iceberg she'd arrived on. "And I'll take you to the Seventh Kingdom."

33

GEMMA

THE ICEBERG WASN'T SLIPPERY—PROBABLY thanks to some type of spell. But the moment I stepped onto it, the gentle rocking made my stomach cramp up. I wrapped my arms around myself, swallowing down nausea as the iceberg floated away.

We'd only traveled for about five minutes before the outline of a boundary dome shimmered in the open ocean ahead.

"This iceberg has been enchanted by our witch," Queen Katherine said. "Anyone on board can pass through the boundary."

Sure enough, the iceberg slipped through the boundary with us on it. As we went through, a tingle passed over my skin.

A small, deserted island had been hidden inside the dome, with a snow-covered log cabin in the center of it. No penguins waddled down to the water, and no seals laid on the ice floating nearby. There wasn't even a breeze. It was so quiet that I could physically feel the stillness.

The iceberg docked into the side of the island. It fit perfectly into the ground, like each were pieces of a puzzle.

I hurried onto solid ground, then looked up at the cabin in question. A soft, orange light glowed out of the windows, the same color as the orbs in Utopia.

I'd expected something grander, like an ice palace.

Maybe, like the huts in the Ward, the cabin was a cover for an underground kingdom.

Without a word, Queen Katherine led us up the snowy path to the cabin. Once we were close enough, I noticed a thin layer of frost covering every bit of the wood.

Queen Katherine reached for the frosty handle of the door, turned it, and walked inside.

I toyed with the chain of my necklace as I stepped through. Because where there was a door, there was a way out.

Three women in heavy animal skins who looked around Queen Katherine's age—in their mid-twenties—sat around a small dining table. By their scents, I could tell that one was a witch, one a vampire, and the other a dragon.

Their scents were complemented by an earthy, meaty concoction brewing in the cauldron over the fireplace.

The fire called to me, the flames leaning slightly in my direction.

"Meet Genevieve, Constance, and Isemay." Queen Katherine pointed to each woman as she said her name. "My loyal subjects in the Seventh Kingdom."

"There are only four of you?" Mira looked baffled.

I was also surprised, although unlike my sister, I did my best to hide it.

Ethan focused on Isemay, the dark-skinned dragon with soft almond eyes. "How did you get here?" he asked. "There haven't been any dragons on Earth in centuries."

"I arrived with the dragons when we first left Ember to explore Earth," she said in a strange accent I couldn't quite place.

"Impossible," Ethan said.

"Why do you say that?"

"Because the dragons came to Earth centuries ago. You don't look a day over twenty-five."

"Incorrect," she said. "I'm twenty-seven."

"It's close enough," he said. "Given that you should be long dead."

She frowned, then looked to Queen Katherine, as if it wasn't up to her to say more.

"Please, join us around the table," Queen Katherine said to the three of us. "We've prepared a hot stew to enjoy while we fill you in on the purpose of the Seventh Kingdom, and our duty as its inhabitants."

I glanced at the cauldron, and while I still instinctively trusted Queen Katherine, I also worried about consuming something when I didn't know what was inside of it.

"It smells amazing," Mira said, apparently not sharing my concern. "I'm starving."

"Wait," Ethan said, and Mira stopped when she was halfway to the table. He looked back to Queen Katherine, and continued, "You told us that you had what we were seeking. We trusted you by following you to your kingdom. Now, I think it's only fair that before we sit down to a meal, you show us that you have what we came here for."

"Understandable," she said, and then she looked to Genevieve. "Go fetch it."

Genevieve stood up—she was tall and willowy, with the classic looks of a Hollywood movie star—and walked into the next room. She returned holding a wooden box with sheer frost covering all sides of it. It was the same size as the gold box in Ethan's backpack that held our half of the Holy Crown.

"Open it," Queen Katherine said.

Genevieve did as commanded.

Inside the box was the second half of the Holy Crown. The small clear crystals and half of a crescent moon on the end were mirror images of the Crown in Ethan's bag.

I wanted to run for the box and take it. But I also didn't want to start a fight with an original vampire, a powerful witch, another vampire, and a dragon. So I stayed where I was, although my eyes remained glued on the second half of the Crown.

"How long have you had it here?" Ethan asked.

"We've guarded this half of the Crown for centuries," Queen Katherine said. "Right after the dragons came to Earth, Isemay came to me with it. She said a fae with omniscient sight came to Ember with both halves of the Crown. He instructed the King of Ember to guard the first half. Then he gave the second half to Isemay, told her to find me, and gave her instructions on what to tell me to do with it."

"The fae with omniscient sight was Prince Devyn," I said.

"He was," Isemay confirmed.

Queen Katherine gave Genevieve a pointed look, and the witch closed the box and placed it on a side table against the wall. "Now do you trust me to sit down to a meal?" she asked. "You know the rules of the kingdoms. Trust must be shown before deals are made."

I nodded, since I'd learned that in Utopia.

Trust was shown by accepting food from your hosts. And I *did* trust Queen Katherine. So I walked over to the table and sat in the chair next to the other vampire, Constance. She was small with strawberry blonde hair, and appeared the least threatening of the three.

Ethan sat in the seat next to me, and Mira took the seat next to him.

"Isemay—get our guests some water," the queen said. "I'll serve the stew."

Within a minute, we were all gathered around the table with glasses of water and steaming bowls of stew.

I picked up my spoon and studied the stew suspiciously. The meat inside was unidentifiable. "What's in it?" I asked.

Please don't say penguin.

"Whale," Queen Katherine said, and my stomach dropped.

They expected me to eat *whale?*

However, I supposed I ate many other fish. And, more importantly, we needed the second half of the Crown. If that meant trying whale stew, then so be it.

I dipped my spoon into the bowl and took a bite. The meat didn't taste all that different from beef.

Queen Katherine nodded after all three of us took a bite. "The four of us have been in this cabin for centuries, guarding the second half of the Crown so we can give it to you," she said.

I looked around the small cabin in horror. "You didn't leave this place for *centuries?*"

"Genevieve and Isemay worked together to safely freeze us until you arrived," she said.

"You mean like in science fiction when people get frozen to travel through space?"

All four of them gave me strange looks.

I guessed if they'd been frozen for centuries, they wouldn't have read or seen any science fiction.

"When people are frozen so they don't age as time passes," I tried again.

"Exactly," the queen said. "Isemay's elemental gift is ice magic, and Genevieve is the ancestor of the most powerful witch who's ever lived—Geneva."

"The witch who gave her life to seal the gap that had been opened between Earth and Hell," I said, since it was one of the big topics in our history lessons. Over seventeen years ago, the demons had come to Earth in the short time the gap had been open. The supernaturals have been in the war to rid the demons from Earth ever since.

Queen Katherine nodded, then continued, "With help from the magic of the second half of the Crown, they created a spell to keep us frozen in time and hidden from the outside world."

"Does that mean you know what magic the Crown has?" Ethan asked.

"No," she said. "But we've been looking forward to your arrival, so we can finally put the halves together and see what happens when the Crown is whole."

I put my spoon down, no longer hungry.

All I cared about was putting that Crown back together.

"Then let's do it," I said.

"One moment," said Isemay, slowly and seriously. "When Prince Devyn gave me the half of the Crown, he gave me an important message about what must happen after the Crown is made whole."

"And…" My heart pounded as I waited for her to continue.

"The dragon king—Ethan Pendragon—must be the one to place the Crown on the head of the Queen of Pentacles. Then, it will gift the Queen with the magic of the fifth element."

"So it's true," I realized, and a wave of excitement—and anxiety—crashed over me. "One of us is definitely the Queen."

"Yes," Queen Katherine said. "It's true."

"What type of magic is the fifth element?"

"We don't know," she said. "We'll find out after the Queen is crowned."

"Okay." I gathered myself, straightened, then looked to my twin. "You can go first."

Mira smiled. I knew it would make her happy to go first.

I also knew that it didn't matter who Ethan crowned first, since only one of us was destined to wear the Crown.

"Wait," Isemay said. "There's one more catch."

"What's that?" I asked.

"Ethan must place the Holy Crown on the head of the twin he truly loves. If he places it on the other twin's head, not only will the Crown be destroyed, but its wearer will die, too."

34

GEMMA

ETHAN PALED AND SAID NOTHING.

"Ethan?" Mira said, her voice small.

"Sorry." He picked his backpack up from the floor, unzipped it, and pulled out the golden box with our half of the Crown. "Let's get this over with."

He refused to look at either me or Mira.

Mira looked like her heart had been beaten with a sledgehammer.

I felt... numb.

It's going to be Mira, I told myself. *He's chosen to be with Mira. They might be having relationship issues right now, but she's the one he loves.*

"Genevieve will put the halves together," Queen Katherine said.

Still not looking at either me or Mira, Ethan took our half of the Crown out of the box and handed it to Genevieve.

She took it from him, walked over to the table against the wall, and took the second half of the Crown out of its icy wooden box. The Crown's crystals glowed, like they were trying to come back to life. But the glow was dim—not quite there yet.

Then Genevieve brought the halves together, and white light exploded through the room. It was so bright that I had to close my eyes. Even then, I could still see the echo of the light behind my lids.

The light died down, and I reopened my eyes.

The Crown was one. Its crystals sparkled and glimmered with an otherworldly light, as did the crescent moon in the center.

Genevieve's eyes were bright with wonder as she stared down at it. "The Holy Crown is whole," she said, and then she pulled her gaze away from the Crown to look at Ethan. "It's time for you to crown our fourth and final Queen."

I could barely breathe as he walked over to Genevieve.

He loves Mira. Mira is going to be the Queen of Pentacles. Mira will receive the fifth element.

Disappointment coursed through me. Because I was more in tune with magic than

Mira. And whatever the fifth element was, I wanted it. My stomach twisted with a sense of *wrongness* at the idea of Mira having it instead of me.

But what was it Hecate had said?

Trust in Fate.

I wasn't going to receive the fifth element. But maybe Fate had something else in store for me. Something that, right now, I couldn't even fathom.

Ethan took the Crown from Genevieve, then spun around to face me and Mira. His eyes were more pained than I'd ever seen them before.

"Wait," said Constance—the vampire gifted with future sight. She'd been quiet so far, and the intensity of her tone surprised me. "The fate of the world hinges on what's about to happen here. We need to proceed correctly."

"What do you mean?" Mira fidgeted and looked back and forth between Ethan and Constance.

Ethan refused to look at her. He refused to look at me, too.

"The two of you need to stand in front of Ethan with your backs against each other and your eyes closed," she said. "Then Ethan will place the Crown on the head of the twin he loves."

"Why?" Mira looked—and sounded—desperate to get this over with.

"To take as much pressure off him as possible."

"There shouldn't be any pressure." Mira squared her shoulders and looked at Constance like she was a bug she wanted to squash. "Ethan's with me. He loves *me*. Which means I'm the Queen of Pentacles."

"That may be the case," Constance said. "But we must follow protocol."

"Fine." Mira stomped across the room and stopped in front of Ethan. She stood perpendicular to him, so her right shoulder was in front of him. "Let's get this over with."

My feet felt like they were weighted down with bricks as I walked over to Mira and pressed my back against hers.

Out of the corner of my eye, I saw Ethan's hands shaking around the Crown.

He shouldn't have been so nervous. There was nothing between me and him other than my unrequited attraction for him and that kiss in Lilith's lair.

He'd had a chance to stay with me that first day we'd met in the cove. But he'd gone on to meet Mira, and then to date her. He'd *chosen* her.

Of course he was going to crown her. He was only nervous because of the second part of what Isemay had said.

If he places the Crown on the other twin's head, she'll die.

By crowning Mira, there was also a chance—a *small* chance—that he could kill her.

Possibly killing the person you loved would be an insane amount of pressure for *anyone*.

But Ethan loved Mira. He was going to crown her, she'd receive the fifth element, and she'd be okay. She'd be more than okay—she'd be the Queen of Pentacles.

It should have been me.

I pushed the thought out of my head, since there was no point in getting upset about something I couldn't control.

Fate had other plans for me. It had to.

"Close your eyes," Genevieve said, and I did as asked.

The next time I opened my eyes, Mira would be a Queen.

"Good luck," I whispered to my twin.

She trembled behind me. "You, too."

The wooden floor creaked as Ethan stepped forward, his delicious, spicy scent growing closer. While I couldn't see him, I could *feel* that he was standing in front of where my and Mira's shoulders were touching.

I sucked in a long breath, reached back for my sister's hands, and held them. Her palms were damp with sweat. She clenched my hands tightly, like she was terrified to let go.

Relax, I thought. *This will be over soon.*

Nervous energy buzzed through me.

I heard Ethan raise his arms.

And then, I felt it.

The weight of the Crown upon my head.

35

GEMMA

My body felt like it was being sliced into pieces. Sliced by the sharp crystals of the Crown.

I screamed, but heard nothing.

And I saw *everything*.

Memories flooded my mind—the memories I'd erased with the potion created by Shivani.

The memories of a life where Ethan had chosen *me*.

The final words he'd spoken to me in that life echoed through my mind.

Centuries ago, most dragons had a Twin Flame out there, somewhere. A mirrored soul they were destined to find, and would search for until they did. We wait to be intimate with anyone until receiving our shifting magic. Because only when we've become whole—when our dragon side unites with our human side—are we ready to find and connect with our twin. Before that moment, even if we met our twin, we'd be attracted to them but we wouldn't know for sure if it was a Twin Flame connection. Our first shift changes that.

And then, the final part:

Every Twin shares at least one element with the other.

Fire.

Ethan and I had always been connected by fire.

But the pain shredding my body apart was so intense that I was going to explode from it. It was like I'd turned to light and had been fractured into a million pieces.

Ethan had crowned the wrong twin.

The Holy Crown was killing me.

I was going to die. The Crown would be destroyed.

Without all four Queens, the world as we knew it would fall into the hands of the demons.

So many people were going to die. And all because—for some unknown reason—Ethan thought he loved *me*.

What had he been thinking when he'd placed that Crown on my head? What must his expression have been?

Had he been looking at me with love? The same way the Ethan from my alternate memories had always looked at me?

Suddenly, the pain was gone, and I was leaning against a wall, in a small bedroom similar in design to the living room of the cabin. I stared down at my hands, surprised to find them intact.

I could still feel the weight of the Crown on my head, and I reached up to touch it.

It was whole.

I hadn't destroyed it by wearing it. More importantly, *it* hadn't destroyed *me*.

So, what had happened?

"Ethan must place the Holy Crown on the head of the twin he truly loves," Isemay's voice sounded from the next room. "If he places it on the other twin's head, not only will the Crown be destroyed, but its wearer will die, too."

I blinked, hit with déjà vu. The world felt like it upended, and I pressed my palms against the wall to make sure I didn't fall over.

No, I thought as I steadied myself. *Impossible.*

The door in the room was cracked open from when Genevieve had come inside to fetch the box holding the second half of the Crown.

As quietly as possible, I walked over to it and peeked through the crack.

Genevieve stood at the wall, next to the table with the second half of the Crown on top of it.

The second half of the fully complete Crown that was also sitting *on my head*.

This couldn't be happening.

"Ethan?" Mira said.

I couldn't see her, but I remembered her expression in that moment. Worried and scared.

I remembered because I'd been standing next to her.

"Sorry," Ethan said, and I heard him unzip his backpack. "Let's get this over with."

"Genevieve will put the halves together," Queen Katherine said.

Ethan's footsteps sounded on the floor, and then he came into view and handed Genevieve our half of the Crown.

My heart caught in my throat, and I could barely breathe. Because everything that I was watching now... it had already happened.

This has to be a dream, I thought. *Something happened when Ethan placed that Crown on my head. Maybe it knocked me out? And now I'm remembering the final minutes beforehand.*

That made sense. Total, complete sense.

At least, more sense than the *other* possibility. Especially since, as I'd learned from the nightshade, I was apparently prone to vivid hallucinations.

Could the Holy Crown have driven me crazy?

I reached for my head to touch it again. Because I was wearing the Crown. But at the same time, Genevieve stood meters away, holding both halves of it. It was here *and* there.

There were *two* Holy Crowns.

Sort of. Maybe the one I was wearing would disappear once the original became whole again.

If that one was the original. Hadn't mine existed first?

Like before, Genevieve brought the halves together. I stepped to the side just before the bright light exploded through the room. If any of them saw me... well, I had no idea *what* would happen if they saw me. But I doubted it would be good.

Especially if *I* saw me.

The light died down, and I resumed my post near the door, watching from the shadows through the crack.

As I knew it would be, the Crown in Genevieve's hands was whole.

The one on my head was still there, too.

Now, there truly were two Crowns, existing in nearly the same space. The implications of that were too huge to comprehend. My brain felt dizzy from trying.

"The Holy Crown is whole," Genevieve said, and then she looked to Ethan. "It's time for you to crown our fourth and final Queen."

I stood totally still as I watched the next moments, knowing exactly how they would play out.

Constance told me and Mira to stand with our backs to each other and close our eyes, to take the pressure off of Ethan.

Constance, the vampire *prophetess*.

Would Ethan have crowned me over Mira if we were both watching?

Given that the Crown would have killed her—*if* I wasn't dead and watching this from some ghost-like limbo, which I still hadn't discounted—I hoped he would have.

In my heart, I *knew* he would have. Because since Ethan loved me, crowning Mira would have been the same thing as murdering her.

So why did me and Mira have to stand back-to-back, not looking at Ethan?

If I got the chance, I was definitely going to ask Constance.

But for now, I had to stay hidden. I had to let these final moments play out the way I already knew they would.

A sense of strangeness floated over me as I watched myself enter the scene and stand with my back against Mira's. I looked so calm and serene.

How had I pulled that off? Because I remembered the anxiety that had been coursing through me in that moment. I'd felt anything *but* calm.

I'd been jealous.

Jealous because I'd thought Mira was about to be crowned as the Queen of Pentacles and gifted with power over the fifth element. I'd been trying to stop myself from getting upset by telling myself that there was another destiny out there for me, but it hadn't changed the fact that I'd wanted to be the Queen.

I'd always been told that I was good at hiding my emotions. Mira had been one of the few who could see through me, and in the past few months, I'd nearly mastered hiding my feelings from *her*.

No one watching would have had any idea of the bitter, jealous thoughts running through my head in those seconds before being crowned.

I leaned forward, since this was the moment I'd been wondering about—what Ethan had looked like when he'd decided to crown me instead of Mira.

Then, other Gemma's eyes darted to the door—the one I was watching through.

I flattened myself against the wall.

"Is there someone else here?" I heard myself ask.

"It's only the seven of us," Queen Katherine said. "Why?"

"I just... thought I saw something."

My heart leaped.

Because I hadn't looked over here before. I hadn't *said* that before.

Just by standing here and watching through the crack, I'd changed what had happened mere minutes ago.

Although given that I'd gotten all my memories back, it felt like it had been so much longer than that. Well, my *sort of* memories. Could they be called memories when they hadn't truly happened?

It was more like I'd gotten my memories of my fake-memories back.

Just when I thought things couldn't get crazier... here I was.

"You're nervous," Constance said to the other me. "Don't worry. It'll be over soon, and all will be well."

Was Constance *helping* me? Not the other me... but the me over here?

Did she know I was here?

Stay still, I told myself, remaining totally flat against the wall. *Don't give the other me another reason to look over here.*

"Okay," I finally heard myself say. Skeptical, but accepting. "Let's get this over with."

I could practically hear the undercurrent in my tone.

It's time to let Ethan crown Mira as Queen.

Oh, other-Gemma. If only you had any idea of what's going to happen next.

Slowly, I moved to peek through the crack again.

The other me had her eyes closed. Mira's back was facing me, but I knew she had hers closed, too.

I saw other-me's lips move as I told Mira good luck. And while I couldn't hear from where I was standing, I knew Mira said, "You, too."

Ethan stepped forward, holding the Holy Crown in both of his hands. He looked at Mira and frowned, his expression pained. Then, he looked to me, and there was no doubting it—his eyes shined with love. Real, true love, just like how I remembered him looking at me in the memories when he and I were together.

My heart stopped, and I held my breath, watching as Ethan placed the Holy Crown on my head.

Other-me flickered a few times, like a failing projection, then flashed out.

"Gemma?" Ethan sounded more fearful than I'd ever heard him before.

Mira spun around, stared at the empty place where I'd been standing, then turned to Ethan. "What did you do?" Anger laced her tone, and she clenched her fists, frost crawling up from her palms to her wrists.

Ethan stared at where I'd been standing, speechless.

Mira zeroed in on Queen Katherine. "You," she said. "You did this." The frost reached her elbows, and wind rushed around her.

"I did nothing," the queen said, and while I couldn't see her, she sounded firm and resolved.

"Then where's my sister? Where's the Crown?"

"Those are questions for your boyfriend. Not for me."

The wind stopped, the air eerily still as Mira faced Ethan. "What's she talking about?"

But Ethan was no longer looking at Mira. Instead, he was focused on the place where I knew Isemay stood. "You told me to crown the twin I loved," he said. "I did what you asked. And it *killed her*."

Smoke floated out of his palms and toward the ceiling.

Fire.

The cabin was made of wood. If he released the full force of his anger, it would all go up in flames.

I couldn't let that happen.

So I reached for the handle of the door, pulled it open, and stepped through. "I'm alive," I said, and Ethan paled, like he was seeing a ghost. "And I think I just traveled back in time."

36

GEMMA

Ethan hurried toward me and wrapped me in his arms. Then he leaned back and cupped my face, his fingers brushing against my cheeks as if he was making sure I was real. "You were gone," he said, disbelief haunting his tone. "I thought I'd killed you."

I stared up into his familiar hazel eyes. There was so much I wanted to say to him—so much I wanted to ask.

"You crowned me," I said instead. "You *chose* me."

He nodded, and his adoring expression said it all.

Ethan loved me.

Wind whipped through the room like a hurricane, and Ethan held me close, steadying me. We both looked to Mira, who was standing at the front of the room with murder in her eyes.

Her lips curled in disgust, and she glared at me like she *hated* me.

"Mira," Ethan said her name steadily, still holding onto me so tightly that I could feel his chest vibrate as he spoke. "I'm sorry."

"Why?" Dark anger seeped from my twin's tone, and the frost crawled all the way up to her neck. "Why did you do it?"

He let go of me and faced her, his hands up as if he was preparing to defend himself against her. "I had to," he said. "I didn't want you—either of you—to find out like this. But if I crowned you, it would have killed you."

"You were supposed to *love* me."

"I do love you," he said. "But I love Gemma, too."

"You mean you love Gemma *more*."

He didn't deny it.

"I can't believe that you—*either* of you—would do this to me." Tears fell from her eyes, turning to ice as they rolled down her cheeks. One after another, they broke off, fell to the floor, and shattered. "How long have you been together behind my back?"

"It wasn't like that," I said.

"Really?" she sneered. "Then what *was* it like?"

I pressed my lips together. Because I barely knew where Ethan and I stood. Where would I even start with explaining it to her?

"It's not Gemma's fault," Ethan rushed to my defense. "She didn't know."

"That doesn't make any sense." Mira raised her arms to the sides and shot icicles through the walls, leaving circular holes in the wood they'd ripped through.

Ethan took a slow step forward, still ready in case he needed to defend himself against her. "I'm so sorry," he repeated. "I never meant for you to find out like this. But if you'll calm down, I can explain."

"You just told me you love my sister more than me, and you want me to *calm down?*" The wind whipped more furiously around her, and she rose up to float a few centimeters above the floor.

She'd never been able to use her magic to levitate before. I wasn't even sure she knew she was doing it now.

I'd never seen her so angry. And I had no idea what to say to her to get her to calm down so she wouldn't lose control of her magic.

Nothing could fix this. And given everything that had happened in the past few minutes, I was in as much shock as she was.

Her eyes snapped to me, cold with anger. "You love him, too," she said. "That's why you've been acting so distant for the past few months. I thought you were just consumed with your new magic. But it was because you were lying to me. And you felt guilty."

Her words were like an icicle through my heart.

"I'm sorry," I said, hating myself with every word. No amount of apologies would ever be enough. "I didn't know he felt the same. I had no way *to* know."

"So the two of you were never together behind my back? Not even once?"

Memories of the kiss in Lilith's lair flashed through my mind.

Ethan must have looked as guilty as I felt.

"I hate you," Mira said, and then she shot a blast of wind in my direction so strong that I flew backward, slammed my head against the wall, and everything went dark.

37

MIRA

Gemma hit the wall, and she slumped to the floor. Somehow, the Holy Crown stayed in place, like it was superglued to her head.

Ethan rushed to her side, visibly relaxing when he realized she was still alive.

I relaxed a bit, too. Because while I truly did hate both of them for what they'd done, I didn't want my twin dead.

But my magic was a storm inside me. And seeing the way Ethan looked down at Gemma—with a deep love I'd never seen when he'd looked at me—made me want to shoot icicles through both of their hearts.

Even that wouldn't cause them as much pain as they'd caused me. They were the two people I loved most in the world—the two people I'd always thought I could trust no matter what.

And they'd betrayed me.

Another wave of ice-cold rage crashed over me, and the wind quickened. All of the others had backed up against the walls, like they were terrified that I'd throw them against one, too. Frost covered my skin like a shield, but even that couldn't protect me from the agony in my heart.

The heartbreak was never going to go away.

I'd never be able to look at Gemma or Ethan the same way again. I'd never be able to trust them.

They were as good as dead to me.

Frost penetrated my skin, begging me to shoot it forward so they could feel the sting of betrayal like I did.

I need to leave. Now. Before I do something I regret.

Unable to look at Ethan holding Gemma as she came into consciousness, I spun around, hurried to the front door, and reached for the key hanging from my necklace.

Where should I go?

Ever since getting my magic, it hadn't felt like I belonged anywhere anymore. All of the supernaturals looked at me like I was a circus curiosity. None of them had dragon elemental magic, like me and Gemma. I was different in Ember, too, since I was half-witch and couldn't shift.

I'd never felt like an outcast before. And I hated it.

There was only one place I'd ever felt truly happy. Only one place that might be able to calm me down before I hit Gemma hard enough with my magic to do far worse than knocking her out.

Home.

I opened the door and stepped into the ivory hall of Hecate's Eternal Library. I didn't even bother to check if Hecate was there before spinning around, opening the door again, and walking into my bedroom.

Relief flooded my body as I inhaled the comforting scent of coffee. It was nighttime in Australia, and the shop was closed, but home always smelled like coffee. The delicious aroma of it was permanently soaked into the walls and carpets.

My room was exactly how I'd left it. The shelves on the walls displayed rows and rows of shoes—the types of shoes I hadn't been able to wear since going on the run, since they'd be impractical in a fight. But Bella had told me she had a spell to make any shoe comfortable, so I definitely was going to pack up my favorites and get her to work her magic on them whenever I saw her next.

I walked to the window, opened it, and inhaled the welcoming, salty smell of the ocean. While it had been nice to be on the water during the journey in Antarctica, it wasn't the same as being here, overlooking the ocean view I'd woken up to every morning for the majority of my life.

I was still looking out when the door to my room creaked open.

I spun around, immediately on guard.

But it was just Shivani—the witch from the Haven who was watching over the café while we were away.

"I thought I heard someone up here." She studied me, and worry creased her brow. "Is everything okay?"

"No," I said bitterly, since there was no point in lying.

"Care to talk about it?"

And just like that, the entire story came pouring out, tears and all. At some point, we went down to the café, and Shivani brewed me a spicy chai tea with the perfect amount of warm milk.

"You've gotten good at this," I said after a few sips, feeling much calmer than I had when I'd arrived. I couldn't put my finger on what it was that Shivani had added to the chai, but it was delicious.

"It's helping you feel better?" she asked.

"No," I muttered. "What they did to me..." I trailed off as another wave of agony crashed over me. The emptiness in my soul couldn't be fixed with a cup of chai tea, no matter how delicious it was. "The two people I loved most in the world betrayed me. I'm never going to be okay again. This pain is something I'm going to have to live with for the rest of my life."

"What if I told you I can take away the pain?"

For the first time since seeing Ethan and Gemma together, a sliver of hope rose in my chest. "You can do that?"

"*I* can't do it," she said. "But I know someone who can."

"Who?"

"She goes by the name the Voodoo Queen. She has a shop in New Orleans. I can teleport us there now, if you'd like."

I'd learned about the Voodoo Queen while studying in Utopia. She was very powerful.

And she practiced dark magic. *Strong* dark magic.

Shivani watched me with an intense hunger in her eyes, waiting for my answer.

"What's in it for you?" I asked.

"Nothing." She blinked, and her expression softened. "Why?"

I finished off my drink, then placed the empty mug down on the table. Another wave of calmness washed over me, and I felt silly for questioning Shivani.

Shivani was from the Haven, and all Haven witches were peaceful. She wouldn't have given me this offer if she didn't believe it would help.

And I needed all the help I could get. Because I couldn't go on feeling so betrayed, unloved, and abandoned. The emptiness in my soul would eat away at me from the inside out, until I was a shell of the person I once was.

The thought of the pain to come hurt too much to bear.

But I didn't *have* to bear it. Not if I went with Shivani to the Voodoo Queen.

"I'm in," I said, and relief coursed through me at the thought of feeling better, soon. "When do we leave?"

"We can go now."

"Do I need to bring anything?"

"All you need is yourself. The Voodoo Queen can handle the rest."

She stood and held out her hands.

"Shouldn't we send her a fire message?" I asked. "So she knows we're coming?"

"Her shop is open," Shivani said. "She'll be there. And she has a very specific way she likes to do these things."

I nodded, unsure why I was hesitating. Taking the pain away was what I wanted.

It was what I *needed*.

Maybe I'd even be able to move on. I doubted it, since I couldn't imagine there being anyone out there more perfect for me than Ethan. But at least it wouldn't hurt anymore. At least I'd be giving myself a chance to be happy.

So I stood and took Shivani's hands, not giving myself another moment to question my decision.

She teleported us out immediately. My stomach swooped as the ground disappeared under my feet, but the feeling only lasted for a second.

We landed on solid ground, and I opened my eyes.

We were in a dimly lit room with no windows. The walls were concrete blocks, and the floor flat cement. It reminded me of the unfinished part of our basement at home. The only furniture inside was a table and chairs, with a pad of paper and a pen on top of it.

And as I looked around, I realized—there were no doors.

My chest tightened.

We were trapped.

"What is this place?" I asked Shivani.

"It's the Voodoo Queen's private meeting space," she said. "Where she performs her most dangerous spells and delivers her most secret potions."

"She couldn't make it a bit more... welcoming?"

"Criminals of all kind come to her for her services. She needs to keep the space as safe as possible, to ensure none of them turn against her."

"And where is she?"

"Upstairs. I have to send her a fire message from this room—with the pen and paper provided—to tell her that we're here, and why. She'll come to us when she's ready."

I sighed with relief that Shivani wouldn't be leaving me in this awful place alone.

As long as she was with me, I was safe.

Shivani sat down and penned the letter. Once done, she folded it, picked it up, and it disappeared in a flame in her palm.

"How long will we wait?" I bounced my leg, anxious to get rid of my heartbreak. I kept seeing the moment when Gemma appeared by Ethan's side, and the way he'd looked at her with so much love...

My heart couldn't bear it.

"The spell is dangerous, but it doesn't take much preparation," she said. "Minutes, if even."

Less than a minute later, an ebony-skinned woman teleported into the room. She wore a patterned purple dress with a matching hairpiece wrapped around her head. She was strikingly beautiful... and there was a dangerous glint in her dark eyes.

She held a large, pewter goblet in one hand, and a matching dagger in the other. "Mira Brown," she said, sizing me up. "Dragon twin of the Gemini prophecy. Shivani has written to me about your plight. The pain you must be feeling..." she trailed off, as if waiting for me to finish the sentence.

"It's agonizing," I said. "I can't live with it. Shivani said you could help."

"Of course I can help." She smiled and placed the goblet down on the table. "Your purpose here on Earth is important. You can't be distracted by such awful feelings. That wouldn't benefit any of us, now, would it?"

"No," I agreed. "It wouldn't."

"This spell is dark, and dangerous," she said. "It's a blood spell. But helping you helps us all. Which is why I'm happy to do it for you."

"Thank you," I said. "What do you need me to do?"

"Just follow my instructions." She held the tip of the dagger to the top of her forearm and cut a deep gash that stopped at her wrist. She didn't flinch, or show even a single sign of pain. Then she held her arm over the goblet and let her blood flow into the chalice.

It was so *much* blood. I wasn't sure how she wasn't passing out from the loss of it.

Finally, she moved her arm away.

The gash knitted together and healed.

"How did you do that?" I couldn't tear my eyes away from the place where the wound had been.

Because witches didn't have accelerated healing abilities like vampires and shifters. That shouldn't have been possible.

"I took healing potion in preparation for the spell," she explained, and she held the dagger out to me, handle first, with her hand wrapped around the blade. "Take a drop from your palm and add it into the goblet."

I did as she said, although I grimaced when I pricked my palm. The blood dropped into the chalice, and the Voodoo Queen picked it back up.

She gazed down into it, then started reciting a spell in Latin. It was like no spell I'd learned during my time in Utopia. It had to have been created by her, or by one of her ancestors.

Wind whipped around her, and a silver glow surrounded the goblet.

The magic felt sinister. Evil.

Dark.

Shivani had told me that this spell was dark magic. But still, it sent a shiver down my spine, like it was warning me away.

Maybe this isn't such a good idea, a tiny voice said in the back of my mind.

I pushed it down.

Because the pain in my soul was too intense. If getting rid of it meant participating in a bit of dark magic, then so be it. And, like the Voodoo Queen had said, getting rid of this pain would allow me to fully focus on doing my part in saving the world from the demons.

I was doing this to help us all.

The silver glow expanded, until it surrounded me. It was icy cold, even to me. It prickled over my skin, and my lungs burned as I breathed it in. Even my bones felt cold.

Unlike my ice magic, which felt comforting and safe, the cold coming from the silver magic *hurt.*

But it didn't hurt as badly as the pain in my heart. Nothing in the world could ever be as agonizing as that.

The silver magic disappeared back into the chalice, and I could breathe again.

The Voodoo Queen stared hungrily down into it.

Then she lifted it to her lips and drank from it. "Perfect," she said, and she handed it to me. "Only take a sip. Anything else will be lethal."

The chalice was heavier than I'd anticipated, and darkness slithered into my palms and through my veins when I held it. I gazed down into the blood inside, inhaling its foul scent. Disgust rolled through my stomach, and I swallowed, unsure I'd be able to get it down.

"What your sister and boyfriend did to you is unforgivable," the Voodoo Queen said, her voice soothing and calming. "I know dark magic can be scary, but it isn't inherently evil. This spell will take away your pain. It will heal your heartbreak. Isn't that what you want?"

"It is," I said, and without further thought, I lifted the goblet to my lips and took a sip. Only a small one, like the Voodoo Queen had instructed.

It crawled down my throat and filled me to the core, the darkness caressing me from the inside out. I'd expected it to be cold, like the silver magic. Instead, it was warm. Welcoming. Like a blanket that had wrapped itself around me and was keeping me safe.

The best part?

The pain was gone. I no longer felt hollow, like I was going to break down at any second. Not even when I thought back to Ethan choosing Gemma over me.

I felt... nothing.

No—not nothing.

I felt strong. Powerful. Calm.

I didn't need Ethan's love to feel complete. I didn't need my sister, either. They never truly loved me, anyway. If they had, they wouldn't have turned on me like that.

But it was okay. Because I was in control of my feelings now. More importantly, I was in control of my magic. I felt it inside me, ready and eager to bend at my will.

"It worked." I stared at the Voodoo Queen in awe. "It actually worked."

"Of course it worked." She reached into her pocket and pulled out two bright red tablets.

Antidote pills.

The color of each antidote pill corresponded to the color of the potion that had created it. And I knew that shade of red from my studies in Utopia.

It was the color of transformation potion.

The Voodoo Queen handed one of the tablets to Shivani, and Shivani eyed it hungrily.

"What's going on?" I should have been panicked. But thanks to the dark magic inside me, I simply waited, calmly, for them to tell me why they were carrying the tablets.

"You've been tricked," the Voodoo Queen said kindly. "And it was so painfully easy to do it."

She popped the antidote pill into her mouth, chewed, and swallowed.

Shivani did the same.

The air around them shimmered, and I was no longer looking at the Voodoo Queen and Shivani.

Two women with pale skin and jet-black hair stood in their places, both of them wearing long white dresses that looked like undergarments from another era.

The one that had been Shivani teleported out, then returned with a long, pewter-colored wand that matched the chalice. A blood-red gemstone sat at the top of the wand, with a few smaller ones below it.

The Dark Wand. And now that she was holding it, I recognized her from the battle in Nebraska.

Lavinia.

The Dark Queen of Wands.

"You pretended to be Shivani," I said calmly. "You brought me here to do…" I turned to the other, taller woman.

Her eyes were a deep, dark red.

The eyes of a demon.

"What did you do to me?" I asked.

"I don't believe we've been properly introduced." She smiled wickedly, her lips the same color as the blood in the chalice. "I'm Lilith. The Dark Queen of Cups."

"The greater demon," I said. "The one who's been tracking me and Gemma."

The one the supernaturals had been trying to locate for years.

The one they were determined to kill.

I should have been scared.

But I wasn't.

"Correct," she said. "And the spell I just performed wasn't to bind your pain, although binding your pain is a lovely side effect of it. Because that isn't any old chalice." She glanced at the goblet on the table and rested her hand on its rim. "It's the Dark Grail. And by drinking from it, you're now bound to me."

"That's why I feel so… numb?"

"It's why you feel so *calm*. So in control. So strong." she said, and I nodded, since that was exactly how I felt. "Welcome to the dark side, Mira. You're going to make a lovely Queen."

THE DRAGON SCORNED

DARK WORLD: THE DRAGON TWINS 3

1

GEMMA

Genevieve leaned over an atlas in the tearoom in the Haven, a pendulum in one hand and one of Mira's favorite sandals in the other. The sandals were one of the few things Mira had in her room in the Haven from our old life, since she'd been wearing them when we'd left home for Utopia.

She'd saved up money for *months* to buy those sandals. They were by some fancy designer, so they cost hundreds of dollars.

It was ridiculous.

Then again, I spent most of my money on hardcover books to display on my shelves instead of buying them as ebooks. So who was I to judge?

Genevieve stared at the pendulum's crystal, putting all of her concentration into the spell.

It refused to move.

Mary, Queen Katherine, Ethan, my mom, the vampire prophetess Constance, and the dragon shifter Isemay watched from the sides. All of them were quiet.

After a few minutes of trying, Genevieve placed the pendulum down on the atlas, and the sandal on the table next to it. "It's not working." She looked at me, her eyes full of apology. "I'm sorry."

"You're the most powerful witch in the world," I said. "How is it *not working?*"

Mira wore a cloaking ring, like the rest of us. But Genevieve thought she'd be able to get past its magic without a problem. She was, after all, an ancestor of Geneva—a witch who'd had magic beyond what should have been possible. If anyone could track down Mira, it was Genevieve.

"Wherever Mira is, she's hidden by magic that I can't get through," she said. "I'm truly sorry. I wish I could have helped."

Ethan walked up to me and wrapped his arms around me.

I shrugged him off. Because if it hadn't been for the secrets he'd kept—mainly, that he loved me instead of Mira—then my twin never would have run off and gone missing in the first place.

After I'd returned to consciousness—Mira had hit me *hard* with her magic, which had put me out for a few hours—we'd left the Seventh Kingdom for the Haven. Everything had been so hurried since getting back that we hadn't told my mom and Mary anything other than that Mira was missing, and that we had to find her.

Now, Mary watched us expectantly. "You clearly have a lot to fill us in on," she said. "But first, I believe introductions should be made."

"Of course." Queen Katherine stepped forward. "I'm Katherine—the Queen of the Seventh Kingdom."

Mary's eyes hardened. "The Seventh Kingdom doesn't exist."

"While small, the Seventh Kingdom does, in fact, exist," Katherine said.

"All of the kingdoms are ruled by an original vampire. Well, *were* ruled by an original vampire," Mary corrected herself, since King Alexander—a vampire who'd been turned by Queen Laila—reigned the Vale after Queen Laila's death. "I know all of the original vampires. You're not one of them."

"I am one of them," Queen Katherine said. "You and I used to be friends."

"You and I have never met."

"You don't remember my existence because I'm gifted with amplified compulsion," Katherine explained what she'd already told me, Ethan, and Mira back in the Seventh Kingdom. "I made you—and all others who knew me—forget about my existence. Then I went with Genevieve, Constance, and Isemay to a small island off the Antarctic Peninsula, where we've guarded the Holy Crown ever since."

All was silent as Mary took it in.

"It sounds like we need to sit down," she finally said. "Because if what you're saying is true, then we're going to be here for a while."

We had breakfast as we filled Mary and Mom in on everything that had happened since we'd left for Antarctica.

"No wonder Mira took off the way she did." Mom glared at Ethan. "You *used* her. And for her to find out like that..." She shook her head, as if unable to find the words. "You broke her heart."

She didn't even look at me.

Did she *blame* me?

"I didn't know," I said quickly. "I was just as surprised as Mira when Ethan put the Crown on my head."

"I didn't want you to find out like that," Ethan said. "*Either* of you."

"One moment." Mary held up a hand, quieting us. "I think we should discuss the Crown's magic. The fifth element."

"Time travel," I said, amazed that it was possible.

"You're *positive* you traveled through time? You didn't teleport to the other room and experience an intense dream while there?"

"I'm positive," I said.

"Then prove it."

"How?"

"Five minutes before you all arrived here, I was sitting down for breakfast in my house," she said. "Go back to that moment and give me this." She pulled a ring off her middle finger and handed it to me.

It was the triple moon, with a moonstone in the center. Eight diamonds surrounded it, and it was set in gold. I couldn't imagine how expensive it must have been.

"Every gemstone is unique," Mary said. "I'll know this one is mine—especially when directly comparing it to itself."

"I've only traveled back in time once," I said. "I'm not exactly sure how it works..."

Mid-sentence, I realized that wasn't correct. Because when I'd traveled back in time, I'd been wondering what Ethan's expression had looked like when he'd crowned me instead of Mira.

The Crown was connected to my soul. I was the Queen of Pentacles—I *commanded* the Holy Crown. It would bring me to whenever I told it to take me.

"Never mind," I said. "I think I can do it."

"Then do it," Mary said. "I'll see you soon."

I closed my eyes and focused on the Crown sitting on my head.

It warmed, like it was listening to me.

Take me to Mary's house, I thought. *Five minutes before we arrived at the Haven.*

Magic burst through me. Thankfully, it wasn't painful, like the first time I'd traveled through time. It was like a cord had released me from the physical world and was bringing me somewhere else.

Unlike teleporting, it didn't happen instantaneously. I flickered a few times, then broke free of the physical world and floated around like a cloud.

I turned solid again, and I opened my eyes.

I was sitting in the same spot, on a bench in the Haven's tearoom.

But now, the room was empty.

I looked at the clock on the wall and gasped.

It had worked. Well, partly. I hadn't teleported to Mary's house, but I'd traveled back in time to five minutes before we'd arrived at the Haven.

Which meant I had five minutes to get to Mary's house and tell her about our impending arrival. No big deal, thanks to the magical key Hecate had given me the first time I'd visited her Eternal Library.

I used the key in the door to the tearoom and stepped into the ivory entry hall of the Eternal Library. The tall, arched ceilings and marble floors stretched out to the double door entrance that led to endless bookshelves full of everything you could ever want to know.

The books had no titles, and no way to search through them. The only person who could locate the book with the information you desired was the goddess of witchcraft, Hecate.

The goddess rarely waited in the ivory hall, and today proved no different.

Not like it mattered, since I wasn't there for information. I was there to take advantage of the other handy trick of the key—its ability to let me leave the Library and walk through the door of any place I'd ever been.

Today's destination?

Mary's house. Not a far journey, since it was across the kingdom, but the key made it faster. Plus, this way I wouldn't risk being stopped by residents of the Haven, which would be bound to happen, given that I was wearing the Holy Crown on my head.

I stepped back through the door, into the main living space of Mary's house.

The Haven's mantra was equality for all. So, like all of its houses for a single person or a couple, Mary's was the size of a one-bedroom apartment.

Just like she'd said, she was in the kitchen, bringing her breakfast and a glass of blood to the table.

Surprise crossed her face, and she set her food and drink down, her gaze focused on the top of my head.

"You found the Holy Crown," she said steadily. "And you're—"

"The Queen of Pentacles," I interrupted, since we had limited time. "It's a long story, but you'll understand everything soon. Right now, I'm here to give you this."

I walked forward and handed her the ring.

She studied it, confused, and compared it to the identical ring on her finger.

I said nothing as I waited for her to put it together.

"Where did you get this?" she finally asked.

"It's yours. You gave it to me," I said. "Well, you're *going* to give it to me."

She continued to look back and forth between the rings, searching for a difference between them. "It's exactly the same, down to the smallest details," she said, and she looked back up at me, her eyes full of questions. "This isn't possible."

"Put it in your pocket for now," I said quickly. "I'm going to arrive in the tearoom with Ethan and some others in about four minutes. When I do, don't mention that I was here."

She did as I requested and pocketed the ring. "Why don't you sit down," she said calmly, and she gestured to the table. "It sounds like we have a lot to discuss."

"Wait to give the ring to me until I say how surprised I was when Ethan put the Crown on my head," I continued, ignoring her invitation to join her for breakfast. "I'm sorry for being so vague, but I promise it won't be long until this all makes sense."

I focused on the Crown's magic and thought, *Take me back to the present.* And *to the tearoom.*

I flickered out and re-appeared in the same place in Mary's kitchen.

Mary was no longer there.

The digital clock on her oven showed it was the same time it had been when I'd left.

Suddenly, two memories overlapped in my mind.

The first was the one that had originally happened—Mary's expression of shock and disbelief when I'd told her that the Crown allowed me to travel through time.

In the second memory, Mary's lips had opened into an O of understanding, and her hand had gone to her pocket where she'd been keeping the ring. Instead of asking me if I was positive I'd traveled through time, she'd calmly handed me the ring and asked me to go back to when she was having breakfast and to give it to her, so I could prove my ability was real.

The second memory—the one of the new reality—layered over the first. The first memory—the one of the reality I'd changed—was still there, although it didn't feel *solid* like the second one.

By giving Mary the ring, I'd erased the timeline where she'd been shocked to learn that the fifth element was time travel and replaced it with a timeline where my visit to give her the ring had clicked into place in her mind.

Kind of confusing, but also pretty cool.

I used the key to return to the tearoom, and Mary's lips curved into a knowing smile.

She pulled the ring out of her pocket and slipped it back onto her finger. "You should have gone back an hour earlier and explained what was going on," she said. "It would have saved me a lot of confusion."

"I wasn't the one who decided to go back five minutes," I said. "It was *your* idea."

She frowned, as if disappointed in her other self's time travel logic. "In the Seventh Kingdom, you teleported to the other room," she said, changing the subject. "So why didn't you teleport into my house instead of going through the Library?"

"I tried." I shrugged. "It didn't work."

She made a sound of disapproval.

"So you walked to Mary's house?" my mom asked. "Did anyone see you wearing the Crown?"

"I went through the Eternal Library."

"You found the nearest witch and got her to teleport you," my mom said, as if she hadn't heard me. "Smart."

"Yep." I nodded, pretending that was exactly what I'd said.

Thanks to Hecate's magic, the only people who knew about the Eternal Library's existence were ones who'd been given keys. Which meant that when someone without a key heard anything about the Eternal Library, their minds replaced what they'd heard with something that made sense to them.

"Very smart," Mary said. "Now, go back again."

"What?" I asked, since I'd already proven that I could travel through time. "Why?"

"I'm curious to see if you can rewrite history again. This time, give me two rings." She removed the moonstone ring again, plus the opal ring next to it, and handed both to me.

"They'll be two of me there," I said. "And three moonstone rings."

I studied the ring in my hand. What would happen when it got back to the present? Would there be *two* of the same ring, since I'd have gone back in time twice? Or would I somehow cancel out the other version of myself—and the other version of the ring? Could I keep going back to the same point in time and change it until getting the result I wanted?

"Couldn't this cause some sort of paradox?" Ethan asked, bringing me out of my confusing, looping thoughts.

"The Crown is a Holy Object," Mary said. "It won't harm itself. And to use it the best we can, we need to learn how it works."

"We can learn how it works later," I said. "Right now, we need to keep searching for Mira."

Genevieve smirked. "You're awfully focused on the present for someone who can travel through time."

I glared at her, then refocused on Mary. "We're finding Mira."

"This will only take a minute," she said. "Satisfy my curiosity, and then I'll help you search for Mira for the rest of the day."

"Thank you."

"But tomorrow, we learn more about the Crown. Deal?"

"Deal," I said, since tomorrow, I intended for Mira to be back in the Haven with us.

So, eager to get it over with, I closed my eyes and asked the Crown to take me back to five minutes before I arrived in the Haven—again.

2

GEMMA

"It isn't working."

I re-opened my eyes, and unsurprisingly, they were all still there watching me. The time on the clock hadn't changed.

"So you can't go back to a time you've already visited," Mary said. "Good to know."

"That seems to be the case." I was unsure if this was a good thing or a bad thing. Probably a bad thing, because it meant that once I went back in time and changed something, I had no do-overs. At least, not from that same point in time. "Now, let's get back to finding Mira. Because I have an idea about where to start."

I told them my idea, and they agreed it was worth a try. Well, *Mary* agreed it was worth a try. Hecate's magic made the others go along with agreeing it was a good idea, despite their obvious confusion.

"I'm coming with you," Ethan said.

I spun around and glared at him. "No."

He stood strong, apparently unaffected by my refusal. "I don't want you going alone."

"I'll be perfectly safe there. Besides, it's not like you can travel with me."

Mary's interest perked up. "That's something we need to test," she said.

"What is?" I asked.

"If you can bring anyone back in time with you or not."

"We'll test it once I'm back," I said, since she was right—it *was* something we needed to know. "Right now, I'm getting my sister."

"You know she might not want to go anywhere with you," Ethan said.

I raised an eyebrow. "And you think it would help if *you* were there?"

"Maybe."

"Wrong. She hates you after what you did."

She hates me, too.

Grief swelled within me, and I tried my best to swallow it down. Because Mira *couldn't* hate me. She was my twin. She could be angry at me—and we'd certainly had our fair share of fights. But she'd never hate me.

She'd also never said she hated me, no matter how bad our fights had been.

She was never going to forgive me for this.

Did I even deserve her forgiveness?

I pushed the thought away. I'd worry about it later. Now, I only had one mission—getting Mira back.

And so, I walked up to the door, put my key in the lock, and returned to Hecate's Eternal Library.

I breathed easier once I was there. Something about the Library was so soothing. It had to be Hecate's magic that filled the air.

The calmness didn't last long, because a second later, Ethan walked through the door.

I stepped back. "I told you not to follow me."

"And I didn't listen."

"Clearly." I crossed my arms, having nothing more to say to him.

"Gemma." His voice was pained as he said my name. "I didn't want you to find out like this."

"You led Mira on for months. You acted like I didn't exist. What the hell was going through your mind?"

"It's complicated." He blew out a long breath and ran a hand through his hair in frustration. "I was confused—until the first time I shifted on Ember."

"The moment dragons know if they have a twin flame."

"How did you know that?" He tilted his head, searching my eyes for answers.

Because another version of you told me in a dream. Or a hallucination. In whatever it was that had happened when I'd been drugged by the nightshade.

At the same time, my heart leaped. Because he'd basically confirmed that he was my twin flame. The connection I felt with him wasn't one sided.

He loved me. And I loved him.

But right now, I was *pissed* at him.

"It's complicated," I said instead. "But we don't have time for this right now. I need to find Mira."

I closed my eyes and focused on the Crown's magic, searching for it in my soul like I had the other times I'd used it.

Nothing was there.

I dug deeper.

Still, nothing.

Take me to the moment Mira left the Seventh Kingdom, I thought, despite the fact that the magic wasn't answering my call.

I opened my eyes, and Ethan was still there, watching me.

"Well?" he asked.

"My magic's gone." I touched the Crown, making sure it was still there despite feeling its weight on my head. "Something's wrong."

"Your magic isn't gone," he said. "At least, not forever."

"What do you mean?"

"We're in Hecate's realm," he said. "And in Hecate's realm—"

"She blocks all magic that isn't witch magic," I finished his sentence, feeling stupid for not putting it together myself. "The Crown's magic isn't witch magic. Time travel is the fifth element. And elemental magic is *dragon* magic."

"Yep." He nodded.

"I can't time travel here." I cursed, since I'd really believed my plan was going to work. "So there's no point in staying here. Let's go back."

"Wait."

I spun around and glared at him again. "What?"

"I'm sorry."

I shook my head, turned away from him, and walked to the door. The sight of him made me feel sick. I couldn't look at him. Not without Mira's final words echoing in my head.

I hate you.

I needed her to understand that none of this was my fault. I needed her forgiveness. To do that, I needed to find her. I was *going* to find her.

And I refused to let my feelings for Ethan distract me from getting my sister back.

3

GEMMA

"We should send a witch to check in on the café," Mom said once Ethan and I were back. "Mira would have needed comfort. She would have wanted to go *home*."

I nodded, since Mom was right. I'd been feeling at home in the supernatural world, but Mira missed our old life and had been plagued with homesickness daily.

"If Mira had gone to the café, Shivani would have told us," Mary said gently.

"Just satisfy me and send someone to check," Mom said.

"I'll go," I volunteered.

"You'll stay right here," Mary said. "Lilith and her dark witches know where you lived. It's not safe for you to go there."

"I won't be there for long."

"Perhaps. But you're a Queen now. You can't risk yourself when there are pawns lined up and ready to put themselves in the line of fire for you."

I glanced down at the floor, deciding this wasn't a good time to admit that I'd already gone back to the café—when Shivani had brewed that memory potion for me.

I looked at the door, half ready to march toward it and go anyway.

Mom spoke before I had a chance. "The first person who talks to Mira should be me," she said. "I'll go with the witch."

"Bad idea," Mary said. "If there are demons watching the café, there's a chance they'll know who you are. We can't risk them seeing you and taking you as bait to lure the twins back to Lilith's lair."

"So I'll take invisibility potion," she said. "With the potion plus my cloaking ring, they'll have no idea I'm there."

Mary looked at me. "What are your thoughts on this?"

"Mom should go," I said. "If there's anyone Mira will listen to, it's her."

It was true, although I hated the fact that I might be sending my mom somewhere dangerous, especially since she had practically no magic.

But the café wasn't dangerous. I'd been there recently, and I'd been fine.

"If Mira isn't there, you'll come right back," I told her.

"Of course."

Mary reached for the pen and paper on the coffee table, wrote a quick message, then looked at me. "Take the Crown off and hide it behind a pillow," she said.

"Why?"

"Because I'm sending for a witch to come here and take your mom to the café, and I don't want her asking any questions. There's a time for others to learn that you're the Queen of Pentacles, and this isn't it."

I removed the Crown and placed it behind the decorative pillow next to me. I kept my hand resting on the pillow, protecting it.

Mary had Genevieve send the fire message, and two minutes later, a witch named Riya teleported into the tearoom with two vials of invisibility potion. I'd had lunch with her a few times when I'd been training in the Haven—she'd always been warm and welcoming.

Mary quickly briefed her on the mission.

"Got it," Riya said, then she took a deep breath and asked, "Has there been any word on Queen Elizabeth?"

The Queen of Utopia hadn't been seen since the demons and dark witches had plundered her kingdom, destroying it and killing everyone there. She'd stayed behind to fight and hadn't been heard from since. We all hoped for the best, but the longer she was gone, the more dire her situation seemed to be.

"The Nephilim army is working hard to locate her," Mary said.

"And we're working on locating my daughter," Mom said to Riya. "Are you ready?"

Riya nodded, then she and Mom drank the invisibility potion and disappeared.

"I'm taking her now." Riya's voice came from where she'd been standing, even though I couldn't see her. "Be back soon."

A few seconds passed.

"Did you leave?" I asked.

No one replied, which I took as a yes.

"While we wait for them to return, we might as well make good use of time," Mary said to me. "Let's do more tests."

From her stoic expression, I could tell she thought I was going to refuse.

"All right," I said, since I was as eager to learn more about my new magic as anyone. And with Mom and Riya at the café looking for Mira, studying my magic was the best thing I could do to help find my twin. "I'm guessing you already know what you want me to try next?"

"We need to figure out if you can take anyone with you when you travel," she said. "Also, I'm curious if you can go to the future as well as the past."

"Let's try that first," I said quickly. "The future one."

She had a good point about needing to see if I could bring anyone with me when I traveled. But what if I hurt them in the process?

What if I hurt *him*?

I glanced at Ethan, since I knew he'd insist on being my test subject.

From the hard determination in his eyes, I was right.

"I'll go a minute into the future," I said, since they did that in one of my favorite movies, *Back to the Future*. "I'll reappear for you in a minute. For me, it'll be like I never left."

I closed my eyes and pulled at the magic inside the Crown.

Unlike in Hecate's realm, its warmth filled me, answering my call.

Take me a minute into the future, I told it.

The magic slipped out of my grasp, then faded away.

I tried again. And again. And again.

Each time, the magic disappeared.

I opened my eyes and looked at everyone in the room except for Ethan. If I pretended he wasn't there, I could pretend my feelings for him weren't there, too.

"I can't travel into the future," I said, and then I looked at Constance. "But you already knew that, right? Since you can see the future."

"I see the future as it will play out without my interference," she said. "If I intervene, I see the new future I've created, along with the one that would have originally existed. I also see the future without your interference, as your magic seems to exist outside the realm of my visions."

"But you knew I was there in the Seventh Kingdom, right? When I was in the bedroom, and the other version of myself heard me move around?"

"The moment you appeared in the bedroom, the future I saw changed."

"And you stopped the other version of me from seeing myself."

"I stopped the other version of you from investigating the room where you were hiding," she said. "I was keeping the original future—the one where Ethan crowned you uninterrupted—intact."

"So you remember *both* possible futures?"

"Yes."

"Interesting," I said, even though it was making my head spin.

"Confusing," Genevieve muttered.

Queen Katherine remained silent, taking it all in.

"It will get less confusing once we do more tests," Mary said. "Take me three minutes into the past."

"Why three?" I asked.

"It's the lucky number of witchcraft."

I stood up to walk toward her, relieved to be taking her instead of Ethan.

"Wait." Ethan stood up as well, and my heart dropped, because I knew what was coming. "Take me. After all, we shouldn't risk a queen when there's a pawn to offer himself up in the line of duty."

"You're not a pawn," I shot back. "You're the King of Ember."

"And it's my job to protect you. I can't do that if you're alone in the past."

"I won't be alone," I said. "The past version of you will be there."

"Which brings up another question," Mary said. "What happens when the past version of you sees the future version?"

"I wouldn't know," I said. "I watched the past version of myself in the Seventh Kingdom, but she didn't see me."

"It's another test to conduct," Mary said.

"It is," I agreed. "But first, you wanted to see if I can bring anyone with me." I turned to face Genevieve, Constance, and Isemay. "You're the only three in here who aren't rulers of a kingdom. Do one of you want to try to travel back in time with me?"

Constance lowered her gaze, like I used to do in lower school when I didn't want to get called on to answer a question.

I took that as a no.

Genevieve stood up and straightened out her white tunic. The gear we'd worn in Antarctica was stifling in the Haven, so while we'd filled Mary in on what had happened in the Seventh Kingdom, she'd sent for Haven whites for us to change into.

"I'll do it," she said. "I'm always down for an adventure."

"Three minutes into the past is hardly an adventure," I said with a small smile. "But thank you for volunteering."

"I'm the most powerful witch in the world," she said. "A little bit of time travel won't kill me."

I nodded, took her hands, then called on the Crown's magic.

Take us three minutes into the past.

The magic filled me, flowed into Genevieve, and we flickered out.

We solidified less than a second later. Genevieve's hands were still firmly in mine, and I opened my eyes, relieved to find her fully intact.

But we weren't in the tearoom.

We were in the hall outside of it.

The door was closed, but if we were three minutes in the past like we were supposed to be, the other versions of ourselves were on the other side.

"Are you okay?" I asked Genevieve, since the first time I'd time traveled had been agonizing.

"That felt more... turbulent than teleporting." She smiled mischievously. "It was fun."

"So it didn't hurt?"

"Not at all."

The pain that first time must have been from receiving my magic—not from the experience of time traveling for the first time.

Good. I hated to think I'd ever have to put anyone in that much pain.

It was also interesting that the two times I'd traveled back to a place I'd been, I'd appeared in the nearest room, where the past version of me couldn't see the current version of me. The two other times, I hadn't moved.

The Crown apparently didn't want me materializing in front of my past self.

But I wondered...

"What would happen if we went inside?" I tilted my head toward the door leading into the tearoom.

"We'd come face to face with our past selves," she said.

"And what would happen when they saw us?"

She raised an eyebrow. "You're the one with time travel magic. What do *you* think will happen when they see us?"

She spoke as if we were definitely going to do it.

"I don't know." I shrugged, then tried to think of the worst possible scenario. "We could cause a paradox, and the world could implode?"

Her expression turned serious. "Then it sounds like we shouldn't open that door."

"I wasn't being serious," I said. "Well, I suppose the paradox is a possibility. But I don't think I would have been given the Holy Crown if I was going to implode the world from opening a door."

"Agreed," she said. "So, what do you want to do?"

"We're here to test out my magic." I moved closer to the door. "So, let's test it."

4

GEMMA

Genevieve stood behind me as I reached for the door, leaving practically no space between the two of us. She was taller than me, so she could get a good view of what was happening by watching over my head. We were like children trying to eavesdrop on the adults after bedtime.

I held the doorknob, then paused.

"Are you going to do it?" she whispered. "Or do you need me to?"

"I can do it."

Not wanting to give myself a chance to hesitate—and also, because our three minutes would be up soon—I twisted the handle and pulled the door open.

My eyes met Constance's, then Isemay's... and then I flickered out.

When I reappeared, the time on the clock was the same as it had been when I'd left. New memories layered on top of the old ones.

"I won't be alone," I told Ethan. "The past version of yourself will be there."

Suddenly, the door opened. I looked to see who was there, but the space was empty.

Embers glowed in Ethan's palms, and he stood ready to attack.

"Relax," Constance said. "Everything's fine."

Ethan stepped out into the hall, checked out both directions, then came back inside. "Unless there are ghosts in the Haven, then someone took invisibility potion and is in here with us." He looked around the room in suspicion. *"Show yourself."*

"No one's here." Constance was as calm as ever.

"Then who opened the door?"

"Gemma and Genevieve," she said. "I saw both of you for a moment, then you flickered out."

"I saw the both of you, too," Isemay said.

"I saw nothing," said Genevieve. She was sitting next to Isemay, which meant she would have been the next person in the room who would have gotten a look at our mysterious visitors.

"You flickered out a split second after I saw you," Isemay said.

"Flickered out," I repeated. "We time traveled. Together."

Mary smiled. "Then it appears that yes, you can bring someone with you," she said. "I was about to ask what happens when a past version of yourself sees a future version of yourself, but it looks like we just got an answer."

"We disappeared right before we could see the future versions of ourselves," I said. "The question is—where did we go? And when did we go?"

"There's only one way to find out," she said, and just like the first time, Genevieve and I traveled three minutes into the past.

We didn't have the conversation about possible paradoxes. I didn't hesitate before opening the door. Instead, I opened it confidently and was forced back into the present right before we would have seen ourselves, appearing exactly where we were right now.

In the present, a second after we'd left.

I stepped through the door, Genevieve right behind me.

Ethan rushed over to make sure I was okay, but I brushed him off and faced Mary. "Time won't let our past selves see our current selves," I said. "Right before it would have happened, we were forced back into the present."

I continued on to tell them about how the two memories had layered on top of each other and that I could differentiate between which one was the original timeline, and which was the altered, current timeline.

Genevieve had memories of both timelines as well.

"This all leads us to a new question," Mary said. "Can you bring *two* people with you?"

"There's only one way to find out," I said, and I turned to Isemay. "Do you want to try to tag along with me and Genevieve?"

Ethan stepped in front of her before she could answer and faced me. "We know you can travel with someone else without harming them," he said carefully, like he was gearing up for me to reject whatever he was about to propose. "I'll travel with you and Genevieve."

"Fine," I said, since Genevieve would be with us, which meant Ethan wouldn't be able to corner me into having a conversation with him that I wasn't emotionally ready to have until I knew Mira wasn't in danger.

He relaxed, the relief clear on his face.

I held out both my hands. Genevieve took one, and Ethan took the other.

Ethan's palm radiated warmth, and it flowed through my arm and into my core. My cheeks flushed as desire hot as fire shot through me, like a flame connecting us together.

No, I told myself, trying to ground myself in the earth to cool the fire. *Don't get distracted from finding Mira.*

I closed my eyes and told the Crown to take us six minutes into the past.

The Crown's magic pulled back, like it was telling me no.

"It's not working." I pulled my hands out of theirs, although the warmth from Ethan's remained. I rubbed my palm against my pants, as if they could absorb the heat. They couldn't. "It seems like I can only take one person back at a time."

Mary nodded, easily accepting this. "Another thought," she said. "What happens if—"

She didn't get a chance to finish, because Riya and Mom teleported back into the tearoom.

Mom's hair was up in a knot on the top of the head, like she always put it when she was frazzled and trying to focus, and her breaths were short, as if she'd been running around.

My heart sank at the panic in her eyes. "What happened?"

"They weren't there," she said. "*Either* of them. I tried to send Shivani a fire message, but it didn't go through."

Grief washed over me. Because if a fire message wasn't going through, it meant one of two things.

Either Shivani was being kept prisoner somewhere, or she was dead.

"We searched every inch of the place for clues," Riya continued, although it was evident from her tone that a possible clue she was searching for was Shivani's dead body. "There was nothing. And nothing was out of place. Whatever happened to her, there was no struggle. And there was one more thing." She turned to me, took a deep breath, and said, "Mira's scent was fresh in her room."

I swallowed. "How fresh?"

"Fresh enough that it seems likely she went there immediately after leaving the Seventh Kingdom."

"I'm going." I reached for my key and headed toward the door.

Ethan was by my side in an instant. "You're not going alone."

Mom sat on the couch, her expression blank, like she was in shock. "You won't find anything," she said. "We checked everywhere."

"You're not thinking fourth dimensionally," I said.

She snapped her head up. "What do you mean?"

"Time," I said, and I touched the Crown to show what I meant. "I'm not going to look for Mira in the present. I'm going to go back in time to the moment she stepped through that door, so I'm there when she arrives."

5

GEMMA

"Good plan." Mom stood up. "I'm going with you."

"No," Ethan said.

"Yes." Mom didn't budge. "Mira will want to see *me*. Not you."

"Mira was out of control," he said calmly. "We don't know how dangerous she might be. I need to go with Gemma, as backup."

"Backup for what?"

"Backup in case she attacks."

"She'd never attack me. I'm her mother." Mom looked at me, like she was waiting for me to take her side.

I wished I could.

"She attacked me," I said slowly. "Back in the Seventh Kingdom. She threw me against that wall so hard that it knocked me out. And we'll be going back to *immediately* after that moment. Ethan's right. We have no idea how dangerous she might be."

"She was angry with you," Mom said. "She wouldn't have actually hurt you."

"Except she *did* actually hurt me." I couldn't believe it was true, but I'd seen the enraged look in Mira's eyes when she'd thrown her magic at me. She was capable of far more than I'd ever given her credit for.

If she lost control and hurt Mom, I'd never be able to forgive myself.

"She was volatile," I said. "Ethan and I will be prepared and can fight back with our magic. You have practically no magic. If she attacks, you won't be able to defend yourself."

"And what if she leaves? You have no idea where she'll go next."

"She won't be able to leave," Ethan said. "I'll block the door."

It made perfect sense to *me*, since Mira couldn't travel through the Eternal Library if she couldn't use her key in the door. But Mom nodded, as if it made sense to her, too.

"She's my twin," I continued, my voice softer. "I love her, too. I'm going to bring her back to us."

Even if that means fighting her with my magic and forcing her through that door.

THE DRAGON SCORNED

Mom said nothing, and I worried she was going to keep arguing with me on this.

"All right," she gave in. "Just make sure to bring her straight back."

"I will," I said. "I promise."

I gave her a hug, then walked through the door and into the Eternal Library. Ethan followed me, but I didn't pause in the Library's ivory hall—I didn't want to give him the opportunity to pull me into a conversation about *us*.

Whatever *we* were.

I stepped into Mira's bedroom, and he followed right behind me.

Like always, I was greeted by Mira's giant shoe rack, where she displayed them all like treasures. It was like a bookcase, but for shoes.

Her window was open, letting in the salty smell of the ocean. And the scent of the ocean was mixed with the warm, spicy one of cinnamon buns.

Mira's scent.

Like Riya had said, it was fresh. So fresh that it was like my sister could be right downstairs.

Even though Mom and Riya had already checked the apartment and café, I raced through the entire place to do the same. The sign on the door was set to closed, and everything was where it should have been. Shivani had been taking perfect care of our home, which I already knew, since I'd been there a few weeks ago.

I raced through as I checked every room, not giving Ethan the opportunity to start a conversation. Once finished checking the basement, I hurried back up to Mira's room.

Ethan followed, not saying a word. At least he was respecting the fact that I didn't want to talk.

He watched me from the center of the room. "What's the plan?" he asked.

"We'll stand in front of the door when we travel back to the past, so we're already blocking it when we arrive. And then..." I frowned, since I didn't want to hurt Mira. "We'll be catching her by surprise. Maybe she'll talk to us."

It was a terrible "plan," and we both knew it.

"We'll see what she's like when she arrives," he said. "If she's out of control, we'll use this." He reached into his pocket and pulled out a dart full of deep blue potion.

Complacent potion.

"Where'd you get that?" I asked.

"Genevieve gave it to me when you were unconscious. She said I'd know when to use it."

Of course she did. Complacent potion was one of the—if not *the*—most difficult potion to brew. Most of the high witches of the kingdom couldn't even create it. It was also highly illegal, although law had sort of gone out the window, given the war with the demons and everything.

I wanted to say that I'd never drug my twin.

But she'd thrown me against a wall so hard that she'd knocked me out. And if this was what it took to get her to the Haven, then so be it.

"Because of my air magic, my aim is flawless." He put it back inside his pocket. "Once we're in the room with her, I'll shoot her with the potion dart."

"You'll shoot her with it *if* she attacks," I said before he could continue. "If she's willing to talk to us, we don't drug her."

"Deal. Then you'll grab her, take her to the present, and get her to the Haven. Once she's back safely, you can return to the moment you left and get me. It'll be like no time passed for me."

"You sure know a lot about time travel," I said.

"I've seen *Back to the Future* a few times," he said. "Great movie. And *Prisoner of Azkaban* was one of my favorites in the Harry Potter series. That was the one with the—"

"Time turner," I finished for him. "It was one of my favorites, too. Along with *Goblet of Fire*."

He gave me a small smile, and for a moment it felt like everything was normal, and we were just two people spending time together, talking about books and movies.

I wanted to grab his hand and pull him into my room so I could show him my bookshelf. There were a bunch of other books there that he'd read and loved, too. And while the Ethan from my nightshade memories had seen it, the *real* Ethan—the one who was in front of me right now—hadn't.

"Wait," I said, the thought of my room making me think of something.

"What?"

"Maybe we shouldn't appear immediately in Mira's room."

"Why not?"

"Firstly, because we don't want to startle her," I said. "But mainly because she's angry because you crowned me instead of her. It might not be a good idea for me to be wearing the Crown when we see her."

"What do you want to do with it? Hold it?" he asked. "She'll still be able to see it."

"I'm going to put it in a bag that I'll be holding," I said. "Remember—Mira came here because she misses her old life. It's a small thing, but if I change into my regular clothes, she might be more willing to talk to us."

"That's fine," he said, and then he stepped to the side, so I could lead us to my room.

This version of Ethan had been in our apartment more times than I could count, but he'd never been in *my* room.

My room was cozier than Mira's—and also messier. Not like I was a slob or anything, but she was beyond meticulous about keeping everything in its place. My backpack was slung over my chair, and my binders and schoolbooks arranged haphazardly on my desk, as if I were rushing to meet the deadline of a project. Which I hadn't been, since we'd been on break when we'd left. I just hadn't totally cleaned up after finals the term before.

Ethan's eyes went straight to my bookshelves.

The urge was strong to walk over there with him and point out my favorites. But I restrained myself.

"I'm going to change," I said. "You can wait out in the hall."

"I'm not leaving you alone," he said. "I'll just turn around in here."

"Nothing's going to happen to me while I change," I snapped, although I immediately felt bad about my harsh tone.

It was just that the thought of Ethan being *right there* while I changed was going to create way more tension than I was ready to deal with.

"Fine," he said. "I'll wait in the hall. But you'll keep your door open."

He stepped out, and I changed into my favorite jeans, a tank top, and a sweatshirt with our school's name on the front—John Astor High. Astor was some super rich American who'd sailed to Australia at the end of his life, and tons of things around here were named after him.

Lastly, I picked the simple brown purse up off my dresser—the one I'd always carried with me. My wallet, keys, and Kindle were inside. The Crown would easily fit in there, too, although I obviously needed to keep it on until we arrived in the past.

I studied myself in the mirror, surprised by how *normal* I looked.

I was also surprised that although I should have been at home in my room, I felt out of place. Like I'd outgrown it for bigger, better things.

Things like elemental magic, time travel, visiting other realms, and being a Queen... even though I didn't actually feel like a Queen yet.

"All right," I called to Ethan. "I'm ready."

He came back in and paused when he saw me.

Tension crackled in the air between us.

"What?" I asked.

"Nothing. It's just, you look so... normal."

"That's the goal," I said, trying not to pay attention to the fact that I'd just been thinking the same thing. "Now, are you ready to get this over with?"

"Let's do it."

With that, I walked over to him, took his hands in mine, and told the Crown to bring us back to the moment after Mira had left the Seventh Kingdom.

6

GEMMA

When we reappeared in my room, everything was the same... except Mira was standing in front of my bookshelf, next to my bed. She was in her Antarctica gear, just like she'd been when she'd left the Seventh Kingdom.

But the rage in her eyes was gone. In fact, when she saw us, she gave us a small smile, like she'd been expecting us. And there was something different about her eyes.

They were a darker blue than usual.

Maybe it had to do with her magic? Were her eyes reflecting the dark emotions inside her?

"Gemma," she said. "Ethan. I knew you'd come after me. How long did it take you to figure out I'd come here?"

I glanced at Ethan's hand. It was near his pocket, but he hadn't reached in for the dart.

"Why are you in my room?" I asked, not bothering to answer her question.

"To snoop around, obviously." She smirked. "To figure out how long the two of you were together behind my back. I figured you'd have written about it in your journal or something."

"My journal's in my suitcase," I said, wondering if our suitcases were still sitting in the living room where we'd left them.

We'd packed as much as possible for Utopia, then learned we weren't allowed to bring our stuff with us. Unless Shivani had moved our bags, they were still in the living room.

"I'll check later." She shrugged, like she didn't care. "Now, back to my question. How long did it take you to figure out that I came straight here?"

Out of all the questions she could have asked us, *that* was what she wanted to know? It didn't make sense.

"We came from tomorrow," I said.

"Interesting."

She didn't sound interested in the slightest.

She sounded... ambivalent.

Her gaze lifted to right above my head. "Nice crown," she said. "It stayed on pretty tightly when you flew through the air. Like it was glued to your head."

"I'm the only one who can take it off," I told her what I'd quickly discovered when I'd woken up in the Seventh Kingdom.

"Convenient."

If she'd asked because she wanted to try to steal it, she seemed unfazed by my answer.

What was going on with her?

I *knew* my twin. And I'd never seen her act so serene and calm. It was eerie, especially given how enraged she'd been when she'd left the Seventh Kingdom.

She'd only arrived moments ago, but I would have expected my room to already look like a tornado had blown through it. Yet, everything was as I'd left it.

"Do you want me to get my journal for you?" I asked. "You can read it. I don't mind."

"No need," she said. "If you'd written anything you didn't want me to see, you wouldn't have offered to hand it over. Anyway," she continued, and she looked to Ethan. "When did you realize you loved Gemma and not me?"

I sucked in a sharp breath, surprised at how nonchalantly she'd said it. And still surprised about how it was *true* that Ethan loved me more than her.

None of it felt real.

"Why don't we go to the Haven and talk about it there?" Ethan said. "Your mom's anxious to see you."

"How would that work, exactly?" She tilted her head, her eyes on my Crown again. "With the time travel and all. Would you bring me there in *this* time? Or would you bring me to the future—to tomorrow, which is your present—and then we'd go to the Haven together?"

I stilled, since I didn't actually know if I could bring someone from the past into the present. I hadn't had time to test it out.

This is why Mary said we needed to do more tests before we left.

Especially since my power technically gave me all the time in the world.

It was going to take me a while to wrap my mind around all this time travel stuff. In the meantime, I was grateful that Mira was cooperating.

Maybe she felt as out of place at home as I did. Maybe coming here made her realize she didn't belong here anymore.

"Mom's already been filled in on everything that happened," I said, not wanting her to know that I wasn't totally sure how the Holy Crown worked. "She's looking forward to seeing you. So I'll bring you to the present—to *my* present. To tomorrow."

Then, once she was back in the Haven, I'd come back and get Ethan.

Our plan was working out way smoother than I'd thought possible.

"Smart choice," she said. "Because given how hard I slammed you into the wall, your past self is currently in the Seventh Kingdom, recovering from that blow to the head. If you brought me to the Haven in *this* time, that means your past self will eventually go there, too. And that would get messy, with having to avoid each other and all of that."

I furrowed my eyebrows, confused. Because Mira didn't read or watch anything with fantasy or science fiction in it. How did she grasp time travel so quickly?

"That's right," I said slowly. "So, does that mean you'll come?"

"No," she said. "You were too late for that."

"What do you mean?"

"I mean that you didn't wake up in time. You see, after a Queen receives her Holy—or Dark—Object, Time writes that moment in stone. Once a Queen, always a Queen. And by the time you were conscious, I'd already been crowned."

She raised her hand and pulled something out of the air next to her shoulder.

A crystal crown.

A crown that matched mine... except its crystals were jet black instead of clear quartz.

The Dark Crown.

She smiled wickedly, then placed the Crown on her head.

By the time Ethan had reached for the dart of complacent potion, she'd already flickered out and disappeared.

7

GEMMA

I RAN to the place where Mira had been standing, as if I could chase her through time.

But I couldn't. Because I had no idea *when* she'd come from. Guessing would be impossible.

"That wasn't Mira," Ethan said slowly, processing what we'd just learned.

I spun around to face him. "It *was* Mira," I said. "But it was a *future* version of Mira. Which means..." I paused and glanced at the door.

"Mira might still be here," he finished my thought.

"The Mira from this present. Before she becomes..." I trailed off again, unable to say it out loud.

"The Dark Queen of Pentacles." It sounded so final when he said it.

"But it hasn't happened yet," I said. "We can stop it before it does. We just have to find her *now*."

I hurried to the door and flung it open, ready to search the entire place for my twin. The first stop? Her bedroom.

She wasn't there... but the warm, spicy smell of chai tea drifted up from the stairwell.

Mira's favorite drink.

I stilled, leaned against the wall, and listened.

Because there were people talking downstairs.

Mira and Shivani.

Ethan stopped walking when he heard them, too.

We listened as Mira talked between sobs, explaining everything that had happened in the Seventh Kingdom to Shivani. She was confessing *everything*.

I pulled Ethan back into Mira's room and quietly shut the door so we could talk freely.

"We'll do the same plan we discussed earlier," I said, being careful to talk softly enough so they wouldn't be able to hear me downstairs.

"What about all the stuff future Mira said?" he asked. "Once a Queen, always a Queen?"

"She went dark—she was probably lying," I said, since I refused to believe anything else. "But *our* Mira is down there right now. We have to save her."

"What about Shivani?"

"We'll save her, too. Demons must have gotten to them. That has to be why they both won't be here tomorrow," I said, easily putting the pieces together in my mind. "But when she sees us, Mira might lose it again. And we don't know when the demons will get here. So the moment she's in eyesight, hit her with that dart. I'll bring her to the future, get her to the Haven, and then I'll come back for you and Shivani."

"If the demons had gotten to them, wouldn't there have been signs of a struggle when your mom and Riya came here to search for them?" Ethan asked.

"Maybe the demons got them quickly," I said. "I don't know. But the longer we stand here talking about it, the more time we lose. Are you in or not?"

"You know I'm in."

"Good."

He took the dart out of his pocket and we tiptoed down the stairs, stopping behind the doorframe when Mira and Shivani came into view.

Mira was holding a cup of chai tea, tears streaming down her face. Shivani sat attentively, listening as Mira vented about what had happened in the Seventh Kingdom.

"He was supposed to crown *me*," Mira said. "He was supposed to love *me*. But no. He picked—"

Ethan shot the dart into the side of her neck before she could finish the sentence.

Her eyes widened in surprise.

Shivani stood and spun around to face the stairs, knocking her chair over. She reached for her dagger, ready to fight.

Ethan and I came down with our hands up to show we weren't going to attack. "It's okay," he said. "We're here to help you."

Shivani wrapped one hand around Mira's arm and used the other to pull a weapon out of the ether.

The Dark Wand.

Steel gray with a ruby crystal on the top, it was the same Wand I'd seen Lavinia use when she'd fought us in Nebraska.

"Too bad I don't want your help." She smirked and shot red magic out of the Wand, toward me and Ethan.

He pulled me down a split second before the magic could hit us, then shot a burst of fire at Shivani.

The fire hit the wall behind where she'd been standing.

Because Shivani and Mira were gone.

Shivani had teleported out with my twin.

I stood there, shocked, watching the wall burn. The flame grew smaller and disappeared, leaving a scorched black circle on the wood.

I wanted to go back and fix it. But I couldn't go back to a time I'd already visited.

"Why did Shivani have the Dark Wand?" I asked instead.

"I don't think that was Shivani," he said.

"What do you mean?"

"I mean that Lavinia would never give up the Dark Wand. Someone would have to kill her and pry it from her hands if they wanted it. And we would have heard if Lavinia was dead."

"So you think that was Lavinia," I said, and he nodded.

I shuddered at the thought of that witch having been in our home.

When I'd come here for the memory potion, had I really been with Shivani? Or had that been Lavinia?

It had to have been Shivani. If it had been Lavinia, she would have taken me, like she'd just taken Mira.

"Lavinia must have gotten to Shivani at some point," he continued. "Used her DNA to make transformation potion so she could take Shivani's place."

"We need to go back in time and stop Lavinia from taking Shivani's place," I said. "If we stop her, she wouldn't have been here today. Then she won't have the chance to take Mira, and Mira won't become the Dark Queen of Pentacles."

"Agreed," he said. "But we shouldn't take on Lavinia alone. We need backup."

"We need the Queen of Swords."

"Exactly. So let's go back to the future, go to the Haven, and get Raven."

I looked around the room—at the fallen chair, the wall scorched by Ethan's fire, and the doorframe that had been cracked by Lavinia's red magic.

If we went back further and stopped Lavinia, then none of this would ever happen.

"Let's do it." I grabbed Ethan's hands, then thought to the Crown, *take us back to the present.*

We flickered out, then reappeared in the present, in the same spot in the café.

Except the scorch mark on the wall was gone. The doorframe was no longer cracked. Mom and Riya could have been the ones who'd picked the chair back up, but there was no way the wall and doorframe could have been fixed that quickly.

The clock on the wall said it was seconds after we'd left.

But what *day* was it?

Unsure how else to check, I hurried up to Mom's office, sat down at her computer, and typed "what day is it" into the Google search bar.

Saturday, March 21. The same day we'd left.

"I don't understand." I sat back and shook my head, trying to make sense of it all.

"I think I do," Ethan said. "Look."

He pulled a dart of complacent potion out of his pocket.

"You had two of them?" I asked.

"I only had one."

"But you used it on Mira."

"I did. But it's back in my pocket, as good as new. Just like the wall and doorframe downstairs are as good as new, too."

"It's like our confrontation with Lavinia and Mira was erased."

"Seems like it."

I shook my head again, not understanding how or why it had happened.

Then the words Dark Mira had said to us replayed in my head, and a sick feeling crept into my stomach.

After a Queen receives her Holy—or Dark—Object, Time writes that moment in stone. Once a Queen, always a Queen.

I reached for the key hanging from my necklace. "Hecate better be in the Library," I said. "Because we need some answers."

8

GEMMA

HECATE MUST HAVE SOMEHOW KNOWN how desperate we were for help, because she was waiting for us in the ivory hall, as serene as ever in her purple gown that reached the floor.

"Gemma," she said. "The Holy Crown looks good on you."

I didn't bother thanking her, or greeting her at all.

"How can I stop Mira from becoming the Dark Queen of Pentacles?" I said instead, getting right to my question.

"Follow me." She spun around and led us into the hall of endless bookshelves.

A woman in a poodle skirt was helping herself to food from the long banquet table in the center—I recognized her from the first time I was in this room. She didn't seem to notice we were there.

Hecate stepped up to the wooden pedestal, and her eyes transformed into galaxies of stars. Smokey, cosmic magic poured out of them and made its way down the hall, tendrils of it breaking off to peruse the books on the shelves. The smoke traveled much farther back than I could see, and it took longer than usual, as if it was reaching deeper than it had for any of my other questions.

Finally, a book flew from the shelves and into Hecate's hands. It was light gray, almost white. And with the book, the mist flew back inside Hecate, and her eyes returned to their normal, deep purple color.

The book opened, and wind blew through the pages, landing on one near the back. As always, Hecate angled the book away from us, so we couldn't read what was inside.

I wondered *why* she wouldn't let us read the books ourselves, but that was a question for another day.

She took a while to read it, looking deep in thought. Finally, she pulled the book closer to her, raised her gaze to look at us, and said, "You cannot stop Mira from becoming the Dark Queen of Pentacles."

I said nothing, waiting for her to continue. Because there had to be more to it than that.

"In the present, Mira has already become the Dark Queen of Pentacles," she said. "Her position as Queen is written in stone—not even Time will allow you to change it. It's the same with all the Queens. If you try to stop them from acquiring the Object that turned them into a Queen, Time will reject the change. The present you return to will be the same one you left, as if you'd never traveled to the past at all."

"Time erased the fact that we went back to help Mira," I realized.

"Yes," she said. "I'm sorry."

Defeat shattered my soul.

My twin was gone. Forever.

But maybe not. Makena—one of the high witches of the Ward—had said that no one but the angels and the demons were truly light or dark. There was light inside of everyone.

Torrence had been able to come back from the dark.

I was going to make sure that Mira would, too.

"Now, Ethan," Hecate said, turning to him. "I take it that you have a question as well?"

"Yes." He stood straighter and kept his eyes locked on Hecate's. "How can I free the dragons from the cuffs that bind their magic?"

"A good question." She faced the shelves, and the cosmic mist floated out of her eyes again.

I wished Ethan had asked more about Mira. He could have thought of *some* question that would help us help her.

But the dragons were his people. He was their king. Freeing them could be the key to defeating the demons.

And if we defeated the demons, maybe we'd have a better chance of helping Mira.

Another book flew into Hecate's hands. This one was such a dark gray that it was nearly black.

Dark magic. I could practically feel the heaviness of it oozing off the pages.

Hecate didn't spend as much time reading the passage inside the book as she had in the one before.

"There's only one way to disable the magic binding cuffs," she said. "You must kill the one who enspelled them."

"Thank you," Ethan said, and we both watched as the books floated off the pedestal, made their way down the hall, and disappeared into its endless shelves.

"Do you know who enspelled the cuffs?" I asked him.

There was no point in asking Hecate—we'd already used up our questions for the day.

"No," he said. "But it's dark mage magic. It has to be one of the dark mages on Ember."

"Got it," I said, and then I turned back to Hecate. "Thank you," I told her. "For being here when I needed answers the most."

"I'm here for you, always," she said. "Even when I'm not here, in the Eternal Library, my magic is everywhere. To find it, all you have to do is to tune into your intuition."

With that, she disappeared into a cloud of cosmic smoke.

Other than the zombied-out witches roaming the shelves, I was alone with Ethan.

Which meant it was time to get out of there. Because as long as I didn't acknowledge my feelings for him, I didn't have to deal with them.

That was how it worked. Right?

"Come on." I turned my back to Ethan and started to make my way to the ivory hall. "We need to get back to the Haven and tell Mary and the others what we've learned."

9

GEMMA

"Mira was able to pull the Dark Crown out of the ether."

Out of everything we'd told her, *that* was the part of the story Mary cared about the most.

"Yes," I said. "She pulled it out of the ether, told us how we couldn't change the fact that she was a Queen, and traveled back to her present—whenever that might be."

For all we knew, the Mira we'd spoken to in my room could have been a version of her from months from now. Or *years* from now, although she didn't look visibly older than she had the last time I'd seen her.

"It used to be that the only people who could access the ether like that were the chosen champions of Mars," Mary said, referring to the half-blood fae chosen to represent the god of war in the annual Faerie Games held in the Otherworld.

Each god gifted their chosen half-blood with magic unique to them. One of the gifts bestowed by Mars was the ability to access any weapon from the ether.

"The Queen of Wands worked with her soulmate Julian—who was a chosen champion of Mars—to create a spell that allowed people to 'store' a weapon of theirs in the ether," Mary continued. "But as far as I know, Selena was the only one who could cast that spell."

"Lavinia is the Dark Queen of Wands," I said. "She could have worked with a chosen champion of Mars to cast that spell on Mira."

"Exactly what I was thinking," said Mary. "But it's important to note that this is a *spell*. Meaning that Selena didn't use her fae magic to do it. She used her witch magic, which was amplified by the Holy Wand."

"What are you getting at?"

"We have the strongest witch in the world here with us." She looked to Genevieve and asked, "If you worked with a chosen champion of Mars, do you think you could cast a spell that would allow Gemma to store the Holy Crown in the ether?"

"Of course I could." Genevieve straightened her shoulders, like she was offended that Mary would think otherwise. "I might not be the Queen of Wands, but my bloodline has genie magic in it. I can do nearly any type of magic."

Mary's eyes widened. "Genie magic?"

"Yes..." Genevieve looked at her like she had amnesia. Then, she turned to Queen Katherine. "What did you do?"

"Like Mary said, you're the most powerful witch in the world," she said. "Well, you were *one* of the most powerful witches in the world, until your bloodline died out."

Genevieve frowned at the reminder of Geneva's sacrifice.

"If people knew you had genie magic, they'd come looking for you," she continued, but Genevieve interrupted before she could say any more.

"You compelled the world to forget about me."

"Yes."

Genevieve took a moment to soak this in. She didn't seem happy about it, but she wasn't raging with anger, either.

"What's done is done," Katherine said.

"It is," Mary agreed. "So, are you willing to attempt this spell?"

"Hold up," Ethan said. "You're asking her to experiment on Gemma."

"The Crown isn't exactly inconspicuous," Mary said. "It's too big to keep in anything but a large bag, and a bag can be easily stolen. This is a good solution to that problem."

Silence descended as they looked at me and Genevieve.

From Ethan's expression, I could tell he wanted me to say no.

But Mary was right. If this spell worked, not only would I be safer, but the Crown would be, too.

"Let's do it." I pretended I didn't see Ethan's jaw clench. Instead, I remained focused on Mary. "I'm guessing you know where we can find a chosen champion of Mars?"

"The Otherworld, of course."

I sighed at the thought of another visit to the Otherworld. The fae might be our allies, but there was something unnerving about being in their presence.

Like I had to be on constant alert for trickery.

Which made sense, since with the fae, one *always* had to be on constant alert for trickery.

"When do we leave?" If we were going, I wanted to get it over with.

"When did you last sleep?"

"Does being knocked unconscious count?"

"It's not the same," she said. "Plus, for you, that was... a while ago."

How long ago *was* it? Time no longer moved for me the same way it used to. The hours that had passed since I'd arrived in the Haven were much longer for me, since I'd been time traveling and spending time in the places I'd visited.

Plus, Mary had a good point. I was tired. And in the Otherworld, I needed to be on full alert.

"Let's rest for the night," I said. "We'll go to the Otherworld tomorrow."

"A wise choice." She looked at me approvingly, as if she were seeing me as a Queen instead of someone who'd been newly thrown into the supernatural world.

But even if she saw me as a Queen, I definitely didn't feel like one.

"I'll stay in your room," Ethan said to me. "To keep you safe."

"No," I said, and he winced, as if I'd physically hurt him. "I'm staying with my mom."

The thought of being alone filled me with dread. It wouldn't be the same without knowing Mira was safe in the room next to mine. And I couldn't stay with Ethan. What could I possibly say to him right now? I had too many emotions coursing through me to keep them straight.

What he'd done made no sense. Why hadn't he been honest about his feelings from the start? If he had, none of this would have happened. Mira wouldn't have gone dark.

My twin sister wouldn't *hate* me.

I felt a pang of emptiness surge through me at the reminder of everything I'd lost.

Thanks to the nightshade, I'd had a taste of what it was like to have Ethan love me, but it wasn't real. Now, I didn't have Mira, either.

The never-ending abyss of dark, painful emotions was too much to process. Especially when I had a mission to focus on.

A mission I refused to fail.

Mom rushed to my side, like she was protecting me. "You'll stay in my room," she said, and I nodded, blinking back tears.

We walked back in silence, and the moment I got in bed, I instantly fell asleep.

10

GEMMA

ETHAN, Genevieve, and I met with Mary in the tearoom the next morning. I'd had breakfast in the room with Mom, and she'd remained positive, assuring me that we'd get Mira back safely, and all would be well. I'd bring Mira back from the darkness, like I'd done for Torrence. I did it once, so there was no reason I couldn't do it again.

I wasn't sure if she'd been trying to convince me, or herself.

Thanks to Earth's alliance with the Otherworld, Mary had portal tokens that led directly into Sorcha's courtyard. She handed them to us and opened the secret door in the tearoom that led to the small room with the fountain that connected our world to theirs.

The token had a depiction of Sorcha's eerily perfect face on one side, and her tall crown on the other. Her crown was larger and more embellished than mine, but it was all for show.

Mine was the one with true power.

I reached for it to touch the crystals, and they warmed, like they were alive.

Alive with *magic*.

We all held our tokens and faced the fountain.

Genevieve shifted uneasily on her feet.

"Are you nervous?" I asked, stunned that someone who exuded such confidence could be nervous about *anything*.

"I've never visited the Otherworld before," she said. "And the fae… they're dangerous."

"They're our allies."

"They have the same goal as us, so they're playing nice," she said. "I don't support the dark witches, but there's a reason they put that curse on the fae to banish them to the Otherworld."

The curse that made them allergic to iron—which made it nearly impossible for them to live on Earth.

"They'll help us," I said. "Just like they helped us get to Ember."

"You mean how they let you walk into their *prison world?*"

She had a good point, since it hadn't cost the fae anything to let us walk into Ember. But I wasn't going to admit it.

"You said you'd help us," I said. "So, are you going to come with us or not?"

"I said I'd work with a chosen champion of Mars to cast the spell on you," she said. "However, I don't see why I have to accompany you to the Otherworld, when you can simply bring a chosen champion of Mars here."

This was taking too long. I wanted to be in the Otherworld speaking with Sorcha already. "Fine—I'll ask her if she'll allow a chosen champion of Mars to come here," I said. "Happy?"

"Yes." Genevieve backed away from the fountain and returned her portal token to Mary.

"Wait," Ethan said. "We should take the token with us. We'll need it to give to the chosen champion of Mars."

"The Empress has her own portal tokens to get here," Mary said. "But you're right. She might try to bargain with it. She might already try to bargain regarding the chosen champion of Mars."

I cursed, since I hadn't thought of that. And bargaining with fae was serious business. They were tricky with their words.

But I was a reader *and* a writer. Well, sort of a writer, if journaling counted. The point was, I was good with words.

I could do this. Plus, I had Ethan's help. We'd figure it out.

I took the extra token from Mary and put it in my pocket. I was back to wearing my Haven whites, and while they were comfortable, I *did* miss my regular clothes from home.

"I'll be careful," I promised.

"You're a Queen," she said. "Your status is equal to the Empress. Remember that."

"I will."

With that, I stepped back over to Ethan's side, purposefully looking into the fountain instead of at him.

I tossed my token into the water.

Ethan did the same.

The water swirled sparkly purple. He took my hand, and together, we jumped through the portal.

11

GEMMA

WE LANDED on the marble floor of Sorcha's courtyard, I let go of Ethan's hand and tumbled right into someone.

A fae with orange wings.

But the fae barely paid me any attention. Because *tons* of fae were gathered in the courtyard. So many of them that they filled the entire space. I stood up, taking in the scene.

The ones in the center cowered together, holding hands with fear in their eyes.

The ones on the outside—mostly ones with steel gray wings—held weapons at the ready, preparing for a fight.

Thumps sounded against the walls around us. One after the other, never stopping.

Then, there were the groans. Deep, inhuman, *hungry* groans. Chills ran up and down my spine at the sound of them.

I'd watched enough episodes of *The Walking Dead* to know that sound anywhere.

Zombies.

They were surrounding the palace. From the sound of it, it wouldn't be long before they broke through.

It was also brighter than it had been the last time I'd been there. A glance up showed me that the protection dome that had been around the city was gone.

The dome must have been obliterated, and then the zombies had piled in.

I searched for Sorcha. Thanks to her white ballgown, it wasn't hard to find her at the center of the courtyard. She stood with her advisor Aeliana, their hands clutched together so tightly that it was like they were holding onto each other for their lives.

I pushed through the crowd to make my way to her. The fae looked at me curiously, but let me pass at the sight of the Crown on my head.

"Sorcha!" I called her name, louder and louder until she heard me.

She spun around, her eyes narrowed in offense—probably at the fact that I hadn't used her royal title to address her. Leave it to Sorcha to care about formalities in a time like this. Then her gaze met mine, and she breathed out in relief.

THE DRAGON SCORNED

The crowd parted as she and Aeliana made their way toward me and Ethan.

"You found the Holy Crown," she said simply.

"What happened here?" I didn't bother answering her question, since yes, obviously I'd found the Crown.

"The boundary dome around the city was created by Selena," she said. "Since she died, it's been deteriorating. It fully gave way yesterday. We've been doing our best to keep the infected at bay, but..." She looked around helplessly. "There are too many of them for us to stop them."

Aeliana looked at me, her gaze steady and calm. "You haven't come to save us."

"I'm sorry," I said. "I don't have that kind of power. I'm not the Queen of Wands. Or the Queen of Swords."

"Not even the Queen of Swords could fight off this many of them," Sorcha said. "They're everywhere—hordes of them. They can only be killed with holy weapons. And since we can't use holy weapons, we're helpless against them."

"The fae can't use holy weapons because of the iron," Ethan said. "But half-bloods aren't allergic to iron. They can use the weapons."

"Half-bloods have no magic or supernatural strength. Only chosen champions are strong enough to kill the infected," Sorcha said. "But there aren't enough chosen champions to hold off all the infected in the realm. If the half-bloods were free, we'd have a large enough army to slaughter the infected in days. But with their magic bound, the half-bloods are useless."

She said the final part in distaste, as if it were the half-bloods' fault that the fae bound their magic at birth to force them into lives of servitude.

"Selena was going to free them," she continued. "If she hadn't gone off on that quest on Earth that got her killed, she'd have already done it, and we wouldn't be in this position now."

Of course.

That was our answer.

"What would you say if I told you I can save Selena?" I asked.

Sorcha lifted an eyebrow. "You can raise the dead?"

"No. But I can change the past."

"I'm listening."

"The Holy Crown's magic allows me to travel back in time," I said, and I quickly summarized what I'd learned so far about my time traveling abilities. I had to raise my voice to be heard over the chaos, but I managed to relay all of it to Sorcha.

I didn't tell her about Mira going dark. We didn't have time for that.

Well, technically, the Crown could give me time for anything. But Sorcha was desperate right now. Which was where I wanted her, so whatever bargain she was sure to propose would be in my favor.

"I can't walk around in the past with the Holy Crown on my head," I explained. "It would bring unwanted attention and potentially make me a target. But if I take it off, I risk it being stolen. I need a safe place to keep it while I'm traveling."

The thumps against the palace walls were getting louder.

Sorcha looked around, worried. "What do you think I can do for you?"

"I need you to command a chosen champion of Mars to come to the Haven with me." I knew from my studies that the fae with steel gray wings who were guarding the outskirts of the courtyard were chosen champions of Mars. "The most powerful witch on Earth has promised to try using the chosen champion's magic to cast a spell on me and the Crown so I can store it in the ether. I have an extra portal token for them to use."

"And in return?" Sorcha asked.

"I'll do everything in my power to save Selena."

"Deal."

No way, I thought, shocked. That was far easier than it should have been. Although maybe not, given Sorcha's current predicament.

I was tempted to thank her, but I held back.

Never thank a fae. Doing so binds you to a favor of their choice.

"You won't regret this," I said instead.

"I know." She turned to the nearest steel winged guard. "Gaius!" she called out, and he hurried toward us and bowed his head to Sorcha.

"Your Highness." He was big and rough around the edges, but soft spoken.

"I need you to accompany the Queen of Pentacles to the Haven," she said. "She'll explain your purpose there after you arrive. You can trust her."

An ear-splitting crack erupted from the other side of the courtyard.

The door had broken open.

Milky-eyed, black-winged, rotted fae-zombies dragged themselves through the opening.

Steel winged fae rushed forward and stabbed the zombies' hearts with their holy weapons. The zombies turned to ash, leaving piles of it where they'd been standing.

Another crack—this time from the side.

More zombies piled through.

My breathing quickened. I had a holy weapon on me, but I wasn't skilled enough to fight so many of them at once. Besides, once I saved Selena, whether or not I stayed to help should be irrelevant.

"Do you have a portal token?" I asked the Empress.

She shook her head no.

But Aeliana had future sight. Surely, she'd known to prepare.

"And you?" I asked her.

"We do not," Aeliana said calmly.

The Empress straightened. "I'll be by the sides of my people until the very end."

Ethan nodded in respect. "A noble choice."

"Now, go." Sorcha motioned toward the fountain. "You can't save Selena if you become food for the infected."

"When we return, this will never have happened," I told her. "The Otherworld will be safe. You won't remember any of this."

"But you'll tell me, so I'll know?"

"I will."

Maybe.

The zombies moved in closer. One of them reached a pink winged fae who'd been pushed to the side, pulled her in, and took a giant bite out of her forearm.

Her scream sliced the air, and my nerves buzzed with warning.

Time to bolt.

I handed the extra portal token to Gaius. He cleared the way toward the fountain for me and Ethan, and then the three of us tossed our tokens into the water and jumped in, leaving the terrified screams, hungry groans, and foul scent of death behind us.

12

GEMMA

The silence when we landed back in the Haven was a sharp contrast to the palace's chaos.

Mary and Genevieve were sitting on the benches in the tearoom, drinking and eating snacks, as if everything were perfectly normal.

Genevieve startled at our arrival. "That was fast," she said, although she wasn't looking at us—she was looking at Gaius.

His wings had gone invisible, since he was on Earth. He eyed her suspiciously, and his huge muscles flexed, clearly on guard.

It made sense, given the strained relationship between the fae and the witches.

Regardless, Genevieve placed her teacup down and smiled seductively. "I see why the god of war blessed you with his magic."

He barely acknowledged her before turning to me. "Tell me why I'm here."

Mary stood, and all attention went to her. "I'm Mary, the ruler of the Haven—one of Earth's seven supernatural kingdoms," she introduced herself. "Please sit and help yourself to whatever you'd like to eat."

"Tell me why I'm here," he repeated.

Apparently, he was a man of few words.

Genevieve huffed in irritation. "It's tradition to break bread before discussing political matters," she said. "By not doing so, you're offending the queen."

Mary didn't like to be called a queen—even though she was, technically, a queen—but she didn't bother to correct the witch.

He glanced at me. "I thought you were the queen."

"I'm a different type of queen," I said, and his brow furrowed in confusion. "Break bread with us, and we'll explain everything."

"The food is safe?"

"I promise."

He hesitated, then said, "The Empress said to trust you. So, I'll trust you."

I stopped myself from pointing out that he didn't have much of a choice, since his realm was destroyed and his only chance of getting it back was to trust me.

He'd learn that soon.

"Thank you." I purposefully used the words that were avoided in the Otherworld. The words only bound a person to a favor for full fae—not half-bloods—but by using them, I hoped to show vulnerability.

He made a soft sound of approval, then sat as far away from Genevieve as possible. She bristled and refused to meet his eyes.

Mary prepared him a plate and handed it to him. He hesitated, then took a bite of buttery naan. It was a good choice, since the Indian flatbread was a specialty in the Haven. As he chewed, his eyes lit up, and he inhaled the rest of it in a few bites.

Mary smiled and placed a full plate of naan in front of him. She also poured him a cup of spicy tea.

He picked up the cup and took a small sip. His lips pursed in distaste, and he placed it back down and took another large bite of naan.

"What type of drink is that?" he asked after swallowing.

"Masala chai," she said.

He took another sip, not looking as startled this time. "Drinks in the Otherworld are all sweet," he said. "Apologies if I offended you."

"No worries," she said. "I understand that this realm is foreign to you. But, now that we've broken bread, we must tell you why you're here."

"We're here to save the Otherworld," he said simply, and Genevieve's eyebrow raised in surprise. "The Empress thought I would be more useful here than there."

"*Save* the Otherworld?" Genevieve repeated, and she looked to me and Ethan for answers.

"We went through the portal and arrived to total chaos," I said, and from there, I told them everything that had happened from the moment we'd entered the Otherworld until now.

After they'd been filled in, we told Gaius our predicament.

"We need to create a space in the ether for me to store the Holy Crown," I said. "Will you help us?"

"The Queen of Wands must be saved," he said. "Of course I'll help you."

"Good," said Genevieve. "Are you both ready to get this over with?"

"Yes," I said, at the same time as Gaius.

"All right," she said. "Obviously I've never done a spell of this nature before. So, I'm just going to go with my intuition."

"Sounds good to me." I'd always trusted my intuition, and since Genevieve was a powerful witch, I assumed she had good intuition, too.

Ethan turned to me, worried. "Are you sure about this?"

"Of course I'm sure." I brushed off his concern, focusing on Genevieve instead. "What do you need me to do?"

"Keep the Crown on," she said, and I nodded, since I hadn't intended to take it off. "I'm going to take both of your hands and try to channel Gaius's magic into you."

"Sounds good."

She stood between me and Gaius and took both of our hands. Then she closed her eyes and started chanting in Latin.

I closed my eyes, too. I didn't like seeing the others staring at me.

Mainly. I didn't like seeing *Ethan* staring at me. It was too tempting to stare back.

As Genevieve chanted, warm magic rushed into my palm and traveled up to the Crown. The Crown tingled with an explosion of light, the crystals buzzing like they were creating magical strands to connect with the Universe.

Genevieve stopped chanting, and the magic receded. She pulled her hand out of mine, and I opened my eyes.

Mary watched us expectantly. "Did it work?"

Genevieve gave her a knowing smile, then turned to me. "Let's have Gemma show us."

"Okay." I reached for the Crown, removed it from my head, and looked to Gaius. This was going to work. It *had* to work. "What do I do?"

"Imagine a cubby next to your shoulder," he said. "Picture it and feel it. Then, reach for it and place the Crown inside."

"You make it sound so easy."

"It is. Give it a go."

I did exactly as Gaius said, and as I held the Crown over my shoulder, I felt the air *opening*. The Crown slid inside an invisible "cubby" and disappeared. Half of my hand was in there, too.

"You can let go of it," Gaius said.

I held my breath. This would be the first time I'd let the Crown out of my sight since Ethan had placed it on my head in Antarctica. I'd even been keeping it on while sleeping.

I breathed out at the same time as I let go of the Crown, and worry tugged at my lungs.

"Good," Gaius said. "Now, reach back into the ether and take it back."

Not wasting a second, I did as he'd instructed. The ether parted as easily for me as it had the first time, and the moment my hand was inside, I felt the Crown's crystals on my fingertips.

I pulled it out and placed it on my head.

Where it belonged.

Every muscle in my body relaxed once it was in place.

I tested the "ether cubby," a few more times, and didn't have any issues with it.

"Glad we got that figured out," I said once I was positive I'd gotten the hang of it, keeping my focus on Mary. "Now... do you have any ideas about how to save Selena?"

"Not quite," she said. "But I know someone who will."

"Who?"

"The people who saw her last. Reed and Torrence."

"Good plan," I said, since at least it was something to start with.

"I'll send a fire message to tell them to come here tomorrow," she said.

"Why tomorrow?"

"Because before we get any more people involved, there are a few more things we need to learn about how your magic works."

13

GEMMA

Torrence and Reed arrived in the Haven the next day, where they met with me, Ethan, and Mary in the tearoom.

Torrence's eyes bulged when she saw the Holy Crown on my head. "I guess you found the other half of it."

"Had to go all the way to Antarctica, but yes, we got the second half of the Crown," I said.

"Antarctica," she repeated. "Sounds like quite the adventure."

"You have no idea."

She looked around, like she was searching for someone else, then refocused on me. "Where's Mira?"

My heart broke all over again at the sound of my sister's name.

Torrence frowned. "I guess she wasn't happy that you're the Queen of Pentacles and not her."

Understatement of the century.

"We should sit down," I said. "Because we have a lot to catch you up on."

Torrence and Reed listened attentively as we told them everything that had happened since parting ways in Ember.

"I have an idea about how to save Selena," I said, and I turned to Reed. "But I'll need your help."

"I'm listening."

"You, Selena, Julian, and the Supreme Mages worked together to find Torrence on Circe's island," I started, and he nodded for me to continue. "I can travel back to when the group of you were together and talk to Selena. I'll tell her what happens, so she's prepared."

"You'll tell her that the Supreme Mages are going to turn on her, killing her and her soulmate?" he said, continuing before I could answer. "Because I don't think that will go over well. Besides, we spent the entire time searching for Torrence on a ship. It was the best way to make sure no witches, mages, or demons interrupted our trip."

"Because they can't teleport onto a ship if they haven't been on that ship, and even so, they can't get there if the ship's moving," I said, remembering what I'd learned while on board the Golden Moon for the Antarctica cruise.

"Exactly."

"You were on a ship the entire time?" Ethan asked.

"We were," Reed said. "As the Queen of Wands, Selena was a target. We didn't want any demons popping in uninvited and attacking."

It was smart.

Unfortunately, it made things harder for us.

Way harder.

"When did you first get on the ship?" My stomach knotted as I waited for the answer.

"Right after Christmas."

I cursed at his answer.

"What's wrong?" Torrence asked.

"I can't travel back to before I received my elemental magic." I'd learned that during the tests I'd conducted with Mary, but hadn't thought it would be an issue, seeing as Selena had been killed *months* after I'd gotten my magic.

"What?" Torrence balked. "Why not?"

"I don't know."

"Well… is there a way you can find out?"

I almost said no, but I stopped myself.

Because there *was* a way I could find out.

"Maybe," I said, standing up. "Can you wait here for a moment?"

Confusion crossed over her features. "Where are you going?"

"To a place where I might be able to get an answer." Without bothering to explain—since there'd be no *point*—I walked over to the door, used my key, and stepped into the ivory hall of the Eternal Library.

I smiled at the sight of Hecate standing there, waiting for me.

Why was she there sometimes, and not others?

I shelved that as a question to ask her in the future. Because right now, we had bigger issues to deal with.

I'd only taken a few steps toward her when the door opened, and Ethan stepped through.

Irritation ran through me. "I know it's your duty to protect me and all, but I'm safe in the Eternal Library," I said.

"I know you're safe here. I also see that Hecate's here." He nodded to her in greeting, and she returned the gesture. "It's better that we're able to ask two questions instead of only one."

I frowned, since his point was a good one, then spun back around to face Hecate. "It's good to see you," I said.

"You, too," she said with a knowing smile. "I assume you're prepared with a question?"

"I am."

"Then follow me, and I'll get your answers."

We walked with her into the hall of bookshelves. It looked the exact same as always, as if the never-ending shelves were trapped in time.

She took her spot in front of the podium, focused on me, and waited.

"My time travel magic is limited—it doesn't let me travel back to before I received my elemental magic." I phrased the start of what I was getting at as a statement, so it wouldn't be confused for my actual question. "How can I travel back to before that moment as easily and consistently as I can travel back to the times after it?"

Hecate turned to the shelves, and the cosmic mist poured out of her eyes and traveled down the hall. It didn't take long before a book soared toward us and into her hands. The book was a soft cream color, and warm, welcoming magic pulsed out of it.

The cosmic mist returned to Hecate's body, the breeze from it flipping through the book's pages until landing on one about three quarters of the way through.

Hecate pressed her lips together in concentration as she read. Once done, she pulled the book closer and looked to us. "The Crown was weakened when it was broken in half," she said. "It's magic won't be at full capacity until it's mended. *You're* able to mend it, but you can't do that until you become stronger. To become strong enough to mend the Crown, you must eat the food of the Heavens—mana."

There was only one place I knew of where mana could be found.

"Looks like we're going to Avalon," I said, and Hecate nodded, as if letting me know it was the right decision.

"Ethan?" she asked.

I didn't look at him. I couldn't. I just... couldn't. It hurt too badly.

"What's the name of the person who enspelled the cuffs that are keeping the dragons on Ember enslaved?" he asked.

Really? He'd asked about the dragons on Ember instead of something that would help us save Mira *again*?

Freeing the dragons can help us save Mira, I reminded myself. *They're our allies. They'll fight with us.*

It still didn't stop me from resenting the fact that he wasn't taking a more direct approach.

Hecate brought forth another book with her cosmic mist. This one was dark gray.

She barely had to glance at the open page to get the answer. "Supreme Mage Ragnarr Bell," she said, and I couldn't help it—I glanced at Ethan to see his reaction.

He froze, shellshocked, like he didn't know what to think. "The King of the Dark Mages," he finally said, although he spoke slowly, like the words were strange and foreign.

"Yes," Hecate said.

"But Supreme Mages can't be killed."

Hecate said nothing.

Yet another question for another day.

"Thank you for all your help," I told her. "Hopefully we'll see you soon."

"Perhaps." She smiled knowingly, then the books flew back to their shelves, and she disappeared.

I spun around angrily to face Ethan. "You *knew* one of the dark mages on Ember enspelled those cuffs," I said. "Why did you waste a question on that?"

"I didn't know exactly which mage it was," he said. "The fact that it's the King of the Dark Mages—a *Supreme Mage*—is huge. We needed that information."

"We *need* more help to save Mira."

"You're angry at me."

"You think?" There was no containing the sarcasm that dripped from my tone.

"Gemma." He reached for me, but I stepped away, and sadness crossed over his features. "Talk to me."

"How am I supposed to talk to you when I can't *trust* you?"

The moment it came out of my mouth, I understood the core of the emotion I'd buried deep inside me.

Distrust.

Ethan had lied to me. He'd lied to Mira. His lies had destroyed all three of us.

How was I supposed to be able to trust him after all we'd been through?

"You can trust me," he said. "I'm here for you, always."

"You're here to protect me physically," I said. "But emotionally? You've…" I paused, searching for the right word.

Hurt me?

That was the understatement of the century.

Betrayed me?

Getting closer.

Destroyed me.

Yes. That was what I felt like inside right now. *Destroyed*. Ripped into so many shreds that I didn't think I'd ever be able to be put back together again.

"I can't do this right now," I said instead, and I hurried out into the ivory hall and toward the door.

I didn't glance over my shoulder to see if Ethan was behind me.

Because if there was one thing I *did* trust, it was that he'd always chase me when I ran.

14

GEMMA

Torrence, Reed, and Mary were eating sugary pastries in the tearoom when we returned.

Mary stared at me and set her teacup down. "She was there."

Apparently, she was able to tell that I'd spoken to Hecate simply from my expression.

"She was," I said.

"Who was where?" Torrence asked.

"The goddess of witches, Hecate," I said, completely deadpan. "She was waiting for us in her Eternal Library, where she used her cosmic magic to find books with the answers to our questions."

Torrence's eyes went blank, then refocused. "I've heard the Haven library is extensive," she said. "Not *nearly* as extensive as the Devereux library, but I'm glad their librarian was able to get our answer."

"What's the answer?" Reed asked, as if Torrence hadn't totally misheard what I'd said.

"The Crown was weakened when it was broken in half," I said. "To fix it, I need to strengthen my magic."

"How do you do that?"

"I need to eat mana."

"Mana can't leave Avalon," Reed said. "It decomposes the moment anyone tries to bring it off the island."

"I know." That was one of the many things I'd learned in my time in Utopia. "We can't bring the mana to me. Which means I need to go to the mana."

"You're coming to Avalon?" Torrence's eyes lit up.

"I'm going to *try* to go to Avalon," I said. "I still haven't gone through the Angel Trials."

"You'll pass," she said, like there was no question about it.

"I thought Harper would pass, too," I said. "We *all* thought she'd pass."

"That's different. I mean, yes, it was surprising Harper didn't pass, given how strong her magic is. But you're one of the Four Holy Queens. Avalon is meant to be your home."

Home.

The thought of finally getting what I'd been missing ever since receiving my magic should have warmed me.

Instead, I felt nothing.

"Home is where my mom and sister are," I said instead.

Ever since leaving Australia, it had been true. I just hadn't realized it until now.

And it's where Ethan is, that annoying little voice in the back of my head reminded me.

"Your mom will enter the Angel Trials, too," Ethan said. "And then, once Mira's back, so will she."

"And then what?" I said bitterly. "The four of us will live happily ever after?"

"We'll be safe," he said, and he turned to Mary. "Bring Rachael here. Also send for three witches, because me, Gemma, and Rachael will immediately go to the Vale so we can enter the Angel Trials."

"One witch," Torrence corrected him. "Reed and I can take two of you. We'll drop you off at the Vale, and then, we'll see you in Avalon."

15

GEMMA

THE CANADIAN ROCKIES were the biggest mountains I'd ever seen, towering high into the starry night sky. The Vale's palace and surrounding towns were built into it, like they'd been born out of the rocks. The palace was near the peak, and the rest of the buildings sprawled out below. Lights glowed from inside of them, the only warmth in the cold night.

I inhaled the crisp, thin air and gazed out at the fresh, powdery snow that covered the mountains. It was beautiful—more like something you'd see on a postcard than in real life.

We'd arrived outside the boundary dome, where Harper and two other witches were waiting for us.

Harper's eyes met mine, and she beamed. Her long, dark hair was shinier than ever, and while she was paler than before, her skin was positively radiant. Also, she was wearing jeans, a black tank, and a leather jacket. I'd never seen her in everyday clothes, and she looked stunning. If she'd walked down the halls of my school, she would have turned every guys' head.

She teleported next to me and threw her arms around me in a hug.

She smelled like a mix of flowers and metal. Witch and vampire. A strange combination, but then again, hers was a strange situation.

She pulled back and studied me—well, she studied the Holy Crown. "The Queen of Pentacles," she said with a smile. "Who would have thought?"

"Definitely not you." I laughed, remembering how frustrated Harper had been during our lessons. I'd had the hardest time getting the hang of my magic.

"Not true." She stuck her tongue out at me. "I always knew you had potential. Especially after you blasted through the rocks to create that escape cave…" She trailed off and looked out to the mountains, her eyes sad.

Because I'd created the cave that allowed us to escape Utopia.

It was the day Harper's kingdom had been destroyed and her mother killed.

"This is where we leave you," Torrence said, and she gave me a knowing look. One that said, *you better pass the Trials, because we need to save Selena.* "We'll see the three of you in Avalon."

"See you there," I said, and then she and Reed teleported out.

My mom wrapped her arms around herself, shifting from one foot to the other on the snow-covered ground. "Any chance we can get inside?" she asked. "All of you might be immune to the cold, but I'm about to turn into an ice cube."

"Of course," Harper said. "King Alexander and Queen Deidre are waiting in the throne room. We'll bring you straight there."

She took my hands, the other two witches took Mom's and Ethan's, and the group of us teleported inside the Vale.

One moment we were in the cold mountains, and the next, we were in the palace, facing a man and a woman sitting on matching ornate thrones. They each wore golden crowns and were dressed like they were attending a black-tie affair. But judging from the more casual outfits worn by the guards and the witches, their attire wasn't the norm in the Vale.

They both stood, which caught me off guard. Because royalty didn't stand for anyone except...

"Queen Gemma," the man—King Alexander—greeted me. "Welcome to the Vale."

Royalty didn't stand for anyone except other royalty.

"King Alexander." I bowed my head slightly. "Queen Deidre."

"It's nice to meet you," Deidre said.

"And you," I replied. "This is my mom. And this..." I paused, unsure how to describe my relationship with Ethan.

My protector?

My sister's ex?

My twin flame?

"Ethan Pendragon." He stepped forward and introduced himself. "The King of Ember."

"The dragon realm," said a man standing to King Alexander's side. "Fascinating. I'm Rohan, by the way. *Prince* Rohan. Harper's boyfriend."

Harper's *boyfriend*?

I looked to her in surprise, and she smiled sheepishly.

No. Way.

Rohan was a vampire.

The supernatural women of Utopia wanted nothing to do with supernatural men.

Rohan must be *really* special to have broken down Harper's walls.

King Alexander cleared his throat, as if he were telling Rohan to mind his place. "Harper has told us much about you and your sister," he said. "But only up to the last time she saw you, when you slayed the vampire who was tracking your dragon magic."

"I know you've come here to enter the Angel Trials," Queen Deidre continued. "However, we were hoping you might stay for dinner. The demons and dark witches pose a major threat to the supernatural kingdoms, and it's important that we share as much as we can with our allies so we can all stay safe."

They wanted information.

After what had happened to Utopia, I didn't blame them. Besides, we'd need as much support as possible when it came to freeing the dragons. The more people we could get on our side, the better.

"We'd love to stay for dinner," Ethan said, apparently having the same idea.

"Wonderful." Deidre beamed. "Dinner isn't for another three hours. Perhaps you'd like a tour of the kingdom beforehand?"

"That would be lovely," I said. "But I'd like to spend some time with Harper first. As you noted, we haven't seen each other in a while. And we have a *lot* to catch each other up on."

I glanced at Rohan at that last part.

Harper's cheeks turned pink.

I never thought I'd see the day when Harper actually *blushed*.

"Of course," Deidre said. "I'll personally see to the start of your mom and King Ethan's tour. You and Harper can join us after you've convened."

"Great." Harper was by my side in a second. "I'll take you to my room."

"We'll see you girls soon," Deidre said, and then Harper grabbed my hands, and teleported us out.

16

GEMMA

"Where's Mira?" Harper asked the moment we landed in her room.

Every organ in my body collapsed at the mention of my twin's name.

"I don't know," I said helplessly, gazing around her room. It was plush, with a king-sized bed with a silk comforter on it, a sitting area for meals, and a balcony that overlooked the town.

It was the total opposite of anything in Utopia.

"What do you mean, you don't know?" she asked.

"I mean that I don't know." I sighed and sat on Harper's bed. "A lot's happened since we last saw each other."

"I can see that." She joined me on the bed, plucked a pillow from the giant pile of them against the headboard, and held it on her lap with her arms wrapped around it. "Want to start from the beginning?"

"Only if you tell me what's been going on with you, too."

"Deal," she said, and from there, we filled each other in on everything that had happened since we'd last seen each other in Lilith's lair.

"Wow," Harper said once we were both caught up on each other's lives. "That's... a lot."

"Tell me about it."

"What do you know about the Dark Objects?" she asked.

"Honestly? Not much." I frowned, since questions about the Dark Objects needed to be added to the list of things to ask Hecate.

"Then it's a good thing I've been looking into them," she said. "Well, that *Rohan* and I have been looking into them. He's been more helpful than I'd thought he'd be."

"Why have you been looking into the Dark Objects?" I asked.

"I'll tell you in a moment," she said. "But first, you need to know that just because someone is the Queen—or King—of a Dark Object, it doesn't mean they're evil."

"There are Kings of the Objects?"

"Rarely. And usually, they don't last for long. Azazel was the Dark King of Cups before Raven killed him."

"Who got the Dark Grail after him?" I asked.

"Lilith."

I sighed, since of *course* the Demon Queen was also one of the Dark Queens. Why should I have expected anything less?

"The point is that just because Mira has the Dark Crown, it doesn't mean she's gone totally dark," Harper continued. "We can still save her."

"How do you know all of this?"

"How else?" She reached for the key hanging from her necklace. "I asked Hecate."

Relief flooded my veins, since Hecate wouldn't lie.

At least, I thought she wouldn't. My gut told me to trust that what she told us from the books was what she'd actually read in them.

"We know that Lavinia took Mira," I said. "And that Lavinia's working with Lilith. The three of them have to be together."

"It would make sense," Harper agreed.

"Have you gotten any closer to figuring out the location of Lilith's lair?"

"No," she said. "I asked Hecate, but even she doesn't know. Whatever magic is hiding the lair is too strong for her to break through."

"So how are we supposed to find them?"

"By using the same technique we did in Nebraska," she said. "By getting them to come to us."

"And how do you propose we do that?"

"By finding something they need. In this case, the fourth Dark Object. The Dark Sword."

"You have it?" I looked around the room, as if she might be hiding it in a drawer or in her closet.

"Rohan and I are working on it," she said. "We were thinking we'd find it to weaken Lilith. Because if we find the Dark Sword and hide it somewhere she can't find it—someplace like Avalon—then she won't be able to get her fourth Dark Queen."

"But we can also use it to draw out Lilith."

"We can," she said, and she paused, like she didn't think I was going to like what she had to say next. "Although I think we should wait until after you've saved Selena, and after we have the dragons fighting on our side. Not like it matters what I think, since we have three—soon to be four—Holy Queens, seven vampire kingdoms, and multiple realms working together. Everyone will have a say on how to find and defeat Lilith, Lavinia, and the demons and dark witches."

"True," I said, since together, there was no reason why we shouldn't be able to defeat the demons. "But how can you know that Lilith doesn't have the Dark Sword?"

"Lavinia told me when I was transitioning into a vampire," she said. "She thought I was trapped there, so she was pretty open with information."

"So you didn't get your gift until after you completed your transition?"

"That's right."

"I'm really happy for you," I said. "I can't imagine you without your witch magic."

"Neither could I," she said. "I'd like to think I would have come to terms with it... but I don't know. I was devastated during those days in the transition when my magic was gone."

"Now you're a witch, *and* you're immortal."

"Stuck as a teenager forever." She made a face. "Just what I always wanted." Sarcasm dripped from her tone.

"It won't be that bad," I said, even though I wouldn't have wanted to be stuck as a teen forever, either. "Luckily, you don't look too young. With the right clothes and makeup, you can easily pass for in your twenties."

"That's what I keep telling myself." She pulled the pillow closer to her chest and looked around the room.

"Are you happy here?" I asked.

"Sure." She smiled, although it wasn't convincing. "Rohan's great. The other witches are warming up to me a bit, although I think it might be because Queen Deidre told them to be more welcoming. It's just…"

"You wish you were in Avalon?"

"Surprisingly, no," she said. "But I do wish I knew why I didn't pass the Angel Trials."

"You really don't remember any of it?"

"None. One moment I was walking through the portal that led to the start of the Trials, and the next I was floating in the rowboat that brought me back to the Vale."

"To the riverbank where Rohan was waiting for you." I gave her a small smile, hoping to lift her spirits at the reminder of the man she was in love with—even if she hadn't put it in those exact words.

"Yeah."

"Do you think you're here because *he's* here?"

"Of course you'd think that," she said, finally smiling again. "You've always been a hopeless romantic. Speaking of…"

"I don't want to talk about him," I said abruptly.

"Okay." She frowned, then continued, "Maybe part of the reason why I'm here is because of Rohan. He's definitely why I wouldn't want to go to Avalon anymore. But I also think I'm supposed to be working with him to research the Dark Sword. I can't explain why… but trying to find information about it *feels* right."

"Witch intuition?" I guessed.

"Maybe. Or maybe I want to feel like I have a purpose."

"You have a purpose," I said, feeling the truth of it deep in my soul. "Everyone does. Besides, I don't think a purpose is something we *have* as much as something we find inside ourselves. And if it feels right to search for the Dark Sword, then I believe you're meant to be searching for the Dark Sword."

"I just wish we could find some kind of lead," she said. "We've traced it up until the early 1900s. After that, it's like it disappeared off the face of the planet."

"Maybe that's it," I said.

"Maybe *what's* it?"

"Lilith has the dragon heart, which is how she tracked down the Dark Wand and the Dark Crown," I started. "But dragon hearts can't track outside the realm they're in."

"So the Dark Sword isn't on Earth?"

"Seems like a strong possibility. Either that, or she already has it, or someone else already has it and is protecting it with a spell that even the dragon heart can't get past."

"All good theories," she said. "I'll look into them."

"Where are you looking?"

"The Vale's library," she said. "And Hecate's. Although Rohan obviously doesn't know about Hecate's. He just thinks I'm *really* good at looking through books." She chuckled, and I did, too, since Harper had always referred to the history books we had to read for our studies in Utopia as the "boring books."

"Speaking of purposes," she said, serious again. "I have a request."

"Name it."

"I want you to bring us back in time to before Utopia was destroyed. And then I want to find Queen Elizabeth and warn her about what's going to happen, so she can make whatever preparations she needs to save my kingdom and everyone in it."

17

GEMMA

"I don't know if I can," I said, and she slumped forward slightly.

"Why?"

"Because if I do anything in the past that makes it so Mira or I don't get our Crowns—or that *any* of the Queens don't get their objects—time will reject the change. I'll come back and everything will be the same as before I left."

"But you don't *know* that saving Utopia will make it so the two of you don't get the Crowns."

"I don't. But that would be a *huge* change…"

"Can we at least try?" she asked. "For me?" Her eyes were huge and desperate, and I understood why.

If I'd lost everything, I'd do anything to get it back, too.

"Of course we can try," I said. "I just don't want you to get your hopes up."

"I understand there's a chance it might not work," she said. "But if we don't try, then there's *zero* chance it'll work."

"I know," I said. "We can try."

She smiled, looking truly happy for the first time since I'd arrived at the Vale, and then we created a plan.

It was rushed, and I doubted Time would accept such a huge change. But I was happy to see Harper happy.

"Let's go now," she said. "We have to be back before dinner. Queen Deidre *hates* when people are late."

"I can time travel, remember?" I said. "I can never be late. No matter how much time we spend in Utopia, it'll be like no time passed in the present. We'll return to the second after we left."

"Perfect," she said, and then she reached for her key and hurried to the door. She put her key in the lock and stepped through before I could say another word—like she was afraid I'd try to stop her.

I rushed into the Eternal Library right after her, glad she was still in the ivory hall when I got there.

There was also someone noticeably missing from the ivory hall—Hecate. Although I shouldn't have been surprised, given how rarely the goddess made her appearances. But still, the chance of seeing Hecate was why we always opted to go through the Library with Harper instead of teleporting to our destination.

"Before we go," I said, and I took a deep breath, unsure how to launch into what needed to be said. "Have you been to Utopia since Lavinia's attack?"

"No," she said. "Have you?"

"No. But I think we need to prepare ourselves for what we're going to see."

"The aftermath of a war zone." She straightened, her eyes hard. "I know."

"Okay. Do you want to enter via the apartment I stayed in while there?" It wasn't a question as much as a statement. Because I didn't know what would happen if we walked into Harper's house, but I couldn't imagine that seeing the place where you'd grown up in shambles would be good for anyone.

I also didn't know if there'd be remains of people who'd lived there inside.

I shuddered at the thought.

But the Nephilim and witches had done "reconnaissance" in Utopia. I hoped that meant they'd cleared out the bodies.

"My apartment was always empty during the days, since Mira and I were in our classes and Mom was working in the bakery," I added, since it was important that no one witnessed our sudden appearance.

The less we changed in the past, the better.

"Good plan," she said, and then she walked up to the door, stuck her key in it, and left the Library.

I followed at her heels.

The scene was as expected—a war zone. Tables and chairs were toppled over. The beds had been pushed aside, as if people had been searching under them. Candlesticks and books had been knocked off nightstands. The wardrobe doors were open, clothes thrown out and strewn around the rooms.

Harper looked around, her expression giving away none of her feelings. "What do we do from here?" she asked.

"I'll take your hands," I said. "It's sort of like teleporting, except we'll be traveling into the past."

"Through time," she said, mystified.

"Exactly." I walked toward her and took her hands. The Crown was already on my head, since I'd worn it to the Vale. No need to hide it in the ether when I'd been making a point of displaying my new position as Queen. "You ready?"

"I'm ready."

I closed my eyes and thought about the time we wanted to go to. The Crown warmed, we flickered a few times, and for a split-second, the ground disappeared beneath our feet.

I let go of Harper's hands and watched as she opened her eyes.

The apartment was back in perfect condition. It was empty of people, but the scent of fresh coffee lingered in the air from when the past versions of me, Mira, Ethan, and Mom had been getting ready in the morning.

"Impressive." Harper gazed around like she was in a museum.

I walked over and put on a fresh pot of coffee, since the strong smell was our best chance of hiding the fact that Harper now gave off the scents of witch *and* vampire.

"Where are your notebooks and stuff?" she asked, getting straight to business.

"I'll get it." I entered my bedroom, where a notebook was placed neatly on top of a giant history book. I picked it up, along with the pencil next to it, and brought them back to Harper.

She examined the sharpened pencil, opened the notebook, then got to writing.

Gemma and I are in her apartment. We need you to come meet us here now—it's urgent. Come alone and don't tell anyone we're here. Also, don't reply to this letter. We'll explain everything in person.

She signed it and folded it. Then she glanced at me. "You should probably take that Crown off," she said.

"Right." I'd become so used to the weight of the Crown on my head that I barely noticed it anymore. When I took it off and stored it in the ether, it was like a part of me was missing. But it was safe there. That was what mattered.

Harper placed the letter in her open palm, then engulfed it in flames. The flames died out, and the letter was gone. Not even ash remained. Because it wasn't a real fire—it was witch magic.

"How long do you think she'll be?" I asked.

"No one ever speaks to Queen Elizabeth like that," she said. "I don't imagine it'll be long."

Sure enough, Queen Elizabeth burst through the apartment door minutes later. The shrunken heads on her belt rustled against each other as she slammed the door shut. "You summoned me?" She stood tall, her nearly six-foot frame towering over us. From the edge in her tone, it was clear she was thinking that whatever we had to say better be good. Then, she froze and asked, "What are you wearing?"

"Gemma's wearing Haven whites," Harper said, even though Queen Elizabeth obviously knew what Haven whites looked like. "I'm wearing civilian clothes, as I've come from the Vale."

Elizabeth narrowed her eyes. "You left Utopia?" She sounded more shocked than anything else.

"We did."

Queen Elizabeth sucked in a long breath, as if she were trying to compose herself. "How could you be so careless?" The iciness in her tone got across one message—there *would* be consequences for this transgression. "The demons are tracking Gemma. You were responsible for keeping her here and giving her lessons to teach her how to control her magic."

"I am giving her lessons," Harper said calmly. "Right now."

"By *bringing her out of my kingdom?*"

Tense energy crackled between the two of them.

"Enough." I stepped forward to stand between them. Yes, we were going for shock value. And yes, I didn't believe anything we did here mattered, since Time would likely reject the changes we made. But it was time to get to the point. "Harper is in the meeting room giving us lessons right now," I said.

Elizabeth's expression changed from anger to confusion. "What are you talking about?"

"Go to the meeting room and check," I said. "We'll be there, in our clothes from Utopia, right now."

She eyed us. "I have guards outside the door," she said, which we knew would be the case. "If you try to leave, they'll attack."

"Understood," I said. "We're not going to leave."

She gave us one final wary look, then left the apartment.

"That went well," Harper said after the door was closed.

"You were goading her."

"I was getting her attention."

"It worked."

"It did." She was silent for a moment, then continued, "What are the chances that this'll work?"

"I have no idea," I said. "But if Elizabeth manages to protect Utopia, so much will change. Mira and I might not end up going to the Haven, which would mean we won't go to Moon Mountain, which means Hecate won't tell us how to find the Crown. Without the Crown, I won't become Queen of Pentacles. If that happens, Time will reject the change."

"But you don't know for sure if that'll happen."

"I don't. Which is why we're here, trying."

She nodded, satisfied, and together, we waited.

Soon enough, Queen Elizabeth burst into the room. Her skin paled when she saw us, like she was looking at ghosts.

She studied us for a few seconds, then said, "You both were in the meeting room practicing using your dragon magic. But you're also here."

"We are," I said.

"Who are you?"

"What do you mean?"

"It's impossible for anyone to duplicate themselves. So whoever the two of you are, you must have taken transformation potion to make yourselves look like Gemma and Harper."

I didn't answer.

Instead, I held my hands to my side and called on my dragon magic, creating an arc of fire above my head. Then I snuffed out the fire and held a hand out toward where a few crystals sat on the center of the kitchen table. I reached for them with my earth magic, and they floated up and toward us, until they hovered between us. I held them there for a few seconds, then returned them to where they'd been on the table.

"I'm the only person in the world with elemental dragon magic," I said. "Harper and I are both in the meeting room and in here with you."

"How?" she asked.

"Because I don't only have earth and fire magic." I reached into the ether, pulled out the Holy Crown, and placed it on my head. "I'm the Queen of Pentacles. And I can control the fifth element."

Her eyes widened as she gazed at the Crown. "What's the fifth element?" she asked.

"Time," I said. "The fifth element allows me to travel through time."

18

GEMMA

"Seriously?" She chuckled, then regained control of herself. "I've lived for over a thousand years. Longer than either of you could ever comprehend. I've heard a lot of stories in my days. But time travel... that's a new one."

"She's telling the truth," Harper said. "We came here from the future. That's why there are two versions of us."

"Impossible."

"I know it sounds crazy. It's easier if I show you." I held my hands out toward Queen Elizabeth. "Take my hands. It's not much different from teleporting."

She stared at my hands like they were covered in poison. "You want me to travel with you through time?"

"Is there any other way you'd believe me?"

"I don't trust it."

"I thought you didn't believe it was possible."

"Perhaps it's possible," she said. "But even if it is, it's not *natural*."

I held in a chuckle at the irony of the fact that this was being said by a supernatural vampire queen. Talk about *unnatural*.

"I'm the Queen of Pentacles," I repeated. "My magic is just as natural as the other three Queens.'"

She eyed the Crown, still not moving forward to take my hands.

I sighed at how difficult she was being, grabbed her hands, and thought, *Take us back to the present.*

I couldn't travel back in time when I was *already* back in time—I had to first return back to the present—so it was our only option.

We flickered out, then landed in the ransacked version of the apartment.

Queen Elizabeth looked around in shock. "What is this?" she asked.

"This is my present," I explained. "And *your* future."

She spun around to face me. "Why would anyone do this to your apartment?"

"It's not just my apartment," I said. "It's the entire kingdom. It's why I came back to find you. I need to tell you what happened so you can stop it."

She walked over to the door, opened it, and left the apartment. I followed her, and revulsion swirled through my stomach at the horrible sight in front of us.

The bridges that had connected the walls of the kingdom had collapsed and fallen to the bottom of the chamber, into the lake and onto the trees and restaurants on the ground floor. Doors had been broken into and left open. The crater at the top of the volcano had been blown open, allowing sunlight to stream into the silent, destroyed kingdom.

Elizabeth stood in the shadows, making sure the sun's rays didn't hit her. Then she turned around to face me, horror splattered across her face, and said, "I'm listening."

"I'll tell you everything," I said. "But I have to bring you back, and Harper and I can tell you there. We're on a bit of a time limit here in the present. Which won't be a problem if we explain in the past."

She stared at me like I'd lost my mind. "Okay," she said, and she walked forward and held her hands out, ready to leave.

I didn't take them. "I can't teleport, so we have to go back inside the apartment and leave from there," I explained. "Your guards are standing outside the door. It would alarm them if we appeared out of nowhere."

She walked back inside the apartment, saying nothing. When she turned back around to face me, she looked me up and down in approval. "I had a feeling that either you or Mira would become the final Queen," she said. "I'm glad it's you."

She held her hands out, and I brought us back to the past.

Harper was standing in the same place she'd been when we'd left, in the center of the room.

"How long were you gone?" she asked, since for her, it would have felt like a split second.

"Only a minute or two," I said. "Enough for her to see what happens."

Harper turned to Elizabeth with hope in her eyes. "You're going to stop it?"

"First, I need to know what 'it' is," she said, and we told her about the attack on Utopia, ending on her decision to remain in the throne room to face off against Lavinia and the demons, and how no one had seen her since.

She was silent as she took it all in.

"What happened after you left?" she asked. "How did you find the Crown and become the Queen of Pentacles?"

As quickly as possible, I told her about escaping to the Haven, going to Ember, finding the first half of the Crown, and then going to Antarctica to find the second half.

"There is no Queen Katherine," she said once I was finished. "Only six of us did the spell to become original vampires."

"Queen Katherine says she was there," I said. "She said she was your friend."

"No compulsion can be that powerful," she said.

"It's her vampire gift," Harper repeated. "Superior compulsion."

"Then her compulsion would have to extend far enough to make everyone who'd ever heard her name so much as whispered by people passing by forget about her—to make them believe there was an entirely different past that this Katherine wasn't a part of," Elizabeth said. "Magic that strong is as dangerous as time travel."

"My magic isn't dangerous," I said. "I'm using it to try to save your kingdom."

"It *is* dangerous," she said. "Because if we change what happens, there's no saying how the future will turn out. It could change so drastically that you don't end up getting the Holy Crown. And, like you said, we need all four Queens to rise for a chance against the demons."

"Once a Queen has a Holy or Dark Object in my present, nothing I do can change that," I explained. "If I make a change that stops one of the Queens from rising, Time will reject the change."

She nodded in approval. "All magic needs limits," she said. "Now, tell me how you think I can save my kingdom."

19

GEMMA

We returned to the present, and Harper let out an anguished cry.

The apartment was a disaster. Everything was the same as when we'd left.

Disappointment filled me to the bones. Even though I'd had a gut feeling that the change would be too huge to stick, I'd *wanted* it to work.

Then I had another idea. One that might actually have a chance of working.

"Teleport me to the throne room," I told Harper.

Before Utopia had been ransacked, there'd been a spell around the kingdom that didn't allow teleportation inside. Now that the protection dome had been destroyed, so had that spell.

Harper took my hands and brought us to the throne room.

Luckily, any bodies that had remained after the battle had been cleared during the reconnaissance mission.

Everything else was in shambles.

Rocks that had broken off from the walls and ceiling covered the floor. The bridge that had connected the entrance to the area with the throne had collapsed into the crevice below. We stood next to the stump that remained of the throne, and the bones that had made up the dragon skull above it were broken and littered around the floor surrounding it.

The place where I'd created a tunnel in the wall had been sealed shut so cleanly that no one would have known the entrance had been there. Anything less, and I was sure Lavinia would have blasted through with the Dark Wand and chased us out.

"Why did you want to come here?" Harper asked.

"Hang tight," I said. "I'll be back in a second."

I flickered out before I could overthink it, and arrived in time to see the tunnel I'd forged in the wall close up.

Good job, past Gemma.

But I had no time to admire my handywork, because chaos surrounded me. Witches stood on guard, facing the only other way out of the chamber—the tunnel I'd collapsed to hold off the demons and dark witches. Bangs echoed from the other side of it, growing louder by the second.

It wouldn't be long until they broke through.

I spun to face the throne, where I knew Queen Elizabeth would be standing.

"Gemma," she greeted me, not looking surprised to see me.

It didn't make sense.

She'd *just* seen me leave the tunnel. Shouldn't she have been confused about how I'd appeared out of nowhere?

But we had no time to waste.

So I took her hands and reached for the Crown with my magic.

Take us back to the present.

We flickered out and landed in the destroyed throne room.

Harper's mouth dropped open when she saw us. "Your Highness?" she asked, as if she didn't believe Elizabeth was real.

Elizabeth surveyed the room. Then she focused on me, her expression grim. "Take me back," she said.

"No."

"I'm the Queen of Utopia. You will return me to my present, where I will fight with my people until the end."

"They're all going to die," I said. "You're going to go missing. There's nothing you can do to save them, or to save Utopia."

"Like you said, I'll be *missing*," she said, her eyes hard. "Not dead. Only a Nephilim can kill an original vampire. You have no idea what the version of myself in your present is doing."

"We assume you were taken by Lavinia," Harper said.

"And for all you know, the present version of me could be in Lilith's lair, working to beat the demons from the inside." She remained focused on me, tall and commanding. Anyone else would have cowered in her presence. But I was a Queen. Which meant we were equals. "Take me back. *Now.*"

"How do you remember I can time travel?" I asked. "Time rejected the change we tried to make. For you, our visit in my apartment never would have happened."

She smirked knowingly. "As you said, Time would most likely have rejected the change if I'd attempted to change the future. So I had a witch create a memory potion for me. Before I drank it, I instructed her to give me the antidote this morning. The morning of the attack."

Harper clenched her fists in anger. "Why?"

"Because I wanted the future to play out as Fate intended—with Gemma finding the Holy Crown and becoming the Queen of Pentacles. I also wanted to remember everything you told me that day in the apartment, in case the knowledge came in handy later."

Harper's breathing quickened, her anger growing visibly. "You didn't even *try* to save our home?"

Elizabeth looked at her sadly, over a thousand years of wisdom shining in her gaze. "The future is what we make of it. But the past is set in stone," she said. "Anything else is unnatural. I have zero interest in messing around with Time."

"You're wrong," I said. "Fate *did* play out as intended—with me bringing you here safely."

"You speak of yourself like you're a god instead of a mortal."

"I'm not a god," I said. "But I *am* the Queen of Pentacles. The Holy Objects were created by the angels. I was gifted my magic to help us beat the demons, and we need the most powerful supernaturals fighting with us to do that. You may not trust my magic, but you don't have to. Because I'm asking you to trust *me*."

Harper moved to stand by my side. "As the Queen of Pentacles, Gemma outranks you," she said to Elizabeth. "If she feels this is the correct course of action, it's your responsibility to do as she commands."

"Is that what you're doing?" Elizabeth tilted her head, challenging me. "Are you *commanding* me?"

I exhaled and smiled slightly at such a ridiculous notion. "If you wish to return to when Lavinia attacked, I'll take you," I said, continuing before she could take me up on it. "However, it's only fair that I warn you—if you'd been successfully working behind the scenes to help us from Lilith's lair, I would have felt the timeline shift when we arrived back here. But I didn't. Which means you haven't done anything in Lilith's lair to change what's happening in the present. And while Lilith might not be able to kill you, there are fates worse than death. So I'm asking you to stay in this time and fight by our sides against the demons. Go wherever you choose—Avalon, the Haven, or the Tower for all I care. But I trust that you're strong enough and experienced enough to do as much good here as you could do there. Like you said, the future is what we make of it. So take this opportunity I've given you, and help us make our future a good one."

She was silent for a few seconds, her stone-cold expression betraying nothing.

"Well," she finally said. "Perhaps you have potential to be a strong Queen after all."

"Does that mean you'll stay?"

She paused, then smiled. "I've always been curious about what life is like on Avalon."

Joy raced through me, and I resisted the urge to jump up and hug her, since Queen Elizabeth wasn't the huggable type.

"Assuming you get through the Trials," Harper said.

"I'm a vampire queen." Elizabeth stood taller, looking every bit like the fierce warrior she was. "I'll pass the Trials."

"I thought I would, too," Harper muttered. "But life doesn't always turn out like we think it will."

"It sure doesn't," Elizabeth said. "And once we're in the Vale, I expect you to tell me how you seem to be both a witch *and* a vampire."

"When did you notice?" Harper asked.

"Back when the two of you spoke with me in Gemma's apartment. Did you really think the smell of *coffee* would cover up your vampire scent?"

"It was worth a try." She shrugged.

"It might have worked on someone with weaker senses," Elizabeth said. "But you should know I'm stronger than that."

"Of course." Harper lowered her eyes in apology. "We were short on time, so we couldn't come up with a better plan."

"Go figure. A time traveler short on time."

"My magic has limitations," I explained. "I'll tell you more about it later. But first, there's something else we still have to do here."

"What's that?" she asked.

I turned to Harper and said, "I hope you know where your mom was when Utopia was breached. Because I want you to take me there."

20

GEMMA

WE STOPPED BACK in my apartment so I could change into clothes that I'd worn in Utopia, then Harper teleported us one at a time to the tunnel that led to what remained at the apothecary.

An entire magma chamber had been dedicated to the apothecary, where the most powerful witches in Utopia had created potions and spelled objects to use both inside the kingdom and for outside trade. Now, broken glass littered the floor, and the shelves had been swept clean.

We walked into the tunnel that led from the main cavern to the apothecary, since appearing in the shadows brought far less questions than popping into the center of a busy room.

"You shouldn't do this," Elizabeth warned. "You've already messed with the past far more than you should have."

"I'm the Queen of Pentacles," I said. "And I can 'mess with the past' however I see fit."

I reached for my magic and connected it with the Crown. *Take me back to five minutes before Utopia's dome is breached*, I thought, and then I flickered out.

Someone walked into my shoulder with enough force to push me against the wall. A witch with brown hair and plain features who I hadn't met before.

"Sorry," she apologized, a hint of annoyance in her tone. "I didn't see you there."

Still facing the wall, I ripped the Crown off my head and stored it in the ether. Then I turned around and gave her a polite smile. "No worries. It happens."

Her mouth dropped open. "You're one of the twins."

"I'm Gemma," I said. "I'm here to speak with Tanya. Do you know where I can find her?"

"Probably at her station," she said, jittery, as if she was meeting a celebrity. "I'm Fiona—one of the assistants at the apothecary. I'll bring you there."

She walked me through the apothecary, which was brimming with life. Large potted plants sat on the floors, smaller ones were in the shelves alongside books, crystals and other witchy items, and others hung from the ceiling. They were all different colors and smelled like a variety of herbs. About ten large tables that reminded me of the ones from science classes at school were placed throughout the chamber, and a few witches stood at each one, brewing potions and casting spells on the crystals.

Fiona led me to a table in the center, where three witches were working. They were so consumed in their work that none of them glanced up.

"Where's Tanya?" she asked.

"She's making a delivery in the saloon," the silver-haired witch closest to her said, not looking up from the potion she was brewing.

"Tannen's?" I asked, recalling the name of the bar Benjamin had taken me to on our date.

That felt like it had been *forever* ago.

"The one and only."

"Thanks." With no time to waste, I spun around, ran out of the chamber and down the tunnel, and stopped at the first door I found—the entrance to one of the restaurants in the main cavern. I used my key and stepped into the Library's ivory hall. I didn't bother checking for Hecate before turning back around and opening the door again.

I entered the saloon through the swinging wooden doors and breathed out a sigh of relief when I saw Tanya sitting at the bar as the bartender—Clara—poured her some whiskey. Tanya looked like I imagined Harper would look in twenty-five years, if Harper hadn't been made immortal when she'd been turned into a vampire. Clara's boyfriend Emmett sat next to Tanya, examining the vials of potion she'd brought over. With his silver hair sticking out in all directions, he looked like some sort of mad scientist.

It was morning, and the bar was far from one of the most popular places in Utopia, so they were the only ones inside.

All of them looked to me when I entered.

"Gemma?" Tanya squinted, as if she wasn't seeing me correctly. "Aren't you supposed to be in the queen's chamber demonstrating your magic?"

"I am."

"So what are you doing here?"

"It's a long story, and I don't have time to explain." I hurried toward her, removed the Holy Crown from the ether, and placed it on my head. "Short version—I'm the Queen of Pentacles, and I'm here to save your life."

Tanya silenced at the sight of the Crown.

I grabbed her hands, and we flickered out and landed in the present.

The saloon wasn't in nearly as bad shape as my apartment and the apothecary. I supposed the demons weren't interested in whiskey. Even the glass Tanya had been drinking from still sat on the bar, nearly full, with dust covering its rim. The only signs that something bad had happened here were the upended tables and knocked-over chairs.

Tanya looked around in shock. "What's this?" she asked.

"I'll explain in a second," I said. "Be right back."

I flickered back to the moment after I'd left. Emmett and Clara were staring at the spot where Tanya and I had disappeared.

Clara hopped over the bar, fangs bared. "What did you do with her?" she asked.

"I saved her life. And I'm about to save yours, too."

THE DRAGON SCORNED

I reached for her and brought her to the present, dropping her off next to Tanya. Then I went back and did the same for Emmett.

The three of them stood shoulder to shoulder, on guard, facing me.

"You said you'd explain in a second," said Tanya. "Now—explain."

"In about ten minutes, Lavinia was going to use the Dark Wand to break through Utopia's boundary dome," I said. "She, the demons, and other dark witches destroyed Utopia and everyone in it. By bringing you here, I saved your lives."

"Great Scott," Emmett said, his eyes wider than what should have been physically possible. "Did you bring us into the future?"

"Forty-five days into the future, to be exact," I said. "Well, it's the future for *you*. It's my present."

Tanya walked over to the bar and picked up the glass she'd been drinking from earlier. She ran a finger over the dusty rim, then placed it back down. "How's it possible?" she asked.

"The Holy Crown gifted me with power over the fifth element," I said. "Time."

"Are you saying that the Holy Crown is a *time machine?*" Emmett asked.

"Sort of. I guess it's a time machine that only I can use. And it's not a machine. It's magic."

"How does it work? How far back can you go? Can you go to the future? How many people can—"

"I'll answer all your questions when I can." I held a hand up to stop him from asking more. "But we don't have time for that right now."

"You're a time traveler," he said. "Shouldn't you have all the time in the world?"

"You'd think. But it doesn't exactly work like that."

"You need to go back," Tanya said suddenly. "Harper was in the throne room. You need to rescue her, too."

"Harper's fine," I said. "A few of us escaped before Lavinia could get to us."

"How could you *escape?*" Tanya's eyes narrowed, skeptical. "There's only one way out of Utopia—through the top crater. The throne room is about as far from there as you can get."

"I used my earth magic to get us out. We went to the Haven, and Mary took us in. A lot's happened in the past forty-five days."

"Like you finding the Holy Crown and becoming the Queen of Pentacles."

"Yep."

"Forty-five days," Tanya repeated. "Harper thought I was gone that entire time."

"You *were* gone." I used the same terminology she had, since it sounded better than saying she'd been *dead*. "All three of you."

"Why did you save us?" Clara asked.

"I did it for Harper," I said. "And since the two of you were also there, I figured, why not?"

"Thank you." She bowed her head. "I'll be forever in your debt."

"Don't say that to a Queen," Tanya chided. "She might hold you to it."

"I saved you because I wanted to," I said. "None of you owe me anything. But Harper's waiting in the apothecary—"

Tanya ran out of the swinging doors before I could finish my sentence, and she gasped at the sight of the ransacked city.

I followed behind her. "None of the spells that were around Utopia are still working," I said. "You can teleport to her. But first, you should know—"

355

She disappeared, cutting me off *again*.

Clara and Emmett joined me in the open hall.

"How are we supposed to get to the apothecary?" Clara asked. "The bridges are all destroyed, and I wouldn't trust the elevators, if they're still there. The only way out of here is by teleporting."

Of course, that wasn't true. But they wouldn't understand it if I told them my *special* way to get around.

"Wait here," I said, already reaching for the key around my neck. "I'll figure it out."

I walked back over to the swinging doors, stuck the key into a hole that didn't exist until the key was inches away from doors, and stepped into the Eternal Library.

21

GEMMA

Hecate wasn't there.

I stared at the door.

Where to from here?

I didn't want to interrupt Harper's reunion with her mom. They could teleport back to the Vale with Queen Elizabeth when they were ready.

But I needed to get Clara and Emmett to safety. And, given that Emmett was human, there was only one kingdom where he'd be safe.

First, I removed the Crown and put it back in the ether. Then I stepped back through the doors of the Library and into the tearoom at the Haven.

Raven stood in the center of the room, her arms crossed over her chest, looking furious. "Seriously?" she said when she saw me. "You're the Queen of Pentacles and you didn't tell me?"

Crap.

She was right.

"Sorry," I said. "Things have been crazy since getting back. Mira... well, she's missing."

"I know all about Mira and the Dark Crown," she said. "Mary caught me up on everything."

"She's the one who told you I'm the Queen of Pentacles."

"Nope. That was Genevieve. Who, by the way, looks an awful lot like her great-great-great whatever granddaughter, Geneva. I don't trust her. I know Geneva went out like a hero, but she was *not* one of the good guys. I know better than anyone, since I had the privilege of being kept prisoner by her for weeks."

"I know," I said, since I'd learned all about that in my studies about the Queens. "But Genevieve isn't Geneva. Did she tell you how I got the Holy Crown?"

"She told me everything," Raven said. "She introduced me to Queen Katherine, too. I don't trust either of them."

"I wouldn't have the Holy Crown if it wasn't for them."

"I still don't trust them."

I shrugged, since there was no point in arguing, given how stubborn Raven was once she'd convinced herself of something.

"I can't stay for long," I said. "I need to get to Avalon."

"Took you long enough."

"I still need to go through the Angel Trials," I said. "But I just got back from a mission in Utopia. I need two witches to go there—to a bar called Tannen's Saloon. There's a vampire and a human waiting there who need to be teleported here."

"They've been surviving in the ruins for that long?"

"Not exactly." I pointed to my head, even though the Crown wasn't on it. "Time travel. Remember?"

"Time travel makes my head spin," she said.

"I went back to right before Lavinia attacked Utopia," I said, and I filled her in from there.

"I can get two witches to them," Raven said once I was done. "But first, can I see the Crown?"

"Of course." I pulled the Crown out of the ether and handed it to her.

She held it up to the light and studied it. "My mom will love this," she said. "She's into crystals and stuff. You'll meet her in Avalon."

"Assuming I pass the Angel Trials."

"You're one of the Holy Queens." She handed me back the Crown, and I placed it in the ether. "You'll pass."

I nodded, since I figured the same. I just didn't want to get too cocky about it, given what had happened to Harper.

"You *need* to pass," she continued. "So you can save Selena."

"Did you know her well?" I asked.

"I only knew her as Jacen and Annika's daughter, back when she had no magic. But she was a kid, so it wasn't like I hung out with her. Then, after she returned from the Otherworld, she disappeared to try to rescue Torrence. And we know how that ended. So I never got to know her after she became the Queen of Wands."

"After I fix this, you won't remember never knowing her," I said.

She frowned. "My memories will be erased?"

"Not erased," I said. "Another timeline will replace this one. A timeline where Selena didn't die. Everything from that moment on will be different."

"So I'll be a different person."

"You'll be the same." I had no way of knowing if that was true, but it was what I needed to say to make her comfortable, and I didn't want to get in a fight about this. "Your life will have been different these past few months, but everything that will happen in the new timeline will be real."

"And what happens to this timeline?"

"I think it disappears."

"You *think?*"

"I only got my magic recently." The days were blurring together, since time no longer passed the same way for me that it did for everyone else. "I don't have all the answers about how it works."

Add "what happens to the previous timelines" to the list of questions for Hecate, I thought.

"But Selena will be alive," I continued. "And that's what matters."

"Yes," she said, although she bit her lower lip, still looking troubled. "I suppose so."

"Anyway, I need to get back to the Vale," I said. "Sorry I couldn't stay long. King Alexander and Queen Deidre are insisting on having dinner with me, Ethan, and my mom before we enter the Angel Trials. You'll send those witches to Utopia?"

"On it," she said. "Then I'm getting back to Avalon. I'll be waiting for you on the dock when you arrive." She paused, then asked, "How are you getting back to the Vale?"

"I have my ways," I said, and then I reached for my key, stepped through the door, and entered Hecate's Eternal Library.

Hecate wasn't there, so I turned around and went back to the Vale. Since I'd been in Harper's room when I'd left, that was where I arrived.

Harper, Tanya, and Elizabeth were all there. Harper's eyes were rimmed with red—she'd been crying.

"Where did you go?" she asked.

"The Haven," I said. "They're sending witches to bring Clara and Emmett there."

"Good." Tanya nodded. "That'll be a good place for them to stay."

"So..." I took a deep breath and looked around at the group. "I guess I'm going to have to tell the others that I went back in time and saved your lives."

"Don't look so worried," Elizabeth said. "You're a Queen. You don't need permission to do anything."

"Weren't you just telling me that you think my power's unnatural?"

"I still think that," she said. "But it's yours to use how you see fit. Don't let the others control you. Make sure not to lose their respect."

"I won't," I said. "But like you said—I'm a Queen. I'm going to be working *with* the other Queens. I'll try to run it by them before I make any big changes to history."

Except that they won't know when I make changes. Maybe there will be things they don't need to know?

I'd deal with it later.

"You're going to make a great Queen," Harper said. "I can feel it."

"I hope so."

"Where's Queen Deidre?" Elizabeth asked. "I should make my arrival in her kingdom known as soon as possible."

"It's not just her kingdom," Harper said. "It's King Alexander's, too."

"Of course." Elizabeth brushed it off, clearly not wanting to acknowledge the male supernatural who also ruled the Vale.

"They're giving my mom and Ethan a tour," I said, and my chest tightened the moment I said Ethan's name.

He was *not* going to be happy when he learned that I went back to Utopia and traveled back in time without him.

But like Elizabeth had said, *I* was the Queen of Pentacles. And while I did intend to work with the other Queens, I didn't need permission to use my power.

"Let's head to the throne room," Harper said. "I'll send the king and queen a fire message to have them meet us there."

22

GEMMA

As expected, Ethan was *not* happy when he heard about my side trip to Utopia.

"What were you *thinking?*" he said for the third time. "You could have died."

I didn't bother responding, since I'd already told him that I'd been thinking that I could save lives—and that I'd succeeded.

"Let's consider it a warm-up for saving Selena," Harper said.

Ethan glared at me. "You should have taken me with you."

"You would have tried to convince me not to go," I said. "We didn't have time for that."

"Enough," Elizabeth said. "What's done is done. Gemma saved me—the Queen of Utopia. She should be rewarded for her actions, not chided. She's the Queen of Pentacles. She needs permission from no one to use her magic."

"She's my twin flame," Ethan said, and chills ran up and down my arms when he said it. *Excited* chills. He turned to me and continued, "Promise me you'll let me know before you do something like that again."

"I can't do that."

"Why not?"

"Because there's no saying where I'll be when I need to travel."

He sucked in a long breath, exhaling slowly as he gathered his thoughts. "Then promise me you'll try."

I pressed my lips together, saying nothing.

"The two of you can continue this conversation in private," Queen Deidre said, her stern tone making it clear that she didn't have time to listen to our quarrel. "Elizabeth and Tanya—would you also like to try to go to Avalon?"

"Yes," Elizabeth said.

"No." Tanya stood proudly next to Harper. "I'm staying with my daughter."

"Very well," said Deidre. "Dinner will be ready soon. There's much we want to learn from Gemma before her departure to Avalon. Let's eat, and then we'll send you on your way."

We filled the others in on everything during the multi-course meal. They were interested in how my magic worked, and I told them everything I knew.

"How do you know that eating the mana will heal the Crown and allow you to travel further back in the past?" Deidre asked.

"I went to Hecate's Eternal Library. She looked up my question and gave me the answer."

Queen Deidre blinked, then smiled blankly. "Wonderful," she said. "I'm happy to hear you have that covered."

Harper smirked at how easily what I'd said had been accepted by the queen.

"Do they truly not have actual food on Avalon?" Mom asked after we finished dessert.

"That's what those who have been there say," Deidre said. "The mana tastes like any food you desire."

"So there's no need to cook."

"Avalon's focus is on training warriors," Elizabeth said. "The fewer other tasks to focus on, the better."

Mom frowned, clearly troubled. I understood why—one of her greatest passions in life was baking the pastries in the café. She loved creating new recipes. Baking had been her job in Utopia, too.

A life without baking would be the same thing to her as a life without reading would be to me.

Meaning, it would be totally and completely unacceptable.

"You're welcome to stay the night," Deidre said once we'd finished the meal. "However, I understand if you want to start the Angel Trials as soon as possible. I assume you're anxious to get to Avalon."

"We are," I said, although I glanced at Harper, sad to be leaving her again.

"We'll see each other again soon," she promised.

"How do you know that?"

"I just do."

I smiled, since I knew what witch intuition felt like. Plus, I eventually expected an update from her about the location of the Dark Sword.

"Also, now you've been to the Vale," she continued. "You can use your key to visit whenever you want. Just don't come *straight* into my room. I'd appreciate if you knocked first."

Pink crept into her cheeks, and I had a feeling I knew what she was thinking—she didn't want me walking in on her and Rohan.

As always when we mentioned the keys, it was like the others hadn't heard anything she'd said.

"I'll call for Prince Rohan now," Deidre said. "And he'll take you straight to the start of the Trials."

Rohan entered the room, and Harper jumped in to letting him know how we'd saved her mom and Elizabeth.

"I have so much to catch my mom up on about what's happened since I got to the

Vale," she said, and the undertone was clear—she didn't want Rohan acting familiar with her until she had a chance to tell her mom about him.

Knowing how the women of Utopia viewed supernatural men, I knew that wasn't going to be an easy conversation. But hopefully her mom would come around and be as happy for Harper as I was.

Rohan escorted me, Ethan, Mom, and Elizabeth down the dark, spiral staircase and to the portal that led to the start of the Angel Trials. Elizabeth stayed as far away from Rohan as possible, as if his pores leaked poison.

"This is where I leave you," he said. "I wish you the best of luck."

"Thanks," I said, and I looked nervously to my mom.

"Don't worry about me." She smiled, pride shining in her eyes. "The Haven has felt like home to me ever since we arrived. If I fail the Trials, I'll return there."

"You're not going to fail the Trials," I said, although the words felt hollow as I spoke them.

"I'm going to try my hardest," she said. "But if I don't pass, then you know where to find me."

I nodded, since I trusted she'd be safe in the Haven. Plus, with the key, I'd be able to visit her whenever I wanted.

I faced the glowing portal and took a deep breath, knowing so much was at stake once I started the Trials.

"Can we go through together?" I asked Rohan.

"One by one," he said. "Who wants to go first?"

"Me," Ethan said, and before any of us could argue, he stepped through the portal, and was gone.

I knew why he'd done it—he didn't want me being on the other side without him there to protect me.

Elizabeth went through next, then my mom, and then I stepped through the bright, glowing light, ready to face whatever waited on the other side.

23

GEMMA

When I awoke, I felt like I was waking up from being knocked out with tranquilizer. My body felt heavy, and my lids didn't want to open. Sunlight bathed me with warmth, calming me so I didn't panic.

Flashes of a dream passed through my mind—a beach surrounded by cliffs, a cave, rolling hills, a dark forest, and a castle in the sky. I'd done something in all those places, but I couldn't remember exactly *what* I'd done. The more I came to, the more the dreams slipped away.

From the light rocking motion, I could tell that I was in some sort of boat. My stomach cramped with nausea, and I groaned. The rocking was barely there, but even that was enough to affect my motion sickness.

The heaviness left my body, and I opened my eyes and pushed myself up.

I was in a rowboat, floating toward a cove of bright blue water. An island with mountains covered with lush greenery surrounded the cove. Puffy white clouds filled the sunny sky, and it was that perfect temperature where you couldn't feel the weather.

Queen Elizabeth was in an identical boat ahead of me, and Ethan was in one behind me. Both of them looked dazed, as if they'd both also woken up from a heavy sleep.

Ethan pulled off the bedhead look like he was a male model getting ready for a photoshoot. But I barely paid him any attention. Because Mom wasn't there. I twisted around, searching for another boat with her in it, but there was no sign of one.

I'd known there was a chance she wouldn't make it to Avalon. I'd tried to prepare myself for it. But I'd wanted to be wrong.

Any hope that Avalon might be a place I'd call home vanished. How could I feel at home in a place my mom couldn't visit?

The boat drifted into an inlet, now so close to Elizabeth and Ethan's boats that the front and back of mine nearly touched theirs. It was like we were on a ride in an amusement park.

Bright green grass grew on both sides of the inlet, and trees with strange white fruit dangling from their thick branches lined the fields. Fae with bright, sparkling wings hung around the trees, picking the fruit and placing it in woven baskets.

At the sight of us, the fae rushed forward and gathered by the riverbank. They frowned as we floated by, then turned around and resumed their jobs of picking the fruit from the trees.

"Don't look too happy to see us," Elizabeth muttered.

As we moved down the river, the fae continued to run to get a good look at us. All of them were disappointed when they got a good view.

"You okay?" Ethan asked from behind me.

I didn't need to ask to know he was referring to the fact that my mom wasn't with us.

"I'm fine," I lied.

We turned around a corner, into a tunnel carved into one of the tallest mountains. Water dripped from the stone, and fire lit the torches along the walls. It should have felt ominous, but somehow, it didn't.

We must have been deep inside the mountain when we turned another corner and floated toward a dock. As promised, Raven waited for us on it. A broad-shouldered man with shaggy brown hair stood next to her, holding her hand. Raven looked up at him and smiled. She seemed happier than I'd ever seen her.

Our boats stopped at the dock, lined up with the fronts of them touching it.

"Congrats on passing the Angel Trials," Raven said. "Welcome to Avalon."

"Thank you." Queen Elizabeth stepped out of her boat and onto the dock with no hesitation. The shrunken heads around her belt rustled against each other, and while the man standing next to Raven glanced at them, he didn't acknowledge them beyond that.

Ethan also stepped out of his boat, then he turned around and offered me his hand.

I took it on instinct, and his grip tightened around mine as he helped me out, as if he was worried I'd pull away.

Which was exactly what I did the moment both of my feet were on the dock.

He frowned, but said nothing.

The warmth that had rushed through me at his touch disappeared. Instinct urged me to reach for his hand again, but I resisted.

"I'd like to introduce you to my mate." Raven smiled again at the man next to her, then refocused on us. "This is Noah."

"Welcome," he said simply.

"This is Queen Elizabeth of Utopia," Raven continued the introductions. "King Ethan Pendragon of Ember. And the Queen of Pentacles, Gemma Brown."

"Good thing I'm getting used to being surrounded by royalty," Noah said, sharing another knowing look with Raven.

It was like the two of them could read each other's minds.

Then I remembered what I'd learned about shifters and their mate bonds. They felt each other's feelings and could *actually* send thoughts to one another.

I was grateful that dragons were an entirely different species than the shifters on Earth. My feelings for Ethan were too intense and confusing for even me to handle. I did *not* want to share my emotions and thoughts with him.

"You're basically royalty yourself, being the alpha of our pack and all," Raven said.

He shrugged, as if being a pack alpha didn't mean much to him.

"Sorry about your mom," Raven said to me. "She'll be well taken care of in the Vale."

"She's going back to the Haven," I said.

"She fits in nicely there."

"She does."

"What do you remember of the Trials?" Raven asked.

I pressed my lips together and tilted my head as I searched through my memories. I knew I'd remembered a bit when I'd first woken up, but now it was fuzzy.

"Nothing," I said, and Ethan and Elizabeth agreed.

"We don't remember much from our Trials, either," Raven said. "No one else has ever remembered anything. But I always ask, just in case."

"How long were we gone?" Ethan asked.

"Only a day. Sometimes the Trials are longer, sometimes shorter. Yours was on the shorter end."

One day. Which meant it was now five days since Mira went missing. Well, five days in the present. Because of my time traveling, I'd lived more than five days during that time. But my mind was spinning far too much by this point to attempt to calculate exactly how much time had passed for me since I'd received my time travel ability.

"The fae watched us as we sailed in," Elizabeth said. "Why?"

"As you know, the Otherworld has been destroyed by the infected fae," Raven said. "The Nephilim are doing our best to search the Otherworld and rescue any fae or halfbloods that have been hiding out. From there, the fae have been entering the Angel Trials. Whenever newcomers come in, the fae hope to see the faces of family and friends who went missing in the Otherworld."

"Which explains why they looked disappointed to see us," Elizabeth said.

"Exactly," she said. "Anyway, Annika wants me to bring Gemma and Ethan to her as soon as possible. Elizabeth, you'll be going with Noah. He'll take you to orientation."

Elizabeth looked at Noah and frowned. "I'll be going with a wolf." The name of his species sounded like a dirty word when she said it.

"I don't bite." Noah smirked. "At least, not when unprovoked."

Raven gave him a warning glare. "We have no prejudices on Avalon," she said to Elizabeth. "All species—and genders—are treated equally. Will that be a problem for you?"

Elizabeth paused, and I worried she was going to say yes and turn around.

"I suppose I'll have to learn to deal with it," she said instead.

"Given that you passed the Angel Trials, I'm sure you'll be able to adjust," Raven said. "Your first chance to do that is now, with Noah. The mages are waiting for you in the orientation room so they can answer as many of your questions as possible."

"I'll have many," she said.

"I expected no less." Raven let go of Noah's hand, gave him a quick kiss, and then Noah took Elizabeth up winding stone steps to the right.

"She's tough," Raven said once they were gone. "Good call rescuing her from Utopia. She'll make a fantastic addition to Avalon's army."

"It was a dangerous call to go back and save her, given that it was during Lavinia's attack," Ethan said.

"Danger is part of being a Queen," Raven said. "It took Noah some time to get used to my running into danger, too. But I was always destined to become the Queen of Swords. He knows I can handle my job."

"Selena was destined to become a Queen, too," Ethan said. "And look how that ended up for her."

We all silenced at the reminder of Selena's death.

"It's going to end up fine for her," I said. "Because we're going to save her."

"Yes, you are." Raven forced brightness into her tone that sounded like desperate hope more than true faith. "Now, come with me. Because there's someone you need to meet."

24

GEMMA

Raven brought us up another set of steps that led into the first floor of what looked like a medieval castle. The halls were huge, with wood floors and giant tapestries hanging on the stone walls.

I would have thought we'd traveled back in time, if it wasn't for the everyday clothing and black Avalon Army jumpsuits worn by the people passing by. They parted to the sides to make way for Raven, watching me and Ethan with curiosity and excitement.

Raven led us up more stairs, to an empty hall on the third floor. We walked all the way to the end, and she knocked on a huge, rounded door.

A woman with hair the same shade of red as Raven's entered. Their features were so similar that it was clear she was Raven's mother.

Skylar Danvers. The vampire prophetess who could use tarot cards to see the future.

"This is my mom," Raven said what I'd already guessed. "Mom, this is Gemma and Ethan."

We all said hello, and then Raven's mom opened the door more for us to come in. We turned into a living room where two people waited on a sofa across from a fireplace. The man was a vampire with dark hair and strong features, and the woman had long brown hair and golden eyes. There were circles under both of their eyes—they looked worn out and exhausted.

Since only angels had completely golden eyes, she had to be the Earth Angel—the Queen of Cups, Annika Pearce. I assumed the vampire sitting next to her was her husband, Jacen.

They stood when they saw us, and when her golden eyes met mine, hope flickered through them.

Without any warning, she ran toward me and engulfed me in a huge hug.

"Is it true?" she asked when she pulled back, her eyes glazed with tears. "You can save Selena?"

"I'll do my absolute best," I promised.

She nodded, as if she had no doubt that my "absolute best" meant Selena would be saved.

The man walked forward to stand by her side. "I'm Jacen," he introduced himself. "This is my wife, Annika."

"Hi," I said. "I'm Gemma."

"And I'm Ethan," he said. "The King of Ember."

"Thank you for protecting Gemma all this time," said Annika.

"I'd do anything to keep her safe."

I stilled at how *sure* he sounded. And I knew he meant it. So why hadn't he been honest with me and Mira from the start? It would have saved us both an incredible amount of heartbreak.

"Where's the Holy Crown?" Jacen asked.

"Oh, right." I pulled it out of the ether and placed it on my head. I was always surprised by how light and comfortable it was.

"It doesn't look broken," he said.

"It was split into two when we found it. Even though it was welded together, it's apparently still broken on the inside."

"Mary filled us in on everything," Annika said. "We have mana ready for you so you can fix the Crown."

She led the way to the small dining table. It looked like it would comfortably seat four people, but it had six chairs crowded around it. The glasses of water were full, and a dish of the strange white fruit I'd seen growing from Avalon's trees sat in the center of the table.

Annika sat down first, and the rest of us followed.

She motioned to the white fruit. "Help yourself."

I reached for a piece of fruit—it was about the size of a mango—and placed it on my plate.

They all watched me expectantly. None of them took a piece of their own.

Was I supposed to pick it up and take a bite, or use a fork and knife?

Since there were place settings, I picked up the fork and knife, cut into it, and took a bite.

It tasted like my favorite grilled cheese sandwich from the café—butter, grease, and all.

I ate until the fruit was gone. No one else was eating—they all watched me, like they were waiting for me to sprout wings or grow a second head at any moment.

I didn't sprout wings. Or grow a second head. But warmth filled my body, my head tingled, and white light glowed through the room.

It came from the Crown.

The light eventually died down, and the Crown buzzed with energy unlike I'd ever felt from it before.

Annika leaned forward eagerly. "Well?"

"I think it worked," I said.

"You *think?*"

"I'd have to test it out to know for sure."

"All right." She gazed out the window at the lush fields and mountains, then turned back to me. "Seventeen years ago, Jacen and I came to Avalon for the first time. Go back to before then and tell us what you see."

THE DRAGON SCORNED

I closed my eyes and thought, *Take me back to a few days before Annika and Jacen arrived on Avalon.*

I opened my eyes in time to see the room flicker out around me—and to see Ethan's angry gaze. He reached for me, but I was gone before he could touch me.

The tapestries on the walls disappeared, and I fell through the chair, my butt hitting the cold stone floor.

"Ow," I said, even though no one was there to hear me.

I stood and looked around, rubbing my tail bone to ease the pain. I'd fallen onto the floor because there *was* no chair. There was no furniture at all. It was just a cold, empty room—a ruined castle. The fireplace was caved in. A gaping space remained where the door had been, leading out into the equally ruined hall. It smelled musty, and a nearly suffocating humidity blanketed my skin.

I walked to the window and looked outside. Gone were the lush fields and mountains. The trees and grass were brown and dead. The overcast sky let no sunshine through, and the water in the cove was dark, murky blue. There were no signs of life anywhere.

It was like I'd gone back centuries—not seventeen years.

But the Crown always listened to my instructions. Which meant Avalon had been in shambles before Annika and Jacen had arrived.

Or maybe, now that I'd eaten the mana, the Crown was too powerful for me to handle. Maybe it *had* taken me back centuries.

I shivered at the possibility.

Take me back to the present, I thought, and the dead island flickered out, replaced by the lush, sunny place I'd originally arrived. The uncomfortable humidity disappeared, and I could breathe again.

I spun around, glad to find the room furnished as before, with a welcoming fire in the mantle. It burned taller at my presence.

The others watched me expectantly. Only a split second had passed for them, so it had appeared like I'd teleported from sitting at the chair to standing by the window.

Ethan stood and gripped the back of his chair. "You should have taken me with you."

"I was fine," I snapped, since after everything he'd done to me, I had zero need or desire to defend my actions to him.

The fire crackled, like it was reacting to the anger inside him. Or inside me. Or both.

"What did you see?" Annika asked.

"It worked," I said. "But either Avalon was in complete ruins right before you arrived, or the Crown accidentally took me back centuries."

She sighed in relief. "Avalon was dead when we first got here," she said.

"How did it change so quickly?"

"When I arrived, I signed a contract, promising myself as the leader of Avalon," she said. "I signed it with my blood. Immediately after the contract was signed, the island bloomed with life, and the castle restored itself. But all magic comes from somewhere. By using my blood to revitalize Avalon, I bound myself to the island. My life force is the heart of the island—it's what keeps Avalon alive. It's why I can never leave."

"What would happen if you tried?"

"I'd be breaking the contract, and Avalon would revert to the way it was before I'd arrived."

I nodded, feeling bad for her. Avalon was paradise, but in a way, it was also Annika's prison.

"Don't look so sad," she said. "I knew what I was getting into when I signed the contract. I'm blessed to provide a safe place for the supernaturals that's safe from the demons. A place that allows us to be the best versions of us we can be. But without Selena here..." She shrugged and trailed off, then snapped back to attention. "It doesn't matter. Because now that you can travel back further than the past few months, you can save her and bring her home."

"I'm going to do my absolute best," I reminded her. "But to do that, I'll need help."

"I'll give you anything you need."

"Then I need you to send for Torrence. Because if anyone can help me strategize about how to save Selena, it's her best friend."

25

GEMMA

We spent the rest of the day brainstorming. The tricky part was that we had to figure out the *exact* right time to travel back to, and the right way to do it, to make as little impact on anything else in the future.

There were a few possibilities, but Torrence was adamant about which one she thought would work the best. So we decided to trust her judgement.

Eventually, we grew so tired that we were going over the same things over and over again without being productive. So we called it a night.

Annika looked warily between me and Ethan. "Do the two of you want shared quarters?"

"No," I said, even though the thought of sharing a bed with Ethan caused a pleasant warmth to bloom in my stomach.

Life would be so much easier if the mere thought of him didn't make my body react the way it did.

"I'd like our rooms to be next to one another," Ethan said.

"No problem," Annika said, and she showed Ethan to the room across from hers, and me to the one next to his. He walked with us as she showed me my room, making sure our rooms were as close as possible. "There are clothes in the wardrobes—enough sizes that you'll be able to find things that fit—and the bathrooms are stocked with all the necessities," Annika said. "Is there anything else I can get you?"

"This is great," I said, since the rooms were fit for royalty. "Thanks."

"See you tomorrow."

"See you." I walked inside and closed the door before Ethan had a chance to say anything to me.

I took a quick shower, changed into the world's most comfortable pajamas, used my magic to light the fireplace, then collapsed into the king-sized, canopy bed. I tossed the decorative pillows to the floor, snuggled under the thick comforter, and started to drift asleep to the soothing sound of the fire crackling.

Then the door creaked open.

Not the door leading to the hall, but the one to my bathroom.

My eyes snapped open, and I watched Ethan step through.

That was why he'd wanted to check out my room.

He wanted to be able to use his key to get inside.

Quickly, I closed my eyes and rolled over. If I pretended to already be asleep, maybe he wouldn't bother me.

"Gemma," he said softly. "I know you're awake."

I rolled over, sighed, and opened my eyes. He was standing next to my bed, watching me, waiting for me to react.

"What do you want?" I asked.

"You've been ignoring me for days," he said. "We need to talk."

"I don't want to talk. I need to sleep."

"And I need you to hear me out."

Anger rushed through me at his insistent tone, and I pushed myself up in bed, no longer tired. "We have a long day tomorrow, and I need to sleep to make sure I'm as alert as possible," I said. "Unless you don't care if demons capture me, like they did with Mira?"

I regretted the words the moment they came out of my mouth, especially given his pained expression.

"Sorry," I said. "I didn't mean that."

"I know." He tentatively moved forward and sat on the edge of the bed, leaving about a meter between the two of us. "But you have every right to hate me after what happened."

"I don't *hate* you," I said. "I'm just..." I paused, searching for a way to express the inner turmoil that had been storming inside me ever since Mira had attacked me with her magic and left the Seventh Kingdom. "We need to get her back."

"We will," he said, even though there was no way he could promise that. Still, it helped to know that he believed it was possible.

"I'm not ready to talk about what happened," I said. "We have to focus on saving Selena. To do that, I need sleep."

"You're a time traveler," he said. "We can go back in time, get as much sleep as we need, then come back fully rested. There's no reason to be deprived of sleep ever again."

"I know." I'd already thought of that. I just wanted him out of my room before he could launch into a conversation where he tried to get me to understand why he'd lied to me and Mira.

Deep down, I wanted to understand why he'd done it more than anything. He was my twin flame. I wanted to let him in, to love him fully and completely.

But what if his explanation wasn't good enough? What if I could never forgive him?

The possibility of having to reject the one person in this world who was supposed to be my perfect match tore at my soul so much that I could barely breathe.

"What I need from you now can't wait," he said.

I sat completely still, forcing myself to breathe steadily to calm the frantic beating of my heart.

I didn't think I'd ever be ready for this conversation. But I was going to have to face what had happened, one way or the other.

It might as well be now.

"Okay." I braced myself for whatever he might throw my way, even though I couldn't imagine an explanation that could justify his actions.

"I want to go back in time and save my father."

"What?" I blinked, caught off-guard by his request.

"You saved Queen Elizabeth, and you saved Harper's mom," he said. "I know it's a long shot, but I have to try to save my dad."

"It's more than a long shot," I said. "If we save your dad, Lavinia won't find the Dark Wand or the Dark Crown. She and Mira won't become Queens. There's no way Time will accept the change."

"We don't know that for sure," he said. "Lavinia might find another way to track down the Dark Objects."

"Maybe," I said, even though it was highly unlikely.

By the look on Ethan's face, he knew it, too.

"I know you don't owe me anything, especially after all that's happened," he said, desperation creeping into his tone. "But if I don't try to save him, I'll never be able to live with myself."

I nodded, since I understood completely. If Mira or Mom had been the ones who'd been killed, I'd try anything to save them. I'd keep trying until so much time passed for me in the past that I was too old and frail in the present to continue trying. I'd try until I either succeeded or died.

Ethan was right—I didn't *owe* him anything.

But I wanted to give him this. If I didn't, I wouldn't be able to live with myself, either.

"Of course we can try," I said, and he released all the tension he'd been holding in his body. "But if we save him, and then Time rejects the change, you realize it's out of my power to do anything more. Right?"

"I do," he said, and then he added, "Thank you."

We held each other's gazes for a few seconds, neither of us moving. Tension crackled between us, and it took every cell in my body to resist moving toward him.

"So," I said, breaking the spell in the air. "I'm guessing you have a plan?"

"I always have a plan," he said, and from there, he told me how he wanted to try to save his father.

26

GEMMA

WE'D BEEN UP for far too long and were too exhausted to get much of anything done. So the first part of the plan was to get some sleep. But not in the present, since we'd be waking up in a few hours to start our mission to save Selena. Instead, we used our keys to go to the Haven.

As always, we checked to see if Hecate was in the Library. Like most times, she wasn't. So we entered the tearoom, I took Ethan's hands, and transported us back to the moment after we'd left for the Vale.

Mary was the only one there. She looked at us and smiled. "You've come from the future," she said simply.

"Yes," I said, and I briefed her on everything that had happened since we'd left for the Vale. "We need to crash here for a bit. Is that okay?"

"You're the Queen of Pentacles," she said. "You have a right to 'crash here' whenever you need."

I nodded, since I'd expected as much. Still, this was her kingdom, and it felt polite to ask. "We'll be in our rooms," I said. "Make sure they're still empty in my current present, since we'll need to pop back there before traveling to the past again."

"Consider those rooms permanently yours," she said. "I'll make sure to never give them to any other guests, so they'll be at your disposal whenever you need to catch up on sleep."

"Thank you."

We used our keys to go to our rooms, and Ethan didn't even try to stay in the room with me. Relief passed through me at his respect of that boundary of mine, and I fell into a deep slumber after my head touched the pillow.

I slept for nine hours straight, then changed into my Haven whites. Ethan was already awake when I knocked on the door that connected his room to mine, also dressed in his clothes from the Haven.

"You look rested," he said.

"I feel it," I said, surprised that after everything we'd been through, it was true. I suspected it was because of the mana and holy water we'd had on Avalon, which provided our bodies with every nutrient they needed to function at their best capacity.

Speaking of food, I was starving. I sent Mary a fire message, and she had breakfast delivered to our rooms in less than ten minutes.

"You ready?" I asked Ethan after we finished eating.

"As ever," he said, and then I took his hands and brought us back to the present. From there, we used our keys to head over to his house in Australia.

It was empty. No one had been there since we'd left, and dust had gathered on all the surfaces.

It felt like so long ago that we'd sat at that dining room table with Mom, Mira, and Rosella and learned about the existence of the supernatural world.

"Glad to see the demons didn't rampage the place," Ethan said, and I nodded, since that was one thing so far working in our favor.

He led me up to his room, which I was extremely familiar with, thanks to the memories I'd experienced of the other life I'd had with him. The huge television, gaming station, and shelf full of books were in the same places I remembered.

"Don't get distracted by the bookshelf," he warned, with a hint of playfulness in his tone.

I couldn't help but smile back. "It's difficult to resist. But I think I can manage a bit of self-control. Barely."

Especially since I already knew exactly what books he owned, and which ones were his favorites. I'd looked through that shelf more times than I could count.

Of course, he didn't know that.

Since he didn't know *me*.

I pushed down the pain that came along with the unwelcome reminder.

"We need to go back to the day before the start of Christmas break," Ethan reminded me.

I connected with the Crown's magic, took his hands, and we flickered out. The next moment, the light shined at a different angle through the window, the bed was unmade, and dust no longer covered all the surfaces.

From the fresh smell of soap coming from the connected bathroom, Ethan had showered that morning before heading out to school. And, only a few kilometers away, Mira and I were walking through the halls, heading to our first class of the day.

It had been one of the last days my twin had felt truly happy.

Even if we saved her—no, *when* we saved her—I'd never have that carefree version of her back. I was sure that what had happened to her had changed her beyond repair.

"Gemma," Ethan said, concerned. "You okay?"

"Yeah," I lied. "It's just strange to be back here."

"I know." From the look in his eyes, I could tell he felt it, too. The stillness in the air of what felt like the calm before the storm.

But it had to be a hundred times worse for him. Because if his assumption was correct, his dad was downstairs, unaware that in a few days, his life was going to be cut short.

I reached for the Crown, ready to put it in the ether.

"Keep it on," Ethan said. "We need proof that we're telling the truth."

"Right," I said, and I placed the Crown back on my head. We'd already discussed that part of the plan, but taking the Crown off when I wasn't using it felt natural. Which was a good thing… except when I needed to prove I was a Holy Queen who'd traveled back in time to share knowledge of the future.

"Let's do this," he said, and then together, we walked down the stairs… where we found his dad and Rosella sitting in the living room with four cups of coffee in front of them, as if they were ready to receive guests.

27

GEMMA

ETHAN FROZE and stared at his dad in shock.

I couldn't imagine what this might be like for him. For the past few weeks, he'd believed his dad was dead. And his dad *had* been dead. But now here he was, very much alive, and apparently expecting guests.

"I've been waiting for this moment ever since bringing you and your sister out of Ember," his dad said, and he motioned to the empty seats. "Please, sit."

I eyed Rosella as we walked toward the couches. She sat straight, her blank eyes revealing nothing.

How did she know we were coming? Yes, she had future sight, but she could only see the future as it was in the current moment. She couldn't see changes I made in the timeline until I'd actually traveled back in time. Which meant that years ago—when Ethan's dad had brought him and his sister out of Ember—she shouldn't have known about this visit Ethan and I were paying them now.

Ethan sat on the couch next to his dad, although he left some space between them. It was like he was afraid that if he got too close, this would stop being real.

I took the chair that faced Rosella.

"You knew we were coming?" Ethan asked his dad.

"Yes."

"How?"

"Prince Devyn," Ethan's dad said the name of Selena's biological dad—the only known fae gifted with omniscient sight. "Haven't you ever wondered how I got the portal tokens that allowed me to take you and your sister out of Ember?"

"Of course I've wondered," Ethan said. "I figured that when you were ready to tell me—*if* you were ever ready to tell me—you would."

"Now's that time," he said. "When Prince Devyn found me in Ember and gave me the portal tokens, he told me that the future depended on getting you and your sister to Earth. I wasn't happy about it—I had a kingdom to rule—but after consulting my advisors, we agreed it was for the best. Especially since I was able to return to Ember whenever I pleased."

He reached for the chain around his neck and pulled one of Hecate's keys out from under his shirt. His key was shaped like a sword, with a dragon wrapped around the body. Green jewels inlayed the top three points of the sword.

"I thought you might have a key," Ethan said. "But how?"

"As you also might have figured out by now, our family line has a small amount of witch blood in it—back from the short time dragons were on Earth," his dad said. "It's enough that we're able to reach Hecate's Eternal Library if we pass her trials on Moon Mountain. The kings of Ember have received keys from Hecate for generations. It's how we've kept what remains of our people safe from the Dark Allies, and how we've pulled off a few rescue missions during that time."

I glanced at Rosella, who was sipping her coffee so casually that it was like she wasn't hearing a word of what Ethan's dad was saying.

She probably *wasn't* hearing what he was saying, since she didn't have a key.

"Due to the nature of the key—the way we can only visit places we've already been—I wasn't able to go to Earth until getting the portal tokens and going to Earth myself," Ethan's dad continued. "After that point, I was able to take care of both my kingdom *and* my children." He looked at Ethan proudly—and sadly. "I'm sure you're making a wonderful king. Our people are lucky to have you as their ruler."

Ethan's jaw clenched. "You know?"

"Yes," his dad confirmed. "When Prince Devyn gave me the portal tokens, he told me that sometime in the future, my son and his twin flame would travel back in time to warn me about my death."

My mouth nearly dropped open. "You knew I'd become the Queen of Pentacles and be able to travel back in time?"

"I knew Ethan's twin flame would be able to travel back in time," he said. "I didn't know her identity—and that she'd also be the Queen of Pentacles—until a few minutes ago when Rosella received a vision that the two of you were here."

I nodded as it all added up. Ethan and I had spent a few minutes in his room preparing to go downstairs. In that time, Rosella's ability would have allowed her to see that we were coming.

"Did he tell you any more than that?" I asked.

"He told me there was no possible future where my death could be stopped. He told me to tell the two of you not to continue trying to save me. There's no outcome except failing, and it will delay you from your true task, which could lead to losing the war against the demons."

I sucked in a sharp breath at the confirmation of what I'd already assumed was true.

Ethan sat completely still, like he refused to believe it.

"Lavinia will use my heart to find the Dark Wand and the Dark Crown," his dad continued, sadly, but firmly. "If she doesn't get my heart, she won't become the Dark Queen of Wands, and the Dark Queen of Pentacles won't rise. Which, as you know, means my death is set in stone."

Ethan's eyes blazed with anger, a burnt orange glow around his irises. "There has to be another way—"

"There is no other way." His dad raised a hand, stopping him from saying any more. "Prince Devyn sees all, and he has confirmed it. I need you to be at peace with the fact that there's nothing you can do to stop this from happening."

The light went out of Ethan's eyes, like this fact had emptied his soul. "When we leave, Time will reject this change," he said. "You'll forget we were ever here."

"Time will only reject the change if the change makes it so the Dark Queens don't rise," his father said. "I came to terms with my death years ago, and will allow my future to play out as fate intended."

"You're not going to do anything?" I asked, shocked.

"Correct."

"Which means the Dark Queens will still rise, and our visit today won't be erased."

"Yes. And whatever we discuss here today will remain in the true timeline."

"We'd remember it anyway," Ethan said. "When we travel, we remember both timelines."

"I know." His father's eyes flashed with sadness. "But now, it will remain in *my* timeline, from now into the Beyond."

Understanding dawned on Ethan's face. "You want this to be goodbye."

"It has to be," his father said, looking relieved when Ethan didn't fight him on it. "Shall we go to my study? There are some things I'd like to share with you, from one king to another."

Ethan nodded, stood up, and followed his dad around the corner, leaving me alone with Rosella.

28

GEMMA

I LOOKED AT THE SEER, unsure what to ask. There was something so ageless about Rosella. It was impossible to explain *what* it was, but somehow, it was like she was all ages at once.

"For you, we haven't met yet," I finally said.

"Yes," she said. "And when we meet in my timeline, you won't know any differently. Everything will happen exactly as you remember."

I nodded, knowing not to question Rosella.

"What's it like?" I asked instead. "To see the future, knowing I can change it so easily?"

She raised an eyebrow. "Has it been easy?"

"Well, no," I admitted. "The future seems pretty stubborn."

She laughed at that. "As you know, I see the most probable future," she said. "That's the future the present prefers."

"The future I can change."

"You're not the only one who can change the future," she said.

"I know." I sighed. "Mira can, too." I still couldn't get the image of Mira in my bedroom out of my mind, with her Dark Crown and eerily calm dark blue eyes.

"She can," Rosella said. "But that's not what I was referring to."

I tilted my head, confused. "Are you saying there are more time travelers out there?"

"You and your sister are the only time travelers who have ever existed in this Universe," she said. "But the two of you aren't the only two people in the Universe who can change the future."

"I'm confused..."

"I'm talking about *choices*," she said. "Everyone can change the future at any moment—with their decisions. We all have free will. We are all the masters of our own futures."

"True," I said, since while it seemed simple, she wasn't wrong.

"You're going to have many important decisions in the future," she said. "Think each one over carefully. At the same time, trust your instincts. There's a careful balance between emotion and logic. Enter that space—a space of perception and insight—and react and make decisions wisely."

"I'll do my best," I said.

"I know you will."

We sat there for about two hours, and Rosella told me stories of her past. She'd lived for centuries and had crossed the paths of many interesting people in her years—many of them meetings of fate that had resulted in positive change for the future. She'd seen so much in her years, and after it all, she believed in our ability to win against the demons, and in my mission to save Selena and Mira.

Her belief in me helped me believe in myself. Not only *could* I do this, but I *would* do this.

Eventually, Ethan and his dad returned to the living room. Ethan appeared deep in thought, off in his own world, processing everything that was happening.

"It's time," his dad said, and he turned to Ethan and smiled. "I'm proud of you, and I believe in you. Save the Queen of Wands, and save the dragons of Ember."

"I will," Ethan said. "I promise."

His dad nodded. "I'm looking forward to hearing all about it when we meet again in the Beyond. Now, go with Gemma and return to your present in Avalon. The future is waiting for you."

29

GEMMA

ETHAN BARELY SAID a word as we returned to the present and used our keys to travel through the Eternal Library back to Avalon. I wanted to ask him what he and his father had spoken about, but I didn't. Those moments were for him to share when—or *if*—he was ever ready.

When we stepped back into my room, he made no move to return to his.

"I've always cared about you both," he said. "You and Mira. Although I also knew something wasn't right between me and Mira. I was so conflicted and torn. I still am."

I pushed down the resentment attempting to make its way up to my heart. Now—so soon after saying goodbye to his father—wasn't the time for me to release my anger onto him.

Then I remembered what Rosella had told me about reacting from a place of wisdom instead of a place of pure emotion. It was true—my emotions had been getting the best of me recently. They were so strong that I'd pushed them down, forcing myself in a space of pure logic.

Neither of those spaces were positive ones. I needed to find a central space—a balance.

A space of wisdom.

The Crown warmed, as if agreeing with me.

"I was conflicted, too," I admitted, since he deserved the truth. Just because we'd come from a place of lies didn't mean we had to remain in a place of lies. "I hated myself for wishing you'd chosen me. I constantly felt like I was betraying Mira. It was awful."

"I constantly felt like I was betraying her, too," he said. "That day in the cove—the day I met you—I didn't want to leave. I have no idea why I left. There was something special about you. Something that drew me to stay. But I didn't listen to that feeling. I should have. If I'd listened to it, so much would be different right now."

I wanted so badly to tell him that I remembered a time when he *had* stayed.

"I would have loved for you to stay, too," I said instead.

"When I continued along the beach and met Mira, something told me to go back to the cove," he said. "We *did* go back. But you were gone. From there, Mira was so warm and inviting."

"She's always been the more outgoing twin," I said. "She's easier to get to know."

"Just because someone's easier to get to know doesn't mean they're more worth getting to know," he said. "Not that Mira's not worth getting to know. I truly do care about both of you. But you're the one I love."

"So why not pick me?" I asked. "If you were more drawn to me after meeting both of us, why not choose to be with me instead?"

"I have no idea." He scratched his head, as if genuinely confused. "I guess I didn't want to hurt Mira or cause a rift between the two of you."

I frowned, since it wasn't enough.

I wasn't sure it would ever be enough. He'd had so many chances to be honest with us, but he hadn't done it until forced.

I wished I could understand. I *wanted* to understand.

But I didn't.

"I should have told you," he said.

"Yeah. You should have."

He looked at me with so much longing that I wanted to run into his arms and tell him it would all be okay.

But I couldn't.

Because I wasn't sure it would ever be okay.

"Will you ever be able to forgive me?" he asked.

I thought of Mira saying she hated me, and the anger in her eyes as she'd used her magic against me. I thought about seeing her in my room when she was the Dark Queen of Pentacles—the darkness I'd felt around her, and how when I looked at her, it felt like my twin was gone.

There was no way of knowing if I'd ever get her back.

Ethan should have been strong enough to tell us the truth. The Ethan I'd loved—truly loved with my heart and soul—had stayed with me back in that cove. He'd loved me, and only me. He'd *chosen* me—not because he was forced to, but because it was as natural to him as breathing.

I wanted that to be our reality.

But it wasn't, and it never would be. Not even I—with my ability to travel back in time—could change the choice he'd made.

He sighed in resignation. "I'm going to take your silence as a no."

My heart broke. "I'm sorry," I said. "I wish it wasn't like this."

"Me, too." Sorrow crossed his eyes, and again, I wished things could be different between us. "Goodnight, Gemma. I hope you sleep well."

With that, he spun around, put his key in the door, and left me alone in my room.

I wanted to go after him.

Once he'd been gone for a few minutes, I put my key into the door and stepped into the ivory hall of the Eternal Library.

Please be here, I thought, and I looked around for Hecate.

The hall was empty.

I cursed and reached for my magic, wanting to throw balls of fire at the marble floor to release my anger. But my magic was blocked, thanks to the spell around Hecate's realm.

Instead, I screamed so loudly that it could have been heard in another dimension. I screamed until my throat hurt and tears streamed down my face. I dug so deep for my magic that it physically hurt—nearly as much as my broken heart.

Once I had nothing more left in me, I laid down and stared up at the details carved in the ivory ceiling.

Would I ever be able to feel whole again? Was I doomed to love someone who only existed in my dreams, but would never be my reality? It felt so wrong, and I hated that there was nothing I could do to make it right.

Could I find it in my heart to forgive him? Would I ever be able to look at him and not be reminded of the fact that my twin flame's decisions had resulted in the loss of my twin sister?

All three of us were broken. And it seemed impossible to become whole again.

Eventually, I forced myself back up. Because while I might feel broken on the inside, there were others who were broken who I could actually help.

Annika and Jacen needed their daughter back.

The *world* needed Selena back.

And I was going to do everything in my power to make it happen.

30

GEMMA

The next morning, Torrence, Reed, Ethan, Skylar, Raven, and I met in Annika and Jacen's quarters. They had a breakfast of mana waiting for us. My mana tasted like one of my favorite breakfasts—French toast and bacon.

Once we were finished, Annika went into her room and came back out with a long, brown cloak.

"Here," she said, handing it to me. "This should keep your identity a secret."

I slipped into the robe and pulled the hood up over my head. "How do I look?" I asked Ethan.

I bit my tongue a second later, realizing that I'd spoken in a friendly way—the way I would have spoken to the Ethan in my dreams.

"Mysterious." He managed a small, teasing smile. "I'd never recognize you."

I tore my gaze away from his, breaking the familiarity between us.

Annika looked back and forth between me and Skylar with tears in her eyes. "I'll never be able to repay the two of you for doing this," she said.

"I'd never ask you to," I said. "The world is at stake. We're doing this for everyone." I glanced at the others. "Are you all ready?"

"Let's do this," Torrence said, and then she took my hands, and Reed took Ethan's hands.

They teleported us to my cove, inside the cave where Mom and Mira had hidden when we'd been attacked by the griffin after getting our magic.

The cave where, in my false memories with Ethan, the two of us had spent time together the day before the ceremony. The cave where I could have sworn he was about to make love to me, despite the dragon tradition that all dragons wait until their first shift, to see if they have a twin flame.

Ethan had been so sure we were twin flames that he was going to defy the tradition of his people.

Torrence flashed out and returned with Skylar, bringing me out of my thoughts and into the present.

"We'll be waiting right here when you get back," Torrence said. "Hopefully, we won't have any memories of Selena ever being dead."

"The only people who will remember are me and Skylar," I said, since for everyone else, time would rearrange around them.

"Do you swear you'll tell us everything once you're back?" Ethan asked.

"Yes," I said. "I promise."

He nodded, and I knew that was good enough for him.

"Us, too," Torrence said, referring to her and Reed.

"Are you sure?"

"I helped you save her life," she said. "I want to know about it."

"And are you going to tell her?"

This was a big cause of debate. Annika and Jacen didn't want Selena to know that she and Julian had died in this timeline. They thought it would be easier on her mental health. And I definitely saw their point.

If there was a timeline where I'd died, I wasn't sure how I'd feel or react if someone told me about it.

But Torrence and Reed thought Selena would want to know.

"I know Selena better than anyone else in the world," Torrence said. "I get that her parents are trying to protect her, but she's stronger than they realize."

"Hopefully I'll see that for myself when I finally get to meet her," I said.

"You will."

We nodded to each other, then I turned to Skylar. "You ready?"

"As I'll ever be." She reached forward, and I took her hands in mine.

Take us to the time after Torrence was taken to Circe's island, when Selena decided to follow her there, I thought to the Crown.

We flickered out, and the sun that had been streaming in through the entrance of the cave disappeared. It was nighttime, and voices sounded from outside.

"I have more power than anyone on Avalon," a young, female voice spoke from across the cove. "And we have no idea what Circe wants with Torrence. The longer she's there, the more danger she's in. So I'm going to Circe's island. I can either drop you off at the Vale first, or you can come with me and Reed. But I'm going, and you can't stop me."

Selena.

It had to be.

"What's it gonna be?" a male voice asked—Reed. "Are you coming or not?"

This was it.

The moment Selena made the decision to go with Reed, find the Supreme Mages, and go on her mission to rescue Torrence.

It was the moment I'd come here to change.

"Fine," another male said. He had to be Selena's soulmate, Julian. "If you're going to Circe's island, then I'm coming with you."

I looked to Skylar and nodded.

Her lips were pressed in a thin, determined line. She was ready.

I tiptoed toward the entrance of the cave, stood as close to the wall as possible, and peeked out.

The three of them—Selena, Julian, and Reed—stood in a triangle at the opposite side of the cove. Selena's long, blonde hair blew in the wind, and with the Holy Wand in her hand, she looked like a goddess. Magic radiated from her so intensely that I could feel it, even from this far away.

Her soulmate, Julian, was as perfect looking as a statue carved by one of the great sculptors of the Renaissance. If she was a goddess, he was a god.

They were made for each other. And together, they looked unstoppable.

If only they knew what was coming next.

"Good." Selena turned to Reed. "You've been to Circe's island. Take us there, now."

"I can only take one of you at a time," he said.

"Right," Selena said. "Take me first. Then I'll come back for Julian."

"All right." He reached forward to take her hands.

No.

I ran out of the cave before I realized what I was doing, hurrying until I was nearly halfway across the beach.

"STOP!" I yelled, and they turned to look at me.

Crap.

I was supposed to stay back in the cave. The three of them would surely recognize me, since they'd stopped in the café earlier that day.

As far as they knew, I was a witch with barely any magic.

It needed to stay that way.

I stopped running and pulled the hood further over my head, glad it was dark enough—and that I was still far enough away—that they wouldn't be able to make out my features.

Skylar was the important one. From their point of view, I was the witch who'd been assigned to teleport Skylar to the cove. Insignificant, and not interesting enough to think twice about.

But I couldn't have let Selena take Reed's hands.

If she had, they'd be gone, and I'd have no way to find them again.

I stood perfectly still, hoping that if I didn't move, they'd be too focused on Skylar to pay me any attention.

Skylar ran until she reached them.

Selena dropped her hands back to her sides and tilted her head, confused. "Skylar?" she asked.

"Selena." Skylar paused to catch her breath. "Julian. Reed."

"How do you know Julian's name?" Selena asked. "And how did you know we were here?"

"I'm a prophetess," Skylar reminded them. "And I need to talk to you before you leave for Aeaea."

Selena said nothing.

Instead, she looked over Skylar's shoulder and focused on me. "Come closer," she said. "We won't hurt you."

Reed and Julian turned their attention to me, too.

Panic rushed through me. I couldn't swallow, I couldn't breathe. All I could do was stare at them, frozen, unsure what to say.

There's a way out of this. There has to be.

No solutions came to me.

"She's new to Avalon," Skylar said quickly. "She's powerful, but shy. But she's no matter. Because I had a vision, and I needed to stop you before it was too late."

31

GEMMA

I held my breath, praying they didn't ask any more questions.

Selena's focus zipped back to Skylar. So did Reed's and Julian's.

"What type of vision?" Selena asked, and I relaxed, able to breathe again.

"You can't go after Torrence," she said. "You have to go back home. Now."

Magic pulsed through the air, the blue gem on the top of the Holy Wand glowed brighter, and thunder roared overhead.

Selena had caused that thunder. It was her storm magic, gifted to her from the king of the Roman gods, Jupiter.

Incredible.

The blue from the crystal shined on Selena's face, and it was clear that the Queen of Wands was a force to be reckoned with.

We *needed* her to fight with us in the war against the demons.

In that moment, I made a decision.

If Skylar failed, and Selena refused to let Reed go on the rescue mission without her and Julian, I'd interfere and tell Selena everything.

It would be incredibly risky to tell her the truth about my time traveling ability.

There would be a chance that Selena's knowledge of the magic I'd get in the future would create such a big ripple that Time would reject the change.

Telling her would be my last resort. It would go against all of our plans.

But I'd do it anyway. What would I have to lose?

"Torrence is my best friend," Selena said, and the wind picked up enough speed that I had to reach up to keep my hood in place.

Selena's storm magic reminded me of Mira's air magic.

A lump formed in my throat at the thought of my sister.

"I would still be trapped in the Otherworld if it wasn't for her," Selena continued. "Why's everyone trying to stop me from helping her?"

Right—the last thing her father, Prince Devyn, had done before taking his own life was to try to get her to not go after Torrence.

She hadn't listened to him.

And she'd paid for that decision with her life.

"I'm not stopping you," Reed said. "I'm going to Aeaea, with or without you."

From his determined tone, I knew he meant it. I also knew he meant it because in my present, he'd told me he'd been about to leave for Aeaea that very moment.

It was only Selena's next words that had stopped him from flashing out right then and there.

"I know," she said. "I'm going with you."

"Then who cares what she says?" Reed said, motioning to Skylar. "Let's get out of here."

If Selena so much as moved her hand to reach for Reed's, it would be time to make my move.

Please don't do it, I thought, wishing I could somehow compel Selena to pick up on my energy and listen to it. *I know it's hard, but think with your head and not your heart. The fate of the world depends on it.*

Selena remained focused on Skylar, studying her like she was trying to read her mind. "Tell us what you saw," she said.

I glanced up at the stars and thanked Hecate for listening to my prayers.

"You and Julian can't go with Reed to save Torrence," Skylar said.

"Why not?" Selena asked.

"Because it has to be Reed—and *only* Reed—who goes after her."

"How do you know this?" Selena crossed her arm, looking skeptically at Skylar. "You don't have omniscient sight. You can only see the future as it's going to happen without any interference."

She had a good point. Because none of us had any idea that *only* Reed should go after her. It just seemed like the best way to make sure Selena and Julian stayed alive, and that Reed still ended up in Ember with Torrence.

Because if Reed and Torrence didn't end up in Ember, the Dark Mages might have killed us when we'd arrived. And if they'd killed us…

Time would definitely reject the change.

"Before I got here, you and Julian were going to go with Reed to Aeaea," Skylar said. "I saw what was going to happen if the three of you followed through with that decision." A lie, but close enough. "Every terrible, awful bit of it. You see, to win the war against the demons, each Queen must fight in the final battle. But if you go to Aeaea, you'll die. Avalon will be no more. The people you love most will be gone."

"My parents?" Selena choked up as she forced the words out.

Skylar nodded, saying nothing.

Fear crossed Selena's face.

I held my breath in anticipation. This could be the moment. Right now, Selena could change her mind—and change the future.

"That's only one possible future." Selena sounded like she was grasping for straws. "There has to be another way. Tell me how I'll die. I can change it. I can do something differently once I get to Aeaea."

No, I thought. *The best way to change it is to* not *go to Aeaea.*

One thing was for sure—the Queen of Wands loved her best friend and would do anything to save her. She and Torrence were soul sisters.

I couldn't blame her for wanting to take action to rescue her. I'd do the same for Mira.

Accepting that the best way to help someone you loved was to sit back and let fate run its course was one of the most difficult decisions imaginable.

"If you go to Aeaea, you'll doom us all." Skylar spoke slowly and surely, like prophets did in movies and television shows. "This moment is the turning point. And you need to go home with your soulmate."

"But *why?*"

Wow, Selena was stubborn. Nearly as stubborn as Raven. Annika had fire in her, too. So did I—literally.

I supposed our determination was part of why we were chosen as the Four Holy Queens.

"Because you're the Queen of Wands," Skylar said. "Your duty is to your people. If you turn your back on them and go after Torrence, the war against the demons will be lost. Their power will grow, and Earth will be theirs."

Chills ran up and down my spine at the terrifying reality of our situation.

Please, Selena, I thought. *Listen to her.*

Wasn't this why prophetesses existed? So they could help change the future for the better?

What good were their powers if the people they were trying to help didn't listen to them?

Fire burned inside me, and it took all my willpower not to run across the beach, reveal my identity, and force some sense into Selena.

But Selena hadn't made a decision yet.

I needed to trust Skylar to make this right. So I took a few deep breaths, calmed myself, and grounded my feet in the sand. The earth calmed my fire, wrapping it in trust and confidence.

I was too far away to see the details of Selena's expression, but this was the longest she'd gone without questioning or arguing with Skylar. The wind stilled, as if Selena had stopped throwing her emotions outward, and instead was focusing inward.

It was like she was absorbing and considering what Skylar was telling her.

"So I can't go after Torrence," Selena said slowly, and relief rushed through me. Finally, she was getting it. Hopefully. "But Reed can?"

"Yes," Skylar said. "However, teleporting to Aeaea with no plan or strategy won't be enough. Circe's an immortal sorceress—an extremely powerful one, at that. He'll need backup."

"What kind of backup?" Selena asked.

"He'll need the help of the Supreme Mages."

The final part of the plan.

The Supreme Mages had been there the first time around. We needed to make sure that this reality was as close as possible to the reality I'd come from. Which meant making sure Reed still got the help of the Supreme Mages, so they could get to Aeaea after Torrence destroyed the island and sentence her to imprisonment in Ember. Reed would follow her, and everything in Ember would play out as it had in the original timeline.

At least, that was what we *hoped* would happen. And, given that Torrence was so consumed with dark magic when she landed in Ember that she wasn't affected by the fact that her best friend had just been killed in front of her, she'd likely behave the same way until we got the first half of the Crown, it absorbed her dark magic, and she left Ember.

"How did you know that so quickly?" Selena asked. "Now that we're on a path to a different future, wouldn't you have needed to look into your cards again to see what changed?"

I nearly cursed, since she had a point. But this was also a good thing. Because Selena had said we were on a *path to a different future*.

Which meant Skylar had gotten through to her, and Selena had decided to take another path.

Hopefully, the path where she didn't go after Torrence.

Skylar stilled. "I'm not the only one who has insight into the future," she said. "I've spoken with others, and I'm speaking with you here and *now* for a reason."

It wasn't a lie. It also wasn't the full truth, but hopefully Selena didn't question it further.

"Is she your source?" Selena turned slightly and looked at me.

I froze, and before I had time to think through what to do, Selena started to walk toward me.

But Skylar, with her vampire speed, was faster. She ran toward me in a blur, took my hands, and said, "Now."

"Wait!" Selena screamed, and a gust of wind blew forward from where she stood.

But my hands were holding Skylar's. So my hood blew back and revealed the Holy Crown that I hadn't placed back in the ether, in case we needed to get out of there quickly.

Take us back to the present, I told the Crown, praying that Selena hadn't gotten a good enough look at me to realize who I was.

Skylar and I flickered out, leaving the dark night behind us and reappearing in the sunlit cove of our present.

32

GEMMA

I BLINKED as my eyes adjusted to the light, and then looked around for Torrence, Reed, and Ethan.

They weren't there.

But only a second was supposed to have passed for them between when Skylar and I had left and now. If they weren't there...

Memories slammed into my mind.

New memories, layering on top of the ones that already existed, until the original ones felt like a dream and the new ones the reality.

"We did it," I said to Skylar, stunned.

She stared out at the ocean, her eyes unfocused as the new memories layered over the old ones in her mind.

"Selena's alive," Skylar said. "But she's not living in Avalon."

"No," I said, and on instinct, I stored the Crown back into the ether. "She's in the Otherworld. Ethan and I met her when we journeyed there to make the ether locker for the Crown. She was ruling by Sorcha's side as Queen of the Half-Bloods."

In my new memories, Selena, Julian, and the freed half-bloods had been fighting the zombies for months. They'd pushed them out of the citadel and the surrounding regions. The citadel had been bright and blooming, and the zombies had never broken through the barrier. There were still zombies in the west, but it was looking like they'd be taken care of soon.

"We never met Gaius, and Genevieve didn't create the ether locker for the Crown for me," I continued. "Selena created it with Julian."

"And your time in Ember?" Skylar asked.

"The same as the first time we were there. As we guessed, since Torrence was dark at that time and her emotions weren't controlling her actions, she didn't act any differently until touching the first half of the Holy Crown. But this time, she didn't return to Avalon to tell Annika and Jacen that their daughter was dead. She went back to reunite with Selena and tell her she was safe."

"The new timeline wrote over the original one." Skylar brought her hands together, her eyes wide. "It actually *worked*."

"It did."

"Now, how are we going to get home?"

"We need to find the nearest door." I reached for my necklace and looked at the stairs winding up the cliff.

The closest door was the one that led inside Twin Pines Café.

"Follow me," I said to Skylar, and I started walking toward the stairs.

"Wait," Skylar said, and I stopped in my path. "What are we going to tell the others?"

It was a good question. Because in the present timeline, the last thing I remembered was having breakfast in Annika's quarters with Annika, Jacen, Raven, Skylar, and Ethan.

After eating, Skylar was going to consult the tarot cards so we could figure out our next move.

Then I'd flickered out, appeared in the cove, and my memories had merged.

"I have no idea," I said. "This is the first time something like this has happened to me."

Skylar frowned, apparently not liking that answer. "They're going to want to know where we went."

I crossed my arms, trying to figure out what we should do.

Torrence didn't want Annika and Jacen to know that Selena had died. So what were we supposed to tell them?

"For what it's worth, I think we should tell them the truth," Skylar said. "But you're the Queen of Pentacles. The decision is yours."

I was still trying to think it through when Torrence, Reed, and Ethan appeared in the cove, at the base of the cliff next to the steps.

"Wow." Torrence glanced at Ethan, who gave her a knowing smirk. "You were right."

I stared at them, startled by their sudden appearance. Especially because given what Torrence had just said, there was only one conclusion I could draw...

"You knew we were here," I said to Ethan, and he nodded. "How?"

It didn't make sense.

In their reality, we hadn't needed to go back in time to save Selena, since Selena had never died. The entire mission we'd just successfully completed didn't exist. Which meant the group of us had never gone to the cove. They hadn't been waiting for us when we'd returned from the past because they hadn't needed to come here in the first place.

"We were having breakfast with Annika, Jacen, Raven, and Skylar, and then the two of you flickered out." He glanced at Skylar, then back to me. "Annika, Jacen, and Raven continued talking, as if nothing strange had happened. When I asked where you were, they were dazed and said they didn't know. It was like the confusion people have when we use or talk about our keys in front of them."

"But *you* realized what had happened," I said.

"I did. And a second later, the memories of the original timeline flooded my mind. I remembered the mission to save Selena, and I knew that in the original timeline, Torrence, Reed, and I had dropped you and Skylar off at the cove."

"That sounds confusing."

"It was," he said. "I asked Annika to bring me to Torrence and Reed, because I thought maybe they remembered both timelines, too. But when I asked them if their memories came back, they looked at me like I was crazy."

"We still think you're crazy," Torrence said.

"There was no time to tell them everything that had happened." Ethan shrugged. "I just told them that you and Skylar were at the cove, that I needed them to teleport me here, and that I'd explain everything once we got here."

"And now we're here," Torrence said. "So—explain."

I thought back to what she already knew. Because in the original timeline, Torrence and Reed only knew that I was the Queen of Pentacles and could travel back in time because we needed their help for the mission to save Selena.

In the new timeline where Selena was alive, we hadn't had to go to Torrence and Reed, since we hadn't needed to save Selena. The last time I'd seen the two of them had been when we'd parted ways in Ember. Back then, we'd only had the first half of the Crown, and had no idea who was going to be the fourth Queen.

Which meant we had a *lot* to catch them up on.

"Skylar and I just got back from saving Selena," I started, figuring it was best to drop it on them all at once. "You see, where I come from, Selena was killed by the Supreme Mages during her attempt to rescue you from Aeaea."

Reed's expression hardened. "Selena never came with me to rescue Torrence," he said. "She was going to, but then Skylar and a witch from Avalon teleported here and warned her not to go. They said if she did, she'd die..." He studied me, and realization dawned in his eyes. "You," he said. "*You* were the witch who brought Skylar to the cove. You were wearing the same robe you have on now."

"Yes." I smiled at how quickly he was catching on. "I needed the hood to hide my identity. Hopefully Selena didn't see me when it blew off in that last second."

"She did see you," Reed said. "She went to check on you in the café. You and Mira were working at the counter, so she figured she'd been mistaken."

"She wasn't mistaken," I said. "I was at the café. I was also here with Skylar while she delivered the message to you and Selena. Like I said, we just returned from that mission. We've been back for about ten minutes."

I stood there patiently, waiting for them to put the pieces together.

"No. Freaking. Way," Torrence finally said, and she turned to Ethan. "You said before that you remembered different timelines. Are you trying to say that..." Her eyes widened, and she refocused on me. "Did you come here that day from the future?"

"I did." I pulled the Holy Crown out of the ether and placed it on my head. "I'm the Queen of Pentacles. And the Holy Crown gifted me with the ability to travel through time."

The Torrence from the original timeline got her wish—the version of her in this timeline learned the details of Selena's original fate.

"Wow," Reed said once we'd finished explaining. "This is heavy."

Ethan raised an eyebrow. "Did you just quote *Back to the Future?*"

"You bet I did."

I looked back and forth between the two of them and smiled, having a feeling that this was going to be the start of a beautiful friendship.

"I'm going to tell Selena," Torrence decided. "She'd want to know that her decision not to go after me was the right one to make."

"And Annika?" I asked.

"I'll leave that decision to Selena."

I nodded, since that seemed like the best way to go.

"So," Ethan said. "We succeeded in our mission to save Selena. What's next?"

"We find Mira," I said. "We'll bring her to Avalon, and I'll take some of the darkness from her, like I did for Torrence."

"How *did* you do that?" Torrence asked.

"I'm not sure. But once we get Mira to Avalon, I'll figure it out."

If she got accepted to Avalon.

Now that she was dark, who was to say she wouldn't be turned away?

I shook the thought away, since it didn't matter. If Mira wasn't accepted in Avalon, I'd bring her somewhere else. The Haven or the Vale.

But what if she traveled back in time while there? We'd be right back to where we started.

The Eternal Library, I realized. *She won't be able to use her dragon magic in the Library.*

I'd tell Ethan the idea later. Together, we'd figure it out.

"I guess now we go back to Avalon," Torrence said. "And from there, I'll head to the Otherworld to find Selena."

33

GEMMA

I WASN'T ready to announce to all of Avalon that I was the Queen of Pentacles, but Annika still gave me a tour of the island, which took up the rest of the day. She was bright, optimistic, and happy—an entirely different person than I'd met in the original timeline.

The island was incredible, and the tour included riding a unicorn across a lake and flying on the back of a wyvern. I could see why Raven thought none of the kingdoms on Earth compared to Avalon.

Avalon was a true, utopian paradise.

But as beautiful as the island was, it could never be my home. Not without my mom—and potentially Mira—there with me.

The entire time I was on the tour, I kept thinking about Ethan. Mainly, how did he remember both timelines, even though he hadn't come with me on the trip to save Selena? The timeline should have morphed around him and erased the original one, like it had for Torrence and Reed. The only ones who should have remembered both timelines were me and Skylar.

Why was it different for Ethan?

Which brought me back to the question that had consumed me since I'd been poisoned with that nightshade—was what I'd experienced with Ethan while I'd been unconscious a dream or an alternate reality, like what I'd theorized with Rosella?

The experience with the nightshade was going to haunt me until I had answers. The emotional agony it had been causing me was unbearable. I'd pushed it down since Mira had turned dark, but now that we didn't have an immediate mission we were trying to complete, the pain had returned at full force.

It was time for me to do something about it.

So that night, I waited for everyone to go to sleep. Then I used my key and entered the Eternal Library.

Hecate stood in the center of the ivory hall, waiting for me. Her gown was as dark as night, and the crescent moon on her forehead glowed as she locked eyes with mine.

"Well done," she said simply.

I almost asked if she was talking about how Skylar and I had saved Selena, but I stopped myself.

Because that wasn't the question I'd come here to ask.

"We needed all four Holy Queens alive to defeat the demons," I said instead.

"Like I said—well done."

That confirmed it.

She knew I'd changed the timeline.

"Shall we?" She motioned toward the doors that led to the room with the endless bookshelves, and I followed her inside.

What more does she know? I wondered as she walked to stand in front of the podium. *Does she know what I'm going to ask before I come here to ask it? What are the limits to the knowledge that can be found in the Library's shelves? Are there any limits?*

So many questions.

But I could only ask one.

"What's the truth behind the visions I had when I'd been poisoned by the nightshade?" I asked.

"I've been waiting for you to be ready to come to me with this question," she said, and then she released the starry smoke from her eyes, its tendrils perusing the shelves.

It returned with a thin, blood-red book. The pages flew open, landing on one near the center.

She glanced at it, then stepped aside, making room in front of the podium. "You need to see this one for yourself," she said.

I inhaled sharply. "I'm allowed to touch the books?"

"I decide what's best seen and what's best told. And the answer to this question is one I feel you need to see."

I walked forward, stood in front of the podium, and looked down at the book. The letters swirled together before I could make out the words, rotating in a hypnotizing vortex that tugged at my skin and pulled me inside until I was falling and spinning like Alice tumbling down the hole to Wonderland.

The world pieced itself back together, and I found myself standing in the living room of the cabin that made up the Seventh Kingdom—the same place I'd been standing when Ethan had first placed the Holy Crown on my head.

This time, the room was empty. It was also brighter than before, thanks to the rays of sunlight streaming in through the windows.

I looked down at my hands—they were pale and transparent, like how they got after drinking invisibility potion. My entire body was invisible. When I walked forward to touch the back of one of the chairs, my hand went right through it. And my footsteps didn't make a sound.

I was more than just invisible. I was a true observer, unable to create any changes in the environment around me.

Suddenly, someone gasped from behind the door that led to the bedroom. It was the room I'd landed in when I'd first time traveled and watched Ethan place the Crown on my head.

Muffled voices sounded from the other side.

I walked toward the door and reached for the knob, but my hand went through it.

I narrowed my eyes at it in frustration. But there was nothing to be frustrated about. Because I wasn't corporeal. So I simply stepped forward and walked through the door, as if it wasn't there. I didn't feel a thing.

Inside the bedroom, Constance was sitting straight up in her bed, her eyes wide.

Katherine, Genevieve, and Isemay were slowly waking up and rubbing their eyes, as if they'd been asleep for years.

No—not years.

Centuries.

This was the moment the four of them woke from the sleeping spell that froze them in time.

Katherine blinked a few times, then focused on Constance. "What's today's date?" she asked.

Constance answered with a date I recognized immediately—the day before my birthday.

Mira and I would be receiving our magic the next day.

But our birthday had been months ago. When we'd arrived in the Seventh Kingdom, Katherine had told us that they'd awoken from the spell that morning, so they'd be there to give us the second half of the Crown.

Assuming the book was showing me the truth, then Katherine had lied.

But *why* would she lie? What did it have to do with the nightshade induced hallucinations I'd had of Ethan?

Katherine studied Constance, who was stunned speechless. "What did you see?" she asked.

"Something horrible," Constance said slowly, like she was still trapped in the haze of her vision.

"Don't leave us in suspense or anything," Genevieve said snidely.

Katherine glared at her. "Mind your manners," she said, and Genevieve huffed and rolled her eyes. Then she refocused on Constance. "Do you need blood?"

"No," Constance replied. "I'm still full from our final meal before we went to sleep."

They all nodded, as if they felt the same.

"Did your vision have to do with the Queen of Pentacles?" Katherine asked.

"It does."

"What about her?"

Constance met the queen's gaze, fear shining in her eyes. "Tomorrow, the twins will receive their dragon magic," she said. "And soon afterward, one of them will die."

34

GEMMA

Queen Katherine was out of bed in a second. "One of those twins is destined to become the Queen of Pentacles," she said. "Is the twin that dies the one who's meant to become the Queen?"

"I don't know," Constance said. "At this point, either one of them may become the Queen."

"Then neither of them can die before that happens."

Genevieve swung her legs over the side of the bed, slow to stand up. "They can," she said. "And according to Constance's vision, one of them will."

"I understand that," Katherine snapped. "But we're guarding the second half of the Crown because we're waiting for the Queen of Pentacles to journey here and find it. She can't do that if she's dead." She faced Isemay, who was the groggiest of them all. "You're the one who spoke with Prince Devyn. He told you to tell us to wait for the twins here. *Both* of them."

"He did," Isemay said.

"Are you sure something didn't get lost in translation?"

"I'm sure."

"Then it looks like we're going to have to go to the Otherworld and speak with him ourselves," Genevieve said. "He'll know which twin is destined to become Queen."

"I'm afraid that won't be possible," Constance said. "Because Prince Devyn is dead."

The three of them silenced.

"How?" Genevieve finally asked. "He's immortal, and he has omniscient sight. He can see every possible way anyone could ever try to kill him, and then he can stop it from happening."

"He chose to end his own life," Constance said solemnly.

Silence again.

"How do you know this?" Genevieve asked. "You're a prophetess. You can see the future—not the past."

"I saw it while sleeping."

"We didn't dream while sleeping under the spell."

"We didn't," Constance agreed. "But I had visions. And the vision I had right now was strong enough to wake me, and therefore the three of you, from the spell."

I watched and listened, as confused as Queen Katherine. Because clearly neither Mira nor I had died.

Constance's vision had been wrong.

Then I thought back to the conversation I'd had with Rosella back at Ethan's house. When prophetesses get visions, it's an opportunity for them to change the future. They must have saved whichever one of us was supposed to die the next day.

But how? And what did this have to do with my dreams of Ethan while I'd been unconscious because of the nightshade?

"Isemay—go fetch some snow from outside, bring it in, and melt it," Queen Katherine said. "I think we should have something to sip on while Constance tells us the details of her vision."

They gathered around the kitchen table a few minutes later, each with a glass of water in front of them.

Unable to sit, I stood next to the table, anxious for Constance to continue.

"I saw the night the twins will get their elemental magic," she started. "Tomorrow night. The blonde twin—Mira—will be gifted with magic over water and air. The brunette—Gemma—will be gifted with earth and fire."

"So they're equally as powerful," Katherine said. "Both of them strong enough to potentially become Queen."

"They have an equal amount of magic inside of them," Constance said. "But one twin is naturally more in tune with her magic and will be more confident using it."

"Which one?"

"Gemma."

"Fire and earth."

Constance nodded.

"Is she the one who dies?" Katherine asked.

"No."

I gasped, although of course, none of them heard me.

Mira had been fine that night. She'd used as much magic as she could, and then Ethan had brought her to the cave with Mom, where they'd been safe until Ethan and I had killed the griffin.

Katherine sat straighter, determination shining in her eyes. "Tell me everything."

Constance started from the moment around the bonfire when Mira and I had been gifted with our magic. She told them about the griffin's attack—how it had swooped down and grabbed our cousin, and how I'd tried and failed to direct Mira on how to use her power over air to try to save her.

No—*I* hadn't failed.

Mira simply hadn't been practiced enough with her magic to know what to do. And who could blame her? We'd gotten our magic *minutes* before all of that had happened.

Constance continued on to tell the others about how the griffin had killed Rebecca, too.

"The twins were losing against the griffin," she said. "I don't think either of them would have survived if Gemma's boyfriend, Ethan, hadn't rushed in from the sidelines to help."

Gemma's boyfriend.

The two words echoed in my mind.

Because Ethan wasn't my boyfriend.

Well, I had no idea what to call him *now*. But on the night we'd gotten our magic, he most definitely hadn't been my boyfriend.

Constance's vision had to be wrong. Because on the day before we'd gotten our magic, Ethan had been *Mira's* boyfriend.

There was nothing the foursome sitting at the table right now could have done after this point to change that.

"Ethan's a powerful dragon prince gifted with magic over fire and air," Constance continued. "He'll try to bring the twins to safety in a nearby cave so he can fight the griffin alone."

"Let me guess," Genevieve said. "The strong twin—Gemma—isn't going to want to sit back in a cave while her boyfriend faces this monster?"

"Ethan wasn't my boyfriend," I said, although of course, none of them heard me.

"Sort of," Constance said. "Kelly's mother—Sasha—will be in shock, unable to move away from her daughter's body. She's a sitting duck for the griffin. Gemma will refuse to leave her there. She'll tell Ethan to bring Mira to the cave while she gets Sasha. The griffin will still be far out in the ocean at this point—where it dropped Rebecca to her death—so Ethan will have time to bring Mira to safety. But he'll follow Gemma, leaving Mira stranded on the beach. He and Gemma will get into a fight as they try to save Sasha. During this time, the griffin will zoom toward Mira, snatch her up, and kill her."

No.

That wasn't what had happened.

I'd gone to Sasha alone.

She'd rejected my help.

So I'd spun around, faced the griffin, and threw as much fire at it as possible. Then, after getting Mira safely to the cave, Ethan had joined me and helped me fight.

But if what Constance was saying was true, then Ethan and I had gotten into some sort of argument about how to help Sasha.

I hadn't turned around and thrown those initial blazes of fire at the griffin. I hadn't slowed the griffin down.

And then Mira—who hadn't been in the cave, because Ethan had followed me instead of taking her—had been standing on the beach, perfect bait for the griffin.

Except none of this had happened.

So why was the book from the Eternal Library showing this to me? Was it another imaginary world, like the one I'd experienced with Ethan after being poisoned by the nightshade?

No, I realized. *This is the world from my hallucination. It's what would have happened there the next night.*

I'd woken up from the "alternate world" the night before Mira and I had gotten our magic. I'd been spending time with Ethan in the cave, mentally preparing for the ceremony.

In the alternate world, this is what would have happened during the ceremony.

In that world, Mira would have died.

If I'd been Ethan's girlfriend instead of Mira, he would have followed me when I'd gone to help Sasha, instead of taking Mira to the cave.

In the alternate world, Ethan's love for me had gotten my twin killed.

"Gemma's magic is strong," Constance continued. "After Mira's death, she'll launch blasts of fire at the griffin and char it to the bones. She's fully capable of killing the griffin alone."

"So you think Ethan should have brought Mira to that cave and left Gemma to handle the situation on her own," Isemay said.

"Since I can only see the future as it will play out at this moment without interference, I can't say what will happen if he takes Mira to that cave and lets Gemma take care of the griffin," Constance said. "I *can* tell you that if Mira's in that cave, she won't be sitting there as easy bait."

But I hadn't fought the griffin on my own. I'd only shot the first blasts. Then Ethan had joined me, and we'd killed the griffin *together*.

Still... I'd shot those first blasts. And those were *strong* blasts. I'd weakened the griffin and slowed its progress significantly.

Ethan had definitely helped. But maybe I hadn't been giving myself enough credit for what I'd done that night.

Genevieve sighed and leaned back in her chair. "It's wonderful to think about what would have happened if Ethan had prioritized Mira's life, especially since it sounds like Mira could have used the extra protection," she said. "But how, exactly, do we get him to leave his girlfriend out in the open like that?"

"I have an idea," Katherine said, and then the world blurred around me like the letters had blurred on the page of the book, and I fell back down the pit before she could say any more.

35

GEMMA

I REAPPEARED in the cave at the cove, in the same ghost-like form. A dozen candles were lit inside, and Ethan and I sat next to each other. He was talking to me with a flame in each hand, and then he snuffed them out.

I knew this moment.

It was my last memory of the alternate world I'd shared with Ethan. It was the moment he'd told me about twin flames.

We looked at each other with love shining in our eyes, as if it was taking all of our self-control not to fall back into each other's arms.

"But I'm not a dragon," the other version of myself—the one from my alternate memories—said. Even though I was only an onlooker right now, I remembered what it was like to be sitting where she was sitting, my arm brushing against Ethan's as I looked into his soulful hazel eyes. "So I can't have a twin flame."

"You'll have dragon magic," Ethan said. "That's what connects twin flames—our magic. Every twin shares at least one element with the other."

"I get my magic tomorrow."

"Yes." He watched me carefully.

I watched the other version of me carefully, too, since what she was about to say were the last words I remembered before I'd been pulled out of the dream.

"Do you think there's a chance—"

She stopped speaking, and her gaze snapped to where I was standing.

I froze.

Was she *seeing* me?

I wracked my mind for an explanation about why I was there, but came up blank. How could I explain what I didn't understand?

Then I heard footsteps behind me.

Someone else was there.

The other version of me wasn't looking at me. She was looking at whoever was walking inside the cave.

I turned around... and there was Katherine, dressed in the same animal hide winter gear she'd worn when she'd met with us in Antarctica. She was ridiculously out of place in the beach in Australia, yet she walked with her head held high—with the confidence of a queen. With her blonde hair that was so pale it was nearly white, she looked like some sort of angel.

"Gemma." Her voice was calm and steady. "Ethan."

They stood.

"Who are you?" he asked.

"I'm someone you're going to meet in the future," she said mysteriously.

"So you're a prophetess." He inhaled deeply. "A gifted vampire."

My other self watched her, mesmerized, clutching onto Ethan's hand. Queen Katherine was the first vampire she'd ever met. She was the first *supernatural* she'd ever met, excluding Ethan.

And excluding Selena, Torrence, Reed, and Julian, given that they'd wiped her—our? —memory of meeting them.

Queen Katherine walked closer and stopped a few meters away from Ethan and the other me. "You're correct that I'm a gifted vampire," she said. "I'm not, however, a prophetess."

"Then what's your gift?" Ethan asked.

"Superior compulsion."

The other me stood strong, and if she was scared, I couldn't tell. "What does that mean?"

"It means that I want the two of you to forget everything that's happened since you met," Katherine said, the melodic sound of the compulsion in her voice hypnotizing as she spoke.

Ethan and other-Gemma's eyes went blank.

Horror sliced through me like shards of glass through my soul.

"No," I said, although of course, none of them heard.

"On that first day in the cove, you didn't tell Ethan your secret," Katherine said to the other me. Then she turned her focus to Ethan. "You got up and continued walking along the beach, where you came across Mira surfing with her friends. You spent time with Mira that day—not with Gemma. Mira's the twin you chose to be with, and the twin you fell in love with. You and Gemma barely know each other. She's only in your life because she's Mira's sister."

She continued on, weaving a tale of Ethan and Mira's relationship. It was a tale I knew well, since Mira had always loved telling me about what she and Ethan did together and how close they were with each other. It was the story I remembered living —it was what had happened in my real world.

As Katherine spoke, the universe shifted around me, like puzzle pieces being pulled apart and forced back into places they didn't quite fit.

"Now, both of you will return home and forget that all of this happened," she said with finality in her tone. "Life will be as I said, and no one will question that it was ever any different."

The jagged ends of the puzzle pieces that made up this new reality smoothed over and locked into place.

My stomach swirled, and I wrapped my arms around it, feeling like I was about to be sick.

This can't be happening.

And yet, it was.

Ethan and other-Gemma's eyes refocused, although they still looked dazed, like they weren't fully present. Saying nothing, they walked out of the cave, not acknowledging Queen Katherine, and not acknowledging each other. It was like they didn't even see each other there.

They turned the corner out of the entrance, and Queen Katherine exhaled, a final whoosh of energy escaping her lips. Then she collapsed and passed out on the sandy ground.

Superior compulsion, I thought as the world swirled around me for the third time that day. *The ability to change the memories of not just the people she was talking to, but of everyone they were connected to as well.*

The ability to change reality as we knew it.

That was my last thought before I was pulled into the pit and fell through, until I landed back where I'd been standing in front of the open book in Hecate's Eternal Library.

36

GEMMA

I SLAMMED THE BOOK SHUT, stormed past Hecate, and hurried through the ivory hall. Fire fueled my blood even though my dragon magic was blocked in Hecate's realm.

This can't be happening.

Except it was. And it made my feelings for Ethan that I'd been fighting for months make a crazy amount of sense.

I used my key to leave the Library, and stepped into Mary's bedroom in the Haven. It was daytime there, so she was sleeping, as expected.

She woke at the sound of the door shutting behind me.

"Gemma?" She yawned, then sat up in bed, instantly alert. "What's going on?"

"I need to speak to Queen Katherine," I said. *"Now."*

I would have barged into Katherine's room if I knew where in the Haven she was staying. There were so many guest rooms that it would be a waste of time to bang on the doors of each one.

Plus, as the Queen of Pentacles, I could do as I pleased. Including barging into the leader of the Haven's room during the height of day and waking her up when I needed help.

"Of course." Mary got out of bed and ran her fingers through her long hair. "Follow me."

She walked me down the path to the guest hotel, glancing at me hesitantly. The only other people awake at this hour were the tiger shifters, who stood on guard in their human forms. They watched me and Mary as we walked, but remained silent, as guards were supposed to do.

The ground rumbled beneath my feet with every step I took.

"Do you care to share what this is about?" Mary asked as we neared the hotel.

"No."

She nodded, as if she'd expected that answer.

We silently entered the hotel lobby, walked into the elevator, and she pressed the button for the fifth floor. She led me all the way down the hall, to the last room on the left.

"This is it," she said, and I flung the door open with so much force that it slammed against the wall.

Katherine stirred in her bed.

The bed frame was made of wood.

I reached for my earth magic and used it to raise the bed nearly to the ceiling, shaking it and dumping Katherine onto the floor. Then I let the bed fall back down next to her with a loud thump, satisfied when she flinched.

"Leave us," I said to Mary.

She left the room and closed the door behind her, shock splattered across her face.

I reached for my witch magic and chanted the Latin for a sound-blocking spell. The magic surged forth from me—more witch magic than I'd ever harnessed before. The walls glowed fiery orange, then dimmed out.

The spell had worked.

No one outside of the room would be able to hear the conversation I was about to have with Katherine.

"Get up," I said to her, and she did as I commanded.

Her pale blonde hair was mussed from sleep, but her expression was as royal and confident as ever.

She knows that I know.

What *else* would I be so raging mad about?

But she just stood there, staring at me with her calm, vampiric gaze. She was waiting for me to speak first.

"You saved Mira's life back in the cove," I started, since that was the one good thing that had come from what she'd done. "Now, reverse the compulsion. Give everyone their memories back. Their memories of the *true* past."

My words hung heavily in the air.

If she was surprised, she didn't show it.

"How did you find out?" she asked.

"I'm the Queen of Pentacles." I didn't want to get into the details of it, because the details didn't matter. "And I'm *commanding* you to fix this."

"I saved your sister's life," she said. "You should be grateful."

"I *am* grateful for that," I said. "Eternally so. But the task is done. Now, give them their real memories back."

"I'm afraid I can't do that."

"You're gifted with superior compulsion," I said. "Of course you can do it."

"My magic has limits," she said. "One of them is that I can't undo anything I've done."

"Why not?"

"I have no idea. But perhaps it's similar to the reason why you can't travel back to the same time in the past more than once."

"What reason is that?"

"I can only guess," she said. "But I've always felt like it was because the mind can only handle so many changes to its perceived reality before going into overdrive."

"You're lying." I couldn't imagine what reason she could have for wanting to keep their memories as they were, but I'd figure it out one way or the other.

"I'm not lying," she said. "I'll drink truth potion and tell you again, if it will help you believe me."

She was bluffing.

She *had* to be bluffing.

"All right." I walked over to the nightstand, picked up the pen, and wrote on the pad of paper.

Send a vial of truth potion to room 535.

I folded it up and sent it as a fire message to the apothecary. There were always witches working in the apothecary—even when the rest of the kingdom was asleep.

I reached for my fire magic and faced Katherine, half-expecting her to run.

She stayed where she was.

"I'm truly sorry for how this affected you and Ethan," she said. "But he's your twin flame. Deep down, he knows he loves you—that's why he crowned you as Queen. I might have erased your past, but the two of you still have a future."

"If what you're saying is true, he'll never remember *falling* in love with me," I said, the truth of it hurting my heart. "And what about Mira? You saved her life, but you broke her soul."

"Would you have preferred it if I did nothing?"

"I would have preferred it if you hadn't played with our emotions by changing our entire perception of the past."

"It was the clearest path to making sure both of you lived," she said. "And it worked. If there was another way, why wouldn't you have already gone back in time to change it instead of coming to me and asking me to reverse it?"

"That's exactly what I'm going to do," I said. "After making sure you're telling the truth about not being able to reverse your compulsion."

"What reason would I have to lie?"

I said nothing, since I was wondering the same thing.

Finally, there was a knock on the door. I opened it and found a young witch standing there with a vial of light blue truth potion.

"Thanks." I took the potion and closed the door before she could ask any questions. Then I marched across the room and shoved the vial in Katherine's face. "Here," I said. "Drink."

She took the vial from me, uncapped it, and I braced myself for her to dump the contents onto the floor. Instead, she raised it to her lips and drank it down.

Her pupils dilated as it kicked in.

"Happy?" she asked.

"Yes."

For the next hour, the potion would force her to answer any question with the truth.

"Can you reverse your compulsion?" I kept the question as simple as possible.

"No," she said without hesitation.

She didn't even try to fight it.

She was telling the truth.

Every piece of hope I'd been holding on to since closing that book in the Library shattered.

But I had one more option. The chance of it working was slim to none, but it was still an option.

I needed to travel back to the past. I needed to stop Katherine before she compelled me and Ethan in that cave, and I needed to convince her to find another way.

If she could pull it off, we'd have our memories back.

If she couldn't, and if Mira died that night in the cove, then Time would reject the change and the true past would be lost forever.

37

GEMMA

I USED my key to leave Katherine's room, and I stepped back in the Library. Hecate wasn't there, since I'd already used my question for the day.

I spun around, put my key back into the lock, and walked into the main room of the cabin in Antarctica. Everything was how we'd left it—including the dent in the wood where Mira had thrown me into the wall.

Fire raged inside me at the sight of it.

But this time, it wasn't anger at Ethan for lying to us and causing a permanent rift between me and my twin. Because Ethan had to have been just as confused and beaten up about his feelings as I'd been.

It was anger at the true person responsible for what had happened—Katherine.

I closed my eyes and thought to the Crown, *Take me back to when Constance had her vision of what was originally supposed to have happened on the night Mira and I got our magic.*

Nothing happened.

I pushed harder.

Still, nothing.

I cursed and used my magic to raise a wooden chair from the floor and throw it against the wall. The chair splintered into pieces.

Why can't I go back to that moment?

I hadn't been there before.

Except… I had. Not in my actual form, but in ghost form. Or whatever form it was technically called when the book from the Eternal Library had let me invisibly observe what had happened here all those months ago.

Time for a new method.

Take me back to when the four of them were in this room and Katherine said she had an idea.

It was the moment after my ghost form had been pulled out of the scene.

I flickered out and reappeared in the same spot, at the moment I'd requested.

This time, all four of them turned their heads to stare at me.

"Gemma?" Constance was the first to speak.

Of course she was—she was the only one who knew what I looked like, since she'd seen me in her vision.

"Hi." I shuffled my feet awkwardly and gave her a small smile.

Where was I supposed to begin with my explanation of everything? There were so many timelines—and now an *imaginary* timeline created by Katherine's compulsion—that it was getting hard to keep track.

Isemay stared at my head like an alien was sitting on top of it. "That's the Holy Crown," she said, and then she hurried into the bedroom—the same place where Genevieve had gone to fetch their half of the Crown when they'd presented it to us. She returned with the frosted box, placed it on the table, and opened it.

Their half of the Crown was inside—exactly where it was supposed to be.

"Impossible." Genevieve's eyes widened at the sight of the half of the Crown in the box. Then she looked to me in confusion. "Why are you wearing a fake Holy Crown?"

"This isn't a fake Holy Crown," I said. "It's the real deal."

"It can't be."

"It is."

"So you're claiming to be the Queen of Pentacles," Katherine said coldly, clearly not believing it.

"I *am* the Queen of Pentacles. And I'm here to give you a warning."

"No," Constance said, and we all looked to her. "This doesn't make sense. I just saw you and your twin in a vision. Neither of you have your dragon magic yet. What little witch magic you have is untrained and useless."

"Apparently not," Isemay said. "Since she just teleported here."

Genevieve sniffed in my general direction. "I don't smell enough witch magic on her for her to be able to do something as advanced as teleportation."

"You're right—I didn't teleport here," I said. "I time traveled."

They all silenced.

I didn't think I'd ever stop feeling the thrill of dropping the time travel bomb on people for the first time.

"I'm here from the future," I started before any of them could get a word in. "I know you just had a vision—one where you saw my twin sister get attacked and killed by a griffin at the ceremony tomorrow night where we'll receive our dragon magic," I said to Constance. Then, I turned my attention to Katherine. "To change that future, you're going to use your gift of superior compulsion to make us all believe that Mira's Ethan's girlfriend, so he'll bring her to safety instead of going after me."

"I haven't even voiced that idea yet," Katherine said. "How do you know all of this?"

"I already told you. I'm from the future. I know all of this because I've already lived through it."

I watched her expression change as acceptance sank in.

Well, not *acceptance*. Not quite yet. But realization that what I was saying might be possible.

"I'm listening," she said.

They hadn't asked me to sit, but I pulled out one of the empty chairs—the one I'd just destroyed in my present—and joined them at the table.

"Your idea goes as planned," I said to Katherine. "After compelling us all to believe that Ethan's dating Mira instead of me, he gets her to the cave safely, and all three of us survive the griffin attack. We learn how to use our magic and eventually make our way here with the first half of the Crown, where I become the Queen of Pentacles and receive the gift of power over the fifth element. Time travel."

"Very interesting." Katherine nodded, as if I hadn't just changed her entire perception of reality as she knew it. "So, if what I'll do is a success, then why are you here?"

"I'm here because Ethan's my twin flame, and you *erased* the months we spent together when we fell in love," I said, venom dripping from my tone. "My twin sister hates me because she thinks Ethan and I betrayed her, even though the relationship she believes she had with him is a lie. So I'm here to beg you to figure out another way to save my sister. A way that doesn't result in such a giant, agonizing, heartbreaking mess."

38

GEMMA

After speaking with Queen Katherine, I said goodbye to the four of them and returned to the present.

The wall was still dented.

The chair was still splintered.

Whatever change Katherine had attempted—*if* she'd attempted one at all—hadn't worked.

Fire rose inside me, swirling around and pleading to be let loose so it could eat the cabin alive. It consumed me, building up until it burst forth in an explosion of orange light, so bright that I wondered if it was visible from space.

Flames surrounded me, heatwaves pulsing all around like I was inside a convection oven. The fire crackled and popped as it ate the wood, the burning remains filling my senses.

Once I'd released more fire than I thought was possible to have inside me, it died down, and I gazed around.

The cabin was ashes at my feet.

The snow on the island had melted, and I was standing on soft, squishy mud.

Panic filled me, and I stood there, shellshocked as I stared at the smooth ocean and snow-covered mountains.

Because there was no door. Without a door, I couldn't use my key to get to Avalon. I was stranded on an island in the middle of Antarctica. I didn't even have a pen and paper to send a fire message to ask Genevieve for help, since she was the only witch in the world who'd been to this island, and therefore, the only witch who'd be able to teleport here to rescue me.

But as quickly as the panic had set in, so did the solution.

I needed to think fourth dimensionally.

Take me back to eight hours ago, I told the Crown, since that was a safe enough time when I wouldn't run into my past self in the Library when I'd asked Hecate about my memories with Ethan.

I flickered out, and in what seemed like a split-second, the cabin reformed around me. It was as good as new, minus the dent in the wall. The only difference from when I was there five minutes ago was that the sun's rays were streaming in through the windows on the opposite side of the room.

Unless I needed to return here in the past, this was the last time I'd see the Seventh Kingdom.

I used my key to enter my room in the Haven. From there, I traveled back to the present, then returned to my room in Avalon. It had only been an hour since I'd left, and everyone in the kingdom was fast asleep.

After my adventures, I was exhausted. But I couldn't go to bed yet.

Not before talking to Ethan.

I changed into my pajamas, then used the key to walk into Ethan's room.

He was awake, reading a book in bed. The moment I entered, he smiled and put the book down. "Everything okay?" he asked.

No.

"I just got back from the Library," I said instead.

"Is Hecate still there?" he asked, apparently figuring out from my tone that I'd spoken with her. "I haven't used my question for the day."

"She's not there anymore." I took a deep breath, then sat on the edge of the bed, leaving not much space between us.

He studied me, like he was trying to see into my soul. "What happened?"

Where could I possibly begin?

I had no idea.

So I leaned forward and kissed him.

He kissed me back hungrily, like he was dying of thirst and I was the liquid he needed to survive.

Love surged through my soul, and time disappeared around me. I wanted this moment to last forever.

His kisses slowed, and he pulled back, cupping my cheek with his hand and looking down at me with the familiarity I remembered from when we'd kissed back in Lilith's lair.

"This has happened before," he said slowly. "Not just that one other time. *Lots* of other times."

Hope rose inside me, and I nodded. "What do you remember?"

"You and me, in your room," he started. "And then in the cave…" He trailed off, and his gaze went blank, like he'd lost his train of thought.

"Yes." My heart beat faster, like it was going to explode with anticipation. "In the cave, the day before I received my magic, when you told me you thought we were twin flames."

"Except that never happened," he said, and I recognized the blank, confused look in his eyes.

It was the way people without keys looked after we talked about Hecate's Eternal Library in front of them.

But he'd remembered. It hadn't been for long, but I hadn't told him about us together in my room or in the cave. Those memories had been *his*.

And I refused to let him lose them.

So I kissed him again, moving closer this time, crawling onto his lap and wrapping my legs around his waist. His kisses became rougher, and with barely anything between us except our clothes, I felt him stiffen beneath me. I reached for the bottom of his shirt and pulled it off over his head, needing to be closer to him.

The closer we were, maybe the more he'd remember.

His hands traveled up under my shirt, my core warmed, and I removed my shirt so my skin pressed against his. I ground my hips against him, wanting *more*.

From the low, rumbling groan he let out, I knew he needed the same.

"Gemma," he said as I reached into his pants and held him firmly in my grasp. After all the months we'd been together, I knew the exact way to stroke him so he leaned his head back and shuddered with pleasure. "We've done this before," he said, and he pulled away, although his lips were inches from mine. "But this was where I always made you stop."

I nodded slowly, remembering all the other times things had gotten this heated between us.

You're going to make me lose control, he'd always said, and then he'd slip his fingers inside me, moving them expertly until relieving me of the pressure building up in my core.

From there, he'd excuse himself, then return once he calmed down, never letting me see him finish. He hadn't trusted himself to get past a certain point around me, and it had frustrated me to no end.

As if out of habit, his hand traveled down below my waist.

I craved the release he was offering. But I used my free hand to wrap my fingers around his wrist, stopping him.

"We're twin flames," I said. "You've had your first shift on Ember. We don't have to stop." I balanced myself on my knees and removed the rest of my clothes until I was naked in front of him. All I wore was the Holy Crown upon my head.

His pupils dilated as he drank me in. "It was you and me together all those months," he said, like he was in a trance. "It was never Mira."

He stared at me in wonder as I lowered myself to my knees and slid his pants off of him. Once he was freed from the remainder of his clothes, I crawled back up to face him, my knees on both sides of his waist, balanced on top of him so there were only centimeters between where he started and I began.

"Katherine used her gift to erase our memories," I said, quickly telling him everything I'd seen in the book. "That's what I just found out from Hecate. But we can complete our bond, and you'll get them back. Permanently."

I didn't know how I knew that.

I just *did*, with my entire heart and soul. Because Ethan was half of my soul. And once the bond was complete, he'd remember it all.

He *had* to.

He breathed slow and steady, like it was taking all of his effort to control himself. "Do you really think it will work?"

I lowered myself down more and grazed myself against the tip of him, teasing him.

From the fiery look in his eyes, he wasn't going to be able to hold out much longer.

"I love you," he said, and then he flipped me over, pinned me down, and slid himself inside me.

I gasped at the twinge of pain as he entered me, forever claiming me as his.

He groaned, a deep rumble in his chest, his eyes locked on mine. "Are you okay?" he asked.

The slight pain disappeared nearly as quickly as it had arrived, shut down by the fire burning inside me. "Yes," I said, and I pressed my hips up against his, my insides throbbing, needing more.

He nodded, satisfied. "I don't care how powerful Katherine is—I'll never forget our past ever again," he said. "I swear it."

Neither of us said any more, no longer needing to speak with words as we moved together, losing ourselves in each other until the world shook and exploded around us, sealing our twin flame bond forever.

39

GEMMA

"The last time I did a tarot reading, I learned that all four Queens would eventually rise," Skylar said to the group of us gathered around the round table in Avalon's meeting room.

The same round table where King Arthur had sat with his knights.

I still had trouble wrapping my head around that one.

Ethan sat next to me, holding my hand. He'd been like this since we'd made love three days ago—never wanting to break contact. It was like he thought that if he stopped touching me, he'd forget our true past.

We'd tested it out, so we knew he wouldn't. I'd been right that sealing our twin flame bond had brought his memories back for good.

The other Queens had been shocked after learning what Queen Katherine had done. A gift as strong as Katherine's wasn't one to be taken lightly. She could change everything we thought to be true, without us being any wiser.

In some ways, it wasn't much different from my own power. Except mine was more dangerous, since it could *actually* change the past, instead of making us believe that a different past had occurred.

Luckily, the others trusted me, because I was the fourth Holy Queen. Queen Katherine was a different matter. But we were going to discuss how to move forward with making an alliance with her later.

Right now our biggest focus was on Skylar, and on why she'd called this meeting. She sat at the seat in front of the fireplace, and the other Queens and I sat around her, with our mates by our sides.

Annika and Jacen looked far more at peace than they had when I'd met them in Avalon. Even though they were immortal, the grief that had been lifted from their souls made them appear years younger. I didn't think Selena had told them that she'd died in the original timeline, and I didn't think she intended to tell them.

Annika and Jacen would never know the lengths I'd gone to save their daughter.

Which was what using my ability would be like—changing lives for the better, without most people knowing that anything had ever been different.

I was a hero in the shadows. And given that I'd never liked being the center of attention, I was totally fine with that.

Raven sat on the other side of her mother, with Noah next to her. The two of them were wildness personified, alert and ready to fight at a moment's notice. I barely knew Noah, and given that he seemed to be the silent, broody type, it might take him a bit to warm up to me, if he ever did at all. Raven's outspoken nature balanced his more reserved one perfectly.

Selena and Julian sat between me and her parents. Selena's magic was so strong that it hummed through the room, like constant noise in the background. She fidgeted in her chair, apparently anxious for the meeting to start. Julian, on the other hand, was still and alert, hyperaware of everything happening around him.

Skylar sorted through her tarot deck and pulled out four cards.

The Queen of Cups, the Queen of Swords, the Queen of Wands, and the Queen of Pentacles. She laid them down in a line, in that order—the order that we'd risen. In my card—the Queen of Pentacles—a woman sat in front of a tree, holding a staff with a pentacle on it, with crystals growing out of the ground around her.

"These were the first four cards I picked in that tarot reading all those years ago," she said. "But there was a fifth card above them—the Unknown Card. Now that the four of you have claimed your positions as Queens, I feel that having your energy with me in this room will be the catalyst to get that fifth card to reveal itself."

She shuffled the cards a few times, then fanned them out in front of her. She took a deep breath, closed her eyes, and picked one from the center.

She opened her eyes, flipped it over, and sucked in a startled breath at the image of a naked woman sitting in front of a tree, holding a bright red apple.

She placed it in its spot above the Four Queens, and I leaned forward to see the words on the bottom.

The Devil.

The woman painted on the card had features similar to Lilith's.

This couldn't be good.

I looked at Skylar, ready for an explanation. But she was staring at the card, lost in a trance. Because when Skylar did a tarot reading, she didn't just glance at the cards. They transformed for her, and she saw *into* them. It was like she was watching a movie that only she could see.

Raven observed her mom, like she was searching for signs in her expression about what she might be seeing. Annika was as calm as ever. Selena continued to fidget, only calming when Julian reached for her hand.

I was so focused on trying not to ruin Skylar's concentration that I could barely breathe.

When Skylar finally looked back up, her green eyes were dark and haunted.

"What is it?" Raven asked.

"The cards have shown me what Lilith has been working toward this entire time. Her end goal," she said. "And it turns out that she isn't the worst we have to fear."

My heart dropped. Because Annika and all of the supernaturals on Avalon had been trying to stop Lilith since I was a baby. If there was someone out there who was more dangerous than she was, how were we supposed to have a fighting chance?

This is why you needed to save Selena, I reminded myself. *The four Queens together are stronger than we could ever be apart.*

"Who could be worse than Lilith?" Annika's question echoed my thoughts.

"Have you met the gods?" Selena asked. "Because they're pretty damn powerful."

"They're also not trying to exterminate or enslave everyone on the planet," Annika said, so focused on Skylar that she barely spared Selena a glance. "Tell us what you saw."

"Lilith has been gathering blood," she started. "Lots and lots of blood."

We already knew this, since the demons had been kidnapping gifted humans for years. They strengthened them, turned them into gifted vampires, then drained their blood. Figuring out the locations of these bunkers, rescuing the humans, and slaying the demons who'd taken them had been one of the Nephilim army's primary goals.

"We know this," Raven said impatiently. "Did you see *why* they're gathering the blood?"

"I did."

"And...?"

"Lilith plans on unleashing the darkest force in the world. One that has been locked inside his own prison realm in Hell for millennia. She's found the location of the rift that leads to his realm, and is going to bathe it in gifted vampire blood. Then, with the help of Lavinia, this dark force will rise."

Shivers crawled up and down my arms. "What type of dark force?"

"The darkest one known to man," she said. "The King of the Demons—Lucifer himself."

THE DRAGON QUEEN

DARK WORLD: THE DRAGON TWINS 4

1

GEMMA

MONDAY, MAY 24 (PRESENT DAY)

I WOKE in Ethan's arms, my back toward him, with his body curled around mine. Warm, safe, and loved. This was where I belonged—with him. It was where I'd always belonged. I couldn't believe I'd ever doubted it.

I couldn't believe I'd ever thought he wasn't mine, and that I wasn't his.

We'd moved into the same quarters in Avalon's castle weeks ago, after learning that the life I'd lived while under the influence of the nightshade was real.

Sleeping beside him each night would have been perfect—if not for the fact that everything else in our lives was falling apart.

Mainly, the fact that my twin was lost to me.

I missed Mira so much that it physically hurt. I knew she was alive—I'd *feel* it if our twin bond was severed—but not a day passed when I didn't wonder where she was, and how she was doing.

"Good morning," Ethan whispered in my ear, lulling me away from my worries about Mira. "How'd you sleep?"

"Good," I said, since I always slept well in Avalon. *Everyone* did. There was something in the water here—literally—that made our bodies function at their best at all times. Still, I loved that he always asked. "You?"

"Same," he said, and his hand wandered down my stomach, sending tingles through my body. "There's only one thing that could make this morning better."

His touch ignited the fire inside me. "And what's that?" I teased.

"I think you know *exactly* what it is." His voice turned low and husky, and I pressed myself back against him, smiling at the feel of how badly he wanted me.

Before we could continue, flames burst forth from the nightstand. They quickly disappeared, leaving a folded piece of parchment where they'd been.

"Ignore it," Ethan murmured, nibbling on the tip of my ear in a way that he knew drove me crazy. "We can look at it once we're finished here."

But I couldn't ignore it.

What if it had news about Mira?

I told him as much, and then I pushed myself up in bed, grabbed the message, and opened it.

It was from Harper.

I have new information about that thing I've been looking for. Get yourself to my room, ASAP.
See you soon,
-Your favorite witch/vampire/all-powerful user of magic

I showed the letter to Ethan, watching as he read it over.

Understanding crossed his hazel eyes at the realization that our relaxing morning together needed to get cut short.

"We have to go." I jumped out of bed and walked over to the wardrobe to get dressed.

Ethan did the same, and soon enough, we were both wearing our black Avalon Army uniforms. There was a bowl of mana on the coffee table, and I inhaled a piece of it quickly, not wanting to be hungry during this meeting with Harper.

I could never focus when I was hungry.

This morning, the mana tasted like one of my favorites—pancakes with maple syrup. I washed it down with some holy water, and then was ready to go.

Once finished, Ethan and I walked to the door together and reached for the keys hanging from our necklaces. We never took them off—not even while sleeping.

Lastly, I reached into the ether, pulled out the Holy Crown, and placed it on my head. There was no need to wear it in front of Harper, but I liked to make an entrance. Plus, with Ethan by my side and the Holy Crown on my head, I felt braver.

Stronger.

Ready for whatever the universe threw my way.

I slipped my key into the keyhole, opened the door, and stepped into the ivory hall of Hecate's Eternal Library. The tall, rounded ceiling carved with swirling patterns of flowers looked the same as always.

But, per usual, Hecate wasn't waiting at the other side of the hall. I released a sigh of disappointment. I hadn't expected to see her there, and I hadn't entered the Library with the goal of speaking with her, but there were still always questions I wanted to ask.

The door closed behind me, then it opened again, and Ethan stepped through. He glanced across the hall, also unsurprised not to see Hecate.

Then he stared down at me, his eyes hungry. "Whatever Harper has to tell us better be important," he said. "Because I was *not* done with you this morning."

My cheeks heated, and I stepped up on my toes to plant a soft kiss on his lips. He groaned and pulled me closer, but I stepped back, my eyes teasing. "Good," I said. "Because I certainly wasn't done with you, either."

We shared a special, secretive smile—the kind that only existed between two people in love. Soulmates. Or, in our case, twin flames.

Then, not wanting to risk getting carried away, I spun around, placed my key back into the lock, and stepped through the door into Harper's room in the Vale.

2

GEMMA

MONDAY, MAY 24 (PRESENT DAY)

HARPER WAS PACING around in her palatial room, waiting for us. Her boyfriend Rohan sat at the table next to the huge window that overlooked the snow-covered mountains, picking at a bowl of fruit. Because the Vale was west of Avalon—nestled in the Canadian Rocky Mountains—it was the dead of night here.

"Finally." Harper let out a relieved breath and stopped pacing. "Took you long enough."

"We were just waking up," I explained, unable to meet her eyes. If I did, she'd totally know what Ethan and I had been up to when she'd sent the fire message.

"Good. Because I had a breakthrough about the Dark Sword. I was finally able to get an answer to a question I needed to ask." She played with the key around her neck, making it clear what she meant—Hecate had appeared to her in the Library. "It led me to some new information, and this morning, it led me to this."

She walked over to her bed, where a large hardcover book lay open to a page in the center. She picked it up and thrust it into my arms. "Here. Check it out."

I glanced at the chapter title, which simply said *The RMS Titanic: Maiden Voyage*.

"What's this?" I asked.

"It's a ship that was a big deal in the early twentieth century," she said. "It took people back and forth from England to New York."

"What does it have to do with the Dark Sword?"

"I was able to track the Sword down to a shifter who boarded that ship for its maiden voyage," she said. "I don't know the shifter's name, but she got on the ship with the Sword in England. There's no record of her since. Which means you have to go back and find her there."

I glanced at the dates of the Titanic's maiden voyage. April 10-17, 1912.

If Harper was correct—which I was sure she was—then I'd be going back to the turn of the twentieth century. Over a hundred years ago. It would be the furthest I'd traveled back in time yet.

The world had been so different back then. How was I supposed to fit in?

But that was a question for later. First, we needed a basic game plan.

"So we should go back to before the Titanic left England," I said. "Find the shifter and get the Dark Sword before she can set sail with it."

"Not possible," Harper said. "I only know that she boarded the ship. I don't know where she was before she got on it."

"Okay," I took a deep breath and thought through it. "So we'll go to New York on April 17. Wait for her to get off the ship, then grab her, steal the Sword, and bring it back to the present."

"Except I don't know *who* she is," Harper said. "You won't know who you're looking for. The moment she leaves the city—which could be immediately after her arrival—we'll be back to square one. And we both know that the dragon heart you used all those weeks ago in Antarctica doesn't have enough juice left in it to track the Sword through the city. It'll be a miracle if it can track the Sword on the ship."

Dread swirled in my stomach at the obvious solution—the one I was trying to avoid.

"We need to go *on* the ship," Ethan said, and nausea hit me just from thinking about it.

After how seasick I'd gotten during the Antarctica journey, I'd sworn never to go on another cruise again.

But shifters couldn't teleport. Assuming this shifter wasn't traveling with a witch—which was probably a correct assumption, given that the different supernatural species hadn't been on good terms with each other in the early twentieth century—she'd be cornered once we found her. And Ethan and I were far more powerful than a shifter. We'd just have to fight her, steal the Dark Sword, escape with it through the Eternal Library, and bring it back to the present.

It was nothing I couldn't handle. Especially with Ethan by my side.

"Exactly my thought," Harper said. "And don't worry—there are herbs that help with motion sickness. I can easily brew up a potion for you."

"Thanks." It would have to be a miracle potion, but I'd try anything.

"So," Rohan said, eyeing us up. "What do the two of you know about life in 1912?"

"Nothing." I shrugged. "Other than that the women had to wear dresses. And corsets. And... well, I guess that's it."

"You're going to have to know a lot more than that if you don't want to draw attention in the past," he said. "And that's the goal, correct? Create the fewest number of changes possible?"

"That's right," I said, since the fewer changes we made, the less likely it would be that one of them would butterfly out and create a change that stopped one of the Queens who'd already gotten an Object from acquiring it. If that happened, Time would reject the change, and we wouldn't have a second chance to get back on that ship, since I could only travel back to the same time once. "But you were alive in 1912, right?"

"In 1912, I was living in India," he said. "Life there was extremely different than it was in Europe. I'm not sure how much I'd be able to help you."

"Then I guess we'll have to find another vampire to help us—one that lived in Europe in 1912," I said. "And given all the connections we have, it shouldn't be hard to find one."

3

GEMMA

TUESDAY, MAY 25 (PRESENT DAY)

Noah, Jacen, and Annika immediately knew the perfect vampire to help us. So the next day, Ethan and I headed to the Haven, ready and excited to meet her.

She waited in the tearoom, and she was drinking a cup of coffee. She had pale skin, dark hair, and light blue eyes. If her scent wasn't the distinct metallic one of a vampire, I might have thought she was a Foster witch.

She placed her cup down on the coffee table, stood, and curtseyed. "Queen Gemma," she said, her gaze lowered to the floor. "King Pendragon."

"Princess Karina," I said. "Please rise."

I smiled inwardly, feeling like I was getting the hang of this whole "being royal" thing.

She did as I asked.

"You can call me Gemma," I said, since no matter how royal I was, I felt a lot more comfortable with people once the formalities were dropped.

She nodded, and since I was of higher rank than she, it was a given that I could drop her title, too.

"And 'Ethan' is a lot less of a mouthful than 'King Pendragon,'" Ethan said, and Karina gave him a small smile at that.

We sat down and helped ourselves to coffee. The holy water on Avalon was refreshing, but it had nothing on real coffee.

"Harper and Rohan briefed me on your mission," Karina said. "And my friends on Avalon were correct—I'm the perfect vampire to help you. Not only did I live in Europe during the time you're visiting, but I've always had an interest in ships. And I just happen to have traveled on a similar voyage from Europe to America on one of the Titanic's sister ships, the Olympic."

"So you'll help us," I said.

"That's why I'm here."

"Good." I smiled, relieved, even though I'd already figured as much. "Where should we start?"

"Easy," she said, looking me up and down. "If you're going to fit in while we're in 1912, we're going to have to get you some appropriate clothing."

4

GEMMA

TUESDAY, JUNE 1 (PRESENT DAY)

Six days had passed in the present.

During that time—thanks to the magic of time travel—we'd spent two weeks in 1912 leading up to the day we'd be traveling to today. And I didn't know what we would have done without Karina, since her vampire compulsion, along with her knowledge of the time period, had proved extraordinarily useful.

She'd gotten us a hotel room in Southampton, which was where we'd be boarding the ship. She'd given us a run-down on what we'd need to know regarding etiquette of the era, and had gotten us fitted for clothes so we'd have everything we needed for the journey.

And we needed a *lot* of clothes. The women on board first class—which was where we'd be traveling, since it would give us access to most anywhere on the ship we pleased—apparently changed their dresses at *least* four times a day. It was ridiculous, but if I didn't do it, I might draw unwanted attention from the other passengers on board. So, Karina had gotten me a month's worth of clothing for a five-day voyage.

I was going to have to spend more time changing outfits than searching for the shifter.

Then there were the hats. They were huge, and so covered with feathers that it was like wearing a bird on my head. To make things worse, women were expected to wear gloves at all times. It took me a lot of tries (and a lot of destroyed gloves) to figure out how to use my fire magic without burning them.

But that wasn't close to the worst of it. Because in the evening, I was expected to wear a corset. AKA one of the worst torture devices known to women. And even though Torrence had a signature family spell that could make any piece of clothing fit perfectly, a perfectly fit corset was *meant* to be suffocating. So the spell did absolutely nothing to help.

Along with clothing, Karina also managed to acquire fake identities for me and Ethan. We'd be traveling as a married couple, given the scandal that would emerge if passengers saw as much as a romantic glance between the two of us otherwise. Karina would be traveling as Ethan's sister. And, luckily for us, forty percent of the Titanic's first-class suites were listed as empty in the manifest, so it was easy for Karina to book us one of those.

Now, we were standing in a back alley in Southampton in the present day, dressed in clothes appropriate for 1912. I didn't feel particularly ready to blend into the time period, but the longer we spent preparing in the present, the more time Lilith had to track down the Dark Sword.

If she found the Dark Sword and got it into the hands of the future Dark Queen of Swords, then Time would lock in the Dark Queen of Swords' fate, and there'd be nothing we could do to change it.

"You ready to get this over with?" Karina asked.

"Ready as I'll ever be," I said, and then I took her hands, told the Crown to bring us to April 10, 1912, and we flickered back through time.

5

GEMMA

WEDNESDAY, APRIL 10, 1912

I DROPPED Karina off in the alley—which had the same exposed brick wall in 1912 as it did in the current day—then returned to the present, grabbed Ethan, and brought him back as well.

I stashed the Crown back into the ether, and we emerged from the alley onto the main street. The air smelled smoggier than it did in the present, which continued to shock me every time we traveled back here.

We passed three women wearing similar hats to the ones Karina and I had on. A man rode by on a bike, and a trolly made its way down the rails in the center of the street. None of them paid us much attention as we walked down the sidewalk toward the hotel we'd been staying in.

Karina had gotten us a two-bedroom suite, and our luggage was in the living room where we'd left it.

She glanced at the clock on the mantle. "Our car should be here by now," she said. "Are you guys ready?"

"As I'll ever be." I took a deep breath and looked to Ethan, who nodded as if saying, *we've got this.*

Preemptively, I reached into my bag for one of the vials with the light orange anti-seasick potion Harper had given me, and took a swig. It tasted like ginger, and tingled going down.

Karina picked up the antique phone on the desk, rang the lobby, and asked them to send the bellboys up for our luggage.

"It's so frustrating to watch them moving our things when the three of us are far stronger than they are," she said with a sigh. "But we must maintain appearances."

That was the mantra of this journey.

Maintain appearances.

The bellboys came for our luggage and took it down the back steps to the lobby.

As Karina had said, a black buggy was in front of the hotel waiting for us. The bellboys placed our luggage on the *top* of the car and strapped it in, and I prayed it wouldn't fall.

Not that I would mind those corsets getting lost in the street.

The driver opened the car door, and Karina and I got in first, followed by Ethan. The inside was small and cramped, but luckily, we didn't have to go far.

As we approached the port, there was a parade of cars on the street. Most had luggage on the top—I assumed they were also full of people preparing to board the Titanic. Many of them would be putting their cars in the Titanic's cargo section to bring with them to America.

We turned a corner around the buildings, and the ship came into view.

The Titanic was one of the largest, grandest ships in the world in 1912. A huge crowd of onlookers had gathered around the port simply to admire it and watch it set sail.

But I had to admit—compared to modern day cruise ships, it was rather small. It must have been half the size of the Golden Moon—the ship we'd taken to Antarctica—and the Golden Moon wasn't nearly as large as some of the mega ships that existed in the present.

"My, how times have changed," Karina said, and I had a feeling she was thinking the same thing.

Our driver yelled at the onlookers to make way, and the crowd parted to let us pass. Most of them were dressed in simpler clothes than we wore, and they craned their necks to try to see inside the car, as if we were celebrities. We had to drive at a snail's pace to make sure not to run anyone over.

Finally, we arrived at the gangway. Karina showed our tickets to the crewmen waiting for us, and they sent a group to tag our bags to have them sent to our room. Then, a steward dressed in finery fitting to serve first-class passengers led us on board and to our suite: B88.

We walked inside, and I immediately retracted my thought about the ship being unimpressive. Because our suite on the Golden Sea—which was one of the most luxurious cruise lines in the present—was bare bones compared to this one. This suite was *ornate*, with paneled wooden walls, velvet canopy beds, a fireplace, crystal lamps, and a full sitting area with plush sofas and chairs. It was like it had been designed for royalty, and it was large enough to host a small party.

"Well," I said as I looked around. "We certainly have enough space to change into all those dresses."

"Back in the day, we traveled in style." Karina's cheeks glowed, as if she felt at home in this time long past. "And this isn't even the largest suite on board."

There was a knock on the door, and a steward delivered the luggage. "Shall I leave these in the servants' quarters?" he asked, and he looked around, as if searching for our servant—which we didn't have.

If he thought this was odd, he said nothing.

"Please," Karina said, and the steward dropped the trunks off in the least lavish room in the suite.

Next, he presented us with a booklet that explained what we should expect on the trip, and a first-class passenger list to browse. Providing the passenger list seemed strange, but I supposed many of them knew each other and would like to know which of their friends were on board.

"Is there anything else I can assist you with?" he asked.

"We're fine for now," Karina said, and once he left, she turned back to me and Ethan. "Time to get started. So how about we head out to the Boat Deck and keep watch for that shifter?"

"Let's do it," I said, and Ethan and I followed her out of the room, ready to nab the shifter and get back to the present as soon as possible.

6

GEMMA

WEDNESDAY, APRIL 10, 1912

THE TITANIC'S layout was nearly identical to the Olympic's—the ship Karina had previously sailed on—so she was easily able to lead us to the Boat Deck. It was the deck where the lifeboats were stored, but more importantly, it was the largest outdoor space for first class passengers to spend time on. It was full of people who'd gathered to take a stroll, mingle, and search the crowd at the dock for any family members who were seeing them off.

On our stroll, we did a preliminarily look-over of the other first-class passengers to see if any of them smelled of shifter. We doubted they would—a shifter traveling with the Dark Sword would likely have a crystal to cloak their scent—but it didn't hurt to check.

Our assumption that we wouldn't be able to simply sniff them out proved correct.

After about an hour of walking around, the Titanic sounded its steam engines, and we were off. I braced myself on the rails, preparing myself for the jolt.

But as we pulled away from port, a miracle happened.

My stomach didn't experience those first cramps of motion sickness.

I was seriously going to have to thank Harper for that potion when we got back.

"You okay?" Ethan asked me.

"Yeah," I said, surprised. "I'm good."

"You look good."

I smiled and felt my cheeks heat. "Thanks."

As the ship left port, we waved to the crowd, even though we knew no one out there. As long as we had the opportunity to live in history, we might as well enjoy it.

Eventually, we were out in the open ocean, and passengers started leaving the deck.

"Everyone is likely going to explore the facilities," Karina said. "Let's head back to our cabin, change, then do the same."

"Do we have to change?" I muttered.

"Do you want to be seen again in the same dress you wore for sail away?" she asked, and she spun around, not waiting for an answer before leading the way back to our suite.

We didn't see anyone who might be a shifter while exploring the first-class areas of the ship, and I was getting the feeling that this mission was going to be harder than we'd hoped.

A bugle sounded in early evening, while we were having tea in the lounge to keep an eye on the other passengers.

Karina set down her teacup and stood up. "Time to change for dinner," she said.

"Did they sound the bugle to let us know it was time to change for dinner?" I asked. What was this—summer camp?

"Correct," she said, and then we followed her back to the room to change. I had her tie my corset as loosely as she deemed socially acceptable, and even then, it barely felt like I could breathe.

"What am I supposed to do if we find the shifter and need to fight her?" I asked. "I'll hardly be of any use if I can't catch my breath."

"Fine," Karina said, and she loosened the corset further. It wasn't perfect, but at least I no longer felt like I was suffocating. "We'll let the others think you might be pregnant."

"You think I look pregnant?" My jaw dropped at the insult.

"Of course not," she said. "But it would explain the loosened corset."

I pursed my lips and glared at her.

"At least it won't cause a scandal," Ethan said. "Since they think we're married."

My heart fluttered at the thought of being married to Ethan, even though the documents had been forged.

Not that marriage mattered to us. The twin flame bond was far stronger than any paper contract.

Ethan held his arm out for me at the top of a gorgeous grand staircase with a stunning clock in the center. "Shall we?" he asked with a twinkle in his eyes.

In his tailor-made suit, he looked like a perfect gentleman. No one would have guessed that he was capable of shifting into a dragon and shooting so much fire out of his mouth that he could burn down this entire ship.

"Of course," I said, and I linked my arm with his, and we made our way down the staircase.

Light poured through the glass dome overhead, and I felt like a movie star going to a swanky party. I'd already walked down the grand staircase, since it could access nearly all the first-class facilities, but it was far more stunning when everyone was dressed like they were attending a fairy tale ball.

The reception room was at the bottom, and we walked through it into the dining saloon. A string quintet played music in the background, along with a pianist, and I relished the luxury.

This was so different from my normal life, and while I felt insanely out of place, I was enjoying it at the same time. Luckily, there were far more important people on board for the other passengers to bother mingling with us, which was ideal, since we needed to affect history as little as possible.

Dinner was an insane, *ten course*, three-hour affair. I'd never been into fancy food—

I'd take pizza or a burger any day—and as I ate, I thought how much Harper would love this. She was the biggest foodie I knew.

Maybe one day, after we won the war against the demons, I'd take her on another sailing of the Titanic so she could experience it herself. On the condition that she made me another batch of seasickness potion.

"Do we have to do this every night?" I asked Karina as the servers took away our ninth course. As supernaturals, we had faster metabolisms than humans, but this was a lot of food, even for me.

It was also taking forever.

"Dinner is one of our best opportunities to listen in on other people's conversations," she said, and I sighed, since it was true. With our supernatural hearing, we were able to listen to people in the tables around us, although they were mainly gossiping about the other passengers on board. It was similar to the talk in high school cafeterias, except with expensive food and way fancier outfits.

There was absolutely zero talk about anything that might give us a clue about who the shifter was, or the location of the Dark Sword.

After dinner, we lingered in the reception room, walking around to eavesdrop some more. Again, we heard nothing useful. Finally, the hall closed, and we were able to return to the suite and change into our pajamas.

"What's the plan for tomorrow?" I asked after we were ready for bed. "Head down to second class and see if we can learn anything useful there?"

"Many of the passengers who boarded in France missed dinner tonight," Karina said, referring to the stop the Titanic made after Southampton to pick up its final group of passengers. "We'll spend tomorrow in first class again to see if we pick up anything useful from them. Plus, today was only half a day. As we saw while exploring, there are many amenities to enjoy in first class tomorrow."

"Is this a mission or a vacation?" I asked, since it was sure sounding like she was treating it as the latter.

"Both," she said, and then she turned off the lights, retired to her room, and we went to sleep.

7

GEMMA

THURSDAY, APRIL 11, 1912

THE NEXT MORNING AFTER BREAKFAST, we walked the first-class halls, with Ethan carrying the shriveled dragon heart in his jacket pocket. The idea was that if the dragon heart was close enough to a room with the Dark Sword inside, it would be able to detect the Sword, so we could get on with our mission.

Either the Dark Sword wasn't in any of the first-class suites, or the dragon heart was out of juice, because we found nothing.

After a walk past the final first-class suite, we headed back to our suite to change for tea. Because of course, it would be totally appalling to wear the same dress to tea that I'd worn to breakfast.

Tea was in the first-class lounge, which was one of the most ornate rooms on the ship. It reminded me of the palace at the Vale, which Harper had told me was decorated to resemble the Versailles palace in France.

We sat down in the plush armchairs at one of the center tables, since it gave us the best chance to listen in on the surrounding conversations. But, as we drank our tea and made light conversation while we eavesdropped, my eyes kept wandering to the beautiful, fully stocked wooden bookcase at the opposite side of the room.

"Go take a look," Ethan said to me. "Karina and I have things covered over here."

I quickly put down my cup of tea and made my way over to the bookshelves. I recognized a bunch of books in there, including *Wuthering Heights, Jane Eyre, Vanity Fair*, and some of my favorites by Jane Austen. I also couldn't help but be amused at the sight of *The Time Machine* by HG Wells.

I was examining the *Anne of Green Gables* collection when someone stepped up next to me.

"Are you a fan of LM Montgomery?" the woman asked.

She was beautiful, with pale skin, dark hair, and soft features. Her dress wasn't as tight around the waist as the other women, and at closer inspection, she appeared to be pregnant.

She was also wearing so much jewelry that I was surprised she wasn't sinking the ship.

"I love *Anne of Green Gables*," I said, although another book near it caught my attention a second later. "But *The Secret Garden* has been one of my favorites since I was a kid."

She studied me for a moment, then let out a lively laugh. "How could you have read it as a kid?" she asked. "It's brand new."

"Oh." I bit my lower lip at the blunder. "I must have confused it with something else."

"Well, if you haven't read it, then you should," she said. "It truly is fantastic."

"I will." I smiled, glad she hadn't pressed further. "Thank you."

"Are you from Australia?"

"Yes," I said, relieved for the change of subject. "Have you been?"

I internally cursed myself for asking, since I doubted anyone on this ship had been to Australia. It wasn't particularly easy to get to in the early 1900s, and in 1912, it hadn't been that long since Australia was the place where the British had sent their convicts.

Then again, she'd recognized my accent. And she was clearly rich. So maybe it wasn't *too* crazy of a thought that she'd been there.

"Not yet," she said. "But my husband has an itch to go. I'm sure we'll make it there someday." She pulled *The Secret Garden* off the shelves and handed it to me. "Take it. I'm sure it'll make you feel like a child again."

"Thanks," I said, and as I examined the pristine hardback, I couldn't help but think about how tempting it would be to take this beautiful first edition back with me to the present.

"My pleasure." She removed another book from the shelves—*The Autobiography of Benjamin Franklin*—and pranced back with it to her table. It was one of the larger tables in the room, and she sat in the center of the sofa that was surrounded by a group of women. They cleared space for her, and from the way they were focused on her, she seemed to be the most popular one in the group.

I clutched the copy of *The Secret Garden* to my chest and walked back to where I'd been sitting with Karina and Ethan.

As I sat down, Karina looked at me like I'd done something extraordinary.

"What?" I asked, since she clearly wanted to say something.

"Do you know who that woman is that you were talking to?"

"You know how many friends I have here in 1912," I said sarcastically. "Who is she?"

She leaned closer, lowered her voice, and said, "That's Madeline Astor. She's the wife of the richest man in the world—John Astor. They love to travel. They're returning back home to America after a long tour of Egypt."

"She mentioned that her husband wanted to visit Australia," I said, and then I realized I knew who they were. Well, at least I knew who *he* was. "They end up going. The street I lived on is John Astor Road, and I went to John Astor High. Tons of things in Australia are named after him."

"Now that you mention it, I remember hearing about their journey there," she said, and then she looked to the book in my hand. "What do you plan on doing with that?"

"Reading it," I said. What else did someone do with a book?

"I suppose you'll have some time to read after we find the Dark Sword," she said, since we had to wait to time travel back to the present until we reached New York. If I tried to bring her to the present while we were on board, we'd end up in the middle of the ocean. "But it would be a shame to miss a minute of this once-in-a-lifetime experience because your nose is buried in a book."

"That's Gemma's favorite place for her nose to be," Ethan said, which earned a smile from me.

"It is," I said. "But Karina's right. We should make the most of this experience. I can always read once we're back home."

"You're taking the book back with you?" From Karina's tone, it was obvious she disapproved.

"Yep."

"What about everything you said about making the fewest changes in the past possible?"

"It's one book." I shrugged. "It'll be fine. Plus, I'm the Queen of Pentacles. If I want to bring the book back with me, then that's what I'm going to do."

8

GEMMA

SUNDAY, APRIL 14, 1912

On Friday, we did the same thing in second class that we'd done in first class—had dinner, eavesdropped on passengers in common areas, and walked by each cabin with the dragon heart to see if it sensed the Dark Sword.

Just like in first class, we finished as clueless as we'd started.

On Saturday, Karina compelled the crew to let us into the cargo area of the ship. There was a *lot* of cargo, and we meticulously searched through each item.

No Dark Sword.

On Sunday morning, there was supposed to be a lifeboat drill, which we thought would be a good opportunity to do a more thorough check of the passengers in case we'd missed some. But the captain canceled it. So we spent the day in steerage, doing the same thing there that we'd done in first and second class.

Nothing turned up.

And Hecate wasn't in the Eternal Library any of those days to answer our questions.

Now, we were back in our suite after dinner, changing into our night robes and trying to figure out our next move.

"The dragon heart is worthless," I said, looking at the shriveled heart in frustration. "We might as well throw it into the ocean for all the good it's been doing us."

"There's still a bit of life left in it," Ethan said. "Not much, but it should have been able to help us."

I shook my head, since if the heart still had life in it, it sure didn't look like it to me.

"I have a question, and you might not like it," Karina said, and we looked at her to continue. "What if Harper was wrong? What if the Dark Sword isn't on this ship?"

"Harper wasn't wrong," I said.

"How can you know for sure?"

"Because she asked Hecate in the Eternal Library."

Of course, since Karina wasn't a witch and didn't have a key, what I'd said went completely over her head.

"So her source was a good one," she said instead.

"Yes," I answered. "Exactly."

She easily accepted this, thanks to the magic of Hecate's keys.

We were sitting around the fireplace—which was actually fake, since a real one would be a fire hazard—when I felt a shift. It was like the world was being pulled apart and pieced back together again.

I *knew* this feeling.

It was the same feeling I'd gotten when I'd watched Katherine change my and Ethan's memories in the cove.

But Katherine was currently in a deep sleep in a cabin below the Antarctic Circle. This wasn't because of her. And there was only one other person in the world who could do something like this.

"Gemma?" Ethan asked. "What's wrong?"

"Mira's here," I said. "And she's making a change in the timeline. A *big* change."

"How can you tell?" Karina asked.

"Because I can feel it."

"So, you can feel where she is?"

"No," I said, and then I looked to Ethan. "Does that heart definitely have some life left in it?"

"Yes," he said. "I'm sure of it."

"Good." I picked the heart up from the coffee table, closed my eyes, and focused on Mira.

She was my twin. Our souls were connected. More than that—our magical objects were connected.

I reached into the ether, removed the Holy Crown, and placed it on my head. The moment I did, its magic flowed through me, filling me with confidence.

The heart didn't have enough power left in it to take me to the Dark Sword. But maybe…

I gathered as much magic as I could, closed my eyes, and pushed it into the dragon heart, like a burst of energy to bring it back to life.

Take me to the Dark Crown, I thought.

The heart pulsed with energy, and an image flashed through my mind.

Mira, on the Titanic, in one of the places I'd been with Karina and Ethan.

When I opened my eyes, Karina and Ethan were staring at me in shock.

The dragon heart in my hands was gray and dead.

"What did you see?" Ethan asked.

"I know where Mira is," I said, and I hurried out the door, not even bothering to put on my shoes before leaving the suite.

9

GEMMA

SUNDAY, APRIL 14, 1912

WE PASSED two first-class passengers in the hall, and they watched us run by in our nightclothes, their mouths wide open at what I supposed to them was a massive scandal.

Not wanting to run into any more passengers, I took a flight of stairs up to the deck below the Boat Deck—the A Deck—and hurried down the first class promenade toward the front of the ship. The outside decks were empty, since it was so freezing outside that the humans preferred to stay indoors. Luckily, vampires had a high tolerance for cold, as did Ethan and I, thanks to our fire magic.

At the front of the deck, I saw her. Mira. She was three decks below, on D Deck which was open space for the steerage passengers. She stood at the railing, carrying a tan woman with wild dark curls. The woman flopped in Mira's arms, looking either unconscious or dead. They both wore the simple clothing of steerage passengers.

A charcoal-colored sword that I assumed was the Dark Sword lay next to my twin's feet.

I hurried down the three decks to D Deck in time to watch Mira hoist the woman over the railing and toss her out to sea.

Mira placed her hands on the railing and looked over it, like she was checking to make sure her job was complete. That woman had to be the shifter. Then, still facing the ocean, Mira reached down and picked up the Sword.

All she needed to do was go to a door, use her key to enter the Eternal Library, and disappear to anywhere in the world.

I needed to stop her before she had the chance.

"Block the doors," I told Ethan and Karina, and then I ran forward, meeting Mira's eyes as the turned to look at me.

She scowled, her eyes full of hate, and she held the Sword at the ready.

But Mira didn't excel in swordplay. She was strongest with her elements.

I reached inside myself to connect to my fire magic, but I didn't call it forward. The

THE DRAGON QUEEN

light would bring attention to us, and I didn't want any humans to check on what was going on and get caught in the crossfire.

"You shouldn't have come," Mira said, and ice crawled out of her hands and up the Sword, turning it into a frozen weapon.

"You can't use that," I said. "You're not the Dark Queen of Swords."

"Its magic won't connect with me, but I can still use it like a regular sword." She leaped toward me, ready to attack, but was blown back by a gust of wind so strong that it slammed her to the floor.

Ethan.

I glanced over my shoulder, and sure enough, Ethan stood in front of one of the doors, palms out and ready to help me against Mira's attacks.

"It's three against one," I said as she pushed herself back up. "You can't beat us."

Her eyes darted around, landing on each of us. She was cornered, and she knew it.

Which made this the perfect time to tell her the truth.

"Do you remember when I was poisoned by the nightshade on Moon Mountain?" I asked her.

She stared at me, Sword out in front of her, not moving.

"I had a vision," I continued. "Of the original version of the past. In it, Ethan and I were together from that first day we met in the cove."

"There were no alternate versions of the past back then," she snarled. "Neither of us had gotten our magic yet."

"Neither one of *us* had our magic yet," I said. "But there was someone else who could change the past as we knew it."

Wind swirled around her, although she made no move to attack again.

"I went to the Eternal Library and asked Hecate about the vision," I continued. "I learned that Katherine, Constance, Isemay, and Genevieve didn't wake from their sleep right before we got to Antarctica. They woke months earlier, on the day before our birthday. Constance had a vision strong enough to pull them out of the spell. She saw us getting our magic the next day, and she saw the griffin kill you."

"Her vision was clearly wrong."

"It wasn't," I said. "Because in the vision, Ethan and I were together. He ran after me when the griffin attacked instead of bringing you to the cave. You were standing on the beach, unprotected, when the griffin attacked."

"No." Her grip tightened around the handle of the Sword, and the wind picked up around her. "He wouldn't do that. He *didn't* do that."

"You're right—he didn't do that," I said. "Katherine and the others in the Seventh Kingdom knew they needed to stop it from happening. They knew one of us was destined to become the Queen of Pentacles, and they needed to keep us both alive. So Katherine went to the cove when Ethan and I were spending time there the night before the ceremony. She used her compulsion on us. She told us that on the day Ethan and I met, he didn't stay with me in the cove. He went on, found you, and ended up dating you. And you know how Katherine's gift of compulsion works. It didn't just change my and Ethan's memories. It changed the memories of everyone connected to us, so we *all* believed that a past that never happened was real."

"You're lying."

"I'm not. Ask Hecate the next time you're in the Eternal Library."

She glanced at Ethan, heartbreak splattered across her face, and then she hurled the Dark Sword at me like a javelin.

I dove out of the way a split second before it could pierce through my heart.

It clanked as it hit the floor, and Ethan bolted toward it. He picked it up, sprinted back to the door he'd been guarding, and used his key to go through.

He and the Sword were gone. He was in the Library, waiting for me to join him, pick a new destination, and bring us back to the present.

But I couldn't leave. Not when I'd finally found Mira.

Plus, I needed to stop her from following him into the Library.

So I spun back around to face my twin. Her palms faced up toward the night sky, creating an arch of ice over her head. The ice crept along her arms, icicles growing from the bottoms of them, and traveled along her entire body. She looked like a frozen sculpture. But still, she could move.

She raised her hands, palms toward me, and sharp icicles grew out of each one.

I still didn't call my fire. I just stood there, eyes locked with hers, waiting.

"Do it," I challenged. "Kill me."

She sneered. "You're not even going to try to fight me?"

"You're my twin," I said simply. "Hurting you is the same as hurting myself."

Wind howled around the deck, and my hair whipped across my cheeks. But I refused to leave her there. I'd already lost her once—I couldn't bear losing her again.

So I stood strong, staring her down, daring her to do it. The ice continued to grow out of her, and the wind blew stronger.

As the seconds passed, doubt crept inside me. Because Mira was the Dark Queen of Pentacles. And I'd seen Torrence when she'd been fully dark, right after Selena had been killed in front of her.

She hadn't been affected by her best friend's death.

I loved my twin. But as much as I wanted to believe that Mira was mentally stronger than Torrence, I knew it wasn't true.

Time felt like it slowed around us, and I braced myself for Mira's attack. I wanted to close my eyes, but I didn't.

Because if my twin was going to kill me, then I wanted her to be looking me in the eyes when she did it.

10

GEMMA

SUNDAY, APRIL 14, 1912

Mira's face contorted in pain, like she was having an intense internal battle.

Then she spun around to face the front of the ship and released her magic into the ocean with a loud scream.

The ice kept coming out of her palms, like there was a bottomless pit of it inside her. Finally, when it seemed impossible for there to be any more magic left, she released the last bit of it and collapsed to the floor.

As she sat up, I ran to her side and wrapped my arms around her in a hug.

She didn't flinch out of my embrace.

But I couldn't focus on her. Because there was something *growing* out of the ocean where she'd thrown her magic. A shadow in the dark night, building on itself until it was taller than it was wide.

The ship sailed closer toward it, and fear formed in my throat at the realization of what we were seeing.

"Iceberg, straight ahead!" a male voice called out from one of the watchpoints behind us.

The ship groaned as it tried to maneuver its way around the giant block of ice, but the iceberg was too close. The Titanic had no chance.

Without some supernatural interference, we were going to hit it.

"Use your magic to melt it," I told Mira.

She raised her hands, but nothing came out.

"I can't." She dropped her arms back to her sides. "I'm drained."

I held up my hands and shot bursts of fire out of my palms. But there was so much ice. Too much for me to melt.

I barely made a dent before the bottom of the ship collided with the ice below the water. A painfully loud screech filled the air as ice tore through steel.

Mira and I stared up at the iceberg and gaped as we passed by. At some point, Karina had run forward to stand next to us, and she was staring at it, too.

Chunks of ice broke off and fell onto the deck.

The screech of ice against steel continued for so long that the sound would be ingrained in my mind forever.

Others hurried out to the deck—curious passengers who wanted to see what had happened. Their eyes were wide as we passed the iceberg and left it behind.

This was bad.

Really, really bad.

We weren't supposed to change history. But now...

"You need to go with Ethan to the Library," Mira said. "Bring him back to the present and get the Sword to Avalon."

I stared at her, shocked. "You're talking like you're on our side."

"I *am* on your side," she said. "Lilith and Lavinia used transformation potion so I didn't know who they were, and they tricked me into going with them to their lair. Lilith is the Dark Queen of Cups. She used the Dark Grail to bind me to her, and she's been controlling my mind ever since."

"Is she in your mind now?"

"Sort of," she said. "The further back in time I go, the less control she has over me. It's like the gap in time weakens her hold. And just now—when I made the choice to save you instead of kill you—I weakened the bond. But it's still there, lingering in the back of my mind. If I return to the present, it'll take full control again."

"So you're staying here," I said. "Until we kill Lilith and break that bond."

"Yes."

"Then I'm staying with you."

"No," she said. "They need you in the present to win the war against Lilith and the demons. You have to stop her from completing her ultimate goal."

"Raising Lucifer," I said.

"How did you know?"

"Skylar saw it in a vision a few weeks ago."

"She's right," Mira said, even though we both knew Skylar's visions were never wrong. "Lilith needs fresh gifted vampire blood to raise Lucifer. She's been turning gifted humans into vampires since the demons rose from Hell, and she's been collecting their blood for the spell to free him from his prison realm there."

"But you said she needs *fresh* gifted vampire blood," I said. "Most of that blood is years old."

"Which is why she needed me," Mira said.

"She's been sending you back in time to bring the blood to the present," I realized.

"Yes."

"Which means she knew what the Holy and Dark Crowns could do all along."

"She did. And I refuse to go back to the present to be her slave again. But once you kill her, I'll feel the bond break. I'll return to the present, go through the Angel Trials, and find you on Avalon."

"You're a Dark Queen," I said. "You don't know if you'll pass the Angel Trials."

She narrowed her eyes, and they flashed icy blue. "I'm going to pass the Angel Trials."

I didn't argue with her, since if she tried to pass the Trials and failed, she'd end up in the river that led to the Vale. If that happened, Harper or someone else who lived there would let me know Mira was there.

"You can't stay here in 1912 alone," I said instead, and I looked up to Karina, who was standing there, listening to us. "Will you stay with her and make sure she's okay here?"

"Of course I will," she said. "Once we dock in New York, I'll get us situated there until everything is figured out in the present."

"This ship isn't docking in New York." Mira picked up a piece of ice and stared at it vacantly.

"What do you mean?" Karina asked.

"The ice ripped through the steel. Right now, water is pouring through the tear and flooding the engine rooms. It's traveling through the bottom of the ship. Sinking it."

"That's impossible." Karina scoffed. "The Titanic is unsinkable."

"The ocean is far more powerful than this ship," Mira said. "The Titanic is going to sink. At the rate the water is filling it up, I give it a few hours, tops."

"Can you stop it?" I asked.

"I can't fix the tear in the steel," she said. "The Titanic is going to sink, and there's nothing I can do about it."

"Then you have to come back with us," I said, but then I realized—Karina would be stuck here, because she couldn't go through the Eternal Library. She needed to be on solid land before I could return her to the present.

"I'm staying in 1912 with Karina, where Lilith can't reach me," Mira said. "There are lifeboats on board, and both of us are immune to the cold. We'll be okay until rescue comes for us."

"There aren't enough lifeboats," Karina said simply.

"Why wouldn't there be enough lifeboats?" I asked.

"White Star Line—the company that built the Titanic—called the ship 'unsinkable,'" she said. "More lifeboats would crowd up the Boat Deck. They removed some of the lifeboats so the first-class passengers could have more room to enjoy the outside space."

"Which means all of these people…" I looked around at the third-class passengers, who were playing with chunks of ice like they had zero cares in the world.

"There aren't enough lifeboats for them all," Karina said. "First class passengers will be prioritized. As for the ones in steerage…" She looked around sadly, not continuing the sentence.

"They'll be left to go down with the ship," I said.

"Yes."

My heart ached for all of these doomed souls. So many of them were going to die because of what had happened here tonight.

Guilt filled me to the core, and I pushed it down to deal with later.

"So much for trying to create as little impact on the past as possible," I said. "If Time rejects the change, we'll lose the Dark Sword."

"As long as we don't directly affect one of the present-day Queens receiving her Object, Time is flexible," Mira said. "It will mold to the changes. And there's no Dark Queen of Swords yet. There's a good chance it will be okay."

"Hopefully," I said. "But I need *you* to be okay, too."

Karina straightened, determination filling her eyes. "Mira and I will be fine," she said. "I'll ensure she's properly dressed so she can take your place. As first-class passengers, we'll have a prime spot on the lifeboats. And if things get rough, I have my compulsion. We're going to be okay. Now, use that Queen of Pentacles magic of yours to get back home, bring the Dark Sword on Avalon, and help kill Lilith."

11

GEMMA

SUNDAY, APRIL 14, 1912

I USED my key to enter the Eternal Library, where Ethan was waiting for me in the ivory hall. He was alone—there was no sign of Hecate—and he was studying the Dark Sword.

It was made of obsidian, and there was a small red gemstone in the center of the handle. As I stepped closer, I felt the darkness pulsing off it. The red gem wasn't glowing, although I had a feeling it would once the Sword was in the hands of its rightful owner.

Relief crossed Ethan's face when he saw me. "I wanted to come after you," he said. "But I had a feeling you'd strangle me if I left the Sword unattended. Plus, I know Mira would never kill you."

"You thought right—on both accounts," I said, and then I filled him in on everything that had happened on the ship after he'd left.

"So the Titanic's going to sink on her maiden voyage, without enough lifeboats, and with many well-known people on board," he said. "That will make history."

"*If* Time accepts the change," I said. "But still, all of those people will be dead."

"I know it's hard. But it's for the greater good," he said. "Otherwise, the demons could win the war and kill far more people than those who will go down with the ship."

"I know," I said, even though I still felt numb about it.

Deciding who would live and who would die was one of the most difficult parts of being a Queen. But it was my responsibility. And like Ethan had said, I believed I'd chosen the lesser of two evils. So I was going to make it worth it.

Which meant getting the Dark Sword to Avalon.

Hecate's realm blocked all magic but my witch magic, so Ethan and I had to go somewhere else before returning to the present. Going straight to Avalon to travel back to the present was out of the question, since in 1912 Avalon was a dead island with no doors, and I needed a door for Hecate's key to work.

"Where to?" I asked him.

"Hm." He scrunched his eyebrows as he thought, since we had to go to a place we'd both been, that had existed in 1912. "Was Twin Pines Cafe around in this time?"

"No," I said. "They didn't build John Astor Road until later."

At the mention of the name of the street where I'd lived, my thoughts went to Madeline Astor. I hoped she and her husband had safely gotten on board a lifeboat.

Given what Karina had said about first class passengers being prioritized, I figured they had a much better chance than others.

"Then I guess the Haven tearoom," he said. "We just have to hope no one's in there when we enter."

"You might want to hide that." I motioned to the Dark Sword. "Just in case."

It was tough, but he managed to slide the Sword into the side of his pants and hide the handle with his jacket.

We used our keys to go to the Haven tearoom… and two people were in there. Mary and another vampire—one with doll-like features, long dark hair, and porcelain skin.

I immediately recognized her from her pictures in the history books.

Queen Laila. The vampire queen of the Vale before she'd been killed by Annika and replaced by King Alexander and Queen Deidre. She hardly looked dangerous—which I supposed was one of the scariest things about her.

Both she and Mary stared at us in shock.

"We're in the middle of a meeting," Mary said, and then she looked at us closer. "I thought I knew all of the citizens of the Haven. Have we met before?"

"Sorry—we were told that you were gone, and we came to clear the food," I said quickly, and then I scurried out of the room with Ethan, put the Holy Crown on my head, and brought us both back to the present.

"Sword still there?" I asked him when we reappeared in the hall.

If Time had rejected the change, it would be gone.

I held my breath as I waited for his answer.

He patted the side of his jacket. "Still here," he said, and he opened it slightly to show me.

Relief flooded my body.

Our mission had been a success.

At the same time, memories of the new timeline overlapped the ones of the original. Ethan's pupils dilated as the new memories filled his brain, too.

Like in the original timeline, Harper had sent us the fire message telling us to come to her room ASAP. But she hadn't needed to bring out a history book to give us information about the Titanic, since the ship was infamous for its tragic sinking on its maiden voyage. We already knew all about it, thanks to the award-winning movie.

Our mission in the new timeline had been to board the Titanic and find the Dark Sword before the ship sank. Karina had joined us both times, but in the new timeline, it was with the assumption that she'd easily get into one of the lifeboats and get picked up by the rescue ship—the Carpathia.

After getting the Dark Sword to Avalon, I was supposed to go to the port of New York City to grab Karina and take her home. But obviously, since she needed to look out for Mira back in 1912, that plan needed to change.

"We did it," I said with a huge smile, and I jumped into Ethan's arms and kissed him.

He swung me around in a circle and kissed me back.

Amidst all the chaos, I was so incredibly grateful that things were finally right between us.

"Ready to go back to Avalon?" he asked after placing me back down.
"Let's go," I said, and then I took out my key and stepped through the door.

12

GEMMA

TUESDAY, JUNE 1 (PRESENT DAY)

THE EARTH ANGEL—ANNIKA Pearce, also known as the Queen of Cups—called a council meeting the moment we knocked on her door and showed her the Dark Sword.

The council met in the castle meeting room, around the ornate round table that had been used by King Arthur and his knights centuries ago. The council consisted of all four Queens, our chosen mates, and Skylar Danvers, the prophetess of Avalon.

The Dark Sword was laid out in the center of the table as we filled them in on everything that had happened in both the original timeline and this one.

"So Lilith is down two Queens," Annika said once we finished. "The Dark Queen of Swords can't be crowned, given that we're in possession of the Dark Sword, and Mira is with Karina in 1912, where she's unreachable to everyone except for you."

"Correct," I said.

"Four Holy Queens against two Dark Queens," Raven said with a smirk. "We've got this."

"Except it's not that easy," Skylar said. "Unless you've forgotten about Lucifer?"

"Right." Raven huffed, sitting back in her chair and crossing her arms. "Him."

"Does anyone even know how to kill Lucifer?" Julian asked. "*Can* he be killed?"

"We don't know yet," Annika said softly. "But we're working on it."

One more question to add to my list of things to ask Hecate next time she showed up in the Library.

"Off-topic, but I have another question," Raven said, and she turned to look at me. "What on Earth's a 'pentacle?'"

I chuckled, since this wasn't the first time I'd gotten this question.

"It's a five-pointed star," I explained. "The five points of the star represent the five elements. Earth, air, water, fire, and spirit. Although in this case, spirit is my power as the Queen of Pentacles—time."

"Got it," she said, and then the double doors to the council room were flung open, and Sage marched inside.

In her skin-tight black Avalon Army uniform, stiletto boots that had most likely been charmed by Bella to be comfortable no matter what, and her long dark hair streaming behind her, Sage looked like a force to be reckoned with.

Annika stood, immediately on guard. "You know you have high standing on Avalon," she said to Sage. "But council meetings are limited to council members only."

"It's calling to me." Sage sounded like she was in a trance. "It *needs* me."

We all watched her in shock as she reached over the table and grabbed the Dark Sword.

The gemstone in the center of the Sword glowed, and red magic swirled around the blade as it came to life. Sage's eyes gleamed red, too, and it was like her entire body was shining with magic.

She held the Dark Sword up high, relishing its power. After a few seconds, the red glow settled down, and she and the Sword were back to normal.

"The Dark Sword," Sage said, studying it with satisfaction. "It's *mine*."

Raven jumped to her feet, Excalibur held up in front of her, ready to fight. Noah stood at her side, his teeth bared, his fingers shifted into sharp claws.

"Whoa," Sage said, and she pointed the tip of the Dark Sword toward the floor. "I'm not going to hurt you."

"You're the Dark Queen of Swords." Raven's voice was calm and steady, although she watched Sage with shock and betrayal.

"I am," Sage said.

"But you're not dark."

"I'm a shifter," she said calmly. "Shifters were created by demons, just like Nephilim were created by angels. Dark magic runs in my blood."

"I know that," Raven said. "But *you're* not dark. You're not *evil*."

Sage remained still, as if she knew one wrong movement would set Raven off. "I've always had darkness in me—just like Noah and every other shifter has darkness in them," she said. "It doesn't make me evil. Just like how Bella Devereux isn't evil even though she practices dark magic."

"But now you're a dark *Queen*," Raven said. "It's different."

"I'm the exact same person you've known since I helped Noah save your life in that back alley in Santa Monica."

Raven lowered Excalibur slightly, although she didn't look fully convinced.

"Torrence uses dark magic," Selena pointed out. "She has control of it now, since Bella's been tutoring her. But the darkness doesn't consume her like it did when she got out of control. She's on our side. Just like Sage is."

Sage shot Selena a grateful smile. "Thanks for believing in me," she said.

"No problem."

Noah's claws shifted back to normal, which made me think he was coming around, too.

"This reminds me of something that Makena—one of the high witches of the Ward—told me and Mira while we were there," I said, and they all looked to me to continue. "She told me that other than the demons and angels, no one is purely good or purely evil. When guided by someone who believes in them, even the darkest souls have the potential to see the light."

"The Montgomery pack is drawn to darkness," Sage said. "My brother is a good enough example of that, given that he teamed up with demons. And I experienced a time of extreme darkness when I was bound to Azazel. But I kept hold of my true self the entire time. I may not have been able to physically fight the demon bond, but I never gave in mentally. That experience gave me the strength I need to fight with Avalon's army as the Dark Queen of Swords."

Raven studied Sage for a few more seconds, and then she lowered Excalibur. "I suppose it's about time I had an equal partner to spar with," she said with a bit of friendly teasing in her tone.

"I can definitely manage that," Sage said lightly.

The two of them shared a smile, and I could tell that things were already back to normal between them.

It reminded me of me and Mira when we forgave each other after a fight. We didn't need to say anything—it was just *known* that everything was okay again. Just like it had been on the deck of the Titanic after she'd thrown her magic at the ocean instead of at me.

Raven and Sage might not be twins, but they were best friends, and that connection counted for something, too.

"The two of you will have to save your sparring session for later," Annika said, and then she looked to Sage and continued, "I need you to find Thomas and bring him here. Because the two of you are the newest members of Avalon's council, and we need all council members here to continue with this meeting."

13

GEMMA

TUESDAY, JUNE 1 (PRESENT DAY)

A FEW HOURS LATER, Thomas and Sage were sitting around the round table, fully briefed on everything that had been going on.

"So, Lilith needs the gifted vampire blood to raise Lucifer," Sage said.

"Correct," I replied.

"And what will happen after Lucifer is released from his prison realm?"

"In the Bible, Lilith is regarded as secretive and conniving," Skylar said, and we all looked to her to continue. "She's snake-like and is often associated with the serpent in the Garden of Eden."

"It explains the snake-like way that she and Lavinia worked together to trick Mira into that demon bond," I said.

"It also explains why she's been leading her side of the war from the shadows," Skylar said. "Lucifer, on the other hand, isn't known for being inconspicuous. Once he's released, he'll likely want us all to know it."

"How do you know all of this?" Ethan asked.

"When I was human, I owned a new age shop," she said. "I immersed myself in the study of all kinds of mysticism."

"'Immersed' is an understatement," Raven said, rolling her eyes. "She was obsessed. *Is* obsessed."

"That's what happens when a person has a higher calling," Skylar said, and then she turned back to Sage. "I take it you had a reason for asking?"

"I did." Sage sat straighter, her eyes taking on a look of hard determination. "As always, we can't find Lilith. Which means we need to get her to come out in the open. Mira told Gemma that as the Dark Queen of Cups, Lilith will lead the ceremony to raise Lucifer. Does anyone have any idea where the Hell Gate to his prison realm is located?"

She looked around at everyone at the table, but no one had any answers.

"I might be able to find someone who does," I said, and then I stood up, walked across the room, stuck my key in the door, and stepped into the ivory hall of the Eternal Library.

Hecate stood across the hall, waiting for me. She wore a purple gown that sparkled with what looked like nighttime stars, and her dark hair glimmered like it was shining under the moonlight.

"Gemma," she greeted me. "You've had quite the adventure since the last time we met."

"You mean how I witnessed one of the most famous maritime disasters in all of history?" I asked.

"I assume that isn't the question you came here to ask."

"No," I said, cursing inwardly at myself for my careless phrasing. "Of course not."

"I figured as much." She gave me a knowing smile, then led me into the endless hall of books, and I asked her my *real* question.

14

GEMMA

TUESDAY, JUNE 1 (PRESENT DAY)

I RE-ENTERED Avalon's meeting room with a triumphant smile.

"She was there?" Ethan asked, but he must have already known my answer, because he jumped up, used his key, and walked through the door.

He came back a few seconds later, looking bummed.

"Was she gone?" I asked.

"Yep."

"Interesting." This was the first time Ethan and I had ever entered the Eternal Library alone. It had never crossed my mind that Hecate would be there for me and then no-show for Ethan on the same day.

"Where did you go?" Annika asked us.

"I needed to double check something," I said simply, and then Ethan and I returned to our seats around the round table without any further questions. "I know the location of the Lucifer's Hell Gate."

"Why didn't you say something earlier?" Raven asked.

"I didn't want to say anything until I knew for sure."

She nodded, apparently accepting my explanation.

"So?" Selena sat forward, impatient. "Where is it?"

"Las Vegas," I said. "Right in the center of the Vegas Strip."

"Vegas," Sage said with a small chuckle. "Very fitting."

The others nodded, and some of them smiled slightly. It was hard to miss the irony of the situation.

"She probably has demons and dark witches stationed there," Raven said. "I could go with the Nephilim army and start clearing them out."

"And alert Lilith that we know the location of Lucifer's Hell Gate?" Julian said, his tone making it clear that he thought that was a terrible idea. "We need a better strategy than that."

"Agreed," said Thomas. "We shouldn't make our presence known. But we can spy on them without them knowing we're there."

THE DRAGON QUEEN

"How?" Selena asked.

"There are cameras in every casino in Vegas," he said. "They're called the Eyes in the Sky."

"You can hack into them," Annika realized. "We can do surveillance from right here on Avalon."

Of course. Thomas was a gifted vampire—his gift was with technology. I wasn't quite sure how it worked, but he could definitely use his gift to tune into the cameras in Vegas.

"I can go there pretty discreetly," he said. "There are supernatural groups of all kinds living in Vegas. Vampires, shifters, witches. All I need to do is touch the walls of the buildings, and we're in."

"And we can talk to the supernaturals who already live there," Raven said. "Get them to keep lookout for us, too."

"This circles back to my original idea," Sage said. "Because eventually, Lilith will go to Vegas to raise Lucifer. Once we get word that she's there, we'll teleport in, ready to strike."

"But she may never go there to raise him," I pointed out. "Remember what Mira said—Lilith needs enough fresh gifted vampire blood to soak the ground around the Hell Gate."

"Our army has been finding the bunkers where the demons are keeping the gifted humans and rescuing them," Raven said proudly. "Saving the gifted humans before she can turn them into vampires is how we've held her off from raising Lucifer for this long."

"And it's working," Sage said. "Maybe too well."

"What do you mean?"

"I mean that we need Lilith in Vegas, ready to raise Lucifer. She can't go there unless she has enough gifted vampire blood to do the spell."

"What are you saying?" I asked, even though I had a pretty good idea of what she was saying.

I just needed her to say it out loud, to be sure.

"I'm saying that we stop rescuing the gifted humans from the bunkers," Sage said. "We let her turn them into vampires, so she has enough gifted vampire blood to go to Vegas and perform the spell."

Horror splashed across Annika's face. "You want us to sacrifice all those innocent people," she said.

"It's been over fifteen years, and we're no closer to finding Lilith than we were back then," Sage said. "This is war. In war, sacrifices need to be made."

"These are innocent people," argued Annika.

"The longer we let this war continue, the more people will be killed," Sage said. "By getting Lilith to Vegas, we can end it sooner than later."

She looked around the table, sizing up who might take her side.

I instantly thought of my time in Ember—when the dragon had sacrificed himself to give us his heart to track the Holy Crown.

But that had been different.

He'd been willing.

These humans would be casualties that could have been saved.

But for how long? The Nephilim army was able to find some of the bunkers and save the gifted humans there, but not all of them. Humans were dying anyway—it was just taking longer than it would have otherwise. Why extend this war when we could kill Lilith before she raised Lucifer and put an end to this once and for all?

"We need to talk about this further," Annika said. "And then we'll do what this council is here for—we'll take a vote."

15

GEMMA

THURSDAY, JUNE 24 (PRESENT DAY)

FOR THE PAST THREE WEEKS, we'd been doing the only thing useful to do in a time like this—preparing for the battle to come.

Because it *would* be coming.

Soon.

Ethan and I were on one of the training grounds when Annika teleported in.

"It's time," she said, and then she took both of us to the council room, where the others were waiting.

They jumped into it immediately once we got there.

"I've alerted the Nephilim army and the witches that it's about to happen," Raven said. "They're waiting for the fire message, and then they'll head out."

"The supernaturals in Vegas have been notified, too," Thomas said.

Sage held tightly onto the Dark Sword. "I can't wait to give Lilith what's coming to her," she said, and then she ran her finger along the flat side of the Sword, like she was petting it. "I'm glad this thing lets me kill greater demons, despite the fact that I'm not Nephilim."

"If I get to her first, I'm taking her down," Raven said. "She's either of ours to kill."

"Then it's a race to see who gets to her first," Sage said, and they shared a friendly, competitive smile.

Annika cleared her throat, and all eyes were on her. "I'd give an encouraging speech on how we've been preparing for this for years, but Lilith isn't going to wait to raise Lucifer," she said, and then she sat down at the table. "Bring me a pen and paper, and I'll get the message to our army."

16

GEMMA

THURSDAY, JUNE 24 (PRESENT DAY)

THERE WAS ONLY one adult on Avalon who couldn't leave the island—Annika.

When she'd first arrived on Avalon and the island was dead, she'd used her magic as the Earth Angel to sign a contract with the island to bring it back to life. It was a contract signed with her blood, which meant her life force was what was keeping Avalon alive.

If she left Avalon, the island would die.

Eventually, the only people left on the island were me, Ethan, Annika, Bella, Torrence, the children who were too young to fight, and the full fae, since their iron allergy made it impossible for them to go to Earth.

Annika looked at me, her golden eyes as serious as ever. "You know your job," she said.

"Yes," I replied. "I know."

Remain at the vantage point.

Observe the battle.

Stay alive.

If we lost, and if I died, then that would be it. There'd be no second chances.

I owed it to the world to remain in the shadows, and to stay alive. That was one of the main things I'd learned from the beginning of my reign as Queen as Pentacles—I was an observer of time, destined to mold it in the shadows. Most would never know how large of a role I played in shaping the future.

I was at peace with that. I'd come to peace with it when I'd returned from saving Selena's life.

"Then go," Annika said. "And return to me with news that we've won this war, once and for all."

Torrence stepped up to stand in front of me, and Bella did the same with Ethan.

"I'll keep you safe," Ethan promised me. "Always."

"I know," I said, and we shared a loving smile.

Then he took Bella's hands, I took Torrence's, and they teleported us out.

THE DRAGON QUEEN

We reappeared on the open-air roof of the Stratosphere—the hotel at the end of the Las Vegas Strip with an observation tower that looked out over the wide street. It was the second tallest observation tower in the Western Hemisphere, which made it the perfect spot for the job I needed to do.

There were a few thrill rides at the top of it, and tourists were enjoying themselves on them without a care in the world.

Humans who could likely become casualties in this battle.

Unfortunately, there was nothing we could do to clear them out without alerting Lilith and her dark army that we knew they were coming. It was another one of those hard decisions—we were putting a fraction of people at risk to save the world.

I hated it.

But it was what needed to be done.

I stared down the street full of massive hotels that was lit by the bright Vegas sun. Lilith had likely chosen to do this during the day on purpose—it made it so the vampires in Avalon's Army had to either stay inside the hotels or be weakened if they went out in the sun. But we had enough Nephilim, witches, and shifters on our side to hold our ground.

She'd also likely chosen this particular day on purpose. Because the normally traffic-packed Strip was devoid of cars. There was a marathon run tonight—it was called Running with the Devil—so the road was cleared to provide safety for the runners.

Besides that, everything on the Strip looked normal. But that was because supernaturals were good at blending in. Thanks to Thomas's ability to magically hack into the camera systems, we knew Lilith's dark witches had been teleporting demons into the hotels all morning.

Which was why our people were stationed on the sidewalks along the street, wearing cloaking crystals to hide themselves from the dark army. Thanks to my supernaturally strong vision, I was able to see a few of the witches and shifters I knew from Avalon.

The people who'd be more recognizable to the dark army—the other Queens and major players—were in the shadows, waiting to emerge when the time came.

"Are you scared?" Ethan asked, bringing me back to the present.

I looked at him, then back at the packed Strip. "Not as scared as I should be."

"Because we're going to win," Torrence said with a confident smirk. "We always do."

"Not always," Bella said, and it was true—Avalon's Army had lost fights with demons over the years. "But we hold our own when it matters most."

"We do," I agreed. "But being a time traveler is strange sometimes. Since I can go back in time and change the present, the present doesn't feel as immediate to me as it did before I became the Queen of Pentacles. It feels more like a dress rehearsal than real life."

"Which is why we're here on this tower," Ethan said. "To analyze the 'dress rehearsal' so we're ready if a second performance is necessary."

"It won't be," Torrence said. "But it's good to know you have our backs, just in case."

"I always have your backs," I promised, and then I heard a strange, soft whirring sound in the distance. I looked out to where it was coming from and saw a pack of black dots rise over the mountains and fly toward us.

Helicopters.

Tons of them.

Horror pooled within me as they reached the Strip, the sounds of their blades growing so loud that it infiltrated my brain. Tourists stopped walking and gazed up, using their hands as visors to block the sun.

The helicopters got lower, and it was obvious that they weren't normal helicopters. Each of them had the outline of a circle around the bottom of it. And on the undersides were what looked like faucets.

"Why are there crop-dusters flying over the Strip?" a tourist asked nearby.

"They're probably gonna make it rain!" his friend said loudly—he sounded drunk. "I hope it's vodka in there!"

Despite the heat, I shivered.

Because there was no way those things were carrying vodka.

"Blood," I whispered to Ethan. "Lilith's going to make it rain gifted vampire blood."

As I said it, the red liquid started spraying out of the bottoms of the helicopters. A giant cloud of red formed above the Strip as the blood rained down from one helicopter, and then the next, and then the next. The blood was so thick that it was impossible to see anything.

It was like a scene from a horror movie.

Screams filled the air.

"Torrence and I need to get a closer look at what's happening," Bella said. "The two of you—stay here."

They were gone before we could reply.

I reached for Ethan's hand and squeezed it. The helicopters were focusing on the center of the Strip, so there wasn't any blood at the top of the Stratosphere, but its metallic scent filled my nose and mouth.

The screams intensified—an eerie chorus echoing out of the red storm.

Bella reappeared next to us. She was covered in blood—her skin looked like it had been dyed red—and blood dripped from her hair. "Our shifters have changed into their animal forms and they're scaring the humans to get them inside the hotels," she said. "They're not hurting the humans, but there are demons and dark witches down there, too. They've already started to fight, but our people are holding them off."

"Where's Torrence?" I asked.

"She stayed down there to help."

Of course she did. Torrence wasn't one to stay on the sidelines.

We stood there for what must have been thirty minutes, watching helicopter after helicopter fly over the Strip and spray blood over the street.

Blue lightning flashed inside the ominous red cloud—Selena's magic.

Bella popped in and out, giving us reports of what was going on down there.

Most of the humans had gone inside and were hiding out in the hotels. Avalon's army was fighting the dark army, and luckily for the humans, the dark army only cared about killing supernaturals. And, according to Bella, our army was slaughtering the dark one.

Maybe I wouldn't have to go back in time for a redo, after all.

Finally, the last helicopters finished raining blood upon the Strip, and the air started to clear.

Bodies were strewn across the pavement. Most of them didn't appear to be anyone I recognized. There were also piles of ashes everywhere.

The remains of demons.

Avalon's army had killed so many of them. And our army was standing strong. Selena, Raven, and Sage stood shoulder-to-shoulder, with Selena in the center, radiating magic out of the Holy Wand. Nephilim, witches, and shifters that I recognized were behind them, weapons drawn and ready to fight. They were all drenched in blood, and they looked terrifying.

They stared up at the helicopters, wind blowing all around as the vehicles lowered themselves down so they were hovering about fifty feet above the street. The helicopters flew in a circle, with the largest one in the center.

A blinding flash of red light exploded from the central helicopter—so bright and painful that I had to hold my hand in front of my eyes and turn around. It was like the entire world was red. Not even closing my eyes or holding my hand in front of my face could stop me from seeing it.

Finally the light died down, and I turned back around.

The central helicopter had landed... and it sat in the middle of a large, red barrier dome.

Selena shot blue lightning out of the Holy Wand toward the dome, but the lightning simply spread out along it and fizzled out. She tried again, and again, with the same results each time.

Raven and Sage tried to wham the dome with their Swords, but they were unsuccessful as well.

The three of them stopped launching their attacks when four women wearing long white robes stepped out of the helicopter, all of them with jet-black hair and pale white skin. I assumed they were Foster witches.

Lavinia followed them. She held the Dark Wand, its red crystals glowing like spotlights next to her.

Next out was a woman with long, flowing hair, and hard, cat-like features. She wore leather pants, a black corset top, and she was holding a metallic, charcoal-gray chalice with both of her hands.

Lilith.

And she was carrying the Dark Grail.

17

RAVEN

THURSDAY, JUNE 24 (PRESENT DAY)

My grip around the Holy Sword tightened the moment Lilith stepped out of that helicopter, and my blood boiled at the sight of her.

I'd been hunting her for over sixteen years.

And now, it was time to take her down.

I ran forward and smashed its blade into the red boundary dome, putting all the force into the blow that I could muster.

Pain seared through me, like I'd been electrocuted. Still, that didn't stop me from trying again, and again, until every nerve in my body felt like it had been fried to oblivion.

"Raven!" someone called from behind me. Noah. He wrapped his arms around me—he must have shifted back into human form and some point—and he pulled me away from the dome. "It isn't working. You're hurting yourself each time you try."

He was right. I knew it.

But it didn't mean I liked it.

"If I have to hurt myself to get to her, then so be it," I said, although I didn't fight to escape his hold on me.

Lavinia smiled devilishly, and the red crystal on the Dark Wand hummed. "You can't break through my barrier," she said.

"Maybe she can't," Sage said from behind me. "But I can."

She ran forward, raised the Dark Sword in the air, and smashed it against the barrier dome that surrounded Lilith, Lavinia, and the Foster witches.

Red electricity burst out of Sage's sword and crackled over the dome, the light so bright that it was nearly blinding. I had no choice but to turn away from it. Once the light died down, I inhaled the charred air and looked to see what had happened.

The barrier dome was gone.

Sage had fallen down to the ground, the Dark Sword in her hand. She sat up, frazzled, but alive.

Thomas zipped to her side, despite the fact that the vampires were supposed to stay out of the sun unless absolutely necessary, and checked to see if she was okay.

Lavinia's lips curled upward, and she pointed the Dark Wand at Sage. "Finally—the Dark Queen of Swords is revealed," she said. "Come, take your place at our side, where you belong."

"I belong with Avalon," she said, and she stood up, ready to fight.

Lavinia changed the angle of the Dark Wand and shot a red beam of light at Thomas.

I ran forward to use my Sword to stop its magic, but Sage was quicker. The red light bounced off her blade, saving Thomas's life. Then Selena was there, and her blue magic collided with Lavinia's red magic, a loud crack filling the air as the beams of light met in the space between them.

Selena's blue magic inched toward Lavinia's red, and Lavinia's eyes narrowed as she fought against her. But Selena was more powerful than Lavinia. She had this.

And, now that I knew my friends were still alive, I turned my focus back to Lilith—just in time to see her turn the Dark Grail upside down and let a thick, oily liquid cascade to the ground.

Its metallic scent was unmistakable—blood. Dark, black, unnatural blood.

It sizzled as it hit the pavement, and horror filled me to the bones.

"*Now*, He will rise," Lilith said, and her eyes flashed red as the black blood crawled over the pavement, forming a sort of sinkhole as it spread out.

Lavinia moved to Lilith's side—she and Selena must have stopped fighting when Lilith dumped the contents of the Dark Grail to the ground.

Finally, the pit stopped growing, and black mist that reminded me of Torrence's dark mage magic rose out of it like steam. The pit reeked of death—like a million demons had been rotting inside of it for centuries. A knot of fear formed in my throat, and I couldn't swallow it down.

Because I knew what was in that pit. *Who* was in that pit.

Lucifer.

But the things that emerged from it weren't shaped like a human. They were dogs. Big, black dogs with eyes that glowed demonic red.

"Hellhounds," Noah whispered from next to me, his voice laced with fear.

He barely had a chance to finish saying the word before I surged forward, dancing around the Hellhounds and swinging the Holy Sword through the air. I sliced off their heads and speared them through their hearts, turning them into piles of ashes around me. I caught a glimpse of Sage in the corner of my eye, and she was doing the same. Selena worked with us, too, using the tip of the Holy Wand as a sword as she rammed it through their hearts to slay them.

I was out of breath by the time all the Hellhounds were dead.

None of them had gotten past us.

I smiled as I looked out toward the Stratosphere hotel, where Gemma stood on the roof with Ethan, watching us win this battle.

But my attention quickly refocused on the pit—because something else was rising out of it. A tall, broad, muscular, naked man. He was four times as big as a human, and his presence made the air thrum with dark, heavy magic. His nails were long, black claws that protruded out of his fingers like ten swords, and I gripped Excalibur tighter at the sight of them.

Once he was fully out of the pit, the ground stitched itself together beneath his feet.

Lilith, Lavinia, and the dark witches gazed up at him, looking as intimidated by his presence as I felt.

But Lilith straightened and held the Dark Grail closer to her chest. "Kill them," she commanded, and Lucifer smirked, like he'd been thinking the same thing.

I ran forward, Sword held high in the air, took a large, leaping jump, and aimed the tip of it at his heart.

The Sword collided with his skin with a crash, but it didn't break through—just like it hadn't broken through Lavinia's barrier dome.

Every bone in my body felt like it shattered on impact. My ears buzzed so loudly that I couldn't hear. It was like someone had struck a gong inside my head, and it wasn't shutting off.

The next thing I knew, I was lying on the ground, Lucifer's claws slashed at my throat, and everything went dark.

18

SELENA

THURSDAY, JUNE 24 (PRESENT DAY)

I FROZE and stared at Raven's body in shock—at the blood gushing out of the place where her neck used to connect to her head. Her head had been disconnected from her body. Her golden-rimmed eyes sightlessly gazed up at the darkened sky, and her skin was paler than ever.

The Holy Sword lay next to her, no longer in her grip.

She was dead.

Raven was *dead*.

It didn't feel real. Because Raven was the Queen of Swords. She was unstoppable. The best fighter around.

But Lucifer had slain her in a single swipe.

If she couldn't kill him, then who could?

The thoughts flashed through my mind in what must have been less than a second. The next thing I knew, a beam of red light shot toward me, and Julian pushed me out of the way before it hit.

"Use the Wand against Lucifer," he said, and then he hopped over Raven's body and picked up Excalibur. He moved in a flash to stand back beside me, and when Lavinia aimed another beam of red magic at me, he used the Holy Sword to reflect it back at Lucifer.

But the demon king simply stood there, *absorbing* the red magic as if it were energy soaking into his body. He even gave Julian what I thought was a challenging smile. As if asking him to bring it on.

I raised the Holy Wand, gathered as much magic as I could, and shot a blue beam of magic out of the crystal at the top.

Lucifer simply stood there, absorbing my magic, too. You wouldn't have even known we were attacking if you didn't see the red and blue laser beams hitting his chest.

Frustration surged through me, and the sky rolled with thunder as I called on the magic gifted to me by the god Jupiter. I gathered more magic than ever before, connected with the dark cloud that had formed above us, and struck Lucifer with a dozen bolts of lightning at once.

I expected a pile of ash to remain in the spot where Lucifer had stood.

But he was still there.

He wasn't even charred. He was just standing there, watching us like we were bugs entertaining him as he waited to squash us.

Not possible.

Lilith cackled from her spot behind Lucifer. "You're unprepared to fight him," she said. "There's nothing you can do that will work. You might as well give up now."

I glanced at Julian, who was still using Excalibur against Lavinia's magic. Sweat poured down his face, his cheeks red with exertion. The Sword hadn't chosen him like it had chosen Raven—Julian wasn't the King of Swords. But he was still able to wield Excalibur. Not as easily as Raven, but he could do it.

"I'm going to need you to keep holding her off," he said, low enough that only I could hear him. Then he glanced behind us, where the others stood in a line, ready to fight. "Sage," he called, and the Dark Queen of Swords flashed to our side. "Let's use both Swords on him at once."

"No," I said. "You saw what happened to Raven." My eyes drifted to where Raven lay on the street in a puddle of her blood. Now someone else lay dead next to her—Noah. There was a bleeding hole in his heart, and one of his arms wrapped around Raven, protecting her even in death.

Sickness rose into my throat, and I forced myself to look away.

"Do you have any better ideas?" Julian asked.

We can leave, I thought, but I didn't say it out loud. Because we were the best bet to kill Lucifer.

We had to try.

Suddenly, the Nephilim were running around us, leaping forward and aiming their holy weapons at Lucifer just like Raven had done.

Just like what had happened to Raven, their weapons did nothing against the demon king. They bounced off him, and the Nephilim fell to the ground one after the other.

Lucifer used his claws to shred them to pieces.

Lavinia aimed the Dark Wand's red magic at the rest of them, frying them one by one.

"Stop!" I screamed, but my voice was drowned out in the chaos.

Before I knew what was happening, Julian and Sage ran toward Lucifer and did exactly what Julian had planned—hit Lucifer's chest with the Holy Sword and the Dark Sword at the same time.

It was no more effective than anything else.

Their bodies slammed to the ground, Lucifer raised his claws to kill them, and then every cell in my body exploded in a red flash of light.

19

GEMMA

THURSDAY, JUNE 24 (PRESENT DAY)

LAVINIA'S MAGIC surrounded Selena in a bright ball of red. She aimed more and more of it at where Selena had been standing, and I held my breath, waiting for Selena's blue magic to emerge—waiting for a sign that she was still alive.

Nothing happened.

Finally, Lavinia let go of her magic.

Charred remains were in the place where Selena had been standing, so twisted that they barely looked human.

Jacen—her father—ran to her side, then was quickly obliterated by Lavinia's magic, too.

Torrence and Reed ran forward, throwing their black, smoky dark mage magic at Lavinia. The two of them together were holding her off—but barely.

Lucifer continued to simply stand there, like the entire bloodbath amused him.

"We have to go back," I said to Ethan. "We have to fix this."

"None of their weapons are working against Lucifer," he said, and his eyes flashed with determination. "Stay here. I'll be back in a minute."

Before I could ask him what he was doing, he exploded into dragon form and soared through the sky until he hovered over Lucifer. He pulled his neck back, then released a blast of fire at the demon king.

Terror swirled inside me.

No.

If Selena's lightning hadn't worked against Lucifer, then why would Ethan's fire do anything different?

I held my breath, watching as he continued aiming his fire at Lucifer.

I was a second away from screaming at him to come back when a sword soared through the sky, heading straight toward him.

The Dark Sword.

It pierced Ethan's chest, and my heart shattered in mine, too.

His neck arched up, a final stream of fire burst from his mouth, and my soul felt like it split from my body as I watched him fall to the ground. The moment he hit the pavement, he returned to his human form.

Dead.

It felt like a fist wrapped itself around my heart, squeezing so much that I couldn't breathe. My chest hurt. *Everything* hurt. The emptiness was all consuming, and all I could do was stand there, frozen, like time had stopped in place.

This couldn't be happening.

This couldn't be real.

But somehow, I caught my breath and collected myself. Because this was just a dress rehearsal.

I'd seen everything I needed to see. And I wasn't going to let this timeline solidify.

I was going to change it.

So I ran to the door that led inside the Stratosphere, put my key in the lock, and stepped inside the ivory hall of Hecate's Eternal Library.

The goddess of witchcraft waited inside, her dark hair draped in waves around her shoulders. "Gemma," she said calmly. "I expected you'd come."

"Nothing they did killed Lucifer." My voice sounded dull and flat to my ears. "They couldn't kill him. They couldn't even hurt him. *Nothing* worked. Not the Holy Sword, or the Holy Wand… and not Ethan's fire." My throat closed up when I said his name.

"There's only one way to kill Lucifer," Hecate said.

I stared at her, amazed that she'd given me information without me asking a question.

She was trying to help me. She wanted me to ask the *right* question. More than that —she'd basically just told me the question I should ask.

"How can we kill Lucifer?" I stared at her, waiting, desperate for an answer.

"I was hoping you'd ask." Her violet eyes shimmered with approval. "Come with me, and I'll tell you." She led the way into the never-ending hall of books and took her place at the pedestal in front. Then she released the smokey mist from her eyes, letting it crawl through the shelves to search for the information she needed.

It didn't take long for a book to fly out—a book so black it looked like a dark hole that led into the ether.

It was the same deep black as the pit Lilith had opened to release Lucifer.

The book settled onto the pedestal and opened to a page near the end.

Hecate barely glanced at the writing inside. "There's only one weapon that can kill Lucifer," she said, her eyes locked on mine. "The Golden Scepter that was once wielded by the Angel of Death. As the most powerful weapon in the world, it can only be wielded by an angel."

"But we can't access the realm of the angels," I said.

"No," she said. "But there's an angel who lives on Earth."

"Annika."

"Yes." Hecate nodded.

Except Annika couldn't leave Avalon. But that was a problem for later. Right now, there was something more important I needed to know.

"Where can I find the Golden Scepter?"

"I've already answered your question of the day," she said. "I'm sorry. That's all the information I can give you."

"I can come back tomorrow," I begged, tears forming in my eyes. "Meet me here tomorrow. Please."

"You have the resources to do the rest of this on your own," she said. "You have strong magic. Use it. Tune into it. Believe in yourself. You can do this."

I wanted to beg her to tell me more. I wanted to tell her that I'd do *anything* for her to give me any bit of information that could help me locate the Scepter.

But I'd been to the Eternal Library enough to know when Hecate was done for the day.

And deep inside myself, I knew she wouldn't leave me with nothing to go on.

So I swallowed down my tears and looked Hecate straight in the eyes. "I *will* do this," I said, and then I hurried into the ivory hall, used my key to unlock the door, and stepped back onto Avalon.

20

MIRA

THURSDAY, APRIL 18, 1912

I'D ALWAYS WANTED to see New York City.

But I never dreamed I'd be seeing it in the year 1912.

The past hour had been a whirlwind. The Carpathia—the ship that had rescued us while we were in the lifeboats after the Titanic sank—had docked at the Port of New York. A huge crowd had gathered to greet the survivors, and Karina and I had pushed through it, quickly getting lost in it.

The first thing Karina had done was bring us to a dress shop, since all we'd had on us when the ship sank were our nightclothes. Now, we were making our way down the sidewalk toward the Upper East Side. The new dress was big and uncomfortable, but wearing it made me feel like I was living in a fantasy world instead of real life. The cars that drove down the streets were all buggies, and instead of modern skyscrapers, the buildings were made of detailed stone and marble. It was so surreal—like we'd been plopped into a movie set.

"We'll stay in the St. Regis hotel," Karina said. "The best hotel in the city."

"And how are we going to afford that?" I had no money on me, and neither did Karina. Everything we'd brought with us onto the Titanic had been lost when the ship sank. "You can't compel an entire company to give us a hotel room like you can compel a dress maker to give us clothing."

"Easy," Karina said, and she hurried over to a well-dressed man walking ahead of us. "Excuse me," she said, and the man stopped to listen to her. When she continued speaking, her voice had a musical quality to it—she was using compulsion. "You're going to give me all of the money you have on you. Then you're going to continue on your way and forget this ever happened."

His eyes glazed over, he removed his wallet from his jacket pocket, took out all the cash, and handed it to Karina. "Have a good day," he said, and he tilted his hat to her, then to me, and continued on his way.

Karina counted the money, turned to me, then flashed me a dangerous grin. "You see?" she said as she put the cash into her pocket. "Easy."

THE DRAGON QUEEN

She continued on her way, and I followed in a daze. Because it had been a crazy few days on the Carpathia as Karina had helped clarify everything Gemma had told me about Ethan.

My memories of Ethan weren't real.

I didn't want to believe it, but I knew in my heart it was true. Because ever since the day we'd gotten our magic, I'd known every time Ethan looked at me that he wasn't the same as before. I'd known something had changed.

Now, I knew what that something was.

Ethan had never loved me.

He'd always loved Gemma.

They were twin flames, and I had no one.

Now, in this new city in a strange time, I felt more alone than ever. But at least I had Karina. Without her, I would have been completely lost.

Karina held her head proudly as she walked past the men in suits in front of the hotel, and I followed her through the revolving doors.

Once inside, I stopped and gazed around in awe at what was definitely the fanciest hotel I'd ever been in. The floors were marble, columns lined the walls, and a crystal chandelier hung in the entrance.

Karina marched up to the desk, and the man working behind it looked up at us.

"My sister and I need a suite," Karina said, using compulsion again. "We'll be staying for an extended amount of time, so book no one else in our room until we leave."

He told us the nightly price, and Karina counted out the bills and handed them over to him.

"We'll pay on a weekly basis," she said, and of course, he agreed. Then he grabbed two keys from behind the desk—two *real* keys, not those plastic cards they use in present-day hotels—and handed them to us. "Is your luggage waiting outside?"

"No luggage," Karina said, and he nodded, as if this was totally normal.

He called for a butler, and the butler led us into the elevator and showed us to the room. He made a huge deal out of explaining everything about the suite, informed us that we could leave our shoes outside our door each night so they could be shined, then saw himself out.

I walked over to one of the windows and looked out at the people walking along the street below.

In New York City.

In *1912*.

This was crazy.

Finally, I looked back over at Karina. "What are we going to do while we're here?" I asked her.

"As much as I dislike it, we're going to have to live quietly," she said. "Make as few waves in time as possible."

"So we're going to stay in the hotel room?"

"We'll limit our interactions with others, but we'll have to leave to get money," she said. "And food. And fresh air. Before the time of air conditioning, buildings were too stuffy to stay indoors all the time." She shuddered, as if the thought of remaining indoors horrified her.

As someone who loved being outside, staying indoors all the time horrified me, too.

"How long will we have to stay here?" I asked, trying to ignore the part of me that never wanted to leave.

Because if I stayed here, I wouldn't have to face everything that waited for me back home.

I'd never have to look into Ethan's eyes and be reminded that he'd never loved me. That my memories of the two of us together were a lie.

I'd never have to see my sister and be reminded of her betrayal. Because at the end of the day, she knew she had feelings for Ethan, and she'd kept her feelings secret from me.

Can you blame her? I thought. *Would you tell her if the situation was reversed?*

I wished I could say I would, but the truth was, I wasn't sure.

"We stay until Lilith is dead," Karina said. "You said you'd know when the bond is severed."

"I will," I said, since the bond was like a thin blanket wrapped around me. Here in the past, I wasn't bound by it. In the present, it controlled my every move.

"Good," she said. "Now, let's get going. There's a lovely bar downstairs, and I need something to drink."

21

MIRA

SUNDAY, APRIL 28, 1912

AFTER ONE WEEK of living in New York City in 1912, I found I didn't hate it as much as anticipated. The dresses were a pain, but the distance from Lilith's hold—and the distance from Ethan—were helping me fight the darkness that had haunted my soul since watching Ethan place the Holy Crown on Gemma's head.

Karina and I spent a decent amount of time at restaurants, where we kept to ourselves. Today, we were on a stroll through Central Park. The sky was covered with clouds, which meant the sun didn't weaken Karina like it would on a bright day. Plus, with the gowns and hats of the era, she was able to cover herself enough that we could go out during normal hours.

In the park, spring was in full bloom, with new leaves on the trees and flowers on the grass. It was strange to feel immersed in nature in the middle of a city. Karina even walked me to a spot in the park where no buildings were visible at all.

Eventually, she zeroed in on the reason we were there—to find a wealthy man she could compel for money. She'd already selected the one she wanted—a young bachelor named William Bradshaw who was one of the wealthiest men in the city. He was the proud owner of one of the world's first compact cameras, and could often be found taking photos on Sunday afternoons in the park. This was a hot topic of gossip amongst the single women in the city, who purposefully timed their afternoon strolls so they could walk past him and try to catch his eye.

He was easy to spot—a man a few years older than me, kneeling to capture a photo of bluebirds on a fountain. His sandy blond hair blew in the wind, and he didn't seem to mind that he might mess up his trousers—probably because he could easily purchase new ones.

When Karina had first told me about him, I'd assumed he'd be high-brow and stuffy, like most of the wealthy men in New York. Instead, he struck me as carefree, artsy, and sensitive.

Not usually my type... but something drew me toward him.

I wanted to know him.

"Pick someone else," I said to Karina, and then I reached for my air magic and created a strong enough wind to blow my hat off my head and straight into the lens of William's camera.

I ran after it, as if I needed to chase the wind, and watched him catch the hat and look around for its owner.

He sucked in a sharp breath when his brown eyes met mine, and I froze in place.

He was one of the most handsome men I'd ever seen.

The corner of his lip curled up in amusement, and he held the hat out to me. "I take it this is yours?" he asked.

"Yes." I reached forward to take it from him, and when my fingers brushed his, warmth flooded from my hand to my heart. "Thank you for rescuing it for me."

He tilted his head and watched me with interest, still not letting go of the hat. "Where are you from?" he asked.

Right—the accent.

There weren't many Australians around here. Even so, my accent was different from theirs, given that over a century had passed between this time and mine.

"Australia," I said, and his eyes widened with interest.

"I've always dreamed of going to Australia," he said. "Taking photos of the wildlife and of the cliffs in the south. I've heard that not even photographs can do its beauty justice, but I'd try my hardest anyway."

"I'm from the south of Melbourne, and I agree—nothing compares to actually standing on the coves that line our beaches," I said, but then I quickly realized that I should have thought before speaking. Because was Melbourne even a city back in 1912?

I should know more about the place where I lived, but I'd never been much of a history buff.

"Fascinating," he said, although from the way he was watching me, it seemed like he found me far more fascinating than my home country. "What brings you to New York?"

I glanced at the hat, which we were still holding between us, and he grinned sheepishly as he released it to me.

"I was spending some time with my sister in Europe." I motioned to Karina, who was standing back, looking *very* irritated. "We came here about a week ago to spend the summer in the city."

"Which ship brought you here?" he asked.

"The Titanic," I said, and, as expected, he leaned forward in further interest.

"I'm thankful that you and your sister arrived unharmed," he said. "And that the wind blew you my way today."

We stood like that for a few seconds, eyes locked, neither of us saying a word.

The last time I'd felt an intense energy like this between a guy had been with Ethan when we'd first met. But unlike those memories with Ethan, what was happening here with William was *real*.

"I'm sorry," he said, shaking his head to refocus. "I didn't introduce myself. I'm William Bradshaw."

"Mira Brown," I said, and he smiled at the sound of my name.

"Mira," he repeated, as if I were a mystery he was determined to solve. "What are your dinner plans tomorrow evening?"

Before I could answer, Karina stalked angrily to my side and linked her arm with mine. "My sister and I are having dinner together tomorrow," she said, an edge of warning in her tone.

"Of course." He nodded. "I wouldn't expect to dine with her without a chaperone."

"Chaperone?" I looked back and forth between William and Karina, confused.

William raised an eyebrow. "Do chaperones not accompany you in Australia while you go out with your suitors?" he asked.

Suitors... another word that caught me by surprise.

William sees himself as my suitor?

"They do," Karina jumped in, and then she turned to me and gave me a small smile. "Mira here simply enjoys toying with people by making Australia sound like an alien planet."

"An alien planet that I can't wait to visit someday," William said mischievously, and then he turned back to me. "I'll pick you up at five?"

"Yes." My cheeks heated—was I actually *blushing* around a guy? "That sounds perfect."

"Where can I find you?"

"We can meet you here," Karina said quickly, at the same time as I said, "The St. Regis Hotel."

I glared at her, annoyed that she wanted us to hide where we were staying, then turned my focus back to William. "We'll meet you in the lobby of the St. Regis."

"I'm looking forward to it."

The butterflies in my stomach flew up to my throat, and my heart leaped in excitement.

I didn't tear my eyes away from his until Karina dragged me around the corner, and she hurried us away until we were out of William's hearing distance. Then she spun me around, her eyes swirling with anger, and scowled at me. "What. Was. That?" she asked.

"I like him," I said, unable to believe it. "After Ethan, I didn't think I'd ever be interested in another man ever again. But... I like him."

"He lives in 1912," she said.

"I realize that."

"He'll be long dead once we return home."

"I know."

She narrowed her eyes, clearly frustrated with me. "*And* we agreed not to make any unnecessary waves in the past," she said. "He's the most sought-after bachelor in the city. What if you're stopping him from meeting the woman who will eventually become his wife?"

"I just used my dragon magic to sink a ship full of some of the most influential people in history," I said. "One courtship is nothing in comparison."

"And what happens when it's time to leave him?"

"Then I'll leave him." I stood straighter, unwilling to back down on this. Because if I was going to be stuck in 1912 for who knew how long, I might as well make the best of it. "What is it that they say? Better to have loved and lost than to never be loved at all?"

It was something like that. And I'd had enough unrequited love to last me for the rest of my life.

"After Ethan, I need this," I said, and I lowered my voice, pleading now. "Please."

Her eyes softened, as if she understood where I was coming from. "Fine," she said. "But I have to accompany you as a chaperone. Otherwise, people will talk. They'll assume you've let William take your virtue."

"My virtue?" I repeated, laughing. "From going out to dinner?"

"It was a different time back then," she said. "But at least you're Australian, so we can pass off your oddities as being because you're a foreigner."

"It seems like William likes my 'oddities,'" I teased.

"Yes," she agreed. "It seems he does. But we'll worry about your courtship later. Because if you don't want to get kicked out of the St. Regis hotel, then we need to find another human to give us his money."

And with that, we were back to business.

22

MIRA

SUNDAY, JUNE 2, 1912

Over a month.

I couldn't believe I'd been living in 1912 for so long.

More than that, I couldn't believe how lucky I was to have met William.

We were sitting in the nicest restaurant in New York, right in the middle of Central Park. It was decorated with tons of greenery, and just like the fountain where William and I had met, it was nearly impossible to tell that the restaurant was in the middle of a bustling city.

William and I were dining at a table in the center of the room. I'd quickly learned that when someone of his status went to a restaurant, they sat him where people could see him, to let everyone know they were dining at one of the most popular restaurants in the city.

A few women at some of the other tables glared at me, which I'd grown accustomed to over the past few weeks. They all wanted William to have chosen them, and they had no idea why he was with a foreigner from the wild land of Australia.

In their eyes, I was lower than dirt.

If only they knew *just* how different my home was from theirs. It amused me simply to think about it.

Karina, of course, sat at a table near the wall, where she could keep an eye on me to chaperone my date with William. She was with a female friend of hers—a vampire she'd befriended in the city. Much like current times, there were rogue vampire clans all throughout America, and Karina was happy to have a friend to hunt with.

I heard the click of the camera, and I realized I'd been gazing out the window at the park beyond. I quickly turned my head to William, glaring playfully. "You know I hate being photographed unaware," I said.

"But it's when you're the most beautiful," he replied. "When you let your guard down and forget there are others watching."

"No one's watching me."

"Wrong," he said. "I am. I *always* am. You shine brighter than anyone I've ever met. Whenever you're around, it's impossible for me to take my eyes off you."

His eyes sparkled when he spoke, as if I'd bewitched him. It was how he always looked at me. With pure, unfiltered love. Like I was the only person on the planet who mattered to him.

Over these past few weeks, he'd quickly become one of the most important people in my life, too.

We might have continued staring at each other forever if the waiter didn't come over with dessert—a chocolate cake for us to share. I picked up the fork to dig in, but before I could, William stood up and dropped down to his knee in front of me.

My breath caught in my chest.

He couldn't be…

"Mira Brown," he said, gazing up at me with pure love. "From the moment your hat blew into my camera lens, I knew you were special. In these past few weeks, I've come to learn just how unique you are. Your spark for adventure is like none I've ever known, and I can't imagine spending my life with anyone but you." He paused, reached into his jacket pocket, brought out a velvet black box, and opened it. Inside was a ring with a single diamond on it—not a large, flashy diamond, but a modest one, although it sparkled with such light that I knew it had to be the highest quality possible.

This can't be happening…

"I love you, Mira," he said. "And I'd be honored if you'd spend the rest of your life with me. So…" He looked down sheepishly, in a way that was so adorably *William*, then beamed back up at me. "Will you marry me?"

Time stood still.

My heart pounded so quickly that I was sure everyone in the restaurant—who were now all staring at us—could hear it.

I couldn't speak.

I loved William—truly, I did. But *married* at seventeen? It was crazy. Like he'd pointed out, we'd only known each other for a few weeks.

Plus, soon I'd leave him forever, and Karina was going to compel him to move on. Just the idea of it made a lump form in my throat, but she and I had already discussed that it was what had to be done.

William would never understand the truth. Yes, he was open-minded… but the truth was an entirely different level of crazy.

Worry crossed his caring eyes, and he gazed up at me in question.

"Mira?" His voice shook slightly when he said my name. "Maybe I should have waited until we were in private. But after I took that photo of you, and you looked so at peace, I thought…"

"It's okay," I said quickly, even though it was anything but okay. "It's just that I can't stay here forever. You know that. I'm eventually going home, to my family in Australia."

"I'll be your new family, here in New York," he said, still holding the box out so he could remove the ring and place it on my finger. "You know how much I want to see Australia. We can visit your family whenever you want."

"You don't understand." My voice wavered, and I stood up abruptly, panic filling my lungs. "It's more complicated than you can imagine. I'm sorry. Sorrier than you'll ever know. But I can't marry you."

Defeat crossed his eyes, and I worried he was going to break down in the middle of the restaurant.

But he stood up, closed the box, and placed it back in his pocket.

"You love me," he said with so much intensity that it was clear he believed it with all his heart. "I know you do."

"I do love you," I said. "But I can't marry you."

We stood there like that, staring at each other in the middle of the restaurant, and people started to chatter quietly around us.

This would probably make the headline in the papers tomorrow.

Australian foreigner Mira Brown rejects the most eligible bachelor in New York.

Once more, William was going to be swarmed with women who wanted to steal his heart. And maybe one of them would.

Jealousy coursed through me at the thought, and then Karina appeared by my side.

"My sister cannot marry you," she said to William. "Now, if you'll excuse us, we must leave."

"Let me at least accompany you back to the hotel," he said, his eyes begging me to say yes.

I wanted to.

Maybe I could talk to him in private. Explain the truth. See his reaction...

"We can get back by ourselves," Karina said. "Have a good rest of your night."

He turned back to me. "You love me," he said. "I know you do."

"I do," I said. "But it's so much more complicated than that."

"Love isn't complicated," he said. "It's either there, or it's not. And you're my one, Mira. You have my heart forever. So if you change your mind, you know where to find me."

With that, he spun around, left a wad of cash on the table, and stormed out of the restaurant, leaving me in total devastation as he disappeared into the night.

23

GEMMA

FRIDAY, JUNE 25 (PRESENT DAY)

I STEPPED into the meeting area with the round table, scribbled a quick note on the pad of paper waiting there, and sent it as a fire message to Annika.

The Earth Angel appeared seconds later. Annika usually dressed casually—in jeans and t-shirts—but now she wore the black uniform of Avalon's Army. Even though she couldn't leave the island, she looked fierce and ready to fight.

"Tell me everything," she said.

I took a deep breath, unsure where to start. "Nothing that happened today is permanent," I reminded her, although I was reminding myself just as much. Without the constant reminder, I feared I might break. "I'm going to go back in time. I'm going to fix it."

"What happened?"

My heart shattered again as I replayed the past few hours in my mind. All I could do was see everyone die, over and over and over again.

See *Ethan* die.

Annika's eyes softened, and she reached for my hand to comfort me. "Let's sit down."

We sat, although so much adrenaline coursed through my veins that I couldn't keep myself from fidgeting.

"Now," Annika said, as strong and as focused as ever. "Tell me everything. Spare no details. And then, together, we'll figure out how to make it right."

"I'll do it," Annika said once I was done.

"What?"

"I'll help you figure out where you can get the Golden Scepter. And then, once we have it, I'll use it to slay Lucifer."

THE DRAGON QUEEN

"That means you'll have to leave Avalon."

Her eyes turned serious. "It does."

"But you're bound to Avalon by your blood," I said. "If you leave…"

"If I leave, Avalon will return to the state it was in when I arrived," she said. "It'll die. Forever. But if I don't do this, we'll have no way to beat Lucifer. The demons will win. All of us will die." Her voice lowered when she said that last part, and she gazed into the fire blazing in the hearth.

"Thank you," I said simply.

But in my heart, I knew she'd volunteer. As Queens, it was our responsibility to do what we needed to stop the demons from taking over our world, no matter how hard those decisions might be. We wouldn't have been chosen by the Holy Objects if we weren't strong enough to make those choices.

"We needed the protection of Avalon as a safe place from the demons," she said. "With Lucifer slain, the island's purpose will be served. *My* purpose as the Earth Angel will be served."

I said nothing, instead staring into the fire with her. Because Avalon was more than a temporary hideout. It was a home to so many people who had nowhere else to go. It was a place where any supernatural could belong, no matter what species they were.

I couldn't imagine—nor could I accept—a world without Avalon.

And that was when it came to me.

A loophole.

In magic, there was *always* a loophole.

"Maybe Avalon doesn't have to die," I said, and hope flashed in Annika's golden eyes. "I can bring people with me when I travel through time. I can bring *you* with me."

"But when you return to the present, isn't it always a second or so after you left?" she asked.

"It is," I said. "But the first time I time traveled—in the Seventh Kingdom—I only traveled a few minutes back into the past. I didn't have to return to the present because time caught up with itself on its own."

She blinked a few times as she processed what I was saying. "As much as I love fantasy novels, time travel has never been my genre of choice," she finally said. "But you're the Queen of Pentacles. If you say you can do this in a way that a version of myself will always be on Avalon, then let's do it."

"I can do it," I said. "And I will. But first, we need to figure out where we can find the Golden Scepter. And I know what we need to locate it."

"What do you need?" she asked.

"A dragon heart," I said, although when I thought back to the old, used heart we tried to use on the Titanic, I knew what needed to be done. "A *fresh* dragon heart."

"You're going to slay a dragon."

"I won't kill one of my people," I said. "But I will go to them and ask for their help."

"You're going to Ember?"

"Yes."

"How?"

"With magic," I said, and then I walked to the door, put my key in the lock, and stepped into the ivory hall of the Eternal Library.

Hecate wasn't there. I hadn't expected anything else, but it didn't stop disappointment from filling my lungs.

But that was no matter. Because now, I had a mission. I had a *purpose.* And I wasn't going to stop until I got the Golden Scepter and made things right.

So I spun around, put my key back into the lock, and stepped into the meeting hall of the underwater kingdom in Ember.

24

GEMMA

FRIDAY, JUNE 25 (PRESENT DAY)

THE MEETING ROOM was empty when I arrived. I took a deep breath and stared out at the sprawling city below, all of it enclosed in a bubble of air kept in place by the dragons with elemental water magic and air magic.

It was beautiful. The existence of the hidden kingdom of Ember was one of the many wonders of the magical world—a way for the dragons to keep themselves safe from the dark fae and mages that had overtaken their realm.

Most of the candles in the shops and apartments were out, which was the only way to tell what time of day it was, given that sunlight didn't reach the depths of the ocean.

I enjoyed the tiny moment of peace, not knowing when I might have time like this to myself again. A moment when there was possibility in the future—when I could change the fates of the battle that had gone horribly wrong.

Because if I failed...

No, I thought. *I can't fail. I won't fail.*

Decision made, I straightened my shoulders, marched into the hall, and walked to the door that led into the quarters of Hypatia, one of the head elders.

A guard waited at the door—a male dragon with deep blue eyes and dark hair who looked to be in his forties. He'd been in the meeting room when Ethan, Torrence, Reed, and I had first been in Ember—when we'd come to find the first half of the Holy Crown.

He lowered his eyes at the sight of me. "Your Highness," he said. "Welcome back to Ember."

"I need to speak to Hypatia," I said. "Now."

"I'll go wake her."

No questions, and no hesitation. Because as the Queen of Pentacles and the twin flame of their king, I was the highest authority in the kingdom.

My heart hurt again at the thought of their king.

Of Ethan.

They had no idea what had happened to him.

Once I fixed this, they never would.

I waited outside the door, not wanting to take advantage of my authority by bursting into Hypatia's quarters. She was an elder of the dragon kingdom, and she deserved my respect.

We likely wouldn't have the second half of the Holy Crown right now if not for her help.

A lump formed in my throat at the memory of how she'd slit the neck of the dragon who'd volunteered to sacrifice himself so we could track down the second half of the Crown. Hypatia was strong and brave—a true leader.

I doubted I was strong enough to do what she'd done.

She came to the door in less than a minute. She wore a silk pink robe, and her gray hair was up in a twist at the back of her head.

Since I'd been crowned Queen of Pentacles, Ethan and I had come to Ember multiple times, so Hypatia didn't have to be briefed on what the Crown could do.

Her eyes crinkled in concern when she saw me, and she opened the door wider. "Come in," she said, and I entered her quarters. Another woman was in there—some sort of lady's maid, and Hypatia focused on her. "Bring us some tea," she ordered. Then she looked to me and asked, "What kind do you prefer?"

"Hot chocolate," I said instantly. "The white kind, if you have it."

"I'm sure Priya can find it somewhere."

"On it," Priya said, and then she left the room, leaving me, Hypatia, and the male guard alone.

Hypatia and I sat down on the sofa. The man remained standing.

I looked to him, unsure if he could be trusted.

"Tarren remains by my side at all times," Hypatia said. "You can speak freely around him."

I'd wanted to speak to Hypatia alone, but I didn't have the energy to fight her on this. If she said her guard could be trusted, then I believed her.

"We lost the war," I said, although as I told her, it didn't feel real. Probably because I knew this timeline wasn't going to remain real. "Lilith used the gifted vampire blood to raise Lucifer from his Hell prison. None of us could kill him. Not Raven, or Sage, or Selena... or Ethan."

When I said his name, it came out as a whisper.

Immediately afterward, there was a knock on the door.

Priya had returned with our drinks. She placed steaming hot jasmine tea in front of Hypatia, and a white hot chocolate in front of me.

"I'll leave you alone," she said, clearly understanding that the conversation Hypatia and I were about to have was private.

"Thank you," Hypatia said, and we were both silent until the door clicked behind Priya.

I picked up my hot chocolate—she'd made it perfectly. But even my comfort drink wasn't enough to calm the anxiety and grief racing through my veins, so I placed it back down, ready to continue my conversation with Hypatia.

"King Pendragon is dead," Hypatia said solemnly.

"It's not permanent," I said. "I'm going to change it."

"How?"

I took another sip of hot chocolate, then told her about the Golden Scepter and the plan I'd created with Annika—how Annika had agreed to leave Avalon to kill Lucifer.

THE DRAGON QUEEN

Suddenly, Tarren stepped forward.

"I'll do it," he said.

"You'll do what?" I asked.

"You need to locate the Golden Scepter. You have no leads about where it could be, and given the destruction that Lucifer and the demons are likely causing on Earth right now, your resources are limited. The best way to find the Golden Scepter is to use a dragon heart. That's why you're here, isn't it? To request one?"

"It is," I said, since there was no point in lying about it.

Still, the thought of what I was asking of them made my stomach roll over.

It's for the greater good, I reminded myself. *Hundreds—maybe thousands—have already died since Lucifer rose. Sacrifices are necessary in times of war.*

But more importantly, it was going to be okay. Because once I fixed this, none of this would have ever happened.

If I was able to fix this.

No, I instantly thought. It wasn't "if." I *was* going to fix this. There was no way that Fate intended the future to end up this way. I'd been chosen as the Queen of Pentacles for a reason.

I sat straighter as confidence raced through me.

I could do this.

Hypatia eyed Tarren suspiciously. "Are you offering to find a dragon who's willing to sacrifice themselves to find the Golden Scepter?" she asked.

"No," he said. "I'm offering to sacrifice myself so the Queen of Pentacles can use my heart to find the Golden Scepter."

She froze, then pursed her lips in dissatisfaction. "You're my head guard," she said. "I need you here. With me."

I looked back and forth between them, and I realized—she was in love with him. And, even though she was likely two or three decades older than he was, I could tell from the way he was looking at her that he fully returned her love.

"Our king is dead," he said. "There's no reason for anyone to know he's fallen. Gemma can use my heart to find the Scepter so the Earth Angel can kill Lucifer. Once she does, this reality will be erased. King Pendragon will still be alive. *I'll* still be alive."

Hypatia still said nothing.

"I have faith in the Queen of Pentacles," he continued. "I know you do, too."

"As do many others in our kingdom," she snapped. "But this is a job for a soldier. A pawn."

"I am a soldier. I serve the Queen of Pentacles," he said, strong and determined. "I want her to use my heart to locate the Golden Scepter. Locating the Scepter is a pivotal part in winning this war—and it's *my* part. I know it deep in my bones." He turned to me, and I could tell by the look on his face that his mind was made up. "The stronger the magic of a dragon, the stronger the magic of their heart," he said. "I was chosen to guard Hypatia because I'm the best there is. Use my heart. Find the Scepter. Let the Earth Angel kill Lucifer to create a new reality—a reality where we take down the demons for good."

I held his gaze, unable to look at Hypatia. Because Tarren was right. We needed a strong heart to locate the Golden Scepter.

His offer was the best I could hope for. It was what I'd come here for.

But this decision wasn't up to me.

"I won't be the one to do it," Hypatia broke the silence.

Tarren looked to her, and his eyes turned gentle. "I'd never ask you to."

It was silent again, and I held my breath, not wanting to interrupt this moment between them.

Hypatia nodded in what looked like acceptance, then refocused on me. "Can you leave us for a few minutes?" she asked.

"Of course." I stepped out into the empty hall, leaving them alone.

Ten minutes later, Hypatia opened the door and beckoned me inside. Her eyes were glassy—she'd clearly been crying.

My heart ached for her nearly as much as it did for my grief over Ethan.

Hypatia moved closer to Tarren and took his hand. "The next time you see us, we won't remember this timeline," she said to me.

"Correct."

"So when it's all over, and you've fixed the past, I want you to tell me what happened," she said. "I want you to come to me and Tarren and tell us about the sacrifice he made in this timeline to help save the world."

I looked to Tarren to make sure it was okay.

"I don't expect glory or validation," he said. "But Hypatia insists, and therefore, I ask this of you as well."

"You have my word," I promised.

"Thank you," he said. "Now, there's one final thing we request."

"Tell me, and I'll do my best to honor it," I said, since I'd learned to never promise something before knowing what a person was asking of me.

"I want you to be the one to wield the blade and end my life."

25

GEMMA

FRIDAY, JUNE 25 (PRESENT DAY)

My blood felt like it froze in my veins, and for a moment, I couldn't breathe.

"You want me to kill you." I prayed I was wrong, even though his request was clear.

"I don't want Hypatia to do it," he said. "And we don't want to involve anyone else in what's going on here. Plus, you're the Queen of Pentacles. It's your job to do what needs to be done to change the present. I'm doing what I need to do by offering myself as a sacrifice. I—" he started, and then he stopped, glancing at Hypatia before looking back to me. "*We* want you to do this for us."

I swallowed, unsure what to say.

Because he was asking me to slit his throat. To watch his life blood drain out of him, and then cut his heart out of his chest after it stopped beating.

My stomach rolled at the thought.

"May I please have a moment?" I asked Hypatia.

"Of course," she said, and then I hurried to her bathroom, making it just before my stomach revolted against me and emptied all of its contents into the toilet.

Once there was nothing left inside me, I swished my mouth out with water from the sink and gazed at my reflection in the mirror. My eyes were bloodshot, there were circles beneath them, and my skin was pale and dry. Exhaustion felt like a living thing, clawing at my insides and trying to pull me down into its endless spiral of despair.

But the Crown on my head glowed with magic, and that magic flowed through me, warming me with energy that I desperately needed.

The magic of the Crown reminded me who I was.

The Queen of Pentacles.

Being a Queen wasn't all confidence and glory. It meant making hard decisions and doing things I'd never dreamed I could do.

The past day had pushed me to my limits. Now, it was pushing me even more.

But the sad, haggard girl in the mirror wasn't who I wanted to be. This timeline wasn't one I wanted to exist in.

I had the power to change it. Plus, once everything was fixed, Tarren would still be alive. I never would have killed him.

But I'd still have the memories of what I'd done. This timeline would disappear for everyone else, but it would still exist for me.

It would still exist for Ethan as well. Thanks to our twin flame bond, he also remembered the timelines I'd changed. We'd learned it from Hecate in one of the few times she'd appeared to us in the Library.

Would he remember dying?

The answer came to me immediately—yes. He remembered everything, so he'd remember dying as well.

He'd also know that I saved him. He was going to ask how I did it. And I was going to tell him everything.

What I was about to do to Tarren wouldn't be a burden I'd have to bear alone. Ethan would help me learn how to live with it.

I *had* to do this. Not just for Ethan, but for everyone.

I was the Queen of Pentacles, and I refused to let the world down. More than that— I refused to let *myself* down.

And so, I cupped my hands together and drank some water from the sink, relieved when it settled in my stomach without coming back up. Then I straightened and stared at myself in the mirror again. There was a strength and determination in my eyes that hadn't been there before.

I can do this.

With that final thought, I walked back into Hypatia's living room with my head held high. I pulled my dagger from my weapons belt—the holy weapon I carried with me in case I was confronted with a demon.

"The Queen of Swords taught me how to do this as quickly and painlessly as possible," I assured Tarren, since while Raven was dangerous with a sword, she wasn't cruel. Then I turned to Hypatia, swallowing before continuing. "But I'm going to need you to walk me through what to do afterward."

Meaning: I needed her to tell me how to cut the heart from his chest without damaging it.

"I will," she promised.

"Thank you," I said, and when I met Tarren's eyes, he stared back at me with deep appreciation and kneeled in front of me.

"I'm the one who should be thanking you," he said, and then he nodded at me, like he was saying it was all going to be okay.

Because it *was* all going to be okay.

And so, keeping my eyes locked with his, I took a deep breath, tightened my grip on the handle of my dagger, and did what needed to be done.

26

GEMMA

FRIDAY, JUNE 25 (PRESENT DAY)

ONCE THE HEART was removed and placed in a satchel, Hypatia and I kneeled before Tarren's body—which we'd covered with a sheet—held our hands together, and spent a few minutes in prayer.

"Your sacrifice will never be forgotten," she finished, and I gave her a small nod of assurance of my promise that in the new timeline, I'd tell them what had happened in this one.

Then I looked up, imagining the ceiling of the ivory hall of the Eternal Library, and thanked Hecate for gifting me with my magic.

Hypatia squeezed my hands, her eyes full of respect when she looked at me. "You're a true Queen," she said, and then she stood up, picked up the satchel with Tarren's heart, and handed it to me. "I doubt the Golden Scepter is in Ember, but there's always a chance. So before you leave, try to see if you can sense it."

I reached into the satchel and held Tarren's heart gently in my hand. I'd cleaned it of blood, and I could feel the magic pulsing out of it from my touch.

In the past, Ethan had been the one to use the heart to try to locate the objects we were searching for. He'd tried to spare me from such a gruesome task.

Now, the strong magic that flowed out of Tarren's heart filled me with further confidence that I could do this.

I didn't know exactly how to "use" the heart, so as always, I tuned into my magical instinct and let it guide me.

Where is the Golden Scepter? I thought as I held onto the heart.

Nothing changed.

I tried again, and again, nothing.

"It's not in Ember," I said, releasing the heart.

"As I suspected," Hypatia said. "But I trust that wherever it is, you'll find it."

"I will," I said. "And the next time I see you, it'll be with good news. I promise."

"I'll see you in another life," she said.

"Another *timeline*," I corrected her, and then I walked over to the door that led out of her room, put my key into the keyhole, and stepped back into the Eternal Library.

If Hecate was there, I already knew what I was going to ask: which realm the Golden Scepter was in. But she wasn't there.

I knew she wouldn't be.

So I used my key to go to a place I prayed was still safe from the demons—the tearoom in the Haven.

It was empty, but still intact. Immediately, I reached into the satchel and asked the heart to locate the Golden Scepter.

Just like in Ember, nothing happened.

Please be in the Otherworld, I thought, as if thinking it could make it true. Because the Otherworld was the only other realm I'd ever been to. Since I could only use my key to go to places I'd already been, it was going to be a lot more complicated if the Golden Scepter was in another realm.

But I'd worry about that when the time came. So I used my key to return to the Eternal Library, and then walked into the courtyard of Sorcha's palace.

In the current timeline, where Selena was alive, the Otherworld hadn't fallen prey to the zombies like it had when she'd died. It was bursting with life again, and there wasn't even a barrier dome around it, since the dome's protection wasn't necessary anymore.

The Empress was waiting for me next to the fountain, alongside her main advisor, Aeliana.

The fountain was drained of water. Which meant if someone were to try to enter through the portal, they wouldn't be able to get through. And when I looked around the courtyard, there was another huge noticeable difference—the fae standing along the walls of the palace all had wings. They were dressed in simple robes similar to the ones previously worn by the half-blood slaves, which made it obvious that they worked in the palace, but none of them had the red circle tattoos around their biceps that bound them to servitude.

Because in the past few months, Selena had done as she'd promised—she'd freed the half-blood slaves. There was still a lot of work to be done in restructuring the Otherworld's economy, but the half-bloods were now being paid fair wages for their work.

But discussing the politics of the Otherworld was far from the reason I was here.

"We know what happened with Lucifer," Sorcha said, not even bothering with a formal greeting. "Aeliana tells me you're working to fix it."

"I am," I said, and then I quickly filled her in on what I'd learned about the Golden Scepter.

"I've never heard of a Golden Scepter," she said. "But I hope for all our sakes that you're able to find it."

"Me, too." I reached into the satchel, wrapped my hand around the heart, and asked it to locate the Golden Scepter.

Nothing happened.

My heart dropped, and when I looked back at Sorcha and Aeliana, I could tell they both already knew what had happened.

"You knew this was going to happen before I even tried," I said to Aeliana, since she was a half-blood gifted with the ability of future sight.

"I did," she said.

"So tell me," I said desperately. "What do I need to do next?"

"I don't see all possible futures," she said. "I only see the future your current decision will lead to."

"And what decision is that?"

"Why don't you tell me?" she asked patiently.

I bit my lower lip and thought for a few seconds. "I guess my next move would be to go to Avalon," I said. "Let the Earth Angel know what's going on and see if she can help get me into other realms, so I can try to find the Scepter in those."

"That sounds like a solid plan." She gave me an encouraging smile.

Hope filled me once again, and more importantly, trust in myself.

"Thank you," I told them. "And I promise you—next time I see you, it'll be with good news."

"I know it will be," Aeliana said. "Goodbye, and good luck."

27

GEMMA

FRIDAY, JUNE 25 (PRESENT DAY)

Annika was pacing in her quarters when I arrived back in Avalon.

Had she been alone this entire time?

Possibly. One thing I'd learned about the Earth Angel during my time in Avalon was that when Annika was troubled, she tended to isolate herself.

She stopped pacing when she saw me. "We've been waiting for you," she said, and then she hurried into her bedroom and told whoever was in there to wake up.

She came back inside with one of the last people I'd expected to see.

"Torrence." I gasped in surprise, and then I ran forward and hugged her. "I thought you were dead."

She pulled out of the hug and gave me a forced half-smile. "I probably would be dead if I'd stayed there."

"You left Vegas," I said, and she nodded. "When?"

"After Ethan fell, Lavinia used the Dark Wand and killed Reed," she said hollowly. "I knew then that our best chance of winning the battle was for you to go back in time and change everything before it happened. Because this timeline can't be the final one. It just can't."

"It won't be," I assured her, and she nodded, like she already knew it. "But if you left soon after I did, why didn't I see you when I got back to Avalon?"

"I went to my mom's first," she said. "I brought her to the kingdom where I thought she'd be the safest—the Ward. Of course, Makena wanted to know everything that had happened with Lucifer. Once I'd finished filling her in and returned to Avalon, you were already gone."

I nodded, since it made sense. If my mom had been in California instead of in the Haven, I would have immediately gotten her out of there and brought her to one of the kingdoms, too.

Although, I supposed none of it technically mattered, since once we were done here, this timeline would cease to exist.

"I did one more thing before leaving Vegas," she said, and I looked to her to continue. "I grabbed the Dark Sword and took it with me."

"How?" I asked, since the last thing I remembered of the Dark Sword was it soaring into Ethan's heart.

"I ran for it and grabbed it." She shrugged, like it was simple. "It was chaos. Then I flashed out before anyone could catch me."

"And where's the Dark Sword now?"

"Here, on Avalon."

"I'm keeping it somewhere safe," Annika added.

"Good," I said. "As long as the Dark Sword doesn't claim another Queen, we have time to fix this."

"Selena stored the Holy Wand in the ether in her final moments," Torrence said. "So we have nothing to worry about there. The only wild card is Excalibur."

"The Holy Objects are on our side." As I said it, the Crown on my head hummed with magic, as if it was supporting my thought. "It won't claim another Queen without giving us a chance to fix this."

"I hope so," Annika said.

"I know so." I must have sounded confident enough, because she nodded and didn't continue the conversation further.

I turned to Torrence. "There's a weapon that can slay Lucifer," I started, but Torrence interrupted before I could continue.

"Annika told me everything," she said. "Did you get the dragon heart?"

"I did," I said, and I filled them in on what had happened while I was in Ember.

They were silent for a few seconds.

"What you did was tough," Annika finally said. "But it was the right thing to do."

"Except the heart hasn't gotten me anywhere so far," I said. "The Scepter wasn't in Ember, it wasn't on Earth, and it wasn't in the Otherworld. Are there any other realms we can get to? Maybe the mages can bring us to Mystica?"

"Maybe," she said. "But I've been thinking. And I've figured out another way to locate the Scepter."

"What way is that?"

"The same way you located the Dark Sword."

I took a moment to process what she was suggesting.

"Are you saying you've traced the Golden Scepter back in history?" I asked.

"There are no written records of the Golden Scepter," Torrence said. "At least, none that I know of. But just because there are no written records doesn't mean there aren't other ways of tracing it."

"What do you mean?"

"She means that some of the oldest supernaturals live right here in Avalon," Annika said. "The fae who left the Otherworld to live here weren't able to fight against Lucifer because their iron allergy makes it so they can't get to Earth. And before the witches cast the spell on them that made the fae allergic to iron, many of them lived on Earth."

I thought back to what I'd learned in my history lessons back in Utopia. "That was over a thousand years ago," I said.

"These holy weapons are older than that," Annika replied. "As are some of the fae who live here. I don't think it could hurt to ask if any of them came across the Golden Scepter at any point in time."

"Any point in time during or before the Middle Ages." I could barely comprehend such a thing. Because I'd thought 1912 was far back to travel.

That would be nothing in comparison to this.

"How is it any different from trying to go to another realm?" Torrence asked. "Because from what I've heard, Mystica is pretty similar to the Middle Ages—except it would be much harder to navigate, since you're not a mage."

"Good point," I said.

"If this works, I think it's a better option than Mystica," Annika said. "And I've already gathered some of the oldest fae to meet with us. They're waiting at the round table."

"I thought the round table was reserved for the leaders of Avalon," I said.

"The leaders of Avalon are dead. Besides, I make the rules here," she said. "So, let's go find out what they know."

28

GEMMA

FRIDAY, JUNE 25 (PRESENT DAY)

About thirty fae waited in the meeting room—far too many for them to all sit at the table. So they were standing, chatting amongst themselves and trying to figure out what could have happened in the battle to slay Lucifer.

They silenced the moment Annika, Torrence, and I walked through the door.

Annika walked to the front of the room to face them. Torrence and I stood by her sides. The chairs around the table remained empty—a reminder of those lost in the battle.

My heart ached from looking at the empty chairs.

This timeline will be erased, I reminded myself, and then I focused on the fae standing before us—the oldest fae in Avalon. From their youthful faces—they all appeared to be in their mid to upper twenties—it was impossible to know exactly *how* old they were.

A woman with gold wings and dark curly hair stepped forward, her gaze focused on mine. "The battle didn't go as planned," she said simply. "You need information from us —ancient information—to go back in time and change the outcome of what happened."

"How did you know?" I asked, since Annika hadn't filled them in on what had happened yet.

"Once you get to be as old as I am, it's not too hard to figure these things out," she said. "None of the other rulers of Avalon are here, which I presume means they were either captured or killed. You've gathered the oldest fae in Avalon to meet with you. You have the ability to travel back in time. Which means there's information you think we'll have that will help you change the outcome of the battle against Lucifer and the demons."

"Correct," Annika said, and she launched into telling them the details. "Do any of you know where and when Gemma might be able to locate the Golden Scepter?"

Most of them shook their heads no.

But the golden winged fae curved her lips into a small smile, like she knew something.

I held her gaze, waiting for her to share.

"I heard mention of the Golden Scepter in a city in Italy where I used to live," she said. "There was a circle of dark witches rumored to have it. But before word could spread, they left and were never heard from again."

"What city?" I asked.

"Pompeii," she said, as if I should have heard of it.

I hadn't. The only cities I knew of in Italy were Rome, Venice, Florence, and Milan.

"What year?" I braced myself for something startling.

"79 AD."

Double digits.

I hadn't braced myself for *that*.

"Ancient Italy," I said, and a slight bit of relief coursed through me, since Ancient Italy was far more civilized than the Middle Ages.

Minus the gladiator fights to the death, of course.

"Does anyone else have any other information?" Annika asked, looking around the room.

No one spoke up.

So, Ancient Italy it was.

29

GEMMA

MONDAY, JUNE 28 (PRESENT DAY)

The golden winged fae—Livia—spent two days briefing us on what to expect in 79 AD.

Now, I was in the meeting room with Torrence, Annika, Livia, and Ruby—a witch who'd been to Pompeii and could teleport us there. Torrence and I wore colorful robes that were popular with nobles of the time. Mine was red, and Torrence's was green. Mine had been fashioned with a large enough pocket to stash the dragon heart, and since the robe was loose, the heart fit inside without being bulky.

Livia reached for the bracelet on her wrist, unclasped it, and held it out to me.

"You really think your past self will believe us?" I asked.

"This bracelet is one of a kind," she said. "It was forged by my soulmate, Atticus." Her voice wavered when she said his name, since he'd died last year in the plague that had overtaken the Otherworld. "He'll be able to identify his own craftsmanship."

"We wouldn't be able to do this without your help," I said as she clasped the bracelet onto my wrist. It was pure gold, so it was heavier than anticipated.

"I'm simply doing my part to make sure the demons don't take over the realms," she said. "The Otherworld included."

I nodded, since it was a sentiment I'd been hearing a lot recently.

Everyone was counting on me—not just to save Earth, but to make sure the demons didn't invade the other realms, too.

And I wasn't going to let them down.

Torrence reached into the pocket of her dress and pulled out two vials of milky blue liquid. "This will last for twenty-four hours," she said, examining the potion with pride. "Are you ready to try it?"

"Ready as ever," I said, since I just wanted to get to Pompeii, find the Scepter, and get back to Avalon.

Torrence handed a vial to me, looked at me with determination, and we clinked our vials together.

"To understanding dead languages," I said.

"Carpe diem." She smirked, raised the vial to her lips, and downed it.

I did the same.

The blue liquid tasted sweet and thick. As I swallowed it down, my head buzzed, and my mouth did, too. My tongue felt heavy for a few seconds, my ears rang, and then, everything went back to normal.

"Well?" Livia asked with a raised eyebrow. "Did it work?"

"I don't know," I said. "Say something in Latin."

"I just did."

"You mean you asked if it worked in Latin?"

"And you replied in it. This entire exchange has been in Latin."

"Like I promised," Torrence said. "The potion makes it so you understand any language someone speaks to you, and that they hear your response in that language, too."

"Impressive," I said.

"Of course it is." Torrence smirked again. "I made it."

Annika looked around at the three of us. "I assume it worked?" she asked.

"Yes," I said, to test it further. "It worked."

"Good."

"Did I say that in English?"

"You did," Livia replied, since she understood both languages. "Now, I wish I could accompany you to Pompeii so I could bring you to the exact place where my villa once stood. But the map I made is a good one, so I'm sure you'll find your way."

"I have a good sense of direction," I said, since being in tune with the world around me was one of the benefits of my elemental magic.

"That makes one of us," Torrence said, and this time, I was the one who smirked a bit.

If I was going to go back to the ancient times with someone who wasn't Ethan, I was glad it was Torrence.

"I'm glad you're coming with me," I said, since one big thing I'd learned through all of this was that life was too short to hold back on voicing appreciation for the people you cared about.

"You better be." She winked. "Because who better than a dark half-mage to help you steal an ancient weapon from a circle of dark witches?"

I almost said Ethan, but I held back. Because Torrence's magic was insanely strong—even stronger than that of a full mage. The only person I'd ever seen with magic stronger than hers was Selena.

Ethan, Mira, and I probably would have been killed by the dark mages guarding the entrance to Ember if Torrence hadn't dropped in and saved us.

"There's no one better," I said, meaning it.

The witch—Ruby—stepped forward. Much like the gem she was named for, her hair was a stunning shade of dark red. "Who's coming first?" she asked.

Torrence stepped forward. "I am," she said.

"No," I said. "I am."

"I see you're already on the same wavelength," Ruby said wryly.

"We don't know what's waiting for us in Pompeii," Torrence said. "And I'm expendable. Gemma's not."

I opened my mouth to refute her, but stopped myself. Because given that this timeline was going to be erased, she was right.

Everyone was expendable but me and Annika, since we only needed the two of us—and the Golden Scepter—to slay Lucifer.

"All right," I agreed, and Torrence looked at me with respect. "You go first."

"My pleasure, *Your Highness*," she said with a small curtsy, in a tone that was both joking and full of respect.

Only Torrence would be able to manage that.

"Now," she said, turning to Ruby. "Let's go to Italy."

Ruby took Torrence's hands, and the two of them flashed out.

I held my breath as I waited for her to return.

What if the demons somehow knew we were going there? What if they're waiting to launch an attack and kill them? What if Lucifer is there?

I swallowed down fear at the thought.

Luckily, Ruby returned before I could think about it further.

"Well?" I asked.

"Well, what?"

"Did everything go smoothly?"

"Would I be here otherwise?"

"No," I said, breathing out slowly. Because of course everything was fine. Lucifer and the dark witches had no way to track us. We were too careful for that. And they had no way of guessing we'd go to Pompeii. They had far bigger targets than that. A random city in Italy wasn't a target at all.

But the vampire kingdoms are.

I pushed the thought out of my mind, since my mom was at one of them. If the citizens of the kingdoms needed to go somewhere else to hide, they would. I had to trust that my mom was in good hands with Mary.

And that she was in good hands with me, given that I was the one fixing this mess.

"Gemma?" Ruby asked, holding out her hands. "We should get going. Torrence is going to be irritated if you leave her waiting."

From the way she said it, you'd think Torrence was the Queen instead of me.

"Okay." I reached forward, taking her hands in mine. "Let's go."

One moment we were in the meeting room, and the next, we were in a quaint Italian city.

A burst of power rushed through me when my feet hit the ground. Because there was magic here. Serious, major, *intense* earth and fire magic.

I spun around and saw where the magic was coming from.

A massive volcano loomed over the city. It overtook the skyline, and the bustling buildings of Pompeii were tiny in comparison. And, most noticeably, the volcano wasn't dormant. I could feel the strength of the magma that flowed in the chambers below, like its fire had an invisible tie to my magic. It was like the magma pulsed with the beat of my heart.

"Mount Vesuvius," Ruby said. "One of the most dangerous volcanoes in the world. Anyone careless enough to have lived on its slopes has paid the price."

"But no large eruptions?" I asked.

"Of course not." Ruby chuckled. "Vesuvius's eruptions are short and small. There wouldn't be cities around it otherwise."

"There're enough magma in there to bury all these cities in ash," I said as I continued to stare at the volcanic monster.

Torrence stepped in front of me, blocking my view of the volcano. "Are you gonna keep staring at that volcano, or are you gonna take us back in time to get the Scepter?" she asked.

I shook my head to snap out of it. "Sorry," I said, and then I reached into the ether, removed the Holy Crown, and placed it on my head.

Torrence's eyes gleamed with excitement.

"You ready?" I asked, even though I could tell by her expression that she was.

"Once we're done with them, those dark witches won't know what hit them," she said, and then she took my hands, her grip firm around them. "Let's show the ancient Romans what we're made of."

I took a deep breath and focused on the Holy Crown.

Take us back to 79 AD, when Livia learned that the dark witches were in Pompeii with the Golden Scepter, I thought, and then the buzz of magic flowed through me, and Torrence and I flickered out.

30

GEMMA

TUESDAY, AUGUST 24, 79 AD

We reappeared on a cobblestone street in front of the entrance of a marble Roman villa. A few people walked nearby—some of them in high quality clothing like me and Torrence wore, and others in more ragged tunics that made it clear they were servants. They blinked and shook their heads as they looked at us, but then their eyes glazed over, and they continued on their ways. It was like they'd had deja vu—not like they'd just witnessed two people materialize in thin air.

Unless humans had magic shoved in their faces, their minds rewired themselves around it to make logical sense of it.

But they could only miss so much. So I quickly reached for the Crown and put it back in the ether. Then I returned my focus to the wooden door in front of me, raised my knuckles up to it, and knocked.

The door opened, and a human man in a plain white toga studied us, taking in our robes that made it clear we were of higher status than he was. "Good morning," he said. "How may I help you?"

"We're here to see Livia," I said simply, as if he should have already known that.

"She didn't tell me she'd be receiving guests."

"That's because we're not guests. We're family." I flipped over my hand, reached for my magic, and a small flame grew from my palm.

His eyes widened, and he stepped back, like he was afraid my fire might burn him. "You're like my mistress," he said breathlessly. "Goddesses."

"Yes, we're like Livia. And we've come a long way to speak with her." I didn't break my gaze from his.

"We need her help," Torrence chimed in, and she raised her hand as a small bit of purple magic swirled around her fingers. "And we'll be helping her, too."

He bowed his head, like he was afraid to look at either of us, and opened the door wider. "Come wait in the foyer," he said. "I'll find the mistress and tell her of your arrival. But first, would you mind putting that out?" He glanced at my palm, where the flame still danced.

"Of course." I closed my hand into a fist to snuff out the fire, then he nodded in approval and moved over so Torrence and I could walk inside.

The foyer had a small fountain in the center, and colorful murals on the walls. There were benches inside, but Torrence and I opted to stand.

"I feel like I'm back in the Otherworld," Torrence said.

"It looks like the villas in the Otherworld," I agreed. "But there's so much fire and earth magic here, so it doesn't *feel* like the Otherworld."

"The volcano is that intense?"

"It's like a monster hiding beneath the surface. If the people here knew how much power it had, they would be long evacuated."

"Sounds dangerous."

"It's fueling my magic. Making me stronger than ever."

"Good." Her eyes glinted with approval, then flashed with darkness. "Because when we go up against this Scepter, we're gonna need as much magic as possible."

We only waited for ten minutes before the man in the toga returned. "My mistress has readied the morning meal for four people," he said. "Please, follow me."

He led the way down a hall and into the atrium in the back of the villa. It was like a smaller version of Empress Sorcha's atrium—open to the sky, with a rectangular pool in the center, and lined with columns. The roof was tiled with red, and the shrubbery was well tended to, although there weren't colorful flowers growing out of them like there were in the Otherworld.

Livia reclined on a lounge chair next to a table covered in fruits, breads, and jams. Her dark curly hair fell around her face just like it did when we'd met, but her golden wings were invisible, since the fae used glamour to conceal their wings while they were on Earth.

A man with light brown hair reclined next to her. Judging by the finery of his robe, I assumed he was her soulmate, Atticus.

Livia waited for the servant to leave before speaking. "Our conversation will be private, thanks to the sound barrier spell my witches have placed around the atrium," she said. "But make no mistake—they are watching us. If you try anything against me, you will regret it."

"We've come here for your help," I said. "We won't hurt either of you."

Atticus eyed us warily. "You're shrouding your scents," he finally said. "What type of supernaturals are you?"

"We're witches," Torrence said, since we'd agreed before coming here to keep it simple. The dragons wouldn't be coming to Earth for centuries—the other supernaturals didn't even know of their existence yet. "Both of us have been gifted with unique magic by the goddess of witchcraft, Hecate."

It was the best story we could come up with to explain Torrence's mage magic and my elemental magic.

"And your names?" Livia asked.

We quickly introduced ourselves.

"Nice to meet you, Gemma and Torrence," she said. "I'm curious to hear why you've come here. But you know our customs. Join us and have a bite of food first."

We reclined on the other two lounge chairs around the tables—I already knew from my time in the Otherworld that the ancient Romans lounged while they ate instead of sitting straight up—and each took a bite of fruit.

Atticus and Livia kept an eye on our every movement.

THE DRAGON QUEEN

"Now," Livia said, and she pushed herself up a bit on her chair. "What is it that you came here to ask?"

"We were told you had information on the location of the Golden Scepter," I said.

She raised an eyebrow. "Who gave you this information?"

"You did."

She pursed her lips and narrowed her eyes. "Come again?"

"This is going to sound crazy, but hear me out," I started, and she waited for me to continue. "Like I said, Torrence and I have been gifted with unique magic from Hecate. My gift is the ability to travel through time."

She stared at me in silence.

"Is this some kind of joke?" Atticus finally asked.

"Not a joke," I said. "Like I told you, Livia is the one who sent us here. Well, the future version of Livia. To prove it, she gave me this to show you."

I removed the bracelet and handed it to him.

He was quiet for a full minute as he studied it. Then he looked to Livia. "Your bracelet," he said. "The one I gave you for your most recent birthday. Give it to me."

She snapped the bracelet off her wrist and handed it to him.

He held them up against each other and studied each detail.

"I know my craftsmanship anywhere," he finally said. "This is the same bracelet I made Livia for her birthday. It should be the only one in existence." He handed both bracelets to Livia so she could see.

She took them and studied them, although for not nearly as long as Atticus had. Then she looked to me. "You're saying that a future version of myself told you to find me and ask about the Golden Scepter, and that she—well, *I*—gave you this bracelet so you could prove you were telling the truth?"

"That's exactly what I'm saying."

"Interesting," she said, and she reclined further back in her chair. "Please, continue. Because this sounds like a fascinating story."

We spent a few hours going through everything with Livia and Atticus. By the time we were finished, it was mid-morning.

Livia was quick to process and believe everything I was telling her.

Atticus was a harder sell, but he eventually came around.

"Where was I through all of this?" he finally asked.

"I mentioned the plague that hit the Otherworld," I said with trepidation. "You fell ill to it."

"It killed me."

"It did. But like I said, I came here to change the future. Now that you know about the plague, you can take precautions to change your fate."

"Simply the information to save Atticus's life would be enough incentive for me to help you," Livia said. "To make things clear, all you're asking for is the location of the dark witches who have the Golden Scepter?"

"Correct."

"All right," she said. "You have done me a great favor by sharing your knowledge of the future. As repayment, I will give you the location of the dark witch circle."

I had a feeling she would have shared their location with us no matter what, but fae were sticklers for not doing anything for free.

"This knowledge will help us greatly," I said, since thanking a fae—even one as kind and gracious as Livia—would bind me to a favor.

"I'm more than happy to share it," she said, and then she told us the location of the dark witch circle.

"As a fair warning, after we leave to find them, I recommend having your witches teleport you, Atticus, and everyone else in your household far away from here," I said.

"Why's that?"

"Because Torrence and I are going to use every magical ability of ours to fight. We'll do *anything* to get that Scepter. And if there's any fallout, I don't want you to be here to suffer the consequences."

31

GEMMA

TUESDAY, AUGUST 24, 79 AD

Livia and Atticus had their human driver take us to the dark witches' villa on their cart, which was pulled by two oxen.

It was a large villa on the outskirts of the city, on the side closer to Vesuvius. Like most of the other villas in Pompeii, it was white with columns, and had a red tiled roof. Nothing about it made it apparent that a circle of dark witches that owned an ancient holy weapon lived there.

Torrence held her hand to her forehead like a visor—it was almost noon, and the sun shined bright overhead. "Are you sure this is the place?" she asked our driver.

"I'm sure."

I reached into my robe, wrapped my hand around the dragon heart, and asked for the location of the Scepter. The heart pulsed in my grip, and I felt a pull toward the villa.

"This is the right place," I said to Torrence, and I stepped out of the cart to face the driver. "Thank you for taking us here."

"I'll wait for you right here," he said.

"We can get back on our own," I said, since the moment Torrence and I got our hands on that Scepter, I'd bring us back to the present. "You should return to Livia's villa."

"Are you sure?" He looked around warily, like he was worried he'd get in trouble for leaving us alone.

"It's for your own safety."

He furrowed his brow in confusion.

This was one of those moments when I wished I could compel people, like the vampires could.

"Trust me," I tried again. "We'll be fine."

My tone must have been convincing, because he nodded, then steered the oxen to bring the cart back into the city.

Torrence and I turned back toward the villa.

"Time for the barrier spell." She rubbed her hands together excitedly. "Gotta make sure the witches can't blink out of here with that Scepter."

"Is there anything I can do to help?"

"It's no secret that your strength isn't your witch magic," she said with a wink. "I've got this."

Before I could reply, she started chanting the barrier spell in Latin. Except this time, because the language potion was making me *understand* Latin, it sounded like she was speaking the spell in English.

Her purple magic gathered around her, then exploded out of her hands in a dome that surrounded the villa. We were just inside the edge of it.

A butterfly flew inside the dome, but when it tried to fly out, it was stuck. That was how prison domes worked—anything could enter, but once inside, they couldn't leave.

Within seconds, the main door of the villa swung open, and two witches dressed in navy robes stood there, staring us down. They both had light red hair—they looked like mother and daughter—and they looked *pissed*.

"Who are you?" the older one asked.

"My name is Gemma Brown." I raised my hands up and created flames that came up from the tips of my fingers, so they looked like extensions of my nails. "I've come for the Golden Scepter."

"We don't know what that is," the younger one said, although from the way her voice wavered, it was clear she was lying.

Torrence's eyes flashed black. "Wrong answer," she said, and then she held up her hands, her palms facing the witches, and blasted black smoky magic toward them.

They didn't have time to scream before they collapsed to the ground.

I froze in shock. "They didn't try to fight us," I said. "Did you really have to *kill* them?"

Torrence rolled her eyes. "I didn't kill them," she said. "I just knocked them out for a few hours, since they didn't seem interested in helping us. Not that we need their help, since we're close enough to the Scepter that the dragon heart can direct you straight to it."

She was right.

I pulled the fire back inside myself, reached into my robe, and held onto the heart.

"Come on," I said, and I marched inside the villa.

Torrence followed quickly at my heels.

The heart led me into the atrium, where a tall witch with light red hair that matched the other two in the circle stood in the center.

She held a long rod with a sharp, pointed golden crystal at the end.

The Golden Scepter.

"I assume you're here for this?" she said with a knowing smirk.

And that was when I noticed—she wasn't a witch. Her eyes were gold, like Annika's.

She was an angel.

Another Earth Angel.

"You assume correctly," Torrence said, and then she blasted her black smoky magic at the angel.

The Scepter's crystal glowed, and Torrence's magic didn't touch the angel. It was like the Scepter had created a barrier spell around her.

"Mage magic," the angel said. "Interesting."

"You know about mages?" I asked, since we didn't learn much of anything about the mages until recently.

"They want the Scepter," she said simply. "And they've offered me a tempting reward if I give it to them."

That's where the Scepter disappeared to, I realized. *Mystica.*

"What kind of reward?" I asked.

"Living on Earth is torturous for me," she said. "All of the humans with their negative emotions surrounding me all the time. I soak it up like a sponge, until it's all I can feel. Emotions like that consume me on a level you can never understand. So in exchange for the Scepter, the mages have offered me a home in Mystica."

"Why do you think Mystica will be any better for you than Earth?" Torrence asked.

"*Anything* will be better than living on Earth."

"Except I *am* a mage," Torrence said. "And I promise you that our emotions are just as strong as the humans. Maybe stronger. I promise you don't want to live there."

"You're lying."

"I'm not."

The angel held up the Scepter and ran toward Torrence with rage in her eyes. From her expression, it was clear that she was aiming to kill.

Torrence quickly moved to the side, so the angel missed her.

Having missed Torrence, she now set her eyes on me.

So I reached for my fire magic, gathered it, and shot two blasts of it at the angel—one from each of my palms.

The fire didn't go straight like it should have. Instead, it diverted *around* her.

I stared at my hands in shock. As I did, frustration rose within me, and I blasted as much fire at her as I could manage. A roaring ball of it surrounded her—enough fire to char her to the bones.

But when the fire died down, she was still there, unscathed.

She cackled when she saw my shocked expression. "Your magic can't hurt me as long as I hold onto the Scepter," she said.

Anger swirled inside me. We didn't have time for this. And I wasn't sure how Torrence and I would do if we tried to use our swords and daggers against an angel wielding the Golden Scepter. Probably not well.

Which meant it was time for Plan B.

It wasn't hard to tune into the power of Vesuvius. My fire and earth magic had been aching to do it since teleporting into Pompeii. There was so much fiery magma beneath the surface that the ground pulsed with it. Within seconds, my magic connected to it, like a magnet that had gotten hold and wouldn't let go.

The ground tremored—a small earthquake. It didn't shake me, but the angel's golden eyes flashed with alarm.

"You did that," she realized.

"I did." I nodded as more power rushed through me, and the world shook again, hard enough for cracks to form in the concrete walls around us. "Maybe our magic can't directly hurt you. But that volcano can."

32

GEMMA

TUESDAY, AUGUST 24, 79 AD

"You can't know that," the angel said.

"Vesuvius is one of the most destructive volcanoes in the world," I said. "I felt the intensity of its power the moment I arrived in Pompeii."

"I'm immortal." She raised her chin higher. "A volcano doesn't scare me."

"I know another Earth Angel," I said. "She's immortal, but she can still be killed."

"She doesn't have the Golden Scepter protecting her."

Her confidence was going to cost her life. I could feel it as much as I could feel the earth and fire connected to my soul.

"Have you ever heard of the Golden Scepter going up against a force of nature like Vesuvius?" I asked, and this time, the world did more than shake.

It exploded with a BOOM so loud that it felt like it shattered my brain. The vibration rose from the ground and rattled every bone in my body. It was like an atomic bomb had gone off.

Within seconds, a black cloud covered the sky, and it was like it had gone from day to night.

Ash.

Flakes of it floated down to the ground like dirty snow, leaving streaks of gray in anything that crossed their path.

True fear crossed over the angel's eyes, and her grip tightened around the Scepter. She looked to Torrence. "Remove the boundary dome," she said. "Your friend might be able to survive the volcano, but you can't."

"I can protect Torrence," I said, since the magma was at my beck and call—I could mold it however I wanted. "But I'm here for the Scepter. If you won't hand it over to me, then I'll pry it away from your ashen corpse."

It was gruesome. But I didn't care. If this was what it took to save Ethan, my family, my friends, and everyone else in the universe, then so be it.

The thought of everyone who would die in the path of the lava made my stomach twist with nausea. But if I didn't do this, there'd be nothing to return home to.

I was sacrificing the lives of an entire city in exchange for saving everyone in the present world. It pained me as much as always, but it needed to be done.

There was another boom, and lightning flashed in the ash cloud overhead.

"Gemma," Torrence said cautiously. "Are you sure you can do this?"

"I *know* I can do this."

"Okay." She moved closer to my side. "I trust you."

I returned my focus to the angel. She was gripping the Scepter so tightly that her knuckles turned white. "I can already feel the lava coming closer," I said. "Hand over the Scepter now, and Torrence will remove the boundary dome. You'll be free to teleport out of here and avoid the disaster to come. And I promise you—it will be a disaster unlike anything you've ever seen."

The ground shook again, like it was confirming my statement. Screams filled the air—cries from all around the city, so shrill that goosebumps covered my skin. Streaks of ash lined both Torrence's and the angel's faces. I was sure mine looked the same.

It was the war paint of the Earth.

Rocks fell from the sky and clattered to the ground. I was able to use my magic to stop them from hitting me and Torrence, but a sharp piece of it sliced the angel's arm. She gasped in pain, and golden blood bubbled up under the cut.

Her eyes glowed gold, and the pointed crystal on the Scepter glowed, too.

I studied her, keeping my gaze locked on hers. "What's your name?" I asked, the question followed by a bright flash of lightning.

"Why do you want to know?"

"Because after you die in this eruption, I want to know the name of the angel I killed."

As I spoke the words, I couldn't believe they were coming out of my mouth. I didn't sound like *me*.

I sounded like a Holy Queen set on vengeance. And while it scared me, it also felt right to embrace the warrior inside me.

My magic felt stronger because of it.

And letting out my rage after witnessing our loss against Lucifer felt like releasing the pain that had been building inside me since seeing Ethan die. It numbed me to it.

"I'm Seraphina," the angel said. "And I'm not going down without a fight."

She ran toward me with the pointed end of the Scepter, but the moment I saw her move, the ground rumbled and shook strongly enough to knock her off her feet.

She smacked to the ground, but kept the Scepter in her hand. It was like it was glued to her palm.

When she looked up at me, her expression was livid.

The Earth was shaking so much that the tiles were breaking from the roof, clacking against each other like shattering glass as they fell to the ground.

Fire exploded from the inside of the house, the flames dancing along the soot-covered roof.

I steadied myself, reached for Torrence's hand, and gripped it tightly as she started to mutter an incantation—the one for the smaller boundary dome around us that could move with us. Only a mage could create a boundary spell strong enough to do that.

The ground continued to tremble, roaring as an avalanche rushed down the volcano.

"You're too late," I told Seraphina, and then lava flowed through the villa, consuming everything in its path.

Everything except for me and Torrence.

It was like we were inside a protective barrier, except it wasn't a barrier—it was Torrence and I using our magic to keep the lava from touching us. I controlled the lava so it didn't hit the barrier walls, since while barrier spells were strong, neither of us knew if they'd been tested against lava before. The boundary also protected us from the heat, which would surely cook Torrence as if she was inside an oven set at the highest temperature.

The lava started to solidify around us, and I created a flame in my palm so we could see.

The air inside the dome was still. It would have been silent, if not for our ragged breathing and pounding hearts.

"Well?" Torrence finally said. "Did it work?"

"There's only one way to find out." I reached for the dragon heart within my robe and asked it to find the Scepter, since it was impossible to see through the lava. Immediately, I felt a pull forward.

"This way." I called on my earth magic and used it to push the lava aside so we could walk through. It hissed and popped as it moved, parts of it still red with heat.

The boundary dome moved with us, and I pushed through the lava as quickly as possible, since the air inside the boundary dome was limited.

We needed to get the Scepter and get out.

It didn't take long before something poked at the edge of the boundary dome—the pointed end of the Golden Scepter's crystal. It couldn't pierce the dome, and the crystal was no longer glowing. But to bring the Scepter back, I needed to have a firm grip on it. So I connected to my earth magic and pushed a little bit more through the rock, revealing the top part of the rod.

A burned, gnarled hand was wrapped around it.

Seraphina's hand.

"Is she dead?" Torrence asked, and for the first time, she looked scared.

"I don't know. But she's not healing." I pulled the Holy Crown out of the ether, placed it on my head, then reached out of the boundary dome.

It was like sticking my hand into an oven. Heat couldn't hurt me, but this was a level of hot that was beyond uncomfortable. Plus, I was getting dizzy. We were starting to run out of air.

So I gripped the Scepter's rod, right above Seraphina's hand. Then I used my other hand to hold onto Torrence's.

Take us back to the present, I told the Crown.

Magic hummed through me, extending to both Torrence and the Scepter, and we flickered out.

33

GEMMA

MONDAY, JUNE 28 (PRESENT DAY)

CRUMBLED RUINS SURROUNDED US.

Gone were the modern buildings that had been in Pompeii when we'd left.

Instead, parts the villa had been preserved to look like they'd been on the day I'd made Vesuvius erupt.

People walked around in touristy clothes—khakis, t-shirts, and backpacks. A group of girls in their twenties gathered in front of a row of columns to take selfies. The frescos on the outdoor walls were maintained well enough that they were identical to what they'd looked like back in 79 AD, although they'd dulled with time.

Most surprisingly, there were plaques on the walls with writing on them. It was like we were in an outdoor museum.

Vesuvius towered in the distance, but instead of one crater, there were two.

An entirely new crater had formed on the top of the volcano because of the eruption.

As I was staring at it, a heavyset couple who'd been outside long enough to have patches of sweat on their shirts approached us.

"Where's the nearest bathroom?" the man asked.

"I don't know," I said on instinct.

"Oh." He frowned. "I thought you worked here." He glanced up and down my robes, and I realized that not only was I still wearing clothes fit for Ancient Rome, but that I had the Crown on my head and was holding the Golden Scepter.

I breathed out in relief that the Scepter had come through time with us.

Torrence pointed at doors that opened to the atrium. "Just through there and to the left," she said, and the tourists thanked her and headed in that direction.

"They excavated Pompeii," I said, looking around in shock. "And made it into a *museum.*"

"Seems that way." Torrence shrugged. "Is the Scepter intact?"

I studied the golden crystal. It wasn't glowing, but it seemed okay. "I think so," I said.

"That's going to have to be good enough," she said, and then she grabbed my hands and teleported us back to the meeting room in Avalon.

Everyone was where we'd left them. But not just *everyone*. Livia was there—with Atticus.

He smiled warmly when he saw me. "Livia and I were careful when the plague hit the Otherworld," he said. "I wouldn't be alive right now if it wasn't for you."

I didn't have time to reply before memories of the new timeline flooded my mind.

In this timeline, everyone knew about Pompeii. It was famous for when Vesuvius had erupted in 79 AD, and it was the location of some of the best preserved ruins in the world. As we'd seen when we'd come back to the present, it was an extremely popular tourist destination.

When Livia had told us that she knew the dark witches were in Pompeii, Torrence and I had purposefully chosen the day of the eruption to travel back to. We figured we could trap the witches in their villa and use the eruption to scare them into handing over the Scepter.

Once we fixed the past and slayed Lucifer, I'd tell them the *real* story about how we'd gotten the Scepter.

"It worked," Annika said when she saw us, and she hurried forward, her hand outstretched to take the Scepter. But she paused when she was inches away. "May I?"

"Of course," I said, and I handed the Scepter to her.

Her hand wrapped around the rod, and the crystal glowed so it was the same color as her golden eyes. "I can do some serious damage with this thing," she said as she studied the Scepter.

"Like slaying the shit out of Lucifer," Torrence said.

"Exactly." Annika nodded and gave Torrence a knowing smile. Then she looked back to me. "You should go change. You can't leave Avalon dressed like that."

I glanced down at my Roman robes, which were covered in soot from the eruption. I couldn't imagine what those tourists must have thought. Probably that I was one of those people who re-enacted ancient times.

"For sure," I said, and I hurried to my room and changed into the black uniform of Avalon's army.

Once dressed, I faced the mirror and studied my reflection. I was a different person than I'd been months ago.

I'd caused enough destruction to turn an entire city into a museum two thousand years later.

I was stronger than I'd ever believed I could be.

But this war was far from over. So I touched the Holy Crown for good luck and hurried back to the meeting room.

Torrence was still in her soot-covered robes, since her part in our mission was complete. She was talking to Livia and Atticus, already telling them about our adventure in Pompeii and how I'd been the one to make Vesuvius blow its lid.

Annika didn't appear to be listening to Torrence. Instead, she was studying the Scepter, deep in thought. "I guess this is it," she said, and then she focused on me. But she didn't look sad—she looked determined. "Time for me to leave Avalon."

"It's going to be okay," I told her. "We have a plan."

"Plans don't always go as expected," she said. "But I hope for everyone's sake that this one will. Now, are you ready to go?"

"I am," I said, and she took one of my hands—holding onto the Scepter with the other—and teleported us out of Avalon.

We arrived in a small house on the coast of Norway—the one the three mages had lived in nearly twenty years ago, before they'd gone to Avalon to help Annika rule the island. We'd chosen the spot because the magic the mages had used to conceal the house was still active. There was a table and chairs in the main room, but other than that, it was abandoned.

A second after we arrived, Annika screamed and keeled over, her shriek filling the air. She was grabbing her abdomen, and the Scepter had fallen onto the floor.

I ran over to comfort her, but she pushed me away.

Her screams stopped, but her breaths were heavy, and her face was covered in sweat.

I wanted to ask if she was okay. But I didn't, since she clearly wasn't. Instead, I stood there, waiting.

She was strong. She could handle this.

Slowly, she reached for the Scepter, picked it up, and stood straight. The gold in her eyes had dimmed, but it was still there.

"My bond to Avalon has been severed." Her voice was pained as she spoke, and her face was pale. She looked like she could fall over at any second.

"You can't fight like this," I said.

"I can't," she agreed. "We get one shot at this. We have to do it right."

"So we rest?"

"Yes," she said. "We rest."

She led the way to the bedroom, which had three twin beds inside. The blankets were coated with dust, but Annika didn't care. She collapsed into one of them, Scepter still in her hand, and instantly fell asleep.

34

GEMMA

TUESDAY, JUNE 29 (PRESENT DAY)

I WOKE before Annika the next day, and my stomach rumbled. Loudly. But not loudly enough to wake her.

With Lucifer released, it was too dangerous to go to any of the vampire kingdoms for food, and I didn't want to risk going to the café either. So I used my key to go to the next best place—McFly's Tavern. Ethan and I had liked to go to dinner there last fall, before I'd gotten my magic.

Last fall felt like *ages* ago.

I didn't have a credit card on me, so I went inside the kitchen and grabbed two burgers from underneath the heat lamp.

A waiter caught me and widened his eyes. "What are you doing with that?" he asked, but before he could approach, I balanced both plates with one hand, reached for my key, and stepped back into the Library.

Just like a few minutes ago, Hecate wasn't there. So I used my key again and stepped into the kitchen of the Norway house, so I didn't disturb Annika. Luckily, the plumbing still worked, and I poured myself a glass of water and downed it.

I was on my second glass when Annika entered the kitchen.

"You got food," she said, and then she walked over to the table, sat down, and took a huge bite out of one of the burgers.

Disgust crossed her face as she chewed.

"What's wrong?" I asked, and the worst possibilities crossed my mind. Did the demons somehow know I'd be there to grab those burgers? Had they poisoned them?

She chewed slowly, then swallowed, like she was force feeding herself. "It's been nearly two decades since I've had regular food," she said. "I suppose nothing can compare to mana."

I chuckled, even though my mana sometimes tasted like the burgers from McFly's, since I loved them so much. "I guess not," I said, then I took my seat and took a bite of my burger.

I immediately understood the problem.

"Well done," I said, and I scrunched my nose. "Don't judge McFly's on this. Their burgers are *much* better medium rare."

"Don't worry about it," she said. "I know you didn't have time to be picky."

"I took the burgers from under the heat lamp and ran."

"Better than taking half-eaten ones from someone's table," she said with a small smile, and we polished off the rest of the burgers in silence.

Her eyes returned to their regular golden glow.

"How are you feeling?" I asked her.

"Ready to go."

We stood up, and just like when we teleported here, Annika took one of my hands in hers and held the Scepter with the other.

Take us back one week, I told the Crown, and we flickered out, reappearing back in the house that looked exactly the same as it had when we'd arrived yesterday.

35

GEMMA

MONDAY, JULY 21 (EIGHT DAYS AGO)

ANNIKA TOOK a few seconds to adjust, since it was the first time she'd time traveled. She seemed relatively unfazed.

"Did it hurt?" I asked, since it hurt *everyone* the first time they traveled back in time.

"It was nothing compared to when I severed my bond with Avalon."

Not a yes, but also not a no.

"It only feels like that the first time," I reminded her. "From now on, it'll feel like teleporting."

"Got it," she said, and then she got straight down to business. "Let's go to the Vale first."

I wasn't surprised she'd chosen the Vale, since it was where she'd lived the year before becoming the Earth Angel.

She took my hands and teleported us outside the Vale's boundary dome. The witches on guard widened their eyes when they saw us, and they teleported us inside without any questions.

Once inside the dome, they went down to their knees and lowered their eyes. "Your Highnesses," the older one said, and then she slowly looked up at us. "What can we do for you?"

"We're going to the throne room," Annika said. "Send a fire message to King Alexandra and Queen Deidre to let them know we're here."

"Of course," she said, and then Annika took my hand again and teleported us to the throne room.

King Alexander and Queen Deidre entered a minute later, dressed in the finery expected of the rulers of the Vale. Their eyes widened when they saw Annika.

"It's true," Deidre said, and she hurried closer to Annika, as if making sure she was actually there. "You left Avalon."

"I did," Annika confirmed.

"But the island…"

"I severed my bond with it," Annika said. "But not in the present. In the future."

"A week in the future, to be exact," I added, and then we told them everything that was going on.

After speaking with King Alexander and Queen Deidre, Annika and I went to the Haven, then the Ward, the Carpathian Kingdom, and lastly, the Tower. The ruler of each kingdom listened closely as we filled them in on what was happening, and they promised to help in any way they could.

The kingdoms didn't always get along—especially the Tower—but against Lucifer, we stood together as one.

Once finished, we returned to the house in Norway.

"That went well," Annika said.

"It did," I agreed.

We stood in silence for a few seconds. Because there was still one place to go—but it was a place I needed to go alone.

Once I returned, Annika would be slightly different from the one I was looking at now.

"Are you sure your witch magic is strong enough for you to teleport to Avalon?" Annika asked. "I can always bring you there and avoid running into my past self."

"Don't worry," I said, and I reached for the key around my neck. "I've got this."

Without any further explanation, I walked to the door that led out of the house, put the key in the lock, and stepped into the ivory hall of the Eternal Library.

Hecate wasn't there.

I was fine with that. Because I was starting to realize that when Hecate wasn't there, it meant she trusted I could handle the situation alone. And she wasn't the only one who trusted this plan. *I* trusted it, too.

I spun back around, put the key into the lock, and walked into an empty bedroom inside Avalon's castle. Before we'd left the island, Annika had brought me there so I'd be able to return. The room was at the end of the hall, and no one had ever lived there.

I removed the folded note from my pocket—the one Annika had already written to tell herself to meet me in the room. She'd said she'd recognize her handwriting anywhere, and I immediately understood why—she had terrible penmanship.

I placed it in my palm and sent it as a fire message to the Annika of this time.

She teleported into the room less than a minute later and studied me suspiciously. "Gemma," she said hesitantly. "I was just training with you on the field."

"You were training with the version of me from your present," I said. "I've come to see you from eight days in the future."

"What happened?"

"In three days, Lilith is going to raise Lucifer," I started, and then I told her all the gory details of what was going to happen in the battle.

"We have to tell the other kingdoms," she said once I was finished. "Let them know to get ready to fight."

"You and I have already alerted them. They're waiting for you to reach out so you can formulate a plan."

"*I* went to see them with you?" she asked, confused.

"You did."

"But I can't leave Avalon."

"Technically, you can. But if all goes well, this version of you—the you I'm speaking with now—will never leave Avalon. The version of you from the future will kill Lucifer."

From there, I told her about the Golden Scepter and the choice she'd make in a few days.

"I see," she said once I'd finished. "It's a good plan."

"I figured you'd think so, since you helped me make it," I said. "But you're not the only one from this timeline who won't leave Avalon for the battle. I took a risk by observing the battle the last time in case I was the only one left alive who saw it, so I could travel back in time and try to fix it. But your future self and I agreed it wouldn't be logical for me to take that chance again. We don't know what happens to my counterparts if they die, and we can't risk finding out now."

"I understand," she said. "I'll make sure she stays back with me."

"Thank you."

"No," she said. "Thank *you*. Without you, we wouldn't have this chance to make things right."

"I'm just using the gift I was given," I said. "Anyone would do the same in my shoes."

"They'd want to," she said. "But when it came down to it, *could* they?"

A lofty question.

"I don't know," I finally said.

"Well, I do. You were chosen as the Queen of Pentacles for a reason. This is going to work. I can feel it."

"I hope so."

Her golden eyes shined with determination. "I won't accept anything other than success."

"Me either," I agreed, since that was why I was here. "I refuse to believe that Fate wants the demons to win. We can do this."

We stood there for a few seconds in silence, taking in the enormity of what was to come.

"I should get back," Annika eventually said.

I wracked my mind for anything I might have left out during our conversation, but I was pretty sure I'd covered everything.

"Good luck," she said. "Tell my counterpart that I know she's got this."

"Will do," I said, and then Annika teleported out, and I returned to the house in Norway, where the future version of her—the one from my present—was waiting.

36

GEMMA

THURSDAY, JUNE 24 (FOUR DAYS AGO)

AFTER THREE DAYS OF WAITING, it was time. Again.

The day Lilith was going to raise Lucifer.

During those three days, a huge part of me had wanted to reach out to the people I loved. Ethan. Mira. My mom.

But I didn't. Because I'd see them all after we won the battle. Seeing them now would only cause pain and distraction.

Those were the last things any of us needed.

Instead, Annika and I had hunkered down in the house in Norway. We tried to think of everything that could go wrong with the plan, and how we'd fix it if it did. We had the gift of being prepared, and we weren't going to waste it.

Annika only left once—when she'd disguised herself and had a witch teleport her to the Vegas Strip to show her where Lilith had raised Lucifer. She'd only needed to stay there for a second to ensure she could return when the moment was right.

The Vegas Strip was so packed with tourists that as far as we were aware, none of the supernaturals keeping watch had noticed her. Even if they'd noticed a rogue supernatural, they'd never guess it was Annika. The last thing they'd expect was for the Earth Angel to have left Avalon. Most people didn't even know it was *possible* for her to leave Avalon.

Finally, it was time to battle Lucifer.

And this time, we were going to win.

37

ANNIKA

THURSDAY, JUNE 24 (FOUR DAYS AGO)

THE MOMENT the fire message arrived, I teleported out of the house in Norway, leaving Gemma there. I'd return for her later. First, I had a demon king to slay.

The Strip was a disaster scene. Piles of ash—slain demons—covered the pavement. Gifted vampire blood had rained down on the entire area, and the metallic scent of it stung the back of my throat so strongly that I was overwhelmed by the taste. It was like swallowing pennies.

And that wasn't the only thing I was overwhelmed with.

Because the pain everyone was experiencing during the battle hit me like a million pins being stabbed into my body at once.

It's all in your mind, I thought. *FOCUS. The world is depending on it.*

Raven and Sage finished killing the last of the hellhounds with their Swords. Selena helped as well, using the Holy Wand as a weapon. She moved with incredible grace—an unstoppable force as fierce as the Queens of Swords.

Pride surged through me at the sight of how strong my daughter had become since claiming her place as the Queen of Wands.

Then a giant, terrifying demon with long black claws rose out of the ground.

Lucifer.

Raven and Sage stared him down, their Swords held high. Selena moved behind them. None of them made a move to attack.

Lilith stood behind Lucifer, and even she looked slightly scared.

"Kill them," she said, and Lucifer smirked as he zeroed in on Raven.

In the battle Gemma had told me about, Raven had used this moment to run at Lucifer and try to slay him with Excalibur.

But she knew better this time.

Now, she stayed where she was.

Instead, I ran toward Lucifer, leaped into the air to fly in an arc toward him, and pulled the Golden Scepter out from the inside of my robes so quickly that he didn't have time to process it as I speared the golden crystal through his heart.

He roared, his eyes glowing bright red, and disintegrated into a pile of ash.

I fell to my knees in front of the pile, holding tightly onto the Golden Scepter.

All the anguish that I'd blocked out when I'd arrived flooded through me again.

This was the reason why angels couldn't live on Earth. Our heightened empathy absorbed all the conflict and pain felt by those who lived here. It was too much. I felt like I was going to explode from the intensity of it.

I couldn't stay here.

Luckily, my part was done.

It was time to get out.

The last thing I saw before teleporting back to the house in Norway were Lilith's angry red eyes as she ran toward me, ready to kill.

38

SAGE

THURSDAY, JUNE 24 (FOUR DAYS AGO)

ANNIKA FLASHED out before Lilith could reach her, and Lilith fell into the pile of Lucifer's ashes.

But while Lilith was powerful, she wasn't the most dangerous force we were up against.

That title went to Lavinia.

Raven was currently facing Lavinia, using Excalibur to deflect the Dark Wand's red magic to keep it from hitting her.

Lavinia's face flushed as she put as much magic as she could muster into the beam of magic.

Raven continued to hold her off.

But Raven couldn't kill Lavinia while she was busy stopping her magic. And after what Lavinia had done to me all those years ago—forcing me to drink from the Dark Grail to become a slave to the demon Azazel—I was ready to get my revenge.

So I raised the Dark Sword, ran toward her in a blur, and screamed as I speared it through her heart.

Her eyes widened when they met mine.

Blood leaked out of the wound and streamed down her white dress.

Magic stopped flowing out of the Dark Wand, and its crystal dimmed.

I gave the Dark Sword one final twist, then pulled it out of her chest, smiling as she fell back to the ground, dead.

Payback. And damn, it felt good.

The Dark Wand clattered onto the ground next to her, rolled out of her limp hand, and rested on the pavement.

I walked over to Lavinia's body, because even though I knew she was dead, I wanted to make sure. Or maybe I wanted to embrace the glory I felt at finally killing her.

But then, a red glow in the corner of my eye caught my attention.

The Dark Wand.

Its crystal was coming back to life.

No, I thought, and I looked back to Lavinia's body. The Dark Queen of Wands was dead. Stone-cold dead.

This wasn't possible.

I looked back to the Dark Wand, confused when the light in the crystal grew brighter.

Then it levitated in the air, pointed itself toward Torrence, and soared into her waiting palm.

39

TORRENCE

THURSDAY, JUNE 24 (FOUR DAYS AGO)

MAGIC EXPLODED INSIDE OF ME, radiating out of my body in the most intense burst of power I'd ever experienced. All of my magic—my purple witch magic, my black mage magic, and my new red magic—wove around themselves and fused together as I became the Dark Queen of Wands.

When the magic settled, I looked around and saw all the others staring at me.

Selena's mouth was wide open.

Sage smirked, then returned to using the Dark Sword to kill any demon nearby.

Reed's dark eyes shined with pride—and love.

But none of them were my concern right now.

Instead, I spun to face Lilith, who looked just as shocked as the others. I pointed the Dark Wand at her and released its magic to create a red barrier dome around her.

I walked toward Raven, and she eyed me warily. She didn't move to attack, although from the way she gripped Excalibur, it was clear she was ready to use it against me at a moment's notice.

I glanced over at where Lilith stood in the boundary dome, her eyes livid as she stared me down, and then I turned my focus back to Raven. "She can't teleport out of that thing," I said. "But I can teleport us in… assuming you want to do the honors?"

A true smile spread across Raven's face as she realized what I was proposing. "You bet I do," she said, and then she took my hand, and I teleported us inside Lilith's prison dome.

40

RAVEN

THURSDAY, JUNE 24 (FOUR DAYS AGO)

LILITH LOWERED her hand that was holding her sword and dropped it down to her feet, next to the Dark Grail.

She looked pathetic.

Defeated.

"Your army wasn't supposed to have the Golden Scepter," she said.

I thought back to the conversation Annika had had with us a few days ago, when she'd relayed everything she'd learned from the future version of Gemma, and said, "I guess we were one step ahead of you."

"Time travel."

"Yep."

"And now you're here to kill me."

"You bet I am," I said, and victory surged through me, even though I hadn't finished her off yet.

"All right." She squared her shoulders and held my gaze, her red eyes blazing with determination. "We both know you've won. So get it over with. I won't fight back."

I frowned. "That doesn't make it much fun."

Her lips curved up into a small smile. "Are you too much of a Holy Queen to kill someone when they're standing helplessly in front of you?"

I returned her smile, amused that she thought she had a chance to survive this. "I'm not *that* holy," I said, and then I raised Excalibur, ran toward her, and speared the Sword through her heart.

41

BELLA

THURSDAY, JUNE 24 (FOUR DAYS AGO)

THE FEW DEMONS that were still alive turned toward Torrence's boundary dome the moment Raven killed Lilith.

Their eyes flashed red, and they teleported out.

They'd lost. They knew it, and they were running scared.

But it was fine. Because no matter where in the world they'd gone, Avalon's Army would find them and kill them. They didn't stand a chance against us.

Torrence raised the Dark Wand, red magic flowed out of it, and the boundary dome disappeared.

My niece had always been kickass. She reminded me of myself more than her mother—my sister—Amber. Now, with the Dark Wand in her hand and her auburn hair blowing around her, she was an embodiment of magic. Like being the Dark Queen of Wands had always been her destiny.

My focus quickly switched to the Dark Grail sitting beside Lilith's ashes. Because the Dark Grail was pulsing with magic. Like it had a heartbeat.

Its heart was beating at the same time as mine.

An invisible cord of magic connected the Dark Grail to my soul. It was the only thing I saw. The only thing I heard.

The pull toward it consumed me.

Barely aware of what I was doing, I started walking toward it. Its heartbeat grew stronger the closer I got.

"What are you doing?" Raven asked, but I didn't answer her.

Instead, I knelt down, picked up the Dark Grail with both of my hands, and stared down inside of it.

You need to drink, the Grail seemed to speak into my mind.

Drink what? I thought back.

Demon blood.

But the demons are all gone...

"Bella?" Raven said. "Are you okay?"

"The Grail wants me to drink from it," I explained. "It wants me to drink demon blood."

Torrence stepped forward to stand beside Raven, and her eyes gleamed with excitement. "You're the Dark Queen of Cups," she said.

"Not yet."

Selena teleported to Torrence's side. "What do you mean?"

"Remember how Annika had to drink angel blood to become the Queen of Cups?" I asked, and she nodded, since everyone knew that story. "To complete the transition, I think I might have to do the same—but with demon blood."

"The demons are gone," she said. "They flashed out when Raven killed Lilith. But I can easily do a spell to track one of them down."

"That won't be necessary," someone said from behind me—Sage.

She walked toward me with a short, blonde demon next to her.

On the other side of the demon was Sage's brother, Flint.

Of course. The demon was Flint's mate. Mara. They'd passed Avalon's trials, but after a few years there they chose to live in the Montgomery pack's mansion in Hollywood Hills instead.

When Mara had mated with Flint, their souls had merged. Which meant that unlike all other demons, Mara had a conscience.

As a member of the Montgomery pack, she was the only demon who'd fought alongside Avalon's Army.

"I'll give you my blood," she offered.

I nearly asked if she was sure. But I didn't.

Because becoming the Dark Queen of Cups was my destiny. I needed her blood. And since she was offering, I had no intention of changing her mind.

"Thank you," I said instead.

"It's my pleasure." She stepped forward, held her hand over the Dark Grail, then used her dagger to slice her wrist.

Her blood was so dark that it was nearly black. It dripped out of the wound and pooled at the bottom of the Dark Grail.

Usually, demon blood smelled like smoke and decay.

Mara's blood smelled so sweet that it sang to me, like a siren's song beckoning me closer.

"That's enough," I said.

She pulled her wrist back and placed her other hand over it. A few seconds later, the gash was healed.

Without any further ceremony, I raised the Grail to my lips and drank.

The blood tasted as sweet as it smelled, and the moment I swallowed it, magic surged from my core throughout my body. My skin buzzed, my vision sharpened, and my hearing grew more sensitive. It was like I'd been supercharged with power.

"Your eyes." Raven gasped. "They're red."

"Red's a good color for me," I said with a small smirk.

"So you don't feel... different?"

"My magic is enhanced," I said. "*Way* enhanced. But if you're asking if I've turned evil, then the answer is no. I think I'm like Mara." I glanced at the demon, and she smiled in return. "A demon, but with a conscience. Because I'm the same person as I was before drinking from the Grail. Just more powerful."

"Sort of like me with the Dark Sword," Sage said.

"And me with the Dark Wand," Torrence chimed in.

"Exactly." I was glad that they'd acquired their Dark Objects before me, so I could have them as backup. If I'd been the first, I wasn't sure the others would have accepted me, given that I was now technically part demon.

It didn't feel real.

At the same time, I'd been a dark witch my entire life. I'd never had any issues with controlling my dark magic. If anyone could handle becoming a demon, it was me.

"What can you do with the Dark Grail?" Raven asked.

The answer came to me immediately. "I can bind people to me, like Lilith did to her," I said. "But don't worry. I'll only do it to people who deserve it."

"And who 'deserves it?'" Selena asked.

"I'd say those demons who teleported out of here with their metaphorical tails behind their legs deserve it first," I said. "I'd love to force them to turn on each other."

"That sounds like a fantastic idea," Torrence said, and the others agreed, too.

"But first, we need to get back to Avalon," Selena said. "I'm sure my mom is dying to know what happened here."

"There is no more Avalon." Mara frowned. "Annika broke her bond with the island when she came here to slay Lucifer."

"She did," I said. "But you've forgotten about the other weapon we have on our side."

"What weapon?"

"Gemma," I said. "Because the Queen of Pentacles had a plan. And if that plan worked, then Avalon should be the same as it was when we left it."

42

MIRA

SUNDAY, JUNE 16, 1912

I WAS HAVING breakfast with Karina in our suite when the familiar feeling of a damp blanket against my skin—the feeling of Lilith's bond—disappeared.

I sucked in a sharp breath as the haze around my brain lifted, and the world grew brighter and more colorful.

Karina placed her teacup down on its saucer and studied me in concern. "What happened?" she asked.

"Lilith's bond," I whispered, as if speaking too loudly would make it return. "It's broken."

"They killed her."

"Yes. That's the only way the bond can break."

Karina's face broke into a smile. "We can finally go home."

I knew she'd be elated. During our time in 1912, she'd told me all about the love of her life, Peter. Both of them were vampires. Then he'd died in the early twentieth century, and she'd traded her memories of him to a fae to have him brought back from the Beyond. But their love was strong. *Soulmate* strong. As he'd told her stories of their time together, she'd experienced all the feelings she'd felt when those memories had happened. They'd made new memories together. And now they loved each other more than ever.

She couldn't wait to go home to him.

But my thoughts went to William.

I hadn't seen him since the disastrous proposal two weeks ago. He'd sent me a letter a few days later, asking if we could talk, but I didn't reply.

I'd been afraid that if I saw him again, I'd regret refusing to marry him.

Karina had promised me that if I didn't see him, my feelings for him would fade. But they hadn't. Maybe two weeks wasn't long enough for feelings to fade, but somehow, they'd only grown stronger than they'd been before.

And now that it was time to face the fact that I'd never see him again, my heart ached with sorrow.

"You're thinking about William," Karina observed.

"Yes."

"As you should, given that it's time we see him so I can erase his memories of us."

"No." The word came out of my mouth before I could stop it.

She raised an eyebrow. "No?"

"I want to be honest with him."

"You want to tell him that you're a witch with dragon magic who time traveled here from over a hundred years in the future so you could prevent a demon queen from mind controlling you in the present?"

I leveled my gaze with hers, hoping to get across how serious I was about this. "I'm not sure I'll ever be able to live with myself if I don't try," I said.

"He's not going to react well."

"You don't know that."

"Humans rarely react well when they're told about the supernatural world. It's too much for most of their minds to handle."

"William's not 'most people,'" I said in his defense. "He's open-minded. He can handle it."

"And if he can't?"

I held my breath, since I knew what she was getting at.

"If he can't, then you can erase his memories."

She smiled, not even bothering to ask what I wanted to do if he reacted well. "All right," she said. "Let's change our dresses, and then we'll call on William."

William was out for his morning meal, so Karina and I waited in the reception room of his brownstone for nearly two hours before he returned.

One of the major things I missed from the present day was cell phones.

Karina and I both stood when William entered the reception room.

His soulful eyes immediately locked on mine. "Have you given my proposal more thought?" he asked hopefully.

"I haven't been honest with you," I said, and his brow knitted in confusion. "But I want to change that. Now. And after I'm finished, it may be you who wants to give your proposal more thought. Or revoke it entirely."

"I assure you that nothing you could possibly tell me could change my feelings for you."

"I hope not," I said, and then I took a deep breath, unsure where to start.

I couldn't find the words.

Instead, I reached into the ether and pulled the Dark Crown out of the air.

William's eyes widened. "How did you do that...?" he asked, studying the pocket of air where the Crown had appeared.

I placed the Crown back inside the ether, and he blinked a few times, clearly baffled by what he was seeing. "It was magic," I said simply.

"An illusion," he concluded, and then he chuckled. "Have you come here to tell me that you're part of a traveling circus?"

"It wasn't an illusion," I said. "It was magic. *Real* magic."

"Impossible."

"Remember how we met?" I asked. "When my hat blew into the lens of your camera?"

"Of course." He smiled. "How could I forget the moment when fate blew you my way?"

"Fate didn't blow me your way," I said. "*I* did it. I controlled the wind to make my hat land where it did."

Another emotion crossed over his eyes—concern.

"You believe you controlled the wind?" he asked cautiously.

"I *know* I did." I reached for my air magic, called on the wind, and had it blow around me and William in a circle, like we were standing in the eye of a hurricane.

His eyes widened. "*You're* doing this?"

"Yes." I snapped my fingers, and the wind stopped.

"How?"

"I already told you. Magic."

"So you're saying you're some sort of witch?" He took a step back, looking slightly scared—but also intrigued.

"I have a bit of witch magic." I shrugged. "But that's not how I controlled the wind. You see, on our seventeenth birthday, Gemma, my true sister, and I were gifted with dragon magic—magic that lets us control the elements. I can control air and water. She can control fire and earth. And we can both control time."

He shook his head in disbelief. "I think we should sit down for this," he said, and relief rushed through me, since sitting down was better than him running away or ordering us out of the house.

We both sat, along with Karina, who'd remained silent thus far. I didn't expect her to be any help.

William placed both hands on his knees, sat straight, and faced me. "I understand the four main elements—air, fire, water, and earth," he said, his voice much calmer than I'd expected. "But what do you mean about controlling *time?*"

"I can travel through time," I said, slowly and seriously. "I know you've noticed by now that I'm different than most of the other women around here."

"Because you're from Australia."

"I am," I said. "But that's not why I'm so different. To be honest, I don't even know much about what Australia was like in 1912... because I wasn't born until nearly a century later."

"What are you talking about?"

"I mean I'm not from this time," I said. "I used my magic to travel here from the future."

43

MIRA

SUNDAY, JUNE 16, 1912

I TOLD William everything from the beginning, when Gemma and I had received our magic at the cove.

He received it moderately well. He was stunned, but he didn't kick me out and tell me to never speak to him again, which I took as a good thing.

"Now that the bond to Lilith is broken, it's time for me to go home," I finished.

"To the future," he said hollowly.

"Yes. To the future."

He gazed out the window, looking troubled. Then he snapped his gaze back to mine. "You're able to bring people with you to the future," he said. "I want to go with you."

"You *what?*"

I'd hoped he'd be open-minded, but that was an entirely different level of acceptance.

"I've never felt like I fit in here." He sat forward, his eyes gleaming with excitement. "I've always felt trapped. But if I go with you to your world—to your *time*—I can have a fresh start. With you."

My breath caught in my chest at the possibility. Because that was what I wanted. A life with William.

But as I thought through the logistics, my heart sank.

"The supernatural world is dangerous," I said slowly. "You're human. Even if you came with me to the future, you still wouldn't be part of my world."

"I can go to Avalon." He squared his shoulders with determination. "I'll enter the Angel Trials and become Nephilim."

"You can't be serious," I said, but from the way he was looking at me, it was clear he was. "You found out about the supernatural world a few hours ago. Now you want to become a Nephilim?"

"I want to be with you," he said. "I've known it since the day I met you. I'll do whatever it takes to make that happen. If you want me to, of course."

THE DRAGON QUEEN

Karina cleared her throat, and we both looked to her.

I expected her to look appalled. To say no immediately.

Instead, she looked interested.

"It's a viable option," she said. "But like Mira said, our world is dangerous—even to the Nephilim."

"You said Lilith was dead," he said.

"The demons aren't the only enemies we've fought, and new enemies will always rise," she explained. "It's simply the way of our world."

"I understand," he said.

She raised an eyebrow. "Do you?"

I said nothing, because Karina was right. There was no way someone could fathom what it was like to fight for your life against terrifying creatures until you had to do it yourself.

"This is my decision," he said, and then he refocused on me. "And yours. If you came here to say goodbye—if you want to return to the future without me—then I understand."

"How are you always so *nice?*" I asked.

"Are the men in your time so terrible?"

I rolled my eyes. "You have no idea."

"Does that mean you'll take me?" He smiled mischievously, like he had a feeling I wanted to say yes.

"What about your family here?" I asked. "And your friends?"

"You're a time traveler. We can come back and visit them whenever we want."

"It wouldn't be that simple," I said. "There are things to consider—like how quickly we'd age. If we pass the Angel Trials—because remember, I haven't entered them yet, either—we could choose to live on Avalon. If we did that, we'd stop aging in our mid-twenties. Your family would notice it if they're aging and we stay the same."

"And if we don't choose to live on Avalon?" he asked.

"Then we'd age normally."

He paused, thinking. "We could tell my family that we've chosen to start a life for ourselves out west," he said, and then he spoke faster, the way he always did when he was excited about an idea. "They've always known I wasn't happy here, so I doubt it would surprise them. We can visit them occasionally—keeping the time between visits proportional to how much we've aged in the present—and they'd never know the difference."

"Hm," I said. "I suppose that could work."

"Is that a yes?"

I looked to Karina. "What do you think?" I asked.

"I promised you that if William accepted the truth, then how you proceed is up to the two of you," she said. "But even so, it was *always* up to you. You're the Dark Queen of Pentacles. You outrank me."

I wanted to smack myself for not realizing it sooner. Karina was so much older than I was—more than a century older—so it was easy to think she was the one in charge.

But this decision was mine, and *only* mine.

So I looked to William, smiled, and said, "I hope you kept that ring. Because my answer is yes."

44

GEMMA

THURSDAY, JUNE 24 (FOUR DAYS AGO)

I WAS PACING ANXIOUSLY in the house in Norway when Annika appeared in the center of the living room.

She collapsed to the floor, although she still held the Golden Scepter.

I hurried over to her and crouched down to be at her level. "What happened?" I asked. "Did you kill him?"

"I did." She smiled, despite how pale she looked.

"Then why are you so…?"

"Weak?" she finished for me.

"Yeah."

"It's angelic empathy. You know how demons lack a conscience?" she asked, and I nodded. "Angels are the opposite. Our empathy is so strong that we absorb the feelings of everything around us. It's why angels live on Heaven and don't come to Earth—or to any of the other realms, for that matter. It's too overwhelming to bear."

"It's another reason why you didn't leave Avalon," I realized.

"One of them. But it's going to be okay. Lucifer is dead. Everything is going as planned."

"I hope so." I took a deep breath, since just because Lucifer was dead, it didn't mean everything was okay. "How were the others doing?"

"They were alive when I left," she said, but then her tone darkened. "As were Lilith and Lavinia. I didn't have the strength to remain there after killing Lucifer. The rest is up to the others."

I pressed my lips together and sat back on my heels. Because I could use my key and go to Vegas right now. I could help the others finish off Lilith, Lavinia, and the rest of the demons and dark witches.

But that would involve leaving Annika alone in an incredibly weakened state. And if something happened to Annika, Avalon would be lost forever.

She'd risked so much for us. My duty right now was to her.

"They can handle it," I said. "I know they can."

"I agree." She squared her shoulders, then used the Golden Scepter to help herself stand back up. Color was returning to her face—like the Scepter was giving her strength. "Now, let's get Avalon back."

I took her hand that wasn't holding onto the Scepter. "Do you need time to rest?" I asked.

"No. I've got this."

With that, she teleported us to the middle of a lush jungle in Avalon. Birds chirped, frogs ribbitted in the small pond ahead, and a waterfall roared nearby. What I could make out of the sky above the trees was bright blue with a few puffy white clouds.

Annika looked around in wonder. "It's like I never broke the bond," she said.

"Because you *haven't* broken the bond," I said. "Well, the past version of you hasn't broken the bond. Not yet."

"But she will."

I nodded, since there was always a few second gap between when I time traveled back to the past and when I returned to the future.

That few second gap was why Annika had never time traveled with me before—not even when I'd experimented with my abilities on Avalon. In those few seconds, she wouldn't be on the island, and the bond would break.

Luckily, there was a loophole to this rule. A way to eliminate the few seconds in between leaving and arriving. I'd experienced it the first time I'd traveled back in time.

"You ready?" I asked her, still holding onto her hand.

"I'm ready."

Take us back to the present, I told the Crown, and then we flickered forward in time.

45

GEMMA

TUESDAY, JUNE 29 (PRESENT DAY)

WE REAPPEARED IN A WASTELAND.

The trees no longer had leaves. The air was thick with humidity, the sky was a depressing gray, the pond was a thick, muddy mess, and silence hung heavy around us.

Avalon was dead.

And then, new memories flooded my mind.

They started eight days ago, when Annika had received a fire message while training us and disappeared. When she'd come back, she'd said that Jacen had needed to speak with her, and had left it at that.

After training, she'd asked me to accompany her to her quarters. She told me she'd been visited by a future version of myself, and then told me everything the version of me from the future had told her.

From there, we'd gathered all the leaders of Avalon around the round table and filled them in. They'd been horrified to hear about Lucifer and how they'd died in the original version of the battle, but they were as determined as we were to change the outcome.

Four days later, when it was time to go to the Vegas Strip, we were ready.

It had killed me to say goodbye to everyone—especially to Ethan. But he'd promised me that things would be different this time around, and I'd believed him.

It took all my willpower not to go with them. But trusting the future version of myself was our best chance of getting everything right this time.

Annika and I had waited anxiously on Avalon as they'd fought.

Then, hours later, they'd returned. *All* of them. Ethan had wrapped me in a hug so tight it felt like he was going to break me.

The only person noticeably missing was Mira.

But I'd told myself that it was okay. She and I hadn't had much time to talk on the Titanic. For all I knew, the version of her I'd seen there had come from further in the future.

I'd simply need to be patient. And when everything was over, if I still hadn't heard from her, I could try to find her in 1912. I didn't want to have to do that, since I didn't want to risk changing anything else in the past, but it was still an option.

In the days that had followed, the Nephilim Army had tracked down the demons that had deserted the battle and killed them all.

We'd beaten them.

All of them.

Annika pressed her fingers to her temples, and she beamed as the memories of the new timeline filled her mind, too. "We won," she said, and she pulled me into a tight hug. "After all these years, it's finally over."

Finally, she loosened her arms around me and looked around the dead forest, frowning.

"This is what it looked like when I first got here all those years ago," she said.

"I remember," I said, since I'd traveled back in time to see Avalon before Annika had arrived. "So, are you ready to bring life back to Avalon—again?"

"You bet I am."

Take us back five minutes, I thought to the Crown.

We flickered for a few seconds, and then Avalon was back to its typical lively state.

"Amazing," Annika said as she looked around.

"It is," I agreed.

The only way Avalon could be alive like this was if our past selves—at least the past version of *Annika*—had remained on the island.

That was the loophole. Since there'd only been one version of each of us in existence for the past four days, I was still able to travel us back to any time in that window.

I'd chosen to take us back five minutes, because this time, I wasn't going to time travel us back to the present. That few second gap without Annika on Avalon wouldn't exist, because we were going to catch up with the present naturally.

Annika paced around in front of the pond. "How much longer?" she asked.

"About two minutes," I replied, because ever since receiving my time travel magic, I had a natural feel for time in general.

She continued to pace silently as we waited.

Two minutes later, Avalon was still intact.

"Okay," I said, and Annika stopped pacing. "We did it."

"Just like that?" she asked.

"The hope was that no change would happen," I said. "So, yes. Just like that."

"And our counterparts…?"

"They're gone," I said, since that was what had happened to my counterpart the first time I'd time traveled in the Seventh Kingdom. "We're the only versions of ourselves that exist right now."

"So, wherever we were, we disappeared."

"Yep. Which means it's time for you to teleport us back to the castle, so we can fill everyone in."

"It's a good thing we already prepped them," she said with a relieved smile. "Otherwise, I can't imagine how we'd begin to explain."

"Tell me about it," I said. "I sometimes even have a hard time wrapping my mind around it myself. But it worked. And in the end, that's what matters."

"It worked," she repeated, and her eyes filled with tears. "Avalon is still alive. Because of you."

"Because of all of us," I corrected her, and then I walked forward, took her hands, and she teleported us to the castle.

46

GEMMA

TUESDAY, JUNE 29 (PRESENT DAY)

JACEN WAS WAITING in the living area of his and Annika's quarters when we popped in.

He tilted his head, his brow scrunched. "That's strange. I was just talking to you, but..." he trailed off, clearly confused.

"But what?" I asked.

"Nothing," he said, and he snapped back to focus.

"Wrong," Annika said, and she ran up to him and pulled him in for a kiss.

I averted my eyes, not wanting to intrude any more than I already had on their private moment.

"So much has happened," she said, and figuring it was safe, I looked back over to them again.

He stared down at her with complete love and adoration. "Does that mean it worked?" he asked with a smile.

Before either of us could confirm, there was a loud knock on the door. I glanced at Annika, since it was up to her to decide who to let into her quarters.

She walked over to the door and opened it.

Torrence stormed inside, holding the Dark Wand. Its red crystal was glowing like crazy.

I knew from my memories of the new timeline that Torrence was now the Dark Queen of Wands. But seeing her in all her glory—and feeling the insane amount of magic that emanated off her—was a totally different story.

She faced me, her eyes a storm of confusion. "I was enjoying some much-needed private time with Reed when I suddenly remembered you and I going back to Pompeii, getting the Golden Scepter from an angel, and you making an entire *volcano* erupt so we could do so," she said, the air around her humming with magic. "But that definitely didn't happen. And at the same time, it did." She crossed her arms the best she could, given that she was holding the Dark Wand. "Explain."

"You remembered it because it happened," I said simply. "We needed to go back in time to find the Golden Scepter because—"

"Because it's the only weapon that can kill Lucifer," she said. "We talked about it in Pompeii. We talked about the battle as if we'd lost it. Except we didn't lose. We *won*."

"I didn't think you'd remember all of that," I said. "It must be because you were there with me. It's the only thing I can think of to explain it."

"It's the only thing that explains *what?*"

I wracked my mind for where to start.

"You weren't a member of the council before the battle, so you don't know the plan we had going into it," I said. "It involved time travel."

"I figured as much." She rolled her eyes.

"I'm trying to explain," I said patiently, since I knew this had to be a lot for her to process.

"Okay." She huffed, and the red crystal on the Dark Wand dimmed, which I took to mean that she was getting a handle on her emotions. "Go ahead."

I nodded, then continued, "You remember one battle, right? The one where we beat Lucifer and Lilith and Lavinia?"

"Yes."

"Like I was saying before, that wasn't the first time the final battle played out," I said. "Because there was another time. A time when we lost."

I waited a few seconds for it to sink in.

"You changed it," she realized. "You went back in time and made sure we won."

"*We* went back in time and made sure we won," I said, and then I filled her in on everything that had happened before our mission to get the Golden Scepter in Pompeii.

47

GEMMA

WEDNESDAY, JUNE 30 (PRESENT DAY)

The majority of yesterday was spent with the council, filling them in on everything that had happened.

Last night was dedicated to Ethan.

I'd never be able to forget seeing him killed in the original battle, and I was going to appreciate every moment I had with him.

We were woken that morning by a loud knock on the door.

I covered our heads with the comforter, but whoever was knocking was insistent. Once it was clear they weren't going to give up, I sat up and let out a frustrated breath.

"Give us a minute!" I said, and then Ethan and I scurried out of bed and quickly got dressed.

I opened the door and found Skylar standing on the other side.

She looked back at Ethan—who was doing his best to hide his annoyance at being woken up—then cleared her throat. "Sorry for the disturbance, but both of you need to come to the dock," she said. "Someone's about to arrive who I know you'll want to see."

"Mira," I said hopefully, and Skylar didn't confirm or deny. She simply moved to the side so Ethan and I could head out of our quarters.

I hurried through the hall and down the steps to the cavern below the castle so quickly that I nearly stumbled over my feet on the way there.

Annika and Jacen were already waiting at the dock, staring out at the still water in the underground lake.

"It's going to be Mira," I said, as if saying it could make it true.

Annika stepped toward me, squeezed my hand, and gave me a small smile. "I hope so."

Finally, after what felt like an hour but what was really only three minutes, a boat turned around the corner.

My heart dropped at the sight of a man I didn't recognize, who was wearing clothes that looked like they'd come out of the early twentieth century. He was gazing around in wonder, like he was seeing the world for the first time. I sniffed to try to pick up his supernatural scent, but he was either wearing a cloaking ring, or he was human.

Why did Skylar wake me up for *this*?

But then, another boat turned around the corner.

Mira.

Her eyes locked with mine, and she stood up in her boat, waving in excitement. She was beaming in a way that I hadn't seen since before we'd gotten our magic, and I knew in that moment that my bubbly, fun, mischievous twin sister was *back*.

I stood on the balls of my feet, barely able to stand still as I waited for her boat to land at the dock.

The crystals of the Dark Crown glimmered as the fire from the torches reflected off them. Mira was also dressed like she'd come from the twentieth century, and I realized that she must not have bothered changing after returning from 1912.

The man's boat reached the dock first, and Mira's followed a few seconds later.

Before I could process that she was truly *here*, Mira bounded off the boat, landed gracefully on the dock, and pulled me in for a huge hug.

I hugged her back tightly, as if afraid she could disappear at any moment.

Eventually we forced ourselves apart.

The moment we did, the man who'd come with her stepped to her side and took her left hand.

Her hand with a *ring* on her finger.

Mira never wore rings on her left hand. She'd always said those fingers were staying bare until she was engaged.

I yanked her hand out of his, and my mouth dropped open at the sight of the massive diamond ring.

"Please tell me this isn't what I think it is," I said.

"You mean an engagement ring?"

"Yeah. That."

She smiled playfully. "So you want me to lie to you?"

"We're *seventeen*," I said. "You can't get engaged at seventeen."

But at the same time, it wasn't the worst thing in the world. Because if Mira had accepted a proposal from whoever this guy was—and, to give her credit, he *was* very attractive—then it meant she was over Ethan.

In fact, she'd barely glanced at Ethan since arriving to Avalon.

"Things are different in 1912," she said.

"You were there for a few *weeks*," I said. "It's not like you're from there. Unless you're planning on going back?"

Sparks of fire buzzed around my fingers at the possibility. Because I'd finally gotten my sister back. She couldn't just leave to go off and live at the turn of the twentieth century with a man she'd met a few weeks ago.

Well, technically she can, I reminded myself.

And would that be the worst thing in the world? If that was what she'd decided would make her happy—and if she'd come all the way to Avalon to tell me—then I'd support her. Besides, I could time travel, too. I could visit her there whenever I wanted.

"Chill." She chuckled, as if she could read my racing thoughts. "I'm staying here. *William* and I are staying here."

I turned to *William* and studied him. He looked only a few years older than us, and his sandy blond hair had gotten ruffled up from the trip to Avalon. If he wasn't dressed in aristocratic clothes, I would have thought he was a bohemian artist.

"It's a pleasure to meet you," he said, holding out his hand for me to shake.

I did, although I was stunned the entire time.

When I let go, my hand immediately found Ethan's.

"I guess Mira told you about… us?" I asked William.

"You mean how she's a witch with dragon elemental magic, and that she traveled more than a century back in the past to wait for you to kill Lilith in the present?"

"All right," I said, surprised by how calmly he'd said it all. "I'll take that as a yes."

He stood straighter and smiled, like he'd aced an exam.

I looked back and forth between the two of them, as if doing so could answer my questions. From the way they were angled toward each other, I could practically feel their love oozing in the air between them.

Annika took a step toward Mira. "Welcome to Avalon," she said with a warm smile. "I'm Annika—the Earth Angel. I'm so glad you made it here safely."

"Trust me—so am I," Mira said.

"Normally we start with orientation…" Annika said, although from the way she trailed off, I could tell she knew that orientation was going to have to wait.

"Do you mind if Mira and I go to my quarters first?" I asked, even though as a Queen, I didn't have to ask for permission to do anything. "So we can catch up alone?"

"Your 'quarters?'" Mira asked, raising an eyebrow.

I supposed it did sound pretty fancy when it was put that way.

"Come and see," I said, and I reached for her hand, leading her toward the stairs. "Because I know you're gonna *love* it here."

48

GEMMA

THURSDAY, JULY 1 (PRESENT DAY)

THE NEXT DAY, Ethan called a council meeting.

It was tight around the table with the new Dark Queens and their partners, but we managed to squeeze enough chairs together. Once everyone was situated, they looked to Ethan, curious about what he wanted to discuss.

I, of course, already knew. Because we'd gone to the Eternal Library last night, and Hecate had given us the final piece of information we needed to do what needed to be done.

Now, we needed to get the others on board to help us.

"As the king of Ember, I have a duty to my people," Ethan started, the confidence in his voice making him *sound* like a king. "Long ago, the dragons lived in peace in our native realm. Then the mages and fae declared Ember a 'prison realm,' and they started sending their worst criminals there."

The others nodded, since this was common knowledge.

"The dark mages and fae—a group that now calls themselves the Dark Allies—took over Ember and turned the majority of my people into slaves," he continued. "The dragons who are free are deep in hiding, but they can't remain that way forever. The Dark Allies must be stopped so we can reclaim our realm."

Everyone was silent as they processed the fact that Ethan was ready to jump into another war so soon after we'd won the war against the demons.

"I assume you have a plan?" Raven finally asked.

"The dragons are strong," Ethan said. "The only reason why they can't fight back against the Dark Allies is because the Dark Allies keep their magic bound with cuffs. These cuffs were created by one of the first dark mages sent to Ember—the Supreme Mage, King Ragnorr. If we kill King Ragnorr, the cuffs will deactivate, and the dragons will be able to use their magic to stand up against the Dark Allies."

"I have no doubt that the dragons are strong," Julian said. "But the Supreme Mages are immortal *and* indestructible. They can't be killed."

"Wrong," Ethan said. "A Supreme Mage can be killed by someone with more magic than they have. In King Ragnorr's case, since he practices dark magic, he can only be killed by someone with more dark magic than he possesses."

That was what we'd learned from Hecate last night. And, after sharing it with the group, Ethan's gaze immediately landed on Torrence's.

She stared back at him, her expression giving away nothing.

"As the Dark Queen of Wands, you're the only person on Earth with more dark magic than King Ragnorr," he said to her. "To free the dragons, I need your help."

Reed moved protectively closer to Torrence. "Even if you succeed, the mages and fae will continue to send their prisoners to Ember," he said to Ethan. "What will stop them from overtaking the dragons again?"

"Ember never belonged to the mages and the fae," he said. "They had no right to turn it into a place to dump their prisoners."

Reed smirked, amused. "You think the mages will stop sending their prisoners to Ember because you asked them nicely?"

"I think we have a lot of powerful people sitting around this table, and that if we approach the fae and the mages, we can come up with another solution. One that *doesn't* involve them dumping all their criminals into a realm with an innocent supernatural species."

"A realm like Hell?" Bella asked.

"Yes," Ethan said. "That would work nicely."

"We just defeated the demons," Annika broke in. "Now you want to open a portal to Hell and risk them escaping again?"

"The portals that currently lead the fae and mages to Ember are one-way," he said calmly. "The Dark Allies have more magic than the demons. If they couldn't break through the portals to escape Ember, then the demons won't be able to break through them to escape Hell."

"And who's going to create these portals?"

This was where the question I'd asked Hecate last night came in handy.

"One-way portals like the ones leading to Ember are nearly impossible to create or destroy," I said. "But if the Holy and Dark Queens of Wands work together, they'll be able to do it."

"How do you know?" she asked.

"Through the same source that told me the Golden Scepter was the only object in existence that could kill Lucifer."

I tensed, expecting her to demand me to explain further.

She didn't. Instead, she gave me a single nod, showing me that she was taking my word as the truth.

"I can talk to Sorcha," Selena volunteered. "Given that Lilith unleashed the plague on the Otherworld that killed a huge amount of fae, I'm sure she'll delight in the idea of throwing our criminals into Hell instead of Ember."

"And the mages?" Annika asked.

"Sorcha is close with our king," Reed said. "If she proposes the idea to him, I'm sure he'll listen."

He said it with so much confidence that no one questioned him.

"But there's still one important factor," he continued. "You said you needed Torrence to kill King Ragnorr." He turned to look at her. "Is this something you're willing to do?"

Her grip around the Dark Wand tightened. "If it wasn't for Gemma and Ethan, then

I'd still be fully dark, I'd still be locked in Ember, and Selena would still be dead," she said. "So you bet I want to help." With that, she turned to me and asked, "When do we leave? And what's the plan?"

"I already have a plan," I said. "I can share it now. As for when we leave..." I trailed off and looked to Annika.

Even though all the Queens were technically equal, it always felt like she was the leader.

"We have much to discuss with the fae and the mages," she said. "We can start working on that immediately. Then, once we come to an agreement, you can do whatever you need to do to free the dragons and give them back their home."

49

TORRENCE

FRIDAY, JULY 9 (PRESENT DAY)

It took Sorcha a week to convince the mages that if we succeeded in overthrowing the Dark Allies, they'd agree to send their criminals to Hell instead of Ember. During that time, the council brainstormed to perfect Gemma's plan.

It involved time travel.

Of *course* it involved time travel.

Understanding time travel was eventually going to be the death of me. Time was supposed to move *forward*—not in every which way and other timelines/universes that Gemma created. But I had my role, and I was ready to play it.

Now, it was just me, Sorcha, and Reed standing in the mausoleum-like thing in the palace of the Otherworld, looking down into the red portal that led to Ember. I held the Dark Wand in my right hand, and the crystal glowed brightly.

Reed placed his hand on my shoulder, and when I looked up at him, he was concerned. "Are you sure you can control it?" he asked.

"I can," I promised. "All it takes is remembering the devastated look on your face when we were prisoners in the mages' dungeon, when I lied and told you I didn't love you."

A shadow crossed over his eyes. "In that moment, it wasn't a lie."

"It was the darkness talking," I said, since back then, I'd been consumed by it. "But you knew I loved you, even though the dark magic was smothering my emotions. Now, I want to be able to give you my heart—all of it. My love for you is what keeps the darkness under control."

"*You* keep your magic under control," he said.

"Maybe. But you make a fantastic incentive."

He smirked, then pulled me close and kissed me. His kiss was hard and rough, but somehow sweet at the same time, which was pretty much Reed in a nutshell.

I would have stripped off his clothes and made love to him right there if Sorcha didn't clear her throat, interrupting our moment.

So I pulled away from Reed, my cheeks flushed from kissing him.

His dark eyes swirled with intensity, like he was hypnotized by me.

"We'll continue this later," I promised. "After I'm back from Ember."

"Come back safely," he said. "Swear to me that you will."

"I swear it."

The Wand's red crystal glowed after I said it, as if confirming my promise.

"Good," he said. "I'll see you soon."

"See you soon," I said, and then I looked back down into the portal.

Like the one in the mage realm—Mystica—the stones built up in a circle around it made it resemble a well. A *deep* well, seeing as there was no bottom in sight.

But luckily, since I'd been down a similar portal before, I knew what to expect. So, not wanting to drag out this farewell any longer than necessary, I stepped onto the ledge of the stones and jumped into Ember.

50

TORRENCE

FRIDAY, JULY 9 (PRESENT DAY)

I LANDED ON MY FEET, my knees bent to absorb the fall, with one hand touching the ground to brace myself and the other holding firmly onto the Dark Wand. I was in the middle of a desert, and the only things breaking up the landscape were the boulders scattered throughout the area. It was bright outside, and the hot sun scorched my skin.

When I righted myself, I made sure the Wand's crystal was glowing brightly, and that black, dark magic covered my eyes.

It didn't take me long to spot the two groups nearby—the dark mages and the dark fae. The fae had wings of all different colors, and the mages wore robes that made them look like Jedi apprentices. Although, given the circumstances, they would most definitely be *Sith* apprentices. Except they wouldn't be apprentices. Because all the mages and fae in Ember were powerful enough to be sent to a one-way prison realm.

The groups stood at opposite sides of the landing spot, and all of them eyed me warily.

A representative of the mages stepped forward. I couldn't see his hair color under his robes, but his eyes were a startling pale blue.

"On behalf of the Dark Allies, welcome to Ember," he said. "I sense strong magic in you."

"You better," I said with a confident smirk. "Because I'm the Dark Queen of Wands. And I'm here to take my rightful place beside your king."

He pressed his lips together, silent.

I bet he hadn't expected *that* one.

"Are you referring to King Ragnorr?" he finally asked.

"Of course I am." I narrowed my eyes. "What other king of our people would I be referring to?"

He sized me up, and another mage stepped up next to him—a female with eyes the same color as his. "King Ragnorr has made no mention of a bride," she said calmly, although I could tell by how tensed she was that she was defensive, and probably a little scared.

"What can I say?" I chuckled, like this didn't concern me. "I like surprises."

Then, someone spoke up from behind me. "Your weapon looks like the Holy Wand of legend," she said, and I glanced over my shoulder to see a fae girl with pale skin and even paler blonde hair. She held her chin high, as if she thought she was better than me.

I spun around to face her. "The Holy Wand has blue crystals—not red," I said. "This is the Dark Wand. And it chose me as its Queen. Which makes me one of the most powerful mages in the world."

"If that's true, then why are you here?"

"What do you mean—*why am I here?*" When I imitated her, I made her nasally voice sound even more annoying than it already was.

"I mean that if you're as powerful as you say you are, how did you get captured and sent here? Shouldn't you have been able to use your magic as the 'Dark Queen of Wands' to avoid being banished in the first place?"

The way she said my title—as if it were a joke—*really* pissed me off.

"She has a good point," the mage with pale blue eyes asked. "If you are who you say you are, and if you've truly been chosen by the Dark Wand, then prove it."

"Fine," I snarled, faced the group of dark fae, and called on my magic.

I blasted it out of the crystal at them like a red laser beam, cutting through their bodies in a straight line.

Some of their mouths were still open in shock when the top halves of their bodies tumbled to the ground next to their already collapsed bottom halves.

All of them dead.

Murdered.

By me.

Disgust rolled through me. Because even though they were criminals, you never knew someone's life story. Maybe some of them had been sent to Ember unjustifiably. Maybe they were just doing their jobs of guarding the portal after Gemma, Mira, Ethan, Reed, and I killed the previous group of guards.

But this was war, and the dragons needed their home realm back. I was their best chance at making that happen. To do that, I had to convince the dark mages that this wasn't an act.

If that meant embracing more of my dark side, then so be it. I trusted myself to rein it in later.

So I inhaled the roasted smell of death, plastered a chilling smile on my face, and spun around to face the dark mages. "Is that enough proof for you?" I asked so sweetly that it was like honey dripping from my voice.

The female dark mage held her gaze with mine. "The fae will be angry with you for killing their guards."

"I'm a mage," I said. "I don't care about the fae."

"We don't care about the fae, either," she replied. "But they're our allies. So we tolerate them."

My magic crashed around like a tsunami of frustration inside of me, and the Wand's crystal glowed red again.

I had to take a few deep breaths to stop myself from doing to the dark mages what I'd just done to the dark fae.

They were so silent that I could practically smell their fear.

It was time to take advantage of that.

Time to let them know that *they* served *me*.

"What part of 'take me to your king' don't you understand?" My voice sliced through the air as sharply as the glass I wanted to pierce through their souls.

I could have sworn I saw the man quiver. "We can't leave the portal unmanned," he finally said. "But my sister will escort you to our palace, and there, she'll present you to our king."

51

TORRENCE

FRIDAY, JULY 9 (PRESENT DAY)

THE BROTHER and sister duo didn't bother to introduce themselves before walking toward me.

Once they were close enough, the woman held out her hand. She was only a few years older than I was.

I glanced at her hand skeptically.

She continued to hold my gaze, showing no ounce of fear. "If you want us to trust you, then you need to trust us," she said firmly.

"Fine," I said. "But if you take me anywhere other than your palace, I'll take care of you like I did those fae. Except unlike I did for them, I'll make sure to take my time while killing you."

She didn't so much as flinch. "You asked us to take you to the king," she said. "I'm offering to do that. You can either accept or not. Your choice."

I contemplated trying to force her into a blood oath. But no—this show of faith would be good.

It would make them think I was truly on their side.

Anyway, if she took me somewhere else, I'd follow through on that promise I'd made her, then return here to show her body as proof that I should be taken seriously, and get another dark mage to do as I'd asked.

"I accept," I said, and then I lowered my hand into her waiting palm.

She flashed us out of there in an instant.

We appeared on the top of a hill that overlooked what I assumed was the sprawling dark mage kingdom. It reminded me of the one from *Frozen*—not the ice palace Elsa had created, but the one in Arendelle where she'd lived with her sister.

Tall stone walls surrounded it like a fortress.

"There's a boundary spell around the kingdom that makes it so no one can teleport directly inside," the dark mage explained, which didn't surprise me, since all the kingdoms on Earth were protected by similar barriers. "We'll have to walk from here."

"Sounds reasonable," I said, continuing before she could walk forward. "Also, I don't know your name."

"That's because I didn't give it." Darkness swirled in her eyes again, but a second before that, I'd seen something I recognized greatly—because it had been the way Gemma had looked at Mira when she'd believed Mira and Ethan were a couple.

Jealousy.

"Do you want King Ragnorr for yourself?" I asked her.

"Of course not," she said, and she motioned to her left ring finger, which had a diamond band around it. She was married. "That Wand, on the other hand…" Her gaze traveled to the Dark Wand gripped firmly in my hand.

"You want power."

"I'm a dark mage," she said. "Of course I want power."

"Then after you take me to the king, I'll ensure you're rewarded," I said. "But to do that, I need your name."

"Freya Kristiansen," she said, and then she looked at me for my response. When I didn't give her one, she asked, "And what's yours?"

"I'm the Dark Queen of Wands," I said simply, and then I looked back to the palace. "Now, let's proceed."

She nodded, and I followed her down the path that led to the stone wall.

The guard at the tall wooden door immediately focused on the Wand. Then he got ahold of himself and looked to Freya. "A new recruit?" he asked.

"This one is special," Freya said, although she didn't elaborate further. "We need escorts to the palace—and an immediate audience with the king."

52

TORRENCE

FRIDAY, JULY 9 (PRESENT DAY)

Freya must have held authority in the dark mage kingdom, because the guard quickly gathered an entourage that marched me to the palace.

Along the way, I spotted servants dressed in rags working along the sides of the streets. Their wrists were cuffed, just like mine had been when my magic had been bound.

Dragons.

They barely paid me any attention as I walked by. It was like their souls had been shattered after years—or likely lifetimes—of slavery.

Eventually, we reached the wide steps that led to the giant front doors of the palace and marched inside.

The interiors of the palace had large rooms, but the decorations were sparser than I'd expected. Most everything was made of some variation of brown stone, which I supposed was because there weren't many other resources in Ember's desert environment to work with. There wasn't much natural light in the palace, either. I felt like I was walking into a giant crypt.

A long hallway led to a giant room where a man wearing a black robe and an obsidian crown sat on a stone throne. He looked to be about twenty-five years old, but his hard, strong features made it clear that he was far, far older than that.

And then there were his eyes. Pitch black, as if permanently consumed by dark magic. There was something so terrifying in them that it made me want to look anywhere else but his eyes, but I stood strong, not wanting to show any signs of weakness.

But even though I kept my gaze on his, I'd already seen the dark mages and dragon slaves along the sides of the room. I wondered why he kept the slaves in there—surely there was nothing they could do for him in the throne room.

Then I realized: they were a display of the power he held over them. He was showing them off as if they were pieces in a museum.

He glanced lazily at the Wand in my hand, unfazed. He'd flicked his eyes so quickly that it was like he couldn't be bothered to move.

Clearly this was a man who'd grown so used to power that he believed himself invincible.

"Who are you?" he asked, sounding bored and annoyed.

"I'm Torrence Devereux—the Dark Queen of Wands," I said. "And I've come here for you."

Before he had a chance to realize what was happening, I raised my Wand and shot a burst of red magic through the crystal. At the same time as my magic fried him to smithereens, I created a boundary dome around myself strong enough to ward off any possible attacks by the other dark mages in the room.

Turned out that it hadn't been necessary, because all of the dark mages were staring in shock at King Ragnorr's charred bones, which were now in piles on the seat of the throne and the floor.

The cuffs around the dragons' wrists clattered to the floor, too. Many of them held out their hands in wonder, and life started appearing in their previously sallow features.

I held the Dark Wand up victoriously. "I've freed you from the dark mages," I said, my voice echoing in the cavernous room. "Now, it's time for you to *fight!*"

Fire, ice, stone, and air launched out of the dragons' hands, and then I flashed out.

I reappeared in the underwater dragon kingdom, in the room on the top of the tower where I'd first met the Elders.

Darius and Hypatia were waiting there—along with Ethan, Gemma, Mira, and Selena.

"He's dead," I said. "And it was *easy*. He was so arrogant that he wasn't even on guard for an attack."

"Or you're so strong that he never stood a chance against you," Selena said.

"Maybe."

"Wow." Her lips formed into an O of disbelief. "Are you actually being *modest?*"

"Of course not," I said, since "modest" wasn't a thing I did. "You should have seen him. He truly believed nothing could touch him. And then I turned him into a pile of bones—on his own throne."

"Nice." Ethan nodded in approval. "I want to hear all about it later. But now, let's move on to part two."

53

GEMMA

THURSDAY, JULY 8 (YESTERDAY)

I HELD Ethan's hands and flickered us one day into the past.

Mira appeared next to us with Selena.

We were in the same place we'd been standing before—in the center of the meeting room on the top floor of the tower. Hypatia and Darius were waiting for us there, looking at us expectantly.

"The plan worked," Ethan told them. "At 3pm tomorrow, Torrence will kill King Ragnorr and free the dragons."

"Incredible." Hypatia grinned.

"Truly." Darius looked to Mira, and then to me. "Your abilities add an entirely new level to battle strategy."

"I'm glad to help free the dragons," I said. "But the real hero is Torrence. She's the one who killed King Ragnorr."

"There are no 'real' heroes," Hypatia said kindly. "There are simply heroes, and I'd say all of you are ones."

I glanced down for a second, because even now, I wasn't the best at receiving compliments.

"While I agree with Hypatia, let's save the congratulations for later," Darius said. "Because this isn't over yet.

"No, it's not," I agreed, and then I walked over to the table, where a piece of paper and a pen were waiting for me.

It worked, I wrote. *And we're on our way to help.*

54

GEMMA

FRIDAY, JULY 9 (PRESENT DAY)

After leaving Torrence the note, the four of us didn't return to the present. Instead, we remained there and helped the Elders prepare the dragons in the kingdom for what was coming next. They'd already been told the plan, but a new sense of hope arose after they learned that Torrence had successfully killed King Ragnorr.

Now, Ethan was flying through the sky in dragon form, and I sat on his back, my hands wrapped around the spikes coming up out of the bottom of his neck. Although I didn't need to hold on as much as I thought I would, since thanks to our twin flame bond, I could feel what movements he was going to make at nearly the same time as he made them. With Ethan, flying felt natural—which said a lot, given that air wasn't one of my elements.

Half of the dragons from the kingdom flew behind us—nearly six hundred in total.

The other half were with Mira and Selena.

The dark mage kingdom finally came into view, and at the exact time Torrence had said it would, the roof of the palace exploded in a flash of red light.

Dragons flew out from the top—more and more of them, far more than were behind us. There were so many dragons that they covered the sky, blotting out the sun so it seemed like night.

Just when I thought there couldn't be any more dragons inside, Torrence rode up on the back of one, her hair flying wildly around her, and her eyes immediately locked on mine.

"There are only dark mages left inside," she said. "Time to burn them down."

All at once, the fire dragons released fire from their mouths—Ethan at the head of the group.

The palace exploded in flames.

As it did, more and more dragons flew up from the rest of the kingdom.

Terrified dark mages ran through the streets, their eyes black with rage as they released clouds of black death magic from their hands. Their dark magic *did* hit some dragons, and I winced as I watched the dragons' bodies fall to the ground and shift back into human form.

But for the most part, the dragons soared over the mages, fueled by their anger as they killed them with ice and fire. Mages flooded past the stone wall surrounding the kingdom and tried to make their way toward the desert, but they were killed, too.

The world burned as much as it had when Vesuvius had exploded over Pompeii, and the air smelled like cooked flesh. The mages continued to try to attack with their magic, but from their terrified screams and continued attempts to flee, they knew they'd lost.

It wasn't even thirty minutes before the entire kingdom was up in flames.

No wonder the mages had insisted on binding the dragons' magic. There were so many dragons in Ember that they didn't have a chance against them otherwise.

Even crazier was that dragons naturally had a peaceful nature. They didn't attack unless provoked. They were content in Ember, and had no interest in conquering other realms. They probably would have lived peacefully alongside the Dark Allies if the Dark Allies hadn't made them their enemies.

Once there was nothing left of the kingdom but ash, Ethan led the hoard of dragons to the portals that dropped people off from the Otherworld and Mystica.

As we got closer, so did another group of dragons opposite us, with Mira and Selena in the front.

Ethan lowered himself to the ground, and I hopped off his back before he returned to human form. The dragons that Torrence, Selena, and Mira were riding did the same, and the other dragons followed suit.

There were so many people in all directions that I couldn't comprehend the size of the crowd. Most of them were dressed in the simple, worn clothes of slaves, and they looked bewildered, as if they weren't sure if this was a dream or reality.

"How'd it go with the dark fae?" Torrence asked Selena.

"Burned them to the ground," she said, and thunder rumbled through the sky, followed with flashes of lightning.

The dragons looked up in amazement, as if the lightning was a blessing from the Heavens.

"Same with the dark mages," Torrence said, and then they aimed their Wands upward and created a sort of magical television screen high enough in the sky that everyone in the crowd could see it. They also created small glowing orbs that buzzed around us like cameras to show us on the screens.

The sight of it silenced the dragons even more.

Ethan faced the orb closest to him, and his face filled the screen. "Ember is ours again," he said, and the crowd erupted into cheers and applause.

He let them cheer for about twenty seconds. Then he held a hand up, and they silenced.

"It's thanks to the most powerful mage and the most powerful fae in the universe that your freedom was given to you today," he said. "And they're going to make sure the dark mages and fae can never come here again."

The orbs focused on Torrence and Selena, and the two of them turned toward the red portal. They held their Wands up toward it, nodded at each other, then shot their magic out toward it.

Red and blue magic collided with the portal, zapping it out of existence.

They made it look so *easy*.

The dragons seemed to agree, given the shocked looks on their faces.

"Rebuilding will take time," Ethan said. "But we lived off the land in the beginning, and for now, we'll do it once more. And as your king, I promise that Ember will never be taken from us again."

More cheers, and again, Ethan held his hand up to silence them.

"I'm happy to announce that I won't be the only one who will help pave our way into a new Golden Age," he said. "Because we wouldn't be here today without help from my twin flame, Gemma Brown. And it's my honor to introduce her to you as my queen."

I held my breath, since this was the part I was most nervous about. Because unlike Ethan, I wasn't a full dragon. Yes, I was gifted with dragon magic, but I couldn't shift.

I wasn't truly one of them.

Would they accept me as their queen?

Luckily, I didn't have to worry about it for long.

Because the moment I appeared on the screen, and Ethan clasped his hand around mine, the crowd once again erupted into approving applause.

I relaxed, but only slightly. Because it didn't end here. There was still a kingdom to rebuild.

But the dragons believed in Ethan, and *I* believed in Ethan.

It was going to take work. But like he'd promised our people, I trusted that we'd lead Ember into a new Golden Age—together.

55

GEMMA

WEDNESDAY, JULY 14 (PRESENT DAY)

THANKS TO HECATE'S keys and the tokens we'd used the first time we'd come to Ember, I was able to return to Earth with Mira, Torrence, and Selena.

Ethan was staying in Ember, because they needed him to lead as king. As his queen, I was going to join him soon, although I did plan to use my key to visit my family on Earth as much as possible. Especially because along with being the queen of Ember, I was also the Queen of Pentacles, which meant I had responsibilities to Earth and Avalon, too.

There was so much for me to do in the future.

But first, I had to say goodbye to my past.

Which was why I was currently in my room above the café, going through my stuff to decide what I wanted to take with me to Avalon and what I wanted to keep around for when I visited Mom. My books were obviously in the box labeled "Avalon," and now I was sorting through my clothes.

I reached for a sweatshirt—one with my high school's name on it—unfolded it, and froze when I saw the name on the front.

Ocean Park High.

No. That wasn't right. I'd never heard of a school called Ocean Park High.

Except as I continued to look at the sweatshirt, new memories layered over the old ones.

Ocean Park High was the name of my school.

Still holding onto the sweatshirt, I hurried into Mira's room. Mom was in there with her, helping her decide what shoes she wanted to take to Avalon, and which ones she wanted to leave here.

I held the sweatshirt up for them to see.

"You should bring it to Avalon," Mom said, misunderstanding my reason for coming in there. "As a memento to your past."

I didn't respond.

Instead, I looked to Mira.

"John Astor died on the Titanic," I said, and she nodded. "Our school was never called John Astor High."

"What's John Astor High?" Mom asked.

"What's the name of the street we live on?" I asked in return, since for me, it had always been John Astor Road.

"The Great Ocean Road…" She sounded baffled, and she looked to Mira. "What's going on?"

Mira smirked and met my gaze.

Then we both looked at Mom, said, "time travel" in unison, and I walked back to my room to continue packing.

56

GEMMA

SATURDAY, JANUARY 1 (FIVE AND A HALF MONTHS LATER)

The day of my and Mira's eighteenth birthday was finally here. Well, the night, since we were born at 10:04 PM.

For our seventeenth birthday, we hadn't known for sure that we'd receive magic. I'd had faith, but that was all it had been—trusting my inner senses.

Now, as I stood with Mira, Ethan, William, Hypatia, and Darius in the desert outside the dragon kingdom, I had a similar feeling. Because at age eighteen, as long as they were in Ember, dragons shifted for the first time.

While Mira and I weren't full dragons, and we'd possibly never be able to shift, I held on to the hope that we'd be able to do this.

The ceremony wasn't as elaborate as the one where we'd received our magic at the cove. In fact, there wasn't a ceremony at all. We just had to stand there, wait for the time of our birth, and see what happened.

Ethan and I stood off to the side, gazing up at the full moon.

"Make a wish," he said softly.

I closed my eyes and did as he said, since wishes made on full moons always felt more powerful than wishes on stars.

Of course, I didn't tell him what I'd wished for, and he didn't ask. He didn't have to. Because right now, we both wanted the same thing.

Rebuilding the dragon kingdom had been going relatively smoothly so far. The fact that our people could control the elements had helped us get a framework in place way faster than it would have otherwise.

Since I was Ethan's twin flame, they respected me as their queen. But the feeling that I wasn't one of them never went away.

The feeling hit the hardest whenever Ethan and the others shifted and I couldn't.

"It's almost time," I said. "We should join the others."

"In a minute," he said. "First, a kiss for good luck."

Then his lips were on mine, and I savored this moment between us, like I did *every* moment between us.

"I love you," I said after pulling away.

"You know I love you," he said, and I smiled, since it was true. Deep down, I'd always known Ethan loved me, and I knew he always would.

Just as I'd always love him.

I glanced over at where Mira and William were standing across the way, staring at each other with as deep of a love as me and Ethan. William had succeeded in becoming Nephilim, and while he and Mira lived on Avalon, he'd come with her for the big night.

"Come on," I said to Ethan, reaching for his hand to lead him toward where Hypatia and Darius were standing. "It's time."

Mira and William joined us, and the six of us stood in a circle.

"One more minute," Hypatia said, as if Mira and I needed someone to inform us of the time. "We need to spread out to give the two of you space."

Ethan gave my hand one final squeeze for luck, then backed up with the others.

I glanced over at Mira—my twin looked positively magical with the crystals of her Crown glimmering in the moonlight.

"We've got this," she said, and I couldn't help but chuckle.

"You sure sound confident for someone who didn't even believe in magic a year ago," I said.

"That was then," she said. "This is now."

I nodded, understanding what she meant. The people we'd been a year ago felt nearly unrecognizable to who we were now. I felt as disconnected to the pre-magic version of myself as I did to the timelines I'd written over in my journeys to the past.

We stepped away from each other, creating ample room for what was hopefully coming next.

The seconds counted down in my head.

Five, four, three, two...

I was looking into my twin's eyes as magic roared inside me, throwing me into the air as my body exploded into its dragon form. And all at once, I felt complete.

Because I was a witch.

I was a dragon.

I was the Queen of Pentacles.

And now, finally, my magic was whole.

FROM THE AUTHOR

I hope you enjoyed the Dragon Twins series! It was such an adventure to write, especially when I mixed in time travel, which made me push myself harder than ever. I hope the *Back to the Future* fans out there caught my many references to the movies.

If you enjoyed the *Dragon Twins* series, I'd love if you left a review on Amazon. The more positive reviews I have, the more encouraged I am to write my next book faster!

A review for the box set is the most helpful. Go to mybook.to/dragontwinsset to leave your review now.

If you haven't read the other three series' in the Dark World universe, I recommend going back and reading them to get the full scope of the Four Queens story. Here are the links:

The Vampire Wish (Annika's story): mybook.to/vampirewishset

The Angel Trials (Raven's story): mybook.to/angeltrialsset

The Faerie Games (Selena's story): mybook.to/faeriegamesset

If you enjoyed the Dark World series, then you'll love the Elementals series, which was my first series to hit it big! CLICK HERE or go to mybook.to/elementalsboxset to grab *Elementals* on Amazon, or turn the page to check out the cover and description.

ELEMENTALS: SNEAK PEEK

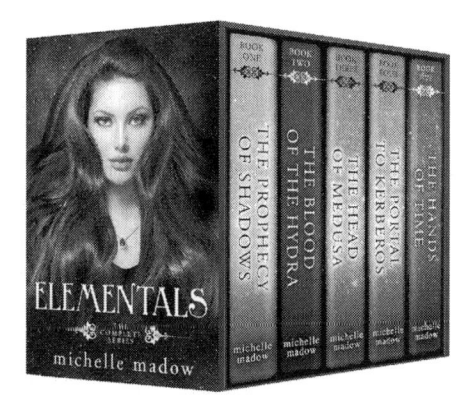

This box set includes all five books in the *USA Today* recommended Elementals series full of magic, adventure, mythology, and romance.

"A must read!"
--USA Today

* A Top 25 Amazon Bestseller in the entire Kindle Store *

Nicole Cassidy is a witch descended from the Greek gods... but she doesn't know it until she moves to a new town and discovers a dangerous world of magic and monsters she never knew existed.

Luckily, one of her new classmates is more than happy to take her under his wing to teach her how to use her magic. His name is Blake, and he's sort of her type: mysterious, possibly trouble.

The connection between Nicole and Blake is instant. There's just one problem: Blake has a girlfriend, Danielle. Rumor has it she harbors a penchant for using dark magic. Especially on anyone who gets near Blake.

As Nicole tries to navigate her mysterious new school—and stay out of Danielle's crosshairs—a new threat emerges: the Olympian Comet. When it shoots through the sky for the first time in 3,000 years, Nicole and four others—including Blake and Danielle—are gifted with elemental powers that have never been seen before.

But the comet has another effect—it opens the portal to another dimension that has imprisoned the Titans for centuries. After an ancient monster escapes, it's up to Nicole and the others to follow a cryptic prophecy in time to save the town...and possibly the world.

This box set includes the entire Elementals series—over 1,400 pages in print. This five book series has been a perennial bestseller since its publication and has garnered over 2,000 reviews on Amazon, 10,000+ ratings on Goodreads, and hundreds of millions of pages read in Kindle Unlimited.

Get it now at:
mybook.to/elementalsboxset

Or turn the page to read the first four chapters!

1

The secretary fumbled through the stacks of papers on her desk, searching for my schedule. "Here it is." She pulled out a piece of paper and handed it to me. "I'm Mrs. Dopkin. Feel free to come to me if you have any questions."

"Thanks." I looked at the schedule, which had my name on the top, and listed my classes and their locations. "This can't be right." I held it closer, as if that would make it change. "It has me in all honors classes."

She frowned and clicked around her computer. "Your schedule is correct," she said. "Your homeroom teacher specifically requested that you be in the honors courses."

"But I wasn't in honors at my old school."

"It doesn't appear to be a mistake," she said. "And the late bell's about to ring, so if you need a schedule adjustment, come back at the end of the day so we can discuss it. You're in Mr. Faulkner's homeroom, in the library. Turn right out of the office and walk down the hall. You'll see the library on the right. Go inside and head all the way to the back. Your homeroom is in the only door there. Be sure to hurry—you don't want to be late."

She returned to her computer, apparently done talking to me, so I thanked her for her help and left the office.

Kinsley High felt cold compared to my school in Georgia, and not just in the literal sense. Boxy tan lockers lined every wall, and the concrete floor was a strange mix of browns that reminded me of throw-up. The worst part was that there were no windows anywhere, and therefore a serious lack of sunlight.

I preferred the warm green carpets and open halls at my old school. Actually I preferred everything about my small Georgia town, especially the sprawling house and the peach tree farm I left behind. But I tried not to complain too much to my parents.

After all, I remembered the way my dad had bounced around the living room while telling us about his promotion to anchorman on the news station. It was his dream job, and he didn't mind that the only position available was in Massachusetts. My mom had jumped on board with the plan to move, confident that her paintings would sell better in a town closer to a major city. My younger sister Becca had liked the idea of starting fresh, along with how the shopping in Boston apparently exceeded anything in our town in Georgia.

There had to be something about the move for me to like. Unfortunately, I had yet to find it.

I didn't realize I'd arrived at the library until the double doors were in front of me. At least I'd found it without getting lost.

I walked inside the library, pleased to find it was nothing like the rest of the school. The golden carpet and wooden walls were warm and welcoming, and the upstairs even had windows. I yearned to run toward the sunlight, but the late bell had already rung, so I headed to the back of the library. Hopefully being new would give me a free pass on being late.

Just as the secretary had said, there was only one door. But with it's ancient peeling wood, it looked like it led to a storage room, not a classroom. And there was no glass panel, so I couldn't peek inside. I had to assume this was it.

I wrapped my fingers around the doorknob, my hand trembling. *It's your first day*, I reminded myself. *No one's going to blame you for being late on your first day.*

I opened the door, halfway expecting it to be a closet full of old books or brooms. But it wasn't a closet.

It was a classroom.

Everyone stared at me, and I looked to the front of the room, where a tall, lanky man in a tweed suit stood next to a blackboard covered with the morning announcements. His gray hair shined under the light, and his wrinkled skin and warm smile reminded me more of a grandfather than a teacher.

He cleared his throat and rolled a piece of chalk in his palm. "You must be Nicole Cassidy," he said.

"Yeah." I nodded and looked around at the other students. There were about thirty of them, and there seemed to be an invisible line going down the middle of the room, dividing them in half. The students near the door wore jeans and sweatshirts, but the ones closer to the wall looked like they were dressed for a fashion show instead of school.

"It's nice to meet you Nicole." The teacher sounded sincere, like he was meeting a new friend instead of a student. "Welcome to our homeroom. I'm Mr. Faulkner, but please call me Darius." He turned to the chalkboard, lifted his hand, and waved it from one side to the other. "You probably weren't expecting everything to look so normal, but we have to be careful. As I'm sure you know, we can't risk letting anyone else know what goes on in here."

Then the board shimmered—like sunlight glimmering off the ocean—and the morning announcements changed into different letters right in front of my eyes.

2

I BLINKED a few times to make sure I wasn't hallucinating. What I'd just seen couldn't have been real.

At least the board had stopped shimmering, although instead of the morning announcements, it was full of information about the meanings of different colors. I glanced at the other students, and while a few of them smiled, they were mostly unfazed. They just watched me, waiting for me to say something. Darius also stood calmly, waiting for my reaction.

"How did you do that?" I finally asked.

"It's easy," Darius said. "I used magic. Well, a task like that wouldn't have been easy for you, since you're only in your second year of studies, but given enough practice you'll get the hang of it." He motioned to a seat in the second row, next to a girl with chin-length mousy brown hair. "Please sit down, and we'll resume class."

I stared at him, not moving. "You used ... magic," I repeated, the word getting stuck in my throat. I looked around the room again, waiting for someone to laugh. This had to be a joke. After all, an owl hadn't dropped a letter down my fireplace to let me know I'd been accepted into a special school, and I certainly hadn't taken an enchanted train to get to Kinsley High. "Funny. Now tell me what you *really* did."

"You mean you don't know?" Darius's forehead crinkled.

"Is this a special studies homeroom?" I asked. "And I somehow got put into one about ... magic tricks?"

"It wasn't a trick," said an athletic boy in the center of the room. His sandy hair fell below his ears, and he leaned back in his seat, pushing his sleeves up to his elbows. "Why use tricks when we can do the real thing?"

I stared at him blankly and backed towards the door. He couldn't be serious. Because magic—*real* magic—didn't exist. They must be playing a joke on me. Make fun of the new kid who hadn't grown up in a town so close to Salem.

I wouldn't fall for it. So I might as well play along.

"If that was magic, then where are your wands?" I held up a pretend wand, making a swooshing motion with my wrist.

Darius cleaned his glasses with the bottom of his sweater. "I'd assumed you'd already started your lessons at your previous school." He frowned and placed his glasses back on. "From your reaction, I'm guessing that's not the case. I apologize for startling you. Unfortunately, there's no easy way to say this now, so I might as well be out with it." He took a deep breath, and said, "We're witches. You are, too. And regarding your question, we don't use wands because real witches don't need them. That's an urban legend created by humans who felt safer believing that they couldn't be harmed if there was no wand in sight."

"You can't be serious." I laughed nervously and pulled at the sleeves of my sweater. "Even if witches did exist—which they don't—I'm definitely not one of them."

The only thing "magical" that had ever happened to me was how the ligament I tore in my knee while playing tennis last month had healed right after moving here. The doctor had said it was a medical miracle.

But that didn't make it *magic*.

"I am completely serious," Darius said. "We're all witches, as are you. And this *is* a special studies homeroom—it's for the witches in the school. Although of course the administration doesn't know that." He chuckled. "They just think it's for highly gifted students. Now, please take a seat in the chair next to Kate, and I'll explain more."

I looked around the room, waiting for someone to end this joke. But the brown-haired girl who I assumed was Kate tucked her hair behind her ears and studied her hands. The athletic boy next to her watched me expectantly, and smiled when he caught me looking at him. A girl behind him glanced through her notes, and several other students shuffled in their seats.

My sweater felt suddenly constricting, and I swallowed away the urge to bolt out of there. This was a mistake, and I had to fix it. Now.

"I'm going to go back to the office to make sure they gave me the right schedule," I said, pointing my thumb at the door. "They must have put me in the wrong homeroom. But have fun talking about…" I looked at the board again to remind myself what it said. "Energy colors and their meanings."

They were completely out of their minds.

I hurried out of the classroom, feeling like I could breathe again once I was in the library lobby. No one else was around, and I sat in a chair to collect my thoughts. I would go back to the front office in a minute. For now, I browsed through my cell phone, wanting to see something familiar to remind myself that I wasn't going crazy.

Looking through my friends' recent photos made me miss home even more. My eyes filled with tears at the thought of them living their lives without me. It hadn't been a week, and they'd already stopped texting me as often as usual. I was hundreds of miles away, and they were moving on, forgetting about me.

Not wanting anyone to see me crying, I wiped away the tears and switched my camera to front facing view to check my reflection. My eyes were slightly red, but not enough that anyone would notice. And my makeup was still intact.

I was about to put my phone away when I noticed something strange. The small scar above my left eyebrow—the one I'd gotten in fourth grade when I'd fallen on a playground—had disappeared. I brushed my index finger against the place where the indentation had been, expecting it to be a trick of the light. But the skin was soft and smooth.

As if the scar had never been there at all.

I dropped my hand down to my lap. Scars didn't disappear overnight, just like torn ligaments didn't repair themselves in days. And Darius had sounded so convinced that what he'd been saying was true. All of the students seemed to support what he was saying, too.

What if they actually believed what he was telling me? That magic *did* exist?

The thought was entertaining, but impossible. So I clicked out of the camera, put the phone back in my bag, and stood up. I had to get out of here. Maybe once I did, I would start thinking straight again.

"Nicole!" someone called from behind me. "Hold on a second."

I let out a long breath and turned around. The brown-haired girl Darius had called Kate was jogging in my direction. She was shorter than I'd originally thought, and the splattering of freckles across her nose made her look the same age as my younger sister Becca, who was in eighth grade. But that was where the similarities between Kate and Becca ended. Because Kate was relatively plain looking, except for her eyes, which were a unique shade of bright, forest green.

"I know that sounded crazy in there," she said once she reached me. She picked at the side of her thumbnail, and while I suspected she wanted me to tell her that it didn't sound crazy, I couldn't lie like that.

"Yeah. It did." I shifted my feet, gripping the strap of my bag. "I know this is Massachusetts and witches are a part of the history here, so if you all believe in that stuff, that's fine. But it's not really my sort of thing."

"Keep your voice down." She scanned the area, but there was no one else in the library, so we were in the clear. "What Darius told you is real. How else would you explain what you saw in there, when he changed what was on the board?"

"A projector?" I shrugged. "Or maybe the board is a TV screen?"

"There's no projector." She held my gaze. "And the board isn't a television screen, even though that would be cool."

"Then I don't know." I glanced at the doors. "But magic wouldn't be on my list of explanations. No offense or anything."

"None taken," she said in complete seriousness. "But you were put in our homeroom for a reason. You're one of us. Think about it ... do strange things ever happen to you or people around you? Things that have no logical explanation?"

I opened my mouth, ready to say no, but closed it. After all, two miraculous healings in a few days definitely counted as strange, although I wouldn't go so far as to call it *magic*.

But wasn't that the definition of a miracle—something that happened without any logical explanation, caused by something bigger than us? Something *magical*?

"It has." Kate smiled, bouncing on her toes. "Hasn't it?"

"I don't know." I shrugged, not wanting to tell her the specifics. It sounded crazy enough in my head—how would it sound when spoken out loud? "But I guess I'll go back with you for now. Only because the secretary said she won't adjust my schedule until the end of the day, anyway."

She smiled and led the way back to the classroom. Everyone stared at me again when we entered, and I didn't meet anyone's eyes as I took the empty chair next to her.

Darius nodded at us and waited for everyone to settle down. Once situated, I finally glanced around at the other students. The boy Darius had called Chris smiled at me, a girl with platinum hair filed her nails under the table, and the girl next to her looked like she was about to fall asleep. They were all typical high school students waiting for class to end.

But my eyes stopped at the end of the row on a guy with dark shaggy hair. His designer jeans and black leather jacket made him look like he'd come straight from a modeling shoot, and the casual way he leaned back in his chair exuded confidence and a carefree attitude. Then his gaze met mine, and goosebumps rose over my skin. His eyes were a startling shade of burnt brown, and they were soft, but calculating. Like he was trying to figure me out.

Kate rested an elbow on the table and leaned closer to me. "Don't even think about it," she whispered, and I yanked my gaze away from his, my cheeks flushing at the realization that I'd been caught staring at him. "That's Blake Carter. He's been dating Danielle Emerson since last year. She's the one to his left."

Not wanting to stare again, I glanced at Danielle from the corner of my eye. Her chestnut hair was supermodel thick, her ocean blue eyes were so bright that I wondered if they were colored contacts, and her black v-neck shirt dropped as low as possible without being overly inappropriate for school.

Of course Blake had a girlfriend, and she was beautiful. I never stood a chance.

"As I said earlier, we're going to review the energy colors and what they mean," Darius said, interrupting my thoughts. "But before we begin, who can explain to Nicole how we use energy?"

I sunk down in my seat, hating that the attention had been brought back to me. Luckily, the athletic boy next to Kate who'd said the thing earlier about magic not being a trick raised his hand.

"Chris," Darius called on him. "Go ahead."

Chris pushed his hair off his forehead and faced me. His t-shirt featured an angry storm cloud holding a lighting bolt like a baseball bat, with "Trenton Thunder" written below it. It was goofy, and not a sports team that I'd ever heard of. But his boyish grin and rounded cheeks made him attractive in a cute way. Not in the same "stop what you're doing because I'm walking in your direction" way as Blake, but he definitely would have gotten attention from the girls at my old school.

"There's energy everywhere." Chris moved his hands in a giant arc above his head to demonstrate. "Humans know that energy exists—they've harnessed it for electronics. The difference between us and humans is that we have the power to tap into energy and use it ourselves, and humans don't." He smiled at me, as if I was supposed to understand what he meant. "Make sense?"

"Not really," I said. "Sorry."

"It's easier if you relate it to something familiar," he said, speaking faster. "What happens to the handle of a metal spoon when you leave it in boiling water?"

"It gets hot?" I said it as a question. This was stuff people learned in fifth grade science—not high school homeroom.

"And what happens when it's plastic?"

"It doesn't get hot," I said slowly. "It stays room temperature."

"Exactly." He grinned at me like I'd just solved an astrophysics mathematical equation. "Humans are like plastic. Even if they're immersed in energy, they can't conduct it. Witches are like metal. We have the ability to absorb energy and control it as we want."

"So, how do we take in this energy?" I asked, since I might as well humor him.

"Through our hands." Chris turned his palms up, closed his eyes, and took a deep breath. He looked like a meditating Buddha. Students snickered, and Chris re-opened his eyes, pushed his sleeves up, and sat back in his chair.

"O-o-kay." I elongated the word, smiling and laughing along with everyone else.

Darius cleared his throat, and everyone calmed down. "We can conduct energy from the Universe into our bodies," he said, his voice full of authority. Chills passed through me, and even though I still didn't believe any of this, I sat back to listen. "Once we've harnessed it, we can use it as we like. Think of energy like light. It contains different colors, each relating to an aspect of life. I've written them on the board. The most basic exercise we learn in this class is to sense this energy and absorb it. Just open your mind, envision the color you're focusing on, and picture it entering your body through your palms."

I rotated my hand to look at my palm. It looked normal—not like it was about to open up and absorb energy from the Universe.

"We're going to do a meditation session," Darius continued. "Everyone should pick a color from the board and picture it as energy entering your palms. Keep it simple and absorb the energy—don't push it back out into the Universe. This exercise is for practice and self-improvement." He looked at me, a hint of challenge in his eyes. "Now, please pick a color and begin."

I looked around the room to see what others were doing. Most people already had their eyes closed, the muscles in their faces calm and relaxed. They were really getting into this. As if they truly believed it.

If I didn't at least *look* like I was trying, I would stand out—again. So I might as well go along with it and pretend.

I re-examined the board and skimmed through the "meanings" of the colors. Red caught my attention first. It apparently increased confidence, courage, and love, along with attraction and desire. The prospect made me glance at Blake, who sat still with his eyes closed, his lips set in a line of concentration.

But he was out of my league *and* he had a girlfriend. I shouldn't waste my time hoping for anything to happen between us.

Instead, I read through the other colors and settled on green. It supposedly brought growth, success, and luck, along with helping a person open their mind, become more aware of options, and choose a good path. Those were all things I needed right now.

I opened my palms towards the ceiling and closed my eyes. Once comfortable, I steadied my breathing and tried clearing my mind.

Then there was the question of how to "channel" a color. Picturing it seemed like a good start, so I imagined myself pulling green out of the air, the color glowing with life. A soft hum filled my ears as it expanded and pushed against me, like waves crashing over my skin. The palms of my hands tingled, and the energy flowed through my body, joining with my blood as it pumped through my veins. It streamed up my arms, moved down to my stomach, and poured down to my toes. Green glowed behind my eyelids, and I kept gathering it and gathering it until it grew so much that it had nowhere else to go.

Then it pushed its way out of my palms with such force that it must have lit up the entire room.

3

The bell rang, and my eyes snapped open, the classroom coming into focus. I looked around, taking in the scuffed tiled floor, the chalkboard covered with writing, the white plaster walls, and the lack of windows. Everything looked normal. Unchanged. There was no proof that anything I'd just felt had been more than a figment of my imagination.

But that energy flowing through my body had been so *real*. I tightened my hands into fists and opened them back up, but only a soft tingle remained. Then it disappeared completely.

Kate stood up, dropped her backpack on her chair, and studied me. "I'm guessing from the look on your face that it worked," she said.

"I don't know." I shrugged and picked up my bag. "I'm not sure what was supposed to happen." I met her eyes and managed a small smile, since it wasn't exactly a lie.

But the energy I'd felt around me was unlike anything I'd ever experienced. Which meant my imagination was running out of control. Because there was no proof that I'd done anything. What I'd "experienced" had existed only in my head. Right?

Kate glanced at her watch. "What class do you have first?"

I pulled out my schedule. "Honors Biology." I scrunched my nose at the prospect. "They put me in all honors classes, and I have no idea why. I was in regular classes at my old school."

"I've got Honors Bio, too," she said. "Come on. I'll explain the whole honors thing on the way there."

I followed Kate down the hallway, although I kept bumping into people, since my mind was spinning after what had happened in homeroom. I'd felt something during that meditation session. Maybe it was the energy that Darius was talking about. And if this energy stuff *was* the reason behind the miraculous recovery of my torn tendon and the healed scar...

I pushed the thought away. There had to be another explanation. One that made *sense*.

Kate edged closer to the wall to give me space to walk next to her. "So, about the honors classes," she said, lowering her voice. "You saw what was written on the board. Each color has a different meaning. Once we learn how to harness energy properly, we can use the different colors to help us ... do things."

"What kind of things?" I asked.

"Let's take yellow—my personal favorite—as an example," she said. "Yellow increases focus and helps us remember information. If you channel yellow energy before studying for a test, it won't take as long to review everything, and you'll remember more. It'll make your memory almost photographic. Pretty cool, right?"

"It does sound useful," I agreed. "Although I'm still not buying all this colors and energy stuff."

"Give it time." Kate smiled, as if she knew something I didn't, and stopped in front of a classroom door. "We're here. Want to sit with me?" She led the way to a table in the front, and I followed, even though front and center wasn't my thing. "I'll help you with the basics after school," she offered. "You got the hang of channeling energy pretty quickly, so it shouldn't be hard. Sometimes it takes the freshmen months to gather enough energy to feel anything significant. It was obvious from where I was sitting that you did it on your first try. That was pretty impressive."

"I'm not sure I actually did anything, but sure, I'll study with you after school," I said. Even though this energy stuff sounded crazy, it was nice of Kate to reach out. I didn't want to miss the chance to make my first friend here. "I could definitely use help getting caught up with my classes."

"Great." Kate beamed. "I'm sure you'll pick it up quickly."

More students piled in, a few of them people I recognized from homeroom. Then, just as I'd started to think it was stupid to hope he would also be in this class, Blake strolled inside, with Danielle trailing close behind.

His eyes met mine, and my breath caught, taken aback by how he'd noticed me again. But he couldn't be interested in me like *that*. It was probably just because I was new. And because, as embarrassing as it was to admit, he'd caught me staring at him. So I opened my textbook to the chapter that Kate already had open, focusing on a section on dominant and recessive genes as if it were the most fascinating thing I'd ever read in my life.

"I told you in homeroom that he's taken, remember?" Kate whispered once Blake and Danielle were far enough away.

My cheeks heated. "Was it that obvious?"

"That you were checking him out?" Kate asked, and I nodded, despite how humiliating it was that she'd noticed. "Yeah."

"I'm not doing it on purpose," I said. "I know that he has a girlfriend. I would never try anything, I promise. But ... have you seen him? It was hard not to at least *look*."

"I know you're not doing it on purpose," she said. "He's one of the hottest guys in the school—I get that. But Danielle doesn't take it too kindly when girls flirt with Blake. Or check out Blake. Or even look like they're *interested* in Blake. It's in your best interest to keep your distance from both of them. Trust me."

I was about to ask why, but before I could, the bell rang and class began.

4

THE OTHER SOPHOMORES from homeroom were in most of my classes, and Kate sat with me in each one, including lunch. I was so behind in the honors courses that I seriously needed whatever Kate said she would teach me after school to help.

"What class do you have next?" Kate asked as we packed our bags after advanced Spanish.

I pulled my schedule out of my pocket. "Ceramics." I groaned. I wasn't awful at art, but I would have preferred a music elective, since music was always my favorite class. "What about you?"

"Theatre," she answered, tucking her hair behind her ears. "I want to be in the school play this spring, but I always get nervous on stage. Hopefully the class will help."

"You'll get in," I said. "Besides, can't you use that witchy energy stuff to convince the teacher to give you the part you want? Or mess up other people during their auditions so they don't get the leads?"

Her eyes darted around the hall, and she leaned in closer, lowering her voice. "We don't use our powers to take advantage of others," she said. "I'll fill you in on everything later. Okay?"

I nodded and followed her through the art wing, resisting the urge to ask her more right now. Instead, I looked around. Student paintings decorated the walls, and what sounded like a flute solo came from a room close by. Kate stopped in front of the double doors that led to the theatre. "This is me," she said. "The ceramics room is upstairs—you shouldn't miss it."

We split ways, and like Kate had told me, the ceramics room was easy to find. Kilns lined the side wall, pottery wheels were on the other end, bricks of clay were stacked in shelves in the back, and the huge windows were a welcome change from the stuffy classrooms I'd been in so far.

I looked around to see if anyone seemed receptive to having the new girl join them, and my eyes stopped when they reached Blake's. He sat at the table furthest away, leaning back in his seat with his legs outstretched. The chairs next to him were empty.

He nodded at me, as if acknowledging me as a member of a special club, and I noticed that no one else from homeroom was in this class. Could he be inviting me to sit with him?

Since everyone from homeroom seemed to stick together, I took that as a yes and walked toward Blake's table, my pulse quickening with every step. I remembered what Kate had told me earlier about Danielle—how she was crazy possessive over Blake—but Danielle wasn't here. And Blake was the only person who wanted me to join him. Refusing would be rude.

He moved his legs to give me room, and I settled in the seat next to him. His deep, liquid eyes had various shades of reddish brown running through them, and he was watching me as if he was waiting for me to say something. I swallowed, not sure how to start, and settled on the obvious.

"Hi." My heart pounded so hard I feared he could hear it. "You're in my homeroom, right?"

"Yep," he said smoothly. "We also have biology, history, and Spanish together." He counted off each on his fingers. "And given that you're in Darius's homeroom, it's safe to say that you have Greek mythology with me next period as well. I'm Blake."

"Nicole," I introduced myself, even though Darius had already done so in front of the class this morning. "I heard that all of the sophomores in our homeroom have to take Greek mythology. Luckily I read *The Odyssey* in English last year, so I shouldn't be totally lost."

"There's a reason we're required to take Greek mythology." He scooted closer to me, as if about to tell me a secret, and I leaned forward in anticipation. "Did you know that we—meaning everyone in our homeroom—are descended from the Greek gods?"

I arched an eyebrow. "Like Zeus and all of them living in a castle on the clouds?" I asked.

"Exactly." He smirked. "Except that they're referred to as the Olympians, and they call their 'castle in the clouds' Mount Olympus."

"So you're saying that we're *gods*?"

"We're not gods." He smiled and shook his head. "But we have 'diluted god blood' in us. It's what gives us our powers."

"Right." I wasn't sure how else to respond, and I looked down at the table. Was he playing a joke on me? Trying to see how gullible the new kid could be?

"What's wrong?" He watched me so intensely—so seriously—that I knew he was truly concerned.

"The truth?" I asked, and he nodded, his gaze locked on mine. So I took a deep breath, and said, "Everything from our homeroom sounds crazy to me. But you're all so serious about it that I'm starting to think you actually believe it."

"It's a lot to take in at once," he said.

"That's the understatement of the day." I flaked a piece of dried clay off the table with my thumbnail. "But Kate offered to teach me some stuff after school, and she's been really nice by taking me around all day, so I told her I would listen to her."

"Kate's a rule follower," Blake said, crossing his arms. "She's only going to tell you about a fraction of the stuff we can do. But stay in homeroom with us, and maybe my friends and I will show you how to have *real* fun with our abilities."

The teacher walked inside before I could respond, and the chattering in the room quieted. As much as I wanted to ask Blake what he meant, I couldn't right now. We weren't supposed to talk about our abilities when humans could hear.

Then I realized: I'd thought of other people as "humans," like I wasn't one of them anymore.

The scary thing was—I might be starting to believe it.

Keep reading Elementals!

Get it now at:
mybook.to/elementalsboxset

ABOUT THE AUTHOR

Michelle Madow is a USA Today bestselling author of fast-paced, young adult fantasy novels full of magic, adventure, romance, and twists you'll never see coming. She's sold over two million books worldwide and has been translated into multiple languages.

Michelle grew up in Maryland, then moved to Florida, and now lives in New York City. She wrote her first book in her junior year of college and hasn't stopped writing since! She also loves traveling, and has been to all seven continents. Someday, she hopes to travel the world for a year on a cruise ship.

Never miss a new release by signing up to get emails or texts when Michelle's books come out:

Sign up for emails: michellemadow.com/subscribe
Sign up for texts: michellemadow.com/texts

Connect with Michelle:

Facebook Group: facebook.com/groups/michellemadow
Instagram: @michellemadow
Email: michelle@madow.com
Website: www.michellemadow.com

THE DRAGON TWINS: THE COMPLETE SERIES

Published by Dreamscape Publishing

Copyright © 2022 Michelle Madow

ISBN: 9798376858080

This book is a work of fiction. Though some actual towns, cities, and locations may be mentioned, they are used in a fictitious manner and the events and occurrences were invented in the mind and imagination of the author. Any similarities of characters or names used within to any person past, present, or future is coincidental.

All rights reserved. No part of this book may be used or reproduced in any manner whatsoever without written permission from the author. Brief quotations may be embodied in critical articles or reviews.

Printed in Great Britain
by Amazon